LINEAGE

LINEAGE

THE DESCENDANTS

BY WILL MCCLINTON

Library of Congress Control Number:		2012905545
ISBN:	Hardcover	978-1-4691-9032-7
	Softcover	978-1-4691-9031-0
	Ebook	978-1-4691-9033-4

This is a work of fiction. Names, characters, places and incidents either are the product of the author's imagination or are used fictitiously, and any resemblance to any actual persons, living or dead, events, or locales is entirely coincidental.

Any people depicted in stock imagery provided by Thinkstock are models, and such images are being used for illustrative purposes only.

This book was printed in the United States of America.

To order additional copies of this book, contact:
Xlibris Corporation
1-888-795-4274
www.Xlibris.com
Orders@Xlibris.com
110950

WHO WOULD EVER believe my parents could be right. Well, especially Mom. I should have listened more closely to our family history. I hope you will at least read this and be wary before it is too late. I am writing this to protect future generations so that they at least have a chance. At not destroying themselves and their loved ones. For there are people, and I use that term loosely, that would seek to destroy you as they have myself and my brother Camel. We are a blended family, as many Arab and American families are. Friends are for life, and family is forever.

The Du Bois and Khalid families have been intertwined in business and family interests since I can remember. Camel's father knew my father before we were born. It was just my good fortune as is happenstance that Camel and I met before we were five years old. It's interesting to note that I was learning Arabic faster than French, and Camel, French faster than English. Our teacher Mr. Arun was a man of Indian descent who spoke his English with a British accent. Go figure. So on occasion my American may slip a little toward British phrasing. I digress.

For my part of the story, it really seemed to start in Rochester, New York. Having been brought there twice at ages eight and eleven to visit with Dad's uncle. My great uncle Theron Du Bois. He was different in a way Mom described as "enlightened." Performing what I would describe as shamanistic rituals. Being raised both Islamic and Christian, I witnessed both sides of my extended families burn incense and chant (just as Roman Catholic priests have done for centuries). So I thought nothing of it at the time. I wish I had paid closer attention at those times uncle Theron had been working those rites.

Have I mentioned that I was raised in the United Arab Emirates? Yes, I have a dual citizenship. Both times I visited Rochester, it was both cold and overcast with gray skies. Being raised so near the equator didn't help my opinion much of Rochester, with its light gray to dark gray clouds blanketing the skies. It's a rare time in the winter to have sunshine. Visiting my cousins in Louisiana was much more interesting. Fun actually, being closer in ages. That and at least it has yellow sunshine with blue skies. But let's not forget humid in the summer, like the Emirates, and hot. It gave us commonalities to complain about.

Both times we visited Uncle Theron, it was never boring. His house smelled of old wood and it was like visiting a museum or is that a mausoleum? In either place I couldn't touch anything. When I complained about that (being a very tactile child), I had to touch everything with my hands vases, paintings, tapestries. You get it. Mom was either yelling at me (only when immediate family was around) or whispering in my ear. "Don't touch that!" Or "Children are to be seen and not heard."

My name is Marc Du Bois; age is of no real importance to me at this time. I was a third-year architectural engineering major who has transferred to the Rochester area. Camel was already here attending college, same major. We were in Rochester for family business interests. When you're born into wealth, the two go hand in hand. The children are expected to assume financial custodianship of trusts and properties. I was a young adult male with life thrust upon me, as you will soon learn. I was still innocent to the dangers of ignorance, just coming into my own life. A friend in Montreal once told me Du Bois is as common a name as Woods is in America. However, as I was soon to learn, Du Bois was anything but if not exceptionally uncommon for those of us from this lineage. Now for the story, where it at least seemed to begin for me.

CHAPTER 1

THE FLIGHT INTO La Guardia from Paris had been boringly uneventful. Something I would wish for in the coming months. Waiting my layover out at one of those busy airport restaurant/bars. People watching as I often like to do. While sipping my coffee, this leggy blonde woman approaches. Coming into my field of vision. Shapely would be a modest description. Towing her carry-on bag along, her other hand loaded with designer names on shopping bags. Stilettos clicking across the marble floor, calf muscles shapely. Herself oblivious to all the men whose heads she turned. Her blue eyes fixed on mine as she comes into the bar. Speaking first to me, she says, "May I rest these here?" Myself tongue-tied for a moment trying to choose a language that would be most effective in charming her. She speaks again. "A vous Francais?"

"Yes," I say, her baggage already dropped as she walks away to the bar. Smooth. My brother Camel would have said something captivating. He was definitely the Arab ladies' man. The bartender walks right past a group of male patrons waving money, to serve her first.

Sitting back down an opportunity missed, but not lost. I've been told I'm pretty easy on the eye myself. Six feet tall dark blue eyes, straight dark almost black hair combed back, olive to *moreno* complexion, being of Cajun heritage. Turning her head to the side glancing to see if I'm still watching her. And I am.

She gives her order to the bartender. "Espresso French roast."

The bartender replies, "Right away," his eyes lingering over her. Then she turns away from him, already talking into her cell phone. Myself having spent a year in Europe studying architecture especially France, honing my language skills. Dad expects me to have at least a passing knowledge of French since it is our heritage. Trying not to be obviously rude and listening in to her conversation. She was chewing someone out because she has to fly commercial instead of Daddy's private jet.

"Dad is going to hear about this!" she says. Pressing end stowing her cell phone turning to sip her espresso. Making a face, she then says, "It's terrible! I said French roast!"

The bartender looking dismayed, replies, "That is the only espresso we have."

"Well, I'm not paying for this mud!" she replies. Walking away from him. Noise of the male patrons resuming calling for drinks. Slipping her arm through Gucci straps and gathering the collection of designer shopping bags. Pulling the rolling carry-on back in tow. Pausing for the briefest of looks at yours truly, confident I'm still following her with my eyes. Winking at me before disappearing into the dense crowd of pedestrians passing by outside. That was the first time I saw her.

CHAPTER 2

THE LAST THIRTY minutes of our approach into Rochester. We were hit with a turbulence strong enough to jar open overhead bins. Causing them to dump their contents on frightened passengers below them. Producing a few screams and yells of fright. Little did I know that this was only the beginning of rough times to come. Believing myself to be worldly and sophisticated, but really having a very sheltered life with my extended family in the United Arab Emirates. Nothing I had experienced could have prepared me for what was coming.

Camel my brother was already living in Rochester. Would be attending the same university I had transferred to. He had arranged for his limousine to pick me up at the airport. I was slightly disappointed he hadn't been there to meet me. The chauffeur after loading my luggage whisked me off to my new home and to meet with Mr. Thornburg, my late uncle's attorney. Also our family attorney for Western New York. I hadn't seen him in years. Wondering what he considered me. A spoiled rich child or a new business associate?

Large wet snowflakes were falling as we glided up East Avenue toward my new residence. A mansard-style mansion built in the 1860s. Complete with a belvedere and widow's walk. Which also had family lore attached to it. Not that I had ever bothered to know more about it. Being a young man of the twenty-first century. Why should I be concerned with an old wives' tale? Much less my family's dusty history. Wasn't it enough I knew the house had been in the Du Bois family since its construction? When once it was a new neighborhood where even George Eastman had chosen to sink his roots? Now that is much more interesting. A multibillion dollar corporation created by my neighbor down the street. Now even that news was as old as the established neighborhood had become from another century.

I was meeting with our family's attorney to sign papers transferring it all under my care. Uncle Theron had been missing for years, presumed dead. Mr. Thornburg to the letter of the law had encouraged this action. It was time I was coming of age, a man. Legal heir to the Rochester part of Uncle's estate.

Robert Thornburg esquire was always on time. The sun was setting in the western sky. One of those beautiful Rochester sunsets with its purples and pinks banded across clouds. Quite stunning if you took the time to appreciate it. As

Mr. Thornburg would have already been reviewing tomorrow's proceedings if it wasn't for this business. There wasn't time for such sentimentality. Pulling up the curving driveway with his large black Mercedes 450 smoothly crossing the cobblestone courtyard. No one there yet checking his console clock sighing. Definitely not like his parents.

Marc catching glimpses of his home through gapes in the canopy of mature beech trees grown massive in the past century. They had thrived since being planted as seedlings. The house was as I hoped I couldn't remember it. Dark shadows surrounding it cast by towering evergreens. What were they called? Yes, hemlocks. Wasn't there a poison made from that? A sliver of the moon is reflected back from round third-floor windows like a pair of cruel eyes watching his approach. In a blink they were gone before he could sight them again. The stretch limousine turns up the driveway. Past gnarled oak trees twisted from harsh winter winds, gray and black in the failing light. Shapes ever changing with the motion of the car. Tree trunks with leathery faces glaring back at him as he passes them. A knot forming in Marc's stomach as déjà vu returns him to childhood memories of long forgotten nightmares. Yes, beginning to remember them all too well now. Passing under the archway connecting the gatehouse to the manor. Into the shadows of a mansard house left empty by its occupant missing now presumed dead.

Old memories from nightmares of falling from the sky only to be captured by nameless faces. Corrupting him in slaveries inescapable acts. Too embarrassing for an eleven-year old boy to discuss with anyone. Especially his parents. Combine that with the threat of death to loved ones in his family if he spoke of these dreams to anyone.

"Sir, we're here."

Bringing him out of his deep memories. Headlamps just penetrating the comfort of the sanctuary. That being the courtyard. His limousine parked beside the black Mercedes. Mr. Thornburg getting out of his car quickly. My chauffeur opening my warm compartment to the chill of an usually cool May night. Gathering myself up I step into my own kismet. Unsure of what is imagined and what if any of this is just a childhood trick. Catching my breath. I can do this. Pushing aside those memories and feelings no longer forgotten.

The darkness of its courtyard warmed only slightly by a yellow light shining from the caretakers' cottage beyond the multiple-bayed garage. Its porch light winking on. Andry hearing all the noise of our arrival coming outside

Mr. Thornburg speaks up, "Marc, you're finally here. I was beginning to fear you were delayed at customs. I trust there wasn't any confusion as happened in the past?" More of a statement than a question. Myself standing taller than him.

"No. Lessons learned."

"Good, I'll get Andry." Robert turns as if on cue. "Andry! Good timing." Andry ambling down the steps of his cottage at an elderly pace. "You remember Marc?"

"Da, uh yes. Many years ago." His Ukrainian accent thick. "How could I forget. You were so angry. Wearing those white robes and that thing on your head with the black rope around it. You refused to speak English. Choosing only to speak in Arabic."

"Yes, that sounds familiar." Thinking to himself, *I had been so angry about coming here.* Now feeling a twinge of embarrassment, glad for the shadows to hide his face. "What a handful."

Andry, "What a brat you were."

The exterior lights winking on being on a timer. Perfect moment for my look of guilt.

Marc, "I guess I was pretty bad."

Andry, "Well, now he is grown up ready to be head of household." I was not feeling as sure as Andry was. The last time I was here I was eleven years old. Forced to come here. My parents both insistent. I could not rally Dad to my side. It was his uncle and mom was unbending. Saying I needed to be familiar with our American family and culture. I was too easily becoming entrenched into a male dominant culture as is the situation with Middle Eastern men. Forcing my thoughts back to the present. Andry and Mr. Thornburg having a quick discussion. Their voices almost lost in the darkness. Keys jingling. My last chance of escape passing with the black limousine silently gliding away fading into the shadows.

Mr. Thornburg, "Well, Marc are you ready to take possession of the house?" Not waiting for me to speak. "It hasn't been lived in for years. So it might be a little neglected for your taste but certainly livable. It won't be like it was abandoned." Meaning that Andry and his wife were no longer able to keep up the estate. They had lived here for decades now in their seventies. Uncle Theron's wishes were made clear by the codicil in the will allowing for them to remain as long as they wanted. Until death if they chose. Maybe things weren't spotless and a few weeds were poking up in the flower beds.

Marc, "I'm sure it will be just fine once I get inside and warm up." The chilled damp air finally sinking through my clothes. Rubbing my hands together to warm them. "I thought it was spring here."

Mr. Thornburg, "Yes, well, May does have its cold days. Come on we'll use the main entrance." Walking on without a glance back at the two of us. Himself not using the side entrance which was closer. Thornburg is still an arrogant ass. Crossing the cobblestone courtyard to the stone path leading around to the front entrance. This path illuminated by low-voltage lighting. Passing through mature rhododendrons and mountain laurels completely obscuring anyone from seeing us pass to the front of the house. Stepping into light from a large wrought iron fixture. Its chains a heavy gauge to support its weight from twenty feet above. Its glass panes coated with years of grime. Standing in front of the massive oak double doors. Andry appearing diminutive by comparison. Jingling the keys in his rough gnarled hands from years of labor as he selects the correct one. Inserting it.

Mr. Thornburg, "Have you deactivated the alarm system?"

Andry, "Uh, da." But thinking to himself, *When was the last time I turned it on?* Unsure of that answer. Having been distracted by his wife's declining health with another hospitalization.

Stepping onto the tiled black and white marble floor of the foyer beautiful even in the dim light. Andry moving away from the two men in search of light switches. With a click light from a crystal chandelier brings forth the mahogany paneling reaching to the second floor. Breathtaking, this home's grand staircase poised curving away a (pied-à-terre). The occasional wall sconce a smaller version of the larger crystal chandelier following the halls on the first and second floors into the distance. Dusty and dull but obviously of exquisite craftsmanship only needing a freshening up. Mr. Thornburg closing the front door silencing the city noises outside. So still inside the house his wheezing on inspiration now apparent. The heavy damask drapes and tapestries absorbing any remaining sounds of traffic. It's like we are not in the city anymore. Andry already down the hall, opening the pocket library doors. Following Andry down the hall Marc taking a moment to admire one of numerous oil paintings decorating the walls. This one a Sydney Laurence of mountains in gilt frame.

Mr. Thornburg, "It's quite impressive. Isn't it?"

Marc, "Yes. It is the work of a true master."

Mr. Thornburg, "There will be plenty of time for you to appreciate your new home." Putting his hand on Marc's arm guiding him. "At per your uncle's request the reading of the will shall take place in the library." Shivering himself. "Andry, light a fire for us. Then you may leave." Pushing aside an old leather-bound book with his thin laptop and briefcase. Booting up the computer for a teleconference with Marc's parents. Each of the three on different continents in separate time zones. His mother Teresa Du Bois in Peru four hours earlier; and his dad Charles du Bois in Iraq a day ahead. Marc looking around the library noting the sixteenth-century Persian rugs. Moving over to another oil painting noting it to be a Max Weyl 1876 of a pastoral setting. Exquisite in its details. Appraising his uncle's home further. Feeling the need to make a crass comment.

"This place is like a museum. I could sell a couple oil paintings like a Laurence or Weyl and wouldn't need a summer job."

Mr. Thornburg his tone sharp, "I don't think so. The provisions set forth by the will are very clear in that matter." Waving his hand for Marc to have a seat at the Federal-period round table. Marc taking a seat. Warmth from the crackling fire reaching him. Both men appreciating it.

Mr. Thornburg, "As per your uncle's directions. Nothing may be liquidated from the estate without approval from the board of trustees of which your parents are on."

"That is correct." Teresa my mother speaking up for the first time.

"Hi mom." Turning to view her image on the screen. "It's good to see you." Giving her one of his charming smiles.

Teresa, "That isn't going to work on me." Smiling back at him. "Are you eating enough? You look thin."

Marc, "Yes, mom. It's the dark clothes." Marc weighing in at 90 kilograms or an even two hundred pounds of solid muscle from weight training, mixed martial arts, with kickboxing a favorite. Not Mr. Muscle and Fitness, but solid.

Teresa, "You look so European, gothic."

Marc, "No. It's cold here and feels more like winter. It was snowing when I arrived and I did just get here from a year in Europe." Mr. Thornburg clearing his throat impatiently.

Teresa, "Your name may be listed on the trust, but I'm still POA and senior trustee. I agree with your late uncle. Families of circumstance don't sell off their assets. It took years for your uncle to put together that art collection." Irritation in her voice.

Marc, "I was just kidding."

Teresa, "I helped him with some of those acquisitions. They are some of the finest representations of Eastern and Western American artists outside a museum." Mr. Thornburg nodding his head in agreement.

Marc, "It would be nice to have the summer off."

Teresa, "No! College is paid for and you have a monthly stipend from your trust fund."

Marc, "Which is paltry compared to Camel's and other friends of mine."

Teresa, "I'm not having some useless playboy for a son. Who is in and out of trouble expecting his parents' money to cover everything. You will have a summer job behaving responsibly like everyone else."

Marc, "Yes, ma am."

Teresa, "I wouldn't think you would be so quick to sell antiquities after your and Camel's brush with Interpol, the U.S. State Department, and UAE and the Iraqi governments."

Marc becoming defensive, "That really was a misunderstanding!"

Teresa, "Don't take that tone with me." Meaning the end of discussion.

Mr. Thornburg looking almost smug holding back a smile. "With that said. Andry is getting on in years and his wife Oksana her health failing. The grounds are becoming unkept as is the house."

Marc, "I'll say. The grounds are spooky and so overgrown. As is this house." Looking up at the cobwebs hanging from the ceiling and chandelier in the library.

Mr. Thornburg, "Then you're in agreement with your mother and I."

Marc, "Well, yes." Looking around the room dragging a finger through the dust on the tabletop they're sitting at.

Mr. Thornburg, "Good. Then it's all set." Marc realizing too late he was being set up. "Andry needs an assistant groundskeeper. You'll be perfect for the job. A strapping young lad with a vested interest in the property. I'll start interviewing housekeepers."

Marc, "What just happened here?"

Teresa, "You agree the manor needs work. Right?"

Marc, "Yes, it does." *What an idiot. I walked right into that one.*

Teresa, "As an architect you'll need to be familiar with garden design."

Marc, "Structural engineering, Mom."

Teresa, "Good work Mr. T." Mom always liked calling him that because he was a heavy hitter legally. "You killed two birds with one stone. People see and use the exterior grounds and its structures. Haven't you seen the green trend in building design? Hong Kong is gorgeous with its city forest. So was the New Orleans garden district. Right where you live now, it's a beautiful street and not just because of the architecture. I believe there was some sort of experimental horticultural nursery at one time. That is why there are so many unique specimen trees of maturity in your area."

Marc, "Great! I'll be the laborer."

Mr. Thornburg, "That's the spirit. I'll continue to manage the household and estate finances. As have been set aside in separate accounts. Until a time when the board deems you capable of handling fiduciary responsibilities."

Teresa, "Exactly what your father and I wanted. Marc, you can grow into his position."

Marc, "Where is Dad anyway? Wasn't he supposed to be a part of this entrapment?"

Mr. Thornburg, "He obviously couldn't make it here. Oh, and there is one more item of importance."

Marc, "I can't believe this. I lived in Europe and went school for the past year—"

Teresa interrupting his griping, "Marc you need to hear this."

Marc, "Yes, ma am. What is it?"

Teresa, "Don't take that tone with me."

Mr. Thornburg smiling, "You have to reside here for one contiguous year. Otherwise your younger cousin Philip the professor will assume responsibility and ownership of the manor."

Marc, "Is he in on this too?"

Teresa, "As a direct male heir. He has been made aware of this. You would do well to know your family history. Every male heir has been required to do this. So are you clear on this?"

Marc, "Yes, ma am."

Teresa, "Have your college transcripts been sent?"

Marc, "In other words am I registered? Yes. I was planning on taking a landscape design course through Cornell."

Mr. Thornburg, "Great, I'll let Andry know he can count on you. When it comes to horticulture, he knows his stuff. It's not just a labor, it's a labor of love. He has brought forth many award-winning gardens here and helped my wife win some. There was a time when the gardens here were on the Rochester garden tour route."

Teresa, "Bob, I didn't realize you were such a big admirer of Andry's."

Mr. Thornburg, "Yes I am but especially my wife."

Teresa, "That sounds wonderful." Looking at Marc. "You're in capable hands. Now Marc, I don't want any disappointing phone calls from Mr. Thornburg. Reporting undesirable incidents at the manor. Even though your father didn't make it to this conference. I know he would agree with me on this. You are to conduct yourself as a respectable young man."

Marc, "Yes, ma am. That was a none too subtle threat. So Mr. T will be spying and reporting on me."

Teresa smiling back at Marc. Speaking to both men. "Well, it sounds like the two of you have it under control." Choosing not to respond.

Mr. Thornburg, "Yes. I've asked my wife's niece Angelique to help find a suitable housekeeper for the estate and of course Marc."

Teresa, "You both know how to reach me through the Sao Paulo Museum. Marc, I'll be incommunicado at least a month at a time. My team and I are following up on rumors of some ruins that haven't been seen since the conquistadors. This could be a significant discovery for my career."

Mr. Thornburg, "That sounds very exciting. Teresa, I hope to read about you in National Geographic."

Marc, "Yeah, very exciting." Sounding very monotone. Thinking, *Now I can be an indentured laborer. My only escape higher education in the fall. Where is Camel? He always knows where to go to have some fun.*

Mr. Thornburg, "How will you locate them?"

Teresa, "I have some contacts in National Security that were testing out advanced mapping techniques."

Mr. Thornburg, "Impressive. You have some good contacts."

Teresa, "Now that you mention it. I owed some big favors to powerful men in Iraq, the National Security Institution, and even Iran. After Marc and Camel's folly. I helped them and they helped me."

Marc, "See, not everything bad came out of that. I can't seem to say I'm sorry enough."

Teresa, "It's called provenance. You will need to say that a few more times."

Mr. Thornburg, "It sounds like you're the one to go to if I want Middle Eastern antiquities."

Teresa, "Yes, if you want to avoid international incidents." Her tone irritated. Going back to the subject. "The technology is used to survey geological layers beneath the earth's crust. It works remarkable well at finding passages and structures covered by centuries of debris and foliage. Let me stop before I give up some secrets. Marc have you heard from your father?"

Marc, "About a year ago. He sent me a card for Ramadan."

Teresa, "Don't sound so excited. At least he remembered you. He forgot our anniversary. Besides, you're in the lap of luxury. I've stayed at the manor. It's beautiful and very modernized."

Marc, "I'm not so sure about modern. We're using a fire to warm the place." Mr. Thornburg picks up a remote control off the table in front of Marc. Pointing it at a wall of mahogany paneling; it slides away to reveal a large plasma screen TV with stereo theater sound equipment.

"Theron spared no expense to have modern amenities installed as planned prior to his disappearance. You have climate zone control for every room. He wanted to bring this house into the new century." Marc's expression questioning. Mr. Thornburg raising his hand to silence him. "There is no point in wasting money heating an empty house or for that matter on just one person."

Marc's mother seeing his exasperation adds. "You have to be mindful of your home's carbon footprint. Living almost on the Tropic of Cancer you will get cold easier. Just dress warmer. Robert would you give us a few minutes?"

Mr. Thornburg, "Of course." Getting up putting away signed deeds into his briefcase.

Teresa, "I know you'll be twenty-one soon enough. There are a few things we should have discussed."

Marc, "I know, keep it zippered or use a condom."

Teresa, "That's good advice but not what I wanted to talk to you about." The satellite connection breaking up making cracking sounds. "It's the Du Bois family history. You're coming of age." Crackling with a loud hum interrupting her.

Marc, "What about it?"

Teresa, "You must take a strong interest in it now. There are dangerous—" Loud humming bursting from the speakers. The computer screen going black. Her image returning snowy. "Don't do anything impulsive. I know how young men can be. Your uncle was supposed to teach you about the family history."

Marc, "Mom don't get all cryptic on me. Our family history is boring. Living in this museum I'm sure I'll come across some of it. Go have fun making new discoveries."

Teresa, "Marc I'm serious. This is important!" Her expression angry.

Marc, "What's so important that you have to tell me now?"

A notification crawling across the screen signal lost. Mr. Thornburg coming back into the room. "Everything good?"

Marc, "Yeah, I guess so."

Mr. Thornburg, "Well Marc, I'll be off. If there is anything more just call me. By the way your friend Camel is dating my wife's niece Angelique. She will be sending over a housekeeper for you. She just called me to let me know she has found someone. I hope this friend of yours treats her well." Looking for Marc to say more.

Marc, "He is a good man, we're like brothers, our families have known each other for years. We grew up together." Marc's bright smile lights up his face. As he hadn't seen Camel in a year. Looking forward to seeing him soon.

Mr. Thornburg, "That's good to hear. Angelique will help you with staffing and meeting the right people here in Rochester. Andry can show you around the house tomorrow to help you get settled. I'm sure you're ready to have some downtime."

Marc, "It has been a busy day. I'm wound up and tired at the same time."

Mr. Thornburg, "You know where the master suite is on the second floor. Your spa is voice activated. I'm a little jealous."

Marc, "Voice activated!" Getting excited

Mr. Thornburg, "Yes. It's completely modern it has chromatherapy in the Jacuzzi."

Marc, "That's great, even Camel doesn't have that yet." *At least I don't think so.* Mr. Thornburg smiling for the first time. At Marc's youthful exuberance.

"Your guest rooms are of equal comfort. I'll be in touch soon." Andry waiting patiently outside the library for Marc to follow him up the stairs. The second-floor hallway covered in thick pile Persian rugs over the hardwood floors cushioning their footsteps. Marc noting good ones like back home. Once again he has an unsettling feeling. At the edges of his consciousness trying to identify what it is. It's so very quiet up here. The sconces on both sides of the hall dusty and covered with cobwebs. A contrast to the dark mahogany paneling. Mom was right. This place will be beautiful once it is cleaned and lived in again. Andry shuffles to a stop outside the door to the master suite. Swinging open the door.

Speaking, "Lights on!" Several lamps wink on around the bedroom suite. A fire already lit earlier crackling in the fireplace warming the room. Its marble mantel white Italian ornately sculpted with wreaths of olive branches its Corinthian columns stately. Heavy burgundy and gold damask drapes closed across Eastern windows. Perfect for morning prayers.

Andry, "Everything is electronically controlled. Including the shower, sauna, and spa tub. You will need to set the temperature settings to your preferences." Marc already becoming familiar with the electronic controls. Pulling off the control panel examining the settings.

Andry, "This was your uncle's room. He was a good man."

Marc, "Yes." Reading instructions on the display. "Difficult to understand."

Andry, "Maybe you found him to be that way because you were so young." Being very insightful. Marc already inside the system preparing to add his voice to the recognition system.

Marc, "You're right." Looking at Andry not recognizing his wisdom. "Thank you for lighting the fire. Why not use the central heating?"

Andry pausing to answer. "Why heat an entire house for one person? When you really just needed the dampness gone."

Marc, "No, really."

Andry, "Some of us can appreciate a time when heating was a luxury."

Marc, "I'm not used to cold weather." Missing his point.

Andry, "I guess living in the desert has its drawbacks."

Marc, "Dubai really isn't a desert city. It's on the ocean." Acknowledging, "Though it is warmer than here and it gets cold but it's not the same."

Andry's blue eyes searching Marc's face. "I'm sure you dress differently there. You must layer your clothes here when it is cold. Covering your head and feet will keep you warmer."

Marc, "That's good advice." Layering at home helps to keep you cool or warm.

Andry, "If you need anything else call me. Otherwise good night." Starting to leave.

Marc, "Where are the central heating controls?"

Andry, "Each bedroom and all common rooms have their own climate control zones. I will familiarize you with them tomorrow. If you don't mind, it's late and my wife needs me." Andry pausing at the door debating whether to speak. "Mr. Thornburg is very conscientious about utility costs. They come out of the household budget. You will find the fireplaces keep the rooms warm especially when the drapes are drawn." Marc looking annoyed by the control Mr. Thornburg will be exerting over him. Andry looking at Marc's short-sleeve shirt. "However the climate control for this room is located next to the bathroom control panel. Just use those controls or the remote until you are set up. Good night."

Marc, "Thank you. Good night."

CHAPTER 3

MAY HAD PASSED into June without much event. I was settling in the house well enough with an occasional strange dream. Something I don't recall doing much of except for those dreams were very erotic. That was probably because I didn't have a steady girlfriend. Camel was insistent I get women and or a girlfriend. I was beginning to believe he was right. He had many women that were interested in him. Being an Arabian ladies' man certainly had its advantages. He and Angelique had decided to be matchmakers. So they had lined up a blind date for me. Something I was not too happy about. How could they know my tastes? But I digress.

People were friendly enough here even after they found out I was Muslim. Ms. Campbell the housekeeper Angelique had arranged for knew her way around the kitchen. It wasn't home cooking but it was certainly good. Once we got past the pork roast incident. After that we were good. She was tough and demanding on the temporary help cleaning the house. Causing us to go through a few. More than a couple young women left in tears after she dismantled them. She wouldn't be satisfied until the right one was hired. I had my doubts as to anyone measuring up to her high levels of cleanliness. That and her critical approach. Still the place was becoming livable again. One morning while I was working outside, I smelled fresh baked apple pie she had set out on the window sill to cool. Cinnamon and apples, uhum. That had my mouth watering for some. Myself and Andry at the rear of the house. That would be the northeast corner, next to the cobblestone parking. Holding the blueprints up, studying the plans for the private garden. Another of my late uncle's improvements moving forward.

Marc, "This is where the new flagstone path will go replacing the brick one."

Andry, "Yes. It will lead out into the secret garden. This path connecting with the path from the back door leading out to it. The old bricks are to be used elsewhere. For the time being stack them on the skids inside the garage. Use one of the empty car bays."

Marc, "I've never done this kind of work before."

Andry ignoring him. "After the path has been cleared and re-graded with sand, you'll scree and compact the sand. The path will be made from Kentucky Crab Orchard flagstone." Marc looking doubtfully at him.

Marc, "I'm supposed to do all of this? I've never laid stone or done this kind of work."

Andry, "That is why I hired a stonemason. He will be coming out to help. Here you will need these." Handing Marc knee pads.

Marc thinking to himself, *I'm the new master of the house yet this senior groundskeeper is my boss.* Feeling the need to speak up, "Between you, my parents and Mr. Thornburg, I'm the cheap labor."

Andry looking impatient with Marc ignoring his comment. Glaring out from under his bushy gray eyebrows his blue eyes piercing. "Once you pry up enough bricks use the wheel-barrel to transport the bricks to bay five in the garage."

Marc, "Anything else boss?"

Andry, "Yes. We will take the seedlings from the greenhouse and start planting the courtyard flower beds. You will plant shasta daisies with zinnias in front of the mountain laurels out in the front garden."

Marc, "I just remembered I have a friend coming over."

Andry, "Good, maybe you can get him to help you."

Marc, "I doubt that. He's from old Middle Eastern money. He will think I'm nuts for doing it myself instead of hiring someone to do this grunt work."

Andry, "It builds character. Your friend is starting to sound like a spoiled rich boy." Just on cue, a black special edition Jaguar convertible races up the driveway, tires squealing. Flashing through the archway sliding to a stop on the cobblestone driveway. Perfectly parked right in front of the two men. Stepping out of the car his six foot plus height and wavy dark hair clipped short. Every bit debonair. Camel Ali Azhar Khalid waves turning to speak to one of his companions. Identical twin blondes looking every bit the part of models. Marc's smile beaming at him. Camel pushing his wraparound sunglasses up on top of his head. Leaning against the car crossing his long legs nonchalantly. Mr. Cool pushing off the car. Marc walks over meeting him half way. Camel bear hugging him. Being the larger of the two men Camel lifts Marc off his feet.

Camel, "My brother. How are you?" Dropping Marc back down. Camel smiling his white teeth. Perfect, his angular jaw strong and dark shadowed as Marc's.

Marc, "I'm good, staying busy. But not the kind of fun busy you are."

Glancing at his guests in the car. Camel says, "A man's got to live before he settles down." Turning his broad back to Marc winking at the two ladies. His black hair thick and wavy. Just the kind of hair women love to touch and run their fingers through. Camel loving every minute of their adoration. Andry waves his hands up having had enough of this reunion leaving. "So this is your new," pausing, "home. Somehow I can't picture you living here. It's a little spooky. Why don't you just paint it all black?" His sarcasm not missed.

Marc, "That's another issue I have to address with Mr. Thornburg the property's financial controller."

Camel, "I'm familiar with that rhetoric. You've heard my dad say it. 'You sons are the guardians of our family.' Meaning no to spending more money."

Marc, "Yes and then he tells us why we can't spend money." Marc being a close member of the family understands. "Enough! Who are these two lovely ladies? And why are they with the likes of you? Instead of with me?" Marc extends his hand to the first twin. "Hi, I'm Marc and you are?"

"Amy," she replies, smiling up at him. "And this is my sister Starr."

Starr speaks up, "Hi, you have beautiful blue eyes. They're like a husky's. Really pretty."

Camel, "They are with me because they want to be with a real man, not a dog." All four of them laugh.

Starr, "Camel tells us he wants to marry both of us."

Amy, "What do you do?"

Camel speaks up before Marc can respond. "You don't want him. He's the groundskeeper's son. He will expect many babies." Both girls laugh, but are not so sure he isn't telling the truth.

Marc, "Where did you meet these two? They're hot." Giving him a questioning look before speaking under his breath. "What about Angelique? Thought you two were getting serious." Camel cocks his head to the right indicating for them to walk. Going up the brick path past the wheelbarrow on its side.

Camel, "We're on again off again. She's very jealous."

Marc, "Is that why?" Looking over his shoulder at the young women.

Camel, "I made no claims, and I suspect she sees other men when it suits her. This place is incredible." Changing the subject. "You don't see this quality of architecture much anymore. Plus the grounds go back a ways. It's a nice piece of land. Mature trees and shrubs."

Marc, "You're right. In this country it's usually knocked down and something new is built. However there is a grassroots trend growing here to restore and preserve the national heritage. So houses like this one have a chance."

Camel, "Good idea. I've seen houses like this one scattered around France. When was it built?"

Marc, "1860."

Camel, "That's new where we come from."

Marc, "Any place is new when you have ten thousand years of history in your backyard."

Camel, "It can be unsettling knowing all those dead people are buried out there."

Marc, "Not here!"

Camel smiles at Marc mischievously. "Not that you know of. This place has a strange feel to it." Both men stare up at the house. "Maybe it's the dark colors it's painted?"

Marc, "It's an old house. There is nothing creepy about it."

Camel, "I didn't say it was creepy. So you were thinking that. Now why would you lie to me, we are family?"

Marc, "I'm not lying." Sounding defensive even to himself. "It just needs a new coat of paint." Thinking to himself, *Now I am lying to myself and him.*

Camel not letting it go. "Did they ever find your uncle's body?"

Marc, "No. He is still missing and presumed dead."

Camel, "So a body was never found." More of a statement than a question. Watching Marc's face closely not breaking eye contact. The two models staring up at the house getting a cold shiver. Camel seeing this as confirmation of his impression. One eyebrow raised.

Marc, "No, it wasn't." Sullen looking not liking to being cornered.

Starr, "Cam, we have to be off or we will be late."

Camel, "I have to go. Duty calls, the ladies have a photo shoot at The Upper Falls. I'll be back. This muscle head groundskeeper can use some direction. He doesn't seem too bright."

Marc, "Only if you're coming back to get your soft hands dirty."

Camel, "Ladies don't like rough hands much less dirty ones." Smiling like a Cheshire cat at his guests, the models settling back in the sports car. Making the black Jaguar peel off down the driveway its tires squealing in the distance. Marc going back to work prying bricks out of the path.

CHAPTER 4

AFTER DINNER, MARC and Camel go outside to enjoy a perfect evening. The temperature in the seventies with clear skies. Walking out to the private garden. Marc carries crystal wineglasses their stems crossed in one hand. The wine bottle Camel places it on the table. Cutting the lead seal and quickly uncorking the bottle of Bordeaux he had brought over as a housewarming gift.

Camel, "So you have to replace all the brick? Even here where we're sitting?"

Marc, "Yes. Uncle Theron wanted it changed. He had one of his architect friends redesign it using flagstone with granite. There will be a low seating wall surrounding us. A pergola on the west side end with pink roses planted in a raised bed behind the seating wall."

Camel, "It sounds very nice. Who is the contractor you've hired to do this work?"

Marc, "That would be me. Mom and Mr. Thornburg decided having me do the work would give me a better understanding of what a working man goes through. Thereby building my character."

Camel, "That is what dad is always lecturing one of us about." Marc nodding agreement. He has heard Mr. Khalid doing just that many occasions. "Usually around the same time he's telling me that I'm spoiled and should remember how hard our grandparents worked."

Marc, "Mom says it will make me feel a part of the home's history. Plus there is nothing wrong with putting in some sweat equity." Camel pours wine into their glasses handing one to Marc.

Camel, "It's not like it's that much work." Turning his head to the side and sizing up the space. "This is a small area."

Marc, "The total area is over a thousand square feet. Then include the two paths, one from the parking court and one from the house to this terrace. That's over four hundred square feet. It's a lot of work." Correcting Camel. "I have to keep up the grounds. It took me all day to get as far as I did. Andry has me power washing the bricks before I store them on the skids."

Camel, "Tough break, dude."

Marc, "Very understanding. What would you know about labor?" Camel ignores his comment. "Taste your wine it's good." Sipping his. "Not more than you do. Like you do this kind of work all the time."

Marc tastes his wine. His expression pleased. Critiquing it. "It's a full bodied and French." Taking another sip pulling air with it.

Camel, "Why don't you let a contractor to do this for you? No one will be the wiser. Then you can stop complaining."

Marc, "I'm sure Andry would tell Mr. Thornburg. You know the rest."

Camel, "Yes, the infamous call to a parent."

Marc, "You know it. I can already hear the speech. 'We're so disappointed...' I might as well get used to being the new servant and start developing character." A gentle breeze rises up warm and caressing Marc's sunbaked skin. Carrying with it the scent of pine from across the terrace. Swaying gracefully boughs of hemlocks with sound whispering through the white pines. Relaxing and peaceful as sitting out in a forest park. Both men deep into their own thoughts. Finishing their wine getting up on an unheard signal time to go inside for fresh apple pie. Shadows long now that the sun is dipping low in the west.

After eating apple pie spiced with cinnamon. They retire to the library for cognac. Marc pours Courvoisier into crystal Baccarat snifters.

Marc, "Uncle Theron always liked the finer things in life."

Camel, "How very true." Swirling cognac in the snifter enjoying its aroma.

Marc, "I can remember a conversation with him about conserving the mature landscape trees. You know he turned down the White House to save one of the trees on this property."

Camel, "Really? That's impressive considering how many people would consider it an honor to have one chosen from their property. Much less tell the head of state no."

Marc, "He did just that. He said it takes decades for a spruce to get that size. They put it up for a few weeks and you have an empty spot for years."

Camel, smiling, "Your uncle was right. I'm liking him the more I hear about him."

Marc, "He said trees this beautiful should be kept alive as long as possible. The White House needs to plant their own. It's in the will. No trees shall be cut down unless diseased or a danger to property or humans."

Camel, "So he was a tree hugger."

Marc, "No, he just realized how majestic they can be. Plus they really do make a property, enhancing the value."

Camel, "That's true. European estates are beautiful with their forests on them. Saving habitats and species."

CHAPTER 5

I WAS HAVING some company over for the evening. Camel was bringing Angelique; they are officially an item together again. Herself an alumni member of a national sorority, she was bringing a friend. It was a setup. All I knew for sure was she was someone I had met before briefly. Which had my curiosity piqued. For I couldn't remember her. Camel reassures me over the phone that she was gorgeous and I wouldn't be disappointed. Just what was supposed to be a very ordinary evening of fun. Young people playing cards and socializing. At least that's what Camel and I were led to believe. However, our lives would all be inextricably changed forever.

Marc answers the side door bell coming from the kitchen. After pulling hors d'oeuvres out of the refrigerator which were prepared earlier for his company. Compliments of Ms. Campbell. Marc opens the door to fog waist high covering the cobblestone and surrounding his guests.

Marc, "Wow! That's different. Angelique you are as beautiful as ever."

Angelique, "Enchante, I'm sure."

Marc, "I still don't understand why you're with the "Beast," referring to Camel.

Camel, "I'm right here."

Marc, "My brother, it's good to see you as always. I just question her judgment."

Camel, "Sometimes I question my own, especially why I would bring my enchanting consort around the likes of you." Smiling equally big at Marc smiling. "This is Melinda. She says you have already met." Marc's eyes round for the briefest of moments with surprise recovering quickly. Melinda gives Marc a demure smile.

"Where is your little knit hat?"

Marc, "It's a taqiyah hat. I don't wear it all the time."

Camel, "So you two have met."

Melinda looks at Marc through her eyelashes blinking at him. "Are you going to ask me in or just stand there letting the dampness soak into my hair?" Marc flashes back to the first time he saw her blonde hair and long legs.

Marc, "Come in please."

Angelique, "I rather like it. It's just like flying into clouds. While they very gently caress your skin with their ethereal touch."

Marc, "I don't recall flying through clouds as so pleasant. I have hors d'oeuvres and refreshments in the kitchen my housekeeper made for us." Leading his guests into the kitchen.

Angelique, "I hope you have some wine. I'm not in the mood for carbonated drinks." Marc having surmised this pulls out a bottle of wine from the built in wine cooler." Will a French Chenin Blanc do?"

Angelique, "So you're not so rough around the edges as I was led to believe." Marc twists the corkscrew in his strong hands quick.

Marc, "What do you mean?"

Angelique, "Well, Uncle Robert is a little critical." Both men listen with full attention. Melinda unconcerned. All the time feigning nonchalance. "He believes anyone raised outside North America is...," pausing, "not so cultured." Marc undaunted, Camel laughing. "I'm sorry you asked." Marc sets a stem in front of Melinda. She picks it up taking a sip. Her face giving a look of approval.

Melinda asks, "Didn't the two of you have a misunderstanding with customs a while back?" Giving Marc an innocent but direct look seeing if she can put him off guard.

Camel speaking up impatient with her games. "Yes. We did and it was resolved to the authorities' satisfaction." His dark eyes narrowing as he looks to Angelique. "Apparently not to your uncle's?"

Angelique, "Well, he is protective of me. Don't take it personally. I am his only niece."

Camel, "Yes. That must be it." Not trying to sound convincing.

Marc, "Shall we move to the library or are you afraid for your reputations? Hanging out with two bad boys?"

Melinda, "Not in the least. I like bad boys. Besides, I've certainly taken issue with customs myself." The foursome walking to the library already paired off. "They can be so boorish. Who cares where you picked up some jewelry? It was paid for."

Angelique, " Enough about past customs misadventures. Let's get this evening off to an exciting start."

Camel, "What did you have in mind?" His hooded brown eyes looking very sexually at her.

Angelique laughs. "Not that just yet. Nature has set the tone outside we're in a spooky old house." Camel pulls the chair out for her at the table where they are to play cards. A shiver races up his spine from the cool air rushing past. Marc holds Melinda's chair not to be outdone. After everyone is settled at the round

Federal period table. Angelique asks, "How about a game of euchre? The winner calls the next game."

Camel, "I'm not that familiar with that card game."

Melinda, "We can teach you as we play."

Marc, "I don't remember it too well either. I haven't played in years."

Angelique, "Then we'll play as couples the first game. Does that sound fair? Then it will be women against men."

Marc, "Yeah."

Camel, "That is fine. I am very good at card games once I pick them up. Some say I have a natural affinity for them."

Melinda, "What you're saying is because you're a man you'll beat a couple of dumb women."

Camel tries to keep a straight face. Failing to as a curl at the corner of his thick lips rises up into a not so subtle smirk. "I wouldn't have put it quite like that, but some of us are more adept at mathematical skills. It's just nature."

Angelique looks at him with a cool expression. "In that case I'll explain the rules and it will be women against men."

Camel, "That will do just fine. Right Marc?"

Marc, "Uh, yeah." Not sounding to convincing.

Angelique, "Good." Shuffling the cards like a blackjack dealer, cards crackling and popping up and back down. Her delicate fingers with long nails clicking against the cards. Angelique offers Marc to her right to cut the deck.

"Cut them deep to make you weep." Melinda comments after Marc cuts the deck. Angelique deals out the cards quickly sailing over the table. Three games later Camel impatiently deals out the last hand. Angelique goes at it alone taking four points for the win.

Camel, "Why don't we play something else that requires more skill?"

Angelique, "And what would that be?"

Marc speaks up quickly. "How about Texas hold 'em?"

Melinda, "I'm game if you are Angelique." Batting her long eyelashes at her partner innocently. Really an exceptional poker player. Her father having played poker for years with her learning to bluff and count cards at his side.

"Winner chooses the next game." After losing a couple more hands the guys become restless. Angelique having bided her time well, says, "Why don't we try something else after a break. There has to be something more exciting to do. Cards can only carry the evening so far. We are young and active. After all we're sitting in a library of an old house. Low fog shrouding it and a large full moon. I'm sure we can find something that will hold the boys' interest."

The women go to the powder room leaving the guys getting up to stretch. Bringing back refreshments more wine for the ladies with milk tea for themselves.

Angelique gives Melinda a knowing look like it's now or never. Why don't we have a séance?"

Melinda's expression goes from bored to excited turning to Marc. Camel none too concerned looks at Angelique. Thinking, *Yes, she is a natural blonde.* His mind racing to what's between her legs, half listening to the conversation around him. Knowing where they will end up.

Melinda, "Come on guys, it's a summer night. We need to liven things up. I don't really feel like going out to a club." Her blue eyes twinkling at Marc.

Marc, "Is that what would make you happy? We play some game where we try to scare each other?"

Melinda, "Great. Who shall we try to contact?"

Angelique, "How about your late uncle Theron. I understand the recently departed are easier to contact." Knowing how Marc would react. "Maybe we can find out what happened to him." Looking over her shoulder scrutinizing her surroundings. Just then a cold chill comes over Marc. Irritated by it he pushes an old book across the round table causing it to shimmer. That wasn't there before their break. Angelique's eyes sparkling with delight she looks to Camel enticingly. "What have we here?"

Marc, "Just some old book I hadn't noticed before. I thought maybe one of you two had put it here."

Melinda, "I think it looks interesting."

Angelique, "Yes. Marc it's yours as the master of the estate. Open it. Could it be your late uncle's?"

Marc pulls the book over opening it. "The first page has what appears to be a family tree. Starting back in the 1600s." Presenting that page to his guests. Angelique keeps her face a mask. Holding back her excitement from Marc as well as Camel.

Angelique, "See what else is in it." Marc turning the pages slowly at first.

Marc, "It's written in French and Latin." Frowning neither language easy him. Moving his right hand over the book. An unseen energy vibrates his hand as a spark snaps off static electricity? Marc jerks his hand back. The book's pages turning slowly but increases in speed until rustling past as the wind blows through them. Then just as suddenly settling to a stop. Melinda watches her breath held. Angelique's icy blue eyes follow Marc's every move.

Angelique, "It looks like a diary."

Melinda, "Are we going to have a séance or read from an old diary?" Camel gulps a drink of his tea stifling his surprise or is it fear? Marc watching his brother's reaction. Hearing his mother's words echoing, "There are dangerous secrets you need to know about our family."

Melinda picks up on their reluctance needing to give the two men a push.

"You both look reluctant, are you afraid? Two big men frightened of ghosts and evil spirits?"

Marc, "No! I'm not afraid. Something happened. Didn't you see it?"

Angelique, "No. I didn't see anything."

Melinda, "Camel. Is the big Arab ladies' man frightened?"

Camel, "Melinda I'm not afraid. I just don't believe in disturbing the dead for silly reasons."

Melinda, "If you're dead. How could you be disturbing them?"

Angelique taking charge. "First of all let's set the mood. Light those candelabras on the mantel. Marc turn off the lights." A cold draft rushes over the group at the table like a well-timed warning. Camel and Marc both stifling a shiver. Already up and across the room Melinda's laughter can be heard unexpectedly. Carrying from over at the fireplace at the other end of the room. Its white marble mantel with its fluted columns reflecting light from the candles in their candelabras igniting suddenly. "Marc dim the lights. You two big men are afraid of ghosts aren't you?" Neither one smiling anymore.

Camel, "Of course not, but I'm not so sure about this séance. Who or what would you be calling?"

Angelique, "It's just a little fun. Ease up babe." Looking at Marc her blue eyes round hinting at excitement. "Your uncle was never found. Let's see if we can contact him." Melinda returns unexpectedly fast from over at the mantel. Under shadows cast by light flickering from the candles. More like a cat in the shadows now standing next to their table. Adding to rising unease felt by two in their group.

Marc, "I don't believe in ghosts. I'm just not so sure this isn't a sin." Not sounding very convincing.

Angelique, "What can it hurt if you don't believe in that stuff." Making quotation marks in the air. "I'm sure you've made bigger sins than this questionable one or at least want to." Referring to Melinda. Marc trying not to look overly interested. "Good with that settled..." Angelique lights the candle at their table. "Let's begin." "Marc are you going to dim the lights? Use the remote."

Melinda adds, "The drapes are open so the full moon will keep it from being too dark."

Marc, "We shouldn't do this. My parents have spoken of indigenous ritual practices—," not finishing because the others' laughter drowns out his feeble attempt at thwarting what was about to happen next. "I'm surprised you are agreeing to this." His irritation directed at Camel.

Camel, "I didn't say I was approving of this." His handsome moreno face displeased not hiding it from Angelique.

Marc slams his fist down against the tabletop. "Enough of this!" Candles flicker around the room as if the force of his demand affected them. Camel looks on approvingly. Melinda's blue eyes stone cold and unflinching.

Angelique as if Marc's concerns were childish. Says, "Fine, we'll do something else." Seizing upon the old leather bound diary. Pulling it across the table with napkin in hand. "What have we here?" Opening the book its pages flutter with a life of their own as her long nailed fingers twist ever so slightly. Marc feels some relief not being comfortable with the idea of a séance. His attention drawn to her. Where did that book come from and how did it turn up? When they sat down it was not there. Was it?

Angelique, "Reduced to reading a diary with poetry in it? Is our host trying to share something with us?" Marc's olive complexion turning dusky across his cheeks.

Marc, "No. I just don't think we should mess with things we know little about."

Camel, "That is ridiculous of course we're not afraid. It's just that there is a lot more in the unseen world than you can imagine." His deep voice rising with concern.

Melinda, "And have you experienced these supernatural occurrences?" Looking very skeptically almost smirking at him. Camel feeling compelled to speak further.

"Some of the older imans would speak of legends about evil, European dark magic. When they didn't think the children were listening." His voice almost a whisper.

Suspicion crosses Marc's handsome face. "You three planned this. You set me up." Looking to Camel. "You're trying to play with my mind. That is so completely messed up. The joke is on you Mr. Khalid."

Camel, "I know nothing of this. I wasn't planning or playing any jokes on you."

Marc, "You're full of it. Don't try to pull one on me." The laughter of the women becomes contagious with all of them ending up laughing.

Angelique, "Very good. Marc you've got us. Now if the two men aren't too frightened. Can we at least explore the book to see what it has written in it?"

Melinda, "Come on Marc. I it'll be fun to see what was in the mind of some distant relative of yours."

Marc smiles impishly beginning to feel foolish. "Go for it."

Camel stands up looking over the pages from across the table. "It's written in French."

Angelique hands caressing the tome. "Yes, it's Old French and some Latin. Interesting."

Marc, "You read middle French and Latin?"

Angelique, "Oui messieurs, a vous tu?"

Marc, "Poorly, but some we've lived on the continent." Meaning himself and Camel.

Melinda, "I'm an MBA, but every good debutante speaks French." Both men give in to their blonde beauties.

Camel, "Then it must be kismet. If it pleases you go ahead. What can it hurt anyway? It's just an old diary." Looking to Angelique, he adds, "I trust we're in good hands."

Angelique, "But of course you are my love." Herself not able to wait any longer. Excitement sending thrills through her. Having waited too long already. "What have we here?

"Mihi spiritum Enkil madatum (mot d'ordre).

"The life force named Enkil I command thee..."

CHAPTER 6

MR. THORNBURG IS back at his office Sunday morning. Reviewing documents from the Du Bois estate. Opening his wall safe noticing a ring box. That's right. Theron wanted his heir to have this. Opening it to view its contents one more time. Trillion cut blue-purple tanzanites set in eighteen-carat gold with Celtic vines twining up both sides of the band ending in platinum leaves. Definitely of heirloom quality. Taking his time appreciating it. Letting his eyes linger over its sparkling stones. Removing the letter that goes with it sealed with red wax. The Du Bois family crest imprinted onto it for privacy. Theron could be so old fashioned at times. *Tomorrow I'll give Marc a call on Monday and drop these off.*

CHAPTER 7

BEING THE THIRD week of June the air is warm outside. A week since the intimate gathering with its unusual amusements. The manor's decentralized climate controls have caused the house to become drafty and cold randomly. Marc positive that something is wrong with the thermostats. One minute the bedroom is comfortable the next he can see his breath.

Sleeping in his boxer shorts. Pulling the covers back jumping out of bed. Rushing over to where the thermostat is located. *Why is it freezing in here?* Incidentally where his flannel robe is also located on the floor. Seventy-two degrees. That can't be possible exhaling a cloud of steam. Able to see his breath this room so cold. Marc calls out, "Floor heat on. Shower ninety-eight degrees." Closing the bathroom door behind him rubbing hands together to warm them up. Dropping his boxer shorts getting into the shower to warm up. The warm water feeling good. Putting his head under the spray. Unobserved something vaporous but human in shape passes in front of the mirror. Hovering there in the reflection of the mirror watching. Vanishing when Marc turns the water off. Reaching for a towel wrapping it around his waist. *Praise be Thy name, it's warm in here.* Marc saunters over to the mirror where the double basin sinks are located. Reveling in the fine black hair having grown up the middle of his rippled abdominal muscles. Connecting all the way up to his chest and spreading out over the large pectoral muscles. Once smooth. Flexing his strong biceps striking a pose. *When did I start to grow chest hair?* Not too concerned. *If this keeps up, I'll catch up with Camel.* Feeling competitive and somehow satisfied at the same time.

After a quick shave and splashing on Tommy Hilfiger. Marc steps into the bedroom which is warmer now. He crosses over to the New England highboy pulling open a drawer to grab a sleeveless tee shirt and cutoffs; the rich smell of cedar fills the air in front of the highboy. The drawers lined with it. Letting his low slung towel slide down exposing courser dark hair. Letting the towel fall to the floor. His member hanging and warm balls swinging as he walks back to the bench at the foot of the bed to dress. Sitting down placing the cell phone beside him from the dresser.

Pressing play while dressing. "Hi, it's Melinda," her voice breathy. "Call me so we can get together for lunch or dinner. I really enjoyed last Friday." Her voice sexy and feminine sending his mind racing. Pressing redial while tugging on his cutoffs before they get too tight all in a noun. Leaving her a message.

"Hi it's Marc," his voice husky. "I just took off your message. That sounds like a great idea. Call me or come by anytime." Hanging up, using his thumb to press retrieve to hear the next message.

"Message 2, received at 4:00 a.m." It's Camel's deep voice.

Deleting the message. I'll call big dog later. He probably isn't up yet. I wonder what flavor of the week he's seeing now. Time to check with Andry for my next work assignment. Sure he has something new for me today.

Marc walks into the kitchen, where Ms. Campbell is busy. "Good morning."

Ms. Campbell, "Well it's about time. I thought you were going to sleep all day. Andry has been in and gone already. He was here at 7:00 a.m. That's when I start."

Marc, "It's Sunday morning, only 9:00 a.m."

Ms. Campbell, "He starts work at 5:00 a.m. The biscuits are in the warmer drawer. You know where to find the jam and butter."

Marc is already biting into a warm buttermilk biscuit. *Um, so good.*

Ms. Campbell, "Ordinarily I wouldn't be working today. The Lord's day to worship 'n' all. But I'm needed elsewhere. So I'm grocery shopping today. Is there anything special you want me to pick up?"

Marc, "Just some Mediterranean hummus and pita bread."

Ms. Campbell, "That's it?" Marc shrugs noncommittally. "Then I'll make a pot roast with vegetables and potatoes. It will be ready by 4:00 p.m. It should be large enough to have leftovers to last you a couple of days. You can make sandwiches, plus there are other frozen meals ready to heat in the freezer. Whichever you choose. I'm off until Tuesday. You'll have to fend for yourself."

Marc, "Having a restful few days."

Ms. Campbell, "No. I volunteer at a convent in Syracuse. I prefer to use my free time helping others. Not just lying around. The gal who usually covers these days is out ill."

Marc, "I'm sure I'll be fine." Choosing not to rise to her comment.

Ms. Campbell, "Yes, I'm sure you will. There are scones in the biscuit tin. Oh by the way. Do you have to keep the house so cold? It was freezing in here when I arrived."

Marc, "It's not me. There is a problem with the thermostats. This has been happening all over the house. I've been cold too."

Ms. Campbell gives him a doubtful look, not one to overlook a chance to comment. "I'm sure Mr. Thornburg will be understanding when he gets the utility bill." Her sarcasm obvious.

Marc all the while is thinking, *And I'm sure you will be only too happy to report this to him.* Instead he says, "Yes, I'll be contacting him Monday. Is there anything you'd like me to tell him?"

Ms. Campbell, "No. I like to speak for myself. I'm off to the store." Picking up her car keys satisfied with having had the last word.

Andry ambles into the kitchen having stayed away while Ms. Campbell was giving Marc a hard time. Speaking, "Finish up your biscuits and let's get to work. The front lawn needs cutting the rhododendrons need deadheading to keep them clean looking. Besides it saves the bushes energy so they are not trying to produce seeds." Marc grabs another biscuit putting it in his mouth then picking up his coffee mug following Andry outside. Where it's already in the eighties.

Marc, "It feels great compared to that cold house."

Andry, "Wait til around noon when it gets more humid. Then we'll see how you feel then. You need to start work in the summer at sunup. That way you have most of the hard work done before the heat of the day sets in."

Marc, "That's great advice but I'm young and I don't care if it's hot outside. Not being disrespectful but I grew up in a desert climate."

Andry, "We'll see." By 11:30 a.m., the front grounds are mowed. Andry was right. The heat and humidity having risen considerably. Marc's tee shirt is soaked through from perspiration all the way into the waist of his cutoffs. His dark straight hair is dripping wet. Time to find some shade and a cold drink of water. Tugging at his shirt which is sticking to his back hot and aggravating. Yanking it over his head pulling his bandana off with it. His muscular chest glistening from perspiration with fine dark hair scattered sparsely over it just visible. Marc looks like a construction worker. Melinda pulls up the driveway lowering the electric window in her white Porsche. Whistling at him. Marc looks up surprised then giving her one of his bright smiles.

Melinda shouts out the window with her best Bronx accent, "Hey, Mack! I'm lookin' for a gardener to tend my private gardens." Marc strolls over pushing a hand through his hair slicking it back out of his face. Looking like a GQ model and very French. His body tan from working out in the sun. Melinda appreciating his chiseled male form. By definition sculpted.

Marc leans over into her open window. "You looking for some help ma'am?"

Melinda, "It's sweaty work but the benefits are good. You interested?" Keeping her D&G sunglasses in place. Using her hand to shade the hot noon sun off her face. Marc stands up straight putting his hands in his back pockets leaning back tightening up his abdominal muscles. Melinda takes a moment longer to glance across at Marc. Not wanting to appear too eager. She pulls her

Porsche into the shade of a towering hemlock. Marc recognizes her hard to get bluff. So he saunters over with long legged slow steps.

Marc, "Yes, ma'am. I am looking for a position with fringe benefits." Leaning against the car looking at Melinda. His face tan high cheekbones made more angular because of the sun. His blue eyes dark and smiling promising much more.

Melinda keeping her passion just low enough not to be over eager. "Um. I love a sweaty man."

"Then you're in luck. Come on, let's go inside. I'm thirsty." Melinda parks her car quickly. Once they're inside the hallway Melinda reaches up pulling Marc's head forward until their lips meet. Heatedly kissing as both of their pulses quicken. Marc enjoying her taste. Her lips quivering against his catching his breath. Bursting through the door Ms. Campbell carrying grocery bags clearing her throat. Startling both of them. Marc's cheeks turning dusky.

Ms. Campbell never at a loss for words. "I could use some help if you two lovebirds could stop for a moment." Melinda in one blink of an eye cutting a glare back at her. Marc's cheeks turn redder. After the groceries are in Marc quickly gulps a bottle of water down. Taking another drinking more slowly. Ms. Campbell was putting groceries away. Melinda looks questioningly at Marc. Her expression changing to a sultry longing look. Marc catching on takes the lead. "Now that you're all set we have some unfinished business to attend to." Ms. Campbell glances dourly in the kitchen mirror at the couple. *Like I don't know what they are up to, business my foot.* Making an "uh" sound not responding.

The two already out of the kitchen and around the corner sneaking a long kiss reigniting the fire that was already smoldering. Later that afternoon lying quietly together in Marc's bed both a little sleepy and relaxed.

Melinda, "I have to get up. I've got studies and a lab practical to get ready for." Not looking at Marc as she slides over to the side of the mattress. Standing up wiggling into her tiny black bikini underwear. Confident Marc is watching. Then leaning over to pick up her cotton summer top off the floor. Looking from the corner of her eye to see him hungrily watching her.

Marc finally speaking, "Yeah, I have to go finish up out front." Melinda smiles at him allowing her eyes to linger on him. Examining his physical appearance taking note. He does have the beginnings of dark body hair but not too much. However, he has a good head of hair thick and a little longer from the last time she saw him, but not thinning on top. Marc believing she is as taken with him as he is with her.

Melinda, "On second thought. Do you mind if I shower first?"

Marc, "No, go ahead." His blue eyes fixed on her. "Why don't we shower together?" His excitement showing beneath the covers. Melinda confident in her control over most men. Why would he be the exception? Why not use such a wonderful specimen of a man. Not really a question at all. If she got into his psyche stronger, then it would give her more control over him. Allowing her to channel all his raw energy. It's almost a shame; they could have been a real power couple. Allowing herself to consider the luxury of his suggestion. Weakening, she gives him a sexy look.

"Sounds good to me." Shivering. "Wow, you really like to keep it cool in here." The moment almost broken, having the vaguest impression of something but not quite a presence near. Casually letting her corn silk like hair fall over her face covering one eye. Turning her head slowly searching for the source, not finding anything.

Marc, " I thought it was me."

Melinda still wary, "Is something wrong with the thermostat?" Two bulges pressing out of her cotton top.

Marc, "Come here and I'll warm you up. You won't need to take that shower. I can heat you up." Melinda gives him a look. Marc gets up taking her hand. "Follow me." Calling out, "Shower on, temperature ninety-eight degrees." Water pours out forming a cloud of steam rising up from the open shower. Both stepping into the warm spray. Marc lifts her up into his arms kissing her. Melinda wraps her legs around his waist. A steamy cloud engulfing them.

Later after their shower while toweling dry. Marc says, "Dinner should be ready if you're interested in eating."

Melinda, "If I stay any longer I won't be able to study." Marc starts to speak, Melinda placing a finger over his thick lips stopping him. "I'll be too relaxed. You know how summer courses are time compressed with frequent tests."

Marc relenting. "Fine," sounding disappointed. "I'll go back to work. Let me walk you to your car." Once they are in the side hallway away from the prying eyes of Ms. Campbell. Melinda kisses Marc goodbye before opening the door to the courtyard parking where she left her Porsche. Their bodies pressed together for one final embrace. Marc holds Melinda in his strong arms gently kissing her lips then working his way down her neck. They feel each other's heat rising again.

Melinda thrilled but not wanting things heating up too much, pushes him away. "I have to go. You are one hot blooded male." Marc places his hand over his heart like he's been stabbed through it. Melinda walks away then turns back smiling. "Call me soon."

Marc, "I will, bye." Standing in the doorway wearing just work boots and cutoffs. He is tough to walk away from. Melinda looks once more from her car as she pulls away. Marc's handsome face set in a very sexual expression unmoving watching her leave. She waves goodbye shifting gears rushing down the driveway.

Marc slips his bandana on going back to work at the front of the property. Needing to finish up for the day. Stomach growling and his appetite ravenous. Pushing on in the heat and humidity still rising with the afternoon sun. Beads of perspiration covering his body. Dripping into his eyes burning them. His back stinging as the sweat runs into the long scratches across it. Pulling his tee shirt dangling from his back pocket to wipe his eyes, burning maddeningly. Then using it across his back pulling it away finding it blood tinged. Surprised at first then realizing something had scratched him. Just miserable the humidity so high. His waist wet with perspiration dripping down between his round firm buttocks, tickling. Ms. Campbell pulls down the driveway in her late model station wagon spotting Marc. *Huh, I would never have expected that he was such a hard worker.*

She slows to a stop calling out, "If you stop work now dinner will be hot." Marc hearing her saunters over. Ms. Campbell continues, "You can finish up tomorrow."

Marc, "I will. I just have a few more things to finish up. Then I'll knock off." Turning to go back to his work.

Ms. Campbell sees his back up close astonished for a moment but recovering quickly. Sighing, speaking under her breath, "Typical male pig. Any little whore that puts out and he's all over her." Turning left out onto East Avenue.

Marc already with the side door open ready to enter the house. Hearing the roar of a sports car he turns in time to see a blur. As Camel's black Ferrari screeches by sliding into a parking space perfectly. Marc speaking to him, "Man, as soon as the food is ready you're here." Smiling broadly his white teeth contrasting with his heavy five o'clock shadow.

Camel, "That's right. It smells great." Pushing past Marc into the hallway. "Um, beef and garlic. When do we eat?"

Marc, "Now."

Camel feeling playful, "From the looks of you, you must have been working outside all day. Right? Or at least part of it." Marc looks at him questioningly. "Who was over? Melinda?"

Marc, "What? How did you know?"

Camel, "Have you looked in a mirror?" Marc turns his head to look over his shoulder using the hall mirror to see what his brother is talking about. "Those scratches look deep on your back."

Marc, "Damn. My back was stinging outside."

Camel, "Perspiration in scratches usually does. Oh, by the way, you stink too." Fanning his nose. Marc ignores his last comment.

"Yeah, Melinda did drop by for a while." Smiling

Camel, "Real good, play it coy. It looks like she was here for longer than a while. And look love bites on your neck."

Marc, "She is hot."

Camel, "She's a tomcat from the looks of you."

Marc, "You were right. She knows her way around the bed. Now let me take a quick shower and we'll eat."

Camel already making himself at home chooses a bottle of Bordeaux from a small wine rack in the butler's pantry. Cutting the seal then twisting in the corkscrew. "Make sure you use plenty of soap on those scratches. You don't want an infection or an ingrown hair. They look a little deep in places."

Marc, "Yeah, I'll be right back." Thinking to himself, *I'm not that hairy. I don't have any hair on my back.*

After dinner Marc and Camel move to the great room. Which faces the garden in the rear of the property. Both quietly absorbed in their own thoughts.

Camel ends the silence. "Is Melinda always that rough during sex?" His brown eyes black pools in the fading evening light.

Marc takes a moment to gather his thoughts. "No. Not that Sunday the first time we were together. Now that you mention it. I had bite marks on my chest." Camel listens intently. "I had to tell her to go easier and she kept telling me to bite her nipples harder. It was a little disturbing. But she is so exciting in the bed." Camel nods his head in agreement. "Today I didn't notice. I was just so horny and into pleasing her. It's almost like I couldn't have stopped myself if I had wanted to. Just couldn't get enough." Camel gives him a knowing look.

Camel, "Yes, I know all too well. It's called being male. I'm that way all the time now. Myself, I like wearing women out. You should try twins sometime if the chance presents itself."

Marc, "How is it you get lucky enough to get twins? But more than one set."

Camel, "Women like me."

Marc, "You are the charmer."

Camel, "Now back to the subject of Melinda. Be careful of her. She may be a sadist and this was just the warm up to tying you down to the bed. Not that a couple of silk scarves around my wrists hasn't happened." Marc looking surprised. "I prefer hands on but if you are going to try that. You really need to trust her. Especially if she's going to tie you up."

Marc, "The more I hear the kinkier you sound. I'm not into all that." Shaking his head.

Camel, "I'm not either but some experimentation can spice things up."

Marc, "What's up with you and Angelique? Everything copacetic with her?"

Camel, "Yes, we've been very hot and heavy. Now that I think about it. Since Sunday she's been using foreign words. Latin maybe in this soft singing voice when we were doing it. It's almost like since that night she let out a side I've never been allowed to see before. Lighting candles and incense. She makes these herbal teas for me to drink before we make love. She said they would make our lovemaking more intense for the both of us. There is no doubt it works. She is like something unhinged when we climax together. She is so giving and so willing to please. She was never that way before."

Marc, "It sounds like you have it pretty good. Melinda burned some incense this afternoon. If it makes her more tractable, I say go for it."

Camel, "To tell you the truth that's not the half of it. The only problem bothering me is she's become too clingy. So I'm trying to let things cool off some. I haven't returned her calls in a couple of days. I went out to Hooters Wednesday night and met these two women. They were in town for a contest. The winnings are to help them pay for premed."

Marc, "I've heard of some creative ways to pay for college. You slept with them both didn't you?" Shaking his head.

Camel, "Yes, I did. You know me. A couple of weeks with the same woman is a long time."

Marc, "You have been seeing her for months."

Camel, "A long time for me. Anyway, I invited them to stay at my place. Friday night we went out together. Then after the contest we spent the night together. Saturday they left to go back home."

Marc, "You are a male whore. Do you ever rest?"

Camel, "Do you? I think I'm sexually addicted. I just can't help myself. Now it's like I'm a magnet. Women just seem drawn to me." His handsome face concerned. Marc is listening so he continues. "I have groupies at the dance club now."

Marc, "That's incredibly hot. What am I saying? Back to the subject of Angelique. She doesn't come off as the type of woman who will put up with that."

Camel, "I can manage her. Besides, what's she going to do to me? If she can't tolerate my popularity, well then, she's not the right one." Changing the subject. "How fast does your hair grow?"

Marc, "I don't know. Why?"

Camel, "Look at mine. You know I keep it short, but it's almost as if my hair grows every time I have sex. Look at this." Raising his shirt up in front to reveal very thick straight black hair covering his abdomen all the way up to his chest.

Marc, "The hair on your head is long for you, but your body? You're Middle Eastern. It's probably just hormones increasing with your age and genetics. Men get hairy as they get older."

Camel, "Like this? Look at you. Your hair is getting long for you. You always looked like an iman's son. Now you're almost a heathen. Are you resting much?" His meaning clear to Marc.

Marc, "I'm not out every night with a different female. Though I'm not saying no to Melinda either."

Camel, "Enough said. I'm staying home tonight. I'm bored with the bar scene. I have been having some strange dreams. Last night was the worst."

Marc, "What are they about?"

Camel, " You remember the twin models I introduced you to."

Marc, "How could I forget them? Go ahead."

Camel, "Well, I dreamed they died in a terrible car accident that Angelique was responsible for."

Marc, "That sounds like a guilty conscience manifesting itself in your dreams."

Camel becoming defensive. "We're not committed. So I don't feel guilty. Besides, I'm sure she sleeps with other men when it suits her. She exerts her right to be independent."

Marc, "So what did she do to cause the accident?"

Camel, "I think she cut the brake lines. I tried to stop her but I couldn't. She kept telling me how it was my fault. That I had to be taught a lesson about control."

Marc, "Angelique would never do anything that got her hands dirty. Much less anything that might break one of her perfectly manicured fingernails. That's how I know it was just a bad dream. Messed up but the truth. Still not like her."

Camel, "You've got a point. She'd hire someone to do it."

Later that evening as Marc is settling into bed. He begins to remember a dream about a women. What was it? Uncle Theron kept telling him something. Stop the powerful force before it is too late? There was something unsettling about her as she kept calling to him in French, "Mon fils, come to me." But Uncle Theron interrupts her. Somehow she is familiar yet still frightening. Her voice soothing almost mesmerizing finding he can't ignore it. Then she reaches out with her long nailed hand for him to take. His uncle's voice loudly proclaiming what? A power? That's what it was. She is trying to control him and if he continues, Uncle Theron won't be able to help him stop it. Marc's eyes too heavy to stay open any longer he dozes off to sleep. So very tired from today.

CHAPTER 8

MONDAY MORNING MARC wakes up sprawled across his bed. Shivering in the air cold enough to see his breath. The covers pushed off onto the floor. Rolling out of bed wearing just boxer shorts he dashes to the bathroom. Checking the thermostat en route seventy-two degrees. Exhaling his breath a visible cloud. That can't be right. Speaking out to the spa system, "Floor heat on. Shower ninety-eight degrees." Closing the door behind him. Steam rising up from the shower. Shivering as he drops his boxers stepping into the welcoming warmth. So nice and warm.

Freshly showered Marc goes downstairs to the kitchen. Pulling open the biscuit tin taking out a couple of scones. Then opening the refrigerator taking the milk out. Opening the gallon jug taking a swig of milk directly from its container. No one there to see him. Its taste bitter. Rushing over to the sink spitting it out. "It's sour!" Washing his mouth out with water repeatedly spitting into the sink.

Andry comes into the kitchen. "Good to see you up. I was beginning to worry. I thought I was going to have to come upstairs and check on you. But I can see you had a late night." Winking at Marc. Seeing the marks on his neck. Marc unsure of what Andry is talking about. Seeing the time on the kitchen clock, 12:15. Surprised.

Marc, "It can't be that late. That would mean I slept half the day away."

Andry, "You are correct on both counts." Checking his wristwatch. "I have made a list of the chores you need to take care over the next couple of days. Since you like to sleep late and I'm up early."

Marc, "Fine," taking the list.

Andry, "First you're going to replace the forsythias that died this past winter. Replacing them with native and Asian witch hazel. This is what your uncle had planned on years ago."

Marc, "My uncle seems to have had a lot of plans that went unfinished."

Andry, "That's true. This particular American witch hazel has orange blossoms and the Asian variety has red. They both bloom in late winter into early spring."

Marc, "This list is extensive. Are you not going to be around for a few days?"

Andry, "My wife Oksana isn't doing well. One of the nurses called from Saint Andrew's this morning."

Marc, "I'm sorry to hear that. I hope she improves."

Andry, "Yes, I am praying and hoping for that also. Bring the plant list to De Ville's Nursery. I trust you can pick out healthy shrubs. Order the cypress mulch sixty bags and nine yards of compost. They will deliver it here."

Marc, "If you need anything, just let me know."

Andry, "Thank you." Being a very private man with that said he turns and leaves.

After returning from De Ville's Marc picks up the local newspaper from beside the side door. Opening it out on the granite counter to read. While he's heating some leftovers in the microwave. He takes a Labatt Blue out of the refrigerator twisting the top off taking a swig. *Oh so good and cold.* Leaning across the stone counter. Reading the front page headline, "Twin Sisters Die in Fatal Car Accident." Skimming down the page. "While two others remain in guarded condition at Strong Memorial Hospital."

Turning to the sports section. "Yankee fans in for a great surprise."

Marc's cell phone ringing pressing the screen to answer the call. "Hello."

Mr. Thornburg, "Hello Marc. How are you?" Sounding his usual smug self. Young people are so predictable. "Andry left me a message. He was having you order supplies for the grounds. I approved the order with De Ville's."

Marc, "Right, how are you?"

Mr. Thornburg, "Oh I'm busy. There is always someone in trouble. I trust you're getting along with Andry."

Marc, "Uh yeah. He thinks I should be up at dawn working. Like I'm on a farm."

Mr. Thornburg, "People get set in certain patterns such as waking up early. It becomes a habit getting up early for work. Something I'm sure you're unfamiliar with growing up as you did. In a palace with servants."

Marc holds his irritation in check out of respect for his elder. Mr. Thornburg continuing with his presumption of correctness. "That seems to happen when you have to work for a living. Then you get older and you're still doing it. Andry was raised on a farm in the Ukraine. I had some distant cousins we visited. They were raised the same. Their father expected them to be up. He had them up before dawn to get chores done before school. As I recall in the summer they wanted the hard labor done before the heat of the day rises."

Marc, "I know. I've heard that speech before. I'm young. Plus I don't care if it's hot outside. Remember I was raised in the desert."

Mr. Thornburg, "I haven't forgotten at all. Then at least recognize this. Andry has always kept that place up for the past forty years. Since he and

Oksana came there. At least before she had her stroke. She kept that house in order and was a great cook. Her homemade potato perogies were as good as my grandmother's. Let alone she made a fine borscht."

Marc, "I'm sure in their day—"

Mr. Thornburg cutting him off. "Andry deserves the respect due someone his age. Your uncle understood loyalty from staff."

Marc, "I wasn't suggesting otherwise. I would never disrespect my elders."

Mr. Thornburg, "Good, as long as we have that understood."

Marc, "As long as I have you on the phone. There is a problem with the climate control. Several of the thermostats need to have their tolerances checked."

Mr. Thornburg, "Why is it too hot in the manor? Ms. Campbell informed me you have been keeping it very cold in there. You need to keep thermostats set at seventy-two degrees."

Marc, "That is the problem."

Mr. Thornburg not letting him finish, "I control household expenses and you will not run up the utility bills."

Marc, "I have not changed them and it is still too cold."

Mr. Thornburg, "I have a service contract with Stevens and Sons. I'll have them out there today. They are very thorough. If anyone can get to the bottom of this problem, it's them.

"Is that all? I'm sure this conversation is drawing to a conclusion."

Marc, "Have you heard anything from my parents?"

Mr. Thornburg, "No. Why should I? We communicate when it is necessary. That could be months to years. As long as everything is going well. You do know how to contact them at their respective embassies in the country they are working from. Don't you do have contacts already set up?" Not waiting for Marc to respond. "I know they don't want to be bothered unless it's something serious."

Marc, "I know. Only if someone is dead or dying."

Mr. Thornburg, "Or their son is arrested for drunken brawling at some dignitary's home. Maybe detained by Interpol and under investigation by INS. You have become mixed up in some shady goings on again?"

Marc frustrated, "That incident at their party wasn't my fault. People shouldn't make fun of other cultures and how they dress." The anger rising in his voice. "You weren't there. Besides, what would you know about Islam? As for the INS incident. That was a misunderstanding we had over import laws."

Mr. Thornburg, "Yes, it is amazing how chock-full the courts are of misunderstandings and confusion over laws. You're right. I wasn't there, but all I have to do is watch the news to get an idea of your...," stopping himself. "Next time use your words, not your fists." Marc very heated now breathing heavily.

Mr. Thornburg takes the silence as acquiescence, so he continues. "Criminal records future employers frown on. They don't care about the why. They just won't hire you. At least at reputable companies."

Marc still hot, "I thought you were influential, as Dad puts it."

Mr. Thornburg, "I don't call in favors for petty crimes or for international criminals. However they do pay my bills. At least the ones I choose to represent." His tone impatient.

Marc, "I'm not planning any illegal acts anytime soon." Glad the cards are out on the table. Always having felt this man the family attorney didn't like him.

Mr. Thornburg, "If there is anything else you wish to discuss, you will need to contact my secretary. I bill out at five hundred dollars an hour." Dismissively the phone connection ends with a click.

Marc is still hot under the collar. "What a dick!" Shouting to the empty house. Slamming his cell phone down.

Later that evening sitting in the library examining the redesigned layout of the private garden. Which Mr. Thornburg had been kind enough to fax over. Marc wonders how many plans did his uncle Theron have that were incomplete? This one having a fourteen foot tall pergola on the west side of the terrace. A stone seating wall in front of it planted with pink roses. Hardy kiwi covering the pergola. The terrace to be circular made from Kentucky Crab Orchard flagstone. Interesting, inset with pink granite at seventy-two degree arcs with a total of five. The first one starting at the north. *What, he couldn't trust me to handle the ordering?* Mr. Thornburg have already faxed it to the local stone yard. Marc's cell rings and he checks the number before answering. It's Andry, so he accepts the phone call.

Andry, "Good you picked up. I'm not going to be coming home tonight." His usually strong voice soft pain choked. "The nursing staff don't think my Oksana is going to make it through the night."

Marc, "Is there anything I can do?"

Andry, "Neyt." Pausing his throat sore from choking back tears. Not being the type of man to show his emotions. "Just work from the list you will do just fine."

Marc, "I know, don't worry about this place. Take as long as you need. Stay with your wife where she needs you there."

Andry, "Thank you for being so understanding. I will keep you informed."

Marc, "Seriously, if you need anything at all. A ride or someone to talk to even at two in the morning, don't hesitate to call me."

Andry, "Thank you, I will. Dasvedonya (Good-bye)."

Marc hangs up the phone sitting at the round Federal period table. Where only a few weeks ago they were having so much fun. Silence of the enormous house engulfing him. The only sound from the rustling of the plans in front of him as the climate control kicks in. Quietly blowing a breeze across them. Life can change so quickly. Marc wonders what he would do if someone he had spent his entire life with was dying. Gathering up the plans to go upstairs and retire to his master suite. His refuge from the world. Not ever remembering feeling so lonely. But first setting the alarm system with its movement sensors inside and outside. So many responsibilities coming from all directions. Emptying his pockets out on the dresser. Then Marc strips down to his boxer shorts. Turning the covers back piling his pillows up. Getting into his soft memory foam bed pulling just the sheet up waist high. Spreading papers out around him on the bed. Glancing at the answering machine with its digital display blinking two messages. Reaching over to the nightstand pressing play.

The preprogrammed voice feminine. "Message one."

It's Camel. "Marc, are we still meeting for our kickboxing workout tomorrow? I have a lot of aggression to work out so watch out. Call me." Beep.

"Message two."

Camel again. "You are not going to believe this. I just read the news online. Do you remember my dream I was telling you about? It came true. I know the accident victims." His voice stressed. Marc deletes the messages, seeing the portable phone not on the charger. Getting out of bed to use his cell. Which he placed on the dresser but never plugged in to charge. The symbols indicating low batteries. *Great!* Retrieving the message waiting for him on that phone.

"Hi stud it's Melinda. I just wanted the last voice you heard tonight to be mine. I'll be dreaming of you. Bye." Her voice so breathy. Marc smiling having a little wicked thought. Turning the cell on keying in under his favorites Camel's number pressing dial. Getting his voice mail recording. So leaving a brief message. Then turning the phone off plugging it into the charger. Getting settled back into bed against the pillows piled against the headboard. Reviewing the plans for the private terraced garden. Getting sleepy with the cool breeze caressing him. After the hot day's work outside it feels incredible. Pages around him move slightly crinkling. His eyes becoming heavy the words and design blur in and out of focus. It's so quiet and peaceful his eyes close. The smart bulb timer winks on and off after thirty minutes. It's a silent warning lights out. Winking off darkness surrounding Marc except for the gape in the drapes where a slant of moonlight is shining through.

Around midnight the temperature in the bedroom begins to drop. Only its digital display on the thermostat bears witness to the phenomenon. Beeping softly as the numbers go down. Almost as someone would reset the temperature lower. Marc's breath slow and steady streaming out forming into a humid misty cloud. A shadowy figure appears hovering at the foot of his bed. Marc's slumbering form unaware of the intruder. Watching thoughtful with conscious intentions. Gliding over Marc's sleeping body. His chest rising and falling in a slow but steady rhythm. Mumbling in his sleep with restless legs moving. Finally still his body betraying him. Paralyzed and helpless as his sleep goes into REM. Only his eyes moving under their lids. The time close now as the dark figure gathers into a seething mass over Marc. Nearly invisible except for blocking out the LED display from the answering machine and the moonbeam. Sinking toward his vulnerable exposed chest. The dark fine hair bristling up as if instinctually reacting to danger on some primal level. Biding its time this malevolent being. Marc inhales. As if on signal the cloud flows into him. His breath stalls as the last of it feels his lungs, his body, and his mind. Wind gathers around them swirling pulling papers up into the air then suspended. His covers sliding off the bed crumpling on the floor. Drapes rippling in the wake scattering moonlight around the room. An eerie spectral form of Marc rising outside his body, light in color.

CHAPTER 9

TUESDAY 7 00 A.M., Ms. Campbell carries a silver tray with coffee in a chambord and fine English china. Shifting the tray to one hand she knocks on the master suite door. Knocking harder after not getting a response quick enough. She pushes open the door. Having taken care of priests. She's not too timid about entering a man's room. Stepping on papers strewn across the floor. Slipping on them so she slows down. The room is too dark to see clearly in and she does not want to trip and fall. Then she steps on the covers beside the bed. Irritated, she places the tray noisily on the table beside the windows. Feeling for the drapery cord giving it a good pull. Morning sunlight flooding the room from eastern windows. Seeing Marc's motionless form with his head buried under pillows.

Ms. Campbell calls out, "Time to rise and shine." His body unmoving. Staring at the fine dark hair across his shoulders running all the way down his spine past the waistband of his boxers. His dad must be one hairy beast. Regaining herself, she speaks louder, "You need to wake up sleepyhead!" Marc wakes with a start. His head jerking sending pillows falling off the bed. Lifting his head up.

Marc, "What time is it?"

Ms. Campbell, "It's 7:00 a.m. and you have a busy day ahead of you. My goodness you like to keep this room cold." Shivering. Marc blocking the sunlight from his eyes with his hand. "My niece will be arriving from London today. She goes to a girls' parochial school. So she has led a sheltered life." Handing Marc the sheet off the floor. Marc not responding so she continues. "I expect you two young men to treat her accordingly. She will be here to help me get this place cleaned and opened up."

Marc sitting on the side of the bed leans over putting his head in his hands. Looking all of hungover to Ms. Campbell. "It's just too much for me to do by myself." Walking away from him picking up clothes off the floor gathering them in her arms. "Breakfast will be ready in thirty minutes. Buttermilk biscuits with turkey sausage and eggs. You'll need a hardy breakfast for today." Walking out the door. Marc gets up letting the sheet fall to the floor stretching his muscular body yawning. Stepping over to the table pushing the plunger on the chambord. The aroma of fresh coffee wafts up to him. Smelling so good. Thinking, *What happened to me?* It feels like he lost a kickboxing match. The scratches on his back already healed completely. Pouring coffee into the china cup. Slurping it to cool it some. *Um, so good, Colombian supremo.*

After finishing his coffee he dresses for the day's work outside. Blue jeans with a sleeveless tee shirt and stuffing a bandana in his back pocket. Rushing down stairs the smell of sage meets him. Marc's stomach growling realizes how hungry he is. Entering the kitchen Marc says, "That smells great! I'm starving. There won't be any leftovers today."

Ms. Campbell, "Breakfast is the king of meals. I love a man with a good appetite. I'm glad you're not one of those pantywaists. Who hardly eat. Dig in." Passing Marc a plate heaped with scrambled eggs and sausages. Pulling the biscuits out of the oven and dumping them into a basket. Placing it beside Marc's plate. Marc is already eating ravenously shoveling in large mouthfuls followed by a hot fresh bite of biscuit. Ms. Campbell smiles proudly. "You need to slow down there's plenty. No one is going to take it away from you."

Spending the better part of the morning spreading cypress mulch and planting summer annuals marigolds, zinnias, and petunias. From graphed out diagrams that Andry designed with every intention of putting the estate back in the Rochester Garden Club tours list. Color and placement to create patterns and shapes. Marc does not have any idea how much thought some people put into their gardens. Of benefit an overcast sky of gray had helped to keep the temperature down but not necessarily the humidity. A small break from the past two days' heat. Yet he still had already broken a good sweat. His bandana was soaked as well as his tee shirt along with the waist of his jeans. His skin was darkening even with an overcast sky being of Cajun descent.

Ms. Campbell comes outside with a pitcher of iced tea. Saying, "Drink some, you have to stay hydrated even on overcast days. It's also lunchtime. Come in and eat while you cool off. You need to keep your strength up."

Marc, "Okay just a few more minutes." Pulling his shirt off to get some air being too warm. His chest hair wet from perspiration dripping off him. His body hair becoming gradually more pronounced.

Camel pulls into the driveway in his red Ferrari from last year. Lowering his window. Whistling at him, then speaking. "You look like a construction worker."

Ms. Campbell, "Hello, Camel. There's nothing wrong with an honest day's work. You should try doing it sometime." The irritation in her voice apparent. Not waiting for him to respond, she turns and walks back into the house. Muttering under her breath, "Spoilt rich foreigners. that's what is wrong with this country." Marc walks over with a long legged strut. Smiling unaware of how striking he looks with his face tanned and his dark blue eyes.

Marc, "Yeah, whatever she said. And why is it you're always on time for food even when you haven't been invited. Especially once the work is done."

Camel smiles and rolls his eyes a little. "It's good Karma."

Marc, "What's so good about you?"

Camel, "Hum, I can find fast women and food." Nodding at him. "The ladies seem to know what is good about me. Does a man need anything else other than that?"

Marc, "You know I can't disagree with you on that. Come on let's eat, big dog. Sweet ride. It still has that new car smell and showroom shine." Marc does a hood slide across. Ready to get in the passenger side.

Camel stops him. "Not like that. You're not. I don't want sweat stains on the leather seats. Besides you need a shower." Pulling off before Marc can object. Leaving him to walk up to the house.

Both young men walk into the kitchen together. Ms. Campbell says, "Lunch is being served in the dining room." Making a face at Marc. Marc gives her a questioning look. "That way you two can talk as young men do, about young women."

Camel, "He's always been a little slow on the uptake." Marc gives him his best hurt face.

Ms. Campbell, "You both could do with being a little slower. If you get my meaning."

Camel, "Now you sound like my second mother."

Marc, "Yes, just like mom."

Ms. Campbell, "Common sense is just good behavior with morals. Living your life fast can come to no good. Mark my words you two." Walking away huffy.

The two men eat ravenously in silence. After a second set of sandwiches are gobbled down,

Marc speaks. "You left a message that sounded important. I tried calling you."

Camel, "I took your message off this morning. Do you remember the twins I brought by the other day?"

Marc, "How could I forget them."

Camel, "Do you remember the dream I told you about? How they died in a car accident. That was the twins. It made the front page story."

Marc, "That's not possible you're making it up."

Camel, "Where is your Sunday newspaper?"

Ms. Campbell clearing away dishes overhears the conversation. "It's in the recycle bin. I'll get it."

Marc, "No, seriously. I usually read the sports section."

Camel, "They were the two people killed in a car accident Saturday night. I couldn't believe it myself until I read their names."

Ms. Campbell returning with the newspaper, "Here you are." Handing it to Marc. "Why are you interested in that horrible accident? Those poor girls and their families."

Camel, "Right here. We knew them, Starr and Amy. It's so incredible to know them alive and now they are gone."

Marc, "It has to be some kind of weird coincidence. That you would dream it and then it comes true. You should try to remember more details if you can. To see how accurate you can be."

Camel, "I'm not sure how much more I want to come back. It was all nonlinear what I do remember. It's all enough to make me not sleep well."

Marc, "Join the club. I didn't sleep well myself last night. This house gets so cold at odd times in different locations."

Camel, "It feels good to me. It's hot outside."

Marc, "I don't mean now. It's always when I'm alone. Just like last night it starts off good. Then it's freezing cold and I have nightmares."

Camel, "Really? What are they about?"

Marc, "I hear my uncle's voice but I can't see him. Telling me something about needing to protect myself from this woman. She's actually a little scary. A darkness surrounds her. Uncle Theron tells me not to trust her."

Camel, "Who could this woman be? Someone from your past?" Marc finds himself annoyed by Camel's lack of seriousness.

Marc, "I have to get back to work." Standing up.

Camel, "No seriously."

Ms. Campbell walks in with the heating and cooling repairmen. Introducing Marc. "This is Mr. Du Bois." Marc extends his hand taking the others' with a firm handshake.

"Adam Stevenson and this is my son Drew."

Camel standing up, "I'll talk to you later." Ready to go out to his car.

Drew, "What seems to be the trouble Mr. Du Bois?"

"Call me Marc, otherwise I won't answer because I'll be waiting for Dad to speak. This place is freezing at times. I don't feel the digital reading for temperature could be accurate."

Adam, "Fair enough." Nodding his head, Drew smiling. "We will check out all of the servers connected to the temperature controls on equipment for each control zone. But I have to say this is a first in the summer with a large house. We usually only get these kind of complaints when its winter."

Marc, "The last couple of weeks I can see my breath when I wake up."

"What did the thermostat read?" Drew asks.

"Seventy-two degrees."

"Your breath sometimes is not a good indicator of that. It's just humidity," Drew says.

"Please just check it out." Looking to Camel, Marc says, "I'll see you later I'm sure. I have a lot to do outside."

Later that afternoon, Mr. Thornburg comes by to drop off the ring and sealed envelope to give to Marc. Walking on the grass to avoid getting his polished wing tips dirty. Thinking to himself when he sees Marc, *Definitely not an heir to a multimillion-dollar estate.* This house being just the tip of the Du Bois holdings in real estate. Marc notices him approaching but does not acknowledge him yet. He's the picture of a typical conservative lawyer. Wearing a navy blue pinstriped Versace suit with starched white shirt and cuffs with his red power tie. Marc's face is dirt smudged dark and stubble covered. His sleeveless tee shirt soaked with perspiration down his chest. Hair sticking out from under the bandana dripping with sweat. Marc looks up to acknowledge his presence.

Mr. Thornburg, "Hello Marc. I see you are hard at work." Holding out the letter with the ring box. Marc pulls off his work gloves reaching for it his hands still dirty. Mr. Thornburg takes a step back so as to not come in contact with him. His expression one of disgust.

Marc answers him, "Yeah, it's hard dirty work. Isn't that the lesson I was to learn from this?"

Mr. Thornburg, "You are to learn responsibility and to respect your family position."

Marc, "Are you familiar with the eighteenth-century table in the study? That's where I sit and work on plans for this place."

Mr. Thornburg, "Yes, I will place it there. Don't forget this ring should be in a safe. This envelope is sealed for privacy for the heir's eyes only."

Ms. Campbell rushes outside with a silver tray carrying iced ice in a crystal pitcher (Baccarat) and crystal tea glasses. "I knew you could use some liquids as hard as you're working. Mr. Thornburg, would you care for some tea?"

Mr. Thornburg, "No thank you. I came by to drop off some personal effects of Theron's. That Marc is to receive. How is the house coming?"

Ms. Campbell, "Pretty well, but it is larger than I was led to believe. And there's a lot more cleaning to be done. I'm going to get some help. Your niece Angelique was kind enough to suggest it."

Mr. Thornburg, "Oh really? She must have overlooked mentioning it to me." His expression softening.

Ms. Campbell, "I'm sure it just slipped her mind. I've sent for my niece from outside London."

Mr. Thornburg, "Did she say where the money was coming from? I wasn't made aware of the increase in household budget."

Ms. Campbell, "She is working for me as a family favor. Since I need the help. Angelique said you wouldn't mind, seeing as to how it's no cost to the estate. Well, maybe some food when she is here working. Due to turn eighteen soon. She won't be any trouble."

Mr. Thornburg, "I hope not. It won't be tolerated."

Ms. Campbell, "She has been in Catholic parochial schools all her life. My late sister's child. She can earn her keep right here. Instead of languishing the summer away in the convent." Her smile almost cruel, catching herself. "Those nuns don't need all the help for free. She can earn her keep right here. While she waits to start college. Besides it doesn't have to be this fall. She can start next year in January if need be."

Mr. Thornburg appearing very satisfied with this arrangement, "When can she get here to start?"

Ms. Campbell, "She'll be her in a day or two."

Mr. Thornburg, "Once she's settled in bring her over."

Ms. Campbell, "She won't need time to settle. I will put her to work right away. There's no reason for her to lie around costing me money. Not when she can be saving us and helping me. Now are you sure you don't want any iced tea?" Pouring a glass offering it to Mr. Thornburg. Leaving Marc to wait for his.

Mr. Thornburg, "Well if you insist." Accepting the glass of iced tea. Marc parched and sweaty reaches for some.

Ms. Campbell, "Not with those filthy hands. Have some manners and don't reach across people. I'll pour you a glass." Marc glares at her. Ms. Campbell disregards him as the lowly groundskeeper.

Mr. Thornburg, "Marc the grounds are looking great. With Andry's direction you're doing an excellent job here. Maybe he can take a look at our place and give you some pointers to help out." Marc eyes him stoically. Mr. Thornburg continues, "These flower beds are original. My wife and her garden club would put this place back on the garden tour route."

Marc, "Thank you but no. Andry and myself have our hands full these days without adding hundreds of people trampling the grounds down. Maybe another year."

Mr. Thornburg, "Suit yourself, but I still might have to hear it from Andry. Now the other reason I'm here for. The historical society has contacted me with numerous complaints about the condition of the paint and shutters. The exterior of the house seeing up close in the light of day. I have to agree. Not only is it hideous for lack of a better word. The place is frightening. If I were looking for a haunted house, I would look no further."

Marc used to his home's appearance by now takes a look sizing it up. "Am I expected to do all that work as well?"

Mr. Thornburg, "No. Of course not. That's not some small home repair project." Chuckling at his hubris, Ms. Campbell having a snicker with him. Mr. Thornburg then says rolling his eyes, "I could just hear my phone ringing already. You live in a landmark house in an established neighborhood. I don't expect you to do any of the restoration." Marc breathes a sigh of relief. "I will have reputable professionals submit bids for this job. A project like that would not be as easy as shoving some dirt around." Marc getting his slight. Mr. Thornburg looks past him at the caretaker's cottage. "What a waste. That could bring in enough income to cover household expenses."

Marc, "That is not really true Andry has been helping me."

Mr. Thornburg, "That's not I what mean. That cottage could be a source of income or tax write off. As it stands now, it's bringing down the value of the house. So it will definitely have to be a part of the estimate. Right along with the carriage house."

A strange feeling coming over Marc. That someone is watching them from the house. The hair on the back of his neck rising up. Disregarding the sensation, he says, "It is lacking in curb appeal."

Mr. Thornburg, "Yes that is the new terminology. I would have thought you would want to be a part of the restoration work. You are still majoring in architecture?"

Marc sets his square jaw. "Yes, I am, but my focus is structural engineering."

Mr. Thornburg, "Good luck with that. Not very many architects get to build landmark skyscrapers."

Marc, "I do know more than how to use a shovel." Starting to get steamed.

Mr. Thornburg, "I will let the general contractor know of your interest. You can submit an application listing your job skills when the time comes."

Marc eager to change the subject, "The granite has arrived but the flagstone is a special order. So it hasn't been delivered yet."

Mr. Thornburg, "Very good. It appears everything is in order. So I'll be off. Don't forget the ring and letter will be in the library."

Marc, "I won't." Mr. Thornburg is turning to leave waving his hand dismissively. Marc shakes his head. *He is such an arrogant ass.*

CHAPTER 10

TUESDAY EVENING MARC already showered. A towel low slung around his hips as he walks out of the spa room and sees the answering machine light blinking. Crossing over to it. His tanned muscular abdomen rippling covered with an ever increasing fine dark hair. More like a stripe up to his chest spreading out. Oblivious to its increasing development. Leaning over pressing the retrieval button.

"You have three new messages," the feminine voice announces. "Message one."

"Hi, Marc it's Melinda," pausing allowing her voice to be breathy. "Call me. I miss you."

"Message two."

Camel's voice. "There's a 'surge' at the Olde Theater of the Arts building Saturday night. Rumor has it's Greek. Put on by Delta Phi Delta and another sorority. There will be at least two women to every man. Sounds like my kind of odds. See you there? Call me."

"Message three."

"Hello Marc it's Angelique. Have you heard from Camel? I hope he is all right. He hasn't been returning my phone calls. Have you spoken with him lately? When you do, let him know I'm concerned about his well-being. I'm not trying to control him. Thank you." *Click*. Marc rubs his jaw. Knowing that this was coming. Picking up the phone to call Melinda. She answers before the ring tone.

Marc, "Hi, babe. I just took off your message."

Melinda, "What are you doing this evening?"

Marc, "Spending time with you. I'm finished for the day."

Melinda, "That's all I needed to hear. I need a break from this research paper."

Marc, "What's the subject?"

Melinda, "Mythological beasts and their commonplace involvement with humans. How they were troublesome and not so easily controlled."

Marc, "I wouldn't mind getting into some trouble with the right human." Speaking playfully.

Melinda, "You can always get into trouble with me. I have a couple of hours to burn. What sort of trouble did you have in mind, Marc?" Her voice soft and sexy almost hypnotic at the same time.

Marc, "Why don't you come over and we'll discover it together." His voice husky with his blue eyes twinkling. His towel pressing outward.

Melinda, "I don't recall you being any trouble at all. Sometimes you have to be bad to be good." Now sounding just a little pouty.

Marc, "I doubt you're bad. Though I'm the one with all the scratches down my back. Not that I'm complaining. You're a real tomcat in the sack."

Melinda, "I wouldn't think you were complaining. I've gotten a few marks you made on me. Enough of this phone play. I'll be right over. Let's make it romantic this time. I'll bring some candles and incense. Bye tiger."

Marc, "Bye." Still holding the phone when the dial tone returns. He snaps out of the enthrallment fully aroused.

That evening Melinda arrives to a catered meal by Tastings. Already set up on the table in the master suite. Drapes opened to the evening garden lit by landscape lights. Mature landscaping creates a forest backdrop with its hemlocks, white pines, and broad red leaf maples leafed out. Path lights and up lights spotting areas of interest. Pulling the chair out for Melinda to sit down. Marc opens a bottle of Chenin Blanc pouring up two glasses. Melinda quietly lifts her head in approval with one blonde brow arched. Finally speaking, "Very nice. I wasn't expecting a meal. How very wonderful."

Marc, "You'll need all your energy for tonight."

After completing their oyster appetizers relaxing. Melinda opens her large Prada bag pulling out candles and saucers to place them on. "The meal was wonderful. Now let me create a romantic setting. I get so tired of white candles. Don't you?"

Marc, "Uh, yes." Looking into her beautiful blue eyes twinkling at him with a longing stare.

Melinda, "Good. Then help me place them around the bed. Center them on these old saucers I brought. Do you mind if we use them?"

Marc, "No. I don't care. That's a good idea." Having not observed the ancient Sanskrit symbols written around the outer edges of them.

Melinda placing a candle and moving her hand around it clockwise three times before lighting it. She speaks softly. "Move the elements. I call on the spirit of fire." Working her way around the circle. Smiling wintery at Marc then giving him some directions. "Put the dishes out for the maid. That smell will distract me." While Marc's clearing the dishes she sprinkles herbs around each saucer counter clockwise placing the fifth candle for use at the foot of the bed on the floor.

Marc's blue eyes dilated to almost black with only the thinnest blue ring around their pupils. He moves over pressing up against Melinda kissing the back of her neck moving down her shoulder. Her expression hard, unchanging, as if she was back in another time and place. When she had no choice but to accept. This being a man she was supposed to love as a child, not a woman. Snapping back to the moment her face changes to sensuous. Guiding his hand away from her.

Marc, "What?"

Melinda, "Fill the spa tub so we can enjoy the experience together. I'll finish up out here. You want everything perfect when we get out of the tub, don't you?" Marc not wanting to leave her continues to caress her back. "Go on. It will be worth it. I promise." Marc steps over to the bathroom spa entrance calling out commands to the system, "Jacuzzi tub fill! Temperature one hundred and two. Circulation when filled." The sound of water gushing into the tub brings a smile to Melinda's hard face. Feeling herself gaining more control over him. Knowing this should complete that process tonight.

"Anything else princess?"

Melinda languishing on the bed stretching her shapely body out. "I brought some aromatic herbs to fragrance the bathwater. I'll add them momentarily."

Marc, "You certainly came prepared."

Melinda, "Well executed... romance can be hotter than a spontaneous act."

Marc, "Doubt we'll make it back to the bed."

Melinda, "You're always up for extra innings, right?"

Marc, "With you always." Already risen to the occasion his pants uncomfortably tight all in a noun. Melinda hearing the swirl of water takes Marc's hand leading him into the bathroom. Steam rises up from the hot water filled Jacuzzi. Melinda casting hand out over the water sprinkling herbs counterclockwise against the bubbling current of water, speeding up. A fragrant scent with earthy undertones wafts up in the air. Marc becoming increasingly enthralled with this new scent added. Melinda hands a sachet of fresh red rose petals to him.

"Scatter these around the water opposite the current. It will help them to mix in better." Melinda pulls off her blouse and then shimmies out of her skirt. Marc following her lead removes his shirt. Melinda watching him pull it over his head. Exposing first his tight abdomen and then his muscular chest. Appraising him. Yes, he is a fine specimen of a male strong in nature. Melinda steps into the center of the swirling current mumbling words softly. Marc not listening to them dropping his pants. Steps up behind her, his excitement pressing against her back as he kisses the side of her neck. His hands roving over her abdomen and up. Melinda chants, "Thrust of sword make strong thy beast of Pan. Let this satyr of my own creation be potent. Bring forth its power I so desire. For the strength of Pan we will need to do our bidding. So mote it be!" Her voice loud and echoing beyond the granite covered walls of that room. Water spinning into a forceful whirlpool rising up past the sides on the Jacuzzi without overflowing. Mist climbs higher carrying with it fragrances. The once clear water now the color of turquoise blue of some deep water port in a tropical paradise. Melinda being no angel of heaven embraces Marc's waist with her legs forcing him inside. Making him gasp with pleasure rippling over him. They sink into the steaming water immersing them as without bottom. Their bodies disappearing beneath the swirling vortex.

Later that night, Marc awakes in his bedroom in darkness. The candles having burnt out long ago. Not remembering getting back into bed. He reaches across the bed for Melinda finding her gone. Smiling contentedly, he dozes off to sleep very relaxed against the soft cotton sheets thread count a thousand plus. His respirations coming slow and steady. In the distance the grandfather clock strikes out the hour of one. The same presence as before gathering into a dense mass, vaporous and tumultuous. Hovering over his quietly resting body. On an inhalation it rushes into his lungs. Spreading throughout his body. Marc unable to catch his breath gasping. Struggling in sleep his hands grasping at the covers. No oxygen for him. This dark being enjoying his strength admiring his will to fight it. Finally allowing him his air. A deep gasping breath is all that is heard in the dark room. Marc moans helplessly still unconscious in the slumber of innocence.

CHAPTER 11

MS. CAMPBELL BUSY in the kitchen punching and kneading dough for her favorite sourdough bread. Thinking to herself, *Just a quick run through.* That girl will have to be able to do these things when she has a household of her own.

Speaking, "I don't know what she expects to get out of college. An archeologist or barrister? She needs something that will keep a roof over her head and pay the bills." Punching the dough again her frustrations directed at it.

"Just like that silly mother of hers. Always dreaming, and what did it get her? Nothing! Just another gal in trouble by some handsome no account. And who was left to take care of everything? It cost me dearly keeping her in private schools. And for what? Now she can pay me back some by helping out for a while. It's the least she can do."

Mr. Thornburg on the speakerphone. "The budget will allow for a small stipend. All young women need a few essentials. Angelique is right."

Ms. Campbell, "We'll see how well she works out." Determined not to just give it to her. "She's had everything provided for her at Mary Regina Girls' Academy. I'm not sure why you want to make her think she needs to be paid for helping me."

Mr. Thornburg, "As I have said young women need a few clothes. Take my Angelique, she loves her new designer clothes. Those young women from her sorority dress in haute couture. The alumni still do."

Ms. Campbell, "Mary is not in the same class as those girls. She needs to learn to be practical, thrifty, if you get my meaning."

Mr. Thornburg smiling, "I do, but to learn to handle money you have to start with a budget. A small stipend would teach her just that."

Ms. Campbell, "Those young women that these two have been dating. Dress less lady like and more tawdry. Not leaving much to the imagination. And I suspect their morals are nonexistent. They are not living right!"

Mr. Thornburg rolls his eyes listening to her. "Young women are always going to be drawn to sexy fashions. Every generation has its risqué styles. When I was younger the men were wearing those vulgar hip huggers. Those certainly leave nothing to the imagination with everything out front."

Ms. Campbell is quiet a rarity but not for long. "I must not remember those. I wouldn't have been allowed to date any young man showing up at the house like that. After our father was gone may his soul rest in peace. Now my younger sister Mary's mother that is quite another story. She always had some handsome Romeo sniffing around. That's the other thing I'm disturbed by. These young women have no virtues!" Getting herself wound up.

Mr. Thornburg, "I know you're not referring to my niece."

Ms. Campbell, "Oh no. Certainly not."

Mr. Thornburg, "Young people are the same throughout time. I believe you are imposing your form of morality on people."

Ms. Campbell, "I don't find it imposing to live by the good book. Mary isn't going to get mixed up in this group with their immoral lifestyles. Much less some other heathen religion."

Mr. Thornburg, "Why don't we put religion off topic for now. I could set up an account with direct deposit to pay Mary from. You can tell her when you're ready. There is nothing wrong with learning to handle financial responsibilities by managing a small income."

Ms. Campbell, "You have a valid point."

Mr. Thornburg, "Good you will consider it. Now how is Marc working out around there?"

Marc awakesns up to sunlight shining through a gap in the drapes. A bright beam cutting across the cold room to his breath creating a misty cloud. The sheet is twisted around his waist exposing his muscular chest. Which is growing increasingly denser black hair. Below the sheet is tented up in a prominent bulge. Tugging the sheet from around his waist swinging his feet over the side of the bed. Then standing up stretching in the semidarkness. After his groan the only other sound heard is the sheet sliding off the bed onto the floor. Moving toward the bathroom his bladder full and member engorged almost painfully so. Calling out, "Floor heat on." Another night of nightmares. Stepping on rose petals scattered across the black marble floor veined with white. Smelling something pungent. Smiling to himself remembering Melinda's visit last night. At least vaguely only bits and pieces. Trying to recall more. Standing back from the toilet letting go. Urine showering down into the bowl straw colored. His own masculine aroma wafting up greet his nose. The sense of pleasure and relief rushing through his body that only males can feel in this condition.

Passing into the kitchen hungry as a wolf. Marc goes right to the warmer where the scent of fresh biscuits is coming from.

Ms. Campbell comes back into her kitchen." Good morning. I see you found the biscuits."

Marc, "Yes, good morning." His voice gruff and deep.

Ms. Campbell, "Andry won't be in today. Oksana isn't doing well."

Marc, "I had heard she wasn't doing well. He left me a lengthy list of projects to follow through on." Ms. Campbell nods her head, busy on the phone after being on hold with the airlines.

After his breakfast of dates with yogurt and biscuits. Marc goes outside to work. Heat and rising humidity blanket him. A large contrast to the cool sometimes cold, dehumidified air of the house. His forehead and arms beading with perspiration. Marc's ever rapidly lengthening dark hair falling into his eyes again. Tired of pushing it out of his face. *When did it ever get this long?* Having always kept it cut short to avoid looking like an infidel. Tying on his blue bandana. His jaw itching rubbing at what felt like a mosquito. Then checking his hand to find only wetness of perspiration. Running his hand over his face feeling more like course sandpaper with its dark thick stubble. The bandana bringing out the dark blue of his eyes. That and his long dark eyelashes. Still very masculine but ruggedly handsome.

By that afternoon the morning's occasional clouds have changed into rain clouds. Finally giving up working outside with boots becoming heavier from mud caking on them making each step feel several pounds more. Marc decides to call it a day. Even though the warm rain feels good against his body having pulled off his shirt earlier. Water running down his face, dripping from his head and body. Standing inside the gardening storage bay now that most of the tools are put away. Watching the rain come down its pattering sound soothing. The life giving moisture refreshing the soil and air. Inhaling deeply so very good this freshest of air cleaned by rain. He can almost feel the life force of nature. Plants all around him awakening taking in moisture and growing. Their energy force strong. The life force powerful yet subtle. He stands looking across this green sea of nature. Drawn to this marvel of life. Walking barefoot off the path on soft green moss. Cushioning his every step. The warm rain as a shower not cold like most of the year. Having spent the better part of an hour wondering through the different rooms of his garden. Taking in each section's particular gifts of beauty and micro-ecosystems. Marc looking more like a hominid between ice ages decides it's time to go in. Life's responsibilities demand attention. Stepping into the cool house with its air-conditioning goose bumps rising up his arms and wet body forcing him to go upstairs.

After a hot shower wrapped in a royal blue terry cloth robe. Marc turns his cell phone on calling Andry at the nursing home. The operator connects him to Oksana's floor. A female answers, "3300."

Marc, "Andry Kunetasava please." Waiting on hold a few minutes.

Andry picks up the phone. "Da? Hello."

Marc, "Hi, I'm calling to check how Oksana is doing."

Andry, "Not too good. But not any worse."

Marc, "How are you holding up?"

Andry, "Tired, but what can I do? I hate seeing her like this and not being able to help her. She is just fading away slowly."

Marc, "I'm sorry to hear that. Maybe she will improve?"

Andry, "Not this time. The doctor believes she has had another how you say, stroke? She is still unconscious. If she does come to. What will be taken from her this time? When this started her left side was already weak and she was having trouble controlling it."

Marc, "What are you going to do?"

Andry, "I'll stay by her side. She made her wishes known. I promised I would follow them. No artificial means of life support. If her heart stops or she stops breathing, nothing is to be done." Trying to sound strong, all the while his heart aching. Knowing that death will be coming soon for her.

Marc speaking just as much to fill the silence and understand. "You mean you'll just let her go?" His voice almost a whisper.

Andry, "That is right. We both feel that way. I'm not going to keep her around as some mindless...," His voice trails off as he chokes back a sob. Tears blurring his vision. Snorting to clear his throat. Regaining some of his composure being a tough Ukrainian man. "Her body won't be kept alive with feeding tubes and people have to clean her like a baby because she is lying in her shit. She wouldn't want to live like that. I promised." His voice softer, "And a promise is a promise. Right?"

Marc, "Yes."

Andry, "Now that the time is nearing, I'm still not ready."

Marc, "You'll know." Trying to be strong for him. "If you need anything just ask me. Something to eat at three in the morning, a ride home. Anything, just let me know."

Andry, "Thank you. We have been married fifty-one years. How will I go on without my Oksana?" Marc unsure what to say. "I'm sorry. I shouldn't burden you with my troubles. You were nice enough to call me."

Marc, "It's no trouble at all."

Andry, "I need to be at Oksana's side. Thank you for calling."

Marc, "Keep me posted."

Andry, "I will. Thank you again. I appreciate you offering your help. I'll be home later to shower and change clothes. Then I'm coming back."

Marc, "All right I will talk to you soon. Bye."

After getting off the phone Marc sits quietly. Looking out onto the garden below him from the bedroom balcony. Feeling sad for Andry. Knowing it is only going to get worse before it is better.

Later that evening Camel calls. Finding him reading in the library.

Camel," What are you doing tonight?"

Marc, "I didn't have any plans. It was a busy day and I had another bad night's sleep."

Camel, "Why, did Melinda spend the night?"

Marc, "No. I don't know what is going on. I'm sleeping but I just don't feel rested when I wake up."

Camel, "What could be so interesting to read that would have you sitting at home like an old man?"

Marc, "I'm reading *Dead Until Dark*. It's actually pretty good so far."

Camel, "Like I said. Why are you reading on a summer night? When you could be out with me. Joey's Bar is having karaoke and it's ladies' night. That place will be wall to wall women."

Marc, "You have a one track mind."

Camel, "All my life."

Marc, "Melinda and I are getting more serious. It's good so I'll pass on tonight. Have you spoken to Angelique? She's been looking for you."

Camel, "No. I'm not that interested in dating her exclusively anymore."

Marc, "What happened?"

Camel, "I don't know. We were very intense for a long time. Then something just changed a few weeks ago. I didn't feel so strongly attracted to her as I had been. You know I was completely into pleasing her. If you know what I mean."

Marc, "Yeah, I do."

Camel, "Then it was like overnight I wasn't infatuated with her anymore. Not that I'm not, but it's been almost a dream come true."

Marc, "Funny that you mention dreams. I've been having some strange ones."

Camel, "What about?"

Marc, "My uncle Theron keeps trying to tell me something about power."

Camel, "What sort of power?"

Marc, "I'm not sure. Every time he starts talking this woman in my dream interrupts him. She keeps speaking French to me. Calling me her son. 'Mon fils.'"

Camel, "That is strange. What else?"

Marc, "My uncle is telling me about a power. To put it back or stop it before…"

Camel, "Before what?"

Marc, "I don't know, too late?"

Camel, "It sounds like a warning. What do you think it could be referring to?"

Marc, "I don't know yet but I will figure it out."

Camel, "Having dead relatives contact you sounds like a warning to me.

"Now." Going back to his subject. "I have more women interested in me than I could have dreamed of. All I have to do is walk into a place. Instead of me working to get some beauty's attention. She get my scent if you will and I have what I came there for in the first place. You won't believe it but there's competition for me. They are literally vying for me to dance, what am I drinking, am I alone. It's almost too good to be true. It's just a matter of picking and choosing."

Marc, "That doesn't really sound any different from when I've been out with you. You've always been easy."

Camel, "You stab me in the heart my brother." His playful sarcasm coming through. Both men laughing. "I don't remember you turning down the attention of any female."

Marc, "Touché. I weep for your newly found condition. Yet I still don't hear anything new. You have always had women after you."

Camel, "Fine, fine." Changing the subject back to Marc. "So what do you think the dreams represent? What power?" Marc listening, so Camel goes on. "Sometimes dreams have a significance. When did they start? You've been dating Melinda for a few weeks now, right?"

Marc serious, "Yeah?"

Camel, "Are you afraid of commitment? Perhaps you are not so intense as you thought you were. What does she want?"

Marc, "She has been very up front. That she is not ready to be serious and that we should date other people. Wow! When did you get so smart?"

Camel, "I have dated a couple of psych majors. It's not like I haven't been accused of a fear of commitment. You know me. I'm still sowing my wild oats. I'm definitely not ready to settle down. So if it's not a fear of commitment then maybe you should talk to an iman."

Marc, "You think so?"

Camel, "Some of the older imans from the deep desert spoke of spirits or demons that try to take control of your mind and body though your dreams."

Marc, "I'm not so sure about all of that. I've heard the same tales as you we grew up together. Even my parents have spoken of old legends from Sumerian times. I didn't realize you took those stories to heart." Trying to come off as logical and modern. Having some doubts of his own just beneath the surface. Not sure whether Camel believes this or is trying to scare him. Long shadows reach across the library now that the sun has set. The house having grown quiet. "Since when did you become so cautious and superstitious?"

Camel, "There is a lot to be said for the old ways of protection and even their warnings." His tone serious and his concern brotherly. "You never talk to anyone in a dream. It's bad luck." Marc becoming suspicious by the last statement. Being so incongruous to Camel's regular behavior.

Marc, "Maybe they are trying to warn me to stay righteous. That I shouldn't let my libido run my life. Desiring gratification all the time."

Camel bursts out laughing. "Maybe it's 'cause I'm a young male. When did you stop wanting women all the time?" Sounding all the part of his playful self.

Marc, "Asshole! I knew it. You were just messing with me."

Camel, "All too easy. You fall for it every time."

Marc, "You did have me going there for a few seconds."

Camel, "Come on man. My picture is in the dictionary next to the definition of Casanova. I was serious about talking to an iman if these strange dreams continue."

Marc, "I'll consider it but not just yet. I don't want to come off as the nut at the mosque."

Camel, "All right, I see work here is done."

Marc, "Bye, don't do anything I wouldn't do."

Camel, "Bye."

Marc settles into one of the damask covered wingback chairs. There's nothing better than a good book and some excellent cognac. Taking a draw off his snifter of Courvoisier. Wishing now he had gone out with Camel. Just then the doorbell to the main entrance rings. Setting down his book. Glancing at the clock on the marble mantel, it's almost eleven. Who would be coming by this late without calling? The doorbell ringing again. Stopping to deactivate the alarm system keying the code quickly on the pad. The bell ringing again. It's probably Camel. It would be just like him always joking around. Marc's smile cut short as the heavy oak door swings open. Angelique's angry face glaring at him.

Angelique, "Where is he?" Her face not its usual reserved beauty. Her light blue eyes round almost bulging with anger.

Marc, "What brings you out at this hour?" Trying to calm her with a little distraction. His voice calm. "If you are looking for Camel, he is not here."

Angelique, "He's been ignoring my calls. When I ask someone to call me because I'm concerned, I expect to hear from him."

Marc, "I told him to call you." Adding quickly, "That you were worried." Angelique's anger over being jilted increasing. Now feeling foolish for having come there. Much less Marc seeing her emotional display. Regaining her composure, pushing back a strand of her blonde hair from her face. Only the sound of her silk Wu dress rustling and shimmering under the light from above.

Angelique, "I won't be calling him anymore. If he needs me, he knows how to find me. When I'm ready to be contacted. Oh, and tell him he left his ring. On my nightstand, the one his father gave him." Impatiently stepping back, her yellow stilettos *peau de soie* matching her dress.

Marc takes in her beauty. "Would you like to come in. I just spoke with him a few hours ago. I'll see if I can reach him. He's been busy with one of his many projects." Marc wondering, did that sound as lame as he thought it did? Almost blushing at being so caught unprepared for this situation. Hating to get mixed up in Camel's women troubles. Knowing this just isn't going to turn out well.

Angelique says, "Oh, do you think so?" Turning her head slightly, her pale blue eyes icy cold. Almost like she was reading his mind. "Do you know where he is now?"

Marc, "He should be home. That's where he was when I spoke to him. He might be asleep by now."

Angelique glares into Marc's eyes. "Do you take me for a fool? That Arab alley cat is out somewhere there are women tonight." Getting an idea. "So he wants to play." Her voice controlled without an accent.

Marc grasps at something innocuous to say, trying to defuse the situation. "He wouldn't play with your emotions. He's just happy go lucky not really the serious type." All the while thinking, *He's a Romeo, tomcat.* Angelique raising her hand to silence him.

Angelique, "You don't need to cover for him. I should have recognized this was going to be necessary at some point. I'll give him what he so desires." Laughing until it was echoing throughout the foyer, more an insane cackle. "How ironic." This more said for herself. Marc not getting her meaning at all. Angelique's anger radiates from her. Stepping forward on one foot reaching up as to caress Marc's face with her long nailed fingers. Grazing his dark stubble covered face. Tiny static electrical sparks crackling off between her nails and his beard. Marc's sapphire blue eyes locking with hers defiantly. Holding himself in check. His reflexes fast from years of martial arts training with a stronger opponent, Camel. Her composure regained, stepping back. "Thank you." Pivoting gracefully on one stilettoed foot away from him. Her stiletto heels clinking down the curving flagstone path. Marc breathes a sigh of relief.

Hearing thunder rumbling distantly as if to mirror her mood. A gust of wind rising up carrying with it humid warm air. Slamming open the heavy oak double doors. Debris whipping past Marc the wind shoving him back unprepared for such a frontal assault. The porch light on its heavy gauge chains creaking and swaying. The large hemlocks nearby having their boughs hit by the forceful wind, causing them to bob up and down creating eerie shadows. Marc struggling to get at least one door closed. Angelique's arms raised toward the night sky. Her long nailed fingers curled looking more like talons twisted into the darkness. Releasing her anger into the clouds above causing them to seethe and roil, lightning streaking outward. Gail force winds howling around her. Shouting at the sky, "Lightning crackle! Thor strike your anvil hotly. Show me your strength light up the night." Jagged branches of lightning cross directly over the manor exploding like artillery cannons booming. The smell of ozone permeating the air.

Marc finally muscles a door closed. Using his foot pushing the sliding lock into the floor. Then pulling the ring of the chain to engage the top bolt sliding into place locking it. Howling winds blowing leaf litter horizontally with dirt and debris pelting his face savagely. His hair blown back with muscles bulging. He forces the other door closed, but not before gale force driven rain hits any exposed skin stinging. Marc's shirt torn and dirt smudged on his face. He leans against the closed doors grateful the storm is locked outside. Thinking to himself, *Wow, that storm came up fast.* Relaxing, believing the worst of it over. Lightning striking the porch light explodes with the brilliance of several suns shining in the entryway windows. Marc jumps and ducks away from the doors shaken. Thunder booms all around the house with lightning flashing like a strobe light. Then just as quickly silent except for rain falling. Marc remembers Angelique outside pulling the door open bracing himself for the worst. Not seeing her anywhere. Hoping she got out of it. But if not, maybe it cooled her off some. Chuckling to himself. Seeing in his mind's eye Angelique doused and dripping wet in her designer clothes.

Angelique inside her Porsche speaking on her cell phone. "Just the weather for my occasion. It will be a foul night for men."

A familiar voice with her educated New York accent responding. "Unless they are faithful and at home with their lovers." The wind outside having stopped just as suddenly as it came up.

Marc hears the distinct sound of a sports car engine being gunned. Tires squealing down the driveway, dumping a gear. Angelique not slowing as she reaches East Avenue tires wailing as her Porsche slides across the wet asphalt paving continuing to accelerate. Slamming it into the next gear. The tires barking once more before grabbing traction. Adding the rotten egg smell of burnt rubber to ozone mixing in the air. *Well, I guess she isn't too worse for the wear, certainly not calmer.* Going back inside closing the door.

Marc halfway up the stairs remembers his cognac in the library. Going back downstairs to retrieve it. Remembering Camel's story about a certain NFL player who it was rumored Angelique had dated him. He was raked over the coals between the press and animal rights people. They crucified him before his prison sentence. Just a few tips about dogfighting and untaxed wagering. Angelique's own identity remaining anonymous. Not once was she ever connected to him.

The thought dawning on him. She is going to want revenge on Camel. Debating on how to try and warn him. Doubting his brother would answer his cell phone. For that matter could he hear it in some noisy club? This certainly put an end to his quiet evening. What the heck it's already over. Just on cue the lights go out across the house. His decision made for him. Great! Marc smacks his shin against a coffee table in the darkness. Pain throbbing across his shin. Once more the quiet night ended. His pain lessening as he limps carefully around the room until finding his bearings in the almost pitch black library. Seeing the room's layout mentally recognizing the offending piece of furniture. Avoiding the impulse to smash it with his fist. Making it over to the table where a candle was left from when they had so much fun that night weeks ago. Playing cards and joking until they found his old family diary. Not able to remember a lot of the evening after that.

Marc lighting candles notices the old tome left untouched. Looking around the room finding his drink where he left it. Why bother with the cognac. He'll be out soon. Picking up the old diary with the candlestick in his other hand. Walking slow and steadily to keep the candle lit. Now only the sound of rain falling and distant thunder. Other than that the old manor silent and devoid of life. His sight aided in illumination from ambient light. Where a drape is parted at the end of the long hallway. Candlelight flickering as he walks casting long shadows across the master suite. Marc lights the candelabras on the mantel. Some the same ones Melinda had used recently to create a romantic mood. But now oddly taking the room back to a previous century. Giving him the unsettling sense of déjà vu.

Picking up his cell phone checking it. Good, the batteries are charged. Turning it on thumbing through the memory dialing Camel's cell going right to voice mail. Marc leaves a message. "Man, are you in for it. Angelique was here looking for you and she is furious. It looks like I'm coming to Joey's. See ya." Ending the phone call. His pulse quickening from the excitement of thinking about going out. That and the lingering scent of Melinda's perfume mixed with that herbal concoction. Sending his blood rushing. Why not meet Camel out? What could it hurt going out for a little while?

Marc heads into his cavernous dressing room setting the candelabra down. Then stripping out of his baggy sweatpants and torn tee shirt. Glancing in the mirror to see his dirt smudged face and tousled hair. Making a quick stop at the bathroom sink splashing water on his face. Then slicking back his dark hair by running his fingers through it. Returning to the dressing room closet to select summer casual clothes for tonight. Choosing navy blue Dockers slacks and a loose fitting blue on blue pattern silk shirt with black loafers to finish the casual look. Not quite satisfied with his reflection, running a hand one more time through his dark hair. Now looking more like a GQ model right off the cover of the magazine without realizing how handsome he cleans up. Masculine and captivating the contrast between sapphire blue eyes and his ever present five o'clock shadow. Slapping on Tommy Hilfiger cologne. *Where the heck is that emergency flashlight?* Finding it at the back of a drawer loaded with junk. Pulling open the drapes to allow some ambient light for later if the power is not back on. Then putting out the candles around the room making ready to leave.

Outside the rain is falling lightly more a mist. Marc revs up his Mustang GT with a roar. The glass packs giving it the extra *umpft*. Shifting into gear pulling out of the garage bay splashing through small puddles on the driveway. At the end of the driveway pausing long enough for traffic. Splashing across one last puddle before turning right toward Alexander Street. Peeling off then merging with traffic before deciding they are moving too slow. Accelerating and weaving past slower drivers. Roaring off into the distance.

CHAPTER 12

APPROACHING THE CLUB district traffic gets heavier and slower on Monroe Avenue. The sidewalks bustling with pedestrians. This part of town dry as if the storm had never blown into the neighborhood. Only blocks away from where there had been gale force driven rain. Stars dimly shining against the background of bright lights with only the occasional wispy cloud in the sky. Moving slower due to traffic and searching for a parking spot. The Mustang engine rumbles steadily like some great cat purring. A testament to its power and engineering. Blue with white racing stripes on the lower quarter panel. A mint 1968 classic not easy to miss.

Warm summer air carrying with it the excited voices of the increasing crowd of young people. Gathering outside Joey's. The line already extending well past the awning in front of the rectangular building. Marc's pulse quickening with the sound of the large bass speakers' *doof, doof, doof* rhythm coming though the walls. His thoughts racing with excitement anxious to get inside where the fun is taking place.

Pausing to allow a black Jaguar to pull out away from a curbside space almost in front of Joey's. What a break. Performing a fast parallel park. Marc knows his car that well. Rolling the manual window up on the passenger side. Allowing him the excuse of a lingering stare. Checking out the line of mostly young women dressed for summer. Their voices chattering with excitement about an up and coming singer performing there earlier tonight. Marc familiar with her unusual name.

Marc steps out of his car stretching his long legs and arms reaching for the sky. Trying to release some of his pent up energy. Adjusting his package for comfort's sake. Strolling up to the line already on several women's radar. His six foot plus and broad shouldered frame moving with feline strength. Smoothly joining the line of mostly women. His rugged tan face causing a couple of compacts to pop open for a quick glance back and a makeup check.

Samantha spots Marc herself a longtime friend of Angelique's and more recently Melinda's. Not one to pass up a handsome male. Leaning forward adjusting herself. As if she needed to adding a flip of her shoulder-length blonde hair. Making it more full. Feeling appropriately sensuous she calls out to Marc waving to him. Marc hears her and smiles looking in her direction. The doormen are letting people out and just about to go in herself. Samantha says, "He's with me!" Waving him up to the front of the line. "Come on. I didn't think you were going to make it." Marc steps up next to her at the front of the line. His buttocks round and prominent from sports, a great view.

The doorman unhitches the red felt rope allowing them both to pass. "You look beautiful as always." Taking her hand up allowing Samantha to twirl around showing off her Dolce & Gabbana ensemble, blue silk. Marc puts his arm through hers before they pass through the door. Her calves exquisitely accented by the four and a half inch heels. Smiling playfully her eyes twinkling. She has the attention of all three men.

The door opening Samantha pulling close squeezing Marc's arm as they walk in together. Both engulfed by the darkness with music pouring over them. The door behind them closing off the world outside. A slow dance ending the music gets louder. Marc like an icebreaker makes his way through the crowd with Samantha following closely. It's wall to wall people. A spot opening up at the bar Marc takes it. Samantha squeezing in next to him.

Samantha, "Handsome as ever." Appraising Marc. "Is Melinda treating you right?" Smiling with an arched eyebrow.

Marc, "Yes, she is incredibly sexual. I have no complaints in that department."

Samantha looks disappointed. "Oh well just checking. If you ever get single or just bored." Giving him a knowing look. "So tell me. Anything new in your life?"

Marc, "No changes. I'm busy with the house all the time landscaping and soon to be restoration."

Samantha, "It's good to know you are good with your hands." Taking one of his rough hands. "I can't say I'm totally happy to hear you are enjoying yourself. Now let's get something to drink. I'm parched already."

Samantha smiles at Marc and then Raul one of the bartenders that night moving over to her. Wondering to herself what it would be like to have them both together.

Raul, "What will it be for the lady?"

Samantha, "Vodka stinger. Stoli. It's the only way to make one."

Raul, "And for you, sir?"

Marc, "Labatt Blue." Raul moves over to the liquor shelves choosing Stolichnaya pouring up hear drink.

Samantha, "So tell me. How serious are the two of you? Will I be hearing about an upcoming engagement?"

Marc, "Slow down. Melinda is very noncommittal at this point. We're not dating exclusively."

Samantha surmises as much asking a probing question. "Is that by your choice or hers?"

Marc, "It's mutual." Not sounding very convincing, adding, "Melinda is very clear about not rushing things. She said we should date other people."

Samantha smiles and nods her head in approval. "Smart girl. But I'm not so sure I'd let you too far off the leash." Raul sets their drinks on cocktail napkins. Marc pulls out his money clip peeling off a hundred dollar bill handing it to Raul.

Samantha, "Here's to mud in your eye." Clinking their drinks together. Marc looks across the dance floor and spots Camel, waving to him. His brother is at the center of the crowded dance floor. Camel's large masculine body moves rhythmically with bestial sensuality. His dark curly hair glistening with beads of perspiration dripping from it. Making his moreno skin shiny with those dark eyes sparkling under the reflected lights. Too busy enjoying the company of his female companions to notice Marc. Finally seeing Samantha and Marc waving back. He leans over his slender blonde dance partners excusing himself. The duo continue after making him promise to return. Camel crosses the crowded dance floor. Realizing how hot he is grabbing some bar napkins pausing to blot his face.

Samantha calls his name, "Camel!" her voice sexy.

Camel responds, "Samantha!" his voice deep and husky. Opening his arms for a hug. "You're more beautiful than Scheherazade. I have eyes for only you."

Samantha stops him. "You're wet and sweaty. I'm wearing silk." Kissing her cheek instead. "If I'm so beautiful, then why are your fingerprints on half the behinds in this place."

Camel pretends to be shocked. Then looks at her like. "Who me?" He then says, "You know you were the only one for me."

Samantha smiles but only half listening by now, herself on the prowl, answering him. "Yes darling, always." Distracted by another male a swarthy brunette tower. So debonair. Dressed in all black with his hair slicked back.

Samantha calls out to him, "Ciao, Mario!" Moving away. Camel reaches out grabbing Marc's shoulders in greeting. Both men pause for the olive-complexioned and silver-green eyed beauty. Her black corn silk hair down her back. Herself not giving pause to the two men. Passing by them as other men parting the way for her. All eyes following in her wake.

Camel, "Marc." Hugging him. "I didn't expected to see you here tonight."

Marc's smile changes to a face of concern. "Have you checked your messages? I came here to warn you."

Camel, "No. I've been busy. Why would you need to warn me?" Looking Marc directly in the eyes.

Marc, "Angelique came by the house tonight looking for you. When she figured out why you weren't returning her calls. She became demented angry. Scary if you had seen her eyes."

Camel, "How did she arrive at that? What did you tell her?"

Marc, "She asked me when I last had spoken to you. I didn't know you still were letting her wait."

Camel speaks calmly, "It's all right, so I haven't returned her calls for a few days."

Marc, "She knows you're seeing other women." Camel looking annoyed with him. "I haven't told her anything." Marc adding, "She doesn't need to be a genius to figure that out. Besides, she knows you well." Shrugging. "If you are not in her bed, you're in some other woman's bed."

Camel, "It's good that it's out. She never wanted to be exclusive and we certainly haven't discussed it. Besides, I know she sees other men. Moss doesn't grow under her feet."

Marc, "You didn't see how psychotically angry she looked. Then something strange happened. A storm blew in with pouring rain and strong winds."

Camel smiles. "Did she get wet?" His look satisfied.

Marc, "I didn't see that. But the winds were strong enough to blow open the doors. I was too busy holding on to them to see what happened to her."

Camel, "Thanks for the heads-up. I haven't noticed anything strange weather but I've been inside." Smiling. "Dancing with those two blondes who are waiting on me to rejoin them." His partners waving to him to come back. "Rochester has strange weather all the time. I wouldn't be surprised if it weren't snowing when we leave." Watching to his dance partners. Marc standing there with his beefy arms folded across his chest disapprovingly.

Marc, "I would be careful with her. You can tell she has a vengeful streak in her. A woman's scorn."

Camel, "Forget her. I'm not afraid of her. What's she going to do? Curse me? It wouldn't be the first time some woman's been angry with me. I'll call her tomorrow and sweet talk her back into bed." Camel's cockiness irritating even to Marc. Looking doubtfully at his brother.

Marc, "Dude, she doesn't come off as the forget and forgive type."

Camel, "It is what it is. Melinda still scratching your back up?" Casually monitoring his surroundings. Watching the gorgeous brunette check out Marc. Herself unaware that Camel has been observing her since she passed by earlier.

Marc, "Yeah, we're good. We can't get enough of each other."

Camel, "Have you noticed with the women in that sorority they don't want any monogamous relationships?"

Marc, "We're all in college. When we graduate we'll all be scattered to the winds. Most of us will be working on our careers before we start making commitments and families."

Camel, "Who said anything about families? I'm certainly not ready for that. Now you are scaring me. You sound too much like dad. We both know what he expects. I'm to marry a nice Muslim woman. A local gal from the UAE or Saudi. Not some high maintenance Christian woman. You?"

Marc, "My parents aren't concerned about the religion. It's just not that important to them."

Camel, "You know my father. If I don't marry someone he's chosen, he'll be angry."

Marc, "I also know he will get past it where you are concerned. Besides, American Christians are more like Sunni and Shiite than any of them realize. It's the same all over again the Evangelical claiming to be moral. I've heard you get kicked out of your own church if you don't vote the way the iman, I mean minister tells you to. How moral can that be?"

Camel, "That is the one thing I do agree with politically, separation of church and state."

Marc, "What most don't realize is that those at the top of the pyramid are the only ones benefiting. There is nothing moral about lying to the peons and just keeping your whores well hidden."

Camel, "Enough political talk. I didn't know you were so cynical. You are starting to sound like an iman."

Marc, "Sorry, I get a little excited."

Camel, "A little?" Leaning over, casually speaking into Marc's ear, "Don't look, just listen. You have an admirer. Remember that olive-skinned brunette with the long silky black hair?"

Marc, "How could I forget her?"

Camel, "Well, she has been checking you out since we have been standing here."

Marc, "Seriously?"

Camel, "Calm down and play it like you haven't noticed her. Come on, I'll get the ball rolling."

Marc, "Don't embarrass me."

Camel, "Do you want to meet her?"

Marc, "Are you kidding? Heck yes."

Camel, "Then follow my lead and come on." Casually moving over to the crowded bar as a Rihanna song comes on. Packing the dance floor.

Marc, "Are you getting it? Angelique is going to be the worst sort of trouble."

Camel not wanting to hear anymore, "Yes, yes. Raul!" calling out loudly. Raul nodding his head busy pouring up a round of kamikazes for a group of guys at the bar. The mysterious dark-haired beauty the subject of many conversations around the area. Some not so nice ones amongst the women.

Raul, "Camel!" The two men knocking fists together. "What can I get for you?"

Camel, "How about a name and whatever that gorgeous brunette is drinking."

Raul leans closer speaking into Camel's ear. Marc tries to listen in but the music is too loud. "You mean the one with those silver-green eyes? Jadon."

Camel, "Yes, is she alone?"

Raul, "Yeah, but don't expect any play. She will see right through a player like you. She's a tough one. Just shoot down pretty boy with his clown friends over there."

Camel, "I didn't ask for your opinion." Peeling off a couple of hundred dollar bills from a large role of them. Sliding them across the bar. "Just tell her the drink is from an anonymous admirer. When she wants to know who it was from tell her old Marc here sent it." Tipping his head toward Marc. Raul eyes Marc up and down.

Raul, "Are you sure about that? She would be a step up for even you, boss."

Camel gives him a glare. "You think so, boss."

Raul speaks to Marc, "You might have a chance but you need to be smoother than these bozos around here."

Camel, "Thanks for the Intel. Later."

Marc, "What are you doing?"

Camel, "I'm giving love a little push. She can't keep her eyes off you."

Marc, "But I'm just here for a few minutes."

Camel, "Well then, just take a few minutes. Melinda is not here and she doesn't want commitments. Go for it." They clink their beer bottles together then taking a swig. Raul leans in talking animatedly with Jadon placing the drink in front of her. She looks over to see who sent the drink. Her eyes more hawk like and piercing. Smiling when she sees who sent it. Marc standing up straight with shoulders back. "You're on man. Later."

Marc, "Wait."

Camel already leaving, "I've got two lovelies out there on the dance floor."

Marc looks back to see Jadon moving gracefully. Her breasts sensuously swaying naturally as she walks over to him. Marc takes a quick look for Camel who is already out of sight gone into the crowd. Men part again as Jadon passes. Heads turning with some leaning over to catch a rear view. Marc takes a quick drink off his beer causing it to foam and spurt on his face. Wiping it out of his eye still burning. Blinking as she walks up to him. Her hand extended. "So you are Marc. What makes you different from these other jerks?"

Marc, "I'm just here for a few minutes." Feeling completely lame, *What an opening line.*

Jadon, "Hi, my name is Jadon." Shaking his hand the chemistry immediately touching them both stirring emotions.

Marc regains some composure. "What a beautiful name."

Jadon, "My father agrees with you." Watching Marc's face to see his reaction. Marc more determined.

"Your accent is Turkish."

Jadon, "Yes, most people in this country wouldn't be able to make that kind of distinction. You're not from around here are you?"

Marc, "No. I moved here a couple months ago." Looking into her eyes at a loss for words.

Jadon, "So are you like your friend there?" Her eyes on Camel dancing with the two blondes. "A different lover every night."

Marc follows her eyes. "Yes, he is. No. No. I'm not like that at all." His cheeks warming up into a blush, grateful for the dim lighting where they are standing. Suddenly tongue-tied.

Jadon, "You can let go of my hand now." Marc lets go. If he could get any more off on this introduction, he wasn't sure how. "Well, which is it?"

Marc, "I'm sorry, you've caught me off balance."

Jadon, "What? Too many questions? Here I thought I saw some intelligence behind those blue eyes."

Marc, "I come here once in a while and no, I don't seek a different woman every night."

Jadon enjoying putting him on the spot. Says, "I'm not sure if you're just saying that because you believe it's what you think I want to hear or are you really sincere?"

Marc, "I wouldn't just say that stuff."

Hearing from the nearby group of guys, "Smooth." Marc glares over their way. His nostrils flaring.

Jadon, "Don't worry about them. They're just jealous you have my attention."

Marc smiles showing his white teeth contrasting against his suntanned face. Speaking, "I like you."

Jadon, "Good." Finishing her drink with a motion of her hand, downing it. "Are you ready for another one? Or would you like to dance?" Camel passes by going up to the bar to order three drinks. Marc stares into her eyes. "What?" her plump lips curling up into a smile.

Marc, "I'm sorry, it's just, you have the most striking eyes I have ever seen. I don't mean to stare." Camel clamps Marc on the shoulder with his large hand. His rich gold and diamond ring sparkling under the pin lights positioned down around the bar. Both men are standing tall pushing out their large pectorals. Even with Marc's shirt untucked Jadon can see his narrow waist. The shirt folding just on top of his round yet squared buttocks. Jadon sizes up the two young men.

Raul calls out, "Camel your order's ready!"

Camel looks at the two of them. "I can see my work is done here."

Marc, "Wait."

Camel, "Time waits for no one little brother. Tempes fugit." Winking at Marc as he moves off. Another young woman is waiting for Camel anxiously. He leans over speaking into her ear. One hand at the center of her back guiding her away. All the while using the other large hand to carry three drinks in it as they move away.

Jadon, "He's quite the ladies' man, but so are you."

Marc, "What are you talking about?"

Jadon, "You have been the subject of conversation with several groups of ladies tonight. Don't play coy with me." Smiling at her compliment and again his dimples showing. That and a flash of his white teeth.

Marc, "Once in a while I go out. I'm too busy for hanging out barhopping. Besides, I've been seeing someone but she doesn't want to be exclusive." Speaking truthfully to Jadon. Herself recognizing the honesty in his face, appraising him further.

Jadon, "Then she is either a fool or just using you." Watching for his reaction to comment, then continuing. "You don't seem like the type to be fooled easily." Her voice softer and definitely more sensuous making full eye contact with his eyes. Marc shifts his weight from one foot to the other. His eyes roving over her olive skinned cleavage lingering before returning to her eyes. "Doesn't Melinda tell you it's not that serious?" Her eyes smiling. Marc not able to hide his surprise.

"How do you know her name?"

Jadon, "We are sorority sisters. Women tell each other a lot about their lovers. She has told me quite a bit about you. How passionate and strong you are in bed."

Marc, "So what else has she told you about us?"

Jadon, "She told me you wouldn't be easy because you are faithful and becoming too involved for her."

Marc expression hurt. "So this was all just a game for you? To see how I would react, social behavior of the male animal." Jadon recognizes the situation is tanking fast. Needing to make her move.

Jadon, "She is not ready to settle down and be a one man woman just yet."

The hurt in Marc's eyes turns to anger. "She couldn't tell me this herself?"

Jadon, "She has. Think about it, she only uses you as a booty call. So stop rushing her."

Marc, "I wasn't aware I was."

Jadon, "Would you sit at the bar next to me? I really don't feel like being hit on."

Trying to hide his hurt, Marc says, "I was leaving but why not?"

Jadon, "At least have one drink with me. Then I'm willing to let you leave." Moving over to the bar with her. Marc unsure why he is suddenly drawn to stay at her side. "Raul, mi hermano dos." Holding up two fingers. Raul moves quickly mixing her drinks. Jadon touching the screen of her cell phone then holding it out to Marc for him to take. "Here this is for you." Looking at her perplexedly. Jadon encouraging him to retrieve the message hands the phone over. Lightly placing her hand on his hard bicep. Questioning himself, *How would she know to give the message to her for me?* Reluctantly listening to the message. Turning away from Jadon. Raul places their cocktails on the bar in front of Jadon. "Put it on our account." Raul nods and moves on to his more anxious customers. Jadon glances over her shoulder Marc's back to her still. She presses a release on her jewel-encrusted ring. Its top lifting up slightly. Taking the drink intended for Marc she sprinkles a powder onto it. Speaking words softly a vortex quickly forms inside the glass dispersing the powder mixing it into the drink. Satisfied, she places the drink back on the bar casually. A smile curling her lips sly and ever so cruel.

Marc listening to Melinda's message. "Hi, babe. I'm tutoring a friend tonight. Hang out with Camel he'll make sure you hook up. He always has a harem around him. I'm just not ready for a serious relationship. You're a sweet guy and definitely hot in the sack. We'll talk soon, bye babe." Marc deleting the message. Placing her up on the bar. His anger rising faster than the hurt of being dumped.

Jadon, "Here you go." Marc downs the drink in one gulp. "Is everything all right?" Her voice pleasant yet managing to be concerned.

Marc frowning, "Yeah. Raul! Another round." His voice deep, "Are you ready for another one?"

Jadon, "I am smaller than you. It wouldn't be wise for me to drink that fast. I could get taken advantage of."

Marc, "Take your time I'm not in a hurry."

Jadon downs her drink, only water. "I'm always up for another one." Raul places two more in front of them. Jadon on impulse moves closer to Marc. Leaning up on her tip toes and reaching up with her long nailed hand behind Marc's neck. Pulling his face toward hers their lips gently touching his. Quickly rippling over his thick lips. Marc responds his tongue sliding against hers eagerly. Hot passionate energy rushing over both of them. Responding to her sensuality his pulse quickening. Her perfume surrounding him. Slowly releasing their kiss.

Mike from De Ville's nursery passes by checking Jadon out, then seeing Marc. "I didn't know you came here. How are you?" Shaking his hand.

Marc, "Good."

Mike glances over at Jadon. "Apparently." Giving Marc a questioning look remembering him with Melinda.

Marc, "This is Jadon. Jadon, Mike, we work together sometimes."

Jadon, "Hello." Her smile curt.

Mike leans to whisper into Marc's ear. "She with you?"

Jadon, "I'm right here and the answer to that is yes, if he is interested."

Marc, "You heard the lady."

Jadon takes Marc's hand pulling him. "Let's dance. Nice to meet you Mike. Let's see how you move big guy."

Mike, "See ya. I'll call you about the order." His voice lost in the loud music and rumble of male voices around the bar. Jadon stays close to Marc as they squeeze through the crowd. One of GaGa's songs starting.

Marc's loaded drink starts to be absorbed into his bloodstream. Feeling warmth and euphoria from the unknown white compound spreading out through his brain and body. Giving him increased libido. His masculine strength with arousal sliding down the leg of his boxer shorts. Jadon moves sensuously and rhythmically with her hips to the music. Her silver-green eyes hypnotic, more like an Arabian princess'. Marc masculine by nature moving his pelvis thrusting with the bass drums pounding. They begin moving in unison slowing with the timing of the music. Marc and Jadon marveling in each other's sensuality. Overhead lights dimmed then flashing and changing colors pulsing to the beat. Heat and humidity rising around all the dancers. Perspiration streaking down Marc's face. Unbuttoning his shirt allowing heat out and cooler air rushing in feeling so good. Inhibitions falling with euphoria pouring over his body. Jadon reveling in his muscular chest covered in short dark hair. Reaching inside his shirt running her hand over the well-developed pectorals, lightly brushing across both sides. Increasing tactile stimulation to encourage nature to arouse within him new feelings. Marc becoming more alive than he can remember.

Jadon, "Your muscles are so hard." Wanting to see more ripping his shirt open buttons popping off. Marc pleasantly surprised by her begins dancing for her. Encouraged by him she moves her hands over his chest with her long nails raking his skin beneath them. Sending waves of pleasure through his body creating ecstasy. Not ever aware of feeling more alive than he is now. His pupils dilating further as the drug she gave him increases its action physically being circulated in the blood. Sending waves of warm ecstasy rushing down his spine. Jadon increases his enthrallment for her. This sensation familiar to times with Melinda. That thought of past comparison overtaken in the moment. Ripples of warmth delighting his senses again and again. Staring deeply into Jadon's silver-green eyes, their colors swirling hypnotically. Pressing against her as a slower lovers' song moves over its dancers.

Marc whispers in her ear, "Come on, my place. I need you." The treble of his voice dropping an octave to bass, growling. His eyes so intensely sexual, no mystery left on the amount of pent up passion she was in for.

Jadon, "I thought you would never ask." Batting her long dark lashes looking innocent and playful. Her eyes twinkling as a mischievous smile comes forth. Marc pulls her closer yet as the music slows. Jadon's hands are on his shoulders as she glances at her watch discreetly noting the time. How perfect the timing exactly 11:45 p.m. Now with the song ending Marc takes her hand leading her off the crowded dance floor.

Outside Jadon takes the lead using the car remote to her red Ferrari convertible chirp. Its doors unlocking with the top opening back. Lightning crackles across the night sky its stars hidden by clouds now. Marc looks up to the sky. "You might want to put the top back up. Looks like another downpour."

Jadon, "Not on us darling, just the party here." Marc climbs into the passenger side sliding the seat all the way back.

Marc, "Whatever you say. Let's go."

Jadon, "Keep that attitude. I'm going to make you one satisfied man tonight."

Marc with his vision spinning laughs one of those deep masculine sounds rumbling like a lion. "I'm counting on it." Leaning over kissing her neck giving her chills. Peeling off away from the curb tires smoking leaving burnt rubber wafting across the crowd waiting outside the club.

Angelique arrives in her white Corvette taking the spot that was just vacated. Stepping out with her long shapely legs extended out. Standing up adjusting her sundress which exposes her taut waist. Walking with a confident stride in her five inch Dolce & Gabbana heels clicking past the line of mostly young women outside Joey's. Unconcerned about the imminent storm rising up following her. Her blonde hair gently swaying with the light breeze pushing in. Passing a couple of women irritated with her arrogance and beauty. Herself seeming not to take notice of them. One comments, "Probably another bar whore." Angelique's face remains unchanged her sky blue eyes becoming strangely remote. Then dangerously hard for a split second. Raising her left hand to brush back a fallen strand of hair back from her face. Her double digit carat diamond ring sparkling when she moves her hand. Making a quick twist of the wrist.

Both doormen recognize her at once. One unclips the red felt rope. The other uses his imposing size to make an opening for her brushing aside patrons at the front of the line. He speaks, "Angelique, come in." his deep voice friendly. She does not bother to acknowledge either of the men. A gust of wind hits the door so powerfully that it slams into the wall inside the bar. Carrying with it bits of paper, gravel, and bar napkins flying inside. Heads turn towards the entrance at the loud bang of the door. Angelique not missing a step continues moving toward her target. The door rebounds shut right behind her just in time.

Rain splatters down pushed horizontally across the line of patrons. A deluge opens up on them like a burst from a fire hydrant. Wetting down the line of patrons especially heavy against the two that made snide statements about her. Leaving their clothes and hair dripping wet. Surprising most with the sudden change in weather. The next wave of wind driven rain sends young women scattering in all directions. Screams of anguish could be heard up and down the street. Along with countless designer pumps running and splashing for cover in the quickly flooding street.

Arriving back at Marc's home in darkness the power still out. Entering the manor through the side entrance. Just inside the doorway with only ambient moonlight under a cloudless sky. Marc takes Jadon in his arms kissing her deeply. She releases the kiss offering her neck for him. He eagerly moves down it with tender brushes of his lips. Jadon moans from the pleasure of his lips caressing and teeth lightly nipping at her neck. His masculine scent mixed with cologne intoxicating to her. Her thoughts swept along, *He is a good man. There has to be a way save him.* Their heavy breathing is the only noise indicating someone's in the shadowy hallway. Jadon pushes Marc away from her needing to reassert who's in control. Having nearly been swept under his newly developing magnetism. Himself unaware of changes wrought by ancient powers of pre-Christian Europe taking effect.

Marc whispers to her, "Boudoir." More a command of need. Taking her hand leading her through the dark mansion up the stairs. Ambient light dimly illuminating the way to their final destination. Where the master suite is waiting and ready. The moon a sliver, what little light reflected between mirrors inside the room brightening it enough to just make out the forms of furniture. Marc easily navigates their way to the king sized bed. Jadon steps up onto the bed turning to face Marc. Now taller than him, she pushes the silk shirt off Marc's large shoulders. Himself anxious but allowing her to feel in control. Stepping off the bed she unfastens his belt. His pants dropping with his boxer shorts to the floor. Enabling comfort to engorgement as his helmeted member springs up to his navel. Making a sound that can only happens with skin against hard muscle covered skin. Jadon delighted with her effect on him not to mention a generous gift from nature. Pushing him back on the bed forcefully.

Marc certainly not resisting her approach, Jadon throws her arms up. Gently her dress lifts up and over her head defying gravity. Exposing her nude Pilates toned body. The dress itself gliding over the back of a chair. Jadon jumps on top of Marc calling out in midair, "Igniculus!" Candles ignite all around the room.

After hours of indulging in pleasures of the flesh both luxuriating in each other's discoveries of the other's mysteries. Jadon insists on moving to the spa tub. Marc in a musk delirium is more than willing. His only focus is on her pleasure and delights. They make their way to the tub already filled with water steam rising off it. Candles positioned on the black granite surround with its gold flecks sparkling from within the stone. Jadon casts her hand out gracefully toward them flames puffing on. Sprinkling herbs clockwise over the surface of the water. Following her hand above the liquid stirring slowly at first but increasing in speed until a vortex forms at the center of it. Pulling everything off the surface down into it.

Jadon steps into the center unafraid. Sinking down until the water washes over her olive skinned breasts bobbing with nipples erect. Looking up into Marc's handsome face with his sensitive eyes, so trusting. Wishing there was some way to save him from the eventual outcome of all this. Knowing there will have to be sacrifices sometimes and the cost will be innocence lost. A small price to pay, well sometimes. Hardening her heart, holding out her hand. "Come, take my hand." Marc accepts it, stepping into the swirling brew completely enthralled with her. Waves crash against the sides of the tub and over his back. Wetting the fine fringe of dark hair running down his spine. Jadon chants, "Elements stir, water sprites dance for thy new satyr. Bear witness to the power of the ancient ones to accept this gift." Marc is so focused on his own passions toward her not listening to what she is chanting. Putting his arms around her sinking into union. The final step of the ritual of supplication is completed. Dark hair spreads thickening and moving up his spine and across his shoulders, forming a thunderbird T on his back. His already fine haired chest filling in to become thick as a pelt of Russian mink fur. Spreading from the center of his chest across his large pectorals and down the center of his abdomen. Creating a strip covering the rippling muscles all the way to his dark coarse patch.

Gently biting her neck and sucking on it. Sending shivers of pleasure through her deep within. Jadon's delighted giggles change to laughter unable to hold it back anymore. Herself unable to resist the power she is channeling finding it too intoxicating. Her laughter echoes against the stone walled room. Carrying it out into the house reaching up into the night. Rainfall mixed with hail coming down now angrily pelting against the windows. Water pouring over the rain gutters completely inundating them. Lightning flashing like a strobe lighting up the interior of the house as if it were daylight.

CHAPTER 13

HOURS EARLIER AFTER Lady GaGa had performed, Joey's was packed. The front entrance door slams shut. Music drowns out the commotion Angelique created at the front of the club. Melinda has worked herself into a perfect viewing position to watch their plan come to fruition. Flirting with her date keeping him focus away from the front of the club and now away from the dance floor. Where the excitement will be taking place soon. Angelique shimmers a glamour over herself becoming a nondescript blonde. Yet resembling on closer inspection one of the women dancing with Camel. Now her eyes green and her clothing dark. Camel unprepared for what was coming. Her gift of revenge unexpected as her arrival, dancing with his companions. His strapping back to the door with danger moving closer every second.

Melinda jokes with her date Brian. Who drives a beer delivery truck for Labatt's. Himself a very muscular yellow blonde, his height 5'10", brown eyes fixed on her. Having wanted Melinda for a long time. Wondering how he finally got so lucky but not really caring about the why. Lustily following her lithe body movements ignoring the gust of wind and commotion moments earlier. Melinda hops up on a bar stool allowing her short dress to ride up. Tugging her dress back down over her crossed legs. Brian's eyes follow her hand to her shapely legs. His gaze roving down to her high heeled feet wearing Jimmy Choo's. Knowing only that they are expensive shoes because she comes from money. Guessing probably they cost more than he makes in a week.

Melinda feels a pair of eyes burning a hole in her head. Excusing herself. "I'll be right back." Before leaving calling an order to Raul, "Two schnapps peppermint." Smiling at the bartender.

After excusing herself from Brian, she slips off through the crowded bar over to her cohort for any final instructions. Intercepting Angelique now a slender blonde. Knowing her preference to use this glamour. Angelique snaps her head toward Melinda, speaking to her, "Everything is going as planned. Jadon has our man. You just need to be on time for a change."

Melinda, "Have I ever let you down?"

Angelique looks at her. "Don't," her voice threatening.

Melinda, "Can't I stay and watch? Besides, it's stormy out tonight I might get wet."

Angelique, "You might want to get your man toy out of here before the party is over."

Melinda, "I will, just not yet." Thunder rumbling louder than the bass speakers mirroring her mood. Rain thrumming against the roof.

Angelique, "See you soon." Her voice pleasantly feminine belying her murderous intentions. Melinda returns to Brian's side, himself having a conversation with a coworker. Raul places the drinks she ordered in front of her.

Raul, "Your drinks ma'am." Winking at her knowingly for she is up to something. Melinda smiles back at him opening her purse removing a small brown vial. Brian's back to her talking. Sprinkling a white powder on one of the shots. Saying a power word the liquid begins spinning into a small whirlpool. Just as quickly stopping. Melinda taps Brian on the shoulder. Handing him the shot as he turns to her.

"Bottoms up." Downing her drink. Both of them stamping their shot glasses down against the bar.

Brian puts his strong arms around her waist pulling her to him. Brian says, "Come on babe let's go somewhere quieter."

Melinda, "Just what I was thinking. Just a few more minutes then we can go. Come on it's too crowded by the bar." Moving them over to a wall by the fire exit. Positioning Brian with his back to the dance floor. Where very soon things are going to heat up quickly. Anxiously awaiting the show. Distracting Brian, Melinda reaches up to pull him closer for a kiss. Brian is eager to accommodate her meeting her lips with his. Kissing wet and deeply.

Out on the dance floor Angelique is working her way closer to Camel. Her anger building the closer she gets to that Arabian dog. Her feet no longer touching the floor except for the toes of her shoes gliding into position. Melinda looks around Brian. Thinking, *Impressive, no one even notices her.* Angelique now at the center of the dance floor behind Camel. Improving on the glamour adjusting it slightly satisfied with her appearance. Anyone noticing would identify another blonde resembling one of the two already dancing with Camel. Raising her arms upward moving with music. Then with a twist of her wrists spreading her fingers sending a spark of blue-white energy streaking across the light fixtures above them. Lightning streaking down from the storm outside. Striking the building at the same time. In that instant she uses both hands to grip her anthem bringing it down with all her anger stabbing Camel in the back. Darkness covering her move, she twists the knife before pulling it out. Camel gasps from the sudden shock of severe pain deep in his back. Followed by excruciating pain in his chest and shoulder. Dropping to him to his knees. Letting out a ragged yell, his breath taken away before more can come out.

Pulling her anthem free dripping with his blood. Then wrapping it in one of his old undershirts stuffed in her purse. Using a second knife she stabs him again before moving away. Nanoseconds later lightning explodes the fixtures showering the patrons in sparks, popping and crackling.

Sending the room into panic with people screaming and scrambling to get out from under the light fixtures, running in every direction. Her blooded anthem safely wrapped and placed in her Prada bag. Then shoving the bloody knife into one of Camel's dance partners' hands. Tripping her into the other one causing them both to fall. The knife being dropped and kicked sending it skidding in the pandemonium. Both women attempt to get up slipping and falling in the warm sticky puddle already surrounding Camel's still, lifeless body.

Panic overtakes logic, evidenced by sounds coming from all over the room. Patrons fall and scream, crashing over furniture. People attempt to get away from the electrical sparks and shattering glass falling. After a delay the emergency lights blink on to reveal in shadowy horror the bloody scene. One of the two young female companions is blood splattered standing over Camel's motionless body. Blood pooling under his prone body spreading out around it.

Beth screaming uncontrollably. Kara her friend struggles up from the floor only to slip in the castoff from the first time he was stabbed with the anthem. Falling face first into warm blood not able to break her fall. She strikes her face against the floor. Momentarily stunned with her nose bleeding, she struggles, flailing with her arms and legs slipping unable to get traction. Slowly she crawls away, her breath puffing between gasps, whimpering. Not able to scream, too focused on getting away from his bloody body. Leaving a trail of dark red blood smudged like an enormous snake had passed through.

Melinda across the room is enjoying herself entirely too much. Watching the spectacle unfold before her. Brian's pupils so dilated, his eyes are black in the dim lighting. His strong arms still wrapped around Melinda. Oblivious to the situation around them. Melinda gently rubs her buttocks against his normal response. Delighted with how well their plan is going. Camel face down on the floor unmoving and those two stupid bitches. Already the prime suspects. Pushing Brian away from her impatient with him. Seeing his look of disappointment. She kisses him deeply meeting his tongue with hers. Then breaking off the kiss, saying, "Come on babe. Let's go." Taking his hand pulling him towards the fire exit door. Already standing open with its alarm ringing. Things couldn't be going better, her mind racing ahead to the next step before ducking out into the rain, laughing.

One of the bar patrons, a resident from a local hospital emergency department rushes over to help the injured male. Immediately begins to assess Camel's condition. Checking his carotid pulse, weak and thready. Amazed he still has one at all noting the volume of blood loss. Respirations shallow and labored. Flipping his cell phone open, dialing 911, while applying strong pressure to the single stab wound using bar napkins. Hoping to slow the hemorrhaging.

Speaking to Camel, "My name is Ali. Can you hear me?" His patient coughing up foamy blood, gasping. Ali calls out, "I need some help here!"

A tall slender dark-skinned women comes over. Concern on her face. "How can I help?"

"Take this call and repeat what I say to the operator." The 911 operator is speaking to Ali at the same time as he is handing off the phone to her. "Tell the operator where to send the ambulance. I have to stabilize him or he is going to die right here," he says. Already handling her part on the phone with the operator. Oolong takes over giving directions and information. Ali assesses his patient's quickly changing condition with his body twisted to the left. The same side as the stab wound, plus the gasping, labored respirations shallow, tinged with foamy bloody sputum. Checking the pulse again, irregular and thready. Pneumothorax.

Looking at the woman. "Can you hold this down? It needs to stay in place over the wound. Keep constant pressure on it at all times."

Oolong kneels beside Camel. "Yes! Just send the ambulance!" Becoming impatient.

"I need a knife," Ali says, looking frantically around at the bar.

"Open my purse." Pushing it toward Ali with her leg. "You'll find one there." Ali lifts out an ivory-handled knife, yellowed with age very old. Then pulling up on the fabric of Camel's shirt, cutting it open all the way down.

"Damn." Impressed with the sharpness of an obsidian blade. Setting the knife down on Camel's back. Keeping it as clean as possible under the circumstances. Palpating his ribs along the left side reaching under his armpit. Taking a pen out of his pocket. Biting down on the end using his teeth to hold on, pulling the insides out leaving a hollow tube. Then picking the knife up again cutting between the ribs causing a grizzle sound as it cuts through muscle. Pushing the knife deeper between his patient's ribs. Camel groan low from pain but not regaining consciousness.

Ali inserts the makeshift tube of the ink pen into the opening between the ribs. Making a hissing sound that allows the lung to re-inflate. The blood bubbling around the tube Ali uses a piece of his patient's shirt to pack it. Camel groans. The wail of sirens approaches in the distance. The young intern satisfied with this triaged step. Reassessing his patient, external hemorrhaging stopped, respirations easier, thorax no longer tilted to the left. Taking a deep breath Ali looks at the knife. Then hands it back to the woman. "That's very old, isn't it?"

Accepting it back, wiping it off before putting it away back into her purse. She looks Ali in the eye before answering him. "Yes, it is." The EMTs arrive pulling the stretcher clattering across the floor. Ali ready to give a report to them, looking over to thank his nurse but no one is there. He searches the crowd of onlookers who have remained with more gathering. Ali begins giving a report to the EMTs. After the stab wound is taped down well and the chest tube secured. He helps the burly emergency trained men turn Camel over and then lift him onto the gurney. Then an IV of normal saline inserted opened on full. Oxygen mask in place and running at two liters.

Police cars slide to a stop outside cutting their sirens off, lights still flashing. The scene inside the bar surreal. Turned over tables with broken glass scattered across the floor. Lighting fixtures shattered some still buzzing and crackling with sparks popping.

Detective Barracks, "Can we get the power turned off to these? I don't feel like getting electrocuted." Detective Arros assesses the few remaining people inside along with the employees. Both detectives are all too familiar with domestic violence. Arros had uniformed men establishing a perimeter with the help of beat cops that have the area as their patrol. The gurney clatters by with Camel's unconscious body on it. The crowd parts for it. Sirens wail as it pulls out of the parking lot heading for the closest emergency room.

Detective Arros, "Did anyone see what happened in here?" Canvassing immediately for any witness in the crowd gathered inside.

Detective Barracks the senior detective takes the lead inside. Having already started questioning the good Samaritan, Dr. Ali Khan, taking down notes. Detective Arros comes inside heading right over to the bartender. Knowing that if anyone saw something it would be him. Plus they know what's going on in the club. Speaking to Raul, he says, " Que passo? So what happened?"

Raul, "That's the crazy bitch right there!" Pointing out Beth sitting quietly her affect flat. Not seeming to register what is going on around her. Staring at her blood covered hands, the blood already drying. Her face smeared with drying blood and her clothes soaked from her fall. Her lip already swelling, a raised area over her eye. Looking more like she had been punched in the face. And so much blood on her dress. How could she not have been the perpetrator?

Detective Barracks, "What's your relationship to the victim?"

Dr. Khan, "I didn't know him." Answering his next question, "I came here to meet some friends. But they were unable to make it. It's ladies' night and I'm here to meet women."

Det. Barracks, "One more question." Dr. Khan waiting patiently. "What did you see?"

Dr. Khan, "I saw that young woman with a knife in her hand." Indicating Beth.

Det. Barracks, "You didn't happen to see where the knife went?"

Dr. Khan, "No. But then I was a little busy." Detective Barracks satisfied for now turning Dr. Khan over to a uniform to get contact information.

Detective Barracks approaches Beth calmly. Choosing his tactics to use with her as he walks over. Having decided she looks battered. So to start slow with her and be a friend. Speaking softly to her, "So what happened to your boyfriend?"

"I don't know," Beth answers Detective Barracks.

"It looks like it got pretty rough. You're all banged up."

Beth slow to respond answers, "I don't know."

Barracks, "How could you not? You have most of your boyfriend's blood on your dress. It was very pretty. How did all of it get there?"

Beth, "It's Camel's blood?" Looking at her hands, taking in that her dress is now soaked in his blood. Registering that something had happened.

Detective Barracks, "How do you think all that blood got on your dress?"

Beth, "Well, he was bleeding."

Detective Arros, "I found it! Get forensics over to document this." Having found a knife under one of the sofa cushions on the floor. Their forensics team started snapping pictures, swabbing blood, gathering evidence.

Detective Barracks, "We're going to need a swab from your hands and dress. You don't mind, do you?" His crime scene technician steps up. "While you're here we need to get a cheek swab." Looking at Beth, "It's just routine with this kind of investigation. We need to exclude you from other contributors."

Beth, "Yes, the knife, he must have been stabbed when the lights went out. I'm sure of it. It was a knife. I had it in my hand."

Detective Barracks, "So then you do remember? You stabbed your boyfriend."

Beth, "No. I didn't stab him. Someone put it in my hand."

Detective Barracks, "Where is that person?" Looking around his movements sarcastic. "Let me tell you what happened. Your boyfriend roughed you up tonight. We can all see what happened to you. Then old tomcat decided he wanted a three-way. Some new meat to kick it up a notch."

Beth, "No, that's not what happened."

Detective Barracks, "When he started working another woman you couldn't handle the competition. This all after your friend slept with your man. Right?"

Beth, "No! Kara and I are friends."

Detective Barracks, "Then you didn't mind sharing him with some other woman?" Beth shocked by hearing him make it sound so sorted and tawdry. "Maybe it was Kara who put the knife in your hand."

"No. She would never do that."

Detective Barracks, "You were both doing him. I think I've heard enough. Stand up, put your hands behind your back." Starting into the Miranda rights.

Beth, "This can't be happening." Tearing up unable to stop the wave sending them streaming down her already tear-streaked face, running through the dried blood.

CHAPTER 14

ANGELIQUE HAD RETURNED home only moments before using only focused thought. Being over one hundred and fifty years old did have its benefits. That and she was the granddaughter of a powerful witch or priestess, as was commonly named. At least before Christianity ruined Europe and a couple of other continents. Her grandmother was alleged to have been more than one thousand years old at her untimely death. Betrayed by one of her male lovers. Something that wasn't going to happen to her ever. Camel came so close to changing her mind. Shuddering to think what could have become of her if that had come to pass. She didn't trust her own coven members. Jadon was too soft and just maybe just a little to reserved to be trusted. She definitely was not easily read. Never trust a traitor. Not even one you've turned from Islam. Then there was Melinda a treacherous New York witch. She definitely had potential, but then she had extorted millions from her own father. That one liked power for the sake of power. Certainly one to never tip your hand to. She would cut it off and offer it back. At a price that is.

She is finishing up writing the ancient inscriptions and symbols inside the double circle. Which surrounded the inverted pentagram with its point in a southward direction. Anxious for her two priestess to arrive back. Needing the power of three along with the energy obtained from satyrs in the making. Placing the scrimshaw hilted anthem with Camel's drying blood at the easternmost point of the star. Symbolizing her betrayal of him. That and a gift to the old powerful spirit of ancient Sumerians. The most important part of this ritual. Would it accept her gift? Only doubting herself for a moment. How could it turn down something so coveted.

Following her grandmother's directions all the way down to the most mundane detail. Only candlelight illuminating the room. Shadows dancing as the flames flicker with a life of their own. Uncovering the large Louis XVI mirror. Having used black silk after blessing it under a full moon.

Angelique hears laughter coming from her boudoir. Her dressing mirror full length. Each woman stepping through it one at a time into the room. Leaving the conjuring room to give her novice witches their final instructions. Before allowing them in, lest they unsettle the elements so carefully called upon before their arrival.

Angelique, "Put on your robes and stop the frivolity. This is not some party mixer. You will need to focus your energy as I have taught you. Adding the energy gathered from your willing male cockles. Soon themselves to be changed forever into forest beasts. Only good for stud until their usefulness is no longer needed."

Melinda, "We have done everything you requested. Allow us our moment of joy." Angelique glares at her. Jadon uncomfortable with this labile woman, her smile gone. Knowing she could kill either of them and not have a troubled night's sleep.

Angelique, "Take your places. Now focus the energy you have gathered. Direct it with your minds when I call for it. Then you will push it into the center of the pentagram." Angelique not one pleased with giving instructions more than once. Both young women at attention listening closely. Waving her hand across the doubly encircled star of protection, the ritual began. Candles placed so they are aligned with the points of the star outside the circles, igniting. Air inside the room becoming very still. The outside world diminishing away from the three.

Angelique gives a command. "Gather round and take my hands sisters." They join hands forming a circle. "Do not step inside these circles." Raising their hands skyward. Walking counterclockwise once around the circles. "Twice more to seal and charge it. For it is the only thing protecting us from what we are conjuring. One wrong step and it will surely kill. It destroys anything it touches until we appease it with the offering. Are we clear on this?" Jadon and Melinda answer yes.

The air in the room is deathly still, as if waiting in anticipation. At first only a drawn breath to be heard from Jadon trying to calm herself. Doubtful, questioning her own courage. Angelique is satisfied that she has them fearful enough to watch closely. She begins. "Bend back time to the millennia's past. Open the darkness from out of history lost." A breeze rises up causing the candles to flicker. Melinda catches her breath. Her thoughts racing. *If she can do this, what could I really learn from her?* Angelique continues her chant. "I call upon the demon, Enkil of Sumerian days gone by. Come forth so we may offer you a gift!" Her voice growing louder as her intention becomes known. The blood crusted anthem rocks slightly. Air flows quicker as something nears them. Cold darkness with icy tendrils reaching out to touch the women. Angelique's voice louder yet. "Enkil of Sumer. I compel thee to come forth! I call upon thee, I beseech thee in my hour of need." Wind howling as a tornado forms inside the circles. Her anthem rising up slowly into the air. Darkness shaping into a dense cloud spun around the vortex.

Angelique, "Accept this vessel as your own!" Changing air pressure in the room causing their ears to pop. Making sounds oddly different. Candle flames extend several inches more like oil flames. Angelique stands strong, defiant. Her blue eyes round insane with hatred and rage. Darkness fills the center of the storm. No longer able to see one another across from each other their candles all going out at once. Taking with them all sound. No light coming from anywhere. Darkness that of a cave with its cold dank breath exhaled, touching their faces. As someone standing too close in the dark watching you. Unspeaking but wanting you to know he is there, seething with anger that is palpable. Cold air brushes against Jadon as it were hands roving down her legs. Unnerving her enough to bring forth an unconscious gasp of fear. Surrounding all with its evil presence until candles on the outer edges of the room reignite. A dark shadowy form inside the circles seething in the clouds. Bubbling upon itself. Yellow feline like eyes, malicious and intelligent. Glaring back at Angelique harder than she could have imagined. Herself determined to make this choice a reality. No going back now.

Angelique's anthem floating up into the maelstrom to where a face should be. Sensing her time to begin the accord. Angelique speaks up, "Yes, smell and taste the blood of our offering. We give this to you willingly. For this we ask only your obedience. Then you may be released to go as you choose." A bestial growl deeper than any normal human male could make, low at first. Rising up in volume until it is a roar echoing throughout the dark house. Making it tremble to its very foundations deep within the earth. Sending a small new crack racing up the subbasement and wine cellar wall. Then taking out the electricity with it.

Enkil began speaking in the ancient tongue of Sumerian. Melinda, "What language is he speaking?"

Angelique, "Sumerian, not that I have ever heard it before or anyone else living today." Thinking of one person who might just have been around long enough. Changing her mind. It will assume our language.

Enkil having listened to them speak changes to modern English. Having discerned it as being a dominant language throughout the neighborhood. His voice a deep vibrating bass that of a large man. "Who is it that conjures me?"

Angelique, speaking in a soft voice, "It is I who calls upon you." Regaining her strength of voice. "Do you not like our offering to you?" Enkil holds back his immediate reaction. To kill them and leave. Curiosity piqued, he decides to go along with their insipid little game. Seeing where it leads.

Enkil, "Yes. Your offering of a strong man of noble character and birth is exceptional." Stretching out his telepathic senses touching Camel's mind. His hold on life tenuous very close to death. The cord of life stretched thin. "You have brought this man as near to death as he can be physically. At any moment he will slip away."

Angelique, "What care you of his dilemma? You may do with him as you see fit. Before that happens will you accept the terms of my proposal? A true gift indeed since you find him so exceptional and of noble birthright." Taking his time to consider her offer.

Enkil, "What is it that you want?" Angelique knows this could be the deal breaker. Pushing ahead. "Your obedience."

Enkil, "Is that all?" Sarcasm thick in his deep voice.

Angelique covering her real motive, "Take him and do as you will. We no longer have use for him."

Enkil, "Then it is you who is doing me a favor?" Angelique relaxes just so slightly. Enkil skilled enough to read the smallest tick of her body movement. Toying with her. "Why such a wonderful gift?" Its reptilian pupils mere slits. Cold and calculating, tilting his head suspiciously.

Melinda becoming inpatient, "We don't need him to interfere with our plans. Just take him." Enkil and Angelique are both angered by her impetuous outburst. Enkil looks at her seething with rage. Forcing her to take a step back. So much anger in his stare as to put heat upon her cheeks. Barely able to contain himself.

Angelique yells at her, "Silence! You fool." Enkil's laughter bounces off the walls. Putting cracks in the plaster ceiling. Jadon shivers unable to contain her fear. Nothing had prepared her for this. Being face to face with evil this strong she would be marked by this for life. Carrying its scar upon her soul, that is.

Angelique, "Do you accept my terms for the gift? Or shall I rebuke you back into the darkness from where you came?"

Enkil, "No mortal witch has ever controlled me!" His voice threatening.

Angelique, "I'm no ordinary witch!" Insulted by his challenge to her. Raising up her hand to brandish an ancient talisman on a gold chain worn around her neck.

Angelique extends her hand to take back her anthem. Enkil holds it in his hand open palmed with long talons curved. Challenging her to take it back keeping balanced there moving before them. Angelique is unable to take it back. Knowing her own limits she redirects him by going back to the purpose for which it was brought before him. "He is yours to do with him what you will. You have a noble man to do as you see fit to use."

He is enjoying watching her anger increase until those round blue eyes are bulging. Not one to give in easily. "A woman spurned. I can sense you were lovers. You seek to destroy a strong man you couldn't control even with your powers." Really getting under her skin now. Stamping her foot, then throwing back her hooded cloak.

Angelique, "Do we have an accord? Yes? He is a manly man. I would think that would be something you could appreciate."

Enkil, "What is it you ask of me?"

Angelique, "In return you come when I call upon you to do my bidding. We both will benefit from this arrangement."

Enkil, "Be warned. Never trifle with me and if I ever find betrayal from you, revenge is a double-edged sword that I will see you suffer beside me. Your soul will know the darkest despair I can visit upon you."

Angelique disregards his statement. "Consider me warned, Enkil."

"Then I accept your gift as payment for now."

Enkil's form dissolves back into a turbulent cloud boiling in over itself. Wind howls at gale forces inside the double circles. Making the very air shimmer from its force. Vanishing with a large blast of cold air gusting over the three women. Their clothes billow back from pressure. Once again, their room is silent and dark except for the smoldering embers of the candles. Jadon casts her trembling hand outward reigniting the candles around the room. Lights come back on in the house. Shining from under the door to the adjacent room. The three of them look at each other. They had done it. Bursting out into laughter.

Melinda, "Now back to business. Jadon have you acquired your part of the ingredients?"

Jadon, "Yes. I have the perspiration of a young satyr. And you?"

Melinda, "Good, yes I do. The skin of a not so innocent man."

Angelique, "Then it is as it should be. I have the blood of a guilty man. We can begin." Their laughter rises up turning into insane cackles echoing. All three cast their hands skyward. Lightning crackles in response streaking across the night sky. Thunder rumbles threateningly outside in the quiet neighborhood.

Melinda, "Now all we need is blood from innocence lost." Looking from one to the other.

Angelique, "I've got that in the works. That vessel will be our final ingredient." Like any good poker player not showing all her cards until the final hand is dealt.

CHAPTER 15

MARC WAKES UP with a startle to hear thunder reverberating inside his bedroom just before lightning strikes one of the old trees causing it to explode. Light brighter than that of the sun for just a millisecond flashing escaping from behind the heavy drapes. Streaking across the room taking with it the last foggy bits of a dream just hanging on. His uncle Theron yelling at him, "Fool!" inside his head. The digital alarm clock displays a cool blue 3:00 a.m. Reaching across the bed feeling for Jadon. Touching only the cool sheets where she had been. Smelling her perfume jasmine still lingering on the sheet and himself. Sending his blood surging with thoughts of her. His bladder full he gets out of bed to urinate. Smiling to himself sleepily padding into the bathroom. Hearing the distant crackling of lightning across the sky. Its thunder muffled rain splattering against the windows. The worst part of the storm had not passed. Slipping back into bed under the covers sleepy and comforted as the storm intensifies outside.

That morning, Ms. Campbell is busily making biscuits along with directing her niece Mary to bring hot coffee up to Marc. Filling the chambord with water that is heated to almost boiling.

Ms. Campbell, "Now be on your way. The coffee will be strong enough by the time you get upstairs." Thinking to herself, being that he is not up yet, *I'm sure that will be just fine.*

Mary carrying the silver serving tray with the Chambord, china, and newspaper. Needing to balance it all on one arm while she knocks on the bedroom door tapping gingerly at first, unsure of herself. Calling out softly, "Hello." Her accent British. Having lived most of her lift in England, just outside London. After a few moments with no response she opens the door slowly. Calling out again, "Hello, are you awake?" All the while noticing an unfamiliar musky scent growing strong the farther she moves into the room. Beginning to understand why he hasn't gotten up yet, let alone heard her. No wonder it's so dark and quiet in here. Making her way slowly as her eyes adjust to the semidarkness. Thinking, what kind of bloke is he? After what her aunt had told her about him. Seeing the outline of a table next to the drapes. Setting the service down feeling for the drapery cord. Finding it pulling them open flooding the room with morning light.

Marc's sleeping form is facedown with a pillow over his head. Moving his leg just enough to cause the sheet to slip. Exposing his back now hairy. It follows his spine all the way down to where the sheet still covers him. This dark straight hair a couple of inches long also spreading out across his broad shoulders. Even the hair on his scalp is several inches longer now also. Mary gasps, startled to be seeing a half-naked man.

Waking up, "Who's there?" Moving fast knocking pillows off the bed falling to the floor. Whipping the sheet back the rest of the way off him. Jumping out of bed. Mary frozen for a second unsure as what to do staring at him. Marc speaks, "Who are you?" Mary blushes red and turns her face away from him. Having never seen a man naked, much less in the morning. As is perfectly natural for young men. Noticing his condition he grabs the sheet off the floor to cover himself.

Mary recovers somewhat but still embarrassed, speaking, "I'm Mary Campbell." Already moving away from him toward the door. Past clothing scattered across the floor some are woman's. All she hadn't been able to see in the darkened room. Marc realizes it's Ms. Campbell's niece. Calling out to her, "Wait! I mean I'm sorry!"

Mary embarrassedly rushes from the room its door slamming shut. Smelling the rich aroma of Columbian roast Marc shrugs the whole incident off, plunging the chambord. Sitting down at the table pouring his frothy coffee in its fine bone china cup followed by real cream. Not that instant stuff. Opening his morning newspaper oblivious to the front page story. Turning right to the sports section to see how the Yankees played last night.

Now that the sports section is completed Marc pours another cup of coffee carrying it with him into the bathroom. Sipping on it. Stepping on rose petals noticing they are scattered across the stone floor. Fragrances of rose and lavender pleasant enough, but another scent catching his attention. This one an unfamiliar scent of something herbal with an earthy undertone. Not so nice but not altogether bad. Following its smell over to the bottom of his spa tub. Picking it up a sachet smelling it closely. That's it. Then chunking it into the waste can. Making a mental note. That's the second woman he has met that used one of those. Huh, it must be something new women are into.

After showering, he uses a thick soft brown towel to dry off. Humming a tune content with life. Stepping in front of the mirror lathering on shaving cream to his face. His back still feeling cool and wet. Turning his head to look over his shoulder using the mirror to see his back. Shocked into stunned silence by what he sees. What the heck? How fast does body hair grow? His back covered from shoulder to shoulder and down the center all to where the towel is wrapped. Long dark hair at least three inches in length forming a large T of straight hair on his back. Resembling a Native American pictograph of the thunderbird. Disregarding his own comparison as preposterous. Wondering who in the Du Bois family was this hirsute. If this keeps up he'll look as hairy as a Persian.

Marc rushes downstairs dressed for outdoor work. Wearing a crew neck tee shirt dark hair curling over it at his throat. Faded blue jeans and a Yankees ball cap on. Entering the kitchen Ms. Campbell looks up from the morning paper. Her green eyes glaring. Marc already knows what's coming. Ms. Campbell, "If you're going to sleep nude from now on we'll leave your coffee outside in the hall. That or you can come downstairs when you're ready. My niece is a young lady."

Marc's cheeks burn red. "I'm so sorry. I forgot she would be here."

Ms. Campbell not one to be interrupted even once when she has something to say, raises her hand. "She has lived a sheltered life at Catholic parochial schools. Under the direction of an order of nuns. You get my meaning."

Marc, "Yes ma'am. Again I'm sorry. It won't happen again."

Ms. Campbell, "I certainly hope not. She is here to help me and learn some responsibilities before going off to college. I would hate to have to call that nice Mr. Thornburg. Being that he is so concerned about expenses. Mary will only be receiving a small stipend. Someone else having to replace her would cost considerably more." Knowing she has the upper hand. Giving Marc a smug look.

Marc, "Why don't I have the coffee downstairs for now." Ms. Campbell satisfied for now.

Marc ready to rush out of the kitchen but not before he is stopped. Ms. Campbell, "Wait! Isn't that your friend on the front page?" Indicating the newspaper on the granite counter.

Marc picks it up reading the headline, "Local College Student Stabbed. Are Violence Increasing in City Clubs?" Marc skims down the story. His pulse quickening as he reads the article. "During a freak electrical storm lightning struck night hot spot Joey's Club. Located on Monroe Avenue outside the inner loop. Reports from witnesses that the lighting system shorted out. Sending sparks showering down on the patrons of the overcrowded dance floor. Panic ensuing when the emergency lights failed to come on. Leaving the establishment in darkness. Creating conditions for the stampede that ensued in the rush for exits." Marc's throat tightens into a knot. "When emergency lights were restored local college student Camel Ali Khalid was found lying on the floor bleeding from an apparent stab wound. Area medical resident gave lifesaving emergent care while waiting for EMTs to arrive. Law enforcement officials are holding two young women. Suspects in the stabbing. Their names are being held. District attorney's office has refused to comment on the ongoing investigation."

Marc drops the newspaper. Turning his cell phone on seeing several missed calls, messages waiting. Fear making his rough hands tremble. Pressing redial off one of the calls getting the hospital. After getting transferred to the ICU nurse but getting nowhere due to HIPPA laws. Finally wrangling out that his brother is in critical condition Marc leaves immediately for the hospital. Confirming to Ms. Campbell she was right, it is Camel. Also that no good can come out of not living right.

CHAPTER 16

WHILE ON HIS drive to the hospital, Marc flashes back to childhood memories of when he and Camel met. Ahmed Khalid, Camel's father made all of his sons live the traditional old way for a month a year. So they wouldn't forget their roots. Thereby living in tents with carpets beneath them. Out in the deep desert under the stars, away from civilization. This was intended to keep Camel and his brothers humble no matter how wealthy they became. This while Dubai was becoming a major metropolis of the future. Marc was there with his dad. Who was working an archeological site. Being two preschool-age boys they became inseparable friends no, brothers. Exploring the desolate location as they grew older as the years passed.

Parking his blue Mustang on one of the upper garage levels. Marc takes the elevator down to get inside the modern hospital labyrinth. His frustration rising with his fears he walks through the maze. How bad could it be? If Camel dies—stopping that thought, but not before causing his throat to tighten up so much it hurts. His eyes mist up from grief. The elevator doors open to a nurses' station with a bank of electronic equipment beeping. Voices of the medical team muffled low. The smell of antiseptic strong. Feeling lost and overwhelmed in the surroundings so unfamiliar.

Nurse Peters, "May I help you?"

Marc, "Yes. I'm here to see Mr. Khalid."

Nurse Peters, "Are you family?"

Marc, "Yes, I'm one of his brothers."

Nurse Peters gets up. "He's in bay two. I'm so glad you're here. We haven't been able to contact any family members yet." Marc listens politely, anxious enough to run into the sealed bay. "He is allowed one visitor for ten minutes every two hours." Seeming to read Marc's thoughts. "He hasn't regained consciousness since his surgery."

Dr. Daas comes over to speak with Marc. His expression grave. "He is in guarded condition. Very lucky to be alive. If there hadn't been a medical resident there at the time of his stabbing it would have been fatal. His heart arrested once around 3:00 a.m. during his surgery. But he seems to be stable for now. He lost a lot of blood. That was a very nasty stab wound." Marc snarls inside, thinking about injuring the responsible person. Dr. Daas goes on, "Whoever stabbed him twisted the knife causing considerably more damage than just a simple wound. Something unusual I noted the shape of the blade was curved like a dagger. Thus allowing it to cause more injury internally from its tip." Marc looks at Dr. Daas and listens closely, his handsome face wrinkling with anger. Giving Dr. Daas pause, not realizing he had been too analytical. Forensic pathology a favorite pastime and being at a teaching hospital. Apologizing to Marc for being too graphic.

Marc, "How soon will we know he's going to be all right?"

Dr. Daas, "Well, his oxygen saturations are good. His collapsed lung isn't accumulating fluids into it and the hemorrhaging into the pericardium has stopped." Marc's face is ashen, his blue eyes rounded with fear of losing his brother. Tears close to coming. "He is strong as an ox and being so young. The next few hours will be critical for him. If he remains stable his chances of recovery improve with time. He was fortunate the dagger only pierced the pericardium. Any closer we wouldn't be having this conversation." Marc feels some relief, but not much.

Marc, "Thank you Dr. Daas."

Dr. Daas, "You're welcome. Go and be at your brother's side." Marc shakes the doctor's hand again and thanks him for saving Camel's life. Starting to walk toward the ICU pod. Dr. Daas speaks up, "Oh, something else. Your brother has been talking in his delirium. The Arabic I understand but he lapses into a much older dialect, the language I don't recognize. Do you know what it is he is speaking?"

Marc, "No. At least not until I have a chance to hear it. He was always the one to pick up on languages much easier than I could." Dr. Daas follows Marc into the pod Camel is recovering in. Hooked up to numerous monitors. Marc takes his brother's larger moreno hand in his own. Camel's hands are larger, but not calloused like his hands. Tears threaten to flow blurring his vision, Marc's body shaking.

Dr. Daas satisfied with Camel's heart rate and rhythm pulls his stethoscope out of his ears. "It's okay to talk to him. Patients that are unconscious can still hear you. He could use a familiar voice to help with the healing process. If you have any questions or concerns just let me know. I'll leave you alone now."

Marc speaks to Camel, "Dude, it's good to see you." Tears beginning to streak down his rough, stubble covered cheeks silently giving in to his grief. Forgetting his embarrassment at putting on such a weak display of emotions. Trying again. "Do you remember when we lost cousin Phil in the desert? And it was the Bedouin sheep herders that found him. We tracked them for hours before catching up with them at that oasis. We both knew if we didn't find him both of our dads would kill us. Remember—"

Nurse Peters comes in. "Sir, it's time to give the patient a rest."

After going through this repeatedly all day into the late evening, in and out of the room, Dr. Daas allows Marc a chair to sit beside the bed. His patient has remained stable. Marc reads to Camel from the Koran, praying for his recovery. By the following early morning Camel grunts out a weak but deep voiced hello in Arabic. Marc sits up smiling warmly. "It's good to see you back with the living."

Camel, "Yes." His mind very cloudy from the pain medication. "How long have you been here?"

Marc, "Since yesterday morning when I found out you were here."

Camel, "It's good to see you." Dozing back to sleep Marc remains at his side.

Later that night, Ali arrives one of Camel's younger brothers. Marc having called home to Dubai to inform the family about Camel's condition. Ali finds Marc dozing in the chair beside the bed with Camel's hand in his. Ali gently shakes Marc's shoulder to wake him. After a quick exchange in Arabic, some of the tension drains out of Marc's face. Happy to see a familiar face beaming at Ali. Ali bear-hugs him squeezing the breath out of him. Marc has forgotten how strong Ali is. All of the men in the Khalid family growing tall and solid. Changing to a serious note Ali questions Marc, "How's he doing?" His young bearded face serious.

Marc, "He is strong. Dr. Daas said he is improving." Ali watches Marc's face for more. "He almost died in surgery. It was a serious stab wound."

Ali, "Who would do such a thing?"

Marc, "The police have two women in custody." Ali gives Marc a knowing look. His face becoming irritated and then accepting, shaking his head. Knowing his brother only too well.

Ali speaks, "It's always the women with my brother. He needs to settle down with a wife. And what about you? Are you still carousing with him?"

Marc on the spot, "Well, I just haven't met the right woman yet."

Ali, "This is what happens when you lead a less than righteous life. Were they fighting over him?" Marc takes pause—how like his father he sounds.

"Uh, no. Yes, the police believe it was jealousy." Not wanting to say more. Ali reads his omission easily.

Ali, "So he was sleeping with both of them?"

Marc, "Probably, if I know him. Lately he's been excessive even for him."

Ali, "And you, my brother, are a step or two behind him in all this... activity." Not really a question. Marc's cheeks redden beneath his dark stubble. His thoughts racing. *This guy is the only one I know besides an iman that can make a man feel like a whore for sleeping around.*

Marc, "No, really."

Ali's eyebrows rise dubiously. Guilt by association. "You both need to settle down."

Marc yawns from exhaustion. "Excuse me, I know you're in matrimonial bliss still. But not all of us are as lucky as you to have found a woman as nice as Aamera."

Ali, "Right, even though I know you are trying to shut me up."

Marc, "I'm serious. When I meet the right woman I'll settle down." Yawning again.

Ali, "Maybe you need to go home and sleep for a while. I slept on the company jet coming over. We can take this in shifts."

Marc, "You won't get any argument from me on that." His look of exhaustion only surpassed by how tired he felt. Marc hugs Ali again. "It's so good to see you here."

Ali puts his hand on Marc's shoulder. "It's good to see you. Finish school and come home. We all miss you two. Get some rest, I'll see you in the morning."

Finishing their good byes Marc too tired to say more he leaves for home.

CHAPTER 17

ARRIVING HOME, MARC finds a note taped on the refrigerator from Ms. Campbell. "Chicken salad is made for sandwiches and potato chips are in the pantry. I hope your friend Camel is all right. I will pray for him. By the way the shipment of stone will be delivered tomorrow morning early. Let me know if you want me to wake you early. We both will be here to get started on the deep cleaning of this house." It is signed Norma.

Tired but still wound up after eating a couple of chicken salad sandwiches Marc pads barefoot down the hall to the library. Deciding a snifter of Courvoisier is in order. That should help him to relax. Calling out, "Mood lights on." Recessed lights come on around the room. Walking past the round Federal table where Angelique had read from the old diary. His footfalls are muffled softly by the fine Persian rugs so soft to the touch of bare feet. Thinking back to earlier the day before how it started. Chuckling a little. If that's the worst thing Mary sees, Camel would be rolling on the floor. A Catholic schoolgirl rushing from the nasty man's bedroom. His mood lifted some.

Passing by the Federal table again something is amiss. Noting the silver candlestick at the center of the table. Where's that diary? Not remembering having moved it. Maybe Ms. Campbell did when she was cleaning. Making a mental note to ask tomorrow. His mood becoming grave with thoughts going back to Camel. Could you believe it? Stabbed at a nightclub on ladies' night. That just wasn't supposed to happen. Picking up his book from the other night, *Dead Until Dark*. Needing a distraction from his own troubles. Sitting down in one of the overstuffed wingback chairs covered in damask fabric. Marc's feet propped up on a hassock. Taking another sip of cognac its heat soothing him as it goes down. Turning to his page where he left off. The grandfather clock in the distance chiming three times. So comfortable and peaceful.

Waking up shivering able to see his breath on the air so cold in the room now. Marc sits forward fragments of a dream still fresh in his memory. Uncle Theron speaking to him again. Something about "protect yourself." Yes, he kept telling him to protect himself from the trouble that was coming. What trouble? Shivering again he gets up from his chair stretching time for bed. Walking past the Federal table only this time the diary is on it. Knowing it wasn't there earlier. How strange is that. It had been a long two days. Picking up the diary before going upstairs.

Settled into bed Marc starts paging through the diary. Searching for where they had been reading from. Parts of it he can't read as it has Latin laced into it and his reading of French not that good to begin with. But what he can understand causes him to become disturbed. Something very unseemly about what is intended by his ancestor. Exhaustion winning out Marc puts the diary in the nightstand not wanting just anyone to have access to it again. An odd feeling for one so open and honest. Turning out the bed side lamp. Falling into a restless and fitful sleep. Dreaming about Melinda and Angelique with another woman. Her face covered by the cowl on her cloak. Behaving strangely and their attire odd. Marc picks up on something else in the darkness with them. Feeling its malevolent presence. Sending fear reaching deep into his dream state. Unable to move paralyzed like a mouse before a cat. Predatory eyes with yellow reptilian irises staring back at him silently, observing, waiting to react to his move. A voice deepest of basses vibrating inside his skull. Penetrating his mind, speaking to him with a strength that cannot be ignored. Though it's language is from one of humanity's elder civilizations, millennia's old. Caught in racial memories too distant to recall to mind. Its speech pattern familiar in a way similar to present-day Arabic, Semitic, and Farsi, recognizable to anyone who has spoken and grown up with them. Marc very accustomed to those languages.

Enkil no longer patient with this young male. His eyes become angrier and more feline with those pupils mere slits. Glaring back at Marc. *Impossible! It's looking at me*. Pulling back in his dream fighting to wake up. Its language English now speaking to him in a threatening voice, "I know you now, boy! You can't escape me." Marc pushes against it too late. Having his body pinned down with its sheer strength overpowering him. Causing an adrenaline rush. Marc fights as hard as he could. Thrashing under his covers being holding him down. *Unk unk unk*. His alarm clock rings with that awful sound. *Unk unk unk*.

Marc wakes up throwing off the covers kicking and punching. Jumping out of bed ready to fight with fists up, his body in a centered stance. His heart pounding ready for it to attack. Nothing there but the empty room with morning sun streaking around folds in the drapes. Trying to shake it off what a dream. His heart still racing beginning to slow. Calming down sitting on the side of the bed. Trying to remember more of this vivid dream. Stretching as he stands up rocking his muscular shoulders to loosen them with his arms up like a boxer. Then cocking his head to the side cracking his neck. His back covered with dark hair, shoulders and across and down the spine still bristled partially. For all intents looking like a Native American thunderbird petroglyph. Not your typical hirsute male. Nature being of its own his engorgement painfully at attention from a full bladder. This dictating what he must do next. Stepping on his boxer shorts on the way to the bathroom. Positioned back a few feet from the toilet. Letting relief go aiming true a urine stream showering down into the bowl. The sensation feeling so good as only a male in that condition can understand.

Dressing for work to go downstairs pulling on his boxers adjusting himself now that he is more able to. Pulling some jeans and a sleeveless tee shirt. Marc touches the screen on his cell phone calling Ali checking on Camel. Ali picks up on the first ring.

Ali, "Hello, Marc. The doctors say Camel is improving enough that he'll be able to be moved out of ICU later today."

Marc, "That's great news. How was he after I left?" Fishing for anything unusual.

Ali, "A few times he was talking in his sleep. It didn't make sense at times. Then other times it was almost like someone else speaking an ancient tongue."

Marc, "Really? Anything else?"

Ali, "I'm sure it was just the ramblings of a delirious mind. I don't know what language it could be. He was always gifted that way, but never very interested in studying anything old. As you well know. Dad could hardly get him to study the Koran much less go to a mosque."

Marc, "How right you are." Changing the subject. "You holding up alright?"

Ali, "I'm fine. When are you coming up?"

Marc, "I have a large delivery of stone coming in this morning. After everything is settled here I'll be up to relieve you."

Ali, "That sounds good, I need some more coffee. So I will see you when you get here. Bye."

March goes downstairs and then into the kitchen. Ms. Campbell is busy cutting open biscuits and placing poached eggs with cheese in them.

Ms. Campbell, "Good timing the stone delivery is here. I made some breakfast sandwiches for you." Pouring coffee into an insulated mug steam rising up. "These will stick to your ribs." Looking at him differently, her eyes lingering. Mary is busy kneading dough for bread. Glancing up to see Marc watching her. She blushes, remembering yesterday's first encounter with him nude. Looking back down at the dough giving it a punch. Her thoughts on Marc. He is handsome even with his clothes on and a day's growth of beard. Sneaking another look while his head is turned. Even the blue-black cast to his beard somehow appealing. Not to mention those thick arms. Marc feels eyes on him. Casually glancing at her with one of his boyish looks through those long dark eyelashes with gleaming sapphire blue eyes. Almost intimidating her with his masculine intensity.

Ms. Campbell interrupts his thoughts speaking to Mary. Snapping her out of her daze. Bringing Marc out of his amorous moment. "You can start cleaning his room. Change the sheets while you're up there." Marc flashes a quick bright white smile at Mary. Causing her to blush again. Ms. Campbell is not amused. "Off to work missy. And you stop looking at her like that. I'm beginning to wonder if you're such a nice young man." Handing Marc his breakfast bagged in a brown paper bag. Marc scoops the mug up leaving.

Out of sight of Ms. Campbell he takes a bite out of one of the sandwiches. The food still held in his mouth, he grabs his package to adjust himself. "Uh uh." Pants getting too tight for comfort thinking about Mary. Her long auburn hair and flawless milky white skin. What a natural beauty. Stepping outside.

Ms. Campbell is alone in the kitchen with her own thoughts. *I'm going to have trouble with him. It's all those wild women he's running around with. He's changing.*

After finishing with accepting the delivery and directing where to place the skids loaded with granite and flagstone Marc cancels his appointment with the stonemason until the next day. Needing time to go up to the hospital to relieve Ali and see Camel. Calling Ali to let him know he's coming soon so he can get some rest soon. Leaving the message on his voice mail.

CHAPTER 18

MARC ARRIVES AT the ICU with Camel nowhere to be found. Having a moment of panic. *Where is he?* Having the worst thoughts possible. Marc rushes up to the nurses' station. "Where is Mr. Khalid?" His heart in his throat, pulse racing.

Nurse Peters, "He's been moved to a private room. It's incredible how fast he is recovering." Smiling at Marc, sensing his relief. "Good things do happen here." Relief washing over him.

After getting directions to Camel's new room. Marc walks in to find Camel sitting up watching TV with IV fluids still running in. His color much better, not that deathly pale anymore. Marc cautiously smiles at him. "How are you feeling?" Turning his head motioning just so. "You know you gave me quite a scare."

Camel his usual unconcerned self speaks. "I'm sore as hell. It hurts every time I move. This tape keeps pulling the my hair on my arm and I'm hungry. They haven't given me any food. Apparently the doctor has to order it first. I'm good and thanks for asking."

Marc, "Now that sounds more like you. Did you see Ali?"

Camel, "No. He's here? You're the first family member I've seen."

Marc, "Yeah, he's staying at your place, I imagine. He'll be relieved to know you're doing so well. Everyone will be. Do you remember anything?"

Camel, "Just that I was dancing and then a searing pain tearing through my back. Then it's all a blur after that. I was told I was stabbed."

Marc, "So do you know why she stabbed you?"

Camel, "I'll tell you the same thing I told Detective Arros. I don't know."

Marc, "Detective Arros?" Marc looking at him with raised eyebrows with an incredulous look on his face. "You were sleeping with both of them. Don't play the innocent victim with me."

Camel, "Oh, so I deserved what I got. Justice served." Putting him off.

Marc, "I didn't mean it that way."

Camel, "Well, you'll be interested to know that Detective Arros wasn't much more sympathetic than you are. He informed me I'm a person of interest in the death of two women. He wasn't here to investigate the crime against me."

Marc, "They know about the twins?" Camel nods his head causing his wavy mane of hair to shimmer under the dull lights. His hair longer than he had ever let it grow. "How could they come up with that?"

Camel, "I'm the common thread between them. I was sleeping with them. But for the record, I just met those two outside the club. They were in line so I asked if they wanted to come in with me and dance. We met for the first time last night."

Marc, "That was two days ago. Not last night. You've been out of it for more than a day and a half."

Camel quiet for a moment taking in this information. "It's been that long?"

Marc stands by the window looking out onto the cemetery below. "Yes."

Camel, "I don't know why she stabbed me." Answering his brother's unspoken question. "We were having fun the three of us. Everything was going smoothly." Questioning himself, *Or was it?* Feeling light-headed, hearing a roar in his ears. Then nothingness. Camel's eyes change with a flash to yellow and predatory. Catlike only infinitely more angry. Marc's back to him looking out at the cemetery below. The view from his hospital room. Literally hundreds of tombstones all different shapes and ages. Mausoleums lined up in a park like setting. Death so near it almost took his brother. His thoughts keeping him distracted. What would his life be like if that had happened? If Camel had died. Camel's voice not his own speaking in a deep bass. "Everything was good until the lights went out. You were having a good time with that beauty from Turkey"

Marc, *Is he serious?* Turning around wounded the hurt on his face.

Camel, "Just do it!" Marc reaches out with his right hand. Camel takes it squeezing it in his large hands saying, "I could promise not to die but we never know when Allah is going to call for us to return. I will always love you my brother and closest friend. Please don't look so fearful. I can't stand that look of pain in your eyes."

Marc changes the subject. "Yeah, I read about the power outage. Lightning apparently struck the building. The power had been out at my place for hours too."

Camel, "Read about it? Weren't you there?" Marc smiles his blue eyes twinkling mischievously. Camel gives him a questioning look. "I didn't see you leave."

Marc, "You're a great wingman. Does that jog your memory?"

Camel smiles a big bright grin. His physical strength returning further. "You went home with that gorgeous, mysterious brunette with the silver-green eyes, didn't you?"

Marc is smiling like the cat that ate the canary. "You never forget a beautiful woman do you?"

Camel, "My brother you know me too well." Reaching over with ease to put on the call light.

Nurse Wahl answers, "Yes, Mr. Khalid, do you need your pain med?"

Camel, "I am as thirsty as the Sahara and I'm hungry. Since we're talking when can I leave?" Marc surprised, yet not really. He is feeling better.

Nurse Wahl, "The doctor will be in shortly to sign orders when he gets out of surgery. Until then you are still NPO. You are receiving fluids and nutrition through the IV. You're not going to dehydrate or starve before the doctor gets here. As for you leaving, that was a deep stab wound. Your sutures need time to heal. So I doubt you'll be discharged anytime today." *Click*, her sarcasm clear in that last remark.

Nurse Wahl speaks to the PA, "Can you believe him? He codes in surgery and a day later is bugging me to go home. This is going to be a long week."

Physician's Assistant Hauser, "Yes, a typical young male."

Nurse Wahl, "Did you read the paper today?" Not waiting for the answer the story to juicy. Ready to dish it out. "He was screwing around with a bunch of different women. Finally he met someone who wouldn't put up with it."

PA Hauser," Is that what the article said?"

Nurse Wahl, "You have to read between the lines. Plus look at him, a big handsome man like that. He's got women all over him."

PA Hauser, "Yes. Some of these younger women are very rough nowadays. Maybe it was gang related?"

Nurse Wahl, "You think?" PA Hauser nods her head.

Marc, "Dude, cool your jets. You have to stay a couple of days to heal. You heard her."

Dr. Daas arrives knocking at the door before walking in speaking. "Hi, how are you feeling today Mr. Khalid?"

Camel, "I'm sore but feeling stronger every minute. When can I go home?"

Dr. Daas smiling, "I'm sure it won't be today Mr. Khalid. Your wound is very deep and cut into the pericardium. Requiring lots of rest to heal safely. You are rushing things a bit to say the least. The body needs to be healed enough before I will consider discharging you to go home. Now let me take a look at it wound. If there are no signs of infection and you remain stable. Well, you are a very lucky man with all the blood loss. I was sure that one of your superior vessels had been lacerated. We still need to monitor those for any possible aneurism. Then we'll discuss a discharge date." Camel sits forward gingerly at first. Feeling a mild pain from the skin pulling as he leans forward.

Dr. Daas, "Carefully. I don't want you pulling any sutures out. It will only make the healing process take longer." Gently peeling away the tape around the edges of the abd pad. Which is soaked with dried blood. The tape pulling stubble on his back where he was shaved for surgery. A thick dark line of hair down his spine fur like and long. Dr. Daas studies it making a mental note very unusual but probably familial. Dr. Daas lifts his eyebrows. At first unable to see the black sutures because of Camel's thick stubble. Then spotting a scar pencil line thin and pale. That scar several inches long running under where the sutures are. Dr. Daas removes the entire dressing to examine the site further. His amazement increasing. Gently touching the skin around the sutures. Speaking his microphone sensitive enough to record tucked away in his shirt pocket. "No arrhythmia, good capillary return, site non-blanching. Skin color equivocal to surrounding tissue. Grossly normal healing for a month old stab wound. But it is not months but two days old."

Dr. Daas, "It looks exceptionally good. Have you always healed this quickly? This is quite amazing. I've never seen anyone heal like that."

Camel, "I don't know, I guess. This has never happened to me before." Dr. Daas looks puzzled. Camel feels the need to elaborate. "Where I've been stabbed."

Dr. Daas, "No childhood injuries?"

Marc, "You fell with the glass bottle in your hand. It broke cutting your palm to your thumb." Camel turns his right hand over to expose a faint scar.

Camel, "I had forgotten about that. It seems I don't scar very easily. Right now all I feel is some tightness in my upper back and shoulder. Moving his left arm back and forth in a slow punching motion. His hospital gown sliding down exposing his large muscular chest. Covered in a thick pelt across it and a long strip running down the center. His chest was already covered but exceptionally now the center with three inch long dark hair going all the way to his groin. Quickly pushing the hospital gown back up.

Dr. Daas, "The wound externally appears healed, but internally I can't say. We need to treat you as if it is not healed. By taking it easy for the next seven to ten days. No strenuous activity or exercise. After that time if you need to you can start some physical therapy. I want to see you in my office in seven days to have the sutures removed. I'll consider signing your discharge papers tomorrow."

Camel, "Can I at least start eating food?"

Dr. Daas, "Yes, of course." Leaving the room amazed yet again how the human body can recover.

"I'm getting out of here tomorrow." His square stubble covered jaw breaking into one of his genuinely happy smiles. Marc feels a real sense of relief the tightness in his shoulders and neck relaxing. After being worried since he found out all this happened.

Nurse Wahl comes in to check his vital signs. "Your BP is 110/70 and pulse, 68."

His late lunch tray arrives one sandwich and soup. Camel examines it not too much but it will do. Looking at Nurse Wahl, he says, "I hope dinner will have more food on the tray. I'm not small in case you haven't noticed."

Nurse Wahl, "I'll let dietary know. Now I have to remove your IV."

Marc, "Since you're doing so well I have to go back to work. Unlike some people who get to lie around in bed all day. It just figures you'd get out of helping me with placing the heavy stone." Opening the cover on the soup for him.

Camel, "Yes. That smells good. You know me, women and food." Nurse Wahl pulls off the tape on his IV line. "Ouch!"

Nurse Wahl, "Put some pressure on that, use your finger." Taping a 2 x 2 folded over the site where the IV was removed from.

Marc, "I'm just glad you're improving. I really thought I was going to lose you."

Camel, "I'm fine. It would take more than some crazy woman to end me. Are you coming back? This television has next to no choices."

Marc, "Yes, this evening. Ali should be back later today."

Camel, "Ali?"

"Remember I told you he's staying at your place. He'll be here soon."

Camel, "Good, I'll have someone to talk with."

Marc hugs Camel carefully saying, "I love you. We're supposed to die old men with our great-grandchildren around us."

Camel hugs him back. "I love you too and I'm fine now. So no more of this syrupy stuff. Go to work." Patting Marc on the back.

Outside in the hall Marc sees Ali. They make a quick exchange in Arabic. Marc is happy to see a familiar face. After smiling at each other for a moment. Ali bear hugs Marc a second time in two days squeezing the breath out of him. Ali all grown up now and strong. Changing to a more serious note. Ali asks, "How is he doing?" His dark bearded face serious again.

Marc, "He's healing remarkably well. Dr. Daas said he could be discharged by tomorrow. That he was very fortunate. The knife wound any closer to his heart or major blood vessels, he would have died."

Ali, "I just can't understand getting that jealous. Since they just met him that night."

Marc, "I don't get it either but at least the two women are in custody."

Ali gives Marc a knowing look. His face becomes stern, shaking his head.

"It's always the same with both of you Marc. Trouble just seems to find you two, slipping into your lives. Are you still carousing with him?"

Marc, "Well, I just went out for a few minutes," Not wanting to tell on his brother. Knowing how lame his half-truth just came off. Taking the hit to cover for Camel. As he would for him. "I haven't met the right woman yet."

Ali, "This is what happens when you lead a less than righteous life. Have you found out anymore as to why she assaulted him?" Ali not misled at all. Everyone in the family knew that Camel and Marc covered for each other, except their father. Who always seemed to be oblivious to their misfortunes or was he? Ali having some insight as a young adult. His brothers not so able to cover their actions with exciting tidbits of close shaves.

Marc noticing how like his own father Ali sounds. "No! Yes. The police believe it was a quarrel." Not wanting to say more. Ali reads this omission easily.

"So he was sleeping with both of them?"

Marc, "He said he wasn't. He was just having fun." Marc thinking Camel had acknowledged his own behavior had been more that of a sexual addict.

Ali, "And you my brother. How were you behaving during all this...," pausing for lack of a better word, "activity?" Marc's cheeks redden a little beneath his dark stubble. Ali getting right to the heart of the matter. The only one besides Ibram their oldest brother to make him embarrassed about unmarried sexual relations.

CHAPTER 19

BY THE AFTERNOON, I had gotten the master craftsman out to help me. Giancarlo was his name. He was from the old country a master at stonework. I was now running the wet saw with its diamond blade on my own. Giancarlo was standing back watching me work. Soon I would be on my own. At least until the time for the private terrace with its intricate detail work to be cut. For a simple path I was approved to go. My fingers were waterlogged and my tee shirt soaked up the front with ground stone (dirt), including the front of my blue jeans. What wasn't wet from the spray off the wet saw then was perspiration. Which was dripping into my eyes causing them to burn. My bandana needed to be wrung out. My back was wet and combined with the heat making all of it run down into the waist of my jeans soaking in. It was June and hot unlike what May had been.

Giancarlo using his free labor yours truly, comments, "You're doing well." Turning the saw off. I was glad for the break. I tend to keep working until the job is done.

"Thank you."

Giancarlo eyes the last stone I'd placed. Putting his level on it. Speaking, "Just as I had thought. Check your level on each stone. You don't want them pitching every which way." Being polite I just listened. "Always keep a little slope away from the center. That way no water pooling or ice forming on your path. Do you understand?"

Marc, "Yes I do." Drying my hands on an old towel.

Giancarlo, "Good. Finish the path to the steps of the terrace. Then you can stop. I may be out of town for a few days next week."

Marc, "What do you want me to do in the meantime?"

Giancarlo, "Make sure the terrace for the private garden is compressed well and the crushed stone is pitched away from the center. So I can start the stonework up there."

Marc, "Will do."

Giancarlo looking at Marc, "I bring some help. The Crab Orchard is heavy but not so hard to cut. Granite is a hard stone to cut. Difficult for even me."

Marc, "I've got it. I'll have it ready when you return." Giancarlo's smile lines cut deeply into his face from years of working outside under the sun. Still handsome with a thick head of salt-and-pepper hair sticking out from under his sweat-stained cap (Yankee blue).

"So I'll see you next week sometime."

By staying focused on the job at hand. I had the first path completed by late afternoon. The other path from the driveway could wait until tomorrow. Grimy and hot I decided it was time to knock off for the day. Anxious to be out of the heat and these wet clothes with a shower needed. Finally I was in the privacy of the master suite peeling off my clothes, which were sticking to my body. Even with the extra hair now. Starting with my soggy tee shirt leaving a trail of clothes to the bathroom. Glancing at my answering machine with its message light flashing. Choosing a cool shower, needing to relax first, then business.

Reenergized from his long cool shower Marc sits on the side of the bed. His towel wrapped loosely around the waist. Leaving exposed well defined abdominal muscles cut and tight with only the center covered by a wide strip of dark straight hair. Pressing the message retrieval button a feminine voice speaks.

"Message one."

It's Camel's voice. "Hi! Angelique called, we made up. When she found out I was in the hospital all was forgiven. So we're on again. I know you think I'm nuts, right? Even I can't believe it. I can't get enough of her. Anyway she invited us to a mixer at her place. It's an alumni and Greek limited guest list. That should be interesting. I know there will be some incredible women there. By the way I'm being discharged in the morning. Call me." *Click*. Deleting the next two messages being from computer generated sales calls.

Marc keys in the numbers for Camel's room at the hospital. He picks up on the first ring. "Hello."

Marc, "That's incredible that you are getting discharged so soon. Much less that you are back with Angelique."

Camel, "I don't know what it is about her. They used an ultrasound or echocardio on me. Anyway they couldn't find any lingering damage. So I'm out." His voice back to his old self.

Marc, "Yeah, like a moth to a flame."

Camel disregards that comment. "She is so fascinating to be around. Plus the parties she throws are unusual. You can make some very good business contacts. She knows people that are incredibly connected and you can only meet them there at her gatherings."

Marc, "Shouldn't you be taking it easy? After all you were stabbed just recently. What, three days ago?"

Camel, "I'm fine. This hospital gets all of the trauma patients. You know, stabbings and drive-bys. They probably had me confused with someone else."

Marc, "Maybe." Not very convinced. "You looked pale almost like death." Not wanting to sound foolish.

Camel, "Be ready to meet some unusual guests." Camel's eyes flicker to predator night eyes with their pupils wide in the dark room. Its drapes closed his eyes eerily more reptilian than feline with their yellow irises. Speaking, his voice dropping an octave to a deep bass. "However I do appreciate your loyalty and concerns. Angelique and I are far from finished." Camel feels himself lost in darkness with sounds muffled.

Marc, "What was that?"

Camel, "It's postnasal drip. It makes my voice deeper you know that."

Marc, "For a moment you sound like someone else."

Camel clears his throat. "No, it's just me." His voice still deep. "Thank you for trying to warn me. She can be very aggressive when angered."

Marc, "You would have done the same for me."

Camel, "You are right. All is forgiven now."

Marc, "I hope so. Angelique doesn't come off as the type to forgive and forget."

Camel, "It's all right. Am I talking to one of my sisters?" Hoping this will irritate Marc enough to change subject.

Marc, "Just an observation. Do with it as you will."

Camel, "I'll keep that in mind."

Marc, "Come to think of it. Their whole group is just off." Trying to put his finger on what it is that makes them so different.

Camel, "In what way my brother?"

Marc takes his time to formulate his answer. "Well, none of them claim to want a relationship."

Camel, "Those are my favorite kind of women."

Marc, "No. It's more than just that. There was something in Angelique's face. A hardened look to her." Camel smiles at Marc on the video phone screen. Making him feel lame. Irritated with his brother for being so dense and cocksure of himself. Marc now grasping at straws. "She doesn't... Her body language doesn't match what she is saying. Can't you see that?"

Camel smiles wolfishly at him. "Psychology 101?" Marc's irritation obvious in his cheeks flushing and thick lips straightening out from their usual Cupid's bow fullness. Camel enjoys getting his goat as only a brother can. Speaking, "All too easy." Marc's frustration quickly gone realizing what his brother was doing to him.

"Maybe she doesn't have a hidden agenda."

Camel, "She is a hot-tempered woman and a little mean. When she doesn't get her way. That's what attracts me to her. Well, that's not all."

Marc not letting it go, "It's just that what she is saying doesn't coincide with what she does."

Camel's voice deepens, his eyes not clear in the image. "Now that you mention it maybe she does have another agenda Marc."

Marc nods his head in agreement. *Finally he's listening to me.*

Camel, "We'll have to be more alert to their subtle actions around us. Keep that thought in the back of your mind. When dealing with any of them. I wouldn't repeat what we have spoken of." The image clears up.

Marc, "Good, I will."

Camel, "So when are you coming to visit me?"

Another voice speaks from the hospital end, "Mr. Khalid, I have your antibiotics here. Also Dr. Daas has ordered one more test. You'll need to get off the phone. They are here now to take you for it."

"What test?" Camel asks. Marc listens to the ensuing commotion, Camel arguing with transportation attendants.

Marc catches a motion out of his peripheral vision. Glances over at the Louis XVI mirror across the room. Without a reflection of the bedroom before it. Blinking once its surface opaque and the next moment seeing images moving inside the mirror. Oddly not that of the bedroom, but some other room's reflection. Marc stands up. "What the heck?"

Camel's concerned voice coming from the phone, "What's wrong?" Marc not answering at first. This causing Camel's pulse to quicken on the cardiac monitor.

"Mr. Khalid calm down."

Camel, "What is it?"

Marc, "It's nothing. For just a moment, I could almost see into the mirror. It wasn't reflecting."

Camel, "Really? What did you see?" His bass voice a low rumble, the telemetry still beeping quicker displaying his excitement. Irritated by this he responds, "You're not supposed to upset people in the hospital." His monitor still beeping quicker.

Marc, "I'm sorry. It must have been the light in here."

Camel washes down the antibiotic tablet with a gulp of water. "I have to go. They're here to take me for another test. I'll see you tomorrow at your place."

"Are you sure?"

Camel, "Yes. I have Ali for a while longer tonight. Just do as I said. Keep that in mind and your mouth closed."

Marc stands up from the bed his towel drops to the floor. Looking back at the mirror one more time to check it. Looking over his shoulder seeing his back. A straight path of dark hair is spread across his upper back and down his spine. Ending at his prominent gluteus maximus. *When did this happen?* On closer inspection his large chest is now covered in not so short black hair from collarbone to collarbone. No longer smooth chested. It's official. He's not going to be smooth without working on it.

Later that evening, Marc settles in for the night. He takes the diary out of the nightstand where it was placed for safekeeping. His family tree in it is remarkable in that it goes back centuries. Many of the Du Bois names unfamiliar as they branch out into the past with other different family names. All having a date of birth but only a very few of them without the date of death. Oddly enough the diary appears to have been written by the same hand over a couple of centuries. Quill in black ink dulled from the passage of time. But still a graceful hand with a florid style. Most assuredly feminine and that of an educated woman.

Marc takes a deep breath and exhales. Talking to himself. "Where did they read from?" Searching for pages unable to recognize which page. The central air conditioning quietly coming on pushing a gentle breeze. Which caresses his shoulder and then blows over the pages. Nudging them a few at a time. His eyes already heavy with sleep, blinking it back. The cool air without humidity feeling so good. Relaxing further. The pages now fluttering seemingly on their own. Marc becoming irritated by this ready to stop it unable to read them. Reaching over to put a stop to this nuisance the pages stop on a passage that is familiar. That's it. The same florid graceful style written in the same hand that had written in French throughout the first half of the diary. Erie sensations of déjà vu passing over him. Then disregarding them as childish.

Reading slowly finding it difficult to follow. Because what is written are instructions for someone that is not a novice. She would not have given too many explanations for fear of retribution from the ecumenical order in control. The cardinal of France then. Marc questions, something about calling upon an ancestor? Mittelschmerz must occur during the season of the serpent? *I must not be understanding this too well. That is German.* Words blurring at times. He keeps having to refocus his eyes to read. Marc's heavy muscled body warm being soothed by the air conditioned breeze blowing across him again. After a hard day of labor under an unrelenting sun. Sleep easily overtakes him this time. The bedside lamp with its Smart bulb winking on and off. Signaling the timer is turning it off. Putting the cool room into a cocoon of slumber. Dream rushing upon dream Marc is swept along. This final one finding himself watching a sensuous blonde woman not of this century. Her hair coiffure high with long curls around her face. Which she keeps hidden by a fan she has attached with a strap to her wrist. Her dress long brushing the ground bowed out at the hips. Her sleeves mid–arm length ending in lace. Walking graciously and speaking to someone of regal station in life. "Oui moi amour." He takes her hand as they stroll through well-manicured gardens. Versailles? Her gentleman companion also dressed for the period. Wearing short pants with knee-high stockings. On his hand a gold ring with a large blue gemstone encrusted with smaller stones surrounding it.

CHAPTER 20

THE NEXT DAY. I want to get finished with laying the flagstones. So I can have a restful weekend. Well, not so restful with the party to go to. I didn't realize it was rave at the time. But I digress. My wet saw placed on a 4 x 8 piece of plywood across two sawhorses. Water dripping off one end and the blueprints were spread out at the other end of the table held open by rocks. Having stopped running the saw long enough to hear that familiar rumble of a Ferrari coming up the driveway. It can't be. Glancing up while I'm on my knees, positioning another piece of flagstone. Camel's smile beaming from ear to ear as he saunters over with his usual long legged strides. Certainly not walking like a man who was seriously wounded days ago. But I was just too happy to see my pal and confidant. Having him back to his old self I did not read anything into it at the time. Getting up and leaving work behind, I meet him across the lawn.

Marc, "You look great!"

Camel, "Never better."

Marc stands there with his soiled knee pads, sweaty sleeveless tee shirt, and large tanned biceps. Hugging Camel until squeezing his breath. Marc releases him upon hearing the grunt. "I'm sorry. Are you all right?" Checking his face concerned.

Camel, "I'm fine. I never felt better." Marc reassured, smiling again. "I should check those blueprints to make sure you are following them correctly."

Marc, "Are you sure you want to chance getting dirty."

Camel looks at Marc's grimy clothes. "I think that chance has already passed."

Marc gives him a look. "Oh well, sorry about that."

Camel, "So I might as well read them over. Besides, I can still smell you on my shirt." Dusting it off. Marc puts his dirty hand on Camel's shoulder.

Marc, "Good, for a minute there I thought you had become one of those white collared, cologne fragrance, soft skinned men. In which case I would have to take you down. At the gym, that is."

Camel, "I think I heard a challenge somewhere in all that rhetoric."

Marc squares his shoulders, pushing his chest out. "Maybe." Camel ignores the coal black dirt on his fine Indian-made linen shirt. "It's incredible. You are one tough man."

Camel, "You better believe it." Examining the completed part of the flagstone path. "It looks professional. Like a stonemason put this in. You did all this work yourself?"

Marc, "Yeah." Waiting for a smart comment.

Camel nods his head in approval. "I'd hire you. You'll have the path completed today."

Marc, "Yes. I'll run the flagstone right up to where the steps begin to the private terrace. Take a look at the blueprints."

Camel leans on the makeshift table. "Interesting," examining the design closer. "Seventy-two degree arcs marked out at five points in the flagstone." Recognizing the shape. "A five sided star in granite. Many cultures prefer to use sixty degrees for an even number. Thus creating a star with six sides."

Marc, "I know. I was surprised to see it used here. Considering the negative connotations so many Christians attribute to it. I have known of instances where people in this country try and destroy them."

Camel, "Anything good can be twisted to evil by religious fanatics."

Marc, "That's the truth. Never mind committing fraud within the banking system. Just don't get caught with whores if you're a married man. Then you're not living right."

Camel arches one of his eyebrows, not in the mood for a sermon on politics and religion. Choosing the high road. "We both have seen six-sided ones used all over the Middle East."

Marc, "I know, it's a beautiful shape. I'm just surprised to see a pentagram used in a garden mosaic."

Camel's eyes change to yellow with their pupils vertical. His voice dropping an octave deeper. Speaking, "Perhaps it is intended for protection." Marc stands next to him, studying the blueprints with him. Camel continues, "The point is facing north. That would be for good seeking protection from something evil." His eyes flash back to normal.

Marc, "You're a well of information today. Not just another pretty face."

Camel, "That's right." His handsome moreno face striking with his five o'clock shadow. Looking mischievously at Marc. "Let us talk about something more interesting than blueprints." Marc looking puzzled. "Tell me about your encounter with your mysterious woman from the other night."

Marc takes a moment. "Well, her name is Jadon."

Camel, "That is a beautiful name. What else? I'm short on imagination so give me details." Marc gives his brother a smug look. "If it wasn't for my skillful maneuvering, you wouldn't have met her."

"All right." Marc gives in having made Camel wait long enough. "She is an incredible lover and so giving." Marcs' blood already surging. His sapphire blue eyes twinkling as his thoughts turn to her.

Camel, "I can see you have fond memories. Don't leave me hanging, go on."

Both men turn to a sound coming from a second story window. Finding the source of the noise. A young woman of fair complexion. Her skin so fair as to be milky white and her hair light auburn. Beating a rug of obvious Persian design with its deep reds and blues.

Camel, "It looks like I have found the real beauty around here. Who is that?"

Marc, "Her name is Mary." Watching her lean out the window. Allowing her long red hair to fan out like corn silk. Her alabaster skin luminescent and unblemished.

Camel, "Are you keeping secrets from me again, Brother dearest?"

Marc, "No. She just arrived yesterday from London." Marc's tanned face becomes dusky. Camel senses a story there.

"Go on." Mary spots the two young men watching her. Blushing, she leans back inside the window. Her aunt Norma watches over her with hawk like eyes, not missing a thing. Appears in the window to see what's going on. Frowning down at the two young men below, her lips drawn tightly and thin.

Camel makes a sound. "Uh." Both guys look back down at the blueprints pretending to be busy.

Marc speaks softer, "She's the housekeeper's niece." The echo of a window slamming closed making him duck slightly.

Camel, "Yes." Not one to let a good story get away.

Marc tries not to notice Camel's piqued interest. Then he finally gives in. "We are to keep our distance from her."

Camel eyes narrow with increased interest. "And why is that, Brother?"

Marc, "Other than having an obviously overprotective aunt, what else could it be?"

Camel, "Indeed." Smiling wryly at Marc. "Well, go on."

Marc, "Our first meeting was after she arrived. It was an awkward morning for both of us. I forgot she would be starting that day." Pausing. "It was the morning after Jadon had visited."

An understanding expression passes over Camel's face. Holding back laughter, fearing he wouldn't get to hear the rest of the story. Camel speaks calmly, "How badly did you embarrass her?"

Marc, "Nothing was left to her imagination. Having been raised at an all girls' parochial school until now."

Camel, "Tsk, tsk." Wagging his finger at Marc. "I'm sure she has had anatomy.

But still not the approach I would have taken. Too direct, you heathen male." Camel unable to hold back his laughter. One of those deep masculine sounds.

Marc laughing along with him. "Yes, it was one of those priceless moments."

Camel, "I would have done anything to see your face."

Marc, "You should have seen hers." Both of them laugh loudly again.

Camel, "Especially her. Raised like a novice and with that pit bull of an aunt. Guarding her innocence."

"Yes, Ms. Campbell gave me the whole lecture on appropriate behavior for young men around young ladies." Camel rolls his eyes. Himself having heard the same lecture on more than one occasion. "Ms. Campbell reminds me of one of those old women who are chaperones. You know the type. Peering back at you through a burka. Convinced your intentions are bad."

Marc, "Yes, the kind that would hit you with a stick or suggest the girl's father should beat you to make sure you are respectful enough to her."

Camel, "What's the word in English? Oh yes, a scoundrel. You are quickly catching up with me, my little brother." Marc's protestations of innocence is interrupted by the rumble of another engine. This one a dark green Ferrari zipping up the driveway coming to a fast stop next to Camel's black one. Jadon steps out of the car wearing a short dress. Exposing her cappuccino toned and very shapely legs. Wearing a pair of four-inch Jimmy Choo's open-toe sling back stiletto heels. Commanding their attention. Taking quick steps across the pavers creating a clicking sound. Letting her long dark hair free after being tied back. Tossing her head shaking her hair loose. Its length well down her back. Looking at Marc with her stunning silver-green eyes. Both men have unconsciously stopped talking to watch her approach. Camel whispers under his breath for Marc to hear, "You lucky dog. You owe me."

Marc takes his work gloves off as he walks over to her. "I didn't expect to see you again. I mean today." His cheeks warming up.

Jadon, "Why wouldn't you" glancing at Camel "want to see me again?" Marc's tanned cheeks turn dusky and warm. Caught off guard by his own mistake. "Or was I just another one-night stand?" Her tone playful but her meaning clear. "Like your brother there is rumored to do so often."

Marc, "It's an unexpected pleasure to see you anytime." Regaining his confidence.

Jadon, "I didn't realize you would have company. Here's my calling card," handing it to Marc. That included her e-mail and fax numbers. A bead of perspiration runs down the stubble covered side of his face. Jadon reaches out blotting at it with her fragranced hair tieback. Its perfume brings back memories of their night together. Making him heady and distracted. Camel stays back as a good wingman should, not competing for her attention. But just barely able to catch the smell of her perfume with its allure.

Jadon, "I enjoy watching men perspire when they are hard at work or just making them do it." Glancing down and back up to his eyes. Satisfied with her effect on him. Marc's jeans becoming uncomfortable and tight.

Jadon, "Call me." Turning and walking away. Sure that both men are watching her walk away. Getting into her car pushing her sunglasses on. Turning the ignition and revving the engine. Shifting into gear and pulling away quickly.

Camel steps up beside Marc speaking. "If you don't call her you're a fool." Marc tucks her calling card into his pocket. Walking back to the table with a little strut in his step.

Ms. Campbell coming outside as the green sports car passes her. Making a guttural sound of disapproval. Walking over in her sneakers. Unsmiling. "It's lunchtime. You two need to come in and eat." Looking Camel over. "You look healthy for a man that was critically wounded a few days ago. At least that's what the news would have everyone believe."

Camel, "I'm fine thank you. The press as always exaggerates everything that is bad. They get better ratings that way." The three of them walk back into the house Norma in front.

Ms. Campbell, "That's all they do. By the way, that girl, as you called her, she will be working here for a while. She is my niece. I say this now because she is off-limits to the both of you." Not turning back to look at them. "And don't try to look innocent because I know you are not." Marc's face set with a sheepish expression and blinking his blue eyes innocently. Camel's handsome square jawed face concerned.

Camel, "I would never do anything to compromise your niece's virtue."

Ms. Campbell, "I would certainly hope not." Turning to look, glaring at Marc right in the eyes. "She wouldn't stand a chance with either of you. My late sister, God rest her soul." Pausing and turning to stop both. "That's my sister's only child and I mean for her to do well. To not be used as some play toy, by a couple of…," catching herself, thinking, *A couple of heathen scoundrels.* "Playboys looking for a fast and loose whore. Am I making myself clear?"

Marc, "We both understand she is off-limits. Right, Camel?"

Camel, "Yes, ma'am."

Ms. Campbell, "Just in case there is any doubt, she is underage." Turning and walking in. Thinking, *That usually scares men off. Not that it had much effect on her father. My ignorant sister soon learned how fickle men can* be. *Unfortunately not until after she was knocked up and unmarried.*

Ms. Campbell making an attempt at being pleasant, "Now go into the dining room where lunch will be served." The three of them walk into the kitchen. Norma busies herself at the stove. Mary pours sugar into tea, soon to be iced. Marc picks up a freshly baked chocolate chip cookie off the metal sheet setting on the granite counter. Camel selects an apple instead from a basket of fruit. Taking a bite out of it. Neither of the men that put off by her speech. Looking at Mary with her cheeks rose pink and dusted with flour. Ms. Campbell turns around seeing them. "Don't spoil your appetites and stop loitering. Out with the two of you. Lunch is not being served in here." The two guys rush out. Ms. Campbell waves her hands. "Out!" Mary hiding a smile.

CHAPTER 21

MS. CAMPBELL ENTERS the room leading the way carrying a tray with large bowls of food on it. Consisting of mashed potatoes with skins mixed in and butter swirled through it. Also a casserole dish with steaming hot broccoli au gratin(white aged Cheddar). Mary brings up the rear with the platter of fried chicken. Ms. Campbell places the tray on the sideboard. Mary places the chicken between the two young men. Its aroma mouthwatering. Ms. Campbell lifts her eyebrows letting that one slide. Instructing Mary, "We serve from the left and remove from the right." Ms. Campbell plates up ample portions of both vegetables one at a time. Handing the plate off to Mary. Her hand shaking a little as she places the first dish in front of Camel, steam rising off it. His eyes round with concern.

Ms. Campbell, "Be careful, that's hot from the oven. You don't want to burn someone." Marc's face friendly and supportive. Before the two women can get out of the room, the two guys are already digging in hungrily. Moments later, Ms. Campbell comes back into the room carrying a basket of buttermilk biscuits. Announcing, "You have a guest."

Melinda walks in confident as ever. Wearing her new summer ensemble in shades of blue. Her blouse cut at the midriff and skirt short, their colors making her eyes bluer. Blonde hair cascading down her back. Completing and making it more effective are white D&G stilettos over five inches high. Clicking against the hardwood floor of the wide dining room. Too impatient to wait for that "old cow Ms. Campbell," disregarding the older woman. Where did he dig that one up? Oh right, Angelique did. Both men rise up from their chairs.

"Don't get up. Marc, I'm so sorry I haven't returned your calls. It's just, I've been so busy these last few days." Managing a brief smile as she walks across the room over to Marc. Kissing him on the same cheek Jadon had touched earlier. Almost the exact place, taking him back to Jadon's soft touch and her intoxicating perfume. Believing herself to be the reason Marc has that longing expression. Seating herself next to Marc at the head of the expansive dining table. Able to seat twenty comfortably.

Melinda speaks to Camel, "You're looking fit." Her expression friendly, smiling at him. But not really so friendly as she is almost smug and knowing. Camel takes note.

Camel, "Yes. I guess you heard about my incident."

"Yes. You certainly don't look any worse for wear." Her thoughts focused on observing him for any changes. Feeling some disappointment at finding nothing apparent.

Camel, "I couldn't be doing any better. The reports were clearly inaccurate. You look as enticing as ever."

"Thank you," she answers, clearly not too concerned with Marc. Having not said much, still perturbed with her for not returning his calls.

Marc, "He does seem to be doing well for someone that was seriously wounded. That woman attacked him with the intention of killing him."

"How serious could it have been?"

Marc not letting her finish, "He was stabbed, Melinda!"

"Stabbed? That was you?" Giving it her best to look surprised and then appalled. "I heard about it on the news. Their take on it was some gigolo had two women fighting over him. I just figured he got what he deserved. Oh, I didn't mean to say it like that. Sometimes words just come out and I say what I'm thinking." Her apology not very sincere. "So where was he stabbed?"

Marc, "In his back!"

"You don't have to be so hostile toward me. I didn't stab him."

Camel having had enough of her toying, "I'm fine. The media in this country clearly exaggerates everything. It was a minor injury. I'm as healthy as an ox." Marc still not completely convinced, remembering Dr. Daas giving his account of the injuries.

Melinda, "Well, thank goodness it wasn't that serious. Angelique wouldn't have an escort for her party. You two well, at least young men get yourselves into all kinds of trouble. No wonder so many die before an old age. Was it some jealous lover?" Her barb getting Camel right where she intended it to.

Camel, "No, it wasn't." Marc wonders, *What is she doing?*

Melinda turns her sweetness and concern toward him. "Where were you during all this?" Her voice educated American, without accent.

Marc on the spot looking guilty, says, "Mary, bring another place setting for our guest. I was at home when it happened."

Melinda's blue eyes hard penetrating and unblinking watching him for his response. Then turning her attention to Mary. Scrutinizing her in the oversized salmon-colored maid's uniform. Dismissing her as not a threat. Then giving her something to do. "Bring me a glass of white wine while you're in the pantry." Turning her attention back on Marc. "When did you get more help?"

"She is here for the summer to help open up the house. Just a job before college."

Melinda, "How responsible." Deciding to mess with Marc's mind just to see his face with that stupid deer caught in the headlights expression. "You were home all night? I tried calling, you didn't pick up." Lying to watch him squirm, moving his feet nervously. Enjoying every second of it. "Didn't you get my message?" Doing her best to look unguarded.

Marc, "I did get a message that night." Struggling to remember what happened before Jadon arrived.

"Oh? If I were the jealous type, I would think you had a woman over."

Marc grasping at anything to move the conversation along, "Angelique came by looking for Camel." Melinda tickled with his misery. Camel silently listening to his own thoughts. Whispering in his mind, *She is a stone-cold liar. Like a cat playing with a mouse.*

Melinda, "I know I called. Didn't you get my message?"

Marc panicking inside, grasping at a thread of truth. "The power went out for several hours. That was after Angelique left."

Melinda, "What time was she here?" Looking suspicious. All the while enjoying herself watching Marc struggle to avoid getting caught.

Camel speaks up, "She was looking for me."

Marc adds, "Right after she left, a huge electrical storm blew in. It was powerful. Nothing like I've ever seen here. Bringing a massive deluge, rain pouring off the roof. Lightning striking with thunder booming across the house. Just after she left."

Camel, "Like you didn't know."

Melinda, "I didn't hear anything about power outages." Playing it close. "Camel, I'm so glad to see you looking so handsome for a random crime victim. Did they take anything?" Working to get him to expose his hand.

Camel unmoved by her overly simple attempt at manipulating him. "It wasn't like that." A voice in his mind whispers to him again. *Wait, when the time is right, she will get what is coming to her.* "I was having some harmless fun dancing with the two women."

Melinda, "Are you sure it was a woman that attack you and not some man? Stabbing someone is so personal." Her eyebrows raised.

Camel, "I wasn't sleeping with them. One of the two just stabbed me."

Melinda, "Maybe she got the wrong impression from you."

Camel, "I was not playing one against the other. I don't have to justify myself."

Melinda, "You mistake my questions. I'm just trying to understand why something like that would happen. That's all. If it's going to upset you, let's just change the subject." Clasping her hands together moving her perfectly manicured French tipped nails. Mary carries in a place setting along with the glass of white wine. Melinda takes the wine glass from her hand. "Finally, you just can't get good help." Taking a sip. "What third world did you have to scour to get her?"

Marc shocked by her comment. "She is from London, England."

Melinda speaking as if Mary weren't there. "Men, a pretty face and they forget about what is important." Looking to Camel. "So it would seem you're just fine after all is said and done." Mary listens from the butler's pantry. *That New York blue blood acts like she is better than all of us. Those two blokes can't see her for what she is.* Aunt Norma's hand grabs her shoulder giving her a good startle. Glaring at her with those hard eyes and dour face. Her thin lips turned down. Indicating silently for Mary to follow her. Not speaking a word until they're out of earshot of Marc and his guests.

Melinda, "Marc you are getting so suntanned. It brings out the blue in your eyes. Letting your hair grow out really becomes you. It makes you look so GQ."

Inside the kitchen Norma Campbell is furious with her niece. Pulling her by her arm the rest of the way into the room. "What were you thinking, eavesdropping. Don't they teach you anything at that hoity-toity girls' school?"

Used to her aunt's brusque approach with her unaffected by her verbal attack. Mary replies, "I can't stand that blue blood, Ms. Sophisticated, with her designer clothes. Speaking with her educated, accent less English. She's manipulating those two and they can't see it."

Norma's anger dissipates some exhaling a deep breath before speaking. "You're right, but men use women like that for one thing. Mark my words, neither of them will every marry her kind."

Mary, "Unless she tricks one of them."

Norma, "There is a word for her type." Scowling. Mary knows it was a time to be quiet and let her aunt speak. Unless she wanted to chance bringing that bad temper to bear on her. Having gotten off lightly, choosing to remain safe.

Norma, "You just stay away from all of them. Know your place and you'll do just fine. That scholarship will take you far." Mary returning to her kitchen duties letting her thoughts wander. Yes, an education will get her away from people like that trust fund snob. Like so many girls forced by wealthy families into parochial boarding schools. Becoming ruthless and cruel to girls of low-income backgrounds. Mary is dicing carrots distractedly. Aunt Norma glances over at her. "You need to pay attention. Are you still thinking about that boy?"

Mary chancing it, says, "Marc's not like her. You can tell he is good, down to earth." Having chosen her words carefully.

Norma, "I've seen enough to know whether it is intentional or not. He'll use you. Then toss you aside without another thought. What will you do after that? You'll be a maid that's knocked up. Lose your scholarship, then what?" Mary's expression still unconvinced with her jaw set. Her green eyes serious looking just like her mother used to. Aunt Norma's patience wearing thin. "You'll be no better off than me or your mother was. Knocked up by some smooth talking debonair type like your father was. Have you ever heard from him? NO! He never even came back to see you after you were born. Much less help pay for your support."

Mary, "Why do you say such things to me?" Hurt, clearly unable to mask her pain.

Norma, "I think it's time for you to clean the paneling upstairs." Slamming her knife down against the counter.

Mary, "This conversation isn't over." Balling up her apron. Aunt Norma glares at her with one of her mean unwavering stares. Challenging her to say more and reap the consequences.

Norma warns her, "Those people run in a fast, loose crowd. They think money can buy them out of their troubles. You watch and see. They'll all be into some serious trouble soon enough." Aunt Norma's face red. "Don't push me girl. You can be so ignorant. Why do you think that young man was stabbed? By some sheer happenstance? It was one of his jealous lovers. I read the news story. He was dancing with two women and probably sleeping with both of them. It's not what was in the news story but what wasn't."

Mary, "Marc's not like that. He's nice. I can tell it." Aunt Norma's smile icy. Sending a chill up Mary's spine. Knowing that her aunt rarely smiled and this wasn't a friendly kind of smile.

Norma, "Yeah? If he is so nice, why was another woman slipping out of here the other morning?"

Mary, "No," her disappointment apparent.

Norma, "Oh yeah. He isn't so nice and little miss in there doesn't have a clue. Didn't you notice that smell up there in the bedroom?" Norma testing Mary, but her face remains unchanged, innocent. Unfamiliar with what her aunt Norma was trying to discover. Norma relaxing just a little.

Aunt Norma, "Well, I guess I shouldn't be surprised. You wouldn't recognize the smell of coitus mixed with male musk. He might try to cover it up with cologne and incense, but I'm not fooled. He's an animal and he'd have you bedded in a moment." Mary knows better than to argue with her aunt when she was this worked up. "You just stay away from him or you'll find yourself back at boarding school. Before you can say Jack Robinson. All I need do is have a quiet word with Sister Ann. She agrees with me on discipline. Do you understand me?" Her threat not too subtle.

Mary, "Yes, ma'am." Her disappointment replaced by hatred. Mary's memories of that minion from hell. Her fear long ago changed to hatred for the nun her aunt had used to make her life a misery. Mary heads toward the back stairs, aunt Norma stopping her.

"First clear the dishes, from the right." Mary goes back into the dining room. Cautiously removing plates from in front of Marc's guests. The three of them are talking animatedly. Melinda takes notice of both men, how their attention casually but definitely stays on Mary, "the maid." Half listening to her. Melinda decides to engage this milky skinned girl.

Melinda, "You must use a lot moisturizers to get that luminescence."

Mary is surprised she was spoken to by the princess. "Uh no." Her large green eyes round with innocence. Forcing Melinda to hold her face soft with an insincere smile.

"It's just dumb luck. I spend a fortune on facials and treatments at the spa. Your skin is so naturally luminescent. Quite beautiful and not a blemish." Mary's cheeks warm up lightly, as she becomes self-conscious with all the attention focused on her. Unsure of how much was a compliment or just an observation. "So many gingers have masses of freckles all over them. I find that disgusting. What do you think, Marc?"

Marc, "I haven't given it much thought."

Camel injects, "They can be very sexy on some women." His brown eyes dreamily glancing at Mary.

Melinda not ready to give up on her yet, "Are you wearing makeup?" Sitting forward, her eyes more like a bird of prey ready to swoop in on its kill. Examining Mary's face.

Mary, "No. I'm not allowed." Realizing her mistake as soon as it left her lips. Melinda smirking. "I mean it's discouraged." Speaking softly, watching the doorway. Knowing any minute Aunt Norma will be out there to embarrass her more.

Melinda, "Who discourages it? How old are you?"

Mary, "I attend parochial school. A very conservative order. Mary Regina Immaculata prevails with strict policies on student attire and conduct."

Melinda, "Do I detect a North London accent?"

Mary, "Yes. How did you know?"

Melinda, "I went to Saint Bartholomew's Preparatory School for Girls. My roommate hailed from north of London. Her family has lived there for centuries. That thrown in with a few others from England. Once you get the ear for it, you can pick out where people are from. Are you British?"

Mary, "Yes. I was raised there. My father was British and my mother American." Her shoulders visibly relaxing. "You went to a Catholic girls' school?"

Melinda, "Yes, an unfortunate event in my life presented me with circumstances I was unable to prevent." Her expression stoic with eyes glacier blue. Mary not wishing to pry continues gathering up the dirty dishes. "So what brings you to the armpit of Western New York?"

Mary, "Ms. Campbell. I mean Aunt Norma. She expects me to assume some responsibility before college. I have a full scholarship to Eton."

Melinda, "Very impressive. My parents wanted the best education without boys around." The two guys hang on every word. "If you ever want company to go shopping or just get out of the house, call me. I'm your woman."

Mary's face lights up. "That would be great."

Melinda, "Marc, you and Camel are coming next week to the alumni mixer." More of a statement of fact.

Camel, "I wouldn't miss it for anything. Even after being stabbed." Looking Melinda in the eyes.

Melinda, "Let's hope that won't be necessary again. Mary, I hope you'll be joining us next Saturday."

Mary, "Really, you're inviting me?"

Melinda, "Of course, us Catholic schoolgirls have to stick together. It would be fun to reminisce." Mary's heart races at the prospect of going to a party.

Marc looks quizzically at Melinda. "I didn't know you went to a Catholic girls' school."

Melinda, "You probably weren't listening when I told you." Turning to Mary, "Guys tend not to listen very closely except when it concerns sex. That's how they end up paying for dinner." Melinda stands up. "Well, I have to be off. Marc, call me. Mary, I look forward to seeing you soon. Let me know when you're ready to go shopping."

Ms. Campbell stamps into the room, interrupting. "The only shopping you're going to be doing is for groceries. You have everything you need already. If you're so good your work is already done, I have more for you to do. Now get to it."

Mary, "Yes, ma'am." Hurrying from the room, dishes rattling on the tray. Both men are standing now.

Camel, "I have to go too. I'll see you later." Winking at Marc.

Marc, "I have to get back to work outside." Their group breaks up.

CHAPTER 22

MELINDA USING HER rearview mirror to check her makeup watches Camel's black Ferrari passing quickly from view. The sound of the wet saw grinding back in use from behind the house. Mary comes out the side door toting a large trash bag in each hand. Seizing her chance Melinda steps out of her car walking gracefully over to Mary. Calling to her softly her voice almost a hiss. Mary sets the bags down placing a finger across her lips to indicate silence. Pulling the bags over stepping into the shadow of the house out of view from the windows.

Melinda, "She shouldn't treat you like an indentured servant. You're her niece and certainly not a child anymore."

Mary nods agreement. Speaking softly so as to not be heard. "Aunt Norma has always treated me that way. She says she doesn't want some spoilt useless child."

Melinda arches her eyebrow. "I know the type. I've had a few stepmothers like that." Raising her voice in anger. Mary flutters her hand to quiet her. Glancing up at the windows above. "I'm sorry. I just can't stand women like that."

Mary admits, "She doesn't want me speaking with any of you."

Melinda, "Why?" Mary pauses, reluctant to say anything. Melinda realizes what it was. "Oh, I get it. She doesn't approve of how we live. The troublemaking rich, spoilt and able to buy our way out of it. Am I right?"

Mary holds her breath afraid to lose a new friend. "Yes."

Melinda opens her purse removing a card, slipping it into Mary's pocket on her maid's uniform. "Hide this from mother superior the guardian of virtue. It has all my contact numbers on it. Call me when you're ready, anytime."

Mary, "I don't know." Looking over her shoulder, conscious of being seen talking with the very woman she was forbidden to have anything to do with.

Melinda, "I know your aunt means well, but to treat you like you are on a parole work relief program? It's the summer before you are off to college. Haven't you earned some fun? You have a scholarship to prove you worked hard for years." Mary has had the same feelings but was afraid to voice them to her aunt.

Expecting her trip abroad to Rochester to be a time of discovery. Making new friends. Not locked in a house with her cruel middle-aged aunt.

Mary, "I'll think about it." Lifting the trash bags. "When you're ready to have some fun use that card. If you decide in time for the soiree, I promise you will meet exciting people many of them your own age. Friends of Marc and Camel's. Your aunt will never have to know. It will be our best kept secret. Memories you will have to get you through those long hours spent studying when at Eton."

Mary desperately wants to go to a real soiree. Many of her more well to do classmates speaking of social events. Where they dressed in gowns and danced the night away, carefree. If only she could manage it. Deciding right then. "I will. I mean call you, soon." Her heart pounding from just the thrill of thinking about doing it. Proving her aunt wrong and defying her another plus. To be going where her sophisticated peers will be present. Marc and Camel, both of those young men so debonair. But to have a chance to spend time with Marc alone, so incredibly sexy. Almost blushing remembering him nude. Her cheeks becoming pink.

Melinda, "Mary where did you go, girl? I think you have some secrets."

Mary, "My aunt must never find out about this. Ever. She would send me to a convent or worse."

Melinda, "Don't you think you are taking that a little far?"

Mary, "No. There is nothing she wouldn't do to hurt me. When she feels I need punishing. She would even decline my scholarship. "

Melinda, "Well then she need not find out. I better go before we are caught. I don't want to be the reason you get into trouble." Melinda looks up at the windows whispering, "Bye."

Mary continuing with her choirs hefting up her overfilled bags. Keeping a steady pace walking over to the trash dumpster beside the garage. Screened by bushes sneaking a long look at Marc working with his shirt off. His muscular pectorals bulging covered with straight dark hair. Thickest in the center passing over his rippling abdominal muscles, wet from perspiration and grime. Focused on the stone he is pushing into the diamond blade of the wet saw. Grinding loudly spraying him with ground stone and water.

Melinda uses her rearview mirror to observe Mary. Seeing patches of salmon color through the bushes. Then using her compact mirror to investigate further what has Mary so attentive. Spying Marc, understanding why she is taking so long. Watching him carry a heavy chunk of flagstone placing it. Everything going as planned. He really is changing. A few weeks ago his body was smooth. Even the hair on his head has been affected. So much thicker and growing fast it will be to his shoulders soon. A smug little expression passing across her face. Shifting into gear pulling away.

Ms. Campbell peeks out a second-story window. Watching Melinda leave, wondering what took her so long. *That one is nothing but trouble for any man that gets involved with her. She is nothing but a rich whore.* Calling out the window, "Mary!" *Where is that girl? She is becoming too much like her mother.*

CHAPTER 23

MARC KNOCKING OFF work, the time is close to six o'clock. His work area already shaded by the tall trees on the west side of the property. Satisfied that his work on the paths is where it should be now after all the delays. Completed right up to where the steps lead to the terrace. Everything ahead of schedule, now he'll be able to have an easy Friday. More importantly, a relaxing weekend. The stonemason will be out next week to help with the terrace and low seating walls. Reviewing in his mind the final steps. A pergola on the west end. Where thorn-less pink roses will be planted behind the seating wall. The west side having been chosen because they will be shaded from the hot afternoon sun. But getting plenty of sunlight in the morning.

Going inside the empty house Marc finds a note on the granite counter written by Mary. Telling him sandwiches are in the refrigerator. Her handwriting so neat and legible. After wolfing down two chicken salad sandwiches, he heads upstairs for a shower. Letting the cool water pelt him savoring the sensation. Just cooling off after being out in the summer heat all day.

After drying off then going downstairs. He settles into an overstuffed wingback chair in the library. His bare feet up on a hassock wearing only his Joe Boxers. Cool air whispering from the central air-conditioning. Time for some light reading and a snifter of Courvoisier. The phone rings, but not bothering with it. Instead allowing it to go to voice mail. Comfortable now, paging through the old diary. Again trying to puzzle out the story. Written in French and Latin, setting it aside in frustration. What the heck. Getting up to see who called. Pressing the play button on the answering machine.

"Hi, Marc." Her voice sexy almost hypnotic. "It's Melinda. I was calling to see if you wanted some company tonight." Feeling his boxers tightening up. His mind rushing over memories of Melinda's body. Hearing another voice in the background familiar. Melinda speaks to her, "What? I can't now. Marc, I'm sorry babe. Angelique needs me for moral support tonight. That Camel did it again. Why doesn't he have the balls to break it off with her. I'm sorry another time babe. Bye-bye." *Click. What did he do this time? He's becoming my cock block.* Marc's hardness pushes past the top of the elastic waistband uncomfortable as heck, pinching. Adjusting himself without much success. Instead looking like an old man with his shorts pulled up too high. Gulping down the snifter of cognac. It burns all the way down helping to distract him from being irritated with Camel, his brother seeming to frequently stir it up. Sitting back down but unable to concentrate on reading. Melinda's voice echoing in his mind's ear, so sultry.

Marc awakened by a loud thud. The diary having slid off his lap onto the floor. Glancing across the library at the clock on the mantel. Almost midnight, having woken from a very bad dream. This one leaving him disturbed grieving after the horrible incident. Remembering part of it about a flight Camel was on. A commercial airliner that clips a skyscraper in Dubai. Shivering, his breath creating a cloud on the cold air. Getting up rubbing his arms to warm them. Time to call it a day carrying the lights' remote control. Pointing it from the doorway switching off all the lights in the library. Setting the remote down on a vase stand beside the doorway. Out in the hallway what a difference in temperature. It's not freezing cold out here already feeling warmer. So much for thermal zone control.

Taking the stairs in the dark every sound amplified throughout the solitary house. The grandfather clock ticking in the foyer carrying up to its second floor. One step creaking under Marc's weight. Hearing another sound, that of fabric rustling as he passes a large baroque mirror. Pausing midstride turning his head. Listening to identify where this noise came from without any drapes nearby. Deciding, *It must be me*. Continuing down the hall to the master suite.

Marc slides under the covers sinking into the engineered foam mattress. So comfortable and soft yet supportive for his tired and aching muscles. Overworked from maneuvering and lifting heavy flagstones into place. Really having needed help from Camel as was planned. But then how could he be expected to do that kind of work after such an injury? Stretching like a big cat, languishing against clean fresh-smelling sheets, reminding him Mary had changed the linens. Smiling softly to himself sleep quickly returns bringing another dream. Only this time it's that woman waiting for him. The one who has become only too familiar to his dreams. It not being possible for him to know her. After all she is from another century, his rational brain still working. Aware of her being in the past because of her attire. Yet still her face remains a mystery. Walking ahead of him in the garden on its path her dress brushing the ground. Her steps slow and graceful with the motion of fabric from her long dress swaying. Fascinated by her Marc follows her closer searching for any cue to understand who this mysterious women was. Observing everything down to the simplest details. Her dress trimmed in hand-sewn lace with sleeves mid–arm length. A fan dangles from her left wrist. Hair platinum blonde elaborately coiffed piled high on her head. Carrying herself with the presence of someone powerful. Her stride purposeful yet regal. Turning as if she has heard something. Opening her fan with a flick of her wrist, just missing seeing her powdered white face covered. The fan hand painted with an Oriental scene obscuring her face from view. Warning feelings, those of dread rippling across his mind. Every fiber of his being warning him to get away from her. *How could she know I'm here? It's only a dream. She acts almost as if she knows I'm observing her.* Their steps crunching against gravel on their path. Moving toward Marc, demurely only at first. Then quickening her step moving right up to him in the blink of an eye. Reaching out with her long nailed hand outstretched. All the while keeping her face obscured from view by the use of her fan. His heart skipping a beat before quickening. Chanting softly something known to him the air around them quivering. Marc frozen in place unable to move his legs.

A male voice frantically calls out in his mind, "Run, Marc!" His voice so recognizable but who alludes him. "Marc! Do it now! Run!" Uncle Theron? Desperation in his voice causes Marc's heart to race with panic. He can't move. What has she done to him? Struggling to make his legs work.

"I can't, Uncle Theron!" Both of them speaking at once. Her in French. What's she saying?

Uncle Theron, "Don't listen to her! Get away before it's too late! You fool!" He must get away, concentrating with all his might to leave. Too late, her hand closing on his right arm with a viselike grip. Nails digging into his the flesh of the bicep. Adrenaline pumping with his heart racing. Suddenly his body unfreezes and like a trapped animal he tears away. Using muscle strength all he has pulling away from her by sheer force. While his hide gives way to her sharp nails digging gouges into his flesh. Ripping across skin, peeling under her sharp talon like nails. Blood coming out in their terrible wake, along with searing pain.

Her words, "Mon fils!"

Waking up gasping trapped under the covers struggling. Marc kicks and fights in the pitch blackness. Throwing them off onto the floor. Jumping out of bed landing on his feet into a defensive crouching posture ready. Swinging his leg out using a foot to reach for the lamp on the bedside table. Bumping it triggering the touch sensor causing the light to come on as it tumbled to the floor. Amazingly not breaking the bulb. A shiver of bestial anger rushes up Marc's spine making the hair on it stand up. How did she know he was there?

His heart still racing, searching the empty room once more before trying to right the fallen lamp. Picking up the lamp with its sensors brightening it more. Setting it back on the nightstand. Calling out, "Lights on." Lights flicker on shining from the maul like opening of the bathroom. Marc's fear abates with his pulse slowing. What a dream. Lifting his tee shirt that was covering the digital clock. Its light always too bright. Hating it for that but glad it doesn't tick, 3:00 a.m. Padding into the bathroom to urinate. Wide awake now.

After straightening out the sheets he begins to make the bed. Not before tapping the cell phone with his foot sending it sliding under the bed. Irritated with this mishap getting down on his hands and knees to retrieve the cell phone from under the bed. Picking it up noting one call missed. Thumbing to retrieve the message. Who would have called this late? Seeing his answer, Camel. Concerned for his recovering brother pressing the play key.

Listening to his message. "I was hoping you were awake. I had the strangest dream. Imagine this, Angelique being a witch."

A feminine voice in the background. "Cam, come back to bed. You said you would cuddle with me until I go to sleep."

Camel, "Yes, just a moment babe.

"Marc and get this. She was the one that stabbed me. How's that for your subconscious playing tricks on you?"

"Cam! I'm cold, come back to bed."

Camel answers her, "I'm coming babe." His voice more of a big cat's purr. "I just thought you might still be up. I'll talk to you soon." *Click*. The dial tone humming.

Marc spreads the bedding haphazardly across the mattress. Sliding under them up to his waist his body still warm. Throwing them off impatiently something about what Camel had said in his message bothering him. Just like a memory not quite grasped, tickling his mind, unable to bring it out. Taking a deep breath exhaling it. Now both of them are having nightmares. Turning the bedside light off with a light tap. The digital clock's blue LEDs casting a wide area of light in the room. That is a problem for someone who has difficulty sleeping. Looking at the time 3:15 a.m. Using a pillowcase to cover the clock up. Satisfied the room is dark enough to sleep in. Lying back against his pillows. Now if only his mind would slow down. Marc's eyes wide open reflecting on recent events. Ever since Angelique read from that old diary. No, what did they call it? A "grimoire." Strange things had begun occurring. Concentrating to remember if anything odd had happened before that.

Camel lies awake staring up at the ceiling. Feeling something was wrong with himself, but just what it was eluding him. Glancing over at the DVR time display 3:15 a.m. Turning over on his side propping himself up on one elbow. Watching his young female guest sleep. Following the slow rise and fall of her exposed chest, sexy yet vulnerable. Wishing Marc had answered the phone. That wasn't all that he had dreamed about. His dreams are becoming more and more sinister. Those two girls he had danced with the night he was assaulted. Both dead now, at least in his dream they were. Unable to shake the image of

Beth hanging lifelessly by her neck from the cell bars. Having used a sheet to do it with. *Why would she stab me and then kill herself? We didn't know each more than a few hours.* Glancing across the room at his own shadowy image in the mirror. Aided only by ambient light from distant security lights. His muscular and very hairy chest just visible. Before his eyes change in an instant to predatory yellow ones. Almost glowing in the dark reflecting light back. Camel's thick lips curve upward ever so slightly, his expression one of lust and hunger. Turning his guest on her side spooning with her. Then entering her causing her to moan softly. Whispering something in a language not heard in several millennia's. At least until a few nights ago.

CHAPTER 24

FRIDAY MORNING ARRIVES with sunlight from the eastern sun pouring into the room. Around poorly closed drapes making his room bright. Marc already awake giving up on sleep. Swings his long hairy legs over the side of the bed. Grabbing a pair of blue jeans off the floor along with a sleeveless tee shirt. Standing up pulling on his pants not fastening the buttons of the Levis' 501s. Then retrieving the pillowcase to check on the time. It figures, 7:00 a.m. and he's up already. On a day he could have slept in, instead he's up early. Carrying his shirt in one hand heading into the bathroom for a quick stop.

Downstairs the rich smell of fresh brewing coffee meets him on the way into the kitchen. Ms. Campbell and Mary haven't arrived yet. But Ms. Campbell being very efficient has the coffee machine timer set. Marc slides his mug under the stream of brewing coffee as it comes out. Then sliding the pot back into place. Taking a sip of the caffeinated black brew on his way outside to examine the finished paths. Outside everything looks great and ahead of schedule. He starts clearing away tools and rock scrapes to allow the lawn beneath them to breath.

Coming back inside later for another cup of coffee, Colombian supremo. Marc notices the note left by Ms. Campbell the day before. "Grocery shopping only on Friday. You'll have to fend for yourself." His perfect weekend shaping up. One just right for the hammock. No one around to find work for him and not a cloud in the sky. The only problem will be finding the hammock in the basement. How hard could that be?

By midmorning Marc is ready to begin his search. Taking the back stairs down into the earth. The manor's foundations set deeply into the ground like roots. Built against bedrock solidly footed. Passing through a notable temperature change. Like passing an invisible wall. Warm on one side and cool on the other. Checking for a light switch standing just inside the basements threshold with floor joints at least eight feet above his six-foot height. Marc estimating the basement's cobweb covered ceiling. His cell phone hooked on his pocket ringing. Accepting the call. "Hello." Its reception poor. Camel, "Didn't you get my message?" His tone impatient.

Marc, "Yeah. When did you get up?"

Camel, "A few minutes ago." Point taken.

"Okay." Marc taking the last step into the basement. Shadows making areas un-viewable. Looking around for a light switch. Feeling around with his free hand to no avail. Camel's heavy breath returning his attention to the phone.

Camel, "Look if this is not a good time."

Marc, "Look nothing. That dream was very disturbing."

Camel, "Why do you have an attitude?"

Marc answering quick and snappy, "I don't! Do you think she could do something like that?" Playing devil's advocate.

Camel, "No." Not very convincing even to himself.

Marc, "You don't sound too sure about that." Sitting down on the steps. Noticing the smell of moist earth mixed with the old house inundating his olfactory senses. Giving in no longer irritated with Camel. After all he is family.

"You saw her that night. What do you think? Knowing her as you do."

Marc, "She was very angry to the point of rage from her jealousy. They caught the woman that did it. Are we talking about the dream or the night in question?"

Camel, "You haven't answered my question."

Marc, "She was angrier than I have ever seen her. As to her state of mind...," pausing to let him think about it. Because he did it again to her just last night. "Yes, she could have done it. There is no doubt in my mind."

Camel, "But she wasn't in the club that night."

Marc, "I certainly didn't see her. That's not to say one of her friends didn't see you and call her." Before Camel could ask. "Not that I can remember much from that night myself. After I met Jadon, I didn't really pay attention to anyone else."

Camel, "It was a strange night. The parts I do remember were before I was stabbed and those are cloudy at best."

Marc, "It's the same for me. The atmosphere was dreamlike, yet I felt so alive and passionate."

Camel, "The more I danced the more euphoric I became. The music seemed to have a life of its own. It affected me on some basal level I was unable to resist."

Marc adds, "The rhythm took control of me. Jadon, she was just so... mesmerizing, her movements. I became caught up on waves of arousal. Something I've never felt before."

Camel, "Like waves of warmth and sensuality caressing my body."

Marc, "Yeah. Jadon held my full attention more than any woman ever has. I was enthralled by her. I have never met a woman more beautiful. When she moved, my body was caressed by her sensuous movements."

Camel makes a "huh" sound under his breath, *Here we go, little brother is getting it bad for some gal*. Only thinking of Marc as his little brother not because of age but being smaller of the two men, not that either were of small build. "It sounds like you have it bad for her." Their conversation turning from serious to a lighter subject.

Marc, "I can't stop thinking about her."

Camel, "What are you going to do about Melinda?"

Marc, "I don't know, with her it's her voice. The effect on me is primal. She captivates me so much I can't stop myself. I know she's spoilt and selfish. But when she uses that sexy, breathy tone…," pausing, images of her provocatively coming to mind. "I just want her." Marc's long legs sprawled open and his broad shoulders wide enough to block the steps he's leaning back on. Letting the cool breeze of the deep basement flow over him. In an effort to dampen his increasing heat. Not finding that to be very effective.

Camel, "You still there?"

Marc comes back from his reverie. "Yeah, I'm still here."

Camel, "You have got it bad. Two women, nothing good will come of this situation. Knowing how you are. If it were me, I'd run with it and not look back, because Brother when it is over they both will turn on you in the end. And it is always the man's fault. Mark my words on that."

Marc, "I don't doubt that but I'm not you, so what am I supposed to do?"

Camel, "Live and learn my brother." Marc takes a deep breath. "I guess you know I went out last night. That urge to prowl for something new. It's just too strong. I met this unusual woman last night."

Marc stops him. "Yeah about that, Melinda was planning on seeing me last night. But instead she had to stay with a friend. Who needed her moral support, we both know who that was. I'm real glad for you. Now you're my cock block."

Camel chuckles. "Tough break." Understanding, *So that's why he had an attitude*.

Marc, "Yeah. How about that?" Standing up, stomping upstairs to look for a flashlight.

Camel tries to keep the laughter out of his voice. "I'm listening."

Marc, "Yeah? When I let all my frustration out on you, I'll wipe that dumb smile off your face in the cage."

Camel, "Yeah? Anytime you want a matchup let me know." His voice very cocksure. "And just for the record."

"Go ahead pretty boy."

Camel, "My smile works on the ladies."

"It won't help you in the ring." Marc's voice a deep growl.

"Moving on to the reason I called. You are not the only one that's been having strange dreams."

Marc, "Go on." His tone more serious now.

Camel, "That woman who stabbed me. She hanged herself in my dream."

"That would save the taxpayers some money." Marc responding out of character.

Camel, "Harsh coming from you."

"I don't appreciate when someone hurts my family."

"I would feel the same way. Now tell me, anything new with your dreams?"

Marc, "I've been dreaming of this woman from another century. She is in the garden of an estate or grounds of something much larger."

Camel, "Like a castle? What else?"

Marc, "She was aware that I'm there watching her."

Camel, "Maybe someone else is there with her. What does she look like?"

Marc, "Her face is always turned away from me or covered by a fan she carries."

Camel, "How is she dressed? What color is her hair?" Camel's eye gleams yellow. Its suspicions aroused with memories entering into his consciousness those not of his own. From deep within his mind too subtle to recognize as coming from someone else. Listening and waiting.

Marc, "The clothes are from the 1800s and her hair is platinum blonde. And it is piled high with some curls around the face. She has the familiarity of someone I know or at least should remember. That would be impossible. How could I know her?"

Camel's voice deeper with a slightly different accent. "Are you sure you can't place her? The hair, is it white? Maybe powdered? Like her face."

Marc, "Yes, that's it. Her skin is white because of powder. She is talking to a man sometimes when I see her. How did you know that?"

Camel smiles. "In the 1800s it was fashionable to use flour to powder the faces of the aristocracy. They also wore large white wigs. Is there anything else you can remember? It may be important."

Marc stops at the top of the stairs. "This sounds foolish but," swallowing, "she has a strong presence of... power about her. She actually is frightening."

Camel, "Do you mean to say her power is evil?"

Marc, "When she calls to me, 'Mon fils,' yes, there is something very malicious in her intentions toward me." The hair on the back of Marc's neck is rising up as a cold chill rushes over him.

Camel, "Say a prayer so you can't hear her. It is bad luck to talk to someone in a dream."

Marc, "I'll try to remember that the next time she grabs me and I can't get away."

"She has tried to touch you?"

Marc, "Not just tried. Last night she grabbed a hold of me with her long fingernails digging into my arm. If it hadn't been for Uncle Theron shouting for me to run. I don't think I would have gotten away. She really had dug her claws into me."

Camel's pupils slits widening in astonishment then narrowing with anger. Speaking his voice dropping an octave deeper to a bass. "Those are the worst kind of dreams."

Marc, "There is nothing worse than feeling trapped and frozen. I couldn't move after she spoke in some language I couldn't understand."

"Bad, very bad." It tries again questioning him. "What do you know of her?"

"Nothing, that is just it."

Camel, "She has to be calling you 'my son' for some reason."

Marc, "Mostly all she speaks is French. How could I be her son?"

Camel, "Yes, that is interesting." Marc experiences another cold draft tickling under his tee shirt over the hair on his spine. Giving him a shiver and raising up his hackles on the back of his neck bristling uncomfortably. Turning around, *Where did that come from?* Camel's deep voice snarling out, "Courtesan!"

Marc, "What? Why is you voice so deep? You some like a different man."

It responds through Camel, "Sinuses, you know, postnasal drip. She was probably a courtesan. One of Louis XV's whores. You know, the worst sort. Jealous women that were power hungry and willing liars for money, lying whores. Willing to stop at nothing until she got what she wanted." Coming off harsh even for himself.

Marc, "How would you know that?"

Camel, "If you had been paying attention during our French history lessons you would have recognized her. As one of Louis XV's most ruthless mistresses or courtesans. She was suspected of setting Marie Antoinette up for numerous extravagant expenses. Diamonds being one of the bigger costs leading to bankrupting the empire. Impersonating her to have jewelry made and accepting it. Leaving Marie to take the blame. At least that is the lore. It is well known they hated each other."

Marc, "Go on. This is fascinating. You sound as though you were there."

"I'm a good listener."

Marc, "Apparently, I should have been listening that day in school. Do go on."

Camel, "Marie Antoinette tried to force her out of the royal court but she had too many allies. It wouldn't be allowed."

Marc, "I can't imagine what she would want with me. Let alone why I would be dreaming of her."

Camel, "Nothing good ever came of her. Never speak to evil in a dream. It will give it power over you. Even worse would be to let her touch you, then having control over you." Marc walks into the kitchen pulling open the junk drawer. Digging around and under tools and papers to find the flashlight.

Marc, "I don't know about all that." Taking out a package of Pop-Tarts, tearing it open with his teeth. Cherry, his favorite. Leaning over the countertop, dropping them in the toaster.

Camel, "Are you still there?" His voice normal again.

Marc, "Yes." Chewing. "When did you become so superstitious?"

Camel, "Are you eating? You need to be taking this seriously."

"I don't know how to take all this. I have always believed that my faith in Allah was all I needed. Now you are talking to me about a world that is more familiar to my parents with their stories made up to frighten young boys. Around an excavation site at night. Tales of the dead with horrific curses on them. I'm not some child you can frighten."

Camel's eyes change back to yellow reptilian ones. Filled with angry and deviousness. Just as they look before he kills a mortal. His voice cold without any compassion. "There are many things of legends no longer believed in this new millennium that still may harm you. Just because they are from ancient times does not make them any less dangerous."

Marc, "Between the ancient beliefs and that voice. One I've never heard you use until now. I find you very disturbing. Where does this come from?"

Camel, "We are from the cradle of civilization. When people settled down and began sharing knowledge." Marc crunches his Pop-Tart nodding agreement. Remembering some of the Bedouin tales out in the deep desert. Told around a fire at night while sipping their milk tea.

Camel, "Creatures no longer believed in this modern world are still dangerous." Marc's hackles bristling along with goose bumps scattered across his dark haired arms. Another shiver passes through him. Stopping in mid bite his mouth becoming very dry. Setting the last chunk down.

Camel, "What? Did I spoil your appetite?" Marc having recovered some but not about to give him the satisfaction of knowing this was getting to him.

Marc, "Come on! You don't believe in that stuff." Changing hands with his cell phone. Gulping his milk tea still too hot burning his mouth and throat all the way down. Inhaling through his mouth to cool it down.

Camel's eyes flicker between his handsome brown eyes back to yellow and predatory. "Some things just want to live. While others relish taking life."

Marc, "What things?"

Camel, "I'll contact an iman about this. You need to investigate the du Bois family history. Keep that book away from everyone. Trust no one, lock it in a safe when you're not studying it." His tone irritating.

Marc hates it when his brother sounds more like an emir. "Hold on. You make it sound like this is my fault. It was your girlfriend Angelique that started all this. It would be fun to conjure something up."

Camel, "It no longer matters who is at fault. Just that we find out what is happening to us." Marc calms down. His brothers rational sound. "Have you read today's paper?"

Marc, "No."

Camel, "Go online and read for yourself." Marc uses the laptop he left on the counter. "Go to the crime section first page. Fortunately it was kept off the front page."

Marc skims to the section. "Okay."

Camel, "Read the article about the apparent double suicide in county jail." Marc reads down the story. Two young women accused in the stabbing and attempted murder of philanthropist Ahmed Hussan Khalid's son Camel Ali Khalid were found hanged in their cells. While both women were awaiting arraignment after the brutal attack. Assistant District Attorney Kunnetza is calling for an immediate investigation into what she describes as a questionable double suicide. Police commissioner angered with these deaths on his watch. While internal affairs move into quick action. Marc whistles. "Now do you really believe that this is just another unfortunate coincidence?" Camel asks.

"I'll make a serious effort to translate the diary. I have it upstairs."

Camel, "Get it and keep it safe."

Marc, "I will. You could be a little more discreet with your bed partners."

"When did you become my conscience? You're starting to sound like Ibrar. Always so sure of what is righteous Islamic behavior."

Marc, "Slow down, brother. I'm not judging you. If this is as bad as you are suggesting, discretion would be wiser and safer until we know what is going on."

Camel, "You have a point. It just would figure. Angelique gets to sleep around with other men. And I'm the one that is punished." Camel not waiting for Marc's insipid question. "I know because I've met a couple of her more recent conquests."

Marc, "Really, how long ago was that?"

Camel, "A few weeks ago. We've always had an open relationship. She wanted it that way."

Marc, "I think she has turned a corner on that one. Unless she is deceiving us both with her behavior."

Camel, "Misdirection is a tool used to control those who will allow themselves to be subjugated. I'll give Angelique a call. It's time to join the game."

Marc, "Be careful, you don't want her to know we suspect her."

Camel, "I will be. Allah Akbar, my brother."

"Allah Akbar." Returning the blessing. "We may need all the blessings we can be afforded."

CHAPTER 25

MARC RESUMES HIS search of the basement for the hammock. Taking the flashlight downstairs this time. Passing though the invisible temperature barrier again. The basement maintaining a more constant cooler temperature than the rest of the manor usually but oddly enough feeling cooler. Shining the flashlight into the semidarkness casting its beam over the walls near the stairs in search of a light switch. There it is flipping the light switch on nothing happening. *Great, the bulb is burnt out.* The musky smell from earth hidden from sunlight insinuating its scent into his nostrils. Light from the flashlight fading into the darkness. Following a long central hall with rooms for storage off to the sides in pitch blackness. Cobwebs increasing in number drooping down from the rafters above dangling. Dust particles scattering the flashlight's beam reducing visibility as Marc continues to move deeper under the old house. White noise ringing in his ears as the last of the outside sounds are cut off.

Streamers of fine invisible spider webs tickle catching on his head. Just enough to give that sensation like something is crawling in your hair. Causing him to reflexively swing at them with his large hands. Marc bats at unseen spiders not liking them at all. Having been bitten before by a large hairy grass spider in Texas. It had jumped out from its hiding place in some lawn clippings on to his bare foot. Sinking its fangs into his skin. Really more frightening because it was unexpected. Becoming jumpy the webs impossible to see in the poor light. His skin touch receptors signaling something is crawling on him. This time brushing against his face putting his imagination into overdrive. Several at once sticking to his hair. Marc frantically dusts his head off sending the flashlight beam swinging wildly. Revealing a switch by chance on a nearby wall. On closer inspection covered in old spider web with dust sticking to it. The switch so long unused it is encrusted with sticky web. Dangling from it skeletal remains white with age of other dead spiders. Wondering how big the spider was that killed them. Using the flashlight to push the button to turn on. Seeing if any lights are controlled by it. Yes, relief as two light bulbs come on. Passing through areas no human has walked in decades from the looks of it. Marc walks past the first bulb making a sizzling electric sound before it goes out with a pop. Seconds later, his flashlight dims. Allowing darkness to close in around him. Along with the tomblike silence of the manor rooted in the earth. Smacking the flashlight against his palm repeatedly. Before its light brightens with one distant bulb still working, but not much benefit. Marc ready to retreat looks back towards the exit out of the basement from where he entered. Lost in the darkest of shadows. No longer visible an optical effect.

This is becoming more troublesome than he expected. All he wanted was to find the hammock and relax. Shining the failing light into a large room off to the side. As luck would have it seeing lawn furniture piled haphazardly. A wooden Adirondack lounger with the hammock on it. What a relief with the flashlight going on and off causing him to speed up and walks smack dab into a spider web clinging to his face and head. Making his heart pound slapping at it. "Get it off me!" Grabbing hold of the wooden part of the hammock. Keeping it away from his body. Watching for anything moving on it. Making a quick retreat out into the hallway. Dim light is better than none. A large black basement spider jumping off the hammock. "What the hell," dropping the hammock on the floor. The spider scampers away into its dark habitat. Marc's adrenaline is pumping making him move fast. Giving the hammock a cursory examination before making a dash for the exit before the light fails. Moving fast now bounding up the stairs two at a time, yanking open the back door with one swift move then chunking the hammock outside. Hastily going outside dusting off his head and clothes.

Using a twig to scrape off white egg sacs of the spider still clinging to the hammock. Satisfied it's free of biting arachnids. Marc takes the new Crab Orchard flagstone path out to the terrace. His footsteps crunching on the compacted gravel surface. Stretching out the hammock between two black walnut trees. Dusting it off. Now to try it out. Rolling into it swaying rapidly. Oh, so relaxing already. Amazing how soothing and comfortable so simple an object can be. Marc settles right in with a warm breeze rustling though the densely grown hemlocks. Their boughs swaying along with the walnut trees. Making his bed float on air. Relaxing closing his eyes to take a short catnap. After all, that was the plan.

Harpsichord music softly carrying in the air. Marc's cell phone on vibrate in his pants pocket buzzing. Just conscious enough to feel his right lateral arm itching. Scratching at it causing it to sting. Pulling the cell out of his pocket. Touching the screen on the IPOD answering the call. It opens to a computerized voice offering lower-interest mortgage loans. Tapping it closed. Waking up more swinging his legs over the side of the hammock. His right arm feeling the sensation of a small insect crawling down it. Slapping at the mosquito his hand coming away damp. What the heck? Looking at his left hand with blood on his fingers. Holding his right arm away from his body to see where this was coming from. Four parallel scratches angling down the outside of the bicep. Huh? Must have happened in the basement.

Dropping down to the ground feeling energized from the nap. Now off to the gym for a good workout. Needing to release some of his pent up frustrations. Feeling his oats, a kickboxing session would be great. But first pump some iron and release endorphins. The same as a runner's high will do. Today his favorite workout routine. Upper body his pectorals with deltoids and always some abdominals. There is nothing like breaking a good sweat.

After getting back from the gym. Marc's pectorals are bulging along with his deltoids. Pumped up like cannonballs. Ready to tackle re-doing of the smaller flower beds by turning and breaking loose the soil mixing in peak and compost. Then finishing them and spreading several yards of mulch. The day a hot sunny July afternoon. Pulling his shirt off stuffing part of it into his back pocket with the rest dangling. It Sways as he walks. Coming from around the back of the manor. Marc sees Mary is unloading groceries from Ms. Campbell's late model station wagon. Mary lifting some heavy bags out with effect. Marc walks over with a masculine strut. Speaking agreeably, "Here let me help you with those."

Mary, "Sure there's plenty more."

Marc's face is dirt smudged with a heavy growth of stubble on his angular jaw. Perspiration running down it. "You were left to do all this by yourself?" Lifting bags of canned goods up making his muscles bulge more.

Mary's cheeks flush. "I could have managed but thank you." Trying not to stare at his well–developed tanned physique. Pausing at his blue eyes Marc smiling. Carrying several bags at once. Her mind racing, a girl could get lost in those deep blue eyes. Watching him walk away the view just as good. Round buttocks solid like a ballplayer's.

Ms. Campbell comes outside. "Oh good, we can certainly use a man. Some of those are heavy. Not that we couldn't have managed just the same." Looking past Marc to see Mary checking him out. Mary turns her head away when she notices her aunt's angry expression.

Aunt Norma eases over to her speaking softly into Marys' ear. "You'd do well to keep your eyes off him. Him and his rich friends are trouble for a girl like you. Mixing it up with a maid. I don't think so. You remember our conversation from earlier? I'll have you back in a convent before you can blink. Are you clear on that?"

Mary, "Yes, ma'am." Hurrying in carrying groceries past Marc coming back outside. His eyes twinkling. Hers lingering over his solid chest. Covered in dark straight hair, very thick. Looking as soft as mink. Wondering how it would feel against her skin.

Norma watches on, her face dour and thin lipped. Her hazel eyes with their pupils pin points threatening with anger. "You need to put your shirt on. That's not appropriate in mixed company. A half-naked male scratched up from one of his lovers."

Marc is surprised by her aggressive approach. But being respectfully polite answers, "Yes, ma'am." Pulling his tee shirt out of his back pocket. Squeezing it on. Finding it a little snug stretching it over his shoulders and chest.

Ms. Campbell, "Thank you for helping. We have it from here. You can go back to work outside." Dismissing him like he's the common help.

Marc, "You're welcome." Raised to be respectful of his elders tolerating brusqueness. That and she has Mr. Thornburg's ear. More than likely reporting everything to him. Otherwise left up to him she would have been dismissed.

Before he can get away from her Ms. Campbell steps out into the hallway that passes the kitchen. Looking up into his face. "Marc, I spoke with Andry earlier. I don't think you know yet. Oksana died early this morning. She had been ill for a long time. Her health declining all in all."

Marc, "No. I hadn't heard."

Ms. Campbell, "I'll let you know when the wake and services are. I expect you'll be going out of respect to Andry."

"Well, yes. He has been very patient with me over the years. I'll be there."

Ms. Campbell, "Good. By the way, we are going to be away until Tuesday." Not feeling the need to tell him why. Marc happy to have the house to himself. She's becoming more irritating with her holier than thou attitude. "I'm making a large roast beef with vegetables and potatoes. That should get you through the weekend. That is if you and your friend Camel don't eat it all in one meal."

Marc ignores her barb, answering her, "That sounds great."

Ms. Campbell, "We're helping out at a convent in Syracuse. As soon as the roast is done," looking at Mary, "and the laundry is finished, we'll be going home." The smell of roasting garlic mixed with rosemary beginning to carry out into the hall.

Marc, "It smells good already."

Mary comes over to the doorway speaking to both of them. "Andry just called. The wake will be this evening."

Ms. Campbell sighs. "It's just well our trip was already going to be delayed. After the wake we will leave." Marc's plans changed now go upstairs and clean up. Ms. Campbell cuts her eyes to the side watching Marc's back. Something so irritating about him.

His appetite stimulated making his stomach growl. Reminding him how little he had eaten today. First a shower and then a shave. Needing a good scrubbing after today's workout at the gym. Plus the dusty basement and labor intensive landscaping. Jogging up the stairs. The hot tub and steam room more appealing by the moment. Walking in the master suite and picking up the remote control turning on music. One of Lady GaGa's songs playing. His thoughts on her. She is so hot, especially in "Bad Romance." Calling out, "Hot tub fill. Temperature one hundred and two degrees. Chromatherapy blue!" Peeling off his grimy wet tee shirt. Making a plopping sound as it hits the marble floor. Going back out into the bedroom pouring himself a snifter of brandy. Swirling it in the crystal snifter. It's aroma rising up inhaling through his nose before taking the first drink. The dark amber liquid sending heat down his throat. Carrying it with him into the bathroom setting it down on the granite counter. Picking up the lighter setting flame to some sandalwood incense that Jadon had left.

Sitting on the side of the tub while unlacing his steel-toe work boots. Pulling them off one at a time then peeling off his damp socks. Fresh air cooling his hot feet. Sliding his sweaty jeans down sticking to his body. That done, moving back over to the granite counter to retrieve his brandy. Pausing to examine how much he had changed. Not bad, a tan line dark at his waist all the way around just above his buttocks. Making a muscle man pose for the mirror. Arms up, flexing his biceps and tightening his pectoral muscles. "Arrrh," teeth gritted. His sapphire blue eyes very striking against his brown skin. Practicing a smile to look charming yet sexy. Back straight, chest out, large solid pectorals now covered in dark straight hair. Especially thick at the center traveling all the way down. Not bad, adjusting to his new look. Helmeted equipment hanging down several inches and thick even at rest. Never had any complaints yet. Besides, he has always endeavored to please first whatever it takes. His thoughts going to Melinda with her short runway and then Jadon with her smooth Brazilian. Those thoughts making his blood surge. Engorgement happening quickly with clear liquid gleaming at the tip. "Shower sixty degrees!"

After shaving then splashing on Tommy Hilfiger cologne burning his face with a little extra to the chest mane to carry the good scent. Marc goes into the cavernous dressing room closet. Choosing a white cotton dress shirt, navy blue suit, and a red tie to wear to the funeral. Standing in front of the full-length mirror, satisfied he looks respectable enough. Putting on his prayer hat feeling complete. It's time to go to the viewing or wake. Whatever it is called. Setting the alarm system before exiting the house.

Marc fires up his blue '68 Mustang the engine turning over with a rumble. Enjoying the sound revving it once more. Yes, it has a hole just large enough to give it some cojones. Appreciating the rumble like a big cat purring. Stepping on its clutch pedal shifting into reverse backing out and then first and second gears in quick succession. Shooting down the long driveway. Popping the clutch making tires squeal out onto East Avenue. Accelerating its 354 horsepower engine roaring off into the distance.

CHAPTER 26

INSIDE THE FUNERAL home, Marc sees Andry surrounded by family members. Being six foot has its advantages. Making his way through the crowd of people to Andry's side. Unnoticing at first over the din of voices not speaking English. His ear adjusting to the multitude recognizing Ukrainian not Russian being spoken.

Andry, "Dyakou (thank you)!" speaking to Marc. Bear hugging him squeezing the breath out of him. Strong for an old guy.

Marc, "My condolences. I'm very sorry for your loss."

Andry's old eyes teary and red, he speaks English this time. "Thank you for being here."

Marc understanding and gracious, "You don't have to thank me. If there is anything I can do for you let me know. Everything at the house is under control. So you don't need to worry about it. Okay?"

Andry, "You are a considerate man for one so young." Other family members move in to speak with Andry. Just having arrived from Kiev.

Ms. Campbell and Mary move over to where Marc is standing. Ms. Campbell squeezes herself in next to Andry. "Are you coming home tonight?"

Andry, "No, I'm staying with Oksana's family for now. I'll be home next week sometime. I'm not sure." Flustered by her question.

Ms. Campbell, "There's a hot meal for you when you need it."

Andry, "Thank you." Trying not to show his annoyance with her. Instead turning to Marc, having made a decision. "It is time I started considering retiring. I'm not up to the heavy workload there anymore."

Marc, "Now is not the time to worry about that. We can talk about that more next week or whenever you are ready to. Don't worry about it."

Ms. Campbell interjects, "Marc is a hard worker and it shows around there. Forget about work for now." Marc becomes annoyed with her crass behavior. Tiring of her always having something to say and being frequently rude. Her sense of entitlement overbearing. Marc finds it difficult not to glare at her, keeping himself distracted. Unaware that Mary cannot take her eyes off him. Finding him so handsome and just comely in that suit. Taking in a silent assessment. Broad shoulders with a narrow waist. Even his coat cropped out at the buttocks. Marc talking with Andry unaware of her. Aunt Norma notices

Mary looking at Marc. Giving her a stern look. The corners of her mouth turned down. Her face marred by permanent frown lines. Mary feels her aunt's eyes burning on her. Casting her eyes down.

Marc speaks with the two women. "I don't think I'll be going to the funeral services. I definitely won't be going to the cemetery."

Ms. Campbell speaks up, "That's all right. Mary and I will make an appearance there. Andry will understand. You at least came here to show your respects. Don't trouble yourself about it. You don't need to go." Keeping her thoughts to herself. *That will keep those two apart. He is quite the looker once he gets some respectable clothes on him. That is, if you're into that outdoorsman look and of course all right with a heathen.* Glancing at Marc's prayer hat. "We'll see you on Tuesday." Marc not really listening to her looking into Mary's eyes. Discovering for the first time how truly green they are. Mary herself lingering on Marc's deep blue eyes. What a dark shade they are.

Aunt Norma notices the both of them. Her tone short, "Come on, Mary, let's pay our respects. We'll say a prayer for Oksana." Guiding her away from Marc over to the casket. Whispering into Mary's ear, "You keep that looking at each other like that and I'll send you back to the convent. You won't leave there until I say you can, even to start college. Do I make myself clear, missy?" Her breath as foul as her face. Not waiting for Mary to answer. "Your eighteenth birthday hasn't come yet. Maybe I'll have a quiet word with the reverend mother. About lascivious and wanton behavior. Reverend Mother and I see eye to eye in disciplining little trollops. Do you understand me?"

Aunt Norma attempts to look pleasant for anyone watching them. Mary answers her aunt in a subdued voice, "Yes, ma'am." Her affect flat as she looks at her aunt. Not daring to let the loathing she feels for this woman show.

Once both of them are kneeling beside the casket praying, only then does Mary allow her true feelings of anger to surface. Her green eyes glaring without a blink her head bowed in prayer. Having learned to hide her emotions for years from her aunt and some of the strict nuns. Sister Mary Regina could be vicious. And never cry out in pain. That only made her more cruel and ruthless. She always deemed crying as a sign of weakness or an attempt at manipulation. The beating would become more forceful and longer. Saying, "Spare the rod and spoil the child. Only the guilty feels the pain of thy staff." Closing her eyes bowing her head concentrating on pushing back painful memories of helplessness. Going deep into her mind where it is safe.

CHAPTER 27

MARC CHOOSING TO take the bay bridge on his return drive to home. So beautiful with the scattered lights at night climbing the hills. Overlooking Irondequoit Bay its quiet dark water below reflecting those same lights. The lakefront air cool rushing in the open windows of the Mustang. His tie already off and shirt unbuttoned refreshing air rustling across his chest puffing his shirt out. Marc's prayer hat off letting his dark hair whip in the wind. *It feeling so good to be alive.* Stars are beginning to come out across the sky over the lake.

The highway diverging south heading on to 590 South. Cool air fading out immediately as though passing through an unseen doorway. The temperature rising some twenty degrees moving away from the lake.

Once inside the house taking off the long-sleeved dress shirt. Glad to be getting out of his suit. Marc's answering machine light blinking four new messages. Pushing the play button while unfastening his pants.

Melinda, "I'm just calling to remind you about Angelique's social gathering next Saturday. Oh, I hope to see you tonight. It's going to be great everyone will be there. Don't miss it." Her voice breathy. *Click*. Message three. *Click*. A hang up

Message four: "Hi Marc. It's Jadon, are you going to this big party tonight? The one at the Olde Theater at the Upper Falls. I hope I see you there. Bye." Her Turkish accent exotic and so sexy. Sending Marc's mind racing back memories of their last encounter making his pulse quicken. Excited to go to a soirée. No, a rave. Never having taken the time to go to one.

Choosing more casual clothes. A royal blue shirt and khaki pants with a pair of brown Dockers. Tucking his shirt in leaving the top button open. The collar too tight to close around his thick neck. Feeling a little self-conscious about the hair pushing out of the open collar. Shaking his head in disbelief. *How did that grow so fast?* From nothing to becoming a bear. Standing in front of the floor-length mirror. *Not bad, if I say so myself. If they don't like it, next*. Ready to leave but something teasing at the back of his mind. What if anything could he be forgetting?

Yes, that's right. Mr. Thornburg brought by the ring. Rummaging through his sock drawer. Pushing aside numerous bar napkins, their sole purpose phone numbers written on them by women. Not here. Where is it? The wall safe.

Moving aside suits at the back of the closet. Spinning the dial on the combination lock. Feeling the tumblers drop into the first of several latches. Pulling its heavy door creaking open. The safe chock full with stacked jewelry boxes, coins, and documents. Taking an envelope out opening it. Sparkling cut diamonds unset. Nice good for emergencies placing it back. If you can't get your hands on cash, diamonds are great currency. There it is removing the mahogany ring box from the safe, opening it. Wow! Its contents sparkling under the dressing room lights. The ring's blue-purple tanzanites glimmering easily with the slightest motion. Marc examining it more closely. The inside band engraved with Celtic runes. His ring exquisite in craftsmanship with vines twining up both sides ending in platinum leaves. At the edge of his consciousness a thought whispers, *Lift up the felt bottom*. Setting the ring aside to examine the box more closely. Turning the box over. No distinctive marking on it. Looking inside giving it more scrutiny. Noting one corner of the felt slightly raised. Pulling up on the felt liner tugging at it. A piece of yellowed folded paper under it falling out. Catching it midair with his left hand. Reflexes honed from years of kickboxing and mixed martial arts training.

Excitedly unfolding the piece of paper to read its hidden message. Recognizing Uncle Theron's eloquent cursive penmanship unmistakable. Having a moment of déjà vu. An unsettling feeling as a cold chill rushes over him. Beginning the message:

> Hi Marc,
>
> If you're reading this message I'm already deceased. This is a powerful ring of protection. It has been bound with good. You are in the gravest of dangers now. Wear the ring at all times. Find the old family bible in the library. Your journey begins with oldest names. You will also find your great-great-grandmother's diary. Really a grimoire. Never use that book or let anyone else take possession of it. It hold powers that could be used against us all. You will come to understand this as you finally begin to learn our family history.
>
> Love,
> Uncle Theron

Marc feeling sad and anxious takes a deep breath exhaling a cloud the air so cold around him. *What the heck? What danger and from whom?* The hair on the back of his neck and arms rising up. Shivering. That air-conditioning acting up again. The thermostat out of whack again. *Now my imagination is playing tricks on me. Allah Akbar! This old house is scaring me like a girl.* Marc puts the ring on with some reluctance. *I don't feel any different. It figures. Uncle Theron with his old mysterious stories about our family.* Muted in the distance the grandfather clock strikes the time. Marc folds the note back up carefully placing it back in its hiding place. Then putting the box back in the safe.

Time to go excited to be going to one of those kind of parties. Wondering how many people will be there. Disregarding his silly feelings from moments ago. Shaking off any doubts. Air-conditioning can't live with it and can't live without it. Glancing over the fax Camel had sent earlier with the directions. A flier that had been circulated around campus. Admiring the details put into the artwork. Obviously the art majors and the drama department will be in attendance. This should be good. The place where it is to take place The Upper Falls district. *Huh, I didn't think anything was there now. Except maybe businesses.* Setting the alarm system before exiting the house.

The night air warm almost hot in the city. Riding with the Mustang's windows down. His anticipation building as he turns on the radio to a rock station. "Sin with a Grin," blasting as he exits the inner loop. Taking a shortcut into the Upper Falls district. Not close yet to the building but traffic already backing up. Droves of young people approaching the building. Voices carrying excitement on both sides of the street. Cars bumper to bumper with loud music playing.

Marc's pulse increasing with the rising anticipation in the air. Young people cutting between cars. Laughter and voices all around him. Inching steadily closer to the building. The pounding of bass drums coming through the walls of the building. Cars double and triple parked. Youth pouring up the steps past large Roman-Greco columns up lit for the occasion. Their acanthus leaves gray to black from decades of burning fossil fuels (coal soot) from neighboring industries.

Parking down the street to avoid dings in the doors of the Mustang and the possibility of being towed. Marc getting out making the car alarm chirp. Joining with the flood of youth going inside the building. Moving past a double set of doors entering the main auditorium. Hundreds of dancers already moving to the loud music. Dancing where once seating for the theater was now removed.

University drama department mixed with ballet and modern dance troupes have the stage staked out already. Couples dancing together in period costumes. There is even a couple of Elizabethan jesters with bells on their hats. Marc pauses to watch a gymnastic routine of running and tumbling into somersaults high in the air. Incredible feats of acrobatics. The air around Marc electric with excitement so strong as to be contagious. Finding it difficult not to join in with the rhythm it is so enticing. Working his way around the crowded room.

Skirting the thicker parts of the packed dance floor searching for a familiar face. His hips having a mind of their own moving to the music.

Marc giving in dancing directly below the stage. One of the dancers from above him notices his ring glowing. Shouts down to him, "Cool ring man!" Then doing a backflip off the stage smoothly landing next to him. A perfect execution from that height.

The man speaks to him, "Where'd you get it from? The drama club?" Taking Marc's large calloused hand to examine the ring closer.

Marc, "No it's mine." The dancer introduces himself, "My name is Gerard, great effect. It looks like tanzanite but I've never seen them do that before. How did you create the effect?"

Marc, "I didn't do anything."

Gerard, "Then it must be the lighting in here. Maybe the laser light is refracting in it." Cocking his head to the side giving Marc a closer inspection. Gerard's short-clipped bearded face giving Marc the old up and down with his eyes very appreciatively. Lingering at his large bulge. Marc pulls his hand out of Gerard's. Gerard smiles lasciviously, offering, "You want to join us? You're hot." Moving his head with a quick nod toward his equally husky dance partner above on the stage. His shirtless smooth body glistening from perspiration. Moving with a completely masculine form thrusting like a stripper.

Marc, "No thanks. I'm looking for my date."

Gerard, "If you change your mind we'll be here for a while." Winking at Marc. Gerard turns and bounds up the steps two at a time back onto the stage. His athletic body familiar Marc studying him. That's right, it comes to him, kickboxing. He's a real bastard in a fight, go figure. Marc examining his ring more closely. Not having noticed it in all the excitement of the evening. The stones in his ring almost glowing from within. Watching laser light reflect off mirrors creating the geometrical shape of a double helix. His ring sparkling now with red twinkles every so often.

By now the building is packed with dancers pushed closely together. The air has become warm and humid from so much body heat. Marc getting past his comfort zone untucks his shirt, opening it a couple of buttons. Continuing his search for one of his friends climbing onto the stage. Standing clear of the acrobatic dancers on the stage. Performing their tumbling routines leaping extraordinarily high into the air. Coming down sticking their landings without giving way knees locked, arm held up high. Feeling eyes on him Marc looks up to see Melinda. Who is leaning on the railing of the catwalk above. Watching the action below from her position in semidarkness. Waving to her Marc rushes across the stage just avoiding one of the acrobats landing. Dodging over to the stairs leading up to the catwalk. Bounding up the steps two at a time excitedly eager to meet up with a friendly face.

Making it to the top rounding the corner smiling. Excited to meet up with Melinda except finding two women smiling back at him, but not the anyone he knows. Oddly familiar perhaps from another place but not taking the time to recall. Confused he looks in both directions only seeing unfamiliar faces. People are scattered throughout this poorly lit space above the throng of youth below. Walking along the catwalk past the two women leaning on the railing. Themselves watching the spectacle below. Marc hears Melinda's familiar laughter coming from the shadows in the distance. Becoming impatient he walks heavily toward the laughter. Marc's two hundred plus muscled body stomping along the planks. Smelling the pungently green scent of marijuana as he approaches a group of people sharing a joint. Laughter peeling from a woman in the group. Glancing at him like she knows him, her expression smug. Marc stares back at her trying to understand why. Melinda not in the group he continues walking past smaller clusters of people talking intimately. Still no sign of her or anyone else he knows. A door opening and closing farther away. His eyes adjusted to the semidarkness he follows the sound. Leading up another set of stairs shorter than the first set going higher into the darkness. Following the back wall of the theater. Coming to a door closed firmly, using some muscle to push into a room lit by ultraviolent light. Going in headlong stumbling over something on the floor.

A voice shouts, "Close the door!" Which snaps shut behind him closing off his exit. The air in the room hot and humid. Marc finds himself pressed up against bodies writhing and moaning. A familiar smell insinuating itself into his nostrils. His eyes adjusted to the faint ultraviolent light partially painted over to make it darker in the room.

Warm hands reach inside Marc's partially opened shirt. Greedily squeezing his firm pectorals. Then his shirt ripped open to the waist. Another hand slides below his waist, grabbing a handful. Marc realizes quickly he's walked into an orgy room. Pushing groping hands off his body to have others replace them. Brushing against the outline of human forms retracing his steps. Reaching back desperately to find the door handle. Touching cool metal of the door. Grabbing the handle pushing it down the door opening a crack. Quickly squeezing back out making a hasty retreat into the cooler air. The door snapping shut behind him. His pulse racing after the surprise of that room.

Marc heads back downstairs to the catwalk. Returning to where the two women had been standing. Observing the spectacle below noticing something odd about the jesters. Their motion. Jumping off the climbing wall like skydivers. Only instead of gravity pulling them to their deaths below on the stage floor.

They fall like gossamer halting right above the floor. Almost floating then standing up and walking back over to the climbing wall. Watching another jester spider crawling up the wall, so lithe, almost gliding up. Marc searches above the light fixtures for thin cables. Unable to find any. Then noting one of the jesters his chest glistening from perspiration under the hot stage lights. He's not wearing a safety harness. Watching them with fascination. How are they staging these stunts? One diving out hurtling spread eagled, slowing just above the floor. Impressive.

Observing one of the acrobats bounding end over end. Leaping into the air farther than humanly possible. What the heck is going on here? Marc having that sensation again when someone is staring at you. Causing the hair on the back of his neck to bristle an unpleasant sensation. Looking down over the crowded dance floor. Spotting Jadon dancing and her dance partner staring back. His eyes unflinching and dark just watching Marc. More handsome than most men there. Even from the catwalk this male very intense and confident in his swagger. Definitely not a student. A true brunette, swarthy and of obvious Middle Eastern descent. His mustache thick and black like his short straight hair. Melinda is dancing next to them confident in her sensuality. Moving to the rhythm of the music turning to look up directly at Marc waving. Signaling for him to come join them.

Marc eases his way down the now crowded stairs. People standing on them, talking and moving to the pervasive atmosphere making his going slow. Wondering, *Who is that with her? A date?* Feeling slighted, his anger rising. When he gets to them, he finds only the women dancing. Their mysterious partner gone.

Melinda, "I'm so glad you could make it. Where have you been?" Laughing delightedly. Hugging and kissing him on the lips. Marc still irritated pulling away. Not ready to give in just yet. Wanting answers to his questions.

Marc, "Where have I been? I've been looking all over for you."

Jadon, "Now you have found us." Marc looks at her questioningly. Jadon changes the subject. "This is my friend Oolong, she's been sitting in on some of my classes. Partnering up with our study group."

Oolong extends her graceful slender hand to Marc. Speaking with a positively beautiful accent, that of Dutch over British, "It's nice to finally meet you. I've heard so much about you." As tall as Marc looking directly into his eyes.

Marc, "It's nice to meet you." Taking her hand, noting its softness but subtle strength. Unavoidably taken in by her genuine beauty. Mahogany skin and slender arms bare except for a silver bracelet wrapped around her right bicep. Her accent intriguing him, Marc comments, "Dutch-British?" Just brushing her hand with his Cupid's bow lips not taking his eyes off her. Intrigued, allowing his eyes to follow her hair a thick red-brown mane long and wavy down her back.

Oolong, "Yes, you are correct. I love your blue eyes especially against your tan skin." Smiling at him with her teeth bright white as his. Marc catches his breath. Not able to take his eyes off her. The blue and purple silk dress flowing as she moves, captivating. Music with ambience and mood all coming together. Her breasts swaying naturally underneath the fabric. Marc tantalized into looking for her dark areola beneath the sheer fabric. Oolong gently takes Marc's face in her hand. Bringing his eyes up to meet hers. Speaking, "My eyes are up here." Looking into his.

Melinda feeling slighted speaks up, "I thought you were going to meet me." Looking ever so pouty.

Marc ignores her not taking his eyes off her companion. "I'm sorry. I didn't mean to stare. You're just so breathtaking."

Oolong, "You did say he was charming. Don't you think you should be giving some of this attention to Melinda? Instead of acting like some bloke?" Oolong reaching for Marc's hand. "I like your ring. Masculine and yet it sparkles very nice. Those are high quality Tanzanites. I'd say about five to seven carats. Did you know they are mined in Tanzania, Africa?"

Marc, "Thank you. I'm not that familiar with this ring. It was left to me by my late uncle."

Oolong, "Your uncle had great taste." Both women examining the ring. Melinda looking but not touching Marc's hand. Avoiding touching the ring at all. Oolong takes notice of this discreetly. Commenting to Marc, "It's an interesting design. Trillion cut stones set with vines intertwined on the outside of the band."

Marc, "Yes, I believe it's Celtic."

Oolong, "Does it represent any ancestral significance to your family?"

Melinda put off by her attention to Marc. Speaking to him, "Have you seen Camel? He's been looking all over for you. He seemed upset by something." Intending to get Marc away from Oolong.

Marc, "No. I haven't. Do you know where he is?"

Melinda, "I believe I saw him headed outside to the courtyard. Something seems different about him. It's almost sad." Determined to get Marc away from Oolong. Looking at her in a new light. "Something has changed. You're different." Not intending to say that.

Marc jokes, "Yeah, I'm fresh and clean now. Ladies, I have to find my brother. Oolong, it was a pleasure meeting you. Melinda will you be here when I get back?"

Melinda, "Maybe," walking off first.

Oolong speaks to Marc before he can leave. Her voice low. "I believe that is a power ring. Intended for protection." Watching Marc's face for any sign of recognition.

Marc, "Protection from what?"

Oolong, "That is the question." Marc looks at her puzzled by her comment. "Go, find your brother. I will be here." Hearing in his mind, *Waiting for you.*

Turning back before leaving to find Camel. "You will be here for a time, right?"

Oolong, "I did just say that, didn't I?" Her presence turning to serious almost mysterious. Marc looks back again before disappearing down a congested hall. Stifling from the amount of body heat making difficult to breathe. The only light coming from outside. Perspiration beading across his forehead with his shirt sticking to his body in places. Moving body to body it's so crowded. The air hot to the point of being oppressive. Its oxygen used up forcing him to take extra breaths to get enough air. Marc starting to feel claustrophobic in the seething mass. The floor damp and gritty from spilt drinks mixed with sweat. Their makeshift bar so near that the smell of sour beer spilt on the floor smells like emesis.

Grateful for the whiff of cool fresh air teasing him. Knowing he has to be getting closer to the exit leading to the courtyard. It has to be less crowded out there. Using those wide solid shoulders to break free emerging outside into the cooler night air. Taking a deep breath of fresh air. Perspiration running down his abdomen and back. His hair wet all the way down now. Needing to cool off untucking his shirt completely most of the buttons missing. Inhaling the fresh air.

People gathered in intimate small groups speak softly amongst themselves. Unlike the roar of voices inside. Peaceful out in the courtyard. Light shining from the top corner of the building. Intended for security outside the walls. Leaving the courtyard with its high cinder block walls with areas of light and deep shadows. From some perspectives the absence of light a true blackness. Like that of outer space. As to the eye unable to make out who or what is present until one in those shadows moves out into the light. Marc wanders from group to group looking into their members' faces closely due to the poor light. Some of these groups smoking pot. While others are just talking and drinking. Marc becoming impatient unable to find Camel. Not ready to give up moving to the farthest corner. Where a tree has outgrown its decorative planter blocking out all the light. Creating an optical illusion of blackness. Keeping anyone choosing to be unseen hidden from prying eyes. Marc steps into the darkness continuing his search for his brother. A pair of reptilian yellow eyes flicker at him. Bunching his fists up stepping into a fighting stance reflexes well-honed from years of training. Lighting bugs suddenly buzzing in a galaxy of their own lights flashing. Relaxing just a little not seeing the large dark form rise up beneath the tree until it was almost too late. Marc's pulse jumps into high speed moving with the speed of youth. Using a left hook connecting with a jaw. Kicking out with his right leg. Hearing a satisfying grunt. Before his next move is executed it's blocked by a strong leg. "Man what are you doing?"

"Camel?" Marc's masculine voice distinctive from a Western Peninsula accent.

Camel's voice comes out a deep bass its irritation not hidden. "Yes."

Marc, "I'm sorry, you surprised me." Stepping up bear hugging his brother in relief. "Why are you out here?" Patting Camel's back hard. His adrenaline rush strong.

Camel's gravelly voice, "It's too crowded in there." Camel pats Marc's back equally hard.

Marc, "What's wrong?"

"Why does something have to be wrong?"

Marc goes right to the point. "Because my brother in a crowd like this with so many women. You're always right in the middle of the excitement. Not in some dark corner, at least not alone."

Camel, "You think you know me so well."

Marc, "Am I wrong?" Not pursuing it, knowing his brother will only get angry. Because he can be so stubborn when he's in a mood like this. "So I hear you were looking for me."

Camel, "I was." Sitting back down on his bench under tree. Lighting bugs flashing on and off, dozens of them.

Marc, "I've been all over this place. Jadon is avoiding me. Melinda is jealous over a woman she introduced me to. Not more than a few minutes ago. And you are in the very last place I would look for you. What gives?"

Camel, "You really are a true friend my little brother. I needed to clear my head out." Taking a deep breath. His sense of smell keen. Picking out Marc's salty, acidic skin, damp with perspiration. "I was getting overheated in there."

Marc, "It is very hot in there." Tugging at his open shirt his chest still damp.

Camel, "I'm glad you are here now. I need to discuss with you some things that have come to my attention. They will affect both of us."

"This sounds serious talk to me. You know I have always been there for you as you have for me."

Camel, "I've been having these dreams as you know. About women that I have made love to." Pausing to gather his strength.

Marc sits down next to his brother on the cement bench. Lowering his voice to a whisper. "Go on."

Camel, "They always die in some horrible fashion."

Marc, "Are you talking about the two involved in your stabbing?"

Camel, "There are at least three more that I know of."

Marc, "Are you sure about that? Maybe it's some strange coincidence."

Camel, "No, it's not!" Raising his voice in frustration. "That is not all I have dreamed about. The other night I dreamed two of my cousins died. My father called an hour ago to tell me they were both missing. After a suicide bombing outside Baghdad in Fallujah. They were last seen before going to the market. Fifty people died there with them. The same as in my dream. I can't believe they are gone. Just like that." Snapping his fingers.

Marc, "Have you ever had premonitions before?"

Camel, "None."

Marc, "Then you don't know they are dead."

Camel, "The women are, I just have a gut feeling they are too. These dreams keep getting more vivid. Like I'm there watching it happen, somehow."

Marc, "Admittedly it's weird." Lowering his voice further becoming deeper, softer, so it won't be overheard. "What other women are dead?"

Camel, "That redhead from a few days ago. I don't know how to prevent them from dying. It's… Something is very wrong." Hanging his head down.

Marc unsure of how to help him suggests, "Why don't you stay at my place tonight?

"If all this is correct then you are going to need family around you. We'll put our heads together and figure out what is happening."

Camel, "How do I know that I won't be putting you in danger?"

Marc, "You need all the help you can get and I'm certainly not afraid." Disregarding his concern. Camel, "Besides, I don't want to spoil your evening. This is what you need to get you out of your shell. That and away from Melinda." Camel going back to the previous subject. "Women can be very difficult to read. Saying one thing and meaning another."

Marc, "It's Melinda's loss. Come on. We have to go back inside to get out of here. You know, I left two gorgeous women to come and find you."

Camel, "To holding my hand. I need to man up."

Marc, "That's the attitude you need. Come back inside and meet her at least. Then I'll make our excuses so we can leave. Who knows, maybe you will change your mind."

Camel, "Really, and what makes you so confident I will?" Already sounding more like his old self.

Marc looks him in the eyes knowingly. "Because I know you, my brother."

Oolong watches discreetly from her position in the large theater for Marc to return with Camel. Their route of approach already determined having to pass the dance floor. Marissa waves to Camel her date pushing her way over to him. Stepping between the two taller men. Saying, "I thought I lost you. Where have you been?" Her expression one of jealous anger. Marc checks her out. Long copper red hair shoulder length with pale flawless skin, petite top, with a pear shaped behind. Marissa sees him out of the corner of her eye. Turning around to Marc. "Stop staring at my ass!" Turning back to Camel. "Well?"

Camel, "We were outside getting some fresh air. Calm yourself." Marissa not placated yet.

"I thought we had a date or are you going home with your boy toy here?" Indicating Marc with a toss of her head.

Camel leans over putting his arms around her. Squeezing her firm ample bottom. Speaking into her ear. "He's my brother and we don't roll that way." Lifting her eagerly into his arms. Marissa satisfied with his response warms up to him pressing herself into his strong chest. Camel matches her voracity kissing her deeply. The atmosphere increasingly a milieu of lost inhibitions. Magic at work here its pull already taking hold on him.

Oolong reaches out touching Marc's shoulder getting his attention. Speaking, "I need to have a word with you." Her long fingered hand graceful gently resting on his shoulder. Radiating heat but something else more subtle. A strength no longer quite human. Undeniable strength but controlled.

Marc turns to her. "What about?" Looking deeply into her eyes concerned. The air is filled with much distraction from music and other things more primal, pheromones of both genders. Easily wrought from such a youthful crowd. The need of genetics overriding logic so strongly. So that all that is left is rhythm with its basal need to move. Oolong finds it difficult to stay focused. Marc moving with the music. Marissa is already dancing with Camel. All but a few not under the charm of this tribal spell commanding movement. All around them youth compelled to dance. The basal drive of drums and hormones enough to entice this sexually charged atmosphere. Then add a spell of desire and lust...

Oolong, "Marc! Pay attention." Holding his shoulders so large and solid.

Marc, "What is it?"

Oolong, "Everything here is not what it seems. Look around you!" Marc glances around them disinterestedly. "Not just here. Look up on the stage and the climbing wall. Have you ever seen such physical feats? Much less how they are descending the wall."

Marc, "I noticed. It's an exceptional performance."

Oolong, "Those climbers aren't wearing a safety harness or cables." Both watching one of the climbers at the top of the climbing wall. Dressed in a vest without a shirt his pants balloon legged, his shoes strange.

Marc, "It's the drama club. So he dressed like a sixth-century Arabian." The climber appears to hang in the air for a moment after leaping from the wall. Effortlessly as a feather would come down to the stage floor below. Except it was a man built for gymnastics, solid muscle and totally cut. Smooth skinned excluding that narrow strip from the navel below. Not attempting to break his fall. Marc finds his body moving again losing interest. So the man is good. Another performer on the stage running. Launching herself into a somersault high above the stage into the air end over end. Landing it perfectly on her feet with arms held up like a gymnast.

Oolong, "Did you see the height she achieved? That is not physically possible. At least not for ordinary mortal humans."

Marc, "It's part of the drama department's special effects. Some of their groups are over the top. Why aren't you dancing?" Marc no longer able to resist the spell's tug. Subtle but gaining strength cast over the entire rave. Oolong unprepared for this large and strong a spell. Her charms unable to resist its effects. Realizing too late that there were many players here. Working together to charm so many.

Oolong, "We need to get out of here now." Already too late for the music with the charmed ambience is caressing and seducing her too, drawn into the trap. It's like an unidentifiable fragrance mixed with a sensation of warmth. Stimulating and giving the sense of well-being. The environment wrapping itself around the crowd.

Marc is moving with the music. Gently brushes the side of Oolong's face with his large hand. His head bobbing rhythmically along with hips masculinely moving. Oolong captivated no longer able to fight the effects of the charged atmosphere joins in with him. The multitude moving en masse. Heat and energy rising with the passions of the youthful gathering. The atmosphere driving itself like the force of a hurricane pulling energy and so much power engulfing all its participants.

Seeming to be several songs later when in reality hours have passed. Marc and Camel are dancing with their shirts off by now. Marc's chest looking like a pelt of wet Russian mink. Camel's appearing like black fleece curled into points dripping. Oolong being strong of mind and soul is the first to come out from under the spell. That and she was cautious enough never to leave anything to chance. Her protective charms being strengthened by the power flowing. She takes Marc by both shoulders forcing his undivided attention. Telling him, "Come on, let's get out of this place." Taking Marc's calloused hand pulling him. Determination her strength. "Get Camel, we have to leave now."

Marc clamps a hand on Camel's large shoulder, telling him, "Let's go. This place is too hot and crowded." Camel nods agreement, taking Marissa's hand.

Her green eyes narrowing suspiciously, "Why are we leaving?"

Camel, "Because it's time. Come on babe, my place."

Her look mean. "Okay."

Finally outside the air fresh helps to clear out their minds. Oolong says, "This is much better. That place was—"

Marissa interrupts her. "Just right. I like it warm when I dance." Marc and Camel exchange a silent glance. Both men walking down the street bare chested. Still cooling off from the heat inside. Marissa sizing Oolong up. Trying to decide if she is trouble and will interfere with her plans. Just what is she there for. Not really sure how she turned up with them.

Where the hell did Melinda disappear off to? Oolong notices the moon being much lower in the sky. Checking her watch. As she suspected, 3:00 a.m. That was some powerful enchantment at work there. The last time she had looked at her watch it was close to midnight. Marc gives her a questioning look. Sliding his arm around her shoulders. Oolong whispers in his ear, "We'll discuss it just not now." Oolong thinking, *He felt it too.* The other, thinking of Camel, didn't seem to notice. Marissa isn't concerned because she is not a part of it.

Camel, "Let's just take my limousine. That way we can all ride together to Marc's place."

Marissa, "What about my car?"

Camel, "You can pick it up on Sunday. Weekend parking in the city is free." The decision made everyone in agreement to his idea. Marc's head still not cleared out completely. It's safer that way.

CHAPTER 28

AFTER GETTING BACK to the manor Marc being a good host shows Camel and Marissa to a guest suite. The walls painted Habsburg blue with gilt trim. Heavy damask drapes red and tan a fabric made in turn of the century Florence. Tapestries and oil paintings hung from the walls. William Parrott landscapes in their original gilt frames. The large bedroom's bed canopied with sheer fabric sashed back to the posts. Marc hands the remote controls over to Camel. Already familiar with their operation. After starting the Jacuzzi filling and the sauna turned on. Leaving his guests to their own devices.

Marc returns to the master suite scented by sandalwood. The scent coming from the spa room. Following the trail of a woman's clothing dropped en route to the Jacuzzi. It's sound gurgling with bubbles water roiling. Oolong up to her neck in hot water relaxing. Sitting up for Marc. Steam rising with the scent of rose petals and lavender. Her long wavy hair tied up high on her head. Rising up just enough to allow her beautiful mahogany toned breasts to bob invitingly. Gently in the swirling water, nipples taut. Proffering her hand. "Join me. It's quite marvelous."

Marc rapidly sheds his clothes with shoes already off. His gender at attention. Oolong says, "I like a man that stands up when he drops his pants."

Accepting her hand slipping into the steamy water. Rose petals and lavender catching on his dark chest mane. "I'm glad I meet your approval."

Oolong, "Oh very much so." Her sensuous thick lips quivering with anticipation. Marc moves over to her grazing his lips across hers before sinking in for the kiss. Fragrances mixing with water vapor rising up around them. Creating a fog to engulf the two.

Each time they are close Oolong has them slowing down. Saying, "We must wait timing is of the essence."

Marc enjoying this game of torture and pleasure from holding back. Finally saying, "What are we waiting for? I'm all about building passion." His blue eyes intense.

Oolong, "Come and let us go to bed now. We are both cleansed by the water. Everything is perfect now." Standing up stepping out of the tub with red rose petals clinging to her dark glistening skin. Marc stands up his hairy chest dripping. Oolong hands him a warmed towel. "You are a very hairy man." Taking another towel. "I'll dry your back."

Marc, "Thank you. It's difficult to get dry."

Oolong, "Does this run in the male family line?"

Marc, "That's an odd question. I haven't given it a lot of thought."

Oolong, "Well, is your father this manly?"

Marc, "No, not this much. Now that you mention it his chest is smooth. It seems like since this summer it's grown very fast. Even the hair on my head grows faster." His hair almost shoulder length.

Oolong, "I like it. You are like a lion." Drying his back her suspicions confirmed. Observing the prominent shaggy thunderbird form it makes across the shoulders and down the spine all the way to his buttocks. His muscular legs hairy too.

Marc takes her hand. "Come on." Leading her to the bed. Several hours later dawn with its first rays of sunlight. Shining on the couple languishing in the afterglow dozing. Oolong insists lovingly on staying in the missionary position. Her sinewy legs still wrapped around Marc's narrow waist. Marc completely relaxed sleep taking him. He drifts into a REM state. Dreaming of a future where he has twin daughters. Their age must be four or five years at least. Happily walking with their mother under a hot tropical sun. Her face radiant from joy wearing a brightly colored cotton dress. Her hair wrapped up in a matching scarf. Both girls cute now, but clearly having good bone structure like their parents. To become stunning women someday.

Sunlight shining brightly now into the bedroom. Oolong wakes Marc up nudging him. "Move over you're too heavy." Prodding him some more. Rolling over mumbling in his sleep. She snuggles up to him. Her cheek rests comfortably against his spinal fur soft as mink.

Marc wakes up reaching across the mattress to an empty bed. Raising his head up from under the pillows hearing water running. Dropping his head back down contently. Oolong walks out of the bathroom. "Good morning." Giving him a bright smile. Marc peeks up with one eye. Turning over onto his back still sleepy. "I have to go my taxi will be here soon."

Marc blinks, his blue eyes round appearing so innocent. "Were you at least going to say good-bye?"

Oolong, "Don't be so dramatic. I knew you were awake." Sitting down on the side of the bed next to Marc. Pulling on her high heels. "That is what I'm trying to do now." Coming off very reasonable.

Marc, "At least stay for breakfast." Sitting up, putting his muscular arms around her.

Oolong kisses him lightly on the lips. "I can't, I have business to attend to."

Lowering her voice. "But we do have to speak privately. When you don't have company." Marc ready to object, Oolong quickly stops him from questioning her. Kissing him into silence. Oolong having seen Marissa out of the corner of her eye walking in.

Marissa, "I hope everyone is decent. I'm sorry. I didn't realize I was interrupting. We were going downstairs for brunch." Looking sharply at the two.

Oolong, "Of course not darling. I was just leaving," standing up. Marc looking confused, knowing he just missed something going along with her. "Here's my buisness card. I'll be in town for a while longer. Call me we'll do lunch."

Marissa, "What's that? Your rates?"

Oolong undaunted by her crass remark. Speaking with her cool Dutch-British accent, "I'm an antiquities collector darling." Smiling at Marc turning to Marissa. "If you're going to barge into another man's room at least have the decency not to smell like a whore." Marissa's green eyes wild with rage. Oolong standing a head taller walking past her as if she was dismissed. There being no further need to speak.

Marc gets out of bed rushing after her. Calling, "Wait!" Oolong turns back. Marissa leaves without a word passing Oolong glaring, seething inside. Marc strides over to Oolong. Looking so virile, his parts swinging. His hair having grown just past shoulder length after last night. Once again confirming what she already knew to be happening to him. Marc speaks, "Stay for breakfast or brunch or whatever we're having today. Who cares, just stay." Oolong weakens considering his offer. His hard body pressed up against her. Allowing herself to rest her cheek against his rough stubble covered jaw. Enjoying their closeness. Running her fingers through his dark pelt covering mountainous pectorals. His rising excitement moving against her dress. The natural glamour from him increasing in strength from the dark spell. Feeling herself losing control to his masculine charms. His presence stronger since last night. Her senses becoming inundated with Marc's aromatic esters. Whispering playfully, "What is it you need to speak with me alone about?" Looking his most charming and sexy. If not for sensing Marissa's dark presence lingering, waiting out in the hallway, listening. Forcing her out of the moment. Silencing Marc with a warning look. A quick move of her head toward the hall.

Marissa, listening just past the doorway out in the hall. Feels Oolong's strong mind reaching out with its energy. Marissa uses her sapphire ring with its charms to conceal her presence from that African witch. Ready to move at the slightest sound so she won't be caught. Her heart quickening catching her breath. Hearing just that, the sound a body makes when moving through air.

Or rather the alteration it causes to the background noise. Retreating quickly back to the guest suite. Marc breaks away from Oolong opening the bedroom door. Stepping out into the hall impatiently. Looking in both directions, the hall empty except for Marissa's perfume with her scent lingering in the air. Marissa stealthily moving back into the suite with Camel.

Marc, "There is no one there but I could still smell her. Just a moment before she was there."

Oolong puts a finger to her lips for silence. Taking Marc's hand encouraging him to follow her over to the nightstand. Picking up the tanzanite ring handing it to him. Speaking very softly, "Now more than ever you really should keep this on at all times." Dropping the ring in his palm.

Marc slips the ring back on his right ring finger. "What do you know of this?"

Oolong, "Shh!" Looking at the marble top nightstand. Pulling open the top drawer. "Just as I thought."

Marc looks over her shoulder. "How did you know that was there?" His voice low and husky.

Oolong, "You really should keep that in a safer place. Wrap it in black silk and lock it up when not in use."

Marc, "You are beginning to scare me."

Oolong, "You are being very careless. Leaving important documents and belongs lying around for anyone to take."

Marc, "That's an old family diary."

Oolong, "It is more than a diary. That book could be very dangerous in the wrong hands. To all of us. I don't know if you are ready for the truth!"

Marc, "Try me."

Oolong, "I'll say this much." Her cell phone rings. "That's my cab I have to leave."

Marc, "What? Tell me."

Oolong answers her cell phone, "Yes, I'll be right out." Snapping it shut. "That is a power ring. It is to protect the owner from dark arts. Your family book there contains powerful thoughts and energies."

Marissa easing back into the darkened room confident in her prowess. Men are such fools. Any male she used sexually would still be unconscious to the world. Pushing the door closed without a sound turning away from it. Their room too quiet she freezes in her footsteps. Listening for the sound of Camel's steady respirations from across the room. Her eyes almost adjusted to the dark now. The bed still too far away in the shadows to see him. Warm air brushing her cheek like someone breathing on her. Causing the hair on her arms to rise up. Fear quickening her pulse as that feeling of being watched courses through her. On some primal level the prey recognizing danger too late. Its form invisible from within the shadows a predator. Except for a pair of eyes in the shadows appearing, brightening quickly angry and yellow with vertical pupils completely predatory. Observing her with cunning in them. Waiting for the moment of maximum fear to pounce. Marissa gasps ready to scream her heart jumping. It moves with preternatural speed. A large hand stifling a scream locked on her throat. Pulling her up and off the floor. Left with her feet dangling on the very air she sought to scream into. Its pupils vertical and wide adjusted to seeing in the dark. Her heart pounding from terror driven adrenaline. Those yellow eyes cold with reptilian emotionlessness causing autonomic systems to respond to fear. Her bladder lets go urine showering onto the floor. Speaking to her ever so softly a hissing sound reaching her terror filled mind. Unable to understand words slowly they begin to register. "I missed you. Where were you?" Easing some of the pressure off her throat. Allowing her feet to touch the floor.

Marissa, "You scared me. I didn't realize you were here and so in control." Feeling herself regaining some control. Deciding now is not the time for truth going on with her lies. "I was inviting Marc and what's her name to join us for brunch."

"How very generous of you. What did they say?"

"Marc didn't answer and she is leaving." Shrugging her shoulders. "I guess she didn't enjoy herself that much." Enkil studies her face perfectly still. "I don't mind entertaining two men over breakfast."

"I bet you don't." Marissa eyeing him as closely as she could in the dark room not sure whether to be insulted or complimented by Enkil's comment. Camel feels the sensation of energy rising up within him. Enkil assuming control over him in his unconscious mind making him feel euphoric.

Marissa already walking away from him. Satisfied with her misdirection. Camel's face twitching ever so slightly. His nose wrinkling up in anger. Marissa says, "Let's go start breakfast. If Marc wants to join us he may. Perhaps he'll stay upstairs for a while licking his wounds." Delighting in her deception to divide the two men.

Enkil reaches out with his hand twisting it fingers spread toward Marissa. His voice commanding. "Shut up!" His timber a deep bass. "Now come to me witch!" Marissa struggles against this unseen urge. *He is not going to treat me like some dog or whore, doing as he sees fit.* Unable to control herself. Anger first then terror rising up making her green eyes widen slowly. Compelled walking over to him submissively positioned. Enkil runs the back of his hand over her delicate neck. Camel no longer euphoric, being a silent witness to what is about to happen. Enkil's eyes cold and calculating. How easy it would be to snap it like a twig. Ending this useless minion's life with her salacious plans. A tear running from the corner of Marissa's eye. Anger exuding from Enkil's presence. An invasive amorphous blackness yet tactile all the same. Twisting around her neck physically. A penetrating coldness reaching inside to her very soul. Leaving her gasping for breath with her heart pounding inside her rib cage. Marissa's pupils dilated from the dark and now terror. What had she gotten herself into? White noise roaring in her ears. She must be losing consciousness. Enkil telepathically disturbing signals to both her temporal and occipital lobes. Causing hearing and vision to become blank. All perception of time gone. Enkil places a suggestion in her memory. Whispering into her temporal lobes, his voice all she is able to hear. "You will feel compelled to speak the truth. When I ask it of you. Pleasure will guide you." Caressing her limbic system.

Marissa blinks, startled Camel suddenly being against her. Kissing her neck roughly nipping at it. His stubble covered jaw like sandpaper scraping her skin. Pushing him off her. Looking deeply into his dark eyes bottomless pools of passion. Camel, "What is it?"

Marissa, "Nothing!" Allowing herself the indignation. After all he is only a tool to be used then discarded. He's not even North American. In control of the situation as always. Men. "I'm hungry and you're scratching my face." End of conversation for her. Camel unaware of anything different. His inner voice telling him to use her for what she is here for. Enkil slipping back into quiet watchfulness.

CHAPTER 29

CAMEL IS ARGUING with Marissa on their way into the kitchen. "I don't understand why you get so moody."

Marissa, "Why do men always say women are moody. When they are not in the mood for sex. All I said is that I was hungry."

Camel, "That's not all I heard you say."

Marc is already busy cooking breakfast. English muffins popping up in the toaster on cue. Marc gives directions to Camel. "Can you butter those and drop some more in?" Marc moves over to the stove. Stirring the scrambled eggs then sprinkling grated smoked cheddar cheese over them.

Camel standing there says, "That smells good." Pinching a bite of cheese. "How did you know when to start cooking?"

Marc smiles wryly at both of them. "After all the noise up there I knew you two would be hungry." Smiling bigger yet.

Camel, "You didn't answer my question." Marissa now smiling.

Marc, "The plumbing makes a distinct sound when the shower is on in that room." Camel crunches on a slice of apple. Nodding his scruffy face in acknowledgment.

Marissa, "Is there anything I can help you with?"

Marc, "Yes, take the sliced fruit and yogurt into the breakfast room. Before he eats it all." Marissa picks them up Camel grabbing another piece of apple. "Are you going to start the muffins or just stand there looking pretty?"

Camel slices open two more English muffins. "I didn't know you could be so bossy in the kitchen." Looking serious.

Marc, "You like your food hot, right?" Marc notices Camel's neck marked up. "It would appear your woman likes to leave a few marks." Examining Camel more closely. Camel moves his lips wryly agreeing by nodding his head. Marc yawns and stretches causing his shirt to ride up his back.

Camel, "Your back is too hairy to see the scratches on it anymore. Aren't cooks supposed to wear hairnets?"

Marc, "In that case I would need to wear a body net these days. Look who's calling the bear hairy."

Camel, "Point taken."

After breakfast Marc comes into the kitchen and finds Camel and Marissa having another little spat. Marissa saying, "If you feel that way then you're the one who is going to lose out."

Camel, "Take the limo and go!" His patience worn thin by Marissa's attitude. "My chauffer will take you back to your car." Marissa not a woman to be dismissed by any man swings at Camel to slap his face. His large arm blocks her faster.

Marissa, "Ouch! Your arm hurt me." Her green eyes infuriated turning and pivoting on her five-inch Manolo Blahnik heels. Passing Marc looking right through him. Her heels clicking down the hall stopping long enough to open and slam the side door.

Marc looks at Camel with his eyebrows raised. "What was that about?"

Camel, "Control brother, control. She believes after one night with her that I'm just going to roll over like some big dog." Marc listening so Camel continuing. "She was expecting me to bring her as a date to Angelique's mixer next Saturday."

Marc looking incredulous, says "Are you serious? Does she know how jealous natured Angelique is?"

Camel, "Right! I'll just show up with another woman at the hostess's home for an alumni mixer. If she didn't want to kill me now, she would then."

Marc adds, "She would be incensed."

Camel, "And who would take the brunt of that rage?"

Marc, "You."

Camel, "Exactly. The big male dog with one of her not so innocent sisters. Marissa just wants to see the sparks fly."

Marc, "Are you still going?"

Camel, "Yes, I wouldn't miss it for the world. But I'm going stag. Are you bringing a date?"

Marc, "Apparently so. I can count on Melinda for this one. Besides, I couldn't bring Jadon. Then I'd be no better off than you. Showing up with another woman. Come on refill your coffee. We'll sit outside on the private terrace. The garden is beautiful out there now."

Camel, "Sounds good to me. I wanted to see your masonry work anyway."

CHAPTER 30

USING THE BACK entrance one of the double doors to go outside. Taking the new path of flagstone multicolored peach Kentucky Crab Orchard. Leading out to the private terrace. Camel notes the close fit of the flagstones. Questioning Marc, "How will it hold up to winter heaving?"

Marc, "No problem. I went two feet down with layers of gravel. Starting with large course stones, working layer by layer up to the top most layer of fine stone. Then I used sand to lock in the top joints. It's all about drainage you know that." Camel nods his head understanding the basic engineering behind it. The new pergola comes into view. Their footsteps crunching on compacted gravel underfoot. Marc's hammock stretched and ready for use. Towering evergreens screening the back of the terrace. A small forest for privacy. Camel turns to look back most of the house hidden from view by the tall hemlocks with their large and lacey boughs. Just framing a piece of the house with its mansard architecture. Leyland cypresses completing the screening on the east side. Only the pergola and a patch of the terrace visible from the house.

Camel sits down on one of the two Adirondack chairs placed next to the glass topped table near the hammock. Speaking after taking a drink of his coffee. "This place is a sanctuary."

Marc, "Then you approve?"

Camel, "Oh yes." Marc is drinking some of his strong Colombian coffee. Both men enjoying the solitude of a Sunday morning. Activity at a minimum in the city neighborhood. Affording them the whispering of a breeze through the treetops. Marc fidgets idly with his ring. Glimmers of blue drawing Camel's attention. "When did you get that?"

Marc, "Just recently. It was a part of my late uncle's estate."

Camel, "May I see it?" Marc removes his ring handing it to him. Camel examines it closely, commenting, "Exquisite craftsmanship." Examining the inscription on the inside of the band. "Are those runes?"

"Yes. I believe they are Celtic."

Camel, "Interesting." His eyes flickering for just a millisecond. "Trillion cut tanzanites set in eighteen-carat gold." Reading the runes. "When did you take possession of it?"

"The other day, Mr. Thornburg forgot it was in his safe. So he dropped it off. Then I had forgotten about it until last night. Funny thing about this ring." Camel hands it back to Marc. Who puts it back on.

Camel, "What is that?" Watching him intensely.

"I found this cryptic message hidden inside the ring box itself." Marc recounts the message.

Camel, "Protection from what?"

Marc, "I don't know. I will have to uncover more of my family history. You know something even stranger?" Camel listens. "Oolong saw the ring last night. She told me to wear it all the time."

Camel, "Why?"

"She said it was for protection."

Camel, "How would she know that? And the bigger question is from what?"

Marc, "She couldn't get to that. Marissa interrupted her and then she was a bitch to Oolong. I suspect she was eavesdropping on us."

Camel, "I don't trust Marissa any further than I can spit on her."

Marc not too surprised by this, confiding. "I don't either, there's something about her."

Camel, "Besides being a troublemaker? I agree, but I just can't put my finger on it." Enkil not having revealed himself to Camel's conscious mind yet. *Smart man.*

Marc, "What danger could Oolong be referring to?"

Camel, "Can you trust her?"

Marc, "She comes off as genuine. There is something about her that instills trust."

Camel, "Find out more about this mystery woman. Where is the danger coming from."

Marc, "I have to meet with her, I'll let you know." The breeze that had been rustling through the trees halts. Camel bristling at this his eyes glinting yellow. His expression suspicious. Enkil senses they are being watched. Not a bird chirping in the stillness.

Camel, "It's just too quiet." His voice deeper.

Marc unaware that anything may be wrong. "That's why I like it here so much. Sometimes it's like being out in the country. On the weekends here with no traffic sounds or noise from people. Only the birds chirping." The garden's tall hemlocks sway again to the warm breeze. A family of cardinals arrives twittering away. Enkil relaxing some knowing it's safe, but keeping his mind open for other energy waves.

Enkil, "Marissa was eavesdropping on you two earlier. I caught her slithering back into our room. She's definitely a liar." Disdain in his voice. "I can't stand sneaks and I hate liars even more."

Marc's face an expression of disdain mirroring his brother's voice. "I knew she had been out in the hall. Why didn't you say something sooner?"

Enkil, "Why didn't you?"

"She was your guest and no harm. No foul."

Camel, "We must communicate sooner with each other. Marissa is not a danger because her actions are as transparent as a cheap silk shirt. Making her easily manipulated." Marc is wide eyed looking at Camel. Seeing a side of his brother never before seen.

Enkil, "As such she serves a purpose for now."

Marc, "I would rather not deal with people like that."

Enkil, knowing their closeness that of siblings chooses to warn him. "My brother you already are. You have been sleeping with at least one. Melinda is the worst sort of woman." Marc silent as Enkil continues to speak, "Angelique and her sorority or is it a coven? They have a secret agenda."

Marc, "And you know this how?"

Enkil not ready to expose himself yet. "Nothing I can prove, but I will figure out what they are after. Then I'll let you know." The hair on the back of Marc's arms rising up as a cold chill except it being summer. Camel's words have a ring of truth to them.

Marc, "Have you been to the mosque to speak with our iman?"

Camel, "I did try."

Marc, "Well, what did he say?"

Camel, "He started lecturing me about my lifestyle. Iman Al-Mohaimeed wanted to know why you haven't been to the mosque."

"It's true I haven't been to mosque in a while. I've been busy around here." Trying not to sound defensive.

Camel, "Yes, I gave him a similar response."

Marc, "What did he say?"

"He said you are never too busy to give praise to Allah. That's when he tugged open my collar. Exposing the marks Angelique had left there." Marc shaking his head already knowing where this was heading. "Then he added, 'If this is what you call busy. Then neither of you are living righteously. That can bring bad things about.'" Marc takes a deep breath then exhaling. "He also said these women could be using dark arts to manipulate us. That would come to pass because we are not living right."

Marc expression one of concern. "He came to that conclusion from the little that you gave? I'm not sure which I find more disturbing. The dark arts part or the fact that you hooked up with Angelique and with one of her retinue. All after you were warned."

Camel, "I'm not so sure there is a difference. I believe they are one and the same. Just for the record, so have you." His expression serious now. "Her allure is impossible for me to resist. She's so hot blooded."

Marc, "That translates into psycho with jealous rage. If you haven't noticed."

Camel ignores Marc's comments. Truer words never spoken. Camel goes on, "Then we have hot passionate make up sex for hours. We do have a history together."

Both men sit in silence each slowly contemplating the turn of events. This new information coming to light. After a time a gentle warm breeze rises up. Rustling the lacy boughs of the hemlocks. A dry leaf skitters across the gravel. Camel's eyes following it. Marc ending the silence. "This all started after Angelique read from that diary."

Enkil, "Yes. After that night in the library." Not surprised at all. "Have you discovered anything more about the diary?"

Marc, "No, but interestingly Oolong went right to where I had it put away." Camel looks at his brother visibly suspicious his moreno face hard. "She told me she felt its presence."

Alarm increasing inside him yet Camel's face calm. "Go on."

"She warned me to keep it in a safe place."

Enkil, "What an odd thing to say."

"Yeah I thought so too. But it was not her warning that got my attention." Camel's irises yellow and reptilian with their pupils narrowing into slits. Marc unnoticing, "She said it could be dangerous to all of us."

Camel's voice deep, Enkil speaking, "Yes, the grimoire." Enkil begins to understand Marc's part in all this.

"Why do you call it that?"

Camel's eyes having returned to normal within thousandths of a second. Enkil still speaking though him. "Grimoire. It's a book of curses and dark magic. Not your usual white magic."

Marc looks directly at Camel. "How do you know all that?"

Enkil, "I must have read about it somewhere during our French history lessons." Bending the truth to cover his knowledge. "You know how the French are always mixed up into something dark. No offense intended."

Marc, "None taken."

Enkil, "Let us retrieve this book and examine it more closely. Perhaps together we can find something to understand what is happening." Getting up leaving the sunny outside to go back into the dark house.

CHAPTER 31

MARC OPENS THE nightstand drawer empty except for condoms and lubricant. Marc, "It was here! I saw it not a few hours ago."

Enkil, "Could Oolong have taken it?" Marc replays in his memory the events of the morning.

Marc, "No. She couldn't have."

Enkil, "Are you sure it was there?"

"Yes, Oolong pointed it out to me. Right here in this drawer."

Enkil looks doubtful, "Then who else could have taken it?"

Marc, "She never actually touched it. Besides she left the room before I did. I know she wouldn't have taken it. She's just not the type." Marc pushes his long hair back out of his face.

Enkil angry, "And you're such a good judge of character." His tone accusatory.

Marc responds defensively, "But you are! At least the women I'm sleeping with aren't stabbing me!" Both men angry now leaning toward each other. Their adrenaline pumping with chests out and shoulders down. Marc regrets having said what he just did. Speaking first, "I'm sorry. I didn't mean that."

Enkil relaxes feeling Camel's brotherly love for Marc. Softening, "No. You are right. I'm no better a judge of character. I've been all over this town like a tomcat. Maybe the iman is correct. I'm not living my life right."

Marc, "I didn't mean for it to come out that way. We have to work together on this. We can't let them divide and conquer us. We are family my brother."

Enkil, "Apology accepted." Both of them calming down. Enkil using his own metaphysical abilities to search outside this physical form. To see outside this body viewing from afar. "We should search this room and if it's not here. Then where else in the house do we expand the search to?"

Marc, "The library!"

After going over every title on the extensive collection of books in the library and coming up empty handed. Then rechecking drawers and cubbyholes anywhere Marc might have placed the book in a hurry. Still no luck. Enkil gets an idea. Speaking through Camel suggesting, "Let us sit at the table where it all began." Marc sits down at the round eighteenth century table. Where Angelique had read from his family grimoire. That name not sitting well with him. Also the same night he met Melinda. It had been so much fun.

Camel, "Now try to remember where you last saw the book." Picking up on Marc's distaste for the name *grimoire*.

Marc, "The last time I saw the grimoire was upstairs in the nightstand. Then before that it was here at this table."

Camel, "Good, go on. Maybe we need to recreate the mood and circumstances of that evening. To help jog your memory."

Marc looks for the remote control for the lights. Not finding it. "It is certainly worth a try. I'll turn off the lights, you light the candles." Marc gets up and walks across the room. Switching off lamps at various locations around the room. Camel's eyes flash to yellow. Waving his hand across the air. Not needing to move physically but enjoying the use of his host's strong and healthy body. Candles igniting on the mantel and at the table in front of him. Camel's eyes flicker back to his rich brown tone.

Marc, "That was fast. I didn't hear you get up." Sitting back down at the table.

Camel, "All to set the mood." Avoiding answering him.

Marc, "Now what else did we do?" Camel sits across the table from him. Reaches out, offering his hands for Marc to take. Marc places his in Camel's larger hands. Not that his are small by any stretch.

Camel, "Now concentrate on the book. It's leather bound, old."

Marc closes his eyes, picturing the book. Getting an idea. Calling out, "Liber!" Both men feel a stirring of cool air causing candles to flicker around the room. Marc's grimoire materializes at the center of the table. His eyes wide with surprise. Enkil not surprised at all. Marc's pulse quickens his voice a whisper. "Do you believe this?"

Camel prays, "Bismillahir-Rahmen ir-Rahim (In the name of Allah Almighty, the beneficent, the merciful). Yes, I saw it. This is very disturbing, yet exciting. Has anything like that ever happened to you before?"

Marc, "No. I would have told you." Thinking of reaching for the book. A shimmering cloud of energy surrounding the grimoire. It then slides across the table to him. Stopping in front of its owner. His blue tanzanite ring sparkling with red glints under the candlelight. Camel swallows, Enkil quietly looking on at Marc with renewed interest. More questions about why he was called upon. Clever witch that Angelique. Marc not sure what to make of this development. His pulse quickened holding the excitement in check. "Well, this is what we wanted. Here it is the grimoire." Enkil calms Camel so Marc will continue on with his fact finding. Interested in where they will lead.

Opening its heavy leather cover. Its first pages names and dates going back to 1525. His family tree laid out over the centuries. The Du Bois family legacy spread out before him. Turning the pages to one name in particular. Penned with a quill, very eloquently and gracefully signed and dated 1750.

Camel becomes impatient. "Can you find where she read from? You'll have plenty of time to research your ancestors."

Marc turns pages, skipping entire sections at a time. "Where is it?" Marc irritated with being rushed. Never having taken the time to review the front with its names. Pages fanning rapidly and then abruptly stopping. Marc not looking up at Camel. "I believe this is it. How is your French? The quill style is very eloquent and feminine."

Camel, "I speak more than I read. How is yours."

Marc, "I was raised with you. I learned to speak but my reading isn't too strong. However I think I can get us some help. You know my cousin Phil in New Orleans."

Camel, "Little cousin Philip, he was always in trouble."

Marc, "Yeah, one and the same one. Except now he is all grown up and teaching Napoleonic law and reads French fluently."

Camel, "That sounds like he is doing well. Maybe a little brighter than I remember him."

Marc, "That was always his problem. He was a lot smarter than both of us and younger."

Camel, "Yes, I remember he was a tagalong. Isn't that what you called him?"

Marc, "Yes, that's good, make sure you bring that up. When I'm trying to ask a favor of him. That will really encourage him to want to do us a favor."

Camel is smirking. "Maybe."

Marc ignores his sarcasm. "He enjoys reading and translating old documents. I'm sure he will be interested in helping us with this."

CHAPTER 32

ANGELIQUE HAS HER main novices present for their part in her current machinations. Melinda and Jadon compelled to the Pittsford home. Dictating orders at the two young women as she would servants. Angelique ready to move forward with the next stage of her plans.

Angelique, "Melinda I need you to engender Mary's trust in you. I need her to be tractable to make this complete blindside work. Everything is coming together quickly now. For years I have been patient with only my dreams keeping me." Not willing to finish her statement. For if she did it would be acknowledging her obsession.

Melinda, "She is so ready for a girlfriend to do something with other than pray and be a handmaid to those useless wombs of heaven."

Angelique chuckling, enjoying her dig at the nuns. "You'll do something girl friendly with her. Force her to hide what she is doing from that nightmare of an aunt."

Melinda, "I'll take her shopping. She will need something to wear to the party I'm going to invite her to."

Jadon adds, "By now she has heard the boys talking about it."

Angelique, her cold blue eyes giving Melinda a shiver. Not ever wanting to be on her wrong side. "She will need guidance from an older sister. Especially useful in helping her choose suitably inappropriate clothes for this occasion."

Jadon, "What will you have me do?" Sounding annoyingly like a princess.

Angelique, "You will continue to run interference." Jadon keeps her expression suitably blank. Angelique being very intolerant of fools and stupidity. Snapping, "Keep Marc distracted. You will help the bartender another sister of course. Being so skilled at misdirection. You can put the catalyst in their drinks."

Jadon, "What time is this all really to begin?"

Angelique, "Give Marc the agent around, say, 11:00 p.m. That should give sufficient time for the desired effects." Turning to Melinda. "I want an Academy Award winning performance of the jealous bitch sort. Marc needs to come to Mary's defense."

Melinda, "This will end our relationship. I'm not so sure I'm ready to give him up." Pouting her lips, Angelique turning her glare on Melinda.

"I don't need your approval, ever. Just follow my directions and you will have what you seek. Besides, he never was yours to begin with. Once you made your accord with me you were always just bait. Nothing more. Did you really believe he would have stayed with you? A vapid spoilt little Christian whore. If he only knew what you were truly about. He would run to the nearest mosque!" Angelique's eyes icy blue and round with anger. Melinda her lip curling up in a snarl at the corner. No one ever got away with treating her like this.

Angelique, "You would be better off making this an accomplishment." Her voice already threatening. "Failure to do so would be unforgiveable." Melinda understanding that." You would do well to remember what happened to Monica?"

Jadon searches Melinda's face, saying, "Forever a whore even in death. The history is already written."

Angelique, "Not that whores don't have their place in the scheme of my plans. But when you're broke and a known whore. What do you have?"

Jadon cautions, "Surely you remember the feeding frenzy of the press. The world's biggest whores eating their young." Her reference to the American free press. Jadon shivers inside. "I'll call Marc and make sure he is here. After all he is central to our plans. If this is going to work out."

Angelique, still glaring at Melinda, "I'll have the stage set. My invitations have already gone out. The elders have been contacted."

Melinda, "The new black sheets made from organically grown cotton were delivered. After they were blessed in an Etruscan cemetery."

Angelique, "The spell room will be prepared for a circle of fire. Once they are joined, there is no turning back. The novices our new sisters turned will help keep our guests entertained."

Jadon feeling a little spiteful, "I'm sure our newest pledge will be delighted to keep Camel occupied." Smiling slyly.

Melinda takes her chance to enjoy a dig at Angelique's expense. "She is such a pretty young blonde," pausing, "girl." Angelique not amused, her face cold and dark. Her blue eyes bulging from rage just held in check. Their laughter silenced by a cutting glare. Looking both women in the eyes, her stare unflinching. Blue-white sparks snapping and crackling off her fingertips. Melinda then adds, "It's all part of the plan," attempting to assuage some of the anger they wrought up by attempting sincerity.

"Camel has to be kept busy," Angelique finally speaks, frowning. "Besides, Enkil is getting stronger in him. Soon he won't be Camel anymore." Melinda places her hand on Angelique's shoulder to comfort her.

Angelique, "I just didn't think it would be this hard to lose him."

Jadon, "We could try and reverse the changes."

Angelique, "Even if I wanted him back, a blood pact once made and then broken would bring revenge against us all. I did not give him to a demon to curry favor. Without Enkil or one like him, this would not be possible. Besides, Enkil is not just going to give up something so coveted as a human body."

Melinda, "It wouldn't be possible to offer him, say, another male body?" Not being able to resist herself, cruel by nature. "You could have your Arabian stud back." Angelique considers this. The muscles around her eyes softening with her pupils widening. Glancing down the corners of her mouth moving slightly up. For just a second fondly thinking of Camel. How good natured and spontaneous he could be. Certainly a man worth keeping around for a lifetime. Jadon goads Melinda with a mischievous look.

Melinda, "Or would he still be a male whore?" Saying this half under her breath but still loud enough for her teacher to hear. Angelique snaps out of her sentimental moment looking angrier. If that were possible with her lips drawn thin. Melinda enjoying hitting a nerve in that heart of stone and cold beauty. "He's got women lined up to fuck him now more than ever. Since you put that curse on him." Angelique's fists clinched at her sides. Nails digging into the palms of her hands bringing forth deep red blood rising over her French tips. The atmosphere in her mansion charged with static electricity. Melinda and Jadon both feeling their scalps tingle. Their hair rising up into the air.

Jadon, "Calm yourself." Her voice soft with quiver. Melinda still defiant as ever watching her.

Angelique, "Why are you both willfully stirring my anger with such relish? Are you not frightened by my rage?" Jadon swallows. Melinda unwilling to show fear in the face of danger. "Both of you were more than willing to stoke him to bring forth his energy." Her jealousy twisting her guts. Jadon is stone faced hiding her fright of Angelique's unpredictable nature.

Melinda is openly disgusted. "This was your idea. You know I'm Wasp through and through. He is certainly not my type."

Angelique glares at her. "Go on! Let me hear what you have learned from all those Park Avenue psychiatrists."

Melinda steps away from her speaking. "You knew he was promiscuous. Is that not why you promoted him to other females in the group? Thus attempting to distance yourself from him. Using him as a tool to channel all that physical and mental energy into one powerful force. All without regard to how he would be changed. Thus creating a satyr. You are cruel beyond comparison. Cursing him not once but twice. So now you have Enkil to deal with who hates you and your bloodline because of Marie."

Angelique, "Now tell me something I don't know."

Jadon, "Well, from some of my Middle Eastern contacts. At the Iraqi

Museum of Antiquities. They have found on clay tablets from Sumer written in cuneiform script of course."

Angelique, "Get to the point. I already know you are well educated."

Jadon, "My contact has found reference to an archenemy of Enkil's."

Angelique, "Do go on."

Jadon, "It is written Enkil betrayed a princess. In doing so she cursed him and became a vengeful demon. Her only purpose for millenniums was to seek vengeance against him. This included his family and the entire household. Destroying all that would have an allegiance to him."

Angelique is seeing a way to bring about Enkil's destruction. All without breaking her pact with him. Her interest piqued.

Melinda interrupts. "You would turn that thing on Camel?" Angelique looks at her un-amused. "There will be other men for you even more powerful. Take Samir, now that's a man to turn."

Angelique, "That's enough!" Brandishing her blood stained anthem. Moving impossibly fast, grabbing Melinda's blonde hair from behind. Her knife pressed against Melinda's left jugular. "You will not insult me again. I will kill you without a moment's hesitation." Melinda is frightened into silence. The sharp blade of the anthem covered in Camel's dried blood over its length pressing into her skin. "If you ever speak to me that way again you will suffer your worst fears long before you die. Ask Jadon how I respond to being trifled with if you don't believe me." Melinda looks to Jadon's frightened face. Angelique releases Melinda's strands of blonde hair remaining in her open hand. Angelique straightens up her composure regained. "Wait until a man stabs you in the heart. Then has the gall to be cavalier about it."

Melinda, "It's happening to me right now. Only slowly and we're the ones making him into a whore. Then I have to give him away to some milky skinned girl. Who wouldn't know now what to do with a man. Except pray."

CHAPTER 33

MARC CALLS HIS cousin Phillip in New Orleans after Camel has left. Phil answers the phone, "Bon jour."

Marc, "Comment allez-vous?"

Phil, "Tres bene. So what has you calling today, Cousin?"

Marc, "I'm," hesitating, then blurting it out, "we're in some trouble."

Phil, "When you say 'we're in trouble,' you mean you and Camel?"

Marc, "Yes. Camel and I have gotten ourselves into something way beyond our knowledge."

Phil, "That is pretty big of you to admit. Do you two need another international lawyer? Or just a change of venue?"

Marc, "You still have that rapier wit." Not laughing.

Phil, "What sort of trouble is it? Certainly you're not going to be a daddy? Tell me in this day and age you are using protection."

Marc, "It's nothing like that. That would be a relief compared to this. I'm not calling about a legal issue either. I need some help translating an old French diary."

Phil, "Now you have my interest piqued. Where did you get this diary?" Relaxing some now that it's not a legal issue.

Marc, "It's one of our family diaries."

Phil, "Why not have one of your girlfriends do it for you?"

Marc, "Do you always have to be so probing with your questions?"

Phil, "Yes, it is my nature. Plus it's my training I am an esquire."

Marc, "I would have thought you would jump at the chance to dig into our family lore."

Phil, "Lore? You said it was a diary."

"Well, it's a diary but also a grimoire." Silence on the other end made longer by the buzzing of electronic distance. "Hello, are you still there?"

Phil, "Yeah I'm still here. Why do I get the feeling this is where it starts to go bad. Do you know what a grimoire is?"

Marc, "I'm beginning to."

Phil, "What have you done and how bad is it? Hold that thought for now. Which of our auspicious ancestors are we dealing with?"

Marc, "It's really a compilation of more than one. The part that concerns us was written by our great-great-grandmother around 1792."

Phil does not like what he is hearing. "You know some of our distant relatives were rumored to be into witchcraft and not the good kind. At least that is the family lore. So how did you come upon this book?"

"We found it here in Uncle Theron's library," Marc answers.

Phil, "We?"

Marc, "Why do I feel like you are cross examining me?"

Phil, "Why do you keep holding back? I can't help you if you don't give me the circumstances about what happened."

Marc sighs a deep breath ready to start. "Point taken. I'm embarrassed to admit we, Camel and I made a blunder. I'm just not sure how big it is."

Phil, "That wasn't so difficult was it? I've never judged you or Camel for your lifestyles. We have known each other our entire lives. You are my favorite and dearest cousins. I would do anything to help you."

Marc, "I know, we feel the same way."

Phil, "Then stop holding back. I can't help you if you keep hiding things from me."

Marc, "Okay, okay. Camel and I had company over. One of the ladies suggested we have some fun by changing things up. We had been playing cards for a while."

Phil, "Let me guess the two of you were losing."

"That's not the point. After taking a break she chose a book from the library. We took turns reading from it."

Phil, "Like a poetry reading?"

Marc, "Yes, but not exactly."

Phil encourages him to go on. "Then how?"

Marc, "Both of the women read the French and Latin with ease. Coaching us with pronunciations at times it was almost like calling to mosque but more musical."

Phil adds, "Like chanting?"

"Now that you mention it."

Phil, "More like a Catholic Mass?"

Marc, "Yes I guess so. Now that you've said it." Marc looking sheepishly.

Phil, "Who told you it was a grimoire?"

Marc, "I'm not sure at this point so much has happened. Strange things around here."

Phil, "Like what? And be specific."

Marc, "Some of the rooms in this house get cold enough to see my breath. Uh,

Camel and I both have been having nightmares. Actually Camel's dreams have been macabre. But that was all inconsequential after Camel was stabbed."

Phil, "Is he all right?"

Marc, "Yeah he's fine now."

Phil, "When did that happen in relation to using the grimoire?"

Marc, "He was stabbed about a week ago. A couple weeks before that."

Phil adds, "Cross examinations always have a way of uncovering the unexpected."

Marc, "More remarkable is his recovery. I stayed at the ICU until Ibram arrived the next day to relieve me."

Phil, "What was he doing when he was assaulted?"

"Just dancing. When one of the women he was dancing with went out of her mind."

Phil, "That is far-fetched. Usually there is a motive other than going berserk. Was he seeing both of them and one became jealous?"

"No, he had just met them that night. Weirder yet, they both committed suicide. While awaiting arraignment in lockup."

Phil, "Now you've gone to disturbing. Marc, whatever you do, don't use the grimoire anymore."

Marc, "We weren't using it."

Phil, "Se je le femme." Marc swallows hearing the seriousness in Phillip's voice. "Do not let anyone have access to that book. A grimoire is a dark book of spells. Dark meaning bad. It's not anything you should be using for amusement or for entertaining women."

Marc, "I realize that now."

Phil, "I thought you were a devout Muslim."

Marc, "I am!" Becoming defensive.

Phil, "You can't dabble in dark arts. What sort of women read Latin and chant. Nuns? I doubt the two of you were entertaining nuns. Unwittingly you have been outmaneuvered."

Marc, "It's beginning to look that way. So will you translate this stuff? We need to know what was done."

Phil, "I'll do it reluctantly. But I have some conditions."

Marc thinks, *Here it comes*, but says, "What's that?"

Phil, "Do not let anyone else have access to our family history. Do not let anyone know of my connection in this. It has to remain secret my involvement."

Marc, "No problem." Relieved the demands weren't bad at all.

Phil, "Yes it is a problem. Reading and putting thought into spells makes them become active. For lack of a better description. I'm going to need help with the Latin translations. I have someone in mind though."

Marc, "Can they be trusted?"

Phil, "Without a doubt. I've known him for a few years. He is an ex-Jesuit and with a little convincing I'm sure he will help us. Now tell me something about these women." Marc recounts who is involved will each of them with a few omissions about himself. "What is this alumni member like that Camel is involved with?"

Marc, "She is a few years older than Camel but she doesn't look it at all. Her uncle is Mr. Thornburg our estate attorney. Mom and Dad have known him for years, you know him. In their opinion he is the greatest. They met him by way of Uncle Theron. If he got any tighter assed, we could hold a right wing fund raiser."

Phil, "So he is established money. How old is this niece of his?"

Marc, "My guess is thirty something. I say that because she has a maturity about her. She exudes confidence but manages to be a very sexy woman. Blonde with blue eyes, something in them almost sinister. Stare right through you with one of her hard looks."

Phil, "What about the other women?"

Marc, "Melinda, from Manhattan upper east side Central Park East. Passion driven, jealous, controlling, and petulant. Did I leave anything out? No, I think that covers it. The opposite of Angelique, except for being a busty. Otherwise blonde and blue eyed, used to making men do what she wants."

Phil, "That includes you?"

Marc, "I'm afraid so. I don't get her. She encourages me to sleep with other women. Then turning jealous, and I know she sleeps with other men."

Phil, "You're all right with having an open relationship?"

Marc, "It wasn't what I have sought out," becoming distracted by powerful feelings of desire for her.

Phil, "You still there buddy?"

Marc, "Yeah, it's just every time she shows up she makes me so enamored and horny, I can't say no." Catching a lite waft of her perfume in that very moment. Marc inhaling searching the air for more even the faintest scent of it. Or was he just imagining that feeling a little heady. "Her perfume, it lingers in the air after she has gone making me want her. Then the look she gives me, her blue eyes twinkle and I'm the only man." Marc feeling like an idiot. Phillip's silence a mute testament to his growing concern. Letting Marc know without hurting his pride.

Phil finally interrupts him. "Copy and fax the pages the four of you chanted from." Coming off very businesslike.

Marc, "I will send you a copy of our family tree. It goes all the way back to the sixteenth century."

Phil, "That would be helpful in determining which relative we are dealing with. If it's that old you should be wearing cotton gloves to keep the oils from your hands off the pages. And don't use a flash or the photocopier. Use your digital camera and download the pictures. Bright light could damage it as well."

Marc, "Anything else?"

Phil, "Don't let anyone else besides Camel know I'm helping you. If our family history has any truth to it…" Pausing. "I wouldn't be too surprised if you two haven't mixed it up with a very old coven."

Marc, "What do you mean?"

Phil, "Some of our older aunts spoke of unusual occurrences."

Marc, "What sort of occurrences?"

Phil, "I have to research this further. It would only be hearsay. But know this, if you are accidently involved in some cult or by design, everyone close to you is in danger."

Marc, "Well, that's just nonsense. Besides, why would gorgeous heiresses become involved with some fanatical group. They are too busy keeping up with haute couture."

Phil, "You doubt this possibility? Camel was stabbed, nearly dying by your own admission. Stop stereotyping people. That's your first mistake. Many cultures have been involved with dark practices long before Islam or Christianity evolved."

Marc, "Now you're starting to sound like one of the Bedouins with their scary tales from the desert. Djinn causing trouble for some unwitting traveler."

Phil, "You never took any of those stories seriously?"

Marc, "No. Of course not. Those stories were meant to entertain and scare young boys into behaving."

Phil, "Both of your parents are archeologists. You can't tell me this comes as a surprise."

Marc, "They are just old legends. Superstitions of ignorant people from before enlightenment."

Phil becoming impatient with his cousin. "Enlightenment of the last two millennia would be the only truth. Anything before that couldn't possibly be real." Not a question but intended to get Marc to thinking. Phillips' approach to Marc as one of his students. "Send the pages. I'm always interested in old French documents. They reveal the laws and attitudes of the time they were written in. Some friends of ours bought a home in the Faubourg Marigny. During the title abstraction the original owner was Creole. He specified in the deed that the home could never be sold to someone white."

Marc, "Wow. I have never heard of anything like that."

Phil, "How enlightened are we if discriminatory directions can be written into property deeds. Only a hundred and fifty years ago.

"Send me the pages and I'll start on them right away."

Marc, "Great." Feeling a sense of relief.

Phil, "One more thing."

Marc, "What's that?"

Phil, "You should be very careful in your dealings with these women. Don't do anything to raise their suspicions. Trust no one."

Marc, "The only one up here I can trust without question is Camel."

Phil asks, "So how is he really?"

Marc, remembering Phillip had a big crush on Camel, says, "He is even more devilishly handsome than he was a few years ago when you last saw him. Lots of women troubles, but they are still lined up to date him."

Phil, "How is your extended family?" Meaning Camel's family.

"His dad is healthy. Wants him to settle down and marry. Still disapproving of his womanizing ways. Even teasing his father about it. We both have positions open with the family architectural firm. Dubai has transformed into a twenty first century capital of the world. Some of the finest architectural designs with the newest engineering feats. I wouldn't pass up an opportunity like that."

Phil, "At least the two of you have your careers on track. It does not seem like much has changed. The two of you back in trouble again."

Marc, "It does seem to find us."

Phil, "I'm still envious of you living in all those exotic lands."

Marc, "They are not really exotic when you are growing up there. As a matter of fact I always wondered what it would have been like to go to American schools. You know I've lived outside this country longer than I have lived in it."

Phil, "I just wish I could have spent more time with the two of you. Your lives have always been an adventure."

Marc, "You visited us in The United Arab Emirates and Peru in those summers. As I recall you were always bored and hot in both places."

Phil, "That's not really true. I only pretended to be bored. I didn't want the two of you to know how much fun I was having. You two were like older brothers to me. So as long as I was with the two of you, it didn't matter where we were. Whether it was a hot sandy dig in the desert or on a mountaintop above the clouds of a rain forest."

Marc, "I never knew that. Camel says hi."

Phil, "Tell him I said hi."

Marc, "I will."

Phil, "You know you two are always welcome down here. Mardi Gras is one big party twenty-four hours a day. Especially the last week of it."

Marc, "I'll keep that in mind."

Phil, "Good, now down to business. Fax me some papers and I'll make time."

Marc, "You should come up here for a visit. Rochester is a lot like East Texas and Baton Rouge rolled together. The East Texas part like where our grandfather lived."

On Phil's end the radio music stops with an announcer breaking to local weather. "It's going to be another sunny day in the Crescent City."

Phil turns it off. "Now that would be boring stuck out in the middle of the woods. I'm really more into the city. At least I was until Katrina came through."

Marc, "Is it still that obvious?"

Phil, "Yes, large sections of the city are abandoned. The city forest destroyed in large swaths. Two century old live oaks that shaded entire streets are now open to hot sun. Everything smells musky like the river. Enough about that. Since there is no such thing as global warming. Right! It's better to spend billions after the fact than to spend a billion dollars on prevention."

Marc, "People up here notice it too. Anyone that gardens or works outside can see the changes from it getting warmer. What concerns me equally is a government that has to legislate the truth in scientific reporting."

Phil, "That should be a concern to us all. Not whatever outcome suits your policies."

Marc, "As long as you claim to be moral and can sound like an evangelical preacher, you must be honest. Right!"

Phil, "You have it. Just for the record, deception is a regularly used and accepted tool of governments."

Marc, "Now that we've ripped the government apart anyone else left?"

Phil, "No. That felt good for now."

Marc, "Yes it did."

Phil, "Fax me pages in blocks of seven at a time. My fax gets a little dicey if you send much more. It was good hearing from you."

Marc, "You too, bye."

CHAPTER 34

MELINDA. "CAMEL'S NOT my type you know that. Marc is and I'm going to lose him after Saturday night. Once he goes to protect her from me. We're all done."

Angelique, "Yes, you will be labeled. There is no doubt about that." Her blue eyes smiling meanly.

Jadon not about to miss a barb, comments, "That bitch on wheels."

Melinda turns around facing Jadon angrily. "Wait, your turn is coming." White-blue sparks crackling across her fingertips more like that of electricity arcing. Releasing a faint smell of ozone into the air. Melinda's body trembles with rage. Holding her angry thoughts at the tip of her tongue, *That olive-skinned bitch thinks she'll come out of this unscathed*. Melinda throws her hands up toward the sky twisting them. Fingers spread releasing her anger into the summer's clear blue topaz sky. Dark storm clouds gather bubbling tremulously. Angelique her own anger roused joins in twisting her French-tipped fingers nails. Lightning jaggedly crackling over the roiling mass. *Caboom,* thunder reverberates outside. Melinda's anger not spent yet releasing more skyward. Charges of lightning streaking across the once cloud free sky making repeated ground strikes. Putting the entire county of Monroe under a storm alert.

Lights in the house flicker humming with an electrical noise. Smell of ozone wafts through the house. Raindrops splatter across the flagstone courtyard in waves of ever increasing intensity. Hail pelts windows banging off wrought iron outdoor furniture. The volume of noise rises as rain and hail collide with cars and roofs. Jadon in tune with nature sensing what is coming next pulls closed the French doors to the courtyard. Wind gusts against them swirling with debris. Power to the entire neighborhood winking out.

Jadon, "Now you have done it."

Angelique shrugs. "That's what backup generators are for." As if to make her point distant generators roar on. Power at her home restored. Angelique looks smugly satisfied. The pleasantest she's looked since they arrived at her home.

Melinda breaks the silence. "Is it going to rain the rest of the day?"

Angelique, "I haven't decided yet." Her lips pouty but her eyes less angry. "Maybe it will be one of those fast moving summer storms." All three of them laugh together their tone evil and maniacal echoing across the house.

CHAPTER 35

MARC PASSES BY a window stopping to check the weather outside as he so often does. Most of his work out there. Lightning streaks jaggedly across a dark sky. Which moments earlier had been clear. Hail is tapping the very window he's looking out from. Rain a deluge overcoming rain gutters pouring off the mansard roof. Lightning flashes like the blinking paparazzi strobe lights. Thunder muffled by the solid walls and some distance. That with heavy drapes helping to diminish the reverberations coming from outside. Marc questions himself. The weather report called for sunny skies, or was that New Orleans weather? Having planned on using the hammock for a time today. It couldn't hurt to have a down pour clean it after being in the dusty basement. Marc is almost always able to find something good to do. Where rainy weather was concerned.

Marc pulls his cell phone out to call Oolong. She answers in her exotic breathy Dutch-British accent, "Hello darling. I've been expecting your call."

Marc covers his surprise. How did she know it was him? "Hi. Would you like to get together for an early dinner?"

Oolong, "That sounds marvelous. Then we could have that private discussion."

Marc, "What kind of food are you in the mood for?"

Oolong, "There is a restaurant on East Avenue I have heard good things about. It's in a hotel?"

Marc, "I know where you are talking about. The food is great there. I live down the street from it." Having been there a few times on dates and with his brother to eat.

Oolong, "Perfect. Then I'll meet you there say around six o'clock?"

Marc adds, "Yes, for cocktails and dinner. Do you need directions?"

Oolong, "No, I'll manage. I have OnStar navigation in my vehicle."

Marc, "Good, I will call and make reservations."

Oolong, "See you at six o'clock."

Marc selects a dark blue summer suit only 10 percent wool. Tailored for him locally at Hickey Freeman. *She would pick a place I have to dress for.* Glad he had listened to his brother and had a new suit cut to fit his extra wide large shoulders. Choosing a blue tie to go with a white dress shirt. Its collar and cuffs crisply starched. Standing in front of the mirror tying his tie. Its color bringing out the sapphire blue of his eyes. Unaware of how handsome he is with his suntanned face. Long shoulder-length dark hair. Which he has slicked back with gel. Looking all the part of a GQ model. His boyish innocence gone now replaced by ruggedly handsome features.

Stepping outside into the warm air and a light, misty drizzle falling. As he heads to his car. Once at the restaurant, the maitre d' greets Marc. "Reservations?"

Marc, "Yes, Du Bois for two. My guest may already be here."

Maitre d', "Ah, very good, sir. She is already seated at your table. This way please."

Marc, *Wow, she got here fast.* He enjoys a few moments to appreciate her from afar unobserved. Oolong is wearing a sleeveless beige dress with a plunging neckline. Exposing her beautiful mahogany skin. That and her shapely cleavage. Noting an unusual pendant nestled between thus allowing his eyes to linger. All the excuse he needed. Diamonds surrounding a large sparkling blue-purple stone. Estimating it to be about twenty carats.

Oolong approvingly acknowledges him as he arrives. "You clean up pretty good, very handsome." Offering her hand to him in one of those dainty gestures that women so often do. Marc takes hers into his large calloused hand. The hand that his tanzanite ring is on sparkling under the lights of the dining room.

Marc, "You look gorgeous."

Oolong, "Thank you. I'm so glad you agreed to meet me. And you are wearing your tanzanite ring."

Marc glances down at her pendant again, his eyes lingering. "I see you wore yours as well."

Oolong, "Yes. This was a gift from my father."

Marc sits down. "It's very beautiful. The details are Celtic?"

Oolong, "It's North African, the symbolism is the same. Vines of life intertwined."

Their waiter arrives. "Cocktail sir?"

Marc already noting his guest is drink white wine. "Do you like red wine?"

Oolong, "Yes, of course darling. I'm just having a Chenin Blanc. As you never know with Americans what they will like." The waiter hands Marc a wine list.

Skimming it quickly Marc selects a well-rounded flavor. "We will have the Châteauneuf-du-Pape."

"Very good, sir." Marc hands the wine list back to him. Looking at Oolong.

"Now tell me what is so mysterious and private that you needed to discuss with me alone?"

Oolong choosing her words carefully. Not wanting to scare Marc off making him think she is some kind of nut. "Are you always so direct?"

Marc, "Yes, unless there is a reason to take it slow."

Oolong, "All right then to the point. Haven't you noticed, say, unusual goings-on?"

"Such as?" Marc being coy.

"Let me put it another way. Odd behavior from people around you that are close?"

"Behavior?"

Oolong, "I thought you wanted direct." Her dark eyes narrowing. "Don't play coy with me."

Marc, "Fine, some of the people I thought were close to me. I'm finding I don't know them at all. Let alone trust. So I'm being cautious in speaking to you."

Oolong, "Good, as well you should be." Marc looks at her for the first time as a possible ally. Trying to decide how much to trust in her. Their waiter arrives with the bottle of wine. Presenting it to Marc for his approval. Glancing at the label, then giving a nod to go ahead. The waiter cuts open the lead seal. Twisting the corkscrew in with skilled motion. Oolong uses the silence to gather her thoughts. "What has changed to make you not trust them?"

Marc, "I haven't yet arrived at an answer for that." Just knowing something about her is trustworthy, unless she really is a good liar. Choosing to go with his gut feeling taking the plunge. "I am frequently woken by this recurrent dream. Where this woman from another time knows me."

Oolong, "A time you couldn't possibly have lived in?" Marc tastes the wine, nodding his approval. The waiter pours each a glass. Then withdraws from the table. Having noticed the serious tone of their conversation.

Marc, "Yes, centuries in the past. The dream is really more a nightmare." Marc sips his wine. Oolong, hers.

"What is happening in these nightmares that you find so frightening?" Marc feels silly for having brought the subject with more pressing issues. Such as the mysterious deaths of several women his brother has been having sexual relations with.

Marc, "My dreams are always about this woman. I can feel her presence before I see her."

Oolong, "Do you recognize her? Describe her."

Marc, "I feel like I should know her. But that is impossible. She is from the eighteen hundreds. A platinum blonde or at least wearing a white wig. Her hair is coiffed high with curls. Her face is powdered white and her dress brushes the ground at times. Oh and her sleeves are mid–arm length ending across the forearms with lacy cuffs." Oolong patiently listens, her eyes intelligent and focused.

Oolong, "What else?"

Marc, "She covers her face with a fan before I can see it. Uh, she has the fan dangling from her wrist. Always as soon as I try to see her face she opens her fan. And recently she is calling to me, 'mon fils,' then reaching out to me."

Oolong's calm exterior is inquisitive but inside becoming one of alarm. "Has she touched you?"

Marc, "It was in the last dream. She grabbed my arm."

Oolong, "What happened when she did that?" Watching his face closely. Marc touches his arm where the scratches had been. Remembering her ferocious grip with her nails gouging his flesh. Forcing him to tear away his arm. While she was screaming, "Mon fils!"

Oolong, "Tell me." Snapping him out of the intense moment. As real as any event in his life. Only it was a dream.

Marc, "It's strange and frightening. She is one scary woman. I was frozen and couldn't move. It took all the power in my mind to wake up to get away from her."

Oolong gathers there was more to tell. "Go on."

Marc, "She had control over me physically, she was in my head. My body wasn't under my control. Then she dug her nails into my arm when she grabbed me. I heard yelling in my dream. 'Wake up!' No, it was my uncle. He was there yelling for me to wake up. When I finally did it really was just a nightmare. Oddly enough my arm was scratched right where she had a hold of me." Marc feeling some relief after being able to tell someone else. "What do you think this all means? It was just a dream, right?" Her dark eyes piercing reading Marc's body language for any signs of dishonesty. Watching his face for the smallest tick of deception. Oolong being very adept at reading people. Using her strong telepathic abilities to sense him. Caressing his mind finding no deception. Only naivety to the point of almost innocence. If you could say that about a twenty one year old male.

Oolong, "I don't know what is going on but whatever it is. I've got a very bad feeling about it."

Marc, "What can I do to protect us?"

Oolong already knows but needs to confirm this. "You mean Camel?"

Marc, "Yes."

Oolong takes a moment to choose her words carefully. "For you, the ring you're wearing will protect you. Most important of all knowledge. Learn your family history. That is where you will find the most protection. For your brother, I'm just not so sure. It may already be too late."

Marc, "What is that supposed to mean?"

Oolong, "The truth about him will be revealed soon enough."

Giving her a dubious look Marc says, "You know, you had me going there for a minute." Smiling. "Seriously. I fell hook, line and sinker. You had me going there with those nebulous answers and veiled warnings. I don't believe in any hocus-pocus. This is ridiculous."

Oolong remaining unsmiling her face very serious. Speaking, "Well, then let me ask you this. Has your hair always grown this fast? Or is this a recent development?"

Marc, "That's an unusual tack but I'll bite." Marc self-consciously runs his hand over his head. His dark straight hair brushing against the shoulders of his suit. Oolong watching him trying to remain serious, but a smile lifts the corners of her lips. "Fine. This is a new development."

Oolong, "What about your body. Have you always been so hirsute?" Pushing him a little. "Is anyone else like you in your family? Your father perhaps?"

Marc, "This is recent. It is perfectly explainable."

Oolong with her eyebrows arched, "Yes?"

Marc, "It's hormonal." Giving in, "At least that is what I thought at first." Their food arrives making them change to a lighter subject. Once the waiter is gone they continue their discussion.

After dinner Marc says, "Do you need a ride back to your place?"

Oolong, "No, I'll be just fine. You have my cell phone number call me. I have done what I came to do."

Marc waiting for the bill. "At least let me walk you out to your car. I'm sure you didn't walk here."

Oolong, "No, that won't be necessary." Getting up to leave Marc standing up too. Oolong walking towards the door. Marc questioning, *Where is the waiter?* Impatient to catch up with her. The waiter brings the bill. Marc signs the credit receipt adding in the tip. Rushing after her outside past other couples coming up the steps. He walks out to the sidewalk looking in both directions up and down the street. Oolong nowhere in sight. *Huh, that was fast.*

CHAPTER 36

BACK AT HOME. Marc is given a lot to think about after his discussion with Oolong. Removing the grimoire from the wall safe in the study. Selecting a comfortable overstuffed chair to read in. Finding it difficult to concentrate after a while laying the book aside. Massaging his forehead a mild headache developing. Pushing his long hair back out of his face again. Enough reading for tonight. Getting up, placing the grimoire back in the safe. Marc goes upstairs to bed after setting the security alarm system.

Friday morning arrives in a pleasant and an unexpected way. Warm rushes of pleasure making him feel incredibly good his breath fast. What a way to wake up. Marc awaken from his erotic dream of Melinda and Jadon. Warm ejaculate pulsing out onto his abdomen and sheets. His dream felt so incredibly real and so good. In his dream they were making love in a ménage à trois. Waves of passionate bliss receding after his intense orgasm. Fragments of his dream dissipating with the morning light. Lying there in peaceful warm bliss so relaxed. After what young men frequently have. Wow. That dream was so real. Now his wet sheets already cooling and sticky. Now he had to get up and shower. Abdominal hair pulling as his bodily fluids dry. Pinching his skin stinging as the hair on his legs pulls away from the skin it's matted to.

After his shower, Marc to pass through the kitchen en route to outside. The coffee machine on a timer his morning coffee already brewed. Its fresh aroma greeting his nose as he enters the kitchen. Pouring it into a large insulated mug, then adding some milk. He continues on to get a head start on the day's work.

By 8:00 a.m., Ms. Campbell and Mary both are busy in the kitchen. Marc comes inside, already sweaty. As July heat is rising outside quickly the air-conditioned cool inside feels good.

Ms. Campbell, "You're up early. Now I don't have to send her up to get you. Breakfast is ready." Marc looks irritated, having not slept well the night before. And not in the mood for a lot of frivolous conversations or Ms. Campbell's sharp tongue.

He answers, "Good, I could eat a horse. Smells good too."

Ms. Campbell, "Mary made her own buttermilk biscuits. Per your request turkey sausage patties seasoned with sage." Mary pulls the fresh biscuits out of the oven their tops golden brown.

Ms. Campbell, "Have a seat." Indicating the stool at the granite countertop. Both women serve up breakfast. Mary dumps hot biscuits into a basket right in front of him. Ms. Campbell places butter and strawberry preserves next to them. Then hands Marc a plate of scrambled eggs. While Mary is blotting the grease off the sausage patties with paper toweling. Marc makes sausage patty sandwiches with a couple of biscuits. Chowing down hungrily his mood improving.

His cell phone rings as he gulps the last bite down. Touching the accepting the call standing up to leave. "Hello. Camel. Yes, I'm going to the alumni mixer." Mary is unable to avoid hearing their conversation. "I don't know why I'm bothering to go. I don't have a date." Talking as he leaves the kitchen to go outside back to work.

Mary gets an idea, excusing herself. Her pulse rising with a rush of excitement going through her body. *Wouldn't it be fun?* Acting on her impulse. Mary takes the card out of her safe place. Safety-pinned inside her bra with some cash. Glancing at it once more mustering the courage with fingers shaking. Dialing Melinda's number secretly from the third floor of the manor. Her mind racing, Aunt Norma would so disapprove. But then she wouldn't know how to have fun anymore. Maybe she should read her Bible some more. Not really needing the card to see the number. She punches in the familiar phone number having looked at it a hundred times. Wanting to call it but not having mustered the courage to follow through with it until now. With her heart racing and listening for any footsteps. Aunt Norma had been known to sneak up on her. Holding the track phone Melinda had given her for just such an occasion. Knowing how bad Aunt Norma would react if she found out. Even if it was only for some shopping and a little girl time. The phone rings on the other end. What if Melinda invites her? No, she couldn't get away from the warden anyway. What if she could? Just for a little while. To be with real people her own age. Normal for once having fun with young people. Not always forced to care for older women. Whose lives had already been lived. The connection made it stops ringing just before going to voice message.

Melinda hears the music of her phone playing. Checking the number screening her calls. Yes, just as planned, but only better. Now she wouldn't have to come up with a cover story. Pausing for few moments longer before speaking. Letting it continue for just a bit more time to increase the excitement in Mary. Knowing full well she's got her where she wants her.

Melinda, "Hello?"

Mary, "Hi, you said to call anytime and we'd go shopping."

Melinda pretends like she doesn't know who it is. "Bon jour? Comment allez-vous?"

Mary feels foolish. Having rushed everything out at once. "It's Mary. You said to call you anytime."

Melinda, "Oh, yes." Pausing to check herself in the rearview mirror. Her smug face looking back at herself so pleased. "Oh yes," whispering more to herself. "Got you."

Mary, "What? You don't remember me?" Disappointment in her voice.

Melinda, "When would you like to do that?" Wind rushing over her as she is driving south on 590. Adjusting her Versace sunglasses.

Mary, "What about this afternoon?"

"Great, I'll pick you up."

Mary panics. "No! No." Calming herself.

"No?" Melinda playing it innocent.

Mary having regained her composure. "I'll meet you."

Melinda, "Very good. Where do you want to meet?"

"I'm not sure," Mary answers thoughtfully.

Melinda, "Why not Macy's parking lot at Eastview Mall. Do you know where that is?"

Mary, "Yes we've passed it on the way to Syracuse. Wait, I don't know how to get there from East Avenue."

Melinda, "That's easy. How are you with directions?"

Mary, "Good I can find my way around London." Trying not to sound like a total loser.

Melinda, "Okay, then you can meet me inside. It's too hot to wait outside."

Mary, "There's just one problem. I have to grocery shop while I'm out."

Melinda thinks to herself, *You have more than one problem.* "That's not a problem. There is a Wegmans grocery store along the way to the mall. You can stop there on the way home. How long do you have?"

Mary, "I have the afternoon off, but I should be home by five o'clock to pick up Aunt Norma."

Melinda, "We can manage that. I can have you back in time. She will be none the wiser. Now get going. The sooner we meet the longer we have to shop."

Mary closes her phone up quietly to avoid getting caught. Aunt Norma calls for her from the second floor landing. Impatiently walking up. "Who was that you were talking to?"

Mary, "It was one of those phone solicitors. I'm going to be leaving soon. Is there anything else you would like me to do before I go?"

Aunt Norma, "Why the hurry?"

Mary, "It is my afternoon off."

Aunt Norma, "You may go. Just be back by five o'clock. I expect to leave here on time. Drive carefully, that car is paid for."

Mary, "I will."

CHAPTER 37

MELINDA ARRIVES QUICKLY being so close to the mall already. Having some time to herself getting a vanilla latte sitting down sipping on it. Her mind wondering, flashing back to her first cousin who used to meet her for lattes. *If he had just stayed out of my business and not exposed my lies. Lies that would have kept my life the same, but no, you changed my life forever. Cousin dearest, didn't you? My parents had to put me in that godforsaken Catholic girls' school.* Stirring her latte taking a sip. *Well, I returned that favor in spades.* It's amazing the contacts you can make at a parochial school. Those gangbangers just needed a little cash and some direction. To send a pretty white boy to Rikers. Then on to Attica. Well, that and a bag of heroin in his sports car. Now who is the hypocritical evangelical with a secret to lie about? Even old money couldn't keep him from being a prison whore. Smiling with a feeling of satisfaction. Glancing at her watch impatiently. Melinda's cell phone ringing.

Melinda, "Hello, Jadon." Getting up walking over to an entrance. Looking outside. "Yes, she is here. How many people are driving 1980s station wagons at East View? I can't stand to look at that milky skinned bitch."

Jadon, "Are you sure you're going to be able to handle this?"

Melinda waves to get Marys' attention. Smiling in greeting to her. "Look, I've taken down cunning businessmen for years. This will be easy. I'll call you later." Cutting the call short hanging up on Jadon end of conversation. Dismissing her cohort.

Jadon, "Bitch!"

Mary waves back smiling radiating happiness. Finally a new friend to spend time with away from oppressive aunt Norma. Melinda waves back smiling thinking, ' the insipid cow in a matronly feed sack.'

Melinda manages to sound friendly and excited. "Come on, girl. Let's go shopping. I know just the store for you."

Mary, "Remember I have to be finished with grocery shopping and be home by five o'clock."

Melinda, "Oh you'll be home by then. I'll make sure of it."

After a light lunch, Melinda guides Mary into a high end store with designer labels. Making sure she has sticker shock. Melinda hands Mary a darling black evening dress, Versace. "You've just got to try this on." Mary comes out of the dressing room looking every bit of stunning. Melinda having to swallows her jealousy. "Let me see the price tag. Oh, I'm so sorry." Turning so Mary sees it as well its price two thousand dollars. Her look of disappointment sustenance for Melinda. Now for the real store.

Melinda, "I know another store that has designer styles at five times less. You don't need these high flying prices to look good. Come on."

Mary, "I hope so." Melinda takes her across the mall to a smaller store.

Melinda, "I shop here all the time. Not everyone can afford two thousand dollars for a evening dress."

Mary, "Are you sure about this store?" The name of which is Flash and Trash.

Melinda, "Absolutely." Leading the way in going over to a rack. Pulling off a short black skirt, sure to be too tight, handing it to Mary. "And this." Handing her a sheer red silk blouse. "It's so you. You'll drive the boys crazy with that. They won't be able to keep their eyes off you." Mary looks very reluctant. "Go on, at least try it on."

Mary comes out of the dressing room feeling completely awkward. Melinda having twinges of jealousy. "My goodness, you have such a nice figure."

The salesclerk, "She sure does. Honey why keep it hidden?"

Mary uncomfortable with so much attention, speaks, "Ms. Campbell, I mean Aunt Norma says I look like a prostitute." Blushing her cheeks becoming rosy. Melinda looks at her. Mary's eyes too innocent to be a whore.

The salesclerk, "You need a red brassiere. It will leave more to the imagination. Not that with your size there is any question. I'll get a bra for you, 44D?" Mary nods yes as if it was regrettable.

Melinda, "That's just bullshit from an old dried up hypocrite who should have been a nun anyway. You have nothing to be ashamed of." 'Not yet anyway.' "You look pretty and at least twenty-one. If you wear that, you will be able to get into any club in this city. All without being carded."

Mary, "I don't know about nightclubs."

Melinda ready to make her move. "You know I'm going to an alumni mixer tonight. It will be great fun. You could go as my guest. It would be so much fun." Mary tries not to look too eager. "Oh I'm sorry. Your aunt Norma would never let you go."

Mary, "I know. If only I could get away from her somehow."

Melinda, "Yes, oh well, it was a good idea for a few seconds. Wait a minute, I have a thought."

"What?"

"No, never mind, you would have to be willing to try it."

Mary taking the bait. "What?"

Melinda easily crafts her next move. "Does she like tea?"

Mary, "Yes Earl Grey is her favorite. She only has it as a treat otherwise choosing a store generic."

Melinda, "I know of this small apothecary with a tea shop attached to it. They have the most marvelous blends of teas. It's all natural. They are sure to have something that would gently help her to sleep. Then you could get away for a time. No one would be the wiser and you would get to wear your new clothes."

Mary, "Aunt Norma is such a light sleeper. It's like living with a prison matron. Nothing gets by her."

Melinda sweeting the pot. "You know Marc will be there and of course Camel. Well there will be other soirées."

Mary's face lights up. Then she plays it down. "Aren't you two dating?"

Melinda, "Marc doesn't want to be exclusive. He said we should date other people and I agreed with him. I'm not ready to get serious and neither is he."

Mary still reluctant. "Ms. Campbell, I mean aunt Norma has bad insomnia. If the tea doesn't work."

Melinda, "You let me work it out. When do you want me to pick you up tonight." Melinda thinking. Sometimes alprazolam with some kava-kava in the tea works even better.

Mary ventures, "It's worth a try."

Melinda, "Good then it's settled. You get her to drink the tea and I'll handle the rest."

Mary, "It's not going to hurt her is it?"

Melinda, "No. I'm sure there is a tea with a natural sedative that is gentle. She'll sleep like a baby. She will probably thank you in the morning. You'll be able to slip out and back in before she ever wakes up."

Mary interrupts Melinda's thoughts. "What sort of tea is it?"

Melinda, "It has kava-kava in it." Seeing Mary's continuing concern Melinda adds, "It's perfectly safe." Knowing full well that it will knock Norma out. The mix of alprazolam and kava-kava is synergistic. Having used it a few times on unsuspecting men. The first time her cousin; otherwise she would never have gotten his car keys. Her aunt will not only sleep but she'll be unconscious to the world. When she wakes up, she'll have a drug hangover in the morning. She thinks aunt Norma is a bitch now. Wait.

Mary, "All right, let's do it."

Melinda, "After we get these clothes paid for we will be off to the herbal shop. Then you can go grocery shopping."

Mary, "About the clothes, I find them a little too provocative. Don't you?"

Melinda finally getting impatient with her. "Look young men like women who aren't afraid to be modern and a little sexy. If you don't want them then just wear one of your matronly dresses. One that makes you look like you should be a novice at a convent. That way you can blend in with the wallpaper and none of the guys will notice you."

Mary becomes defensive. "I'm not familiar with this style of clothing. I've heard other girls whispering about whores."

Melinda looking injured her eyes misting a little. "I'm sorry. I thought you wanted my help. But since you don't trust my taste I'm wasting my time. If you change your mind call." A tear rolling down Melinda's cheek.

Mary, "I'm sorry all I ever wanted was a friend. A big sister to be a confidante. You are so pretty. No, beautiful and sophisticated. I'll trust your judgment on this."

Melinda brightens pulling a tissue out of her Prada bag. Gently blotting her tears so as to not ruin her makeup. "Good, now let's finish this ensemble. You will need your underwear to match the bra. Then you need a pair of shoes."

Mary, "I hadn't thought about shoes."

Melinda looks at Mary's feet. "What size do you wear?"

Mary, "Size 7."

Melinda, "Perfect, I'm the same shoe size. I have a pair of Manolo Blahnik sling backs that will be perfect for you." Melinda looks at the salesclerk. "Ring her up, we need to go." The bill comes to more than Mary has counting out all of her cash and still short. Melinda expecting as much pulls out a credit card. "What's the point of having a credit card if you don't use it. Consider it a gift from a big sister." Smiling so genuinely at her.

Mary, "No. You can't. I promise I'll pay you back."

Melinda, "Don't worry about it my father has more money than the pope. He will just pay the bill when it comes in."

Mary, "No one has ever done that for me. You are too kind." Hugging Melinda. Her blue eyes stone cold for just a moment.

Melinda, "Now you go change." Mary pauses. "Yes?"

Mary, "I can't believe aunt Norma doesn't want me around you."

"Really, why is that?" Her voice soft.

Mary, "Well, she says you and Marc's friends don't live your lives right." Realizing she didn't want to tell her everything. Leaving out the part about "no good coming of them."

Melinda's pupils narrow her face glowering. "Because I don't sit at home holding my Bible? She needs to join the twenty-first century. Women don't have to be demure anymore. We can go after what we want."

Mary trying to minimize damage. "She says I'm too young and sheltered to be running with your crowd."

Melinda, "Well that's just ridiculous! You should be sitting with that hausfrau. Go on and change."

Mary, "What time is it?" Panicking looking for a clock.

Melinda, "Relax it's only three o'clock. After we pick up the herbal tea you can go grocery shopping. I'll make sure you the directions for the tea. Make sure you hide the clothes at home. I'm sure anything youthful will be frowned on by your aunt." That last part said leaving a bad taste on her tongue. Smiling as Mary goes to the dressing room. Melinda making a quick call using her cell phone. Pressing Angelique's pre-programmed number getting her answering machine. "Everything is going as planned. Our guest of honor will be present." Hanging up sliding her phone back into her purse. Mary comes out of the dressing room her green eyes sparkling. Her auburn hair down around her shoulders framing a delicate featured face with milky toned skin glowing and unblemished. Beautiful in her youthful innocence. Melinda despising her more than ever.

CHAPTER 38

AFTER GETTING THE herbal tea and Mary on her way. Melinda calls Jadon using her cell while heading north on 590. Turning left at the Pittsford exit. Getting Jadon's voice mail, "I need your help. We have to pull together something for tonight. I'm sure you're the right woman for the job. Call me." *Click,* hanging up planning her next moves. Smiling with a satisfied look on her face. Warm air rushing over her scarf covered head driving with her convertible top down. Glancing at her own reflection looking back with Versace sunglasses.

CHAPTER 39

MARC FINISHES EARLY as planned. The pergola built and positioned ready for the low seating wall planter. Where the fragrant thorn-less pink roses will be planted. This weekend will be great. No work and a party tonight. A hammock to use all weekend. Marc walks toward the house sees Mary pulling in parking the late model station wagon back from grocery shopping. Wearing her new sunglasses she is able to check him out without being so obvious. Catching her breath as he saunters over to her. His body moving like some big cat. Smooth and graceful, muscles rippling under that soft looking chest fur a deep brown. His tee shirt off upper body muscular and sun darkened. At least that which is exposed to the sun. Marc had been to the gym earlier that day; his muscles still pumped adding sweaty from the hot sun and hard work outside.

Marc, "Here I'll help." Stepping up always thoughtful toward women reaching for grocery bags.

Mary smiles at him from behind her new sunglasses. "As well you should. What good are all those muscles if you aren't going to help out?"

Marc, "Hey! I work around here too." Marc noticing something different about her, *Hum, she's more attentive.* Lifting the heavy bags out of the station wagon. Making his cannonball shoulders and biceps bulge. Getting into the kitchen setting the bags down on the brown granite countertop. Ms. Campbell turns around raising an eyebrow. Her hazel eyes hard with their pupils narrowing to pinpoints jaws set. Marc notices her glowering look. Pulls his tee shirt out of his back pocket sliding it over head snug fitting. Dark straight hair pushing out its crew neck. Cutting her eyes around to catch Mary sneaking a last look at him.

Ms. Campbell, "Take your sunglasses off when you're in the house. It's rude." Ignoring Marc for the moment. Directing her attention to Mary instead. "You finish bringing in the groceries. I want to leave soon for home." Then to Marc, "You may go, shower or whatever it is you need to do. We have it from here." Dismissing him but not before giving him a look of disgust. Marc not hiding his irritation with her. His blue eyes staring at her for a moment longer. His stubble covered jaws tight. Leaving to go upstairs without a word. Thinking to himself, *That old biddy is nothing but if she isn't miserable all the time.* Stomping up the stairs heavy footed in his steel-toe boots. That and some anger.

Refusing to have her boss him around. Marc puts on some shorts and goes back outside to the private garden. Pulling off his tee shirt dropping it on the table. Hopping into the hammock and stretching out with his heads behind his head. Its rocking motion combined with the warm breeze and shade create a soothing and very relaxing sensation. Dozing off to sleep in the peaceful garden. Surrounded by towering hemlocks and Leyland cypresses.

Waking up several hours later after a disturbing dream involving the alumni. Veils of sleep making the dream fragments unclear. His final dream was of a brown skinned man in his early twenties. Wearing a loincloth similar to what the Egyptian men wore in such a hot climate. The young man being broad chested and very hairy. Almost familiar for some reason. Trying to warn him, speaking in an ancient language. Middle Eastern in origin but much older Hittite? About something that he doesn't want Marc to do. This man grabs both Marc's arms in desperation. Squeezing them in almost a panic. Yelling at Marc and shaking him. Marc yells back at him. "I don't know!" Waking himself up startled flailing his arms. Shadows long leaving the garden shaded. The sun far in the west now. Marc swings his legs over the side of the hammock. Feet touching down on the gravel. Stretching, his tall muscular frame rested, but what dreams. Heading into the house using the new flagstone pathway. It's time to clean up for the party.

CHAPTER 40

ON THE APPROACH to Angelique's home in Pittsford "on the hill." Parking is tight with so many cars. The crew of valets parking cars having used up everything close. Marc hands his keys to the 1968 Mustang to one of the valets finding a spot close. Squeezing the blue Mustang in between two dark Escalades. His sports car lost between them. Walking past one expensive car after another. Jadon's black Ferrari, Camel's red Aston Martin, a couple of Jaguars, several Mercedes-Benz, and of course Hummers. What he liked to call tanks. Music drifting softly through a lush densely planted privacy screen of Canadian hemlocks. Towering blue spruce are up lit by landscape lights. Angelique's white Federal style mansion coming into view with its six fluted columns. Her house trimmed in white with black shutters opened. Revealing the exquisite landscaping to guests inside. A couple of lacy-leafed blood red Japanese maples. Beautiful very old specimen trees with landscaping lights on them. Several more wolf eye dogwoods their variegated leaves reflecting light from perfectly positioned down lights. Crossing the expansive cobblestoned driveway appearing more like an imports dealership. So packed with foreign cars shiny and new. As he gets closer to the mansion Marc has a sudden feeling of déjà vu. Not ready to go inside more fascinated with how Angelique's grounds were landscaped. He follows a cobblestone path that in appearance is more like a Roman highway from somewhere in Europe rather than Western New York. Its stones perfectly fitted and worn where carts would have passed over it for centuries. Dogwoods with variegated leaves planted along this path light reflecting off them making darkness brighter. The winding path going around a corner of the house passed a second brick chimney. Leading into a private vignette with wrought iron seating arranged facing a water fountain. The sound of water bubbling down over its three tiers inviting one to stay and relax. Taking a moment sitting down on one of the wrought iron chairs. An ornamental tree showering white blossoms over Marc like soft snowfall so tranquil and serene. Not wanting to give that moment up. Then feeling foolish he gets up and walks back up the path. Ready to join the festivities of the evening.

Before Marc steps on to the porch security is already coming out of the shadows on him at the door. Already having him identified with a facial recognition software moving back. The door opened promptly by one of the extra maids on duty. Angelique not far behind ever the gracious hostess greets Marc. "Bon jour monsieur." Handing him a crystal champagne flute (Baccarat). A flute in her other hand raised festively. Poised wearing a black Jimmy Choo dress décolletage accented with a black pearl necklace. As if his eyes needed leading. Finishing her ensemble with five inch heeled Manolo's open toe sling backs.

Angelique, "I'm so glad you could make it. Come in." Checking Marc out. "Mon dieu se beau. Le sol on your skin making you even more handsome. If I didn't already have a date Melinda would be in trouble." Handing the champagne flute to the maid standing near ready for orders.

Marc takes the hand she has proffered. "As always you are breathtaking."

Angelique, "*Enchante* and he's got a mind." Flirting with him. "Julia and Melinda are bartending in the billiards room. You know your way around." Passing through the crowded living room. Its low roar of voices sounding more like a session of the United Nations. So many different languages being spoken. Marc at ease with the international flavor to the gathering. Having grown up in Dubai the crossroads of the world. Many of her guests wearing their own nation's attire saris, robes, and turbans. Most eyes following his entrance into the room discreetly of course.

Making their way past dignitaries, Marc sets his champagne flute on the passing waiter's tray. With only a polite sip taken not to offend the hostess. Angelique releases his hand. "I trust you can find yourself the rest of the way to the bar. Where I believe Camel is still playing a game of billiards." Leaving him to greet another male guest. Calling to him, "Samir!" Marc glances at this very handsome swarthy man. His black mustache the same color as his eyes. Something familiar about him, but he is too excited to be concerned. The man watches Marc from across the crowded room.

Samir speaks to Angelique, "It seems you may very well pull this off. The triumvirate will be awaiting your success."

Angelique, "Yes, I always complete what I start."

Samir, "Failure was never a concern."

Angelique, "Don't you mean acceptable?"

Samir, "What you are putting into motion if you fail could bring down heaven's fury upon us all. Your failure was never an option."

CHAPTER 41

ACROSS THE HOUSE in the billiards room Marc ambles through the doorway almost filling it. His six foot broad shoulder frame hard to miss. That with his long dark straight hair now just passed his shoulders even more noticeable. Jadon is playing billiards with Camel, just managing to keep her short dress down. While casually watching the doorway for Marc's arrival.

Jadon calls out, "Hi, Marc!" Striking the cue ball. Its target made sinking the ball she smiles. "You look dapper." Flirting. Camel looks exasperated having just lost again to her. Hanging up his pool stick.

Marc, "Hi you look as ravishing as always." Jadon's moss green dress complimenting her silver-green eyes sparkling. A champagne cork pops hitting Marc in the back of the head.

"Ouch!" He turns to see where it came from.

"Oh, sorry," Melinda says. Then she adds, "You know how they can get away sometimes. Are you all right?" The corners of her mouth turning up just a little.

Marc rubs the back of his head. "Yeah. I'm fine." Looking sheepish. "I didn't see you over there."

Melinda smiles wryly. "Now you do." His blue eyes give her a mean look. Melinda offers, "Glenlivet rocks?"

Marc, "Yes with a splash." Moving over to the bar where she is helping out. Melinda is wearing a short black dress with a plunging neckline revealing her cleavage. Marc's eyes are roving up and down. Not hearing Camel speaking.

"Hi!" Clamping a large hand on Marc's shoulder. Then he says, "Hello," looking at one of the new pledges standing at the bar. Camel having a fascination for blondes. Her accent heavy with a Southern drawl. Not himself his face serious.

Marc, "Hi." They shake hands. "Why the serious expression?"

Camel, "It's concern." Dropping his voice lower speaking so only Marc hears him. "What are you doing?"

Marc, "What? What do you mean?"

Camel, "Be careful, or do you need a hammer upside your head?" Turning his head watching Jadon's approach. Melinda sets Marc's drink up on the bar in front of him.

Marc, "Oh gotcha." Jadon slides up to the bar beside Marc. Handing him his drink.

Camel, "I'm not in the mood for a lot of people. But I did promise Angelique I would be here. And you asked me to be here too."

Jadon clinks Marc's glass with hers. "You two need to loosen up," She says. Looking at Camel she adds, "You are usually the party guy everyone wants to dance with." Handing Camel his drink. "Bottoms up." Downing her shot. "Come on. I'm not passing up on the two hottest guys at the party." Taking both of their hands and pulling them toward the music coming up from the basement. Where the dancing and loud music are. Samir intercepts the three of them by crossing their path. Jadon sees Angelique's hard look, only fleeting but getting the unspoken message. Shifting her gaze across the room to the clock. Excusing herself saying, "I'll be back." Seeing the questioning looks of the two men. "I have some hostess business."

Meeting Melinda and Angelique upstairs. Angelique says, "Is she coming?"

Melinda, "Yes. Everything is under control." Adding, "She will call me using her track phone. When she's able to slip away from that nightmare of an aunt. I'll leave and go pick her up at the bus stop near her house."

Jadon, "How appropriate. The help is waiting to help us by being our gift. I can't wait to see her."

Melinda, "She will look like a Lyell Avenue streetwalker." All three laugh with malicious delight.

Angelique, "Stay focused," cautioning. "Once you get her here make yourself scarce. Until time for the performance." Her face becomes serious eyes hard pupils narrowing. "Come to the spell room. We need to work a little magic on Aunt Norma." Both young women follow her into the dark arts room. Angelique casts her hand out across the room. Igniting candles she has placed for this occasion. Standing at three of the five points of an inverted pentacle. Angelique places a note written by Norma Campbell with some of her hair from a brush and some of her blood at the center. "Now concentrate ladies. On that cruel matronly woman. Focus your thoughts on this idea. Give her this suggestion, whisper it into her mind. Take the alprazolam with your tea. Nothing more." All three whisper the thought. Their intended Norma is to hear in her mind.

Ms. Campbell is sitting in her reading chair. Sipping the tea that her niece bought for her today. Enjoying it. Thinking maybe all her hard work is finally paying off. Mary might just actually become a decent Christian woman. Unlike that whore of a mother she was born to. *My sister, well, she got what she deserved. Now I'm raising her daughter the way she should have been raised. No easy way for her even if she is bright. I better go check on her. She is probably still watching TV.* Setting her teacup down getting up and going upstairs. Moving quietly as she always does easing up on her niece. Then walking into Mary's room without knocking. "It's time to turn that off and read your Bible."

Mary is startled by her silent approach and sudden entrance into the room. "My program will be over in a few minutes." Her tone irritated.

Aunt Norma, "You need to turn it off now. I don't like your tone and don't look at me like that." Her anger rising. "It's my home. As long as you live under my roof you'll do as you're told!" Mary gets up and switches off the old black and white TV set.

Aunt Norma, "Now I'll never get to sleep without aid. Get your Bible, girl! Start Leviticus! We'll discuss it tomorrow." Stamping out of the room leaving the door open. Going to the medicine cabinet taking out one of her alprazolam 0.5 mg tablets. Taking it downstairs with her to have some more tea. Her anger dissipating some sitting back down. Sipping her tea washing down the tablet. *I'm certainly deserving of a good treat. Even if it is from that ungrateful little sinner.* Picking her book up again, *Christian Heritage*. Yawning glancing at the clock just after nine o'clock.

CHAPTER 42

MINUTES EARLIER. UPSTAIRS at Angelique's home. Jadon removes the black fabric covering the mirror in Angelique's dark arts spell room. Angelique herself already focused on her intention. Casting her hand across her scrying mirror. Chanting, "Show me now what I seek. Mirror of truth bring forth the location. So that I may see her. The cruel one I so choose to control." Her own image with her two consorts in the background wavering, then dissolving. Their view now into Norms' living room and of her sitting in a worn easy chair while reading.

Angelique whispers as to Norma's ear, "Check on that girl so disrespectful. Now you will need something for sleep. Drink some more of that delightful tea it will help." Norma sets her book down going upstairs. Giving Mary her orders for the evening. After which stopping off at the medicine cabinet. Then coming back down to the kitchen.

Minutes later Jadon looks into the living room. Sees Ms. Campbell dozing in her chair. The book she was reading sliding off her lap to the floor with a dull thump. Mary comes into the room. Gently touching her aunt's shoulder. Telling her to go to bed.

Angelique breaks her concentration. Moving her hand over the mirror in the opposite direction. Thus the view in the mirror dissolving back to her own.

Melinda, "Well, are you satisfied?"

"Everything is going as planned. She will be calling soon enough."

Looking to Angelique, Jadon always the worrier asks, "How long will she sleep?"

Angelique, "Norma will get a good night's rest. However, I wouldn't want to be around her when she wakes up."

Jadon, "Why?"

Angelique, "As Melinda could tell you she will have a drug hangover. Knowing how moody and miserable she is on a good day. If I were Mary, I wouldn't want to cross her. At least not for a few hours until her head has cleared out. Now continue as planned." Melinda's cell phone rings.

"I'm the bartender so I better get into position," Jadon says. Her pulse quickening with thoughts of the impending fireworks to come.

Melinda lets her phone ring knowing it will increase Mary's anxiety.

Answering her phone on the third ring. "Hello, is everything all right? Good I'll be on my way." Mary nervously questioning her. "Of course you'll be home long before she wakes up." Rolling her eyes.

Angelique walking away with Jadon going over instructions. "You have the doses ready for our two guests of honor?"

Jadon, "Yes." Angelique not looking back as Melinda catches up with them. Locking the door to her suite. Everything blessed and charged. Not wanting some unwitting guest disrupting the sanctity.

Angelique, "Melinda once you have returned. I'll receive her as any gracious host would. I don't want her to feel ill at ease. You are to circulate and attach yourself to the elders keeping them amused. I'm sure a girl of talents should be able to do that." Angelique adds as an afterthought, "Watch yourself with Samir. He is a real ladies' man. He could charm the diamonds off a rattlesnake's back. If it were still long enough..." Not completing her comment out loud. 'and fuck it.'

CHAPTER 43

MARC AND CAMEL are enjoying themselves circulating amongst the guests. Visiting with old acquaintances both men feeling like they are being observed. Exchanging a glance that says more than they could speak about with so many ears around them. Camel notices a small group of Sunni Persians speaking intimately with a Romanian dignitary and his wife. Conversing softly amongst themselves the entire group pausing for a moment. Looking at Camel and then Marc knowingly almost excited. Marc turns his head away from them whispering to Camel, "Did you see that?"

Camel, "Yes."

Marc, "What was that all about?"

Camel, "I don't know, but I have a feeling after tonight a lot of things will be revealed." Looking distant.

Marc, "Revealed?"

Marissa moves up near Camel. Positioned herself craftily so he would pass before he saw her. Having used the taller Romanian dignitary to stand behind. "Hi handsome." Reaching up for a hug and a kiss. Camel leans over accommodating her.

Marissa, "I haven't seen you in days." Her thick red hair up in a French twist. Striking against her green blouse.

Camel, "I know, I have been busy with family interests." All the while moving them back toward the bar area.

Jadon, "Another round gentlemen?" Smiling up at Marc giving him a blink of her long dark lashes with those enchanting green-silver eyes. Pausing remembering his drink. "Glenlivet, rocks with a splash of water."

Marc finds her flirtations infectious smiling back. "Yes but make it a double. I don't want to be back so soon."

Jadon, "You don't want to be around me that much?" She says playfully.

Marc, "No. It's not that. I just wanted a good drink."

Jadon, "I was just giving you a hard time." Julia working next to her. Unable to keep her face neutral glaring at Camel with Marissa. If her thoughts could be heard: *The bastard. He's all around town like some tomcat.* Jadon reading Julia's look speaks up to defuse the potentially explosive situation. "And what is one of our invaluable hostesses going to have?"

Marissa, "Vodka stinger." Julia recovers quickly, retracting her nails now reminded of her function. Blinking innocently and managing a smile for the happy couple, Camel and Marissa. Julia sweeps her long corn silk like red hair away from her face with a hand. It's length mid back. Marissa recognizes Julia at the same time as she does. Julia rushing from behind the bar with a peal of laughter. Her black dress's décolletage dangerously close to spilling its full pale white contents. The men look on as the two women are hugging. Jadon not missing a perfectly timed distraction. Presses the release on her ring tapping it sending sprinkles of the tasteless white compound to falling over both of their drinks. A small vortex swirling up mixing it into the contents of their glasses.

Jadon, "Here you go gentlemen." Handing them their drinks. "Drink up!" Clinking glasses with them downing her false shot (tea). Jadon spies a friend of hers coming from around the bar over to her. Sarah hugs her, another redhead. Both men look at each other. Camel winks at Marc approvingly. Marc knows what the other is thinking. Camel really likes redheads with their milky white complexions.

Melinda appearing next to Marc. Speaking, "I've missed you." Hugging him closely kissing him on the lips. "I love the smell of scotch on your breath." Smelling his breath. Taking hold of his hand, they move away to a more private location.

Angelique arrives with Mary in tow. Introducing her to Jadon. Asking her, "Would you like a glass of wine or something else to drink?"

Mary, "Oh, uh, I don't drink alcohol."

Angelique smiles. "I'm sure one small glass of wine with friends isn't going to corrupt you. I won't tell anyone if you won't." Mary unsure. "Hold on to the glass and have just a sip on it every now and then. You can nurse it all night. That's what I do. I certainly couldn't maintain my poise as a hostess if I didn't."

Mary relaxes a little. "Well, I don't know."

Angelique, "Look." Her voice edgy. "You're dressed like a woman tonight act like one. No man is going to be interested in a child. Just hold it and sip." Mary giving in and accepts the glass of white wine Jadon has poured for her. Angelique and Mary both women looking for Marc, for different reasons. Angelique speaks under her breath, "Where does that little witch Melinda have him?"

Leaving Mary standing alone next to the bar. Wearing her new clothes hoping to impress a certain male. In her sheer red blouse with a red lacy bra and a short tight black skirt. Teetering on the four inch black Manolo Blahnik that Melinda had provided her with. Actually the highest heel she could walk in without falling. Even with this pair it was dicey at best. Angelique seeing her discomfort goes to her and says, "You look beautiful don't worry. Now arch your back and stand straight."

Mary complies looking more like a Barbie doll all grown up very shapely.

Marc with Melinda on his arm passes back into the billiards room. "Now that everything is under way I would like a glass of wine," Melinda says. Moving them over to where the bar is and coincidentally where Mary is standing alone. Using a tissue to wipe off her lipstick on Marc's lips. Saying, "That's not really your shade. Hi Mary you look gorgeous. Doesn't she Marc?" Turning to him. Marc's eyes are almost black now his pupils are so dilated. Leaving only the thinnest ring of blue exposed. Himself already feeling the effects of the compound slipped into his last drink. His body heat rising along with his libido. Readily agreeing with Melinda unable to take his eyes off Mary. Her light auburn hair long and thick trailing down her back. Her skin flawless and milky white. Other men turn already watching some less than discrete, Camel included. Gazing upon her with his black eyes undressing her. His swarthy and ruggedly handsome face appraising her.

Mary blushes unaccustomed to so much attention from men. Finishing her wine in a couple of gulps. Jadon already has another glass poured and ready for her. Says, "Here honey your glass is empty." Winking at her smartly.

Marissa, Camel's date gives him a nudge to get his attention back on her. He glances at her half listening. "Yes." Giving her a very intense sexual look into her eyes. His wavy dark hair usually short clipped has grown out and is pulled back in a short ponytail. Making his face more masculine and angular. Cocking his head to the side enjoying the view. Marissa endeavoring to have his full attention, finally succeeding. Causing her jealous anger to dissolve into an evil smile. Holding out her hand for him to take saying, "Come on let's go downstairs." As they're leaving, Camel sneaks another look at Mary. Nodding his approval to Marc as he passes. Marc sees this as encouragement to take another lusty look for himself.

Melinda seizes her chance everything falling into place perfectly. It's now or face a lost opportunity. She reaches up to grab Marcs' handsome sun-bronzed face. His reflexes fast using his arm to block her hand. But not before her long nails graze the skin, still not scratching it. His rough stubble having protected it. Melinda made even angrier by hurting her arm when it hit his large forearm block. "I'm not going to put up with my date undressing other women with his eyes. Right in front of me! Look at her! She's dressed like a whore! Is that what you want? Some Lyell Avenue streetwalker!" Her voice loud and carrying across the once noisy billiards room. Now all play at the tables ceased.

Julia behind the bar calls out, "Mary." Melinda takes a quick step over to Mary. Slaps her across the face hard. Mary cries out startled dropping her glass of wine; it shatters against the hardwood floor. Guests in the immediate area step back. Others gathering forward to see what just happened.

Marc immediately protective of Mary positions himself between the two women. Being very defensive on Mary's behalf says, "Melinda what are you doing!"

Mary, "Why would you do that? I thought we were friends!" Her eyes sparkling with tears gathering. More embarrassed than hurt from the spectacle she has become with so many watching her.

Melinda, "Friends? You are nothing more than a man-stealing tramp! Look at you feigning innocence." Throwing her champagne around Marc's broad upper body. The drink splashes down the front of her blouse and skirt.

Marc shouts, "Stop it! You're acting like a jealous maniac!" Their altercation having rippled out into the other room. Now a crowd of guests have gathered in the doorway from the adjoining room. Watching the scene unfold.

Melinda, "I can see who you are siding with! Little Ms. Innocent!" Her face twisted with rage.

Marc, "Babe it's not like that." Melinda swings to slap him across the face. Her hand blocked again, she turns and stamps away with her fists clinched at her sides. Her stiletto heels clicking loudly with all noise ceased, digging divots left in the hardwood floor. The knot of onlookers parts rapidly for her to pass. Marc takes a clean bar towel from Jadon. Gently blotting Mary's face and silk blouse. Her new blouse ruined by the champagne. Fighting to hold back tears, *Don't let them see you cry.* Her feelings hurt from Melinda's words. Marc folds Mary into his strong arms. Comforting her in his muscular hard arms just holding her. Mary buries her face in his chest crying. Too embarrassed to look at the crowd.

Jadon is delighted trying to stifle a smile. What a performance from Melinda. *I knew she was an Upper East Side princess, but what an engaging show.* Ducking her head in an effort to hide her smile trying not to look too pleased. Angelique watches from afar. Waiting for her time to step in and help Mary out. Her own cruel blue eyes smiling. While the rest of her face remains stone cold.

Angelique speaks to her guests, "The excitement is over! Go back to enjoying yourselves." Angelique comes over to Mary's aid. Speaking softly to her, "Are you all right?" Insinuating herself between them, nurturing. "Marc I have it from here." Taking Mary under her wing putting her arm around her shoulders. Speaking to both of them. "She just needs a moment and to freshen up. Come on, let's get you a little privacy." Marc hovering protectively. Angelique gives him a warning look cutting her eyes around towards his. Marc does not challenge her but is not backing off. "I'll show her to the second floor powder room. It's more private." Angelique takes charge guiding Mary away out of the billiards room past the kitchen. And then up the back stairs away from the crowded lower floors of her mansion. Taking her down a dark hallway mahogany paneled. Lit by a crystal chandelier wall sconces sparkling down on them from above the high ceilings sixteen foot. Their light lost against the paneling. Sounds from the party below muffled. Mary already beginning to relax some. Angelique pushes open a door leading into a posh modern bedroom suite.

Angelique, "These are my private quarters." Answering before Mary can ask. "That way you can freshen up in some peace and quiet."

Mary, "Thank you." Angelique directs her into the bathroom. Mary still frazzled yet oddly warm, beginning to relax further. Less fazed by the whole incident. Finding the lights in the bathroom too bright. Turning the dimmer switch lowering the lights. Blotting her face with a cool damp washcloth. Noticing how very soft it is. Then sitting down on the commode to pee. How good it feels not realizing how much she had to go. After washing her hands Mary comes out of the bathroom. Noticing the bed covered with a black duvet with ancient symbols woven into it. The sparkle of gold silk thread apparent in the symbols making them very beautiful. A dark blue Persian rug beside the bed with silk woven into it. These threads sparkling like distant stars of the night sky. Mary notices for the first time that the room is lit by candles and fragranced with myrrh. Angelique's maid appears with a silver tea service and tray with fine china on it set for two. Angelique breezes in directing her where to place it. Pouring them both some handing a cup to Mary.

"Here this will help soothe your nerves." Angelique places her lips against the cup appearing to take a sip. Mary takes a sip from hers finding it hot and bitter. Her hostess noticing her expression. "After a couple of sips it's less bitter. I usually drink this after a trying day. It's an old family recipe from my grandmother." Smiling at Mary. "Go on drink some more." Sounding motherly and innocuous. Mary sipping more finding what Angelique had said to be true. Drinking more deeply the bitter taste subsiding.

Angelique, "Now let's get you out of those wet clothes." Getting up moving over to her dressing room. Returning carrying a black silk robe handing it to Mary. "You go right back in the bathroom and change. I don't want you catching cold." Sounding more motherly than she ever would feel towards her or any child for that matter. Only too easy. *So why not be nice to this girl? She is going to give me exactly what I wanted.* Only just a little while longer after decades of patience being her only sustenance.

Mary becoming increasingly tactile more than she would ordinarily have been. The tea having its intended effect. Certainly more suggestible. Mary stands in the en suite spa unfastening her red lace brassiere. A Victoria's Secret knockoff her blouse ruined. Examining it with detachment she would never have had if it were not for the compound in her tea. Sliding on the silk robe so incredibly soft and caressing her skin as it moves. Luxuriating in it as she steps out into the bedroom. Angelique looks at the blouse. "That's a shame, champagne will stain silk. Sit down and finish your tea, angel." Her voice soothing, engendering trust. Patting the bed beside her. Her face a mask nearly choking on that last work. Certainly not one she ever wanted to use again, except if used in deception.

Angelique, "Are feeling a little more at ease?"

Mary complies sitting down but strengthening her resolve. "Yes. I don't think I want to go back to the party. Can someone take me home?"

Angelique, "I'm sure that can be arranged. What happened between you two? You were thick as thieves earlier." Mary finishing her tea. Angelique was right it's better with each taste. Feeling very soothed and much calmer now even a little slower to respond. Her affect becoming flatter no longer upset. Not a trouble on her face.

"Oh yes. She became jealous over Marc."

Angelique, "He is quite handsome."

Mary, "She said they weren't serious. And they aren't even exclusive. All I was doing is talking to him. I wasn't coming on to him."

Angelique, "Well, Melinda can be a bit territorial. I'm sure she feels badly now. Plus she has had a little too much to drink. By tomorrow she will be apologizing for the spectacle she made of herself."

Marys' attention span diminished examining the robe she is wearing more closely. Yellow gold runes scattered amongst constellations. Recognizing the twelve zodiacs from her astronomy classes. Odd she would notice this at all. Moving her black silk robe to examine one across her breast. That one unfamiliar to her. Mary observing, "You know those runes on the duvet are also in the china pattern."

"Yes, they are the same," Angelique answers, her face soft with contentment.

"It's quite fascinating and beautiful. I've never seen them used in a china pattern before."

Angelique, "No?"

"This china looks to be quite old if I do say so myself," Mary observes.

"They were my great-grandmother's made in another century," Angelique adds.

"I don't recognize this constellation," Mary says. As she becomes more confused and light-headed from the herbal tea with the compound mixed in it.

"You wouldn't be familiar with that constellation dear. It has not been seen in millennia. It was one from the zodiac known as the serpent." Her tone more that of a teacher instructing a child. Angelique changes the subject. "It's a shame so much is ruined by what time takes from us." "That is an odd thing to say for one so young. You almost sound like one of the elderly nuns I care for in Syracuse." Mary says having a moment of clarity. Angelique getting a deeper insight into the intuitive intelligence of this young women. A real shame that she wasn't one of her novices unlike the other two. Especially Melinda with her shortsighted and petulant nature. She will never be a great sorceress.

Mary leans back across the duvet with the room shimmering softly. Giving her the sensation of floating gently above the bed. "Thank you."

Angelique, "No. Thank you."

Mary, "This family recipe of yours is helping. You are so kind. I'm terribly sorry for the scene downstairs."

Angelique, "That was nothing forget about it. If that is the worst thing that ever happens to you, well, just forget about it." Trying to minimize the situation. "Don't worry about it. Haven't some of the girls at boarding school gotten frisky?" Mary listening to Angelique's voice continuing on calming and soothing almost melodic. Her voice moving between foreign words and some just audible but musical and sweet. Mary is at a suggestible mental state. "You know, Marc does seem to be showing you quite a lot of attention tonight. Or is it more than just tonight dear?" Her insight so helpful in tone. Time to plant her seeds of seduction the moment of realization coming to fruition. Having the natural patience for a mature woman well beyond a hundred years of age. Mary answers slowly, thoughtfully. "I hadn't noticed it that much. He always seems so into her every time she comes around. Do you really believe—?" Stopping herself from saying it.

Angelique surmises her unvoiced question, plans within plans it's so good when hard work bares out the final goal. Now to finish manipulating this upstairs maid. "Well, they were lovers at least until tonight. He certainly seems smitten with you. He couldn't take his eyes off you." Angelique manages a sincere expression for Mary. Using this altered mental state to manipulate her further. "And it's not like she isn't seeing other men. Why does she have to get them all? Don't you deserve some love?"

Mary feeling empowered says, "He is so ruggedly handsome. He would make a smart match if I say so myself." Becoming more confident as her pupils dilate to where the green is almost black.

Angelique, "Melinda isn't really interested in him anyway. She is just a tart! She's seeing other men you know." Sounding more like a confidante. Her accent becoming slightly British.

Mary, "Is she really?"

"Oh yes. She's one of those Upper East Side princesses. Does anything she pleases," Angelique answers.

Mary, "He'd be the only man I would ever need."

Angelique, "Well after her childish stunt tonight he is certainly going to be available. Besides, didn't she leave with another of her boyfriends?" Before Mary can respond she adds, "How are you feeling now?" Her tone concerned and attentively looking at Mary. Unable to recognize watchfulness.

Mary, "I'm feeling much better now and calmer." Leaning back against the headboard of the bed. Setting the empty cup next to herself on the soft duvet. "I'm a little warm." Fanning herself with one hand.

Angelique, "That's good angel make yourself comfortable. Now I have to check on my guests wait right here. I'm sure there is someone waiting anxiously to see how you are doing." Marc pacing out in the hall.

Mary, "I doubt he would want to have anything to do with me after everything that's happened tonight."

"Oh, I wouldn't be so sure about that. I bet he is anxious to know you are all right."

Mary, "It's so warm in here."

"Loosen the robe." Angelique tugs it open the top exposing pale milky skin. Unblemished by freckles. Made all the more pale by the robe's dark color contrasting with her skin. Natural cleavage that goes with a full figure. Her plans are going like clockwork. Knowing full well as she gets up crossing over to the door that when she opens it Marc will be waiting on the other side. Having noticed his pacing outside in the hallway moments earlier. Carrying the silver tray and her special china teacups rattling as she balances it on one hand to open the door. Stepping out into the hall. Closing the door quickly behind her.

Marc waits anxiously outside the room. Jadon has been out there with him keeping him occupied. Nothing left to chance Angelique feigns concern. "Oh good you're here."

"How is she doing?" Marc asks. His tanned skin and dark stubble covered face concerned. Marcs' beard so heavy now that he would always have a five o'clock shadow. Carrying his coat over his arm and tie loose. A little too warm for comfort but attributing it to the crowd. A lot of people forget to compensate with central air-conditioning.

Angelique, "Much better now. She wants to see you. Here I'll hang your coat up." Unbuttoning the second button of his shirt and tugging his tie off. The silk sliding quickly from around his neck. Allowing his shirt to open. Dark hair spilling out at the top of his shirt. Angelique says, "I'll put it in your coat. She is fine and asking for you." Smiling sincerely.

Jadon looking concerned, says, "We'll leave you two alone duty calls. If you need anything just let us know." Marc is already moving past her into the candlelit room. Jadon closes the door after him quietly.

Mary propped up against pillows on the black duvet. Her milky skin luminescent where it is exposed through the gap in the robe. Marc's eyes rove over her shapely chest then back up her eyes incredibly sexy looking. Marc sits on the side of the bed next to her. His weight causing the mattress to dip slightly. Gravity does the rest her body sliding over causing their thighs to touch.

"Hi. Are you all right?" Marc says. His voice a rich baritone.

Mary, "I'm much better now. I'm so sorry. I didn't—"

Marc stops her. "It's not your fault at all. I don't know what to say. She has never acted like that before and she has always made it clear we're not exclusive. Repeatedly." Both become aware of their thighs touching. The spark of sexual energy charged rippling over both of them in waves of warmth. Marc's breath catching in his throat as he looks into her green eyes for recognition. His mind already racing how silky smooth her skin looks. Allowing his eyes to follow the robe down to the small gap. Blood rushing to his organ making the way he's sitting uncomfortable. Mary looks into his blue eyes. Reaches up to tenderly brush a hand against his cheek razor stubbled. Rough as she had suspected this blue-black coarseness of manhood. Marc's five o'clock shadow pronounced and making him more swarthy under the candlelight. Her mere touch of his face sending rushes of excitement through her in this uninhibited state. Their brew the tea recipe having its true intended effect. Her face flushed and warmed as waves reach deep into her body. The aphrodisiac having its timely planned results. Along with some unforeseen side effects, being those innate abilities that have lain dormant. Only needing a gentle push to come to the forefront.

Unsure of herself lightly running her fingertips over Marc's thick cupid lips. Lost in his intense deep blue eyes with desire rising. Marc's skin radiating heat strong enough to feel without touching him. Her simple touch against his lips raising his fever of carnal desire ever higher. Causing his body to release airborne pheromones impossible to detect overtly. Her body unconsciously responds to them as she inhales them. Marc reads her signals subtle though they may be the right ones. His pants painfully tight now. Leaning forward gently brushing his lips against hers. His mouth already watering as he parts her moist lips with her tongue meeting his. Encouraged he slides his hand inside her robe. Caressing her marble white yet soft breast delicately rubbing its light pink areola. Marc's hand creates the sensation of extra fine sandpaper brushing against her soft skin. His fingers rough from all the recent stonework. Mary's tactile senses heightened by the compound and enthralled by his pheromones. She is completely reduced to a quivering mass of tactile thrills unimagined before now. By the one man that could do this to her. Marc from the day she met him kind to her. Innocent in the way that young men are before numerous encounters with women jade them. Leaving only one thing on their mind.

This is everything she always dreamed of and more. Since the day she met him. He would be her first and only true love. Remembering only now dream of dreams it was finally happening. Waves of euphoria mixed with warmth rapidly rushing down her spine. Increasing as he softly kisses her neck moving down it. The black silk robe teasing her skin as it slides off her shoulder. Marc follows the fabric down with his lips. Mary feeling just a little vulnerable with her chest exposed. But trusting this man so carefully touching her. Unbuttoning Marc's shirt increasing the heady smell of cologne mixed with his own masculine chemistry intoxicating. Engulfing her olfactory senses which in turn signals her limbic system for pleasure. That with the occasional brush of his stubble covered jaw as he kisses just under her pale areola. Scratching her sensitive skin but not too coarsely. Causing her to moan from deep within her throat. A breathy feminine sound rising up out of her mouth. Unable to repress this sound. No longer caring about who might hear it. Marc stops long enough for her to say no. As he would never force a woman.

Mary looking him in the eyes responds, "Yes," in a deep breathy womanly voice she's never heard before. Yet it is her own voice. Marc needs no further encouragement ripping open his shirt the rest of the way buttons flying off it. His broad muscular chest covered by a thick but soft dark brown pelt. Mary's eyes follow his hands as he stands up unfastening his belt. Pants dropping to the floor relieving some of his discomfort. His boxers tight he pulls them down for relief from confinement. Mary stares at his helmeted organ in all its unfolded reach above his navel. Not quite sure herself what to do, but not frightened either.

Marc watching her carefully lies down beside her. Avoiding rushing her and not wanting to have their first time over in seconds. Cupping her face in his hands both of them looking into each other's eyes. Could she be the right girl or is this just lust? Their lips touching moving to open mouth kissing, passionately and deeply tongues together exploring. Marc heated with desire rolls on top of her using his strong hard legs. Mary gasps a whisper in his ear, "Slowly my angel." Her body quivering with excitement and apprehension. Marc's hard muscular body pressed against hers. Surprised at how soft his dark hirsute chest with the band all the way down his abdomen feels against her skin. Feeling his hard pulsing strength with its own heat against her. Not having joined yet.

Downstairs the party goes on with the true intended party guests having gathered nearby upstairs. Chanting an incantation as the Louis XVI mantel clock chimes the time. Along with the grandfather clock in the billiards room. New pledges are giving their allegiance to the sorority. Some more knowledgeable of their actual intended membership. Helping to pull energy in the house to a fevered pitch. The culmination of all their efforts happening at once, clocks chiming, music booming, pledges chanting, the tremulous sky outside rumbling in warning. Excitement from intentions made known to all the powers beyond mortal perceptions. Stirring from out of distant planes. Causing the fabric of time to bend. One from the cull to be torn from it and released again. All of heaven to bear witness.

Angelique delights in the fruition of years of planning finally coming together. Finally having her one true chance at the ultimate power. Now all of the elders would have to give her the respect and deference that was her due. Even Samir wouldn't be able to hold her past misfortune against her. He would have to acknowledge her accomplishment. That arrogant Arabian bastard so confident and disdainful of her. His square jaw set in disapproval. As if they weren't equals having been lovers. Admittedly he is much older but not her superior.

The elders gathered around completing the circle around the inverted pentacle. In the adjacent room its ceiling no longer visible. Instead the clear night sky with its stars flowing through the constellations blurring past across the heavens. Odd not only because of the speed they are passing by. But strange in that their direction is reversed. If it were possible the sun would be rising in the western sky. Accelerating into millennia past within a matter of seconds. Until an ancient constellation reappears, rejoining the twelve representing the zodiac. Then just as quickly the night sky slows back to the crawl of regular time movement. This long lost constellation of the zodiac, the serpent, having drifted away from Sol's galaxy from the expanding universe. Angelique using herself as the thirteenth person in the coven representing the serpent.

Upstairs Mary's eighteenth birthday is arriving. As she cries out in pain and pleasure. Finally having the man of her dreams. How else could it be? The two of them as one in complete sync to her passions. Then his, Marc unknowing of that one fact. However having been altered psychosexually just a nudge and physical training for this explicit purpose all culminating at this moment. Gentle enough to enter even with his size and still plenty of natural moisture to spare. Driving and focusing their fevered pitch of release not once but repeatedly. Their energy being channeled by him with direction coming from the group in the next room. Needing all of them to control his strength gracefully and gently, yet so precisely to the source of life. Spirals of his own energy pulsing against a ripe ovum to push ovulation that a woman can feel. Mary gasps from the microsecond of pain that is her Mittelschmerz. Unaware of what just happened to her. This not a sensation that had occurred to her before or would again and be conscious of it. Now only their driving needs exist.

CHAPTER 44

JADON AWAKENS MARY hours later. Quietly so as not to disturb Marc. Handing her some casual clothes that were put away by Melinda expressly for this occasion. The ride home for Mary is one of excitement. Charged from her experience with Marc. Her cheeks are blushing with a rose pink cast to them.

"You are positively glowing." Jadon observes. Mary smiling placing a hand to her cheek. Still unable to believe it actually happened.

Mary, "I cannot remember ever being this happy." Her cheerful delight infectious enough for Jadon to forget the unpleasantness of her true intentions. Those of betrayal destroying what could have been a genuine friendship. Unlike that of her current associates. Early morning light just beginning to brighten the street in patches. As dawn breaks through the thick foliage of the mature trees. Her own joy short lived as the car slows before her aunt Norma's house. Mary's happiness changing to dread followed by outright fear. Just now beginning to realize how late she was getting home. Acid rising up in the back of her throat. Jadon pulls the car over a few houses away from their destination. Cutting the headlights off. Letting the engine idle coasting over to the curb in neutral as close as she would dare. Observing the lights still off at aunt Norma's' house. The entire street quiet except for her heart pounding in her ears. That and the soft purr of a high-performance engine. Sunday newspapers still lying in driveways where they had been tossed earlier.

Mary sitting in the passenger seat for a moment longer. Dreading getting out of the car a chill rushing over her. Not from cold air but her reality upon her pushed by kismet all too real for comfort. Making her hand tremble as she starts to reach for the door handle. Bracing herself time to be strong. Only the thinnest slice of happiness and joy from one night spent with Marc all she may ever have. Wishing for a lifetime with Marc. Strengthening her resolve to face what could be coming. Questioning herself which door to use. Which one would aunt Norma will be least likely to catch her coming in through so late. If she wakes her up shuddering at that thought. Life will be an absolute misery.

Jadon feeling so sorry for Mary. Knowing how her own father would react. If she was caught sneaking in. Feeling helpless herself to stop the chain of events that were already unfolding. Having been set in motion years ago. The time not right yet to do more unless she puts everything in jeopardy. Which has been so meticulously constructed. *We all have our parts to suffer for the better good.*

Jadon ends both of their silent ruminations. "Do you think she is awake? The lights aren't on in the house."

Mary, "She's a light sleeper if she isn't already up." Not finishing her thought. She couldn't dare to hope for one more hairsbreadth of salvation. Guilt mixed with fear prevailing. How could she have been so careless to fall asleep afterward.

Jadon, "Would she leave the lights off?"

"Yes, she wanders around the house with the lights off frequently. Saving on the electric bill, you know. Besides nothing fires her up more than letting me think I got away with it. Then busting me with all her vicious glory," Jadon now really feels bad for her. Trying to be encouraging yet only wanting to get the hell away from here.

Jadon, "Maybe she won't be awake yet." Sounding lame even to herself.

Mary, "Yes, maybe." Reaching for the door handle her hand already begun to trembling. Forcing it not to shake. The door release clicks open barely audible but even that is loud with her heightened senses.

Jadon, "Good luck." Mary slowly steps out of the low sports car. Soreness from last night a reminder of Marc. Pushing the car door closed quietly. It was thrilling to have him in that way. He was all male. Her happy memory fading with the thin wisps of early morning. As the shadows lighten with increasing speed. Mary sneaks across the street like a burglar. Acid burning in the pit of her stomach. Fear mixed with dread pumping her adrenaline higher yet. Walking lightly up the sidewalk of the sleeping neighborhood. Quiet except for her breath and an occasional footstep. Echoing across the neatly clipped lawns causing her to wince. Easing up to the house listening for any signs of movement inside. Peeking through a window in the living room. No lights on yet everything still. Just maybe she isn't awake yet. Perspiration dampening her simple cotton blouse. Pausing at the corner of the house. Which door to use? The front or the side door? Choosing the side door. The living room has those first few floorboards by the door. Those could be creaky if you didn't step just right knowing how light aunt Norma sleeps, why chance it? Going instead to the side door. Gently inserting her key into its dead bolt. Turning it slowly hearing it click open. Freezing in place, again listening for any sounds from inside the house. Nothing, satisfied it's safe to go in. Pushing the door lightly which will not budge. Damn door the humidity must have expanded it. Putting her shoulder into it hitting it with a bump. It swings open fast. Mary stumbles in after it trying to prevent it from slamming into the wall. Aunt Norma standing there; Mary lets out a startled gasp. Aunt Norma's face glowering with anger.

Norma, "Thought you'd sneak in didn't ya?" Not waiting for her to answer. "I can't stand little sneaks. Where have you been all night?" Jadon's white sports car passes by gaining speed. Aunt Norma spots this expensive vehicle before it's passed. Mary recovered from the initial shock of her aunt surprising her coming in. The beginning of her worst nightmare coming to pass. Fear of a different kind spreading through her mind, the unknown. What would she do to her?

"Well? What have you to say for yourself?" Aunt Norma demands. Switching on the overhead light. Her aunt's face ugly on a good day, but under this light every deep wrinkle a crevice with her cragged neck like a Shar-Pei. Anger twisting it into something even uglier if that was possible. It becomes ruddy with the corners of her mouth turned down into those prominent frown wrinkles rutted into her cheeks. A hard life and miserable from it.

"I was out with a friend. I didn't realize it had become so late." Mary grasping at an answer. Her voice soft and almost childlike but undeniably feminine. Just like her mother's. Making Norma angrier.

"With a male friend!" Norma says. Not a question.

Mary desperate, "No! I spent the night at a friend's. A girlfriend's it was Jadon." Giving more information than necessary like all poor liars. Unable to hide the guilt after just lying to her aunt. Never really having developed that talent. Unlike so many of her classmates having learned how to alibi themselves. Twisting up a story skillfully like Melinda could leaving nothing to chance getting caught.

Aunt Norma eyes her face closely. "You should have called." Using the pretext of concern to smell Mary's breath leaning closer. "I smell alcohol and men's cologne on you. You're lying! You weren't at a girlfriend's at all, were you? Look at me." Reaching out taking hold of Mary's chin turning her head to the side examining at her neck and then face more closely.

"You have whisker burns and love bites on your neck." Her fair complexion having given her away. Norma releases her grip. "Get in the house before the neighbors see you coming like some whore!" Mary rushes past her aunt heading toward the stairs to go to her room.

Aunt Norma, "Where do you think you are going! I expect an answer. Who were you with?"

Mary, "I was with Jadon we spent the night together." That not being a total lie.

Aunt Norma, "Lying to me will only make me more angry." Her arms folded across her chest patting her foot waiting for Mary to speak.

"I'm eighteen now. I can sleep over—"

Norma interrupts her. "You're a liar! Just because you are eighteen doesn't make it legal in this country. I knew you shouldn't have been raised in Europe. I have to call the police back and let them know who gave you the liquor.

"Well? I want the truth! You spent the night with a man. And he gave you alcohol under age? Who was he?" Mary refuses to answer her fearing Marc would be blamed. Locking herself down emotionally, her affect flatting. Norma smells the cologne on Mary. Trying to rattle her. "That cologne familiar. I'll figure out who it was."

Mary blushing now, saying, "No." Her eyes downcast towards the floor.

Norma, "You look just as guilty as your mother did. When she had been out carousing with men. That's how she was with your no account Brit father. I won't have you behaving like a whore! Not under my roof."

"I'm not!" Mary tries to defend herself but not well at all.

Aunt Norma, "Don't take that tone with me! If you're not going to say who it was then get upstairs and get dressed. Put on your maid's uniform. It's Sunday. Since you were out sinning you can make atonement by working for the day. That basement at the manor needs cleaning out."

Mary halfway up the stairs, "I need to freshen up."

Aunt Norma, "Don't bother with showering. You can wear your boyfriend's sweat on you until you're done working tonight." Yelling up the stairs at her. "We're leaving in the next few minutes. Now go!" Mary already withdrawing into her mind behind high walls that she built years ago used to protect herself. Just as she would when Sister Ann was doling out corporal punishment. Directly from Aunt Norma's instructions. That and Sister Ann's own philosophy right out of the Bible. "Spare the rod and spoil the child." Those trust fund girls might get away with everything, but a few of you were going to be righteous.

Norma's head is pounding from a drug hangover and she is feeling mean. She wants to be a sinner; then she can do penance. "Hurry up and get in the car!" Yelling again.

CHAPTER 45

MARC WAKES UP to a darkened room with his arm across her waist. Feeling the warmth of Mary's body next to his pressed against him. Her body moving ever so gently, moaning softly. Wanting nothing more than her wrapped around his full length as he lightly kisses her neck. Angelique's house quiet after the celebration having lasted until sunup. Turning over into his strong arms locking on to his lips kissing and taking it in. Melinda delights in his surprised expression. Marc lets out a quick breath, not speaking unsure of what happened last night. Thinking, *What the—? How did she get here?*

Melinda takes it all in enjoying herself. Says, "Hello, tiger. You were incredible last night. So attentive to my needs. So driven to please. I don't think I've ever had so many orgasms." Smiling her blue eyes devious. Leaning in nipping his thick bottom lip. Pulling away giving a giggle. Enjoying his confused expression her reward. That and of course his thick hardness pressed between her legs. Melinda rolls away from him getting out of bed nude.

Melinda, "You smell incredibly masculine and of sex. This room is strong with its scent." Marc becoming heady from arousal. Shower water running in the background bringing him back. Completely having missed her departure into the bathroom. Melinda's nude body steps in front of the floor-length mirror. Shifting her hips side to side appreciating the image. Her glamour becoming ethereal, dissolving back into the real image of the woman creating it. Smiling back at herself ever so delighted with herself. Pushing short blonde hair back from her face a smug and contented look on it. Moving her hands over her face and body restoring her glamour. Melinda calls out to Marc, "Are you coming? I'm getting lonely in here!" Marc gets up quickly letting the sheet fall onto the floor. His hairy olive-skinned buttocks contrasting with his sun-bronzed brown back and equally hairy legs. Not wanting to appear over anxious, he strolls into the master bathroom spa. Unnoticing of his black hair well past shoulder length, thick and mane like.

Stepping into the shower right into an embrace. Energy shimmers over his body as water splashes on it. Melinda runs her hands over Marc's back, kissing his chest, biting just hard enough to reach the skin beneath. Gathering energy as she stimulates him into higher musk yet. Adoring his power, allowing him to enter her warmth, thus increasing his energy further. Marc unaware of her true intentions. Going on as he is lost in passions' lust seeking only the higher level of physical sensations. All to please her and then himself through her. His altered desires increasing the longer he is under her spell. She knows at some point there will be no return to normal human male satiation. But then after all, there have to be some sacrifices to achieve her ultimate goals.

Melinda finally pulls free from him under protest as he wanted more of her, herself satisfied. "Oh well." Leaving him to finish his shower as men have from time immemorial. Water spraying over his large shoulders giving them high pressure pulses from special heads. Sending waves of pleasure onto his skin. Not needing to turn water spraying from multiple jets striking his upper body. Then lingering on the armpits with his solid arms raised above his head. The warm rush of water feeling ever so good streaming down his body. So like a summer's warm deluge of rainfall. Finally deciding he has had enough of this hedonistic pleasure. Hunger pains driving his next actions. Ravenous like a primal creature of mythology. Needing sustenance after all the physical exertion overnight. Toweling his long hair just enough to keep it from dripping. Then running his fingers through it like a comb to get it out of his face. Grabbing another from the towel warmer to dry his body. The first towel too wet to do much good.

Stepping in front of the floor to ceiling mirror. Almost not recognizing himself. His dark hair much longer than it was the day before. *Huh, it seems to grow every time I have sex.* His angular jaw dark from thick stubble giving off a blue-black sheen. Marc's sapphire blue eyes sparkling mischievously. As his mind wonders back to his dream of Mary from last night. It was so real. Her auburn hair like corn silk brushing across his chest. And that soft milky white skin of hers under his hands. All this sending blood rushing south. Standing beside the bed he can almost smell her perfumes' light scent of flowers (four-o'clocks). Sitting on the bed pulling on his socks her perfumes scent is even stronger. Turning and looking at the bottom sheet in the center are dried rusty colored smudges. What the heck? Then noticing a piece of lavender lacy material just under the black duvet at the foot of the bed. Same as in his dream of Mary but she had on red lace lingerie. Putting his face to them smelling perfume with a womanly scent. Pulling the duvet up off the floor seeing the same golden yellow runes woven into its fabric.

Questioning himself, was she here? Stunned and yet happily surprised. Getting up and pulling his pants on. Then seeing red underwear on the floor. Examining it, Mary's? The question teasing at his memory. Before stuffing the red lacy lingerie into his pants pocket. Déjà vu creeping into his consciousness with that unsettling sensation moving over him. *Could this have happened again to me? What the heck is going on here?* Rushing downstairs not taking time to button his shirt just on flapping behind him. Ready to confront Melinda.

The house spotlessly clean and empty as if no one had been there the night before. Walking through several rooms devoid of anyone. He finds Angelique drinking coffee in the breakfast nook off the kitchen. Looking ever so pleased with herself.

Angelique, "Coffee darling?" Glancing over to the maid. "What a marvelous party if I say so myself." Marc searching for Melinda, his anger rising.

Marc, "Where is she?"

Angelique, "Sit, have some coffee." Nodding her head for the maid to approach and pour his coffee. "Who darling? Melinda?"

Marc, "Who else?"

Angelique, "You could be asking about Mary or some other debutante."

"What happened to Mary? She was here?" he asks.

Angelique takes a sip of her coffee a smug but satisfied smirk on her face. Looking to content. "Which question do I answer first? Melinda, well she had to leave. Something about studies and a research paper due. Sit, please Marc." Marc gives in needing some coffee to clear his mind. The scent of dark French roast superb, obviously imported. Angelique continues, "There you go, slow down for a moment. My gathering was a smashing success. Everyone enjoyed themselves."

Marc gives her a dubious look. "Really? What happened to Mary?"

Angelique, "She went home. Jadon gave her a lift." Marc relaxes some. "You were quite the party favorite yourself," Angelique adds.

Marc drinks his hot coffee a little too quickly, burning his mouth. "Yeah? Nice party. What I can remember of it, but strange."

Angelique ignoring his comment goes on. "I had fun. Didn't you?" Taking another sip of her coffee before setting it down. Making a clinking sound that of fine porcelain. Marc watches her face closely knowing she is leading up to something he didn't remember.

Angelique, "After all, how many women did you bed last night?" Marc takes pause with the coffee cup frozen at his cupid lips trying to remember. Angelique enjoying herself entirely too much playing her catty game with him. She continues, "At least three I know of, maybe more. You are quite the stud. I guess men can be whores too." Marc swallows before putting on his poker face. Getting onto her game unwilling to give her any more satisfaction. That last statement of hers making him unable not to react to. Last night was all a blur more like a dream. But somehow this was all beginning to feel more than just a coincidence. Like a setup and he was just a pawn to be used and then sacrificed. As happens to all pawns, they are expendable once their use has been served.

Marc, "Yes, you're right. I'm certainly not complaining." His thick dark hair beginning to dry falling forward. Using his large hand to push the long corn silk but dark hair back out of his face. Thinking, *What the hell is all this about?* Even his body was a mystery. His hair had never been long like some heathen's. Maybe his beard but that had been full since he was twelve. After all he was a devout Muslim. He didn't need to shave. That was this American no Roman custom.

Angelique, "That is a beautiful ring. When did you get it?" Her icy blue eyes narrowing as she loses her smug content expression.

Marc, "This? It was part of my late uncle's estate."

Angelique, "Odd uncle Robert never mentioned any jewelry. It's very beautiful, I wouldn't wear a heirloom like that just anytime. It could get damaged or lost." Staring at the ring from afar feeling its' power emanating from it. Discreetly keeping her distance avoiding asking to see it up close. Why hadn't she noticed it before upstairs? It must have been cloaked somehow.

"I'll keep that in mind." Marc answers. Drawing her attention back.

Angelique, "Since it is a family heirloom you should take care to preserve it for your progeny." Changing the subject not wanting to arouse Marc's suspicions about the ring. "You keep this up and you may catch up with Camel. Oh but then you haven't had any die yet. Have you?" Her smug look returning.

Marc looking her right in the eyes across the table from him. Answers her, "No." Unsure how to respond to this revelation. How did she know about that? Have the police made the connection? His tan face becoming a shade paler. "What are you talking about?" Marc feigning ignorance

Angelique, "Come now, you're his brother and close confidant. How could you not have heard these same rumors circulating. I have my sources and they are telling me that some of Camel's casual love interests have been turning up dead. Under mysterious circumstances and not just a few." Taking another sip of her coffee managing not to take her eyes off him. Marc attempting to remain stoic and unreadable.

Angelique, "You haven't heard about their deaths? He just may need a good trial litigator."

Marc, "No! If I had, I wouldn't be at liberty to discuss something that serious and of a personal nature."

"Not even with his girlfriend? One who is a close family friend of yours as well? At least I think of you as a dear friend." Avoiding saying "a trusted friend." That would be an outright lie. "Sometimes you have to be careful of who your known associates are. At least that's what uncle Bob says." Her threat clearly directed at Marc.

"This coffee is almost good. I prefer a Columbian grown bean not roasted so darkly. Are you offering uncle Robert's services as a litigator?" Returning a backhanded comment.

Angelique's pupils narrowed. "When did I suggest that?"

Marc standing up. "You didn't. I have to leave now. I'll show myself out." Checking his pockets for his keys.

Angelique, "Your keys are in the foyer. Where I had the valet place them after you remained upstairs. After all most of my other guests went home." Marc gives her a questioning look.

Angelique, "While you were detained."

Marc, "Yes right." His mind flashing back to parts of the night. Beginning to remember more.

Angelique, "Thank you for coming to our gathering. You helped make *le rite de passage* a complete success. Without you it just couldn't have gone as devised." Her round blue eyes icy and cruel. Whatever did his brother see in her?

Marc, "Anything to be of help." Thinking to himself, *That was an odd thing to say.* "You have a nice day. As always it was interesting conversing with you."

Angelique, "Yes likewise. With you there is always more than just another handsome face. I'm sure I will see you soon." Marc begins to understand there was subterfuge here artfully disguised. Himself and his brother ensnared and this time there would be damage. Lifelong that much he was sure of.

Closing the solid oak door after him. *Sooner than you will ever know.* "I don't know how anyone with so much potential could be so oblivious to what is going on around him." Jadon appears a shimmer from out of a Louis XVI mirror in the adjacent dining room.

Jadon, "Aren't most men?"

Angelique, "Yes that is true as a rule but not always. Some are intelligent and not so self-absorbed. Those are the ones you have to be careful about." Changing the subject. "You are getting good at that. Just be mindful, listening in sometimes you can get your feelings hurt or worse." Looking right through her.

Jadon, "I don't usually pick up on what other people are thinking when I'm traveling." Clarifing herself as not ease dropping.

Angelique, "I wouldn't make it a habit around here." Making a mental note to herself. To watch out for that one. She's getting stronger every day now. Add that to intelligence with cunning making for a deadly combination. *I may have to retire her sooner than later.*

Angelique, "Come on let's go to brunch at the Brook House. I could go for a stiff Bloody Mary. How about you?"

"That sounds perfect. Certainly not a Virgin Mary," Jadon agrees.

Angelique, "Well, not anymore."

"You could say we did have one last night. At least Marc did." Both of them laugh at their crass double entendre.

CHAPTER 46

MARC WALKING DOWN the cobblestone driveway feeling exceptionally relaxed. His classic 1968 Mustang parked under the shade of mature Sycamore trees branching from both sides of the street. This area kept cooler because of them on an otherwise hot sunny day. Getting into his car turning the engine over with a deep rumble. Checking the time almost noon on a Sunday. His stomach gurgling to remind him he hasn't had anything to eat since yesterday. Suddenly becoming ravenously hungry. Planning that after breakfast the hammock will be the perfect way to spend such a day. Relaxing outside wearing shorts and a tank top or no shirt at all. Since the house will be empty. Heck, being that it's Rochester. He could lie around in the back gardens nude being that it is legal. Not that it would matter. It's so completely private back there no one could see him anyway.

Arriving home pulling in the driveway he sees Ms. Campbell's late model station wagon. Parked near the side entrance. Pulling into one of the garage bays closing the electric doors. *Huh, I thought she was off today.* Hoping as he comes in through the side entrance she won't be around to see him. Passing down the hallway quietly before nearing the kitchen. Hesitating for just a moment leaning back peering in quickly. Seeing no one speeding his pace to get upstairs and change into comfortable summer clothes. Still wearing his dress clothes from last night. Nix the nudity out back. Not that he really cares if she saw him without clothes. But it would be better not to hear the complaining about moral behavior from that old witch. Wondering if Mary had come in to work with her. Ready to go search for her but having second thoughts. Not wanting to embarrass her or arouse the suspicions of her commandant aunt. If indeed something had happened between them. Why had she left? How had Melinda replaced her without him knowing? Last night had to have been a dream, but it was so real. Still remembering the light sweet scent of her perfume on her skin. That was so creamy and so very soft to the touch. His thoughts making him become aroused. Definitely not a good idea to go look for her. Wait and see.

Marc changes into a comfortable pair of carpenter shorts and an old white ribbed undershirt. Gathering the family bible and grimoire to continue his search for clues as to what's going on. Stuffing both books with extra writing paper and pens into a book bag. With it slung over his solid cannonball shoulder.

Choosing the back stairs to go unnoticed and retreat outside. Guarding his peace and quiet by taking the stairs lightly. If that is at all possible for a two hundred pound male all muscle to do. The strong smell of bleach wafting up to hit his nose as he comes down the back stairs. The smell coming up from the basement. Nodding his head. It could use a good cleaning. Assuming Ms. Campbell must be down there cleaning. Passing piles of old junk and garbage bags just inside the door. Taking the opposite direction going out one of the back doors using the new flagstone path. Leading out to the private terrace garden where the hammock is already set up.

Finally settled into the hammock swaying Marc pulls the books out of his book bag. The grimoire has smoky wisps curling up from it. Thinking it must be dusty the way sunlight was catching the particles. Disregarding the angle of dappled sunlight. Choosing the bible first reading over the oldest dates and names first. Their dates starting in the early sixteen hundreds. As expected most of the names are French. One name appears familiar, a Marie Jeanette Lametz le Noir. How could that be? She was born over two hundred years ago. Not in the sixteen hundreds. Marc skims the names for another Marie le Noir. Several Maries but not her. It must be a mistake. How could his great-great-grandmother have been born more than four hundred years ago?

Marc tries to envision what she was like. Her name written so gracefully and sweeping. Someone well educated had entered her name. People don't inscribe names with that style anymore. Reading down the list of names to the present. His uncle Theron M. Du Bois, along with his own and cousin Phillip Du Bois. Growing drowsy in the warm afternoon heat under the dappled shade. That and the occasional breeze to sway the hammock. Feeling so soothed and relaxed just content. Marc tosses the bible onto the round tabletop. Tiled in shades of blue Arabian in pattern but French in the wrought iron frame. Taking a long drink of his mint iced tea. Setting the glass carefully back on the table while swaying from the hammock.

Now for the grimoire. Opening the old leather bound tome. Searching again for where Angelique had read from paging through the book. A light breeze rises up blowing across the book sending its pages fluttering. Annoyed with that putting his hand down stopping it abruptly. He skims over the page reading the cursive written French. Gracefully scripted and oddly similar to another's handwriting. His mind drifting back to last night. "Busy" would be putting it mildly. Marc's eyes growing heavy and his body so warm, he blinks back sleep. Tugging his undershirt off now, blissfully comfortable. Was it true that last night he had finally made love to Mary? Marc's eyes becoming heavier with sleep that he tries to blink it away. Where was that passage she chanted from? His chin drifts down touching his chest. A light breeze brushes over his cashmere soft chest pelt. As if the very air was grooming and caressing him with its warmth. The pages turning slowly at first but rapidly increasing in speed. As an unseen force pushes them faster until they are fluttering. This very sound rousing him from his sleep. Stopping as chosen just as abruptly the page where his search would begin.

Reading there a name that is foreign and strange to him but somehow it is familiar. That strange name Enkil. Shade covering part of the garden now. In the late afternoon it's peaceful and quiet. Just the occasional rustle of leaves. Mimicking the patter of rain in the upper part of the trees surrounding the secluded garden. Marc keeps trying to focus his eyes on the page. Coming back to that name Enkil. Repeating it softly to grasp at it. Marc says it louder with a more Arabic pronunciation, "Enkil." Just before sleep overtakes him in this warm and safe place. The hammock swaying gently.

Confusing dreams of people and places from other centuries come and go. Daylight giving way to darkness outside. Another warm and clear summer night sky with its denizens winking into view. Stars of late July rising across the sky. Orion's Belt far to the south Ursa Minor rising.

Marc wakes up with a start from that some dream again. Where the blonde women is calling out to him, "Mon fils!" Her native tongue French. Only this time he saw her powdered white face. Her name is Marie. Swinging his legs over the side of the hammock letting them dangle.

Wow, I slept all afternoon. Slowly coming to realize something is not right. Sensing the presence of someone else in the darkest shadows watching him. Right there in the garden with him. Hair at the nape of his neck and arms rising up. It's been waiting patiently for him to wake up. Marc becomes alert all at once. Dropping out of the hammock. Landing solidly on his bare feet being dug into by the sharp course gravel. The grimoire falling to the ground thudding. Already in a defensive crouch his hands up and ready for an assault. Adrenaline pumping Marc straining to see, instead hearing the crunch of gravel under foot turning his head towards the empty blackness. Knowing it is there coming.

"Who's there!" Marc shouts out. Movement imperceptibly from within the shadowy blackness hidden by the starlight. A figure moves toward Marc. Only discernible by the absence of what is around it.

"You're trespassing!" Marc's voice a low growl. Ready to fight this large unrecognizable male form. Male because of its broad shoulders.

Marc, "Camel?" His large shadowed figure just an outline visible under the starlight. "You scared the hell out of me. Asshole!" Shaking from the effects of his adrenaline rush, not fear itself. Marc relaxes his stance, straightening up.

A deep bass voice answers, "You called for me. I'm not Camel."

Marc looks at Camel under the starlight. What game is he playing tonight?

"Okay. Good to see you." Ignoring the game. "I wanted to talk to you about last night. There is something strange about Angelique and her alumni, with those sorority sisters. At least some of them. I believe they are up to something bad." Seconds pass by in silence. Marc steps from one foot to the other. Searching the ground around him for his shoes. The same deep bass voice comes from Camel. At first Arabic sounding, but then much older ancient in fact. Marc listens to its phonetics similar but not quite. Picking out a word or two but unclear of what is intended.

Marc, "Speak Arabic or English!" Becoming impatient with this game of his.

Camel, "Yes, you are right. They are up to something very bad. Since they are daughters of darkness. Witches, as you would name them in this millennium."

Marc, "Stop kidding around. I am sure that you find that voice most effective. If you are trying to frighten one of the fast women you usually go for. As far as witches are concerned. Is not Wiccan philosophy harm none? These women are just wicked."

Camel, "Yes, you are right about that. There is much more going on than what is fronted."

Marc, "I didn't know you were so old fashioned, superstitious. I don't buy into that evil witches conjuring and casting spells. That is just—"

Enkil interrupts with his deep bass voice becoming louder. The irritation toward Marc hard to miss. "I am not Camel! This is his body standing before you that is true. But I am not him!" Waving his hand toward the tiled tabletop. A bronze candleholder materializing with lit candles on it next to the Christian Bible. Marc is startled at first recovering quickly.

"Nice," Marc says nonchalantly. Then adding, "I was getting tired of standing out here in the dark. That's a pretty good trick. Come on Camel stop with the crass magic tricks."

Enkil starting to fume. "You need more proof. I will give it to you in abundance." His voice echoing into the small forest.

Raising his large arms up toward the night sky. Releasing his anger charged energy flashing up into the stratosphere. Creating a colorful aurora borealis shimmering in emerald green with shades of blue before it descends into a lower level of the atmosphere. Creating clouds that are roiling violently over themselves rapidly spreading out over the star filled night sky. Darkening out all light from the heavens above. Putting the two men into a pitch blackness that is so deep that the candles on the nearby table are just able to illuminate the immediate area closest to them. Their faces no longer visible to each other. Enkil speaking in Sumerian chanting with his fingers spread wide twisting his wrists, hands pointed at the deepest night. Commanding down his fists clinched tightly a bolt of pure white energy. Faster than sound crashing into the gravel beneath their feet. Marc reacts in hundredths of a second jumping into the hammock. Shielding his eyes from the brightness of a plasma bolt, pure energy. Its impact followed by the sound catching up to it. Roaring, making the earth tremble shaking the trees, hammock, and Marc helplessly.

Now the entire terrace lights up brighter than the surface of Venus. Just as rapidly the light dims followed by magma orange light surrounding stones as they materialize. Spreading out cobblestones covering the gravel in all directions. Marc opens his eyes fascinated watching this creation become a completely finished terrace. Appearing as it had been there for centuries in some Old World garden of the Mediterranean. Camel is unharmed by this energy. Just as suddenly it was begun, it is ended. Heat radiating outward dissipated from energy used. Thunder erupts out into the night. Echoing across the quiet neighborhood. The clear night sky again filled with stars horizon to horizon. Winds rising up blowing across the Phoenician stone terrace cooling it. Stopping just as abruptly before putting the candles out, making them smolder, but quickly back to flames.

Enkil's yellow irises glowering predatory and angry like a big cat's. Their pupils' vertical slits unblinking glaring back at Marc. Looking at his friend unsure of himself. What to say or do. Memories rushing to mind from childhood stories. Told around fires at night out in the deep desert. Teasing at his memory. Whispered tales from an old Shiite iman. That used to visit them at his parents' archaeological site. Legends Marc's father would speak of. Camel's dad telling them stories of what could happen to boys that were bad. All of these thoughts rushing too quickly through his mind. Having disregarded all of those tales as just myths. Both he and Camel sure they were nothing more than stories to scare little boys into behaving.

Marc loosens the tight lock of fear on his vocal cords. Making his voice deep. Not going to show fear to this—abomination?

Marc, "Who? What do you want of me?" Turning his head to the side, pushing up his anger. Defiant in his manner. Enkil smirks and raises his eyebrows. Beginning to like this human's moxie. Not having been around any humans in centuries.

Speaking in his deep bass voice, "Enkil! You conjured me! What is it you want? Besides your feet to not hurt from the sharp gravel under them. And this work to be completed. As specified on your blueprints." Marc sits in the hammock his long hairy legs dangling. Looking down at the smooth stone now below his feet. Wondering if it's safe to stand on. This has to be some colossal dream. Which he was going to wake up from any moment.

Enkil, "It is safe for you to step down on it. I would have never allowed you to be hurt. At least not by accident."

Marc, "You can read my mind?"

Enkil, "Your face is easily read." Marc relaxes for a split second. Enkil continues, "Yes, usually mortal men are all too common in their thoughts. For some, not clearly as others for some reason. Your mind is not completely open to me, irregardless. Were you not complaining about your bare feet hurting against the gravel? Along with having to do all this work by yourself?" Marc does not answer but thinks it to test Enkil.

"Yes," Enkil answers for him. "Now you have both. Plus you have this fine Phoenician stone in your garden."

"I didn't know I conjured you," Marc says. Stepping down from the hammock cautiously, one bare foot at a time. Onto the cool smooth stone.

Marc, "The last thing I remember is reading your name." Was he saying it questioning himself? Enkil's yellow feline eyes seem to soften. His face remaining hard, nearer to anger.

Marc, "What are you?"

Enkil gives him a snarl, white teeth bared. "If you don't know, witch, then you'll have to figure it out for yourself!" Enkil suspicious of Marc's intentions. Unable to freely hear his thoughts as so many other men before Marc. Many has he killed over the millennia past. For bothering him with their foolish dreams of power and trying to control him.

Marc tries another tactic. "What do you mean by witch? I'm just an ordinary man." Enkil asks himself, *What game is this one playing?* Marc is unwavering in his innocence. As Enkil reads his body language and facial expressions. Unable to pick up anything from Marc's mind of covert intentions. Enkil gives Marc an annoyed look but it changes to one of surprise. Then just plain mean with his yellow eyes their pupils narrowing to slits.

Enkil, "Perhaps I judged you too harshly. Apparently the two of you have been unwittingly supplicating yourselves to a coven of sorceresses." Marc is dumbfounded.

Enkil, "Or to use your vernacular, you have been doing a group of witches."

Marc, flustered, "We haven't been worshipping them or anything else! We pray to no other than Allah. We're both good Muslims." Marc's outrage at such accusations strong. Enkil's face softens into a smile. If you could call it that. His eyes still hard and calculating lips in a sneer.

Enkil, "How often are the righteous the last to know they are the minions of evil. Doing its bidding blindly while claiming their innocence. Once their deeds are laid open for all to judge. What a different story you will tell." His tone condescending.

Marc's ego stings from Enkil's statement. Defending himself, "I may not be the most devout but—"

Enkil interrupts him as if his words are unimportant impatiently speaking. "What have you been doing for these women? Besides giving them your sexual life force. All the while worshiping their bodies. How many women do you know of who curry sexual favors with the same men amongst themselves freely? Sharing the two of you like the whores you have become." Enkil sees him flinch having hit a nerve, grinning at Marc. Whose anger is rising quickly but determined not to give Enkil the upper hand. Instead trying to learn more.

"What sexual force?"

Enkil, "Every living creature has a life force. That energy is raised during reproductive cycles. In humans it can be heightened or channeled with the right guidance." Enkil notes to himself, *This one is sharp, not so easily riled*. He has learned how to redirect his anger.

Marc, "How is this energy manipulated?"

Enkil, "Now you are asking the correct questions. I will answer them. You both have a bad influence on you." Marc unsure of what he means. His expression quizzical.

Enkil, "Surely you have noticed the physical changes. Look at you!" Enkil reaches over grabbing a handful of Marc's chest hair tugging at it. "It's a pelt." Releasing it. "You are heathenish, becoming more an animal with each encounter. Soon it will be too late."

Marc, "Are you saying I am bewitched?" Shaking his head in disbelief, swallowing with a gulp. Making his Adam's apple bob up and down.

Enkil, "I would say yes. You are bewitched. From a spell that has been wrought over you. It's diabolical. Every time you have intercourse with these witches you are changed a little more."

Marc, desperate, "But how?" Marc's eyes round.

Enkil, "They have been given access to a very powerful and devious spell. To use on the two of you. It is changing you two into sexual animals called satyrs."

Marc, "Satyrs?"

Enkil speaks as he would to a child patiently so far. "If you are going to repeat everything I say we're going to be here for a long while."

Marc, "How are you so sure of this?" Enkil's eyes glow yellow with hatred for witches. Having a long history with them one of betrayal.

Enkil, "Look at your body. Are you not becoming ever increasingly hirsute?"

His lip twitching up in disgust. Preferring the smoother and softer perfumed bodies of females.

Marc, "I just didn't know what to attribute this all to."

Enkil, "The hair on your head increasing in length each time you have sexual relations. As does the amount of body hair thickens. They are using the two of you. To what ends I don't know yet."

Marc, "Why us?"

Enkil, "Good question. Could be just bad luck. But I have an idea there is more to it than just bad luck. Understand this, no good will come out of any of this."

Marc, "What can I do to stop this spell?"

Enkil, "To stop it from reaching the inevitable conclusion you must stop having sexual relations with these... women." Pausing as though it were difficult to speak of them. "Don't give them anymore of yourself. Camel will no longer be providing them with anything. Their diabolical machination can have no further effect on him." Having ended the effects on his host. "However, nothing short of breaking this curse on you will end it."

Marc, "What of Camel?" Enkil smiles with Camel's most devilish grin white teeth flashing and his most debonair look. Enough to warm some of the coldest hearts.

Enkil, "He is right here, for now." Laughing with one of those masculine deep bass tones that only men have. Plus some rumbling across the terrace causing the stone beneath Marc's feet to tremble. Using more than just laughter to do that. The true extent of his powers unimaginable. Marc glances at the grimoire, averting his eyes quickly. Wondering if there is something in it to send Enkil back. Enkil easily reading Marc's face. You didn't need to be a mind reader to know where his line of thinking was going.

Enkil, "You should focus on how you are going to circumvent what this coven has set in motion." His tone cold with controlled anger. Surprising Marc by how easily read he was. Changing what he was thinking of to prevent Enkil from gaining more insight.

Enkil, "They are a very powerful coven. Camel tells me they are well connected and probably international, as you say in this time."

Marc's concern deepens. "Is Mary one of them?"

Enkil, "No. Not yet. She is a conduit for their means to an end. As you are." Looking at Marc more closely. Enkil's expression changes to one of realization crossing his handsome face. A smirk turning up the corners of his mouth.

Marc, "What is it? You know something I can tell. They haven't harmed her have they?" Enkil smelling the air similar to a blood hound getting a scent. Stepping closer to Marc.

Marc, "Well? Answer me!" His angry blue eyes staring into Enkil's unflinching yellow eyes. Enkil's smile becomes bigger.

Enkil, "To my knowledge she is just fine, except tired. You smell of innocence lost." Marc's cheeks blushing visible even under the candlelight. "You are holding back, clouding your mind to me. Hide a little as you choose, but certain things are impossible to cover up. You can't wash that away so easily man animal."

Marc, *He couldn't possibly smell innocence. What is he talking about?* Enkil watches Marc's face and body reading them like an open book. These young ones are so ignorant. Becoming impatient, folding his large arms across his chest.

Enkil finally speaks, "You smell of coitus mixed with blood. How unwittingly you were manipulated into furthering their plans." Marc's moreno cheeks dusky. His mind rushing back to the previous night's events. Trying to remembering how Mary didn't behave.

Marc, "Damn, I was so caught up in the passion of the moment. I didn't consider it could be her first time. Why didn't she tell me?"

Enkil, "That is something you will have to take up with her." Inhaling the air again taking a deep breath. "Yes, I like that smell. So does your brother Camel. It's arousing him. This all takes me back many was the day." Chuckling at Marc's apparent ignorance. Leaving him stinging from his own foolishness laid bare. That with being the crux of a private joke so amusing to this… thing. *How much can he read my mind?*

Marc, "I won't be so easily deceived from now on."

Enkil, his face stern. "They will allure you, entice and charm you to reach the final objective."

Marc, "That won't happen now that I'm onto them."

Enkil shakes his head. "You are already spellbound. All any of these women need do is draw on her charm. Which she already has over you. The enthrallment will immediately ensnare your mind. And you'll be there to satiate her every desire because it is your basic need to do so. That is a consequence of your folly"

Marc, "How are you so convinced of this?"

Enkil smells the air again before answering. "Inhale the air deeply around you. Then tell me what it is you find." Marc breathes in the air with his sense of smell heightened. Catching his own musky male aroma but noting a faint but distinctly feminine scent like a perfume to him. Whom does it belong to? *How am I able to gather all these different scents?* Coming back to the immediate subject of importance.

Marc, "I showered this morning apparently not well enough."

Enkil, "As you are changed physically that will include your other senses." Marc finally begins to understand the ramifications.

Marc, "I'll be led like a goat to the slaughter."

Enkil, "Literally when they are finished with you. History has incidents recorded of men being killed for being too hirsute."

Marc, "I don't know of any such events."

Enkil, "When the Romans murdered the Arabic men in Jerusalem. They killed all men with full beards." Marc rubs his course and dedicatedly stubble covered jaw.

Marc answers, "That was because they weren't Christians. The Roman soldiers went crazy on a killing spree, racial cleansing."

Enkil, "Was it now? Why would they be suspicious of the men that were not at war with them? They were just living their daily lives."

Marc, "That is history. It's common knowledge."

Enkil, "History is what the rulers say it was. Believe me, I was alive in that time. A coven used misdirection to cover their ill-gotten powers. There was dark magic behind all of that. Many innocent men, fathers and sons, lost their lives to hide what was in play there."

Marc, "How will I be able to protect myself from all this?"

Enkil, "There is your family book." Waving his hand toward the grimoire. "Read it. I'm sure answers lie within."

Marc, "Will this all go away if I break the enchantment?" Marc's expression grim, faced with so many extraordinary circumstances. His whole system of beliefs had never dealt with supernatural beings at least evil.

Enkil chuckles at him. Then answers, "How does a man go back to being a boy?"

Marc, "What does that mean?"

Enkil, "I wouldn't cockle any more women of that coven." Just the mention of these women now having an effect on him. Marc's expression distant his entire body heating up. Consciousness going to lascivious thoughts quickly rushing blood to specific body areas. His mouth wet and his pants painfully tight. Adjusting his package. Enkil's reptilian eyes inhumanly cold with their pupils wide, ready to speak. "Now you know your weakness. Don't let them control you through it." Marc uncomfortable in his highly aroused state.

Enkil, "Know this. You are only of value to them as long as they need you. It is not just your energy they are after."

Marc, "I was thinking about what you said. If this can happen to any men then why us?"

Enkil, "That is the question indeed. Until we figure out that answer you will be at a serious disadvantage. Once they have what they need from you, you will be expendable." Marc having the same thought. Enkil's face softens or was he just imagining it?

Pauses long enough for Marc to take in his warning. Satisfied he continues, "I'm leaving now. It's been more than two hundred years since I spoke this much to one man." Enkil moves toward the low seating stone wall. His body fading quickly to a shimmer of light as on water. Marc left standing alone, his bare feet against the smooth stone terrace. Candlelight flickering gently with the warm breeze. He looks up at the late night sky with its stars, Ursa Minor shifted to the eastern horizon.

Heading down the flagstone path toward the empty house. Looming up in the darkness with its steep-angled mansard rooftops eerie in the shadows. Entering through the back door with stairs leading to two directions one the dark basement. A cool breeze blows from below the earth carrying on it the fresh scents of bleach and Pine-Sol. Turning away from it to go upstairs a few steps. Choosing to take the hallway past the kitchen more familiar. His bare feet padding along against the hardwood floor in the darkness. Not having bothered to turn on any lights. His steps muffled every once in a while by thick Persian rugs. Marc can't but help notice the silence throughout the house. Arriving at the foyer with its grandfather clock ticking. After setting the security system taking the stairs.

Finally getting to the master suite. Pulling his shorts off letting them drop onto the floor. Enjoying the cool air against his exposed body parts. You don't really notice how warm and constricting everything can be until it isn't. Going right to the en suite spa calling out to the voice activation shower controls, "Temperature ninety-eight degrees, on!" Stepping into the warm spray lathering up his chest hair more like a lion's mane except it is soft as the finest mink. Difficult to get it wet all the way down to the skin. Trying to scrub away the greasy perspiration and uncleanness he was feeling from being completely used. In every sense of word. Using a lufa sponge as best as he could to scour away any hint of the night before. Lathering up soap on all areas some needing more than others and some just too hirsute to scrub. Satisfied with that rinsing off working his fingers through his past shoulder-length straight dark hair. Then repeating the process for his chest pelt. Sufficiently rinsed he just lets the warm water run. Adjusting the spray to a rain shower Marc leans against the wall. Letting it flow over and down his back. The reflection in the mirror revealing how far the spell has progressed. Hair is all the way down his back especially on his spine and across the shoulders.

Unaware at this time of a pair of beautiful eyes watching him from the other side of the mirror. Having an unsettling feeling that someone is watching him. He calls out, "Shower stop!" Moving immediately into a fighting readiness for an assailant without being obvious hands at defensive. No one there he listens hearing only the water dripping off him. Reaching for a towel feeling foolish only seeing his own reflection in the mirror. He almost doesn't recognize himself. Looking more like a man animal of Greek mythology. Shaky from the adrenaline's after effects starting to towel dry. Only now it takes a couple of towels to do what once took one. How could this change have taken place so quickly? He certainly didn't invite this or did he? Padding out onto the marble floor outside the shower. Feeling warm and relaxed until the cool air hits the wet hair against his skin. Causing a shiver giving him the urge to shake off.

Coming out of the bathroom the answering machine has several new messages on it. Not feeling up to dealing with any of them. Marc tosses his towel over the machine before sliding under the covers into bed. Still damp but warming up not able to fall asleep right away. Thinking back over the recent turn of events. Everything Camel, no, Enkil had said. Hearing Ibram's condescending words of warning about sleeping around with infidel whores. His inevitable criticism. "Now look what it's gotten you. Both of you tainted marked by your sins." Punching his pillow. Who wants to hear, "I told you so"?

Slipping into a restless sleep filled with dream after dream. About women at the party. Melinda, Jadon with others all erotic with all of them using him. Unable to resist their advances demands for him to pleasure them. Circling the edges of all this, Enkil's warnings to resist, 'keep to yourself.' How could he with a harem offerings of gorgeous women. Frightening at times as in one dream he is a centaur. In another he changes into a goat. That which Angelique cuts the throat of in celebration of her success. Of what? The last dream Melinda again hot as ever. She is astride him squeezing him and twisting. His jaw set holding back refusing release. Finally unable to stop. "Oh, OH!" Waking up as he is climaxing ejaculate spraying out under the sheets. His respirations deep warm waves of pleasure rippling through his body.

What a way to wake up stretching languidly. Turning toward the drape covered windows still dark outside. Grabbing the towel off the answering machine using it to wipe up. Sleepy and relaxed it is still dark out. Rolling over onto the dry side of the bed going back to sleep. This time the temperature in the room drops low enough for his breath to come out in clouds of humid vapor. This dream of uncle Theron warning him, "Control the power! You must before it is too late to make things right!" His sleep moving to REM stage dreaming of Mary. Her soft pale skin like moonlight with light auburn hair tickling across his chest. Looking at him with those lovely emerald green eyes. Their color that dark green of centuries ago mined in Brazil. How gentle he had been with her, slow not rushing or forcing. Allowing her to become ready. Yes she was tight like a glove but lusciously wet.

His dream changes Mary replaced by Melinda. "No!" Speaking in his sleep. "Come back!" To late she is already gone, not really her at all. It's Angelique and she is a wild woman. Screaming for more biting his thick neck and digging her long fingernails into his back. Raking them down his hairy back deep enough to reach the pale flesh below scratching it. Lost in rapture Marc is unable to refuse her. She has him right where she wants him. Under her sexual spell a slave to her. Bringing him close repeatedly then stopping at his threshold. Keeping him paralyzed except for his vocal cords. Now on his back Marc's only release to howl at the heavens. With her stars spinning past faster and faster until accelerating into a blur.

This time sunlight is beaming around the edges of the drapes. Marc wakes up to wet and cold sheets against his legs and lower abdomen. "What the heck?" Moving to get up his body hair sticking to his skin. The hair matted in places pulling as he moves stinging. Smelling musky and of the alkaline fluids of male discharge drying on his body. Standing up from the bed. Those dreams were so erotic and real. It was like the women of his dreams were in this very room. Truly the only one that had been in his bed here at the manor was Melinda. "No, there was also Jadon." The air cold enough to see his breath. Giving him reason to hurry on into the bathroom spa. Not seeing a lacy piece of lingerie at the foot of the bed just barely sticking out from under the sheet.

Moving quickly over checking the thermostat. Its reading a normal setting of sixty-eight degrees. *Why is it so cold in here?*

Calling out, "Lights on master bath! Floor heat on!" Moving into the bathroom pulling the door closed. "Spa tub fill ninety-eight degrees!" Needing to clean up again. Between his smell and the matted hair pulling and making the skin sting. Becoming aggravated rubbing at his hairy muscular thigh in an effort to keep the skin from pulling when he moves. Not effective at all. The only good thing is the marble floor warming up and he's already warmer with the door closed.

"What color to use for chromatherapy?" the system prompts.

Choosing he says, "Purple," as the color shines on under the bubbling water. Marc's skin pinching as he steps into the soothing hot water sinking under it completely. His head popping out with steam rising off the water. Pushing his dark hair back out of his face giving the appearance of a GQ magazine front cover. Looking every bit Cajun with his dark hair and deep blue eyes. That with the olive to moreno skin tone. Soaking for a while before using a washcloth and his fingers to work out the matted areas of hair on his abdomen and thighs. Satisfied his skin is no longer being pulled standing up dripping. He pulls a warmed towel off the rack to begin drying off.

CHAPTER 47

STANDING IN FRONT of the vessel sink. A large bowl mounted above the granite vanity with its surrounding bank of mirrors. Marc notes his beard grown in full and heavy. Not one of those men that can get away with skipping a day. *Forget it, I'm not shaving again.* Applying deodorant liberally to his armpits. Then splashing on Tommy Hilfiger to his face and chest. Dressing with comfort in mind. Choosing boxer shorts and some old 501 jeans. A knock at the door distracts him out of his thoughts.

Marc, "Come in!" Ms. Campbell crosses the master suite. Carrying a sterling silver tray with a chambord on it for his morning coffee. Placing the tray on the table beside the windows facing the garden.

"The stonemason is here to help you finish up out back," Ms. Campbell announces as she pulls open the drapes. Marc eager for his morning Java steps out of the dressing room walk-in closet. Norma turns around startled by his physical appearance without a shirt on. Not recalling him looking like a beast but not surprised. Most men look like what they are, animals. Her expression quickly changes to one of irritation and disgust. Marc defiantly leaves his shirt off plunging the French press ignoring her. Then pouring his coffee into the bone china cup steam rising up. Letting it cool for a moment while pulling on a tee shirt. Then taking a sip of good strong coffee (Colombian supremo) savoring its rich taste.

Ms. Campbell unavoidably smells his cologne, 'with as much as he uses.' At least he smells good. Its fragrance almost familiar a nice scent for him disregarding her thought. But too hairy and he needs a haircut. Moving over to make the bed. Gathering the sheets up until seeing the stains and damp areas. Making a sound of disgust under her breath but still loud enough for him to hear. Herself not caring and wanting him to know she finds him disgusting. Marc gets a sense of satisfaction. Chuckling to himself not saying what was on the tip of his tongue. *What's the matter? Has it been that long since you've been with a man?* Finally speaking to her, "I'll be down soon." Standing by the windows engrossed in the verdant garden below. A view of just the terrace visible in part. Enough to see its completed Phoenician stonework. Definitely not a bad dream. Not that any of his dreams last night were bad, for a man animal. We'll see about that latter part.

Having already forgotten about Ms. Campbell. "This bed will need changing." At least until she spoke with her usual curt tone.

"Yeah, whatever." Marc dismisses her. Not really listening to her with much more important matters on his mind.

Ms. Campbell leaves the room muttering under her breath. "I shouldn't have to deal with that filth." Seizing on the idea Mary can do it. She wants to be a woman of the world. Here's her chance starting right now. Taking care of men and their needs. Well at least the end result of it. Thinking snidely to herself. Walking into the master bathroom to gather up towels from off the floor irritated in their state of use. Coming back out into the room glaring at Marc.

"Apparently the master suite needs cleaning again." Her tone sharp. Thinking to herself, *It smells like a men's locker room in here*. Opening a window letting a rush of fresh summer air. Marc focused on his own troubles doesn't notice her anymore taking a drink of his coffee. Ms. Campbell picks up a pile of clothes mixed with towels off the floor. Holding them at arm's length away from her making a sour face as she walks out of the room. Passing Mary out in the hall. "You can clean it once he goes downstairs."

Marc meets with the stonemason outside.

Giancarlo, "Wow you were busy. All of the work is finished on the terrace. Are you sure you haven't done this before? That Mr. Thornburg was wrong about you?"

Marc, "No, but I had some help from a friend." Thinking, *If I told him, he would just think I was crazy*. The less said, the better.

Giancarlo, "Whoever your friend is I could use someone like that on my crew. The attention to detail is old world master craftsmanship."

Marc tries to play it down. "I know. That's why I asked him for help."

Giancarlo, "You changed the type of stone and the color of the granite. That black granite pentagram with the gold specks gleaming looks great. It reminds me of my grandfather's barn in Pennsylvania. They used them to ward off evil spirits. Who designed it?"

Marc, "My uncle."

Giancarlo, "It's a tip of the hat to the old world." He walks over the terrace examining the cuts and spacing between joints. Setting his level down. "Nice, a very slight pitch away from the center. That'll keep rain and snowmelt from pooling." Marc thinks, *I guess Enkil thought of everything when he made it*.

Giancarlo, "I already have my crew packing up our equipment. Now we're ahead of schedule. Which is great. We have a large job in Pittsford to get started on."

Marc, "Good for you." Very noncommittal.

Giancarlo, "This stonework is really top-notch. Like the old stonework done a century ago by Italians. If your friend needs a few extra bucks have him call me." Trying to wrangle a name out of him.

"I doubt he needs more work."

Giancarlo still examining the stone terrace under his feet. Recognition hitting him on the kind of stone used. "I wouldn't have used something so expensive outside." *Phoenician stone. Huh. Rich people, go figure.* Marc already gone accepting a delivery from De Ville's nursery.

Marc examines the delivery of Chinese peony bushes. The red blossom type with smaller growing azaleas that have yellow gold blossoms to go in front of the peonies. The low seating wall to have light pink roses behind it. Very fragrant but wickedly thorny wondering if that was such a good place to put them. Close to people but a good sunny spot for them to grow in. They will just have to be maintained.

Hours later breaking a good sweat Marc is wiping the perspiration off his brow taking a moment. Now for the easy part. Planting the sedum in between the rocks of the south low seating wall. Once grown in they will create a cascading effect. Passing by the table next to the hammock. Where the Bronze Age candleholder still remains. The candles long burnt down wax dripped over them. His books right where he left them last night. Very careless. Anyone could have taken them. Gathering them up placing them in separate compartments of the book bag also left outside. Taking his precious cargo back up the flagstone path into the house. Mary coming out dragging a heavy black plastic garbage bag. Marc quickens his pace to meet her.

"Hi! Here I'll take that," Marc says smiling. Taking it from her hands easily swinging it over to the side with one arm his bicep bulging. "What's in here your favorite rock collection?" Marc teases her.

Mary is enjoying his attention smiling brightly. "No just rubbish from the basement." Her green eyes sparkling and a slight flush coming to her cheeks. Marc's smile looks devilishly debonair. Thinking of their night together. Looking into her eyes innocent compared to those of the other women. She is special. Mary glances over her shoulder afraid of being seen.

"I have to get back to work." Her smile gone.

Marc, "You can't stop for a moment and talk? What's with the maid's uniform?"

Mary, "Ms. Campbell, I mean aunt Norma insisted I was to wear this." Before Marc can ask she adds, "To remind me of my place here."

Marc, "Your place? This isn't some century past. I was hoping to ask you out on a real date." Mary thrilled on the inside. Her face lights up unable to hold back her excitement. Both of them turning to a noise coming from inside. Her face becomes stone all expression of happiness gone.

Aunt Norma appears around the corner on the stairs from above. Stamping down the stairs noisily. "Have you finished in the basement?"

Mary, "No, ma'am."

Aunt Norma, "Stay right here for a moment." Then speaking to Marc, "Are you coming inside?"

Marc, "Yes, I've finished working outside for the day. I'll be working on some research in the library."

Aunt Norma, "Since he is coming in from outside is the master suite cleaned? Those linens needed changing they're soiled." Wishing she could say what she really thought, *Filthy*.

Mary, "No ma'am. It's not completed."

Aunt Norma, "Well then get back up there. You can finish upstairs work first. Unless you need me to find more for you to do." *What was that all about?* Marc looks at Mary about to say something. Mary gives him the slightest turn of her head saying no. Mary is already going back up the stairs. Ms. Campbell is glaring at Marc. *What a disappointment he has turned out to be. To think I believed he was a nice young man at one time.* Marc passes her on the stairs. Ms. Campbell smelling his cologne, now mixed with perspiration. That which makes everyone's scent unique with their body chemistry. His being very masculine evoking sensuality. Herself pleased by the fragrance so familiar. He always smells so good. Recognizing the scent. It was him.

Her anger boiling up she yells, "Mary! Come here now!" Mary cringes at that tone. The pit of her stomach knotting. Knowing she's in trouble again.

Aunt Norma, "Get down here now!" Mary taking the steps slowly to face her tormenter. Her affect flat looking down to where her aunt is standing on the landing. Norma is glaring at her.

Mary, "Yes ma'am."

Norma enraged to the point of wanting to slap her. "So he's the one you defied me with." Mary's expression aghast. *How did she know?* Norma becoming angrier upon seeing Mary's reaction. Stamping up the steps and getting right in her face. "He's a pig. You wasted yourself on that, that... heathen!" Mary not answering her staring back at her defiantly. Normas' green eyes fiery now. Challenged by this determined to get a reaction from her.

Norma, "I can see you have no remorse for your sins that you have committed. Just like your mother, the whore!"

Mary glares at her aunt right in the eyes. Her own green eyes narrowed to points. Dangerous hate for this woman claiming to love her but is only too willing to be cruel. Norma feeling her sense of power over this love child slipping away. A constant reminder of her pain of betrayal. Mary then says, "My mother wasn't a whore!"

Norma no longer able to contain her rage replies, "Oh yes she was! She ran off with my fiancé. Then leaves you on my doorstep." Her face twisted with hate. Mary finally understands why her aunt was too cruel and unforgiving of her. *She has every reason to hate me. She blames me for her miserable life.* Mary detaches herself from the anger and hurt. Her face a mask, affect flat, no longer responding to her aunt's hateful words.

Ms. Campbell enraged further by Mary's seeming indifference to her angry words. Swings her hand up slapping Mary's face hard. The strike loud, carrying up the stairwell.

Norma, "Clean that filthy suite! Now you'll be able to see just what kind of animal he is. Get out of my sight! I'll have a word with him later."

Mary, "You can say whatever you want to him. I don't care."

Ms. Campbell draws back to slap her again. This time Mary blocks her swing. Saying, "If you ever strike me again, I'll have you arrested for assault."

Ms. Campbell, "You're going back to the convent or the street. I don't care which. Come to think of it, I'm going to give Eton a call. As your legal guardian that will be out."

Mary, "You can't do that!"

Norma, "Just watch me. When they find out what an immoral girl you are, you'll be withdrawn." Stamping up the steps past Mary. Leaving her dust covered face streaked with tears. All her dreams destroyed along with the chance to escape from her cruel aunt.

CHAPTER 48

MARC IN THE library is taking messages off from the answering machine. His cousin Phil has left two messages. One time calling from his office at Tulane stating it was urgent. To call him back as soon as he got the message. Camel having left two messages also. One no more urgent than the last.

Camel, "It's important call me." Marc thinking, *You bet it's important.* Remembering last night after Enkil's visit with his demonstration of the massive amount of power he welds. Transporting thousands of pounds of Phoenician stone. That and his warning about the coven. *Yes, I'd say it was important.* Just then a blast of cold air blows over him. Giving him a chill causing the hair on his arms to stand up. Darn climate control. Hearing Enkil's deep voice resounding in his head the warnings. What is Enkil? Male yes but what? The answers lie in the grimoire and the past.

Reaching over picking up pages in the fax machine. Reading over the first page from Phil. "I enlisted the help of a friend, Father Broussard. Well, actually he is an ex-Jesuit priest. To help with the translation of the Latin passages. This grimoire is not only a book of spells but also a diary. Some of it is written in a code to confuse anyone just reading it. I hope you don't mind that I brought in outside help. He is a friend that I trust implicitly. One of the passages is some sort of sexual spell. Father Broussard, I mean Paul, tells me it is a transformation spell. Used to control men by turning them into satyrs. At least eventually through repeated sexual intercourse. Could you imagine if this really worked? Like men need their libidos increased and then using it against them. Here is a portion of the translation for you to read over. Let me know what you think."

Marc checks the time these pages were sent hours ago. "Hi Marc, Paul Broussard you really have gotten yourself into something dangerous. Some of these rituals predate Christianity. I've only read of Babylonian references to some of these forces. Much less the incantations that seek to call upon and control them. These documents are transcribed from the oldest known civilization. Meaning they are from Sanskrit writings and cuneiforms. You need an archeologist that has an understanding of Sumerian culture. What I do recognize is that even a madji would be challenged to direct one of these forces. A novice would be at great risk of possession. That being the least of your concerns. Though that alone would be reason enough for me not to pursue this. However since you were not the one unleashing ancient forces on an unsuspecting modern world. Beings that were unseen in millennia would have devastating consequences."

Marc sets the last page down. A cold chill raising the hair on the back of his neck and arms. What is Angelique after? His realization of how intelligent and deeply manipulative she was. To have gotten this far with her plans. She would have had to be planning this for years. Long before he lived in Rochester. Noticing the air around him having become very cold, seeing his own breath. What the... The phone rings startling him. Snatching the phone up.

"Hello."

His cousin Phil on the other end. "Good you're home. I was getting worried."

Ms. Campbell storms into the library yelling at him. "How dare you! You filthy heathen. Taking advantage of my niece using her for your depraved sexual needs. I won't have it!"

Marc stammers, "I,I didn't know... I wasn't trying to."

Ms. Campbell, "Liar! You knew what you were doing. She was infatuated with you!"

Phil, "Is this a bad time?"

Marc not answer Ms. Campbell quickly enough. "She's underage did you know that?"

Marc, "I know she is eighteen. You're not going to pull that one on me." Not having meant to say it that way.

Ms. Campbell, "So you did know. This was all planned wasn't it? You and your decadent, filthy rich friends. All just some game to seduce a naive young girl."

Marc, "It wasn't like that. Our drinks were spiked with something."

Ms. Campbell, "So you gave liquor to an underage girl?" More of an accusation than a question.

"Real smooth cousin. Alcohol and a just legal girl mostly," Phil says.

Marc, "It wasn't like that!" answering Phil but Norma believing it was her.

Ms. Campbell, "What was it, a good time had by all?"

Phil, "I'll call you back."

Marc, "Yeah that's a good idea." *Click*. "I didn't plan on any of this. Everything just got out of control."

Ms. Campbell, "You were in control when you seduced her. What was she doing underage drinking at a party you and your friends would go to?"

Marc, "I didn't know Mary would be there." As if it just sank in.

"You gave her drugs?" Her voice loud.

Marc, "I didn't know the drinks were drugged!"

Ms. Campbell, "Let me get this straight. You gave liquor to a minor and you didn't know it was drugged? Is that right?"

Marc, "Yes, I mean no!"

Ms. Campbell, "Don't you yell at me. I don't have to take that from you!" Mary hearing the commotion races downstairs.

CHAPTER 49

ANGELIQUE UPSTAIRS IN her home. Pulls with a flourish the black silk fabric covering her scrying mirror. A large baroque Louis the XVI mirror. Staring into the eyes of her own reflection. Her icy blue eyes hard and cold. Time to monitor what she put in motion. How is it progressing? Chanting, "Mirror. Mirror. Bring forth what I seek. Bend distance so I may view the meek." Her frightening reflection dissolves rippling away. As another room slowly comes into view. Angry voices carrying into her own room. From the library at Marc's home its image rippling then clearing. Perfect, what great timing. A ringside seat to view the misery from. Her thin lips curling into one of her wicked smirks. Ever so satisfied with herself. Her plans falling into place as dominoes would, one after the other.

On the other side of the mirror Mary rushes into the room. "I'm not underage anymore. I won't allow you to speak to him like that. Twisting his words like you do me!" Norma surprised by her outburst. Turning her attention to Mary.

"So that just makes it..." Norma warms up. "a willful disregard for the good book and the law. You were brought up better at least I thought so. I won't tolerate that kind of behavior while you're living under my roof. Drinking and fornicating like those decadent Europeans. I should have never left you with so much freedom."

Mary, "The only decadent person here is you. You're a cruel sadist!" The harshest thing she could think of to say to her aunt. Still not wanting to be to disrespectful.

Aunt Norma turns to Marc. "The drinking age for alcohol consumption is twenty-one in this country. I wonder what that nice detective Mr. Arros would say about this." Marc's look of fear exactly what she was looking for, continuing. "I'm sure Mr. Thornburg will be delighted. To hear about how the new master of the manor is making it into a den of iniquity. Combining alcohol and under aged girls. What would he have to say about that?"

Marc, "I have had enough of you with your disrespect."

Norma disregarding him, "Mary get back to work! I don't have to respect you with your heathen culture with those filthy rich whores you call friends. No good will come to any of you!" Her wrinkled face weathered beyond her years twisted. Norma's thin lips turned down making the white peach fuzz on them stand out her green eyes narrowed. But still managing to have condescension on her face looking up at Marc's. Very satisfied with the reaction from him. His cheeks flushed with anger.

Marc, "You are the reason people hate Christians. You are nothing more than a self-righteous asshole. Get out! You're fired!"

Norma, "You can't fire me. Robert, Mr. Thornburg hired me. He is in control of this estate." Marc catches on to her familiarity with his attorney. So she was reporting to him as he had suspected.

Back at Angelique's. The intercom buzzes in her bedroom next door to the spell room. Causing her concentration to waver. Her own reflection reappearing in the mirror. "Damn!" Walking away from it. Pressing the intercom button taking it off privacy. "What! I said I don't want to be disturbed."

Her butler unperturbed by this outburst announces. "Ms. Jadon is here to see you."

"I'm busy!" Having a second thought. "Send her up!"

Jadon startled by Angelique's brusque approach. Snatching her into the room and locking the door behind them.

Angelique, "Maybe you can be of some help to me. Since you are here come on. This is too good to miss." Rushing back to the mirror excitedly. Standing in front of it trying to calm herself, concentrating. Jadon joins her easily focused. The image returns to the manor library.

Marc angry yet in control now. "It's my money that pays your salary. So I do have a say in who works for me. You are fired, get out! You cruel witch."

Norma Campbell not used to being one-upped. Angry to the point of being incensed yells at Mary, "Get in the car we're leaving!"

Mary, "I'm not going anywhere with you. I've had enough of you." Her expression one of terror gradually changing to one of resolve. Trembling on the inside Mary unwilling to give back to her tormenter power over her.

Aunt Norma, "You dare to defy me? Get in the car now!"

Mary, "No. I don't have to be treated this way anymore by you."

Aunt Norma uses her last trump card. "You get in the car now or I'll throw you out onto the street. Just like that strumpet mother of yours was."

Mary, "You don't care about me, not really. I'm just a reminder of what was done to you. A mistake left on your doorstep."

Norma, "That's right. Even your father didn't want you. You believe your new boyfriend here is going to care for you. Once you're knocked up you'll be of no use to him at all. Rich men don't marry the maid. All they do is use them for sex. Moving on to the next little whore. I'll fix both of you. First I'll tell Mr. Thornburg. Then I will go to the police. What will they make of alcohol being served to minors. Where illegal drugs are being given out?" Mary unaware of this new information looks at Marc.

Marc, "It wasn't supposed to happen like that."

Mary is horrified. "You knew I was drugged?"

Marc, "Yes. I mean no! Not until the next—"

Ms. Campbell not letting him finish speaking to Mary, "Now what do you think of him? I wonder how much it will cost your Pittsford friend to hush it up? Wait until the scandal gets out. I'm sure one of those press whores from *Extra* will eat the story up."

CHAPTER 50

JADON NOT BOTHERING to look at Angelique's face. Already knowing her little smirk is replaced with rage. Angelique says, "That old troublemaking crone." Speaking under her breath. "You are not going to have the chance to ruin my plans.

"What to do?" speaking to herself. "Let this play out. An opportunity will present itself." Calming herself. Jadon ready to speak. Angelique raises her hand to silence her. "Watch and learn."

CHAPTER 51

MARY. "YOU WOULDN'T do that to us."

Aunt Norma, "Hum, my ungrateful whore of a niece and her Casanova lover." Pretending to think about it. "You lose." Turning around to leave.

Mary, "Where are you going?"

Norma, "I'm leaving. I've been fired." Staring cruelly at Mary. "Don't bother with coming back home. I'll burn your clothes so you will have no need to ever return to my house. How do you think the scholarship committee will feel about all this? I guess I will be busy for the next few days."

Mary, "Please don't do this to me!" Her dreams of college being destroyed. She could never pay for a school like Eton.

Aunt Norma, "Watch and see. When he's done using you for what's between your legs you'll be just like your mother was. Knocked up and on the street!" Mary bursts into tears.

Marc yells, "Get out!" Norma stamps away on the hardwood floors. Slamming the side door. Wheels squealing out in the driveway. Marc puts his solid arms around Mary to comfort her. Mary buries her face in his chest.

CHAPTER 52

ANGELIQUE BACK IN place views the situation through her scrying mirror. An opportunity will present itself; all she needs to do is watch and be ready.

Angelique, "How perfect. Keep their attention misdirected. A tragedy can be quite useful in making someone more traceable. That old Christian bitch has served my purposes well."

Jadon whispers, "Maybe she wouldn't have been so cruel if she had a man once in a while."

Angelique, "True."

"But then that hasn't changed you. You're still cruel as ever," Jadon adds before thinking. Angelique gives her a dirty look. Then smiles at her. Sending a chill down her spine. Giving her a wrenching sensation to her lower abdomen with the blood rushing away. Angelique so enjoying the reaction she invoked in her young minion. Turning her attention back to aunt Norma. Focusing her mind on the late-model station wagon. Detaching her consciousness from her body. Astral projecting through the mirror.

Following the sound of tires squealing outside a microsecond later Angelique's ethereal form is sitting beside Norma on the front seat of the station wagon. Ranting to herself loudly furious with Mary unaware of her new passenger. "I'll show that insolent girl and her tawdry friends. Just how much trouble an old bitch can cause." Angelique shimmers outside the fourth dimension that of time. Everything appearing to slow down. Norma's simplest actions that of her movements slowed to where seconds are like minutes. Angelique delighted with herself for the moment because anything was possible. But only able to perform this feat of power for a few seconds. All she would need to exact retribution against this vile creature. If she used any more time the energy so carefully collected from soon to be satyrs would be used up. Requiring more to be gathered from other men. Not that she wasn't willing to destroy other men along with their families lives. Time was precious now for it would take years to recreate all that was needed.

Turning to Norma she speaks to her. "Yes that is certainly true. You could create quite a disturbance for me. Nothing that uncle Robert couldn't squelch. I'm sure you could get some tongues wagging. There are a few that would relish seeing me taken down a notch or two. But sadly for you I don't tolerate being crossed, ever. So now it is time for you to get back to being useful. One more time." Angelique begins chanting. "Make a gift of light so bright. Blind her sight. Let her see her own demise for my delight." Angelique's ephemeral form shimmers into present time. Norma feels a presence next to her. Hearing a voice whispering, then plain as day seeing something out of the corner of her eye. Moving her head toward the sound to see Angelique's cold stare glaring back at her.

Norma, "What in heaven's name?"

Angelique, "Oh this is not in heaven's name, dearie!" Twisting her long nailed fingers claw like. Shouting, "Make it fast and go forth!" Angelique's laughter what could only be described as insane. Her laughter echoing back and forth inside the car. Norma feels the accelerator drop out from under her foot. Depressing to the floor sending the station wagon careening over the small knoll in the driveway. Norma struggles to keep her vehicle under control as it races down the driveway. Mashing the brake pedal frantically without effect. Light reflecting into her eyes as the end of the driveway comes. Stomping frantically on the brakes with both feet still not slowing. The blinding lights reflection out of her face Norma turning the steering wheel. The station wagons tires skidding on the asphalt. Just as an urban waste disposal truck is rushing up the road. Norma screaming in terror seeing the truck too late. The truck driver seeing her coming just not able to do anything more jams on his air brakes. Truck tires howl against the asphalt road. Only too late, metal twisting and groaning. Norma's scream drowned out by the carnage. Glass explodes on the passenger side. Broadsided. Her head strikes the windshield as her car is turned over and dragged under the truck. Plumes of sparks spray out before her vehicle is crushed under the large truck grinding to a halt. Smoke rises up from both vehicles. The only sound is of hot metal pinging.

CHAPTER 53

ANGELIQUE STARES BACK at her own reflection in the mirror. Its elegant baroque gilt framing a bow with ribbons belying its true use. Her icy round blue eyes cruel on a face of beauty, but on her hinting of insanity. No longer able to hold back her delight. Bursting out into laughter again. Clutching at her abdomen hurting from laughing so hard. Stopping to catch her breath. "Oh my lord. That felt so good." Jadon watching on quietly, studiously. Holding back her deep feelings of disgust. Angelique lifts the black silk fabric with her taloned hand. Flings the cloth up and back over the ornate mirror covering it. Leaving the room. After all, "company is waiting."

CHAPTER 54

MARC HOLDS MARY to comfort her after such a vicious attack by her aunt. Following his convictions he makes a decision. "You're more than welcome to stay here until you start college. You have a scholarship to Eton, right?" Trying to encourage her.

"Yes, I do. If she doesn't destroy that." Mary's eyes tear up again. Marc squeezes her against his solid chest to comfort her. Mary presses her face into his chest. His tee shirt becoming wet from her tears. Bending his neck down resting his chin against her head. Only wanting to protect her. His face touching her long auburn hair. Its scent smells good. Her long hair brushes against his hands feeling as corn silk. Her body pressed against his so warm and soft in all the right places. His mind goes back to Saturday night. Setting sensations of arousal flowing quickly becoming engorged. Using the last bit of self-control he breaks the embrace. Mary looks up at him so sadly not realizing why he pulled away.

Marc, "Don't worry about the clothes." Directing the subject away from what just happened. "We will get you new ones."

Mary, "Thank you. I guess you'll have a charity case for a while."

Marc, "I don't feel that way at all. I'm serious you are more than welcome here. No strings attached." Realizing this may be harder on him than her. Having to keep to himself with his current situation.

Mary, "Thank you but I don't have much money."

Marc stops her with a hand wave dismissing her thought. Adding, "I do and it's the least I can do for you. Considering all the trouble my so called friends have created in your life." Thinking to himself, *And my life*. "Come on let's get out of here."

Outside sirens are wailing in the distance. As they are getting into Marc's Mustang.

Mary, "That sounds close. Those sirens are always so frightful. You always know something just awful has happened."

Marc not too concerned, "Or something. They just come out it seems." Letting his mind go with the flow. It would be convenient if that old crone Ms. Campbell was out of the way for a while. It would serve her right. Something to keep her hospitalized for a long stay.

"Marc it's close." Bringing him out of his fantasy. "I hope no one is seriously hurt."

Marc, "It's probably some asshole driving fast and reckless." Crossing over the small knoll, the wreckage coming into view. Slowing their car to a stop at the apron of the driveway. Looking on at the scene unfolding on East Avenue.

An almost unidentifiable car crushed under the front of a sanitation truck. The smell of gasoline and antifreeze wafting in the hot air. Fire rescue crews already at work using the jaws of life to cut away wreckage. Causing the faux wood panel on the station wagon to move. At that same moment both of them recognize the vehicle. Mary screams, "Oh no!" scrambling out of the car. Marc faster than humanly possible is out of the Mustang. Grabbing her before she rushes out into the street. Pulling her into his body an instant before a car narrowly misses hitting her. An onlooker too busy trying to see as much as he can. Marc makes a quick obscene gesture at the driver. Traffic behind the accident already backing up. Police cording off all traffic stopped.

Mary oddly quiet looking very distant. Marc says, "There is nothing we could have done. I'm sorry." Mary blinks back tears leaning against his solid chest. Marc spots Detective Barracks talking with uniformed police. Searching for his partner Detective Arros, 'King Cock', god's gift to women. Locking eyes with him from across the street. Great, now there will be more questions. Assuming his best poker face. Never let them see you sweat. *I'm sure somehow this will be my fault. Here we go,* detective Barracks glancing his way.

Detective Barracks speaking loudly, "Don't let that truck driver leave. I want a word with him."

Detective Arros struts across the street toward the two. His black hair slicked back slowly walking as confident men can do. Allowing his large thighs and round buttocks tight in his pants to draw attention. Testosterone filling the air as the two men size each other up for another round.

Detective Arros, "That's bad. I hope it wasn't anyone you knew." Studying Marc's face watching it for a reaction.

Marc answers, "It was her aunt."

Detective Arros, "*Lo cento,* my condolences miss."

Marc knows what was next. "Norma Campbell, but as to why she was in such a hurry, I don't know why." Mary looks up at Marc her face guilt-ridden.

Detective Arros not missing anything especially that look. "How did you know she was in a hurry?" Arros's intense dark brown eyes unflinching. Marc not caught off guard. And certainly not wanting to have everything brought out for scrutiny especially by the police. One more strike for an increasingly dubious reputation.

Detective Barracks picks up on the tension. Quickly choosing to be the devil's advocate. "Why do you two look like you got caught with your hands in the cookie jar?" Arros sees Mary's cheeks redden into a full blush.

Marc visibly irritated, "Well, there's no skid marks." Sounding very defensive.

Detective Barracks, "That's true, but it could also mean her brakes failed."

Detective Arros, "Or she could have been upset about something and been distracted." Letting the unspoken question hang on the air watching their reactions. Marc releases his arm from around Mary's waist. Arros follows a hunch about Mary. Her tear streaked cheeks and red eyes. Obviously not bereaved about her aunt. That and her tears wouldn't have had time to dry leaving salty streaks on her face. Looking all of thirteen or fourteen at the moment.

Mary feels obliged to speak her British accent educated. "We were having a family disagreement."

Detective Arros, "That so? It must have been a very heated disagreement." Reading into their body language. Mary too familiar with Marc for it to be casual. Standing close reaching for his hand. "So what was the argument about? Enlighten us." His square jaw set a blue-black shadow across his clean shaved face.

Mary, "It's personal."

Marc, "You don't have to tell them anything without a lawyer."

Detective Barracks, "That didn't take very long at all. Why would you need a lawyer?"

Detective Arros, "Your accent is British right? Don't you call them barristers? How old are you? Was this all about rich boy here doing the underage maid? Did Auntie go ballistic when she found out?"

Marc, "She is eighteen."

Detective Arros, "I wasn't talking to you."

Detective Barracks, "Do you have proof of that? Such as a driver's license. What's your date of birth?" Mary gives Marc a frightened look before answering him. Barracks flips open his notebook, paging back. "Isn't she a little young for you? I know you're of drinking age, in college right? You and that Camel are pretty tight. Where has he been? Lying low since he was stabbed by one of his harem girls." Not really a question.

Marc, "You seem to have all the answers. You tell me."

Detective Arros becoming aggressive now. Stepping up into Marc's face. "If we had all the answers the body count wouldn't be rising around you and your... boyfriend. Do you really like women? Or is it just a front? Is that why so many young women are dead?"

Marc lunges into Arros's face. "Take that back!"

Detective Barracks stepping between them. "That's enough!" Pushing the two men apart.

Detective Arros, "You want to add assault of a police officer to your charges? Come on! I'm not a petite woman."

Barracks pushes Arros back. Saying something into his ear. Then louder, "Enough, we'll get them, but not like this." Detective Barracks turns back to Marc. "How long have you been intimate with Ms. Campbell here?" Marc's look of surprise is perfect, another question answered. Detective Arros enjoying watching him squirm.

Marc pauses for a split second. 'It's none of their business.' Attempting to nip this in the bud. "Since she turned eighteen."

Arros, "Smooth. So you waited until she was legal, what this weekend?" Marc's poker face is gone now and he's angry. Detective Arros hitting a nerve. How quickly he made him sound like a predator. Glaring back at him.

Marc, "Do I need an attorney?"

Detective Barracks, "Maybe." Speaking to Mary, "You have heard about this one and his partner, right? Everyone knows they share women. Are you all right with that?"

Mary's expression one of hurt, but she still comes to Marc's defense. "Those are just rumors." Marc seething inside now. His sapphire blue eyes the tell with their pupils narrowed. The muscles in his jaw tight from gnashing his teeth.

Detective Arros, "Is that it?"

Marc, "Do we need an attorney present?"

Arros, "Do you?" His Puerto Rican heritage prominent in his handsome moreno face. Intelligent dark brown eyes intense. Muscles rippling under his dress shirt from years of pounding weights and wrestling in the local police department club. Definitely a ladies' man with a gift bulging below. He couldn't stand men that take advantage of young women. Trying another tactic. "How's your friend Camel? That was a remarkable recovery after a near-fatal stabbing." Not expecting Marc to answer, so he continues. "Funny thing, both of those women are dead now." Detective Arros looks at Mary. "You should be careful chica."

Marc snarls, "What's that supposed to mean?"

Arros pauses for effect. "Just that women seem to wind up dead around you two party boys." Marc's cheeks are becoming dusky under his tan skin. Shifting his weight really wanting to punch him for that last comment. Detective Arros reads him. "You got a problem with me?" Stepping in closer to Marc unflinching. Marc looks down into his face being just a shade taller. Those eyes intelligent daring him to make a move. Each young male challenging the other. Shoulders down with chests out evaluating how to take the other down. Mary and Detective

Barracks are both watching the younger males. Barracks enjoying a good fight, Mary afraid for Marc.

Detective Barracks flashes a grin at Mary speaking, "All right, enough of the pissing contest." Neither man taking their eyes off the other.

Marc, "Why are you two here?"

Barracks, "I like that, to the point. The bar your friend was stabbed at is near here. We were investigating your friend's stabbing. Look what we come across. Another death of questionable circumstances." Mary's eyes misting up.

Marc, "We didn't see anything. Is it all right if I take her back into the house? This has been very rough on her." Marc looks at Detective Arros. "If that's all right with you, Detective." His voice sarcastic.

Detective Barracks, "Yeah, go ahead." The clatter of wheels and metal banging. Getting everyone's attention as the gurney with a body bag is pushed into the back of the ambulance.

Mary softly gasps at the sight. The finality reaching all of them from across the street.

Detective Barracks, "We'll need her full name and address with phone numbers where we can contact you. For more questions. You have my deepest condolences, Ms. Campbell."

Detective Arros, "We already have your number." Marc eases Mary toward the car and into the seat. Then gives her information to the police. Concern etched on his handsome face as he steps into his Mustang. Reaching over resting a hand lightly on her shoulder. Mary quiet and withdrawn looking away, not responding to his touch right away. He turns the engine over; it rumbles to life. Dual exhaust glass packs making it sound tough. Easing it up the driveway in reverse.

Detective Arros speaks to Barracks, "That's a sweet ride." Taking in the size of the manor. Whistling. "Have you gotten a look at that house?" The belfry rising above the treetops. Dark clouds thick looking like a taloned hand reaching down toward it.

Detective Barracks, "Yeah, old money."

Detective Arros, "No. I get a real bad feeling about that place. It's spooky." Shaking off a shudder.

Detective Barracks, "What, are you afraid?"

Arros, "Me? No way." Looking back up at the house where its belfry stands. Having sworn he saw a pair of evil yellow eyes watching him from its windows. "*Mi abuela* warned us about the evil—" Stopping himself.

Detective Barracks, "You and your island superstitions. What, is it another of your grandmother's stories?"

Detective Arros, "Never mind. I just wouldn't hang out around here at night." Rumbling coming from the gathering clouds. Lightning streaking across them as they move closer.

Barracks, "And not a minute too soon." The crushed station wagon is pulled onto a flatbed wrecker. Rain splatters onto the hot asphalt road. Steam rises up in the patchy sunlight.

CHAPTER 55

MARC WALKS MARY into the library. "Is there someone you need to contact?"

Mary, "I'm not sure. She was all the family I had."

Marc, "I'll put a call in to Mr. Thornburg." Unfortunately as he had come to suspect pressing speed dial. Ms. Campbell was calling Mr. Thornburg pressing display to see numerous outgoing calls were made to him. His secretary answers the phone informing Marc that Mr. Thornburg is in court with a client. After giving her the message to call him he hangs up. Marc pours Mary a snifter of cognac handing it to her. Unsure of what to do next for her. Going back outside to see if anything else is needed. Opening the side door to Detective Barracks standing there.

Detective Barracks, "Good timing. A family member is going to have to ID the body at the morgue."

Marc, "I'll go with her."

Barracks, "There's no one else?"

Marc, "No."

Barracks, "She's going to need someone strong for her. To get through all this. Not just for the good times."

Marc, "I'll be there for her. Is there anything else?"

"No, that's it for now." Marc ready to close the door Detective Barracks stops him. "Oh yeah. You never said what you were arguing about." Looking more closely at Marc's appearance. Sleeveless tee shirt (a wife beater), soiled from sweat and dirt. His face unshaved for at least two days. Smelling of cologne mixed with a strong masculine scent. Thick dark hair curling over the top of the crew neck. Detective Barracks already getting a bead on his type. Marc looks him in the eyes. Giving him time to make his judgmental assessment.

Marc, "I didn't say we were arguing."

Barracks, "Right. You know some things are transparent. Like a cheap silk shirt you can see through it."

Marc, "I'll keep that in mind."

CHAPTER 56

MARC COMES BACK into the library expecting to have to help Mary through all the arrangements. Mary is on the phone. " Thank you, bye" Marc gives her a questioning look.

Mary, "That was a friend of aunt Norma's and mine as well, Sister Mary Frances. She's going to help me out with the funeral arrangements. At least what hasn't already been taken care of."

Marc, "I'll help you with whatever you need."

Mary's affect distant almost distrusting. "I need to get back to aunt Norma's house. I need to clean up and have some time alone to myself. To collect my thoughts. You understand?"

Marc, "Yeah, I get it. I'll drive you home."

Mary, "No! That won't be necessary. Sister Mary Frances is on her way over to pick me up."

Marc, "Is there something I did wrong? You're acting different."

Mary, "Besides my only family member being dead? After the absolutely worst argument we have ever had?"

Marc, "I understand that but there's something else, isn't there?"

Mary tries to work into it. "Sister Mary Frances says it is inappropriate for me to stay here. You being an unmarried man and no other women in the house."

Marc, "That's a load of bull."

Mary, "It's not just that."

Marc, "What is it?"

Mary, "I'm not comfortable here. Especially now after everything that's happened. I have a lot to think about."

Marc feels a little paranoid. "It's not because of what the detectives said? Those are just lies and rumors."

Mary, "I don't want to get into all of that right now. But yes. Those detective are perfect strangers. Yet they're saying the same things as aunt Norma warned me about. Even Melinda warned me about you and Camel."

Marc, "Surely you don't believe all that? You've seen me around here. I'm not a womanizer."

Mary, "Yes, I have and it makes me take pause."

Marc feeling helpless to defend himself. "I don't know what to say."

Mary, "Say nothing. If you really are concerned about how I feel in all this, you'll give me the time and space I need." The delivery side door bell rings.

Marc, "You'll call me and let me know you're all right?"

Mary, "Yes, I will. You are attending the funeral, right?"

Marc, "For you of course." The doorbell rings again. Marc moves over to hug her good bye.

Mary steps back. "I have to go." Watching her leave wondering what made her completely change. Strange.

Checking the answering machine in the library. Finding several new messages its light blinking. Pressing the play button to retrieve the first message. "Marc, it's Camel. I had another of those bad dreams. This time it was about that mean housekeeper of yours. She dies in a car wreck. A large truck smashed into that old station wagon with her in it." Pausing to think goose bumps rising up on Marc's arms. *What the hell is going on?*

Camel, "It seemed so real. Wouldn't that solve a lot of your troubles. Anyway, call me." *Click.*

Message two, Melinda using her breathy voice. "I haven't heard from you since Saturday night's soiree. I miss you. Sorry about getting jealous. You know I can get a little possessive. Call me and I'll make it up to you." *Click.*

Marc speaks to the machine, "Yes I'll rush to do that. You witch." Still having difficulty getting his mind around that fact.

Message three: "Marc it's Mr. Robert Thornburg. What's going on? I've had two detectives come by my office. Asking a lot of questions with serious implications. I expect you to call me tonight. Is this thing working?" Now half speaking under his breath. "This is my third call. It must be this infuriating weather. Hello? I'll be home after 6:00 p.m." *Click.*

Marc, *Great, now he's involved.* More lectures on discreet behavior and the right associates as friends.

Message four: "Marc it's Camel are you all right? Call me it's important." Pressing redial, Camel picking up on the first ring.

Camel, "Hello, is it you?"

Marc, "Yes. I just got your message."

Camel, "Praise be to Allah. Did you stop Ms. Campbell from driving?"

Marc, "No. It's already too late." Silence.

Camel, "What do you mean?"

Marc, "You're the one that had the dream. She's already dead." Speaking softer. "I know you tried, but I didn't get your message until it was too late."

Camel, "Why is this happening to me. I just don't get it. Nothing like this has ever happened to me before."

Marc, "I think I have some answers for you. We need to meet right away. We've become involved in something unbelievable."

Camel, "What are you talking about?" Marc takes a moment to choose what to say to his best friend. No, really a brother to him.

Marc, "Tell me what you remember about being here last night. When you were here with me."

Camel, "I know I wasn't there with you. I was home last night."

Marc, "You were here. Except it wasn't you."

Camel, "What does that mean? I was home entertaining last night."

Marc, "When? I mean at what time?"

Camel, "In the evening. You're starting to sound like a jealous, I don't know girlfriend. Uh, like Angelique." His attempt at humor not very good.

Marc, "I was at home too, but you were here for a while. We talked quite extensively about what has been going on. Do you not remember any of that?" Testing him to see how much Enkil allows him to know.

Camel, "We did? No. I don't have any recollection of seeing you at all since the night of the party."

Marc, "Just come over now. We have to plan and prepare for what is coming."

Camel, "Are you in trouble with the law? Our family has excellent legal contacts. But you already know that."

Marc, "It's not a legal issue, yet. More importantly the outcome will affect the rest of our lives."

Camel, "You come off so serious. Just tell me."

Marc, "This is not something I will discuss over the phone. It requires a face to face. Okay."

Camel, "Okay." Hearing the concern in Marc's voice. "I'm on my way."

Marc, "Good."

CHAPTER 57

NOW TIME TO call cousin Phillip in New Orleans. Getting Phil's machine, leaving a message to call him back using Marc's cell phone. As he'll have it with him. Passing a mirror on the way upstairs. Catching out of the corner of his eye images blurring and changing, except not of reflections of the manor's interior. Disregarding it as an optical illusion caused by his own movement. Who doesn't see blurred images at the edge of their vision?

Once in the master suite spa Marc strips down in front of the mirror. His tanned face peering back at himself. For all intentions looking like he hasn't shaved in days. Heavy stubble all the way down his neck. Meeting the crush of hair from his chest. Pushing his long hair back out of his face. Now well past his shoulders its color dark brown. Straight like corn silk and shiny yet mane like in that it is so very thick. Realizing just how bad he needs a haircut. *I look like a heathen or a Cro-Magnon man.* Staring at himself, so hirsute at twenty-one. It would have to be those witches. Maybe what Enkil was saying last night was true. And if that is true? Shaking his head, not ready to acknowledge the rest of what is coming. That is, unless they are stopped. His frustration coming out. "Shower on, ninety-eight degrees!" His voice echoing off the stone walls. Marc's back turned to the mirror presenting hair across his large shoulders and down his spine. Meeting at his bulging gluteus maximus. Round yet narrow with dimples on the sides that males can have. When they have a truly masculine figure.

Camel arrives while Marc is in the shower. Letting himself in with his set of keys. Knowing the code to the alarm system, deactivating it. Stopping by the kitchen making himself a sandwich. After all he is family and hungry. Wolfing it down grabbing a can of pop. Snapping it open on the way upstairs gulping some down. Hearing Marc still in the shower with the water running. Camel takes a seat at the table with a view of the garden below. Letting out a large belch. Appreciating the lush arboreal structure of mature trees with large lilacs screening the lower heights. Just able to see part of the private terraced garden with its stone steps leading to it. The long pergola in place on the west side somehow familiar. When did he finish it? Sweet.

Water from in the shower is no longer running. Marc steps out of the shower toweling his back. Glancing at Camel through long wet hair hanging over his face. Camel not missing a chance to tease

Marc. "Dude! You sure you're not Persian or Greek?" Marc continues to dry off ignoring his comment. Wrapping the towel around his waist using a hand to push his long hair out of his face.

Marc, "When did you get here?"

Camel, "Just a few minutes ago." Taking a long drink of his pop. Marc lathers on shaving cream to his face. "I thought my back was hairy but you've got me on that one."

Marc, "Yeah right, the pot calling the kettle black."

Camel feeling playful encouraged by his brother's lack of defense. "No seriously. What gorilla was your mother sleeping with?" Laughing all too pleased with himself. Taking a bite out of his second turkey sandwich.

"Your father!" Marc answers him. Both of them laughing Marc setting his razor down coming over to the threshold of the bathroom. Shaving cream on half his face. "This is a side effect of the spell that was put over me." Indicating his chest (more like a pelt of thick and luxurious mink) which is still damp moving his hands down it. Camel follows his hands all the way down hairy legs matted and wet.

Camel still not taking it seriously says "You don't need a spell to look like that in my family. As you well know most of my uncles and our brothers are hairy." Taking another bite out of his sandwich.

Marc, "I'll be out in a minute."

Camel, "Since when did you start believing in spells?" Cracking open another can of pop. "That terraced private garden looks intriguing from here. When did you finish it?"

Marc, "You will see that soon enough." Washing the remaining shaving cream off his face. Then splashing liberal amounts of Tommy Hilfiger cologne on his face and body. Marc passes out of the bathroom spa nude to go into the dressing room. Not being shy as they grew up together. Spending time in the deserts of Dubai and other parts of Arabia. Tents being close quarters. Pulling on a pair of boxer shorts and then carpenter shorts with all of its pockets. Leaving his new tee shirt off from a local beer representative. Enjoying the comfort of air against his exposed chest.

Marc glances at his cell phone. One missed message checking it. Yes, Phil had called while he was in the shower. "Come on we'll go to the library and take a conference call."

Camel, "Who are we conferencing with?"

"You remember cousin Phil in New Orleans?"

Camel, "Yeah." Giving Marc a questioning look.

"Come on." Taking the lead heading downstairs.

After both men settled in the library comfortably in wingback chairs. Marc presses redial on Phillip's call. "Hello?"

Marc, "Hi, it's your cousin in Rochester."

Phil, "It's about time. I've tried to leave several messages. Your phone system keeps going out of order."

Marc, "I'm not surprised. My cell and the home phones have been out of order on and off."

Phil, "Take it from me every call but one got through."

"We have had some bad thunderstorms. The phones and power have been knocked."

Phil, "You may have some damage that the phone company needs to check out."

Marc, "I'm going to turn the volume up and switch to speakers. You remember Camel? From your summers with us in the UAE?" Camel steps forward in view of the webcam.

Phil, "Yes. How are you?"

Camel, "I'm good considering everything."

Phil, "I'll say so improving with age." Managing to flirt with him. Phil having had a big crush on Camel for years. "You don't look to have been seriously wounded recently."

Camel, "I'm good as new thank you. What have you found out from that old book?"

Phil, "That old book is called a grimoire or a book of shadows." Both young men look at each other. "Good, I'm glad I have your attention because this is serious," Phil says. "Do either of you understand just what that 'book,' as you call it, is?" Phil takes their silence as a negative. "It is a book of spells combined with a diary." Camel and Marc speak at once.

Phil, "Wait! It gets better, Marc. One of our female relatives started it in 1600s. She kept writing in it for over two hundred years."

"That's impossible," Marc says.

Camel not missing the distinction, "One of your distant relatives was a witch."

Phil, "Now you're getting on track. Marc it's the same handwriting for over two hundred years. She uses runes to identify herself by. We're working on the name." Seeing that Marc was impatient to speak Phil adds, "Hold on I'm not finished. I spoke with our great-great-aunt Croisant. She lives in Shreveport in a nursing home. Mentally she is still very cognizant for one hundred and two years old. She said family legend has it this grimoire was written by one of our distant great-grandmothers. Then used by a cousin of ours to gain power and money. After which she disappeared and the grimoire was believed to be lost. Finally she said it was dangerous. If anyone found it, they need to understand it is evil and should be locked away or buried in hallowed ground."

Marc, "Why not destroy it?"

"Good question. I asked that also. She said it was cursed and that it could not be destroyed."

Marc, "Then I'll just burn it."

Camel, "Good idea."

Phil, "Not so fast. That's not all she said. Aunt Croisant said it couldn't be. That the one who tries will find themselves cursed."

"Cursed? What will happen?" Camel asks.

Phil, "She didn't know but she said to leave it alone. Anyone who has tried to use it, well no good has come to them."

"I don't know if I buy into all this cursed nonsense," Marc says.

Camel, "Really. Really?" Marc looking annoyed with both of them. "Look at you."

Phil, "He's got a point. You're starting to look like a bear. And not in a good way."

Marc ignores that last comment. "What else can you tell us?"

Phil, "I have a Jesuit friend helping me with the Latin translations. This ancestor of ours and a couple of other Du Bois family members were straight out evil. Marie le Noir was using demonic powers to enslave the King Louis XV for her twin sister Madame du Barry"

"Oh come on," Marc says. Not believing his cousin.

Camel, "Which one?"

Phil, "Louis XV. It gets better. Madame du Barry slandered a member of Marie Antoinette's family infuriating her. She's the one who Louis XV had the million dollar diamond necklace commissioned for not Marie Antoinette."

Marc, "That was just a legend. That never really happened."

Phil, "She impersonated her and accepted it."

Marc, "Are you serious?"

Camel, "So you're saying that a distant relative of yours Madame du Barry set up the royal family and inadvertently caused the French revolution?"

Phil, "I'm saying I've got a smoking gun here. Some of this actually confirms stories from that time. The French government is known to have gone into massive debt because of Marie Antoinette's spending on jewelry."

Marc, "Which she denied all the way to the guillotine."

Phil, "Right! Because she did not order the consignment. It is certain she never took possession of that necklace. That other priceless gems were never found in her belongings"

Camel, "Does she say where she hid the jewels?"

Phil, "No. However she does refer to having them before she was attempting to flee to London. Madame du Barry never made it. She was arrested and later executed by guillotine. However Jeannette la Noir fled to London. Where you know the Hope Diamond was sold a few days after the French government wouldn't be able to lay claim. A large blue diamond sold from London. It's quite exciting reading." Camel, "Is there more?"

"That's as far as Paul has gotten," Phil says.

"Who's Paul?" Marc asks.

"He is the ex-Jesuit priest that is helping me with the Latin translations," Phil says.

"It would be incredible to find all those diamonds," Camel says.

Marc, "We need to get back on track."

Phil, "Right you are. Marc tells me there have been a few unexplained deaths occurring around you. A number of women you have been sleeping with are dead." Camel gives Marc a stern look. Marc nods his head to go on. Giving him a reassuring look that it's okay to spill all the story.

Marc, "That's why I have you here. I had two detectives asking questions about you. And now I'm on their radar with Ms. Campbell's sudden death."

Phil, "Someone else is dead?"

Marc, "Yes. The housekeeper is dead."

Phil, "That's too close, you have to protect yourselves. It's gotten into your home."

Camel, "What, no remorse?"

Marc, "What has gotten in?" Then speaking to Camel. "I'm not happy she is dead. But you don't know how extremely mean and twisted her mind was."

"Who?" Phil asks

Marc, "The housekeeper."

Camel, "She found out you slept with her niece, right?"

Marc, "Yes, but that's not the issue. She went all Christian extremist on me. You know how they are in the Southern part of this country."

Phil, "It's not just Camel. You are both up to your necks in this." Everyone speaking at once.

Marc yelling, "Quiet! I can't hear myself think."

Camel, "Was she of age?"

Marc, "Yes."

Camel, "Then she was just of age. You have nothing to worry about. In Europe legal is fifteen."

Phil, "We're getting off topic again."

After Marc and Camel bring Phil up to the present. About everything that has been going on. The strange dreams both of them have been having. Along with the physical changes in appearance. Phil is finally ready to speak. "You two have been playing around with a powerful book of spells. Haven't you both learned from the Koran or the Bible? How powerful words are." Even from online his young face is visibly concerned. Both of his cohorts listening reflectively. Trying not to let their embarrassment show. Phil being the youngest of the three. Yet coming across more wise and worldly.

Phil, "Letting a powerful witch such as Angelique..." Camel ready to object, Phil cuts him off, raising his hand toward the camera. "That is what she is have no doubt. This wouldn't be my first encounter with one. Certainly not so directly. She sounds to be very vengeful. Being a practitioner of the dark arts it goes with the territory, Camel. One of the cute rhymes that you allowed them to use. We just translated is a ritual of possession. Which bestows the intended person with dreams of premonition."

Camel, "How is that possible? I just cannot believe this is happening."

Phil, "Believe it and learn. Those dream premonitions may become of some use. If you act on them quickly enough."

Marc, "This is so incredible. If I weren't right in the middle of this I would assume it was a tale. Told to scare young children at night."

Phil, "You have to understand that what is happening to the two of you is real. And it will destroy you if you don't master it." Camel shakes his head. Marc looking lost.

Phil, "Has the demon made its presence known to either of you?"

Camel, "No!" a loud response.

Marc, "Yes." His voice low barely a whisper. Camel eyes him suspiciously his brown eyes frightened. A stark contrast to his usual devil may care handsome face. Beginning to feel that the gist of Marc's next comments coming way too slowly are going to affect him. Marc has never seen Camel so scared.

Phil, "Go on. It's time to come clean." Sensing their rising fear as his own increases. His closest family members before him. Encouraging Marc to continue.

Marc, "I've seen the being and he is incredibly strong. I mean powerful." Camel watches Marc intensely.

Phil, "Could you be more specific? When did you see him?"

Marc, "Last night in the garden. It appeared before me from out of the shadows."

Camel, "Is that why we are here having this meeting?" His normally deep voice wavering.

Phil surmises what caused it to come to Marc. "What were you doing to conjure it?"

"You conjured it?" Camel says.

"I was just reading from the book. I was tired and having trouble pronouncing the name." Marc sounding defensive. "I fell asleep saying its name. All right! It… he said I was calling for him." A cold rush of air blows over the three of them. Being in different parts of the continent and still causing the hair on their arms to rise up. Phil involuntarily shivers.

Camel, "You fool! Why would you say a demon's name out loud?" Speaking out of fear more than a question.

Marc becomes more defensive if it was possible. Made by the sting of his brother's words. "I was falling asleep. All I was trying to do was to pronounce another word from that book, okay?"

"Grimoire," Phil corrects him.

Marc glares at Phil. "So I kept rereading the same line over and over again. As I was falling asleep. When I woke up in the hammock he was there. Waiting for me in the darkness. He stepped out of the shadows." Camel's look of horror passes to fright. Twisting Marc's insides up with pain from guilt. Knowing what he was going to say next to his brother would be much worse. Camel remembers what his brother had said earlier about having seen him last night. Knew he was holding back something bad. Watching him closely waiting as the sense of dread rises up inside his intestines. The truth close now.

Phil softly coaxes Marc, "What is it?" His cousin always so honest and not very good at hiding hurtful information. Tension increasing for him even at this great distance. This had to be bad news.

Camel, "Come on, say it." Regretting that it came out so gruffly.

Marc looks Camel in the eyes. "It was in you!"

Camel angrily, "That is not possible!" Everyone speaks at once.

Phil, "Shut up! Let him speak."

"I would know," Camel says.

Marc, "He was there."

Phil asks, "Camel do you have any memories of this?"

Camel, "NO! Of course not. This is not something I would forget." Feeling like he was the butt of a bad joke.

Phil, "Not necessarily until it is ready to reveal itself."

Camel, "How do you know so much?"

Phil, "I'm working with an ex-Jesuit priest. Are these premonitions always in your dreams?"

Camel not so easily convinced. "Dreams yes, always." Becoming angry. "Come on this is some childish attempt at messing with my mind. You think because I'm Arabic I'm some superstitious nomad that's uneducated. You can't trick me so easily!" Standing up from his chair angrily ready to leave.

Marc, "Wait! Hear me out. I am not playing some childish joke on you. This is serious and it affects both of us." Camel not so convinced anymore. Watching Marc's face for any sign of a smile. Then he would know it was a prank. "Please listen to me," Marc pleads, Camel reluctantly sitting back down.

Marc, "After you hear what I have to say. Then we can go outside and you can see for yourself the power that is involved."

Camel, "This had better be on the level." His handsome face not its usual easy going anymore. His forehead furrowed with deep lines of concern.

Phil, "All right go on Marc." His own curiosity roused.

Marc, "It was Camel but not your voice. His is much deeper, a bass actually. He spoke with an accent. Now that I think about it at first he spoke another language. One that I have never heard before." Camel sits but is very uneasy with the story that was coming out.

Marc goes on to explain how at first he didn't believe Enkil either. At least not until he conjured stone pavers. How they spread across the ground rippling out from a bolt of lightning. Having followed the blueprints improving on the design. But using more rare materials. Phoenician stone and black granite laced with gold throughout it. Causing it to sparkle under the moonlight. Like twinkling stars.

Marc, "The stonemason was here this morning. He said it was old world master craftsmanship at its best." Both men listen intently. Marc encouraged by their silence to continue. "He had never seen such quality work and asked me who had done it. So he could hire him for some future projects coming up." Camel becomes intrigued with this tale. "I've been around enough archaeological sites to recognize Phoenician stonework. He must have taken it from ruins on the western shores on the Sinai." Both men talking at once.

Camel being the louder of the two says, "I want to see this terraced mosaic that I created. That is what you are telling us." Looking dubiously between Marc and Phil on the other end of the webcam.

Phil, "You didn't tell me about that."

Marc, "I haven't had time. Something has been happening to me all day to the present. I did leave messages for both of you to call me."

Camel, "You should have tried harder. Why didn't you tell me sooner about this...," pausing. He didn't want to use the words coming to mind ("devil" and "possession"). "Being!" Marc at a loss for words. "Why can't I remember anything about this?" Camel asks.

A voice comes from behind Phil. "Because the possessed don't usually know they are."

Phil startled bangs his knee letting out a gasp from pain. Marc and Camel stand up alarmed and concerned for Phil.

"Who the hell is that?" Camel asks.

Phil, "Jesus, you could have let me know you were home."

"Hi, Paul Broussard here. I am so sorry Phillip. I thought you heard me come in."

Phil, "Here is the ex-Jesuit I was telling you about. That is helping me translate the Latin. He also has been pretty helpful in interpreting the runes."

Camel, "How many people know about this?"

Marc, "Just the four of us." Sneaking a glance at Phil. To see him confirm this with a nod of his head.

"You two young men," Paul Broussard speaks with authority being the oldest of the four almost thirty, "have gotten yourselves involved with some extremely dangerous people."

Marc, "Tell me something I don't already know."

Paul, "This grimoire is the worst sort of dark magic. It's almost unimaginable how far powers like these could reach. No one is safe in your families."

Marc, "We didn't know the people we considered friends were so corrupted."

Paul, "I only have a few people I consider true friends. And I can count them on one hand." Sounding more like Camel's dad by the minute. Paul continues, "We have like minds with genuine interests. For the betterment and preservation of humanity. You certainly cannot say that about these friends of yours."

"We were just having fun. Trying something different out to amuse the ladies." Marc sounding foolish.

Camel speaks up. "It was Angelique. She was the one that suggested we do something different."

Marc adds, "As a matter of fact she was the one who discovered that book in the first place."

"Yes, I remember. You practically handed the book right to her." Camel's voice accusatory.

Marc, "Thanks, like I don't feel bad enough about all this."

Paul, "What do you mean she discovered it? How did she find the grimoire?"

Camel, "It was on the table when we came back from the kitchen."

Marc, "I don't know. It was just on the table. Our dates suggested we read from it since we didn't want to have a seyonce."

Camel, "Strange things started right away." Putting his big hand to the side of his head. Trying to picture that night. As if somehow running his fingers through his dark hair would trigger his memory speaking, "Angelique placed her hands over the grimoire and its pages fluttered open to the section we read aloud from."

Marc, "I thought it was just the air blowing the pages. At least not until much later at the time she just held her hands over it."

Paul, "Thereby giving her express access and as much as permission." His expression exasperated. "I can't believe you considered this fun." Both men feeling guilty. "You're mixed up in powers beyond your abilities to control them. Camel besides these dreams do you have any memories intruding into your consciousness that don't seem quite like they are yours?"

Camel answers, "No. I don't have someone else's memories." Disbelief in his voice.

Marc, "Well that's not really true. You have memories of a demon named Enkil. Whatever he is." Paul yells at Marc, "You never say its name! Or any other unholy creature's name. Unless you are conjuring it." Camel's eyes flash to yellow and then back to normal. All too quickly for any of them to notice.

Marc, "I'm sorry I didn't know that."

Camel, "This is ridiculous. There is not anything in possession of me." Standing up, slamming his sizeable fist like a judge's hammer against the tabletop. Bringing everyone to silence. Understandably upset and ready to leave. "This is some colossal joke, isn't it?" Camel says, his dark eyes fiery with anger. Marc unsure of what to say next. Knowing how his brother can be once he is angered. Not easily pushed to the edge.

Marc, "I need your help with this one." Speaking to Paul, "Is there anything I can do to help him remember or to demonstrate to him what is going on here?"

Phil, "Show him the stonework outside. It sounds impressive."

Marc, "It's beautiful beyond anything I could have imagined."

Camel, "Show me."

Paul, "We can continue this later. Camel this being will reveal itself to you in due time. You both need to know this. The longer it inhabits a host the stronger it will become. Making it more difficult to drive out of him." Paul speaking to Camel, "You are going to have your faith tested. It will be all you have to keep your sanity. Hold on to it with all your might."

Camel, "How are you so sure of this?"

Paul, "Every man it your condition has his faith challenged. Allah will be the one to get you through this." Both sets of men separated by hundreds of miles. Somber in their looks between each other. Their silence broken by the crackle of static. A rapidly building thunderstorm rumbling in the Crescent City.

Paul continues, "Now Marc what effects are you presenting with?" Marc swallows, as a slight rush of blood to his cheeks colors them dusky.

Camel gives him a condescending glance and then comments, "Now you can have yourself exposed." Marc pauses before speaking. Not relishing the idea of admitting to an ex–holy man be that as it may. His personal life of which he has become extremely horny and promiscuous.

Camel answers for him. "He is as horny as a herd of goats and becoming just as hairy." Marc gives him a dirty look. "Well, it's true isn't it?"

Marc, "Yes, he is correct."

Phil, "That wasn't so bad was it?" Marc gives Camel another dirty look.

Marc, "Next time I'll just bring you to confession. Then you can speak for me." Camel smirks with a satisfied look on his face.

Phil, "All right. You two need to stick together now more than ever."

Paul, "That is correct. What we have learned is that this is a ritual to gather sexual energy from men. Which at your age is very strong. It's like picking ripe apples there for the taking."

Phil, "Once the spell is completed neither of you will be human anymore. You have stopped having sex with this women, right?"

Paul, "Let us be clear on this matter. These are no ordinary women they are witches. And I don't mean Wiccan nice do no harm to anyone. These are the kind legends are told of. If what we are translating is true. The frightening reality is a vindictive and jealous woman who set up Marie Antoinette. Destroying her and her family."

Phil, "You have stopped right?" His meaning clear.

Marc, "Uh, well yes, sort of."

Camel, "Now that's not really the truth is it?" Marc looking very guilty. "You tapped that virgin didn't you, big dog?"

Paul, "What virgin?"

Phil speaks to Paul, "I told him to cool his jets. He wasn't supposed to have any physical relations with any of these women."

Marc, "She's not one of them. They were using her just like us."

Paul, "You know this how?"

Marc, "She's a good Catholic girl."

Camel, "Just how good was she?"

Marc, "Shut up!"

Camel, "Very touching, Brother. I guess we have our answer."

Paul, "Assuming this is true. You are still following them into what is still yet a larger plan. This is a new development. Where is this young woman now?"

After bringing everyone up to date on what happened, Marc says, "She is staying with one of her nun friends at the cloister.

Paul, "She may still need protecting."

Marc, "That is why I asked her to stay here with me."

Paul, "Not such a good idea. Who is going to protect the two of you from each other and these witches."

Marc, "I did stop after the night of the party. So much happened that night. You remember Camel. They were so mean to her and...," pausing.

Camel looks him in the eyes. Searching his face. "Yes we both were easy targets. You especially. Your Melinda attacked Mary. Throwing her drink on her then slapping her face. You rushed right in to protect her."

Marc, "Yes, I did." Feeling like an idiot now. "Angelique had her waiting in the bedroom for me." Remembering how enticing Mary looked that night. In her silk and lace undergarments once the robe had slid off her. His pulse quickening at the thought of her green eyes so round and sensuous. Her milky white skin luminescent. Able once again to feel her soft flesh under his rough hands. His respirations coming quick and heavy.

Camel, "Marc! Back to earth!" Pulling Marc back out of his reverie and lust.

Phil, "Is what I think just happened there?"

Camel, "Yes, my brother is behaving as a bull in musk."

Paul, "She can't stay with you. If mere thoughts of her arouse you that much. What's going to happen when she is alone with you?" Marc ready to object. "Add that to some outside influences and you'll be powerless to stop yourself. She needs to stay at the cloister," Paul says. Marc accepts his advice reluctantly at first. Paul then adds, "I can make some calls if you need to help facilitate this."

Angelique returns to her mirror to spy but also to enjoy the view. After all, where is the fun in creating unexpected trouble if you can't watch it? Her mirrors image ripples out as drop of water striking a still pond. Casting her hands over the Louis XVI mirror. "Someone is blocking me from viewing. What is going on over there?" Her blue eyes round and bulging with rage. "Someone will pay for this!"

Paul, "You may have unwittingly aided them in their plans. Now that we are onto them. You must abstain from sexual relations with any woman."

Marc, "I don't understand why this is happening to us." His frustration evident in his young face. His eyes no longer youthfully naive.

Paul, "Patience and time will reveal their hand. We have already gained some insight into what they are after."

Marc, "Does this abstinence include masturbation? Because if it does not I'm in trouble."

Paul, "I believe that should be safe enough."

Marc, "What about the erotic wet dreams I keep having? They are powerful."

Paul, "Are they the same women from the coven in them?"

Marc, "Yes. Also I have discovered..." Himself embarrassed to admit this out loud. Everyone waiting for him to finish.

Paul, "Yes," encouraging him gently to speak.

"Well, when Melinda or Jadon requests of me, I don't know. Something comes over me."

Camel, "Tell us what happens?"

Marc, "They have so much allure, I find myself completely captivated. I cannot deny them. My beguilement is so strong. There is no self-control left in me." His cheeks hot from the blood rushing to them so forcefully. Camel nods his head in agreement. As if to say, *I could buy that*. "You know what I mean?" Looking to Camel for understanding.

Camel, "Yes." Avoiding admitting any more than he had to about the same feelings. At least those he did have until recently. When did he start having more control?

Paul, "I believe we are way past being shy about these matters. We are all men here speaking openly. You are what is called bewitched or enthralled."

"How do I fight that?" Marc asks

"Usually a strong faith combined with prayer. When was the last time either of you went to mosque or church?" Marc and Camel mumble at once.

Paul, "I didn't get that. When?" Putting both men on the spot forcing them to come up with an answer.

"I'm not sure. It couldn't have been that long ago," Camel says.

Marc, "It's been a while since I have prayed." Acknowledging, "Longer since I've been to a mosque."

Paul, "You both need to go to mosque. And some prayer to Allah would be of benefit. Especially with circumstances becoming so dire. It sounds to me like you both have exhibited poor judgment. Much less than behaved righteously."

Marc, "Are you saying we brought this on ourselves?"

Paul, "No, but caution from now on would be wiser. Until this spell is broken Marc. If masturbation helps you have control over yourself I don't see any harm in it. Especially if you gain more resistance to their charms. Then do it. Camel you may need an exorcism to drive this demonic being from you."

Camel, "I am not comfortable with the idea of some ancient Christian ritual being performed over me." Glancing at Marc for support.

"Possibly your iman will have something more suitable from the Koran,"

Paul suggests. "But understand this much. You run the risk of never being free from it. The longer it stays with you if you will," Paul speaks more sternly.

Marc, "I'm not going to let that happen to my brother. Some infidel witches aren't going to beat us. We are educated Muslim men." Camel gives Marc a look as if he was a worldly man. Not the eyes of a man only twenty-one years old.

Paul, "Pride cometh before a fall. I caution against sexual relations with any women. To the both of you until these issues are resolved."

Marc, "I'm not proud. I'm just not beaten and I won't stop until we both have our lives back."

Paul, "Keep that resolve. You're going to need it. I have a feeling your faith and soul are going to be challenged in ways you can't imagine yet. If this is as far reaching as I suspect. We will all be tested by fire."

Phillip looks to Paul, his young face concerned. Seeking reassurance from his partner. Paul himself of French descent but a blonde with intense blue eyes. Unwavering in strength and his stubble-covered jaw set in resolve with the muscles tight. Phillip has never seen him look fervent. Himself feeling a sense of dread building in the pit of his stomach twisting it. The seriousness of their predicament felt on both ends of this distant communication. Static crackling in the background. Silence being the only solace they have. As the storm that truth has shown to be gathering around them builds like a hurricane pulling clouds to it quickly. Silence like death ringing in their ears no longer a comfort.

Phil anxious to shake this feeling speaks first. "Finish scanning and faxing that section from the grimoire. We will continue translating and searching for answers." All of them grateful for the distraction from their own thoughts.

CHAPTER 58

CAMEL AND MARC sit quietly after disconnecting from the conference call. Taking in the ramifications of this new information. Finally Marc stands up. "Come on let's go look at your master craftsmanship." Camel follows him quietly.

Stepping outside taking the flagstone path with its rich peach tones. Camel appreciates the work Marc had put into it. Taking the three steps up onto the terrace. It's like stepping into another time. The age of the stone with the attention to detail is breathtaking. Camel speaks, "It's beautiful." Examining the spacing. "It is like a mosaic." The late afternoon sun already off the terrace. With only the rustle of leaves and a glimpse of the mansard roof seen from where they are standing. One could believe they were in some distant European forest.

Camel working his way around the entire terrace examining its inlaid stonework. Every bit as beautiful as some of the mosaic tile patterns in the old mosques. Exquisitely fashioned. Camel satisfied look to Marc genuine appreciation of the workmanship.

Marc, "Do you remember any of this? Anything at all from last night?"

Camel takes his time in answering. "I'm just not sure. This hammock seems familiar." Staring at the bronze age candleholder with beeswax dripped down with the faintest scent of honey.

Marc, "You were standing right there." Excitement showing on his face. Pointing at the place where Enkil had stood.

"You were here." Camel guessing where Marc was in the hammock.

Marc becomes disappointed. "Yes. That is where you told me told me about Angelique along with the others being witches. How they were using both of us to gather our sexual energy or power. That is created out of desire and passion."

Camel listens. "Go on."

Marc, "When I didn't believe you to be Enkil, that is when he conjured this stonework to prove who he said he was." Marc realizes too late for as soon as he used Enkil's name, Camel's eyes changed, and so did his demeanor.

Enkil, "So we are back here again. Why?" Looking into Marc's eyes and face. Trying to read him. Marc keeps his best poker face in place. Unwilling to give any indication as to why they were there. "Very well." Enkil moves up to Marc so quickly that in one blink of an eye both of Enkil's large hands are placed on either side of his head.

Unable to move Marc panics. "What are you doing."

Enkil, "Taking some knowledge. So you want Camel to know about me?" Understanding now what Enkil was doing. Also that he would be unable to lie to him. At least not easily.

Marc, "Yes. I don't want to become a satyr any more than Camel does. We have to break this spell."

Enkil, "You think that I would help you?" Taking his hands off Marc's head, satisfied with what he has sensed. That and Marc's response.

Marc going with a hunch looks Enkil in his predatory yellow eyes frighteningly inhuman. Glaring back at him more that of a panther's equally cold and unreadable. "I don't think you want some mortal witches controlling you any more than we do." Camel's ruggedly handsome face distant. Marc becomes close to panic. Maybe he had overplayed his hand. A sly smile crosses his brother's face with those angry yellow eyes.

Enkil, "That was very insightful. They won't be soon. Camel is no longer affected by their simple spells." His disdain for the witches apparent. "Why should I help you?"

Marc, "A common enemy."

Enkil, "I like the way you think. But if you're going to try and manipulate me, you will need to do better than that." Marc's spark of hope fading. "What makes you think they are mortal?" Marc's surprised expression pleases him. "You are a child in a world of manipulation."

Marc thinks fast. "Because they conjured you. They will always be trying to control you. Is it not better to have an ally? Than being some witches lackey." Enkil's eyes becoming angry." Marc continues, "No really just a lap dog castrated and impotent just neutrally watching on."

Enkil's eyes becoming angrier with his jaw tight. Marc having hit the mark. "Helpless really, waiting until it is no longer of value." Enkil glaring at Marc now. "I'm not so sure of your neutrality. You will always have an interest in this one's life. To be neutral is to be without gain." Marc's insides twist again; Enkil has seen through his ploy. "Yet you are right. An ally in this fight would benefit both of us. I will consider your offer. Now I will take my leave." Enkil's form shimmers and then vanishes. Leaving in its wake a warm breeze. Moving Marc's ever-increasing long hair across his face.

Left standing alone the crickets pickup their nightly song. As fireflies winking on create streaks of light across the darkening shadows of dense growth surrounding him. Marc walks back to the house along the Crab Orchard flagstone. Illuminated by landscape lights that weren't there before. Enkil is quick to learn the newest features of this century. Still in all Marc appreciating his attention to detail.

CHAPTER 59

MARC CHECKS THE answering machine. Which always seems to have messages. Retrieving the first one. Mary calling to say she will be staying at the sister house. Next, Mr. Thornburg. He will be contacting a local housekeeping service. After his wife screens candidates sending them over for Marc to interview for replacement housekeeper.

While sitting in the library after studying the grimoire. The grandfather clock hammers out its deep sound carrying from the foyer down the hall. The only other sound in the manor other than his own breath. Concentrating on the information he had just read. His phone rings startling him out of his silent ruminations. Debating whether to let the machine take the call and just listen to who is calling. Marc recognizes the country code on the caller ID. Iraq. Grabbing the phone up not quick enough to prevent the message from starting.

"Hi Marc it's your dad."

Marc, "Dad!" Not intending to yell into the receiver.

Charles, "Your message came across as urgent. What's going on?" Marc glad to hear his father's friendly voice.

"It's so good to hear your voice," Marc says.

Charles, "You knew I was out in the deep desert at a site. I'm working with a group to preserve historic antiquities. Through location and dedication of land areas."

"I don't know where to begin," Marc rushes to speak.

Charles, "You don't sound any worse for the wear. What could be so important? It's very dangerous to travel here. Especially into the cities. You know that from the news. If you're keeping up with world events." His annoyance apparent in his voice. Marc all too aware of how his father hates being interrupted from his life's work by the trivialities of others.

Marc, "Dad, I'm sorry but I really needed to speak with you."

Charles, "Well? Go ahead then, you have my attention. What is so important?"

Marc, "What do you know of our family history?"

Charles, "You called me about that? Now?" Impatience rising in his tone. "You couldn't be bothered when myself and your uncle Theron tried to talk to you about this. Unfortunately your uncle Theron is gone now. He knew a lot more of our family lore than I do."

Marc, "I'm having some problems here. Our family lore, as you call it, could be of some benefit to know." Marc stalls, having difficulty getting to the point. Already expecting his father to be less than understanding.

Charles, "Why the sudden interest? This couldn't wait until after Ramadan?"

Marc, "No, Dad."

Charles, "There are increasing numbers of pilgrims now. Making it more dangerous than ever for foreigners to travel. I can't just leave at the drop of a hat."

Marc, "A set of events have set in motion circumstances that I'm struggling with to understand." Pausing, unsure how much to tell his dad without sounding foolish.

Charles, "Wow. I guess that expensive education paid off. You sound more like an evasive politician than I care to recognize. So what is it, you need money?"

Marc, "No, Dad, that would be simple."

Charles, "Of course not. You have a trust fund. Plus money from your great-uncle Theron's estate."

Marc, "You're making this more difficult to explain." Beginning to wish he hadn't bothered to call his dad at all.

Charles, "Have you gotten some girl pregnant?"

Marc, "No! It's not like that!"

Charles, "Don't raise your voice at me. Just tell me and be done with it!"

Marc, "What do you know about our ancestor Marie Jeanette Lametz le Noir?"

Charles, repeating her name, "Marie Jeanette Lametz le Noir," not remembering too much about her. Except, "Family legend has it that she practiced *the dark arts*." Charles placing heavy emphasis on those three words. "Marc seriously? That could have been because in her day someone considered her a fast and loose woman. I wouldn't place too much value in those kind of old family stories. I couldn't possibly remember any of the specifics about her. You have at your disposal a vast amount of information on our family right there in that library. All you have to do is take the time to research it."

Marc, "I already have started."

"Watch your tone with me," Charles says.

"Dad, I don't have one. I was just hoping you had some knowledge of her."

Charles, "Your cousin in New Orleans, Phillip would be your go to man. You remember him, don't you?"

"Yes, I have already enlisted his help on this matter. He was always interested in our family legends." His voice less irritated.

"Phil has investigated numerous ancestors with unusual finds. He's a law professor at Tulane. I always knew he would do well for himself." Charles's voice almost proud of his nephew.

Marc, "Yes." His voice dry, a little too short for Charles.

"You don't have to begrudge him his expertise. He worked hard for his degree in international law and his law degree. The Napoleonic Code is required to practice law in Louisiana. I believe he has another degree also in French language."

Marc, "Yes, he does."

"How's he doing?" Charles asks.

Marc, "He's good, happy with his career teaching and he is partner in a firm." Charles chuckles softly only too happy for the son he never had, or so Marc felt. Charles hears his son's impatient catch of breath. Chooses not to continue with the sore subject of his successful first cousin. Marc waits in irritated silence for his dad to give Phil more exaltations.

Charles, "You know Theron did mention something about the occult. Giving some reason I don't remember. How some of our family members are drawn to the dark arts."

Marc pulse quickens. This was the reason he had called Dad. "Yes?"

Charles, "Nothing, I don't remember. Theron even suggested that your uncle, my twin brother, was attracted to the occult. It was his involvement in that is what led to his untimely death. I never bought into that nonsense." Marc's moment of excited hope gone. "You're not involved in the occult with their ridiculous practices are you? Not that I would believe any of those stories and legends. I need empirical hard scientific proof." Marc has not answered his father yet. Charles is fully aware of his son's lack of a response to his question. Pressing him for an answer. "Now why do you want to know about our ancestor?"

Marc chooses to take the plunge. "We've been having some problems here." He explains about the night they found the grimoire. How Angelique had used the book. Charles listens patiently, holding his comments until Marc has finished his story.

Marc, "Dad, Camel has changed. He really conjured or made Phoenician stone pavers appear. Completing the terrace here." Marc rushes on, "I'm changing physically. I've become hirsute now and I'm always horny."

Charles, "Hold on for a minute. You are a young man, and French. At your age that is all I had on my mind."

"Dad, it's not like that," Marc says.

Charles, "Come on, most men think about sex all the time. As far as body hair, we may not talk about it much. But a large portion of us become hairy the older we get. Besides, it was really the only difference between your uncle and myself. If it weren't for that we would have remained identical."

Marc, "This stuff is thick like some kind of animal pelt."

Charles, "I'm afraid it just may be that way for you. My twin brother your uncle Anton had a hairy body. When he was younger he didn't. That just comes with age for some of us."

Marc, "Don't you think it was weird that only he was hairy? This really is so much more. I can't believe you don't get it."

Charles, "It's okay. Some women don't mind a bear in their bed. You sound almost hysterical. You can have laser hair removal. What about Camel? Doesn't he have quite a bit?"

Marc, "Yes, but his isn't as thick as mine now."

Charles, "Marc, you know Camel has always been a trickster. Are you sure he isn't playing some elaborate stunt? He always liked setting up."

Marc, "This is no trick. It would have been impossible to do all that." Charles is doubtful. "Besides, my body has changed over a matter of weeks and days not years."

Charles, "Maybe you need to see an endocrinologist. Excessive body hair with increased sex drive could be a sign of a hormonal imbalance. I'm not a medical doctor. You need to get it checked on."

Marc, "I'll put that under consideration but I'm sure it is not anything a 'doctor of medicine' will be able to resolve."

Charles, "You get that streak of stubbornness from your mother. Once she has an idea in her head, she is like a pit bull and won't let it go. So you believe you have been affected by some pagan ritual?" Almost laughing at the preposterousness of that thought. Marc's father not completely able to keep the laugh out of his voice. Marc's silence a mute testament to his irritation. "At your age all I could think about was sex and women. And how I was going to combine the two. Most men your age have a steady girlfriend or a wife."

Marc, "I do, or I did have one."

Charles, "Are you promiscuous?"

Marc, "Dad!" uncomfortable where the conversation was heading.

Charles, "Dad nothing. Most women will not put up with a man that's sleeping around. Are you practicing safe sex?" Not waiting for him to answer. "Always use a condom. The AIDS epidemic is increasing worldwide."

Marc, "I've had sex education."

Charles, "That's evasive. You have been using protection with these women, haven't you?"

Marc, "It started out that way, but no I don't always." Their conversation heads in the wrong direction. "That's not why I'm calling."

Charles, "You could be paying for a mistake like that for the rest of your life. Let alone the matter of assets they have to go after now. Open your eyes and think with your big head not the dumb one. A child could be used against you."

Marc, "I'm aware of that, but it's not about money. These women all come from money. We're getting off the subject. You obviously aren't taking what I say seriously." Marc's snapping at his father.

Charles, "I know this, you will not take that tone with me."

Marc, "Dad, I'm sorry. I didn't mean to snap at you."

Charles, "I am taking you seriously. But you have to rule out the most overt reasons. Before you assume a condition that is affecting you…," pausing, "is due to some pagan ritual predating Islam."

Marc, "I have, Dad." Resignation in his voice. Knowing his father doesn't believe him.

Charles, "Camel has always been a joker. Playing jokes on you and his family. Wasn't it Ibrar who was always being irritated by his numerous pranks?"

Marc, "Yes, you are correct."

Charles, "I wonder how Camel's father would feel about this. The two of you fornicating all these women. Behaving as lascivious… cockles."

Marc, "Why don't you just say it? Male whores."

Charles, "You are certainly speaking as common as one." Continuing his train of thought. "Ahmed is a very old school religious man. He would not approve of one his sons or godson behaving as such."

Marc, "I haven't forgotten that."

Charles, "His father wouldn't tolerate an infidel as a friend to his son. Much less in their home at one time. Your mother and I both agreed. A formal religious education from an iman would benefit you even though we are both Christian. Have you been to a mosque or church since you have been back in the States?"

Marc, "Uh, yes, once or twice." Becoming defensive. "I have been busy working as set forth in the trust. The grounds here had fallen into neglect, so has the house. Mr. Thornburg makes me account for every penny. I have to do most of the work here to save money for the manor account."

Charles, "That's wise of him. How else do you think families of wealth keep their money? Enough said on that. Sometimes it helps to speak with someone more mature, wise. Who can lend some of their own insight to a situation. That's why I asked if you had spoken with an iman or even a priest."

Marc, "Phil brought in a priest for some help. And we will both be talking to an iman soon."

Charles, "Good. It almost sounds like you two are mixed up in some extremist Christian sect. Those kind of people are the most dangerous. All anyone has to do is look around here in the Middle East. To see the damage religious extremists can do."

Marc, "Right, but, Dad—"

Charles cuts him off. "Look at American politics to see the same. People are more worried about a politician's sexual partners than they are about financial responsibility to their country and themselves."

"Dad."

Charles, "No, you listen. America is in trouble too. Any country that has to legislate the 'truth' with regard to scientific results is in deep trouble from within."

Marc, "If people don't recognize that their elected officials give themselves everything they want. While the majority believe that it's not them. It's always someone else, 'them.' What can I do about it? I'm a structural engineering major with a minor in botany."

Charles, "I don't know. They need to stop worrying about who is having sex with whom. Would be a good start."

Marc, "I've been working with plants and gardening for as long as I can remember. In many different temperature zones. We who put our hands in the soil can recognize global warming. Now enough politics. I'll search the library and with Phil's help discover our family history."

Charles, "If I think of anything else, I'll be in touch. Oh, talk to your mom. She was more into our family history than I was. She worked closely with your uncle Anton for a time."

Marc, "I didn't know that. When was that?" Charles pauses for a moment. His pain renewed as memories of his twin brother rush back to him. How close they were as twins often are.

Charles, "Up until shortly before his death."

Marc, "I'm sorry, Dad. I didn't mean to bring up painful memories."

Charles, "Son, sometimes that is all you have left."

CHAPTER 60

LATER THAT EVENING Melinda calls while Marc is busy reading from one of several books. All opened and spread around him on the library table. Its lamp the only light on in the enormous house. Even more books spread around the periphery on varying subjects spiritual possession, Arabian mythology, theological views on supernatural occurrences. One area of interest spectral displacement, where a spirit possesses the physical body of another and pushes that person's spirit out. Shuddering at the idea of losing his brother to that one.

Marc screening his phone calls pausing from his work to listen. Melinda's voice soft and throaty. "Hi Marc. I have some free time this evening. Call me we'll get together and make some… noise. Bye." Evoking a strong response with just her sexy voice. Marc's pupils dilating his pulse quickening with hot blood rushing down. Struggling with himself not to pick up the phone before she hangs up. Damn, she is one sexy woman intoxicating his mind flooding it with memories. Releasing endorphins. How good he always feels with her. Her warmth against his skin, the two of them pressed so tightly together. Melinda's exotic perfume engulfing his olfactory senses. Breaths quickened. *How is she doing this to me?* Reaching for the phone, no longer able to deny her his animal lust. *Click*. Anger rising up quickly. Chiding himself. *Why didn't I answer it sooner?*

The phone rings once again. Grabbing it up. Not letting her get away this time. "Hello." Speaking very husky, masculine.

"Hello? It's your mother. Why are you answering the phone like that? Never mind. I received your message."

Marc flustered, "Mom?"

Teresa, "Obviously you were expecting someone else. Your message sounded urgent. Are you all right?"

"I'm fine."

Teresa, "Is Camel all right?"

"We are both physically healthy," Marc says.

Teresa all too familiar with her son. His choice of frasing raising her concerns. "Well, spit it out. You did call me."

Marc, "Something has been… is happening to us both."

"Yes." Her voice becoming inpatient.

Marc, "I believe this has to do with the Du Bois family past."

Her interest piqued she replies, "Really? Enlighten me."

Marc does not have to see her face to recognize her tone. When her hazel eyes narrow and that cool tone emerges, watch out. Trying to decide where to start his explanation. "What do you know of the Du Bois family history?"

Teresa, "A significant amount. Could you be more specific? Such as, oh I don't know, like which century. Do you have any particular person in mind?" Becoming suspicious, knowing how young men tend to blunder into trouble beyond their abilities to cope with.

Marc, "How about the eighteen hundreds, Marie le Noir. What do you know about her?" Taking the plunge.

His mother shivers from a sudden chill to the air in her room sweeping over her. At the same time the bulb of the lamp on the nightstand explodes. Then the lamp topples over hitting the floor breaking. "Well, isn't that interesting?" Teresa is undaunted.

Marc, "What's that, Mom?"

"First, why don't you tell me what brought on this sudden curiosity about her. Of all your father's relatives to be inquisitive about." The air in her room becoming charged with static electricity. Causing her simplest movements to crackle and spark. Marc begins his story about how it started as a double date. They were just trying to amuse their lady friends. Now everything was moving frighteningly out of control. Her suspicions are confirmed, but only much worse than she had thought. Marc is finished with how much he was willing to tell his mom without becoming embarrassed.

Teresa finally speaks, "Documents I've come across and diaries that your great-uncle shared with me" as close as an 'I told you so' that she would give him "describe her as an evil, if not vengeful woman. Stopping at nothing to get what she wanted. Even cursing people that she felt wronged her." Marc has a sinking feeling that this was going to get much worse. "Definitely not someone you crossed and lived to tell about it."

Marc, "How so?"

Teresa, "People around her, including family members died untimely deaths from unusual accidents. Especially her enemies. I would describe her as a witch. Though none ever did. I suspect they were too frightened of her to do so."

"Do you believe all that?" Marc asks.

His mother chooses her words with care. "There almost always is a grain of truth to legends."

Marc admits more. "Now that I think of it, Angelique was the one who found the grimoire."

Teresa, "Stop! How do you know this book is a grimoire?"

Marc, "Cousin Phil told me so. Along with a priest friend of his."

"Why would you ever let someone you didn't know well perform rituals from a pagan book? Are you serious?"

Marc, "We thought it would be fun. It was just for entertainment. I know that sounds dumb now."

Teresa, "It's beyond that. It's irresponsible no dangerous. Are you not a devout Muslim?"

Marc, "Yes ma'am." Not expecting this angry reaction from his mother.

"You performed rituals without knowing what purpose they were for or what they could bring about?" Her frustration with her son rising.

Marc, "I'm sorry. I don't know what else to say. I trusted Melinda and Angelique. How could I know they were after something?"

Teresa, "So you gave them full control of a book of spells. How very naive, for a pair of young men who are supposed to be well traveled and educated." Her voice angrier than he could remember except for the antique imports fiasco. Not much can top calls from the State Department and Customs. Except irate Iraqi and Iranian national treasures officials.

Teresa, "Marc, are you listening to me?"

Marc, "Uh yeah. I mean yes ma'am."

Teresa, "You can't be airheaded, now focus."

Marc grasps at an explanation. "They understood the Latin and Old French."

Teresa, "You spent a year in France. *A vous franchise?* You couldn't figure out the Latin from word derivatives? It's the basis of all Western languages. French being the least changed from the source."

Marc, "Mom, getting angry now isn't going to help matters."

Teresa, "Don't try to manipulate me. It isn't going to work. I'll be as angry for as long as I want to be. Are you clear on that?"

"Yes ma'am."

Teresa, "You've been taught to respect other cultures and their practices. Your father is equally negligent in this for obstructing your education of the Du Bois family history. He still insists on empirical data over faith."

"It's already done." Marc speaking softly trying to project calming.

Teresa, "You can't just play with unknown rituals. Not in this family." Taking a deep breath in and then letting it out. Using breathing techniques to calm herself. Knowing she can be of more help if she is centered, relaxed. "So what incantation did these women use on the two of you?" Sounding calmer even to herself.

Marc, "Uh, well, the first part I found out was to control a man." Pausing not wishing to go further with that part of the information.

Teresa, "Go on. It can't be all that bad."

Marc, "It's some sort of sexual spell."

Teresa already sees a darker use to this. "What else?"

Marc, "It changes a man into a satyr."

Teresa, "This would be funny if it wasn't so serious."

Marc, "Right."

Teresa, "As if a woman needs a spell to control a man through sex. I suppose you two thought it would be fun. To have women controlling and using you as sex objects?"

Marc, "We didn't know that was the purpose of those incantations. It was difficult to follow what was being said. They were speaking Latin with medieval French and back to English."

Teresa, "And what did you think about that?"

Marc hears her trap but is unable to avoid it. Feeling incredibly foolish. "I thought they were very learned."

Teresa, "Yes, most university women speak and understand Middle French and Latin." Her sarcasm hitting the target.

Marc, "You are right Mom as always."

Teresa, "Tell me something about these two women."

Marc, "Melinda is working on her MBA with a minor in linguistics."

"What's her last name?" Marc gives her the Van der Vittel. Teresa taking a moment says, "I know that name it's Dutch. Her family comes from old money. As in families that were living in New Netherland before it was New York. That name is familiar for some reason, enough about her. What of this gal Camel is seeing?"

Marc, "Her name is Angelique. She has a degree in political science and French history."

Teresa, "So Angelique is an older woman. Is there any reason you're not giving me her full name?"

"Gremillion."

"She is an alumni member of a sorority that Melinda is a member, correct?"

Marc, "Yes. Also she is not that much older than Camel."

Teresa follows a hunch. "That you know of how old is she?"

Marc, "I don't know."

Teresa, "What does she do for a living?"

Marc, "She's independently wealthy, I never thought to ask. She sponsors an internationally recognized sorority. They just had a cocktail party. Where pledges were accepted from all over the country from some very prominent families"

Teresa, "Gremillion is an old Louisiana name you don't recognize that name?"

"Ah, no," Marc answers.

"You haven't told me much about what is happening to you. Be specific." Her tone authoritative.

Marc knew this was coming swallowing his embarrassment. "Besides all the strange goings on around here..." His mouth dry choosing to just go for it. "My body is physically changing I've become hirsute. Every time I have coitus it becomes hairy. The hair on my scalp grows longer each time much faster than normal. I heal quicker and I'm physically faster than I used to be. It's like I go into musk around these women. You know, like young male elephants. They are irresistible and I can't be satiated. Oh and Camel is possessed by a powerful spirit. Phillip's friend, an ex-Jesuit, says that Camel will probably have to have an exorcism. To get rid of the demon. There, it is all out."

After a considerable pause Marc asks, "Are you still there?"

Teresa answers him. "Yes, I'm still here. I was taking in what you have just told me. That's a lot to get my mind around. If you will forgive me the moment."

Marc, "Yeah sure take your time. What do you think?"

Teresa, "How did two intelligent well educated Muslim men get yourselves so embroiled in an obviously very powerful coven of dark witches? Isn't adultery a sin in the Koran?"

Marc, "Yes ma'am it is."

Teresa, "I just needed to hear that from you. You're sure about Camel?"

Marc, "Oh yeah. Enkil the spirit that is in possession of him physically, took Phoenician stone and completed the terrace with it. He read the blueprints from my mind. Actually improving on Uncle Theron's design. Putting a beautifully detailed pentagram in it. The workmanship is superb."

Teresa, "I'm not sure which disturbs me more. That you don't appear frightened of this spirit. Or that you sound impressed with its abilities."

Marc, "Well, with his abilities he did save me a lot of work." Said with a tone of appreciation.

"I am frightened by Enkil," Marc adds quickly. "What am I supposed to do? I believe he can be a strong ally."

Teresa, "Hold that thought. What direction is the pentagram pointing?"

Marc takes a moment to think about it. "It's pointing north. Why?"

Teresa, "If it were inverted it would be used for evil. As it is now this would indicate to me that your djinn is willing to be on the side of good."

Marc, "Now that we have that settled. What can I do to stop all this?

"Djinn?" What his mother said finally sinking in. "Djinn."

Teresa, "That's right djinn. We don't have anything settled. You allowed use of spells from your grimoire that delves into ancient religions without knowing what they do. That is what happens. How do you put a djinn back in the proverbial bottle?"

Marc, "I didn't bring him forth."

"If not you, then why did it appear to you? You accepted and were bequeathed charge of the du Bois family legacy. You are the head of the family in direct lineage. Your father has passed on that responsibility to you. He is the senior spokesperson but you are now the next in lineage. That came with your uncle Theron's estate." "Do you understand now?" She asks.

Marc, "Not quite." Teresa, "Let me put it another way. The grimoire is yours as head of the family thereby you are the owner and responsible for how the contents are used. You allowed its use to conjure a djinn." "I'm responsible for that?" Marc says incredulously. Teresa, "Yes, your book, your home, your allowing its use." "That's why does everyone keep telling to put the power back in the bottle?"

Teresa, "Who is everyone?"

Marc, "I keep having these dreams. One of them where uncle Theron keeps telling me to put the power back before it is too late. Something to that effect."

Teresa, "What did you think he meant?"

Marc starts to feel a little foolish. "Why do you answer every question I have with a question?"

"To make you think," she answers.

Marc, "So you're telling me that it really is my uncle?"

Teresa, "Why wouldn't it be? You're playing with witches and you have conjured a djinn. You were his favorite nephew. He was heavily into the occult. And I don't mean dark magic or something evil."

Marc, "I had no idea."

Teresa, "You don't know what I'm talking about, do you?"

Marc, "Not really."

Teresa, "White magic with some Wiccan beliefs. The old religion of Europe before it was repressed. No, crushed by the new order. There are so many things that this Christian culture of ours has destroyed. Well, not really yours. Since you're of the Islamic faith. But the same in their intolerance of the older religions. The Wiccan philosophy is slowly coming out of the shadows. 'Harm none.' Take your pentagram for instance. Its point is in the north direction. Thereby it is for good. Not used for malicious intentions. As your uncle intended it to be used." Marc listens in quiet awe. *How does she know all of this?* Native Americans with their love and respect of the planet as a whole were very much like the old European religion for the good of the planet. As well as respectful of women and motherhood.

Marc becomes impatient; she has to be coming to a point soon. His mother hears this in his sigh. "You look at your hand and that's all you see. There is much more there an energy field surrounds it."

Marc, "I know that."

Teresa, "Apparently not. Or you wouldn't have been playing with spells. Some of the energy from you goes into the intention of the spell you are sending out."

Marc, "I don't understand what you mean."

Teresa, "Let me try this another way. When you conceive of an idea there is energy created with that thought attached to it. Then it goes out with an intention attached to it."

Marc, "We didn't have any intentions."

Teresa, "You are not getting it. Those women you two were having casual relations with and attempting to amuse them. They did."

Marc, "Alright, I understand their part. This is getting deep."

Teresa, "They are not simple women by any stretch of your imagination. They had this planned for months, if not years. This is not something that just happened."

Marc, "How can you tell that from just our conversation?"

Teresa, "It clearly demonstrates strategy with subterfuge. Just as politicians maneuver the public with religious misdirection. To put themselves into office. You have to look beyond the surface. To see what are they really after."

Marc, "How do I figure that out?"

Teresa, "A book was supposedly chosen at random from your library. You must learn all you can about the du Bois family history. I can't help directly with this one. It is your path to lead the du Bois lineage forward. However you have to your advantage the knowledge of generations before you."

"How do I have that? In the library?" Marc begins to understand his mother.

Teresa, "Now you are using your mind. Start searching for answers in our family history." Rumblings of thunder reverberating over the high altitude city of Lima. His mother feeling the air become charged with static electricity. The very dry mountain air holding the building energy. Static crackling over the communication link with her son. "You did get a ring from Mr. Thornburg that was left to you by your uncle?"

Marc, "Yeah, I have it on now. Tell me about?"

" Your uncle said it was a power ring that will protect you. He had it made from stone of Eden. I never saw him without it after he had it cut."

Marc, "The stone of Eden?"

"Yes. Once a stone of Eden is cut and fashioned with the vine of life intertwined around it, the wearer is said to be protected from witches and demons."

Marc, "This conversation is taking a direction I never was aware of."

Teresa, "Only because you didn't bother to listen to myself or your great uncle. We both tried to start teaching you."

Marc chimes in, "Our family history right?"

Teresa, "Exactly. Now let's hope for both of our sakes it's not too late." Marc startled by her directness. "I have the utmost confidence in your innate abilities."

"What abilities?" he asks. Static crackling louder breaking up their conversation. Marc repeats, "What abilities?"

Teresa, "It's time to lift the binding spell. So you can at least protect yourself."

"Binding spell? What is going on that you haven't told me about?"

Static electricity rises so strongly in her room. That her hair is floating out like a Tesla experiment. Lightening streaking across the sky followed by thunder reverberating off the surrounding buildings into her room. Deafening her from hearing Marc. "I believe someone or something is trying to prevent us from finishing this conversation. Put the ring on a chain around your neck if you are not going to wear it on your finger." The sky over Lima darkened from ominous clouds. Lightning crackling over them connecting to the ground repeatedly. Its noise booming off the mountains up into the heavens above. Unseen are the wind shears pushing down inside the writhing mass of clouds growing darker. The noise of the growing storm increasing in volume. Satellite reception going in and out. Clouds gathering over East Avenue into the south wedge. Lightning streaking across the sky of Rochester barking louder.

Marc, "Where else do I find information to help me here?" His voice fading in and out.

"Find the Wiccan section in the religions of the library. You need to start reading and stop running the streets," Teresa says.

Marc, "I know, stay home and keep it in my pants. Dad already told me that!" Having to yell to be heard.

Teresa, "Well, isn't that how they were able to get to you? Through your indiscriminate behavior. Though I wouldn't have put it so crudely. Leave it to men to make it sound more uncouth."

Marc, "Let's not dwell on the past."

Teresa, "We need to get off the phone."

Marc, " I know, I've heard it's dangerous to use them during—" Lightning strikes the transformer outside exploding in a volley of sparks. Marc drops the phone microseconds before the electricity can find the path of least resistance, his hand. The percussion rattles the windowpanes its noise so loud. Seeing electrical sparks come out where his ear would have been smoke rises up from it. What a way to end a conversation. That was too strange to be a coincidence. *Damn, both my parents are criticizing my behavior. I'd be embarrassed if it weren't for the seriousness of the situation. Not something I wish to discuss with my parents again, at all.*

CHAPTER 61

AFTER WHAT SEEMED like hours of creeks and groans from the house. Rain and hail pelting it from out of the southern sky as summer storms do. Those noises made more distant by the library being at the heart of the house. That and with its heavy damask drapes pulled closed. All affording Marc the sense of safety and comfort in this room. Having read through various chapters in Wiccan books. Grasping the philosophy of "harm none" and placing Post-it notes to mark pages of interest. Rituals and methods of protecting one's home. Uneasy with some of these rituals being a devout Muslim. Needing to speak to a holy man to inquire what wouldn't be a sin to use.

The most disturbing book wasn't Wiccan. Untitled and leather bound it looked like a first edition from the Gutenberg Press, very old. It described using mirrors as portals to spy on your enemies. One chapter expressly on using your astral body to travel through the mirror effectively. Thus enabling the user to wreak havoc on your enemies. That one giving Marc a feeling of unease. His mind wondering, *Is that possible?* There are literally dozens of mirrors in this house. Some easily over three hundred years old. Remembering back to a couple of instances where a mirror such as the one on the grand staircase or in the library didn't seem to give back a reflection. Questioning himself, *Am I being paranoid or had this really happened?*

Unwilling to take the chance Marc settles on a Wiccan book. To read its chapter on how to cleanse and charm your mirrors. Wash them with mugwort and cover them. That would take hours to do. Plus where is he going to find mugwort? Also it's not just the mirrors that need protection. The thresholds and windows need guarding from unwelcome guests. Calling for other herbs and supplies. *Great, I'll just call the corner drugstore. Hi, I'm whipping up a little spell of protection and I need a cup of mugwort. That will go over big, another nut calling the pharmacist.*

There has to be some place. An apothecary where a herbalist would sell supplies. Thinking back on what his mother had said. "You have always had some natural abilities. How else do you think you and Camel survived. The two of you nearly died or were almost killed on numerous occasions. That you two always survived managing to get out of the trouble. You don't think it was just money and lawyers did you? That last business venture should have gotten you both charged under international law." Rumbling thunder softer now its sound coming from out of the east. Meaning the worst of it had passed.

Standing up from his Louis XVI desk using an ultramodern chair with its black mesh fabric and lumbar support. Marc walks back to the religions section of the library. There has to be something more on herbs. Glancing over the Wiccan section going back to occult. Seeing a well-used, heavy-bound book. Titled *Herbs, Not Just Don Quixote Can Fly*. Reaching up pulling on the book. Thus causing an entire section of bookshelves to pivot back into the wall. A gasp of dank cool air rushes out at him. Standing there surprised and unsettled. Having never heard of a secret passage in this manor. Let alone a trick lever giving access to it. *What the heck another secret?* His view limited to only a few feet with just the ambient light behind him from the library. That light rapidly lost in the long unused passage leading into darkness. The hair on his arms blowing as cooler air from deep within the earth rushes past him. Leaning into the opening his eyes adjusting to the darkness. But still he is only able to just see to a portion of the way in. Where steps disappear into a cavernous opening down into blackness.

Marc's pulse quickens with excitement. Needing a flashlight to explore this new discovery. He rushes over to the Louis XVI desk hurriedly rummaging through its drawer. Searching for a flashlight that he remembered seeing earlier. Having made a mental note of it after the storm had started. *There it is!* Grabbing it up and giving it a test switching the light on. Satisfied, now into the secret passageway. Shining the light into the darkness dust particles like snow reflecting light back at him. Almost dizzying his heart racing as he begins. The journey of exploration and searching for the truth. Moving down the secret hallway cool air rushing past him. Carrying on it the smell of damp earth with something else. This passageway undisturbed by human intervention for years. Giving Marc the unsettling impression of walking into an open grave. Passing farther down the cool rough-hewn stone hallway. Along the wall sconces where candle wax having dripped down like stalactites from decades of use. Now only covered with cobwebs using it for tenuous support. Marc reaches up brushing away cobwebs. His six-foot height putting them onto his head. Looking closer at the vaulting ceiling to discover the thick tangled mass. Not wanting to bring that down on his head. *Where is this in the house?* Blueprints of the house coming up in his mind. North side his memory photographic. Hearing a noise coming from behind him in the library.

Melinda's voice. "Marc?" She can't be allowed to find out about this. Marc turns around quickly. Accidentally grazing the sconce with his broad shoulder. Triggering a spring mechanism, it softly clicks into place. Loosening a chunk of dust covered cobwebs, sending them falling onto his head and face. Marc hates spiders from a couple of bad experiences. Panicking, brushing his hands wildly to get it off his head. The only route of escape closing. His fast movements causing more spider webs to fall. Giving him the tickling sensations of spiders crawling on him. Instinctively swinging the flashlight up in his other hand. Causing its old filament to weaken. His only source of light winking out. Marc stands in total darkness with no one in the world aware of where he has disappeared to.

CHAPTER 62

MELINDA CONCENTRATES ON the antique mirror before her. Smiling with inner satisfaction to herself. The student surpassing the instructor. At least she can do this by herself. She's able to see into the library at the old du Bois estate, its room silent.

"What's going on over there?" Speaking to Angelique. "It doesn't appear that he is at home."

Angelique, "Keep searching for him. More importantly, what is keeping us from viewing him when we want to? He might be onto us." Her paranoia rising and thus her mind racing.

Melinda, "I wouldn't get too concerned just yet. Marc and his brother are as dumb as a box of blocks."

Angelique, "Even the dimmest-witted male eventually will come to suspect something is afoot."

Melinda, "As long as one of the ladies and I use that noun loosely is able to manipulate the two of them. As males are so easily done through sexual behaviors. Then we have nothing to worry about." Melinda redirects her attention on the mirror scrying. Following her own suspicions Jadon's living room comes into view. Angelique not so convinced formulating an alternative move. Just in case always having plans within plans allowing for unforeseen opportunities. Remaining flexible is always the best way to achieving a goal.

CHAPTER 63

MARC ENGULFED IN darkness, commanding his mind to calm itself. After being satisfied that nothing multi-legged is crawling on him. He smacks the flashlight against his palm. Its beam of light cuts across the darkness. Still adrenaline pumped, quickly retracing his steps back to where the doorway was. Ending up at a stone wall devoid of any way to open it. Anxiously running his hands over the wall along mortared seams. Telling himself to calm down. *I'm not trapped. I'll just use my cell phone and call Camel for help.* Reaching into his pocket where it always is, empty. *Just figures!* Remembering it's on the desk where he emptied his pockets. *Great!*

Telling himself to remain calm. Taking a deep calming breath. Focusing his mind. How did this all start? What caused the door to close? Shining his light down the hall back to the wall sconce. Retracing his steps reaching up touching the wrought iron wall sconce. Smooth and cool to touch pushing on it. Hearing the soft click of a release mechanism as the secret entrance to this passageway pops open. Calming relief washing over him.

Marc listens at the doorway for any sounds. Not quite convinced the coast is clear. Easing open the door further. Still holding his breath ready for Melinda or one of the witches to appear. He steps back into the room scanning it quickly. Walking over to the desk checking the answering machine. Collecting his cell phone no new messages; but he had heard her voice. How was that possible? After making a sweep of the manor finding it to be empty. Now satisfied he resumes the exploration of the secret passageway.

Moving past the place where all the trouble began. Marc finds himself standing at the top of stone stairs curving away into blackness. Panning his flashlight to see how far this path leads. His light lost before he can see the bottom. With no railing on the right side to prevent a fall to surely what would be a painful death below. Dying slowly broken and helpless in the deep earth. Not his plan today or ever to become another family legend. This one the same as the last with a missing heir. What if he finds uncle Theron's smashed skeletal remains down here? Disregarding those morose thoughts for what future will he have. If he does nothing to fight the evil that has been wrought against himself and his brother. Or possibly even their families now.

He begins the first step on one of many journeys into the unknown. His life already changed forever; childhood is over. Needing to leave naiveté along with innocence behind. Silence ringing in his ears which comes from being deep inside the earth such as a cave. The sounds of his footsteps made gritty by sand the color of beige to light pink. A finer grit sand which you reach once you get below the top soil in this part of the country. Marc moves down the steps ever mindful of an edge dropping off into the black abyss. Focusing his mind on something other than fear of falling. Knowing the geology of this area of the country he must be passing well below ground into the earth. Out of cell phone range truly on his own. Reaching back in time to when glaciers deposited sands before topsoil had formed again healing the scarred planet. Passing through an invisible barrier of temperature. Confirming his awareness of traveling deeper into the earth. The air much cooler musty but not stale.

Now at least two stories below ground. His only companion the sound of his breath and gritty footsteps. At last the winding stone stairs reach an end standing before a cavernous room. Its ceilings high and vaulted in the old ways. Looking more like the inside of some lost cathedral of France. Rather than some mysterious catacomb under a home in Western New York. The flashlight not able to illuminate the ceiling to well. Its beam spread too thin.

After getting over his initial surprise Marc shines his light into a vestibule. Its entryway flanked by two columns. White marble with veining of purple through them. Sculpted in the classical Roman fashion fluted towering up to at least sixteen feet. At the end a set of heavy oak double doors slightly ajar. Pushing them open further, feeling closed in being underground. Marc begins to explore what appears to be some kind of library with an apothecary. Literally thousands of books lining its shelves with equally too numerous to count jars covered with cobwebs and thick dust. Noting a large medieval table octagon shaped with its eight pairs of legs. Scattered across its top books opened as someone had just been reading them. Numerous candles burnt down in holders on the table. Picking up a box of kitchen matches. Marc takes one striking it against the box igniting it. Lighting several candles on the table which cast long shadows across the room. Warm light nonetheless in a cold silent place without any sounds from the modern world above. For some reason he feels at ease here almost familiar. Like your favorite recliner. So very comfortable in this place. But how so? He had never been here before this day.

Being able to see better so more comfortable with his exploration. Marc shines his flashlight over the shelves nearest to him. Reaching past leather-bound tomes for a dark blue glass jar from rows of them. Similar to the type used early in the last century in hospital apothecaries. Using his thumb to scrape away thick dust to read the label. Arachnid *Loxosceles reclusa?* Wondering to himself, *Isn't that some kind of spider?* Yes, arachnid is spider. Running his fingers down the side of the jar. Smudging the dust, then shining light through the glass. To reveal its contents of three spider carcasses on their backs with their legs curled into themselves. Setting it back quickly. Who or why would someone collect something like that? Selecting another one from a lower shelf. *Hottentotta judaicus* (Israeli black scorpion). Searching the *M*'s for a bottle. Just as he had suspected. Mugwort amongst other unfamiliar names alphabetical in arrangement.

Carrying the bottle of dried Mugwort back over to the reading table. He sets the bottle down examining a few of the books closest to him. Written in German, *Sefer Ha-Qabbalah. Huh,* skimming through the book written 1854. Its leather binding well-worn. Turning the flashlight off. No longer needing it to read by with all the candles lit. Other books written in Hebrew, French, Latin, Arabic. Marc's eyes settle on what looks like a diary. Opening it to see the strong cursive style written in uncle Theron's hand. *Wow, I never realized how diverse his education was.* Thinking back to what his mother had said. "It wasn't just Mr. Thornburg who was instrumental in smoothing over his and Camel's business debacle. Who would have guessed the Syrians could use keffiyeh scarf as part of a front for smuggling. But with Uncle Theron's astute guidance a few well-chosen Aramaean and Byzantium artifacts could assuage angry Islamic nations. Never mind the fact that it would be an honor and a distinction for both of their families. How is that for turning lemons into lemonade?

His feelings of sadness is like a yoke around his neck. Uncle Theron would have known what to do in this bad situation. Pushing his feelings of loss away for now. Paging through the diary divided by subjects? Spells of protection, glamour's, blessings, and divinations. Paging back to spells of protection. Mirrors: To prevent others from using your own mirrors in your home to watch you, you must cleanse them. Mixing two tablespoons of dried mugwort into eight ounces of blessed water. Concentrating on positive thoughts, stirring clockwise. You will wash the front and back of the mirror to be protected. Then you should cover it with black fabric when not in use. This is especially true for scrying mirrors. Covering other mirrors once they are blessed will aid in maintaining privacy. This will also prevent accidental use. Marc exclaims, "Allah Akbar! There are mirrors all over the house." Realizing how much time this task of blessing the mirrors is going to take. Also with considerable reservations with using a possible pagan ritual being a devout Muslim.

Thinking back on Ms. Campbell how determined she was going around uncovering all the mirrors and cleaning them with ammonia. Reading further, never clear the mirrors with ammonia or other cleansers once they are protected. This will negate the protection you have afforded them. The thought crosses his mind. Could that have been the reason all the mirrors were covered up?

Remembering back to when he first moved into the manor. All of the mirrors were covered. Slowly opening the top on the jar of mugwort to examine its contents. Good, it is ground and almost full. Not sure of how much he will need. Picking the jar up as he blows out the candles. Taking in the deathly quiet with its pitch darkness. Unnerving just to think. No one would ever find you here in the dark so far underground. You couldn't be heard if you were calling for help.

Turning on the flashlight. Mental note, *Get more candles and perhaps some lanterns*. Starting the return trip back up the twisting stone stairs. Passing out of the cooler air into warmer letting him know he was approaching the main floor back aboveground.

Reaching for the wall sconce giving it a twist to the left. A shaft of light opens up in the wall. Followed by a rush of air pushing past him into the library. Everything gathered in his arms with only a finger to spare. Carefully tugging at the book resealing the secret passage. Unloading it all on the round table. Where all the trouble began or so it seemed until now. Looking sheepishly at his own reflection in the mirror. His cell phone begins to ring reading the display her all too familiar number.

Marc accepts this call to avoid suspicions. To a very sexy voiced Melinda speaking, "Hello."

Marc, "Hi."

Melinda, "You haven't been returning my calls. Is something wrong?" Convinced she has him under her thumb like every man she encounters is eventually. She continues without waiting for his response. "I saw the news. It's horrible what happened to Ms. Campbell. Such an unexpected accident. How is Mary taking the loss of her only living relative?"

Marc, "She is broken up over it but she keeps her feelings hidden. She is not easy to read at all."

Melinda, "Some women are good at that. I never could hid my emotions very well."

Marc, "No." His tone full of sarcasm.

Melinda chooses to ignore that one. Having an agenda for her call. "So where have you been? You're so dusty." Looking at him not only with her cell phone but watching him through the mirror from behind.

Marc, "Busy. There is a lot to do around here." Very noncommittal.

Melinda, "Are you able to make a little time for me?" Using her soft feminine voice, pushing her charms into it making sexy overtones.

Marc's ring glows lightly. Already becoming disarmed by her. His pulse quickens answering back in a husky deep voice. "I always have time for you. When?" Shaking his head fanning its mane of dark hair across his face hiding his eyes. Thinking, *What am I doing?* The urge rising up so strongly for her overcoming good judgment.

Melinda continues her flirtatious banter. All the while skillfully using her mesmerizing voice with such ease, a natural at this. Marc swept up in her soothing yet provocative tones. Thoughts of such lasciviousness controlling his mind and body.

Marc growls, "Come on over I want you."

Melinda, "I'm in my car. I'll be right over." *Click*. Dropping her cell phone back into her purse. Marc looks at the dark blue jar and diary on the table. Then glances around the room to reorient himself. What was it that I am supposed to be doing? Staring at his own reflection in the Louis XVI mirror. His mind still cloudy but not so lost in her ardor. Hiding the mugwort along with the diary in the nearby desk drawer.

The side door bell rings. Marc goes to answer it swinging it open. Not expecting Melinda standing there having arrived so quickly. "I was in your neighborhood." Marc smiles only half listening to her explanation too busy checking her out. Melinda eats it up.

"I was shopping at a boutique on Park Avenue." Twirling around. "Do you like?"

Marc still smiling, but his dark blue eyes longing. "Very much, come in." Brushing past him as she walks by all the encouragement it takes. Marc grabs her forcefully pulling her into his strong arms, kissing her deeply. Not so forcefully as to hurt but just aggressive enough to make his intentions known. Lifting her up and using a foot to close the door. Not noticing his tanzanite ring glowing a deep blue. He carries her into the library setting her on the sofa like a precious china doll. Pulling his shirt off exposing his muscular chest covered in a dark rich pelt. Melinda stares at her handiwork. All the more excited by the changes that have taken place since she last examined him.

Melinda still with her clothes on lies back on the sofa. Striking a sensuous pose rubbing one leg against the other. One knee higher than the other her eyes fixed on Marc's sensuous lips. That's all the signal he needs to send a flush of hot blood rushing. He strips off his pants. His erection springs up to his hairy rippled abdomen. Melinda stops him with her hand up. Taking her sweet time long enough to let her new summer dress slip off the shoulders. Before letting it hit the floor. Marc onto her toying with him takes his time. Bracing himself over her with his strong arms and legs not touching her. Only his long soft silky hair brushing over her skin. Giving her shivers. No longer willing to wait wrapping her arms around his neck to force him to her. Marc holds back for a second longer, the satyr in him enjoying seeing her need, desperate for him to give her gratification. Her soft aquifer weeping from anticipation, allowing for coupling, immediately sinking down. At least until the thicker part of him is slowed down while stretching her. Melinda in rapture and Marc totally into his need.

After their first orgasm remaining connected lying in each other's arms. The satyr is now completely under her control. Only desiring more to pleasure her. Melinda heady from the belief of herself having so much control. Letting him have his way as she might a pet. Unaware as he takes on his new role under their influence that she is being overtaken by his strong pheromones. Becoming enthralled herself. Thinking how soft his body hair has become. Running her hands over his chest. Luxuriating, how incredibly like Russian mink. His chest is like having her own mink blanket, with, "Oh, oh."

Later that evening having moved upstairs to the master suite. This time it's less urgent at least for him. Marc is completely into pleasuring her using his stamina. However she finds something is not quite the same. Melinda cannot tap into the energy force they are creating. Feeling its intensity yet unable to channel it. Marc's tanzanite ring unnoticed as the stones are pressed up against her skin. Stopping her from gathering their energy. Marc's dark hair a fuller and thicker mane now. Having grown longer again it is well past his shoulders and down his back.

Melinda's cell phone is programed to ring with music. Its song coming from the heap of clothes on the floor beside the bed. Tapping his shoulder Marc knows what she wants without speaking. Sliding together over to the side of the bed. Being taller having the longer reach of the two. Grabs the source of the noise handing the purse to her. Melinda accepting the call answering impatiently, "Hello! I'm a little busy right now." Knowing who it is calling without seeing the phone number displayed. Marc focused on the physical sensations, not stopping.

Angelique, "I can see that!" snapping back at her. Melinda looks over Marc's broad back at the mirror across the room. To see Angelique's glaring face staring back at her. Those blue eyes bulging and round with rage. Her voice in stereo coming from across the room and the cell phone. "Something is wrong!"

Melinda, "Yes. Oh, I know."

Angelique, "I'm not receiving any of his energy. How long have you been there?"

Melinda glances at her watch. "About two hours." Her enthrallment from Marc abating now with her anger rising at this interruption. Hitting Marc on the shoulder. "Stop! I'm not in the mood anymore." Speaking into her cell, "This couldn't have waited?" Pushing against Marc's solid body. "Get off me." His embrace becoming a bear hug tightening his hold on her. As he increases his efforts kissing and gently biting down the side of her neck. Melinda ignores Angelique, choosing Marc. *Why waste a good time?* Bites on Marc's neck, this being all the encouragement he needs increasing his pace. Besides, he is too large a man to shove off her.

Angelique, "Finish up and get back over here. Now! We need to correct this. I want all the energy we can get before he is—" Stopping herself from speaking over the phone. The cell in Melinda's hand quiet she ends the call, dropping it on the floor.

Angelique looks into her scrying mirror. To see her room reflected back along with her own glaring face. Not amused. *That little witch! She not only hung up on me. She blocked me!* Screaming out in rage.

Melinda, *Damn, he is persistent.* Giving in to her own needs twisting her hips up on him, meeting his thrusts. Both of them carried over the edge.

Breathing heavy Marc so relaxed and sleepy now. Melinda pushes on him. This time rolling off her with a pop. Marc tries to cuddle. "Come on baby."

Melinda, "I've got to go. I said I could only stay for a while." Marc turns over going to sleep so very relaxed. Melinda gets up grabbing her clothes on the way to the bathroom. Having missed her cell phone under the sheets on the floor. Closing the door behind her. The sound of running water Marc's clue to investigate. Using only his eyes checking the mirror first. Seeing only the room reflected back. The coast is clear rolling out of bed, Marc picks up her cell phone. Pushing in the last call received. Just as he had suspected. Angelique's private cell number in the memory. What to do next? Placing the phone back on the floor where he found it. If he confronts her she'll just take control of him with her sexual spell.

Hearing the shower stop. No time to do anything panicking for a second. He gets back into bed in the same position he was in before. Pretending to be asleep. Calming himself, making his respirations slow and easy. Melinda dresses quickly as she comes out. Lifting up the sheet spotting her cell phone. Then rushing out of the room. Marc lies there giving her sufficient time to leave the manor. Then he gets up and pulls on his boxer shorts. Going downstairs to lock the side door. A quick look out the kitchen window. Melinda's car is gone. His mind completely clear of her allure. Making rounds on the other doors and setting the alarm. Now that the manor is secured against normal physical assailants. Time to get to work on protection from metaphysical manipulation.

Going into the library to retrieve the directions and supplies. Once settled in the kitchen seeming to be the most natural place for this. Marc places a large crystal punch bowl (Baccarat) out on the granite counter. He begins by saying a prayer facing the east. With that done he focuses his mind on what it is that he has to do. Protection of himself and the occupants of the manor. Pouring spring water that comes from deep within the earth into the punch bowl. He mixes in mugwort making a solution and in a smaller bowl making a paste.

Reading from the diary, cleanse the mirrors front and back with the solution. Using the paste to draw a protective symbol such as a crescent moon on the back. This process takes several hours to perform. Marc has not realized how many mirrors the manor has. Covering some of the less used mirrors and ones that could be used strategically to monitor his activities with black fabric. Knowing some of them may need to be taken down and stored in one of the third-floor attic rooms for its isolation.

Standing in the library after putting away his supplies. Marc takes it all in witches, sexual spells, intrigue, and then possession. Surrounded with memories the clock ticks down then a soft whine from a compressor of the air-conditioning coming on. The manor built within the earth and rising up three floors above him. Oddly quiet for even this place. White noise ringing in his ears almost as loud as it does when he has a high fever. Defiantly not ill but trying not to feel overwhelmed. What to do next? *If they are not onto me, they will be soon enough.* How far are they willing to go to protect what has been planned for years. Perhaps what may have been in the works for decades. If the truth is ever to be found in all this. The grandfather clock bangs out the late hour. Snapping Marc out of his deep reverie. Having lost track of time the late hour upon him. Needing to get cleaned up and go to bed. Knowing tomorrow will bring with it fresh ideas. Choosing to walk up the main stairs past the grandfather clock. Its steady rhythm a comfort.

Taking a long hot shower, Marc attempts to wash Melinda's perfume, her very scent, off his fur to get ready for bed. Making a mental note to pick up some crème rinse to soften and groom with. The lufa sponge didn't work so well being so hairy now. Finding his abdominal fur a wide stripe down his center that becomes matted and knotted when it's not brushed out. Feeling more like some Persian show cat. Which needs regular brushing to maintain its luxurious coat. This irritates him all the more. Being that he was a low-maintenance male.

Comfortable in bed with the sheets laid over to the side. Being much too warm to be under any covers. Sleepy and ready to dose off except for light wafts of Melinda's perfume distracting him. It's not only intoxicating but arousing. Finally he gets up and changes the sheets. The only way he will get any sleep. Eliminating the scent of her mixed with perfume. Scent being one of the strongest ties to the reptilian part of the brain.

CHAPTER 64

WAKING UP AROUND noon, refreshed from some well needed rest. Especially after the past few days. What more could be thrown at him?

Dressing then heading downstairs starting the coffee machine the timer not set. Marc goes out the side door to retrieve the newspaper. For some odd reason needing the finality of the printed word, not an electronic image. Paging through it on the way back to the kitchen turning to the obituaries. There it is Norma Campbell deceased. Skimming over the column to his area of interest. Survived by her niece Mary Campbell last known living relative.

Pausing long enough to take a drink of strong black coffee. Marc leans across the granite countertop reaching for his cell phone on the opposite side. Taking another sip of his Columbian brew before calling Camel. Activating the cell open with his thumb. Pressing the memory recall button again using his thumb. Taking comfort in Camel's sleepy answer. "Hello."

Marc, "You're not up yet?"

Camel, "I am now. Angelique and I made up last night."

"Oh?" Marc's tone says it all. "I thought you weren't going to have sexual relations with her anymore." Not trying to hide the irritation in his tone.

Camel becomes defensive. "I thought you were not sleeping with Melinda anymore."

"You know about Melinda?" Marc surprised

Camel, "Yes."

Marc, "But how did you find out so fast?"

"Enkil let me know they were trying to use their sexual spell again. Angelique thought she was all slick. Seducing me again and being in complete control of Enkil. However after a couple of hours I have to give her credit for trying. I was repeatedly satisfied. She was not too happy. She became so moody because she couldn't draw off our energy." Camel fighting to keep the laugh out of his voice. "I'm not quite sure how that works. Enkil hasn't explained it to me. I feigned exhaustion. So while she thought I was out she contacted Melinda." Marc understanding it now. Camel continues, "Who I might add appeared to be having a real good time. Not too happy about the interruption. Well, not that you stopped. By the way I think you have the Persians beaten now. Your ass is very hairy."

"Ordinarily I'd say forget you." Marc laughs as only a large man can with a deep-chested sound. "I won't argue with the truth." Both of them laugh at his expense. Laughter feeling so good after not having done it in so long. Marc feeling empty once they stop. The seriousness of their situation paramount. "So then you have seen how they are able to monitor us." More a statement than a question.

Camel, "Yes right into your bedroom. You two were passionate. If I didn't know any better, little brother. It looks like you had her under your ardor."

Marc, "Thanks for the critique."

Camel, "It's not a critique. Enkil saw it too."

Marc, "Great now I've got an audience in the bedroom."

Camel, "You've had one for a while we both have." Marc not the most comfortable with this new development. Camel knowing his brother too well. "Besides, you have nothing to worry about. Porn star." Camel snickers. Marc, "That's not funny! Voyeur. I think I've taken care of that problem."

Camel, "How so?"

Marc, "I need you to come over and then I can go over it with you."

Camel, "I have to tell you, it's very impressive to watch Angelique scrying. By the way you know that is not all she can do with a mirror."

"What else can she do?" Marc questions afraid of the answer.

Camel, "She can astral project through them. That's how she was able to get Ms. Campbell. I know this because Enkil told me." Anticipating Marc's next question.

Marc, "So what is the purpose of this energy they are after?"

Camel, "That is the answer we need to find. Along with some other things I'm curious about."

Marc, "Go on?"

Camel, "How were you able to resist Melinda?"

Marc, "I wasn't completely able to but it could be the ring I was wearing."

Camel, "What ring?"

Marc, "The one that I that I showed you." Camel does not respond. "It was my late uncle's I told you about it. Mr. Thornburg had been holding it for me. Then I had it in the safe here and forgot about it. Until recently. When I spoke to Mom she remembered it. Said it was a power ring."

Camel, "Yes now I remember, so what makes it special?" His tone dubious.

Marc, "Well? It's the tanzanite an earth mineral that channels power from the goddess. What I have been able to read so far which isn't much more. The ring also has Celtic runes for protection engraved into the band. Mom said," trying to remember her exact words.

Camel, "Go ahead what else?"

Marc, "There are Celtic vines of life intertwined around the outside. I don't know why but it is believed that it imbues the wearer with protection from dark magic."

Camel, "It could be working."

Marc, "Hum, since I've been wearing it? I cannot tell if there has been anymore changes. Except my hair continues to grow faster."

Camel suspects there is more to it that Marc isn't telling him. "That's all? Come on, I know you. You're holding something back."

Marc becomes slightly shy to say what it is. Camel presses him for the answer but is pretty sure he already knows it. "Come on, it's me you're talking to." Enjoying teasing him with one of his weaknesses. Not really a weakness at all.

Marc, "Fine! I know you just what to hear me say it. Every time I have sexual contact with a woman, my hair grows longer. It's well down my back now."

Camel holds back a laugh. "There, that wasn't so bad now was it now? I was half expecting you to say you were turning into a goat or something."

Marc ignores him. "Didn't you have this problem?"

Camel, "I was, but Enkil is protecting me now. So no further changes will happen to me."

Marc, "It's called a satyr."

Camel, "A what?"

Marc, "You know, like Pan, the god of the forest and promiscuity."

Camel, "When did you become a wellspring of occult knowledge? Melinda talking in her sleep? Not that from what I saw she was getting much sleep."

Marc covers his embarrassment with indignation. "When I was left with the impossible task of saving us. This has not been easy for me. You haven't been much help."

Camel, "Easy! I'm just kidding you. Enkil and I are both helping you."

Marc, "I'm sorry. It's just that it has become so difficult. The more I delve into my family history the more questions are raised than answered. It's beginning to look like all the trouble we're in now is my fault or at the least leads back to my family somehow."

Camel, "I don't blame you for what has occurred against us. We are responsible in some small part. But you are right about the machinations. This has the sense of something that was started long ago. Just now it is starting to speed up my brother. We have to be united in this fight not divided."

Marc, "She doesn't sleep over anymore. Melinda does have the ability to seduce with her voice." He confides

Camel, "Then we will find a way for you to resist it."

Marc, "There may be something in one of these books."

Camel's voice drops an octave deeper to a bass. "Isn't it just like a witch to use a man at his most vulnerable, turning basic needs against him?" Both hearing a story behind that comment. Enkil having been quite changes the subject. "I can feel the power of this ring. It has stopped the progression of the spell on you but not reversed it. So what is your plan?" Marc swallows the lump in his throat. Caused by fear of losing Camel to this being. Holding his spiritual brother captive. This abomination, becoming angry with it. Marc feels the slightest tickle of air movement near him. Causing the hair at the nape of his neck to rise up. Enkil then asks, "Well?" His voice coming from right behind Marc. Jumping startled at the unnatural speed Enkil moves without any indication he was about to do so. Enkil impatient as always where mortals are concerned. His predatory yellow eyes glaring challengingly at Marc from up close and personal. Marc's hands clinched into fists with his body already having slid into readiness for a fight. Enkil reads his body language not intimidated by this. Moves past Marc his back to him taking a seat facing him. As a CEO would taking a boardroom meeting.

Marc, "I'm using information found in some old Wiccan books."

Enkil, "How so?"

Marc, "The mirrors throughout this home have been blocked. Made inaccessible to Angelique and her coven. The same will need to be done at Camel's estate. I have the instructions written out along with the supplies gathered for this." Handing the instructions to Enkil, who reads over them before speaking.

"Good, disrupt their communications portals. Using the older religion of Europe. Nice touch. You know it was a much kinder religion than Christianity. You are more resourceful than I would have expected." Marc relaxes a little.

Enkil, "Now how are you going to send me back?" Marc's eyes give away his thoughts. Enkil not one to let his guard down nor let his soldiers relax. "I know you are thinking about it. Camel keeps thinking about it. You two are as close as brothers can be. Short of sharing the same womb together."

"I... I," Marc stammers.

Enkil, "Don't lie to me. You will only insult me if you do."

Marc, "A Jesuit priest said it may take an exorcism to extricate you." Not wanting to hide too much. Seeing as to how he can read some of Marc's thoughts.

Enkil, "Good, very good. I like that. You're being honest and to the point. An exorcism, that takes me back. I would relish a good one. Especially with an old priest performing it. They are so ready to die for an innocent lost soul. Does he know it will be for a heathen? Or how you say it now, non-Christian."

Marc, "That has been given only the briefest of discussions. So you have been extricated before in this manner?"

Enkil, "I'm sure this will come due all in good time." Smiling at Marc, looking his absolute most frightening. Marc unable to maintain a poker face. Mentally noting that he didn't answer his question.

"Yes, one last bid. The ultimate good deed. What great fun I will have crushing another feeble attempt. I am really coming to like this body." Pumping up Camel's large chest and flexing his biceps. Large from hard workouts at the gym and made faster with Enkil's reflexes. Not that he wasn't already from years of martial arts training with his brother at his side. "Have you seen one before?"

Marc, "No. Only at the movies."

Enkil, "I'm not one of those insipid minions. Destroying the flesh while torturing a soul. You know in some cultures an abomination is killed. However your Catholic ritual can be so much more personal. When you are there." His laughter loud and deep. Echoing off the walls of the library.

Marc's hair on his neck and arms rising up. As cold chill rushes deep into his core. Marc angered by his own fear. "Enough! If you are not going to help me then let me speak to Camel. We have to fight together otherwise we are lost."

Enkil's angry eyes are yellow slits with his face an arrogant mask. "How right you are. So you know I have been helping you, man animal. You will need my help increasingly. Don't forget that!" The yellow winking out of Camel's eyes returning to his normal dark brown. Just as Marc is hit by a blast of warm air pushing hard against his body. Forcing him to widen his stance to keep from being blown down. His long straight dark corn silk hair whipping in the wind. Papers flying off the desk with books toppling to the floor, paintings moved to hanging sideways on the walls.

Camel, "*Moi frère*! You've got some brass balls on you." Smiling at his brother with renewed pride. "What do we need to do next?"

Marc, "Good, he's gone."

Camel, "Not really. He is just allowing me out. So don't disparage him. He still knows what is going on."

Marc, "Anyway, we need to get these spells broken or maybe"—getting an idea—"we can trick one of them into removing it."

Camel, "Angelique is not going to fall for anything. She's very crafty. That witch has been around for a long time."

Marc, "What? She looks to be in her thirties at most."

Camel, "Try much older decades, it's just a hunch. No it's a feeling. No wait, one of Enkil's memories. He's telling me she is at least one hundred and fifty years old."

Marc, "That's not possible. Is it?" Doubting himself.

Camel, "People all over this planet are living past one hundred. We are dealing with the supernatural. Do you have any doubts about that?"

Marc, "No. Getting back to the more immediate issue. One of us needs to target Jadon or Melinda, maybe even one of the lower order novices."

Camel, "I don't believe any of the novices would have access to that information. Uh" correcting himself, "abilities we need." Their plan coming together. "It would have to be Jadon or Melinda with me keeping Angelique distracted for a while. If you get my meaning." Camel smiles his most sly and lascivious expression. His handsome face with white teeth showing a devil may care. "I'm always up for a challenge. However this is going to get dangerous very quickly. They already know something is wrong."

Marc, "It is a chance we have to take. If we don't...," letting his thoughts trail off. "Do you think Enkil could help us find out what it is they are after? He doesn't seem to like them very much."

Camel, "You are right about one thing. He hates them. I get the sense it's something in his past dealings with Angelique's ancestors. So yes, I believe he would help us."

Marc, "I get the same impression. Is he with you all the time?"

Camel, "No. He leaves for periods of time but they are becoming less frequent. I'm afraid if we don't find a reason for him to leave he will keep my physical body. He is very pleased with it." Camel's face very grim.

Marc, "Yes." Marc's face equally grim. "Can you hear me when I'm talking with him?"

Camel, "Sometimes it's like having two minds in my head."

Marc, "Since you are that close to him, he obviously has some access to your memories. Do you his? What can you learn from him?"

Camel, "Occasionally I see images. They are his memories. Some of which are very strange. I don't understand them. Memories are like digital data storage except with organic systems every time you retrieve them. They get overwritten causing them to change slightly. He is thousands of years old. Thereby his memories are of different centuries sometimes from past millennia. Then sometimes it's like I'm sleeping, no floating in darkness." Camel pauses, his brown eyes round from sadness. Marc listens on his eyes quickened with fear.

Marc's curiosity piqued, he says, "Give me an example of a different century."

Camel, "Well..." His hand grazes the blue-black stubble covering his chin. "One is of the French court. They are wearing those big white wigs and speaking French of course."

Marc, "Before the revolution?"

Camel, "Yes most certainly. It's the court of Louis the XVI."

Marc, "You're certain of this?" Marc recognizes another piece of the puzzle. Not sure it is wise at this time to speak of it at this time.

Camel, "Yes Enkil indicated that much. I'm not sure why he is around at this time. I believe one of the courtesans was conjuring him."

Marc becomes excited. "Totally great! What else? Give me another example. This time from an older time." His face lights up just like when the old storytellers wove an intrigue around the fire out in the deep desert.

Camel smiles at their fond memories. "It's another time, much older, pre-Islam and pre-Christian. The language is very old I'm not familiar with it. Enkil says its Hittite." Marc listens quietly as Camel recounts the memory.

They discuss what Camel can glean from Enkil to formulate a plan against the coven. Enkil has returned and is not opposed to helping serve up some revenge.

CHAPTER 65

THAT FOLLOWING AFTERNOON they meet at the funeral home where Ms. Campbell is in repose. It's a closed casket as the damage was too extensive to repair. Mary is standing with a group of nuns. She almost blends in with them. Herself wearing a long black dress with her head covered by a black mantilla. It's very old fashioned long and of handmade lace beautiful. Her emerald green eyes are red from crying.

Marc and Camel are dapper in dark suits. Heads covered wearing their prayer hats. Both coming over to Mary to give their condolences. Camel stepping up first gives her a big hug. Speaking softly his voice a rumble, "I'm so sorry for your loss. She'll be waiting on the other side for you to join her someday." Mary smiles flatly thanking him. Thinking to herself, *I hope not. Aunt Norma should be rotting in hell. For as mean a bitch as she was to me and apparently to Mom also.*

Camel, "I can see you are at a loss for words."

Mary, "Yes."

Marc steps up and hugs her taking in her scent. His pupils dilating neither missing a beat. Her eyes search his blue eyes quickly. His expression one of concern and sadness. Speaking in a deep soft voice, "I am so sorry for everything that has happened to you." Taking one of her hands. They move away from Camel and the nuns to have a quiet conversation.

Mary speaks first, "I don't blame you for any of this. I wanted you as much as you wanted me. You were the perfect man for my first time." Her face clears of sadness becoming resolute. Her eyes twinkling for just a moment. Standing this close to Marc, his cologne mixed with his masculine scent brings back fond memories for her. Working outside with his shirt off laughing. Handsome and sincere a killer combination. Finally understanding what other young women at school had been talking about. Definitely not the pretty man look. Marc's features chiseled with high cheekbones. Mary's face hardens again ending her assessment of him.

"She was beyond cruel to me for as long as I can remember." Referring to her aunt. "There's something not right with Melinda. I wouldn't trust her if I were you."

Marc, "I know. Now is not the time to go into it, but we do need to talk."

Mary, "They manipulated us into that situation. Melinda knew I had a big crush on you. I believe we were drugged."

Marc, "I know that now, but what was the purpose?" Getting that sensation over his skin when something is crawling on it. Casually turning his head in the direction where the nuns are standing. A piercing set of blue eyes unblinking, hard to the point of coldness. Watching the two of them. Her wimple and veil obscuring the rest of her face.

Mary, "Yes I feel it too." Not looking in that direction. Taking his hand and shaking it. "Thank you for being here. We will talk later I'm sure." Marc puts on his poker face. Surprised but grateful she has some good insight.

Andry comes in as the two young men are leaving. He nods to Marc giving it some direction. Marc already pausing to speak with him.

Andry, "I'm glad I found you."

Marc, "What is it?" Already having a good idea where this conversation is headed.

Andry, "There are too many memories of Oksana at the manor. I just can't do it anymore. I need to get away from there. So I'm moving in with my niece and her family."

Marc, "I understand. If you need to talk to someone call me anytime or better yet just come by and have some coffee."

Andry, "This just brings it all back." At a loss for words but the feelings of loss obvious.

Marc, "You do what you have to for your own well-being."

Andry, "Thank you, I knew you would understand."

Marc, "If you change your mind there will always be a place open for you." Andry thanks him again before disappearing into the crowd.

Camel, "What was that about?" As they are going down the steps outside having that feeling again of eyes boring into his back. He glances back to see those same blue eyes glaring at him. Their hate palpable.

Marc, "He's not staying on property. I knew it was a matter of time before he left with his wife dying."

Camel, "No. Not that. I meant why are you acting so strange?"

"Because we are being watched. Don't look, keep your eyes on me."

"Is it the coven members?" Camel asks.

"I don't know, but don't let on I told you."

Camel, "All right. Then what is going on between you and Mary?"

"Come on, I'm not talking here," Marc says. After they're out in the parking lot he explains about why Ms. Campbell was treating Mary so badly all along. After Saturday night her treatment of her became insufferable toward her.

Camel, "That explains a lot. The sins of our parents are visited upon their children."

Marc, "Is it the children's fault that their parents wronged people?" His tone becoming angry. "It does explain the religious extremism and her cruelty."

Camel, "Just proves any religious extremists are the same, wrong."

Marc, "Yeah. As long as you're right you can do anything in the name of Allah, God, or Jehovah because it's your religion."

Camel, "You know I wouldn't have expected it from her. She was so nice to us."

Marc, "No, she wasn't. She was a two-faced nut. The Europeans had it right when they ran all the Christian extremists out of Europe. The only problem is now all their descendants are here and they're still nuts."

Camel, "Wow. I guess I know your opinion on that subject." Both men get into their sports cars Marc's blue Mustang and Camel his black Ferrari. Camel has two a red and a black one.

That evening Marc and Andry have a long visit over coffee. Whereby Andry explains his decision to move in with his niece in Florida. Marc reassures him per the proviso of the will he is welcome to come back with or without the provision. Andry would always be welcome.

Once Andry leaves Marc being keyed up goes back to studying his great uncle's diary. Cross-referencing names and information with other books. Now surrounding him on the library table in the manor. Its halls still and dark as evening passes into the night.

CHAPTER 66

ANGELIQUE HAS CALLED a meeting with her top members of the league. Graduates with affiliations strongly bound to her. Having selected and nurtured them into positions of great affluence and power. These women only too willing to aid her in her time of need. Herself working to gain back the respect with a position of power in the triumvirate. Its members numbering in the hundreds with some of them the ancients. Save for a few who are millennia old. The oldest having survived destruction caused by their own boredom. Having created intrigues that warranted intervention from higher celestial beings. Once in a while nothing more than a spurned lover or an apprentice gone power hungry.

Melinda and Jadon take their seats at a long table in Angelique's power room. Its table more like a boardroom. Large enough to seat thirteen and just as tense. Angelique having called an emergency meeting. Very suspicious that someone or something (Enkil) is interfering with her plans. All of the members gathered now seated. The last arrival late having been pulled from a political fund-raiser. Her blonde hair impeccably coiffed still wearing her signature red dress.

Angelique cuts a glare at her before continuing her inquest. "Why else would the energy be blocked? Melinda, have you been able to speak with Mary?"

Melinda, "I've left messages at her aunt's home and on her cell phone the one I gave her. She hasn't returned my calls. Now she has it turned off." Angelique looking even more impatient. "I even apologized. Telling her how sorry I was for being jealous of her and Marc." Her tone sarcastic rolling her eyes. "The little witch won't return any of my calls."

Jadon feels the tickle of her familiar brush against her neck. Where it's perched a yellow finch twittering softly so as only she can hear it. Opening her compact to retrieve the message. Jadon's lips curve ever so slightly with contentment, reporting off, "She is surrounded by nuns at the funeral. After which she will be returning to the sister house."

Angelique, "Very good. At least someone can do what I ask of them." Glaring at Melinda. "Thank you. You both may leave, now" Dismissing both off her low-level consorts.

Melinda irritated and unaccustomed to being dismissed remains seated. Angelique addresses the group. "Something strong is about. I can feel it has been hindering the smooth flow of my plans. Also I'm starting to suspect a very powerful witch is behind the scenes. Attempting to manipulate circumstances." Angelique speaks to Jadon. "I want a meeting called of all the inner-circle sorority novices." Her blue eyes round and bulging with anger just held in check. Others around the table all too familiar with that look. Jadon shudders inwardly not allowing the others around the table to see her fear. Whispering softly to her familiar. Sending it back trapped inside the mirror of Mary's compact. Where it will wait once again until its release when she opens it. Hopefully at the convent house giving them access.

Something there in her memory she just can't quite reach yet. Having that sensation you get when you know the answer but it just isn't coming to your conscious mind.

Angelique, "Jadon are you listening? You seem very distracted." Watching her closely.

Jadon, "Yes. I was considering what you said. It rings of more than just coincidence." Angelique nods so Jadon continues, "Are you sure that demon Enkil isn't working against our plans?"

Melinda injects, "I thought you had him under your complete control."

A deathly silence comes over the room. Angelique glares back at the both of them from across the table. Her anger at the edge of uncontrolled. "No demon is ever under your complete control. Only a fool would believe that. You two are still here. Why? Have you already scheduled my meeting with the novices?" Melinda ready to protest. "Good-bye." Dismissing them again. Melinda slides her chair back. Jadon is already up and going out the door.

Angelique takes a moment to ask herself. *Why would he go against me?* Taking it personally this affront. He's been more than cooperative up until now. Being most helpful with Marc and certainly more than willing to take on Camel's strong will.

CHAPTER 67

AN HOUR AFTER the emergency meeting standing outside the closed doors to the power room. Melinda says, "I still can't believe that? She dismissed us like common servants." Jadon is unwilling to comment. Knowing the walls can have ears. Especially with a room full of vengeful witches next door. No joke intended. Melinda however the consummate Upper East Side princess. Fearless in her direct disregard for the danger. "I can tell Enkil doesn't have Camel all the way under his control. She is the fool. His good nature still comes out."

Jadon, "That is true I saw how nice he was to Ms. Campbell."

Melinda, "She was so easily manipulated by him. She had a soft spot for the big bear."

Angelique standing quietly behind them listening. For how long neither was sure. Having chosen to speak, "Religious extremists are human. Thereby have weaknesses making them easy to manipulate. They are not just righteous they are convinced. Making them all too easy to misdirect. We only have to look to politics to see numerous examples of this. A well-placed 'whore' can do so much good." All three laugh easing some the tension from earlier.

Angelique, "I'm still curious as to how she found out. Not that the problem wasn't remedied quickly enough." Looking at Melinda with an arched eyebrow knowingly. "Dear old aunt Norma won't be interfering with my plans anymore." Melinda too quiet. Fearing this line of questioning.

Jadon, "Yes, well problem eliminated."

Melinda, "If we are done here, I do need to be on my way. I have found a more than suitable replacement for our uses. I have a date with a new man toy. He's on the lacrosse team. His energy will be a powerful new addition to wield."

Jadon, "If he survives the spell."

Melinda, "If not, oh well. At least the sex will be worth it." Her lips pouty.

Jadon, "You're such a whore." Giggling. Angelique smiles her entire face softening into beauty. Making it all so easy to understand how Camel became enchanted by her.

Angelique, "Since when has that been a flaw amongst our little family? If he lives you will be sharing him anyway." This time they all laugh. Except her eyes, Angelique watching Melinda closely. Noting her laughter to be a little forced. A twinge of jealousy flashing across her face. *Yes, I'll bet tarots to dollars. That one is the one who put Auntie in harm's way. Revenge is best when it is least expected.*

Angelique, "Before you are off to get ready for your date. I need the both of you. For a time then the two of you may be off." Following her into the spell room with a fire already lit. Flames licking hungrily around a black cast-iron cauldron. Smoke rising up the chimney. "Now gather round. We will form a circle outside the pentagram." Walking east to west counterclockwise nine times. "Come forth elements of air and fire. Accept these gifts I offer thee. Protect us with a barrier from this creature's reach." Casting a sachet of dried herbs with ground spider into the fire. Poisonous hemlock with black widow spider known for killing their mates (the males) right after copulation. "Chant with me," Angelique directs her minions. "Cauldron smoke let it rise up guiding thee and provoke this one so dark. Bring her forth one who is forgotten. So that you may smote your enemy of mine." Air around them beginning to stir gently at first. Embers sparking up into the air between the two circles of protection. Wind rustling at their clothing and hair tugging as if there were hands unseen in it. As it gathers in strength. Angelique is speaking alone now, "Ardor the one who will see what we cannot. Come forth from ancient times long past. I beseech you. Vengeance shall be thy gift for all concerned."

Candle flames flicker in between the double circles. Which hold back danger for the three conjuring it. Lightning crackles across Rochester's cloudless sky. Clouds form massing upon themselves tremulously. Blocking out starlight and the moon. Blackening the earth below as substations fail. All being joined in this spell of darkness. Thunder rumbles like a timpani building. Its sound carrying from distant and close locations. A storm gathers in its strength with Angelique's every word.

"Andor we stir thee from your long sleep. Andor we beseech thee in this time of our need." Each time her unholy name is spoken thunder booms louder their hair whipping on the wind. Flames beneath the cauldron lick out from the sides wildly. The room becoming hot and humid.

Angelique, "One thing more." Holding a stiff, wrinkled blood-dried piece of fabric in her hand. Waving it through the air. "Smell the blood of the one we seek vengeance on. Andor!" Angelique becomes angry and rash in her jealous behavior. Spits into the cauldron with some of her spittle sizzling on its side. "Know the one who commands you!" Dead silence ringing in their ears engulfs the room. Not the slightest breeze moving the air now fetid with the stench of brimstone increasing. Grey smoke starting to rise up in pulses from inside the cauldron. Then twisting into streamers flowing over to the center of the pentagram. Where they form helical strands shimmering with a neon green of the Paraiba tourmalines in smoke rising up twisting back on themselves. Higher and higher until meeting after three turns to form a dark apparition. A pair of angry red eyes glare out of the dark ethereal cloud. Slowing seething into itself to form a humanoid shape. A shrill sound bursting from it. Certainly not human. Making its human subjects wince in pain. This sound morphing into an ancient human dialect. A language unheard in thousands of years.

Melinda, "What's it saying?" Impetuous and disrespectful as always.

Angelique, "Silence!" Andor stares at Melinda unblinking. Jadon desperate to go unnoticed, recoils stepping back. Andor speaking Sumerian but changes languages quickly. Skimming forward to more current human languages. Choosing next Hittite and then Old Persian. Still no response from them. Andor becomes impatient with these three ignorant witches. Knowing their type from past experiences. Angelique becoming concerned. "I can't lose her." Speaking French, then Arabic and back to English. Andor finally hears enough to identify their English language. Yes hearing that Old English and Saxon tribal tongue interesting how they were mixed. Now those were some admirable savages. Not that she didn't recognize now what the others became.

"Who has called me from my dark slumber? I have killed fools for less."

Angelique regains her composure. "It is I who called upon you master of vengeance." Bowing her head in deference to Andor. Watching her with those gleaming red eyes. Narrow-slit pupils indicative of some night predator.

"I offer you a gift to do with as you see fit." Tossing the piece of fabric with dried blood across the double circles at the dark hominid form. The instant it passed through the protective barrier embers spark flying off in different directions. Then gravity defied frozen in midair this piece of ruined dress shirt remains suspended there. Darkness the absence of any color snatching this token offering from the air. Fingers curling around it made longer by sharp talons. At first a scratching is heard but then becomes obvious. That of fabric tearing as the sharp nails rip through as the hand they are attached to becomes visible. Closing around it making a sickening crumbling sound as dried flakes fall off. Andor brings it up to smell it before tasting it with a red tongue lapping over the stiff fabric. Turning its head to the side with recognition. Letting out a bestial growl edged with hate. As its form vaporous engulfs it greedily.

Angelique, "It is one of your own. That I fear has betrayed us."

Andor, "And that affects me how? You're just a coven of witches." Angelique's eyes become round and bulging with rage. At being admonished by this being. Her beautiful face twisted up in anger. Concentrating her rage, blue-white sparks begin to crackle across her fingertips. Ready she releases it as a bolt of energy. Which then disperses crackling and popping around the dark apparition. Causing it to dissolve into a cloud of charged ions. Making it howl as a wounded animal. Speaking through gritted teeth. "I will kill you for that!" Andor says

Angelique unmoved by this threat. "Good, I have your attention now. I need your sight and hearing for now."

Andor, "What is it you are seeking?" Hissing out a reptilian sound. Her dark pupils narrowed to slits within ferocious red eyes. No humanity to be found in them.

Angelique, "Do we have an accord?"

Andor, "Yes." Her voice a hiss. Chewing on the fabric to release the taste of blood wetting it from her saliva.

Angelique, "Find him, watch and report back to me. Kill no one, yet."

Andor, "Find him I will." Savoring the taste of Camel's blood. Taking in his essence thus perceiving him. Her presence reaching out across distance. "Um, he is Arabian. I will enjoy this man." Her eyes widening with understanding a smirk curling her lips. "He is your lover." Not a question but a statement of fact. "Before all is done you will pay me in what I choose. For now you are indebted to me."

Angelique, "He will be your payment and nothing more. When I say we are done and not before. For you surely can be sent back to hell where you came from."

Andor smiles at her. "You do drive a hard bargain witch."

Angelique, "Good now go. I will call for you when you are needed." Dismissing Andor like any other common servant without the respect that is due her. Treating her as such a very dangerous mistake. Something she isn't and should never be confused with is a servant or an equal. Being powerful and commanding of others. Andor unaccustomed to being dismissed in this manner. Her bilious dark form expands, slamming into the invisible barrier provided by the double circles. Casting off sparks against it.

All three women feel the cold energy testing the strength of their barrier. Its clouds dissipating but not before hitting them with a blast of cold air. As a warning for all those who bear witness. Wind rushing out in all directions extinguishing candles and the cauldron fire. Darkness engulfing them with the fetid smell of brimstone. Its foul odor causing Jadon to gag. Angelique unmoved by this display of power casts her hands outward. "Ignitus!" Commanding all of the flames to reignite. Fire under the cauldron explodes back to life.

CHAPTER 68

A NEW DAY finds Marc busy with more chores. First to protect the manor from uninvited guests. Using holy water from Rochester's new cathedral and dried lavender and rosemary from the kitchen garden. He cuts up the herbs and sprinkles them with the holy water around all thresholds and even some of the interior doorways. The library entrance and the secret doorway behind the shelf. Stopping only long enough to call Camel. His call going to voice mail. Marc leaves word for him to contact him.

Returning to work in the kitchen preferring the granite countertops to cut stainless steel on. Hence not using an antique table to get scratched and gouged by sharp metal. Cutting out crescent moons, stars, and other shapes to hang outside off of shrubs and low-hanging limbs. Using the shiny, reflective surfaces to vex and confuse creatures sent to spy. Including inquisitive witches.

Marc hears the distant squeal of tires against pavement. Followed by that all too familiar rumble of a Ferrari outside the kitchen windows. Continuing to cut the heavy gauge metal with tin sniper's. His hands aching from using muscles unaccustomed to this kind of work. Anticipating Camel to stroll in any moment with his usual masculine gait. Instead hearing the doorbell chime. Yelling from the kitchen, "Come in!" Nothing happens. If the door is locked why doesn't he use his key? Camel pushes the button again. Marc yells a second time for his brother to come in. Finally setting the snipers down and walking around and out to the door. Marc pulls open the door which was unlocked. Strange.

Marc, "It was unlocked. Why didn't you come in?"

Camel, "Enkil could not enter the house without you allowing him to enter. You have it blocked. He is telling me you have been busy since we were last here." Camel remains outside putting his hand out speaking.

"Yes, I can feel it myself."

Waiting for Marc, "You must make an opening in the protective field you have created," Enkil's deep bass voice speaking. Marc looks unsure what to do. So Enkil instructs him. "Push the herbs aside. Then trace a portal out with your power hand of the doorway. While envisioning it." Marc follows the directions. Once this is done Camel is hesitant to enter still. His expression irritated hiding the twinge of fear. Having never had this happen before.

Marc expression one of questioning. "Well? Come on dude, come in. The three of us have work to do." Camel steps across the threshold into the house.

Enkil instructs Marc further. "You need to close the opening you have made. So that no other uninvited...," pausing to choose his words, "guests may enter." After closing the door and the threshold leading them into the kitchen. Marc peers out one of the five windows through a gap in the curtains. Satisfied no one is watching, he pulls the curtains together but not before putting a match stem between two of the blinds. Affording him a view to discreetly peek out from.

Camel, "A little paranoid are we?"

Marc, "You could do with some after everything that has happened."

Camel shrugs. "True. Now what is it you wanted to give to me?"

Marc, "I'll explain that shortly. First I could use some help cutting out some more charms." Handing a pair of metal snipers to his brother. Camel looks doubtfully at the shapes already cut out.

Camel, "Enkil says the charms you are cutting do work to confuse spirits. At least the weaker ones and maybe some witches." Closing his eyes for a moment, opening them again. "He especially likes the blue-purple gazing balls you've placed around the garden." Marc nods his appreciation at the compliment.

"Thank you." Cutting a metal spiral. "My hands are aching and sore from using muscles unaccustomed to this kind of work."

Camel's eyes flash to yellow his pupils vertical slits. His appearance frightening but still ruggedly handsome, wise beyond his years. Setting down the cutters. Enkil waves his hand over the metal causing it to creak and pop. Numerous different shapes detach right out of the metal. Rising up into the air, spirals, circles within circles spinning. Marc about to speak but Enkil silences him. While giving them a little tweak with his other hand. Wires attaching to the shapes creating mobiles of constellations spinning in midair. Marc takes a short quick breath. Holding back his delight at the artistry before him.

Enkil, "These charms are good but if you really want something to confuse and misdirect try these. Cut crystals like the ones of chandeliers appearing suspended in midair. Sparkling as they dance under the light from the recessed illumination of the kitchen. Light refracting colors in all directions. Touching everything with its beauty. The three of them marveling in silent awe at something so simple yet exquisite.

Enkil, "Now you could use some modern metal abstract sculptures outside." Waving his hands for dramatic effect. "Place the crystal charms in sunny windows around the house. That way light can shine through them." Enkil is now outside Camel's body looking him directly in the eyes.

"You have some serious intentions placed within this house. It is very strong." Marc nods, pleased with himself. He and Camel knock fists together.

Camel, "Yes! You did it brother!" Genuinely happy his white teeth flashing.

Enkil's yellow eyes unchanged serious. Speaking now that he has both of their attentions.

"Do you have witches in your bloodline?" His eyes cold. Wondering why he hadn't suspected this before. Waiting to hear Marc's response.

Marc, "Uh. The more I investigate into family history. Uh..." His tan cheeks become dusky. "Quite a few of my ancestors were...," searching for a better word unable to find one.

Enkil's impatience increases. "Just say it!" Marc becomes a little uneasy. Knowing how much Enkil hates them.

"Yes, sorcerers." Camel is surprised and impressed by his brother's use of semantics. All too aware of how Enkil feels about witches.

Enkil, "I felt it the first time we met. I should have realized it wasn't the coven. You were the one that conjured me. Only a strong witch could have brought me forth." Camel is determined to run some interference between Enkil and his brother.

"Can we have some time to discuss this new development?" Glad his father had made him go to a boardroom meeting or two. That and unfortunately needing legal representation on occasion.

Enkil, "Yes you should talk to him." Turning to Marc, "You may not have been raised as one. But you are what you are." Staring Marc down with a hard look. "Before I acquiesce to take my leave make sure the two of you keep your guard up at all times. Without doubt you will be under attack from the most seemingly innocuous things. Hear my warning." Taking one last look at Marc. He should have recognized what he was. Shimmering away, both men feeling the slightest breeze against their faces as Enkil leaves. His energy field tickles their heads and arms like a gossamer spider web ever so gently brushing the tips of their hair.

Marc, "Did you feel that?"

"Yes," Camel says.

Marc, "Does that happen every time he leaves?"

Camel, "I hadn't noticed. He doesn't leave my body very often." Marc gives Camel a concerned expression.

Camel, "I know, but there is nothing we can do right now."

Marc, "Come on. Let's get these put up around the house." Both young men take a moment longer to look at the charms. Sparkling and floating on air unattached to anything.

CHAPTER 69

THEY SPEND CONSIDERABLE time choosing which windows would be most effective to hang the remaining charms in. Having just placed the last one then moving to the library. Where they sit and drink hot tea. "You seem to be taking all this magic and witchcraft very well. Like a duck to water." Camel says. Marc pulling off his shirt to expose an animally hirsute upper body. Thick with straight dark brown almost black hair covers his still very muscular chest bulging beneath. From the center of his chest disappearing below the waistband like mink fur in the winter. Naturally long and satiny soft with strong curving muscles beneath. His pectorals and deltoids still impressive.

Marc, "I was getting warm with that on. You know I used to be smooth. Have I beat you yet?" Camel lifts up the front of his shirt. Almost but not quite as hirsute.

Camel, "Okay." Letting go of his shirt covering his rippled abdomen hair covered. "It looks like you win." His smile showing pearly white teeth while cocking his head. As if to say, *Oh well, tough break*. "Enkil has stopped the progression of the spell. It no longer acts on me."

Marc, "Great for you. American women don't like bestial men."

Camel, "So don't marry one. I won't have that problem with an arranged marriage she will not have a choice."

Marc, "Are you still going through with that?"

Camel, "We will see."

Marc, "Maybe I'll marry a nice Middle Eastern Muslim woman as well."

Camel, "You could. After all you were raised Muslim as well as Christian. My father would be happy to help you get a wife from a good family. Or wives if you choose. You certainly can afford the expense of more"

They both sit in silence letting their thoughts roam. Marc about a harem. Being an American but having a dual citizenship. Would he be allowed to have more than one wife? Even if he is Muslim. His thought becoming more intimate on Jadon, Melinda, and Mary. All three being his wives. Finding himself becoming excited at that idea. Camel's thoughts of having a couple of wives also. Looking at Marc, he punches him on the shoulder. "Man you too?"

Marc, "Yeah. I was thinking about what it would be like to have a home for a harem.(A place in the house for your wives.)"

Camel, "Come on." Standing up. "I need a workout and I feel like putting a hurt on someone."

Marc, "You have thirty pounds on me."

Camel, "What? Are you afraid I'll mop the floor with you?"

Marc, "You are on big dog. First I need to pump some iron."

Walking out to their cars Camel says, "Enkil is not into physical work. Yet he likes my tight body." Both men run to their cars. Camel just getting into his car first. Smoking some rubber to beat Marc to the gym.

Being an upper body day they spot each other at the bench press.

Camel encourages "Push it! Feel the burn, one more. Come on." Marc's pectorals tight and burning from lactic acid buildup.

Yelling, "Ah." Two hundred and forty pounds smacking into the metal rack. Perspiration dripping off his face.

Then they do a brutal round of kickboxing. Marc using every skill he has picked up over the years. Even having pinned Camel to the mat a couple times. Still finally losing but not before perspiration is dripping off both men. Bare-chested deodorants long gone. The ring smelling more of a locker room. A crowd of men gathered watching them fight yelling. Each of them with his own supporters to cheer him on. When the fight over the group disperse.

Marc, "You stink!"

Camel, "And what, you don't? You smell like a goat herder."

Marc smiles brightly. "Yeah, I do. It feels good to sweat."

Camel, "There's nothing like it. Getting endorphins pumping that make you feel good. Now how about that soak in the Jacuzzi?"

Marc, "I thought you'd never get to it." Pulling off his soggy blue bandana along with rubber bands letting his thick mane free well down his back.

Camel, "Tough talk for the man who just lost."

"Next time," Marc says.

CHAPTER 70

AFTER THE VENGEANCE demon has left Melinda asks a question that is puzzling her.

"Angelique, why did you call it 'master'?"

Angelique, "You should use flattery to enlist its help. Demon or Djinn whichever you choose to call that being. Giving it the appearance of being obsequious will get us what I need. All of their kind want to be worshipped." Becoming angry with Melinda's blank look. Choosing to elaborate. "Males always believe they are in charge. You have no further to look than Camel or Marc. Both believing they control us with their sexual prowess. When all along we are using them for the energy they created in unadulterated bliss. Ignorant to what was really happening to them. Only too eager to have one of us submit to them. Did the chemicals on your hair stay on too long?" Her sarcasm acidic.

Melinda covers her irritation and rising anger toward Angelique by attacking Jadon verbally. "You didn't know either." Jadon's smug expression unchanged. Looking back at her smirking. Refusing to take the bait.

Melinda's anger internalized beginning to slip out in the form of blue-white energy. Crackling over her fingertips. Releasing it toward the sky in a burst. Blinding white energy streaking across the night sky in microseconds. Exploding out, jaggedly branching over the few clouds in there. Releasing a second bolt on top of the first boom. Forcing a cloud to expand rapidly with negative and positive electrons separating. A lightning bolt jumps from this cloud discharging energy toward the ground. Striking a tall tree ripping off a chunk of it. Looking as if it was split with an axe. Melinda is enjoying her release of anger. Turning to Angelique, "Will there be anything else you require of me, master?"

Angelique unmoved by her display. "That will be all, for now. Thank you." Dismissing her. Melinda digging divots into the hardwood with her high heels clicking. Passing through the door with a shimmer, appearing outside next to her car. Too angry to be impressed with her evolving power.

Jadon excited. "The power we have gained from them is growing in us, increasing our abilities."

Angelique, "Yes as I said it would."

Jadon, "I wouldn't alienate her. She is becoming powerful. It is of a benefit to us not to have her against us."

Angelique, "If I thought for one moment she was against me. I would slit her throat myself and use her blood as a gift. To that bitch vengeance demon. Enough about her." Walking out of the room.

Jadon thinking to herself, *If I wanted to get back at Melinda, I would make her suffer by trapping her astral body as a reflection in a mirror.* Giggling to herself. Remembering back to a rival that died in coma. It was all so easy. People always assume because she is the quieter one that she is not as capable. Aren't they always so surprised?

CHAPTER 71

MARC SOAKING IN the chromatherapy Jacuzzi with his brother Camel across from him. Having agreed on blue as their color for now. Hot currents mixed with lavender scented bubbles come from all directions. Compliments of Oolong. Relaxing in all of this scented hot water up to their scruffy necks. Adjustable jets pulse against sore achy muscles from the pain of combat needing to relax. Marc allows his mind to drift back to the match. Does it seem they are physically stronger? When he hit Camel with both his feet to the chest, it threw him into the ropes. He was airborne before slamming into the ropes. His lips curled slightly into a smile of discreet satisfaction. Yet he recovered, redirecting the force back at Marc, making him bounce when he hit the mat. Knocking his breath out of him leaving him gasping for air.

Camel reading his face, speaks first, "Did it appear to you that we fought with more power?"

Marc, "I was thinking that too. The last time I ran through that routine at the gym, Javier was pissed off at me." Javier being one of Marc's sparring partners in the same weight class. "He said I was using excessive force. Like it was some kind of tournament."

Camel, "Yes, Sergio was particularly vicious. When punching my midsection." Tightening his sculpted abdominals. "Now that you mention it." Taking a moment to reflect. "He was cursing at me, something about a hairy bastard!" His expression unchanged. Both men nod their heads stoically. Then break out into mean spirited laughter.

Marc, "You were kicking the heck out of me."

Camel, "Me? You were vicious, finding the smallest openings to strike hard." Languishing in the hot lavender scented water. Floating up on his back enjoying the caressing sensation caused by rivulets of water pouring off his body. Then submerging letting the hair sway sensuously in the water. Simultaneously both of them sitting up to attention at a slight noise. More an echo of a presence than a sound. Marc looks to Camel.

"Did you feel that?" His hair at the nape of his neck rising up.

Camel, "Enkil tells me there is a demonic force outside trying to gain access to this house."

Marc stands up in the Jacuzzi water showering down. "That didn't take long."

"It seems to be confused," Camel says smiling. "The charms are deflecting light at it. It can't see beyond them into the house."

Marc, "Good. It cannot gain access to the house without an opening being made for it to enter, correct?"

"That is correct." Camel's voice comes out in a deep bass. Enkil now in control again. "It has been sent here on reconnaissance. They want to know what has happened to prevent them from drawing off your energy. There is no need to fear it yet," Enkil says. "I'm sensing some derision amongst the witches. We should be able to put that to some use."

Marc, "I think I know the one who could be turned. She has a kindness that she hides from the others. We might be able to work that in our favor."

Enkil, "That is good because this demon would rather just kill Camel. She hates strong men."

Marc, "What?"

Enkil not having intended to give them so much information about this new opponent redirects the conversation. "Fear not for your brother's life. It cannot harm him. At least as long as I am around to protect him. That should be something for you to consider in your haste to get rid of me. Now with that said, I have no intentions of letting this choice male body go to waste that way. I will deal with her soon enough. You two need to devise a plan to help move matters into our favor. I can't be the only one challenging their defenses."

Marc, "Interesting you should mention that. We have been bouncing some thoughts around and have come up with an idea. It still needs working out."

Enkil, "Good. Camel, you get me out of the house and I will keep the vengeance demon occupied." Then Enkil says to Marc, "He will be right back." Camel disappears for a second. Marc blinks once and he is back in the Jacuzzi. Camel has been returned in a standing position. Wobbling to catch his balance.

Camel, "I hate when he does that." Marc reaches out to steady him water still coming off him. "Thanks."

Marc looking like a wet bear dripping. Expressing his wishes, "Wouldn't it be great to have all of them out of our lives. I would be able to take my shirt off without feeling self-conscious outside." Looking down his chest both of their eyes following the wet pelt all the way down.

Camel, "Don't you mean your smooth body back? So the ladies will ogle over you."

Marc, "Yes." Flexing his upper body. Making his thick pectorals mountainous and biceps bulge.

Camel, "I don't want to burst your bubble, but Enkil said that some of the changes wrought by this kind of dark magic can be permanent."

Marc, "Seriously? Which changes would that be?" Stepping out of the jacuzzi over into the shower. Barking out commands to the electronics, "Temperature ninety-nine degrees. Rain!" Water falls from the ceiling like a hot summer shower.

"Are you using Irish Spring like I suggested?" Camel asks.

Marc steps under the water. "Yes. It really does help cut down on the musky smell longer." Marc all the while working crème rinse down to his scalp. Then pouring it on his chest, kneading it in deeply.

Camel, "Well, you may shed some of your body hair but I wouldn't count on that much." Marc pauses to give him a mean look. Camel shrugs a shoulder along with a noncommittal tip of his head to one side. As if saying, *Oh well, another tough break*. "Your back will still be furry but at least it won't have that thunderbird look, maybe. Plus you will keep your strong sexual appetite."

Marc looking disappointed, putting his head under the shower adjusting it to a more concentrated spray. "And on the plus side?" Marc asks. Letting the water spray his chest.

Camel, "You maintain your very strong sexual appetite."

Marc, "You said that twice. That's the only positive in this?"

"Uh, yeah," Camel says.

"What about you?" Marc says.

"I won't be as hairy as a Persian like you," Camel says chuckling, Marc not amused. "Enkil is not concerned about my heavy body hair. As I've told you he has stopped the progression of the dark magic against me." Marc relaxing a little. "However, because Angelique gifted me to him as payment. I will never be apart from him unless he so chooses." Marc lets out a deep breath he didn't realize he was holding. Camel reads him as only a close family member can. "It could always get worse."

"Yes," Marc says, nodding agreement. "At least we're not going to change into a beast unable to control ourselves."

Camel, "Another plus." Relief showing in his ruggedly handsome face with its blue-black stubbled sheen.

Marc, "I guess I can always shave and wax."

Camel, "Wax? Are you nuts, as thick as this is?" Grabbing a handful of Marc's chest hair. While he's toweling his mid back length mane of hair.

Marc hollers, "Ouch! That pulls my skin!"

Camel lets go. "It's a fucking pelt. You're just going to rip it off with hot wax?" Marc gets his point. "You can't keep your face smooth. So how are you going to do it with your body?"

Marc's hand is already grazing his rough stubble-covered jaw. "I don't know," Marc says.

Camel, "Men who wax their backs as the Russian Jews are inclined to do get a very rough stubble on their backs as it grows in. You have seen them at the gym."

Marc, "It was just a thought."

Camel is not finished yet. "A lathering of crème rinse when you shower makes it soft. Ladies may not like it when they see it. But once they feel how soft it is, they love it. Take it from me." Camel steps into the shower after calling out, "Temperature ninety degrees."

Marc, "Is that the ones you've paid for or the ones you have seduced?" Camel ignores his barb, dunking his head under the falling water. But not before farting out a big cloud.

Camel speaks, "I'm sorry, did you say something?"

Marc steps away wrapping his towel around his waist holding his breath. "Uh, it's like sewer in here." Both erupt into laughter. Marc walks over to the bank of mirrors with their protective hex marks written on them in mugwort. These mirrors set against the granite counter. Two separate vessels set above the counter each with a spout coming out of the mirror. The one Marc is standing at with the mood LEDs on blue. Making the water color an electric blue as it comes. From right out of the mirror. Deciding not to shave tonight Marc orders the water off. *What's the point?*

Camel over in the shower calls out, "Water off." Grabbing a warmed towel. Drying his head first his hair much shorter than Marc's but still thick enough to lose a hand in. Needing an extra towel himself to dry his body. Starting with the dense pelt of black on his chest.

Marc, "Jadon is the one I could get to."

"You think so?" Camel says.

"I need to approach her without drawing any suspicions," Marc says, forming a plan.

Camel stops his toweling. "You call her, needing her help. Possibly only something a woman would have insight into."

Marc, "That's good. No wonder you bed so many women."

Camel, "Then you use the dark spell against her. Seduce her. When she is under your satyr ardor, have her remove the spell from us both."

Marc, "Are you sure that will work?"

Camel, "Have you forgotten? We now have strong pheromones. Get her under your ardor."

Marc, "You think that would work on her?"

Camel, "You did it to Melinda."

Marc remembering his night with Jadon. *This won't be difficult at all, getting charged up over her. That should start the releasing of pheromones.*

"Angelique and Melinda are very close friends for years," Camel says. Then he adds, "She has to feel a little on the outside. Plus they are very competitive amongst themselves. She'll have something to prove."

Marc, "I think you are onto something."

Camel, "Those two are mean-spirited. She would want to rub it in their faces her success. Where they had failed."

Marc, "My cover could be advice on drapes for the living room. I need a woman's help in choosing a good color and fabric. After all, I'm a red-blooded male. What would I know about that?"

Camel, "That's good. By the way, Enkil believes she is hiding something."

Marc, "Any ideas what that might be? Maybe it's something we could use to enlist her cooperation."

Camel, "None whatsoever, but now you're thinking."

Marc, "I don't like that idea about choosing drapes."

Camel, "Then come up with something else."

Marc, "I've got it. I dreamed about her dying in a freak accident and I want to discuss it in person. Being concerned for her safety. She could meet me somewhere of her choosing."

Camel, "That is good. You still have to bed her."

Marc, "I'm attracted to her." Going back to his story, "She drowns in a flash flood. I'll be wearing my ring for protection."

Camel, "You could try for more."

"How so?" Marc asks.

"While she is in the throes of passion, planting the seeds of doubt against the other women. See how strong are your satyr abilities."

Marc, "Justice served!"

Camel, "Right! When was your last time with a woman?"

Marc knows where he was headed. "Saturday past. So my pheromones will be high." Ruminating about Jadon. Her beautiful cappuccino-colored skin so soft and perfumed. Stretching languidly, his towel slipping down just hanging on his hips. His arousal rising quickly.

"Hey, slow down the intentions are good," Camel says. Both men indulge in their thoughts of women becoming aroused. Even with cologne on the air their is a cloud of male pheromones mixed subtly with it.

Marc, "Okay. This could work."

"Call her. Let us see how it goes," Camel says.

Marc picking up his cell phone from off the counter, never very far away.

Formulating his story further making a decision regarding Melinda. Using his thumb to skim down the memory finding her number. Pushing send.

Jadon answers, "Hello." Her voice sexy with her thick Turkish accent. Knowing it was Marc calling.

"Hi. I need to talk to you about something important. I know this is going to sound silly, but I had a bad dream where you were in it."

Jadon is suspicious. "What happened in this dream?"

Marc, "I would prefer to meet with you in person. It's not something I care to discuss over the phone. You just let me know where you would like to meet. Preferably some place private."

Jadon smiling to herself, a knowing look spreading across her face. "Oh, and you are frightened for me?"

Marc, "That and I feel something is wrong with me. I need a woman's opinion."

Jadon convinced she is onto his less than subtle play. "Some place private, Hum." Pretending to give this some thought. "How about my home? Would that be to your liking?"

Marc, "Sure, that would be great. Somewhere we won't be disturbed."

Jadon, "I can assure you we won't be disturbed here. Meet me, say in one hour. I planning on freshen up."

Marc's voice husky, "I'll be there." Ending their call not wanting to sound too desperate. "Well, it's all set. I'll be leaving soon. What are you going to be doing tonight?"

Camel, "Me? I'm going out. Some lucky ladies are getting a love machine. I'm as horny as a herd of goats." Rising to leave.

Marc, "Be careful, no witches."

Camel, "Enkil won't allow that. Besides the spell will no longer progress for me. Remember I'm protected now. You are the one who needs to be careful. They are already suspicious if they are sending out spies."

Marc, "I'm counting on that." Camel looks worried for his brother's safety searching his face. Marc feels the need to elaborate. "If the spy witnesses me seducing her and she ends the spell. Reporting back to the other two creating a point of division amongst their happy family."

Camel, "What if the demon doesn't witness the betrayal and report back?"

Marc, "It is still a win-win. Because they will know a traitor in their mists. Driving a wedge between them." His tone hardened with anger. Camel looking at his brother closely unsure he likes this change in him. Deciding whether to say anything.

Camel, "I don't know if I like the new harder you."

Marc, "Do I have a choice?"

Camel, "No. I guess not. If this works Angelique will be incensed with rage."

Marc, "Melinda will be angry to the point of being irrational and hopefully, start making mistakes in judgment."

Camel lets out a soft whistle before speaking. "Angelique will retaliate. She may kill her."

Marc, "That would be unfortunate, but Jadon made her choice long before I met her."

Camel, "Good luck. I'll ask Enkil to watch out for you. He seems to like you. I'm not sure why being a heartless demon."

Marc, "Whatever the reason, I'll accept the help from anywhere at this point."

Camel, "Allah Akbar, my brother." Crushing Marc in a bear hug as he would a man before going off into war.

Marc, "Allah Akbar." Knowing he will need all the blessings of Allah he can get. Hugging Camel back, breaking the hold by patting his lifelong friend on the back. No matter how this all works out they will always be friends, even unto death. Then becoming stoic, focusing his mind on the task at hand.

CHAPTER 72

ARRIVING AT JADON'S home, a stunning old Victorian on a side street off Main street. An East Side neighborhood, very established. His blue Mustang shinny from another application of wax rumbling up her driveway. The car has cojones, a V8 engine not like they make now. Marc admires the attention to detail that was put into the home's restoration. Three stories of house set amongst old specimen trees. As was the custom decades ago in Rochester. The house painted in vibrant purple and red accents. Its landscaping immaculate. Large rhododendrons green and thick surround the first floor. Cosmos flowering in brilliant colors echo the colors of the house in the main flower bed.

Ringing the doorbell Marc is surprised by Jadon answering the door herself. Instead of one of the maids. After welling him in she guides him into the parlor with its high ceilings trimmed with large crown molding. Exquisitely restored and painted. Indicating for him to take a seat on the rectangular midcentury sofa low to the floor. Herself going to the kitchen to put some tea on. After having offer refreshments. Giving Marc time to admire the oil paintings hung around the room. Landscapes before the impressionistic movement. Immediately recognizing several artists' works. A William Parrott of mountains in Oregon.

Jadon clears her throat to get his attention. "You like classical oil paintings?"

Marc, "Absolutely. This one makes me feel like I'm right there in the mountains."

Jadon, "Yes, it is breathtaking. Most of these in this room my brother helped me to collect. As you can tell they have a strong masculine influence. Cream for your tea?"

Marc, "Yes, thank you."

"Sugar?"

Marc, "No, thank you." Jadon pours herself a cup. Marc pretends to take a sip. "It's very good. I don't recognize the tea."

Jadon, "An old family recipe." Sipping hers. Just as the telephone rings. Marc grateful for the chance switching their cups around, giving Jadon the cup intended for him.

Jadon leaves the room to take the call in private. Expecting it to be

Angelique calling. Already aware that Marc is there. Knowing how she watches everyone.

Marc notes her lipstick on the edge of his cup. Quickly using his thumb to rub it off. Transferring just a bit back to her cup. *Let's see how she behaves with her own herbal tea.* Hearing Jadon raise her voice. Snapping at the caller, she speaking Hindi. "You fool, I don't want anything!" Jadon comes back into the room taking her seat on the sofa next to Marc. He takes a gulp of the tea trying to appear nonchalant.

Jadon, "So tell me. What is it you wanted to talk to me about so urgently that you couldn't discuss over the phone?" Taking a sip of her tea.

Marc stalls her. "I hope that call wasn't important?"

Jadon becoming slightly anointed. "No! I mean it was some outsourced salesperson. I thought I had all of those telemarketers blocked."

Marc, "They always find a way to get through." Looking into her grey-green eyes. "I'm concerned for you." Taking another drink of his tea. "This is really good. Indonesian?"

Jadon drinks some more of hers, holding the porcelain cup with a dainty hand. "Yes, it is. Mostly white tea with a mix of my own herbs."

Marc, "I don't know how to say this but to be out with it." Jadon raises her graceful arched eyebrows. "First I had that nightmare where you drown. It was so real."

Jadon is unmoved so far. "They can be life like but I wouldn't get too concerned over one dream."

Marc, "That's just it. It was not just one dream. Melinda said some things that concerned me about you. She said you weren't working out here." Jadon watching his face intently, so he continues. "She said you were transferring to another university by fall. I hope that isn't true."

Her grey-green eyes their pupils narrowed unable to hold back her rising anger with fear. *Could they be getting rid of me?*

Marc, "Is there anything I can do to help you adjust? I don't want you to leave." Using his most innocent schoolboy face.

Jadon, "When did you hear this?"

"It was after the party," Marc says. Pretending to think about it more. While tugging at his collar distractedly and becoming warm, loosening his tie. "Is it warm in here?" Glancing longingly with his most sexy expression. Working her with his dark blue eyes twinkling. "I think about you all the time. How sensuous your voice is. The one time we spent together."

Jadon sets her empty teacup down. "Yes?" Feeling flushed herself. " It does seem to be a little warm in here." Marc finishes his tea in a careless gulp. Jadon reaches over "Here," pulling his tie off in one quick yank. Unbuttoning his shirt down some allowing its dark crush of straight hair out. Wanting to touch it so shiny and luxurious. Thinking to herself, *It has to be soft. I'll show both of them. Get rid of me.* Believing it to be time to take control of the situation. Reaching inside his shirt running her hand over it. Even better, soft as mink pushing her hand through it. Deciding to find out how thick it is. Digging her long nails more forcefully to get down to the skin below. Sending shivers through him. Releasing pheromones mixed with his cologne making a unique scent. Wafting around him and thereby up her nostrils. Jadon takes pause; he so is very desirable and masculine. Ensnaring herself with her own weapon of seduction; that and with some karmic justice of her own creation. The satyr.

Finding herself becoming helplessly attracted to Marc. His curse or natural senses picking up on her quickening physiology, that of increased respirations and heart rate. Marc slowly unbuttons his shirt further. Thus exposing more of his body to the air to carry more pheromones on the current. Jadon's senses immediately react, her body already betraying her. *He smells so good,* her nostrils flaring, body temperature rising, struggling within herself to maintain control. The battle already lost. Such a great body so virile. Marc slides his unbuttoned shirt off. Jadon watches it fall to the floor. Her eyes returning to those thick Cupid's bow lips. Leaning over toward him knowing in that instant that it is too late to change what was happening. *He tricked me.* Marc brushes his lips against hers, then pulling away tantalizingly not kissing her. Only igniting her heated desire more. Marc gently slowly kisses down the side of her neck. As a rush of sensation followed by a moan escapes from her.

The herb tea is taking effect, allowing her to become mesmerized by his masculine pheromones. This hairy beast of a man able to do as he pleases with her self-control gone. He knows she is his for the taking. Reading her body's responses puts him into rusk. Enthralling her more with his scent and touch. Marc's only mission to pleasure her forgetting the reason he is there. Well, not really.

Speaking softly whispering suggestions in her ear. Now that the herbal tea has opened up her mind to some gentle guidance. Marc finds himself enjoying this role reversal. After himself and Camel were so thoroughly deceived. Then used as cockles of some past coterie. This last thought sparking just a little anger in him. Making it all the more imperative to succeed.

Jadon's inhibitions fall away lost. Opening up to his questions about the coven's plans. Caring about them yet unable to deny him the answers. His drive to titillate raising her enthrallment only to encourage her willingness to divulge dark secrets. Marc devours her supple cappuccino-toned body with kisses and nips. His teeth just grazing her skin.

Marc whispers into her ear between love bites to her neck, "They are just using you." Jadon listening, Marc continues, "Angelique will kill you when she is done with you."

Jadon lets out her hidden suspicions, "I know, I've never trusted either of them."

Marc, "You know Angelique and Melinda have been deceiving you. You're just a means to an end."

Jadon, "Yes. So has Melinda used you, your little Ms. Upper East Side."

Marc holds back his surprise at this statement. "What do you mean?"

"You know it already in your heart. She will stop at nothing once she sets her mind to it."

Marc, "Both of them are murderers aren't they?"

Jadon, "No one crosses our coven, ever." Marc strokes her abdomen with just the tips of his fingers. His thoughts straying. *She is so gorgeous with her long dark hair and those eyes. She would bear beautiful children. If only she could be trusted.*

Marc, "You should break from them."

Jadon, "I can't. They would never let me live."

Marc, "You must do it gradually, be subtle. Not to arouse any suspicions."

Jadon, "Go on." Marc's lips graze over hers, his course stubble-covered jaw scratching her. "Break the spell on myself and Camel."

Jadon, "I can't, they will know it was me."

Marc, "How will they find out if we don't tell?" Kissing her deeply, causing her to moan from his stretching of her. Gently nibbling and squeezing with both hands. Her rapture rising, she claws at his back. Nails digging into hair there. Keeping her hanging on to the edge, unmoving.

Marc, "End this darkness that you have put on myself and my brother. Please, do this for me."

Jadon breathing heavily, her decision made. Whispering, "Show me how much you need me."

Marc, "Chant it now and I will give us what we both desire." Jadon begins chanting in Latin. Marc then tells her, "Say it in English."

Jadon, "Remove what has been done. Spell of passion disperse on the four winds. I command it!"

Marc's eyes are glazed over the spell acting on him. Driving his need for her warmth around him. Perspiration wicking through his pelt to make her chest slick. Jadon's voice changes speaking in a language unheard in millennia's. His thoughts too distracted by her charms and his own duplicitous intentions to notice. All of these affecting his mind's clarity. After all, she is one incredible women. Fluent in several languages obviously using another. Making her even more exotic drawing him out to his edge of climax. Jadon pauses for a second gasping for air. Her irises changing to red with their pupils vertical angry in appearance those demonic eyes. Powerful is her nature flipping his two hundred pounds of solid muscle over onto his back with the slightest of efforts. Marc realizes somewhere in his hormone-clouded mind something is not right. She is almost like a different woman, but uh, silky warm sensations override the analytical part of his mind. She feels so very good and her perfume jasmine engulfs the air around them. *When did she start using that scent?*

Jadon leans over biting and kissing his neck. Sending thrills rushing through him. Giving his chin a firm bite. Not enough to break the skin, mind you. Just enough to create firm pressure. Twisting on him, she's in control now. Dragging her long nails over his soft, thick chest hair (like mink). Following the curves of his pectorals. Digging her French-tipped nails into what she was seeking. His large areola to the nipple. Squeezing it and twisting his nipple between her nails. He is being driven mad with pain and pleasure from so many places.

Speaking with a feminine voice breathy from passion but no longer a Turkish accent. Just when both of them are at their peak. "How do you know Enkil?"

Marc catches his breath. "What, who?" Unable to speak further. Warm waves intensely consuming them both in climax. Satiation and blissful relaxation soothing them into a quiet time. Jadon still lying a top him with muscular arms wrapped around her smaller body. Each listening to the other's heart beats slowing. Their respirations easy and steady no longer quick.

Marc wakes up in a panic not in his own bedroom. Calming quickly seeing Jadon resting quietly beside him. Easing off the bed noiselessly. Giving the floor a glance checking for clothes. None found. He walks nude through the air-conditioned house. How good the cool air feels heading back towards the parlor. Enjoying the sensation of bare feet on the numerous Persian rugs scattered along the way. So soft and resplendent, especially the ones with a high silk thread count. Bringing back fond memories from childhood racing barefoot through the palace.

Stopping to gather up clothes strewn across the parlor floor. Dressing rapidly not wanting to discuss what happened with Jadon. Just in case she has some remorse for what she has done against the coven.

Safely on the road and not feeling any different. Marc wonders whether Jadon followed through. His mind is still clearing out the fresh summer air blowing into the windows of the Mustang. Heading north on 590 at 70 mph. What did happen back there? Jadon behaved as someone else. Pushing himself to remember back through the clouds of ardor. He was in control until—? His memory a little fuzzy after they were in the bedroom together. Having a strange feeling coming over him. Feeling very uncomfortable with the déjà vu he was experiencing. Could the demon they had conjured taken control? Thinking back to what Enkil had said. He had called it a female before he changed the subject.

Oh shit, something did happen. Missing his turn at Goodman Street. Having to take the inner loop to get home. Turning right onto East Avenue.

Finally home Marc goes upstairs to shower. Shedding his clothes as he walks. Leaving a trail of his clothes scattered across the marble floor in the bathroom. Once he is in the shower lathering up his thick chest and body hair with Irish Spring. Knowing if he doesn't he'll get more than just a little of that musky smell back. Especially after that incredible session with Jadon. He already smells of sex mixed with his greasy perspiration.

After drying off, he finishes up with a good dousing of Tommy Hilfiger. Camel was right. The combination of the two does work well to keep him smelling fresh for hours. That and of course a strong deodorant.

Hungry he goes downstairs to search the kitchen for something to eat. First checking the refrigerator which is almost empty. Except for clabbered milk and some overripe tomatoes with fluids pooling under them. Closing the door and opening the freezer. Good taking out two chicken potpies. Peeling open the boxes giving the directions a quick glance. Cutting slits in their tops and placing both in the microwave. Popping open a can of Pepsi-Cola the last one. Drinking this while he waits for the microwave to do its work. Leaning on the brown granite counter its surface cool. Determining he needs some groceries in here and a housekeeper. Surveying the condition of the kitchen with dishes piled up in the sink.

CHAPTER 73

THE FOLLOWING MORNING Marc sitting in the formal dining room. Seated at the head of the long mahogany table with room with nine chairs on each side, easily seating twenty. Its high ceiling sixteen feet with two crystal chandeliers sparkling centered over the table. Drinking his strong black coffee from a fine bone china cup. Absentmindedly examining the unusual pattern. Cobalt blue with gold painted trim. Wishing he had gone to the local grocery store for milk and a good loaf of bread.

Instead he pulling over the cornucopia that he had brought in with him earlier. When he came into the room with his coffee, half awake. Picking through the grapes and finding a pomegranate. Smelling its skin, then peeling it open and taking a bite. So sweet and flavorful. Having finished the sports section of the *D&C*, opened on his laptop. While drinking his second cup coffee skimming back to the front-page headline story.

"Rapid Lake Effect Storms Cause Power Outages to Eastern Monroe County." Rainfall totals of up to nine inches in one hour were measured. Heavy isolated downpours inundate the Irondequoit Creek tributary system. Causing flooding to parts of the creek system into Ellison Park basin, with water depths of up to twelve feet reported to cover Blossom Road. These sudden fast-moving electrical storms seem to appear over the eastern side of Monroe County. Resulting in power outages as yet again to Pittsford and the immediate surrounding communities. Local stable Heberle with horse riding was flooded. Forcing the rescue and release of horses. When the stables and home of owners of Heberle were swept from its foundations. Subsequently forcing the closing of Browncroft Boulevard due to debris and high water. Which in turn limited rescue efforts.

An even darker side to events was the report of a Ferrari swept from Blossom Road near Powder Mills Restaurant. Which was also sustained damage from floodwaters of Irondequoit Creek. The car was near Powder Mills heading west. When it was swept from the road. As recounted by the surviving passenger and companion. College student and lacrosse captain Helmut Stein survived after swimming to safety. Where he had clung for hours waiting for rescue. The Irondequoit Search and Rescue Team pulled him from the branches of a tree. His female companions two other local university students were not so lucky.

One was found inside the car where her seat belt failed to release. The owner of the car is missing and presumed drowned. Officials believe her body may have been swept into the estuary. Where they will broaden the search and recovery efforts into the marsh that connects to Irondequoit Bay. When the flood waters have drained off some. Both young women's names have been withheld until family members can be contacted. One death confirmed so far with another expected. *How many lives will this flash flood claim?*

Marc reading into this story. That weather occurrence rings of unnatural manipulation. Remembering back to the night Angelique had been looking for Camel a few weeks ago. Now she and her little group are continuing to destroying lives. When it hits him a sick feeling deep in his gut. Could that missing women be Jadon? She does drive a Ferrari. No. *They couldn't have found out about our plan.* Anguish quickening his pulse. Thinking back to their encounter last evening. Where her voice had changed along with her behavior. Remembering how easily she repositioned them. Reaching for his cell phone music blasting from it starling him. Recovering quickly seeing Camel's familiar number displayed. Accepting the call touch the screen.

Answering grumpily, "What?"

Camel, "Wow. Get up on the wrong side of the bed?"

Marc, "Sorry, the phone startled me."

Camel, "Have you seen the morning news?"

Marc, "Yeah. I'm reading it online. I'm pretty sure one of the drowning victims is Jadon."

Camel, "Which means they are onto us. Did she break the spell?"

Marc, "I can't tell yet."

Camel's turn to be annoyed. "That's a yes or no answer."

Marc, "I don't feel any different. So I just don't know."

Camel settles down using another tactic. "Tell me from the beginning and leave nothing out. I want all the hot details."

Marc recounts what had happened with his switching the tea. "As planned I had a telemarketer friend from Mozambique call her. Using a routed call to look familiar to ones she has received a few times before."

Camel, "You had access to her private phone records?"

Marc speaking casually, "After our run in with the State Department and Persian Antiquities Ministry, I have a few contacts now."

Camel smiles approvingly. "Go on."

Marc continues his story. "You know how suggestible their concoction made us. I had an evening of bliss and she did end the spell."

Camel smiles wolfishly. "I'm not sure which I'm more impressed with your manipulation of her or your contacts. You know you only broke a few laws, federal and international."

Marc, "Haven't they been working outside higher laws all along?"

Camel, "Right you are my brother. You don't have to defend yourself to me."

Marc, "She agreed to work her magic while we were, you know."

Camel, "Yes." His dark eyes sparkling knowingly. Waiting to hear some tawdry tidbits.

Marc's tone becomes serious. "Something unexpected happened after she had completed her chanting during intercourse." Camel quietly listens thus encouraging Marc to continue his view of the turn of events. Concern creeping into his mind Camel listens closely. Marc continues, "Her lovemaking changed. It was like being with a different woman. One more experienced in the ways of the boudoir."

Camel, "What else?"

"Uh, her voice had a decidedly different accent." Marc anticipating his next question adds, "It wasn't Turkish. Somehow familiar but I don't recall where I've heard that accent before. It was unusual, plus her personality changed. She became more self-confident. No actually more sexually aggressive."

Enkil is now listening closely yet remaining in the periphery of Camel's mind. Having taken charge of his host's body. Secretly so as not to alert either men of his presence. Feeding the next question to Camel. "Yes. Were you not frightened at this?"

Marc looks at his brother's face on the phone. "No. Why should I be?"

Camel, "Just curious, go on."

Marc, "She was completely in control. She just rolled me over onto my back like it was nothing. Jadon is petite. Yet she was so aggressive and strong." Enkil listens on his suspicions increasing. "For a split second there I thought her eyes changed."

Camel sits up to attention. "How so?"

Marc, "Like Enkil's except red." His memory clearing more. "Then she asked me how I knew Enkil."

Camel, "Strange considering she was a part of conjuring him into our lives." Marc's turn to feel something is not right with his brother. Monitoring him more closely but not overtly. Camel continues, "More importantly, why didn't you say anything about this to me until now?"

Marc, "My memory has been cloudy since last night. I must have gotten some of the drug when I was kissing her."

"None of this frightened you?" Camel asks.

Marc, "No. Now that you mention it. It was just more exciting." Looking sheepishly back at his brother. Camel gives him a disdainful look. "Has Enkil said or noticed anything different about us?"

Camel, "He has been amazingly quiet since we last all met to put your plans into effect. I haven't heard his voice in my mind." Enkil listens with excited interest.

Marc, "It would be great if this curse has been lifted."

Camel, "It would be great to get back to being a normal university student again."

Marc, "Will that ever be possible?" Unsure of anything ever being the same. Certainly their innocence to life was gone forever.

Camel's handsome face serious and distant, finally responding. "You are probably right but at least we would be rid of the evil that Angelique and her crew has brought upon us."

Marc, "Only a small piece of it. There is much more we have to deal with before we are safe. I am sure that we have only scraped the surface of what she has planned."

Camel, "In that event it wouldn't hurt to have some additional insurance. Enkil isn't around all the time."

Marc gives him a playful remark, "Now you're using that big head of yours. I have the blessings written out and the herbs I have bagged up for you to take."

Camel, "I will pick them up soon, longhair heathen. Are you sure you're not Persian? With that rug on your body I'm not so sure about you. I didn't think Frenchmen had such a heavy suit."

Marc, "Maybe it comes from your father's side of the family."

Camel, "Maybe." Both of them having a good laugh at each other's expense. Enkil's vaporous form facing away from Camel, searching outside his palatial home with its walled gardens. Using his telepathy to reach out across the surrounding neighborhood. *When will she make her appearance?*

CHAPTER 74

LATER THAT EVENING Angelique is ever the perfect hostess entertains a coterie mixer with Melinda having brought a novice her name Barbara. Who is interested in pledging to join their sorority. She will be shadowing Melinda. Unaware of how dark the intentions are behind having this quasi-formal yet informal cocktail party.

Melinda pours a beer up from the tap conscious of Barbara's watchful eyes. Melinda releases the jeweled top on her ring. All while managing to flirt with one of their unsuspecting male guests of honor. Sprinkling ever so quickly a dash of white powder into the beer. A small vortex swirling inside the frosty mug giving it a good head. Bubbles rising above the glass. She releases the lever sliding it over to Helmut Stein, who in turn clinks his mug with hers. Taking a large draw off the cold beer. Himself preferring warm beer as is custom in Germany. But what the heck a pretty fräulein serving his beer. Blinking her baby blue eyes at him with less than innocent intentions in them. Causing him to take another large draw off beer.

Music piped in a not too loud heavy metal song. Angelique herself would have preferred something more soothing. Needing her anger assuaged after having been betrayed. *Such a pity. That girl had real potential, innate powers. Given some time she could have rivaled even myself. Well, maybe not that much.* Her ego cutting the compliment off. *Traitors, however they come about, have to be dealt with harshly or else the others…* Sensing Enkil's strong energy nearby snapping her out of her quiet reverie. Smiling to her guests casually scanning the room as she walks through the group. Her five-inch Manolo Blahnik's accentuating her lovely calves. That and a raw silk dress matching her shoes. Casual eloquence seeming to float across the room. Male eyes always admiring her feminine attributes. Angelique whispers into Barbara's ear.

Melinda gives a German cheer, "Go Zie handsome." Flirting with Helmut and giving him her most sexual look. Unflinching when she looks him in the eyes. Hers twinkling with promises of more excitement to come.

While Angelique is entertaining a running back from another local college. Placing her hand on his broad muscular shoulder. Having to reach up because he is so much taller than her even with heels on. His brown eyes dreamy, fascinated by this gorgeous woman paying him so much attention. Looking down at her, his shaved head smooth and brown. Speaking to her with a Georgia accent his voice a deep base that of a large man, matching his appearance. "Thank you ma'am," after she hands him another rocks glass of sour mash whiskey. Angelique enjoys this game of conquest so much. The chase half the fun.

"My name is Angelique not ma'am," She says. Holding out her arm for him to take so he can escort her. "Just as you requested. How is the whiskey?"

Robert, "It's good, ma'am. I mean Angelique." Himself having been raised to be respectful of all women. Not finding it easy to dispense with formalities.

Angelique, "Excellent. Now tell me about yourself." Her cocktail napkin slipping from her hand dropping to his feet. Stopping him from picking it up for her. Leaning over adding to her decotage. Feeling his eyes fixed on her. Perfume gently caressing his olfactory senses. Straightening back up her napkin retrieved. Allowing the fabric of her silk dress to brush against his pant leg as she rises up. Swaying to steadying herself by placing a soft hand on his strong arm. Robert's pulse already quickening downing the whiskey. Angelique smiles at Robert satisfied with her effect on him. Knowing her glamour has enticed him. He wouldn't have needed the ancient compound if seduction was all she intended. Her allure so powerful now only one of the oldest of the elders could resist it. But plans well laid are to be kept unless one wants to invite failure. Which could never be allowed to happen again because of a man.

Angelique, "Well now where were we? Oh you need a refill." Snapping her fingers at one of the waiters circulating with a silver cocktail tray. "Another whiskey for my guest Robert."

Robert, "Thank you ma'am."

Angelique, "You really don't need to be so formal. My mother was a 'ma'am.' Your mother was a 'ma'am.' Do I look like I'm your mother or anyone else's for that matter?"

Robert, "No ma'am. I mean no, Angelique." His brown cheeks becoming ever so slightly dusky.

Angelique, "Do they all grow so big where you come from?" Robert smiles his white teeth bright against his dark skin. His smile making his cheekbones more angular. So naturally handsome and unaware of this, Angelique appreciating him. *Yes, an innocent male. I will so welcome his individuality to our fold. Maybe these two will be enough to complete what is needed. In either case, what great fun it will be to watch the changes happen to him. Evangelicals, you have lost another to my side.*

CHAPTER 75

CAMEL ARRIVES AT the manor around noon. Passing a grey haired woman on her way out the side door. Glancing at him, her face wooden unreadable. Wearing a gold chain around her neck with a cross on it. Noting her pear shaped figure once she has passed. His lips ever so slightly turned up in a smile. Back to his happy go lucky self and definitely a behind man. Walking into the library finding Marc not so happy. As he pushes a stack of papers for potential applicants across the desk in frustration. More faxes arriving, Mr. Thornburg's secretary having already set up interviews for him. Beginning this morning.

Camel, "You don't look too pleased. Aren't you looking for dour and strict?" Trying not to smile but the harder he tries it just breaks open. Into a big white teethed smile, chuckling at Marc's expense.

Marc, "I'm not. I don't want another one like Ms. Campbell." Not smiling. "You seem to be taking particular delight in my difficulty." Even more irritated at his brother's continued happiness.

Camel, "Sorry. I'm just feeling like my old self again. What service are you using?"

Marc, "The ultraconservative and opinionated one. Then he screens them before ever sending a potential to me." Meaning Mr. Thornburg.

Camel, "Maybe you do need the grandmotherly type to care for you. Look at you. You haven't shaved in what appears to be days and you need a haircut plus," smelling the air, "you smell like a sheepherder."

No longer able to hold back a smile laughing with Camel. Marc replies, "You sir, smell like a perfumed Arabian whore."

Camel, "Thank you. I'll take that as a compliment." Choosing a chair across from Marc to sit in. "Why don't you just use my housekeeper until you hire a new one. She knows you. When was the last time you had a good home cooked meal?"

Marc pauses to think about it. When was it that he had a good home cooked meal, United Arab Emirates style. "Not since you had me over to dinner."

Camel, "That's been a while."

Marc, "I've spent more time in fast food places than here. So I'll take you up on that offer. She isn't going to get nervous about all the stuff going on around here, is she?"

Camel gives his best smile, bright white teeth against his olive brown skin. Saying, "What? You are concerned about your less than prudent behavior and what a servant will think about it? We're two young men in America. We can do what we want. Sure she is a prude but you can bring all the infidel whores home you want. She is not going to say anything. You will just get her disapproving looks." Camel breaks into a laugh at Marc's serious expression.

Speaking from his irritation with Camel, "You're just being a dick."

Camel, "I've been called worse." Enkil's attitudes overtaking his own. "Household staff stay employed by using discretion. Not by imposing their own brand of morality."

Marc shakes his head. "Who is in there? My dad?"

Camel, "Hire another Ms. Campbell. Then you better make sure you hide all your condom wrappers."

Marc, "Okay point taken. I have to talk to Mr. Thornburg about the housekeepers he has been sending me."

Camel, "Good finally you are making sense. This place looks like it could use some help." Looking around the room at dirty clothes on the floor. Several glasses and coffee cups left around the room. "If this room is any indication."

Marc, "Yes, well, that would be great. When could she start?"

Camel, "She hasn't agreed to it yet and she is only on loan. You can't have her. I know she can help find some staff for here and organize them. This place will sparkle. Plus she stays to herself or at the mosque. If not her then who else?"

Marc, "I really don't want another old Christian hypocrite judging me in my own home."

Camel, "Well then here's your answer. Nahadeina may be disapproving but she is not cruel. As long as you don't unnerve her by using unseemly magical powers. She knows her place and will keep her mouth shut and do her job."

Marc, "Is that not what you expect from a wife?"

Camel pauses to think about his response. "No, but she does need to be receptive in bed."

Marc, "Come on let's continue to research occult protective rituals."

Camel, "Why don't we pray first. It's not like we can't use all the help we can get." Marc's prayer rug already in the library. Both men face east and kneel. Marc on his prayer rug and Camel on one of the older Persian rugs. Which actually is an expensive prayer rug with Arabic writing where his head will touch. Woven with silk threads interspersed throughout it sparkling even under the low lighting of the library. Camel's forehead touching where the prayers are woven in. Both men praying quietly.

CHAPTER 76

AFTER SEVERAL HOURS of studying from the Koran. Satisfied with their religious faith observed. They both continue with the old leather bound tomes from the seventeenth and eighteenth centuries. What would become known in present times as Wiccan books. Searching for rituals of protection. Enkil has returned and is explaining how to bring forth intentions. To push energy into these rituals. More for Camel's understanding but Enkil finding it interesting. That both men are comfortable with this approach of mentally infusing themselves into fields of energy for protection. Camel nods that he is satisfied with Enkil's explanations.

Marc begins gathering up supplies for Camel to take home. Herbs and black candles that he has set aside for him to take home. The doorbell rings ending their lesson. Marc already watching out for the delivery from De Ville's nursery. Getting up to answer the door. Enkil ready for an attack having moved outside Camel to see who could be there. Marc says his good-byes to both. Needing to examine the delivery of perennials. Andry's last design with colors for the new flower bed that Marc had dug. To contain royal blue delphiniums and purple foxglove (*Digitalis*) with midnight red hollyhocks and white ones for depth in the flower beds. Or as Marc would say, dramatic effect. After inspecting over two hundred plants and accepting the delivery and seeing Camel off. It is finally time to start planting them anxious to get started. One last thing to do. Calling Mr. Thornburg to cancel the afternoon interviews. Having a busy afternoon of planting ahead.

Marc talking Mike from De Ville's into helping him with the large amount of planting to be done. Mike is a six foot two blonde with a beard the same shade as his hair. Very muscular from hard work one of those natural builds. Seems more than eager to help Marc out. Talking with him while he organizes the flowers before placing them. Watching Marc appreciatively in his tight jeans (bubble butt) and white sleeveless tee shirt with his thick patch of black hair pushing out at the neck. Marc is focused on the work at hand. His chemistry mixed with his cologne a veritable cloud of natural male pheromones. Even the honeybees seem to hover longer around him more than an ordinary man. Taking in his scent before going to the flowers. A few choosing to hover and alight on his thick hair. Unaware of this attraction they have to him.

Marc comments, "I thought you were staying to help." Mike blushes from his own overtness and underlying attraction. Something he had never had before, at least not for another man. Not against it just not for him.

Mike, "No, I just remembered a lot of other work I have left to do."

Marc, "Maybe you need to take a break and get out of the sun. Your face is kind of flushed."

Mike, "Yeah, maybe I'll do that. Bye." Marc wonders to himself, *What got into him*. Turning back to study how he was to begin.

Mike walks quickly back to his truck. Stopping before climbing into the cab to sneak one last glance. Talking to himself, "Damn, what the heck has gotten into me?" Starting up the truck depressing the clutch and pushing it into gear. Making the truck lurch forward.

CHAPTER 77

MARY AFTER LENGTHY discussions with her aunt's friend an older nun. Sister Mary Lark has decided to return to London while her aunt Norma's will is probated. Moving up her plans to attend Eton in the fall instead of in the winter. The scholarship committee in agreement with her plans. After all, it had been her aunt Norma who had insisted they move her admission to January. So she could have time with her before being pressed with studies. What a lie that was. Aunt Norma had her come to America to be an indentured servant. Making her labor from sunup until sundown. Having never understood why her aunt was so hard on her until now. After her aunt's shocking revelation. That she was the love child to her aunt's fiancé and sister. *Well, no wonder she hated me.* A constant reminder of her betrayal by both of them. But still in all it wasn't her fault. This she would have to think about in more detail in the future. Moving away from the past for now.

That whole situation with Marc a little embarrassing. Even though the only nice people she knew outside the convent were Marc and Camel. She would miss them and just maybe Rochester. After all it was the place of her first taste of real independence. Still needing to speak with him to clear the air before leaving town. Mary picks up her cell phone sliding it open. To call Marc getting his voice mail. So leaving him a message to call her.

Later that evening Marc comes in from the July heat outside. The cool air-conditioned temperature refreshing. After hours of labor but still a labor of love working outside in the gardens. His work boots heavy he stops walking as a clump of dirt slides out in front of him. Recognizing his boots are caked with dirt in their thick treads. Stopping where he is in the side hallway. To unlace his steel-toe work boots pulling them off. Using one dirty hand pressed up against the wall. Leaving a grimy handprint to his astonishment, not having thought about how dirty he was. Dropping his moist sweat-soaked socks right there. Padding barefoot over the hardwood floors. At least part of him felt refreshed. Longing to strip off his perspiration soaked clothes and get comfortable. Instead thirsty going into the kitchen for a can of pop. Cracking it open, gulping cold thirst quenching Pepsi. Stopping long enough to wash his hands over the dish filled sink. Before heading upstairs he goes into the library to check the answering machine.

Retrieving Mary's message to call her becoming excited. Pressing redial waiting while the phone rings at the convent. After six rings a voice message comes on. It's a woman's voice very dry educated, yet congenial. Marc's voice husky and low unaware of his masculine need coming across on the machine. Having been days without female contact unintentionally focusing his persuasive satyr tone into the message. Not realizing how strongly provocative his tone will come across to whomever takes this message off. Long finished with the usual cordialities.

Mary is brought to the phone to hear his message by one of the older nuns. Who appears less than amused by her caller's masculine charms. Looking at her with unrequited anger and disapproval. Mary embarrassed as a first reaction, then holding her temper in check. Having spoken with Melinda earlier. For which she unexpectedly gave her some eye opening insight into Marc and his "harem." As Melinda described it littered with the hearts of dozens of young women he had thrown aside. His approach that of, "Love um and leave um, Byron." The infamous poet and seducer from British history.

Marc, "I need to meet with you. You won't believe the information about the turn of events in our lives that I have to tell you." Half listening to his husky tone as her anger increases. Thinking back to what Melinda said: "You were nothing more than a feather in his cap. Being his next conquest extra points for a real virgin." Melinda's tone so cold with her upper east side Manhattan accent. Mary thanking the sister for letting her hear his message.

Time enough to address that big scoundrel. *He thinks he can call me up being all sexy man seductive and I'll just fall into his bed*. Mary's face flushed, her pale complexion so easily reddened when she is angry or embarrassed. But this time definitely anger. Pushing in his number on her cell phone's memory. Marc answers on the second ring.

"Hello? I'm so glad you called me back."

Mary, "What is it you wanted to talk to me about?"

Marc, "I wanted to go over with you in person. Some important information that has come to light. You need to be made aware of for your safety."

Mary, "What sort of information is it that you cannot tell me over the phone?" Her tone cold.

Marc pausing something not sounds right with her. "Well, it has to do with Melinda and---"

Mary, "So it's true you are back in Melinda's bed." Her throat tightening with pain. She had gone from infatuation to quiet adoration over the past couple of months. Actually believing he could love her. "I was a virgin, you seduced me for game."

Marc, "It wasn't a part of the plan. Melinda and her friends had a hand in it. I mean, they planned it." Everything was coming out wrong.

Mary, "How could I have so easily believed you were the one. Then to hear you admit it."

Marc, "I'm not admitting to it. I didn't have anything to do with it."

Mary, "Are you serious! Not a part of it? You did it! Without you there wouldn't have been anything happening."

Marc, "That's not what I mean. I'm trying to tell you about them."

Mary, "I already know about them and your pathetic little game. Melinda explained everything to me. She warned me about you before all this went down. I just didn't have the good sense to listen. This was all just some twisted game you two men play. Using a woman's feeling to get what you want. More sex."

Marc, "But—"

Mary cuts him off. "I already know Melinda is a stone cold bitch!" Marc pulls the phone away from his ear. Her anger getting the best of her for a moment. Then calming herself some. "So are her dear friends Angelique and Jadon. Are you going to deny you slept with Jadon again also?"

Marc, "How did you ---? I did that to protect us. They were using us. I haven't figured out to what ends, but you have to believe me when I say I am innocent. Melinda has been planning this for a while."

Mary, "You are nowhere near innocent. There certainly isn't anything innocent about Camel. To imply this about yourself would mean you believe me to be a fool. Is that what you are saying?"

Marc trying another tactic. "I'm not back with Melinda. You need to listen to me. They are witches!" His tone brusque and loud.

Mary, "No. I don't have to listen to any more of your lies. You are not going to pull me back in with some outrageous story about Melinda and her friends. Being a coven of witches. That seduced two innocent men. What I do believe in part what Melinda told me was true. I haven't heard you deny that you bedded Jadon. Again!"

Marc is angry with her now for not giving him a chance to explain. "What's that?"

Mary, "The two of you are decadent sex-freak rich boys." Her British accent becoming stronger. "How is it that you Americans say it? You're just tapping a few hos in your stable."

Marc, "I never would have touched you if I had known. You are not so innocent in all this. You wanted it as much as I did." His anger lashing out at her. Sorry he had said it as soon as it came out.

Mary, "You're right. It's always the women's fault isn't it? You Muslim men always blame the women."

Marc, "That isn't fair bringing religion into this."

Mary, "Oh right, it's no different with Christian men. The women is always labeled the whore. You men are just the victims of nature."

Marc tries to calm the situation. Choosing another direction to warn her. "That is not how I feel."

Mary, "Melinda warned me about you. That you would give me some ridiculous story and if I didn't accept it. You would blame me for what happened. To think I believed you were a nice guy."

Marc, "I'm not blaming you for what happened. I'm trying to warn you."

Mary, "Consider me warned. Don't call me again ever. I'm leaving for London as soon as I can get aunt Norma's affairs in order. I'm out of here!" Ending the call almost breaking the phone so angry with him. Marc winces as he pulls the phone away from his ear. That didn't go as he expected.

How the hell did that little manipulative witch get to her so fast? She had to have planned this days ago. Every step of our conversation was anticipated throughout. Am I that predictable? Maybe it's for the best that she leaves this country. She would be one less person for me to worry about a retaliation against. Especially if they knew how he felt about her. Coming to that realization himself. They had killed several young women for being associated with Camel. Would his punishment be her death? If he was right about Jadon. Convinced Enkil was telling the truth Ms. Campbell never had a chance. Once she got in their way she was expendable. How long before Camel or himself for that matter get in the way? Are plans already in motion to replace the old guys with new ones? *How can I jam a wrench in their gears?* His feeling of being out maneuvered and played hard getting under his skin.

Wanting some revenge for having Mary turned against him. That and being so easily duped. The empty silence of the manor ringing in his ears. White noise his only companion making it seem like a fever is upon him. Shadows darkening with the twilight engulfing him. Standing alone in his cavernous library with the ceiling reaching up three stories. Gone are the setting sun's last rays over the mature forested grounds outside the manor.

CHAPTER 78

MELINDA CHECKS ON the progress of her handiwork. Needing to call Mary to see if Marc has been in communication with her. More importantly, was he able to sway her or are they still allies? Listening to the phone ring. Anxious to know so she can report back. Now that she is the underboss. At least feeling powerful like one.

Mary picks up. "Hello."

Melinda, "How are you holding up?"

Mary, "I'm fine. You were so right about him."

Melinda, "Oh?" Delight spreading across her face.

Mary, "Marc blamed everyone but himself. He even tried to give me some lame story."

Melinda, "Some men always try to lay the blame elsewhere. What did he try to say was the cause?" Unable to hold her mind back from hating this redheaded moron. So easy to make them all dance like a marionette.

Mary takes a deep breath before starting. "He tried to tell me some cock and bull story," pausing, "that we all were being manipulated by witches. Along with something about being unable to control himself a victim in all this. Just used for sexual favors. I don't know I just stopped him from telling any more lies."

Melinda oddly quiet speaking at last. "Wow. That's quite some story. Did he say who these witches were?"

Mary, "Yes. I'm almost embarrassed to say." Melinda waits for her response with the seconds passing like minutes. "He said it was you and your friends. Angelique with other select girls from the sorority."

Melinda, " What did you think?"

Mary, "Such an outlandish tale utter rubbish. I hung up on him." Melinda almost wishing she had believed him. Giving her a chance to go after that stupid girl.

Melinda, "That's so like a man. When they are caught with their pants down. They will come up with some outrageous stories. Did he say why this was being done?"

Mary's turn to sound impatient. "No. I wouldn't let him continue with his lies. I may be naive but I'm nobody's fool."

Melinda, "You sure surprised him no doubt of that." Rolling her eyes at the other end.

Mary, "Whoever heard of gorgeous witches."

Melinda, "Imagine that." Stifling a giggle. "Even I wouldn't have bought that story and my roots are blonde." Now for her next bit of acting. "He's been giving me some tall ones for a while now. I believe I'm the one who has been naive." Melinda admits, "I thought he loved me." Her voice hushed carrying a sorrowful tone. Stifling back tears, swallowing.

Mary, "I am sure we are not the only ones taken in by him." Being strong for both of them. Anger flickering in her green eyes. The set of her tight jaw resembling her aunt. That which only a few close family members would recognize. Her mother being one of them.

Melinda enjoying a good performance well executed. "I am just so sorry that I took it out on you. It should have never been you. The one I took my jealousy and hurt out on. I am really so very sorry." Laying it on thick.

Mary, "It's water under the bridge. Excluding once or twice you have always been nice to me. No beyond nice like a sister to me. I should have listened to you. You are a good friend." Melinda so content with her deception, feeling smug. Now to bring it to a finish. So that light skinned bitch will never trust him again. "Now that we are both onto him, he won't possibly be able to use us for his scorecard. Camel will have to share women from his stable. I know the points won't count as much not like him landing a virgin." Realizing too late she hadn't wanted to share that part. Mary's breath catching in her throat on that last comment. Anger overcoming tears of disappointment and pain. Embarrassment making her cheeks blush red. Asking herself, *When did I tell her that?*

Melinda fills in the awkward pause quickly. "He and Camel just use women for sex. Marc picked up those subcontinent ways from his brother. I won't allow him back in my life."

Mary, "We have the misfortune to have found out how far he will go to get his way." Her voice raspy from choking back tears.

Melinda stifles a moan heartfelt by Mary. Someone used to suffering in silence. As Robert the running back from the previous day's mixer. Softly kisses down her neck his thick lips and hot breath sending waves of pleasure to her brain. Becoming impatient taking her nipple in his teeth gently tugging at it. Melinda gasps catching her breath covering her response. "What doesn't kill us makes us stronger," speaking up.

Mary believing this to be emotional pain. "Are you all right? Do you need me to come over for moral support?"

Melinda covers Robert's mouth with her hand. "No, I'll be fine. It's just going to take some time." Sounding damaged, all the while holding back laughter. "I'll be fine. Don't worry about me. Bye-bye."

Mary not taking the hint, "Keep a stiff upper lip love. Try not to cry over a lying dog."

Melinda, "I will try just give me some time. Call me once you're settled in London. I'll come for a visit, bye-bye." *Click*. Hanging up before she laughs in Mary's ear. Melinda bursts out into a maniacal laughter echoing. Robert unable to hear the true cruelty in it. So like music to Robert's ears all the encouragement he needs to resume kissing her neck. His dark brown eyes almost black. Due to his pupils being so dilated from the herbal brew Melinda has given him. Looking on his ruggedly handsome features making it all too easy to enjoy this new male. So strong pulling her atop of him. His large hands roaming down her back caressing it. Making her desire increase while keeping her mind detached. So she can harness and direct his animal energy, desire to its fullest. Repeatedly.

CHAPTER 79

NAHADEINA THE HOUSEKEEPER to Camel's palatial home. Good natured wise and remembering changing his diapers. Having been on staff in his father's home in the United Arab Emirates when he was an infant. Finding it odd to be cleaning all the mirrors throughout this home with this herbal wash of mugwort. She watches Camel with mounting concern. After he covers two of the Louis XIV mirrors. That he had been so excited to buy at auction two years ago. Now covering them? After having demonstrated how to use this wash on the backs and fronts of the mirrors. Burning candles and incense that she is familiar with. It helps to cleanse and purify the home. But this other ritual feels somehow untoward.

Camel has the other servants busy sprinkling salt and herbs around windows. At all entrances to the mansion. Somehow missing the large balcony adjoining the master suite. Which overlooks the high walled garden below. Servants busy throughout the estate even the groundskeeper (Anri) and his staff given special instructions. To add lavender to the plantings along the driveway and at its gates. And of course around the jasmine planters growing on the south walls and pergola. Where it more sheltered from winter's cold.

It isn't until later in the evening that Camel notices that Enkil has returned. Smelling the aroma of tobacco and finding it smoldering in his father's old hookah. Left from a previous visit. Speaking to Enkil inside his head. "You know I don't smoke. Behavior like that will attract unwanted attention to us. A possession charge could cost you this fine body you so covet!"

Enkil, "That isn't going to happen. I have already taken care of it. Your thinly veiled attempt to frighten me only exposes your own fear."

Camel, "You will leave one of these times and not be able to get back in. Then I'll make sure you go back to hell, or wherever it is you came from."

Enkil, "Empty words for one who has no power over me. I will leave when I choose and return as it suits me. You will never be able to prevent that. You belong to me from now and forever!" Neither of them hearing Nahadeina's approach. Camel turns angrily toward her.

She looks at the hookah speaking, "Camel, are you smoking in the house again? You know how it affects Aziza. She has allergic asthma." Looking at him critically.

Camel, "I forgot, apologize to her for me. It won't happen again."

Nahadeina not finished yet, "I'm surprised at you. Your father just had heart surgery. Smoking is very bad for the heart."

Camel picking up the hookah, "I'll be sure to use the balcony in the future." Taking it through the open French doors placing it on the table outside. Which overlooks the high walled garden below with its towering Leyland cypresses and Canadian hemlocks. Their graceful boughs swaying with a gentle breeze. Even a couple of bald cypresses tall and leafed out with their delicate lacy leaves in the mix. All creating a dense barrier against the outside world. Inside this sanctuary of nature.

Cardinals and yellow finches twitter in the background. Its breeze carrying with it the scent of jasmine. Growing from the green and white veined arabesque marble urns. Carved by artisans from centuries long past. The fragrant scent of jasmine caressing the air around him on the balcony. Five large arches framing the direction of Mecca in the east. Giving it a surrealistic feel out of time from an ancient palace. Heightened more by the echo of water falling into a mosaic tiled pond surround. Making the low seating wall perfect to enjoy the serenity from. Equally breathtaking from a distance covered in shades of blue. Especially mosque blue so vibrant yet relaxing with the sunlight reflected sparkling off the water.

Lilies with dark pink blossoms perched just out of the water. With its urn fountain bubbling the sound enhancing a sense of tranquility, true serenity. How long had it been since he enjoyed something so simple as this. Leaning on the balustrade taking in the ambience. His large build body taking up a portion of the framed view inside the arch. Enkil feeling a sense of pure joy that nature gives. Along with her calming effect which is engendered in this beautiful place. Moving back to a table in the shade. Taking up the hookah puffing on it savoring the taste of dried apples mixed with tobacco a sweet taste. Allowing his thoughts to roam.

Such an archaic yet relaxing practice. Wondering why the Sumerians his own people never developed this. Releasing a puff of smoke watching it rising up. Changing directions twisting toward the wind chimes now tinkling in a high octave a complete scale Zen.

This breeze increasing in strength along with the wind chimes' volume. No longer in successive order, becoming discordant. As the chimes bang together frantically. Enkil glances causally into the direction of the wind. Blowing out smoke across a face as yet to be seen. Decidedly feminine, himself holding back a smile.

Enkil lifts an eyebrow before speaking. "I was just wondering how long it would take you to come to me." His brown eyes twinkling mischievously before they change to his true yellow cat's eyes. Hard and calculating a true predator. Where the smoke had passed a form effusive and vaporous, gradually taking shape inside a darkening maelstrom. Its shape feminine and petite yet statuesque, before taking on a human form. An olive complexioned beauty of high cheekbones. Almond shaped silver-green eyes sparkling from deep pools of intelligence. Not to be mistaken with longing. That of a woman used to reading men for what they are. Hair dark and long crimped into waves falling to her waist. Her lips full almost pouty, yet her stance and demeanor one of a woman from the highest station of court. Clothed in silk fabrics of purple and royal blue befitting her once noble position in life. Her silks cascading and draped in the ancient fashion over her voluminously shaped figure. That of an hourglass difficult to hide such femininity.

Enkil taking it all in. She was one gorgeous woman for any age. His dark eyes lascivious with their pupils widening. Unable to hide his wanton lust for her. And knowing she is eating it up that he can want but not have. Struggling not to smile at her being a natural flirt. This only makes it more difficult not to do. Giving in he breaks into a wide smile genuine his white teeth bright against his moreno skin. Ending the silence between them.

"Andor you can still take my breath away with your beauty." His voice deep, husky, almost loving. Cocking his head to one side. Andor not expecting to evoke this strong a positive reaction to her presence.

Andor, "What makes you think I have come for you?" Enkil ignores her mild anger. She always was a proud woman.

"How long has it been?" he asks.

Andor, "Since 1786, July. You do the math." Allowing her anger with him to dissipate for now. Her face becoming even more beautiful if that were possible. "I see you have yourself a man capable of giving you all the carnal pleasures you so enjoyed."

Enkil, "Yes. I see you're still angry after thousands of years." Reaching out for her arm.

Andor immediately stepping back in anticipation of his move. "I see you are still boringly predictable. Always wanting a woman you can't have."

Enkil, "And who would that be?" Her almond shaped eyes becoming angry glaring at him. "Let it go." Enkil speaks softly, "You helped make me more of what I am now. Than I ever could have been. My precious vengeance demon." Andor's face softens. "How many men's lives have you destroyed by now?"

Andor, "Only the promiscuous unfaithful dogs that most men are." Stepping closer to Enkil. Running her hand over his broad chest. Enkil allowing her closer yet she finds his new scar where he had be stabbed only a few weeks. "What's this from? Already right into your old ways of hurting women?" Rubbing the scar through the linen fabric. Making lazy circles around it. Enkil refusing to rise to her baiting of him. "He has already been stabbed to within inches of death by a supposed jealous lover. Definitely a man of your type."

Enkil reaches up, softly brushing her cheek with his large hand. Looking into her eyes searching. "Who could ever compare to your ageless beauty?" Andor basks in his genuine adoration, momentarily forgetting her anger with him. Sitting across his lap with her arm draped behind his neck. Staring into his eyes to see them softening to deep pools of unknown waters. Jasmine's scent lingering in the air around them. As the breeze has died down the air still with expectation. Even the wild creatures silenced for the two of them. Watching and waiting for the outcome. Leaving them both to their memories transporting them back. Thousands of years to a sunny tropical land. Where date palm fronds rustle in the wind. Carrying on it a waft of myrrh and frankincense smoldering in a censer of bronze. Molded in the likeness of Ishtar, goddess of fertility and war setting on the stone terrace. Enkil kissing her fully yet gently so as his full course beard wouldn't brush burn her soft skin. Inhaling the scent of jasmine oil compounded with other essences for her skin. A unique fragrance made for only a queen by the royal astrologer. Andor enthralled with the man she loves deeply. It was their honeymoon.

Andor recovers from their shared memory first. Anger flashing across her beautiful face. How dare he touch her. Pushing Enkil's hand away from her face as it dissolves back into its true present form. Cold and calculating their irises red with vertical pupils that of a nocturnal carnivore. Her nostrils flaring angrily, jumping up out of his lap. Turning to face him.

"What a handsome and strapping lad you are this time. Not one of those cockles of the court with their white powdered faces and wigs." Andor laying into him with her sharp tongue. Knowing just what to say to get to him. Enkil glares at her Andor continues, "That takes me back. Whatever happened to that merchant from Arabia?"

Enkil, "Why are you here?" Avoiding her question.

Andor, "I so loved the French court for their judicious use of the guillotine. It's so final. Bad boys are gone with a chop." Moving her hand down in a chopping motion. Her human form still desirable those eyes no longer silver-green. Now her eyes are predatory with their vertical pupils dark against red irises gleaming. Her lips turned down in a snarl. "You remember that day I said good-bye, don't you?"

Enkil, "Again with this dredging up of the past." Yawning, not attempting to hide it or giving her the satisfaction of reacting to her barb. "They don't use such devices in this time. So I guess you will have to be disappointed." Smirking at her showing some white teeth.

Andor, "Lethal injection is too easy like falling asleep. Cyanide or electrocution would be my choice for a pretty boy such as yourself."

Enkil, "That is not going to happen!" Her persistence beginning to get to him.

Andor, "If these young women you're known to consort with continue to die. I will not be that far off the mark, especially with a little help. Those detectives could string together enough evidence to find themselves an Arabian mad dog killer. Oh that's right, a sociopathic serial killer." Her turn to smirk.

Enkil, "So you are aware of what they call you in this century." More an affirmation than any answer she would have given him. "Are you the one behind those murders?" Knowing very well she isn't, but questioning her as such will anger her more.

Andor's lips no longer pouty now stretched thin. Her anger quick to rise but she is not going to give him more satisfaction. "You know I don't kill innocent women. Even if they are foolish enough to be seduced by a brute." Acid dripping from her words. "How many scorned lovers do you already have in this time?"

Enkil, "Apparently one you're here."

Andor, "An exceptionally powerful one now. She seems to want to rectify her mistake."

Enkil unsure as whether she is talking about herself or Angelique, "The mistake was hers not mine."

Andor, "Men are always the victim. Never responsible for whom they are copulating with. Is that right?"

Enkil, "One mistake five thousand years ago and I'm still paying for it!" Slamming his fist down against the table as he stands up. His chair falling back as his deep bass voice booms across the peaceful garden. Eyes gleaming yellow predatory and fixed on Andor. Herself unyielding to his angry display. Defiantly glaring back up at him being shorter. Andor allows a smirk to cross her lips really more of a sneer. Satisfied she had gotten the response she was seeking.

Enkil's loud anger filled giving all of the household staff pause. Everything deadly quiet even the sparrows silently watching from their hiding places amongst the leaves of the bushes. The hawk giving up its chance for a well fed garden sparrow. Flying away from its hunting perch some forty feet up in the hemlocks. Enkil's jaws tightly clinched and his right eye beginning to twitch.

Andor speaking in a calmer tone. "At last a genuine admission of guilt from the king." Turning her back on him disrespectfully, taking a few steps away. Household noises resuming throughout the estate. After no more shouting is heard from Camel. A leaf blower wails on.

Cook and Nahadeina give each other a glance. Unspoken words of caution passed between them. Nahadeina questions whether she should check in on him. Believing him to be alone not having seen any guests arrive. Usually Ahmed his butler would have let staff know there was company. But more importantly, who could make him that angry? He has always been so easygoing. Let alone to display such temperament. Only one woman could make him that angry. That cruel infidel, Angelique. Shuddering at the thought of having her to serve. Cook glaring having the same thought. Throwing the meat on the outdoor grill.

Andor turning around to face him. "I see your tastes have not changed much over the centuries. Turkish tobacco in a hookah...," smelling the air carrying on it aromatic spices. Mouthwatering with the scent of roasted fowl. "And roast emu." Walking back toward him slowly, sensuously. Her form all woman breasts swaying under silk garments. Draped as only a new wife would to rouse her husband's attention. Covering her head and face with only her silver-green eyes showing. Enkil's anger long past, watching her move with fascination. Snapping out of her beguiling motion becoming wary of her charms. Struggling not to respond to her allure. Andor stands so close he can feel her heat. Let alone smell her intoxicating perfume. Its name, 'Desert Secret', long since lost to modern times. Most of its ingredients exotic since the last millennium. Camel's body betraying both men as mind and body heat up, pants uncomfortably tight.

Enkil, resisting her, "What is the nature of your visit?"

Andor, "Always to the point." Glancing down at his apparent discomfort. Giving her some satisfaction from his response to her. Walking over to the balustrade leaning out to look down at the outdoor cooking area. "That's supposed to be modern?" Speaking in Sumerian.

Nahadeina and Cook both hear her unusual language looking up to see her. Andor's veil down just enough to reveal her olive complexion. That combined with her silver-green eyes. Her beauty breathtaking. Cook gapes at seeing such beauty as only an Arabian woman could sire. Understanding why Camel's anger could be so easily raised and how he is still keeping such company. Gorgeous women, thinking about his wife when they were younger. "Huh, she is still a scorch."

Nahadeina, "What?" Hearing him speaking under his breath.

Cook, "It's nothing." Sneaking a glance back up to the balustrade. Andor allows her scarf and veil to slip down resting on her shoulders. Regal with long dark hair crimped as was the way in Persia long past. Dark blue and purple silks shimmering on the light breeze. So warm out now, Cook feeling perspiration beading across his forehead. Andor watches him below grilling the meats and vegetables.

"People of this age are rediscovering some of the old ways are quite good." Speaking her high Sumerian dialect. Enkil answering her back in their native tongue of Sumerian. Standing next to Andor watching Cook below. One of his servants arrives carrying a tray with foods and dishes. Setting places for two at the table. Uncovering the grilled emu along with a platter of fresh fruit and sizzling escargot in garlic butter right from the oven. Righting the overturned chair.

Enkil, "Join me. The emu is lightly smoked before it is grilled. Just the way it was in the day." His voice trailing off.

Andor selects a small piece of emu. Tasting it before acknowledging his generous invitation. "Even smoked with olive wood. Nice touch. What are these? "Andor waits for him to pull out her chair. Enkil pushes her chair under her perfectly executed as a gentleman.

"They are called escargot cooked in butter with garlic." Taking his seat. "Use this device to hold one while you pull it out."

Andor, "Uhum, very good." Enkil ready to eat digging in. Andor enjoys the unexpected time of normalcy. Looking at his handsome face. No longer seeing Camel but Enkil as he was so long ago. His joy of foods and life. Watching her cautiously through thick black eyelashes as some men have naturally. Her eyes that silvery green again so loving. Remembering the first time he saw her. She was directing one of her servant girls. Which soap root to dig up out of the shallows of the river.

"So what are your plans for Camel?" Bringing him back to the present. Before he can speak she silences him by reaching over placing a finger over his lips.

Andor, "I know what you saw at the river that sunny morning. It's written on your face. The river is now called the Euphrates. What a strange name for such a once beautiful place." Enkil reaches out to Andor at the same time. Softly squeezing her petite hand. Pulling her over onto his lap with her legs over the arm of the chair. He grunts moving his legs to adjust himself. Enkil feels Camel's body responding to her warm body pressed against his. Nature being as it is she feels his hard body. Her eyes flickering between human and demon.

"Yes?" Enkil says, his voice deep and husky.

Andor, "You certainly have picked yourself a healthy one." Standing up quickly. "I don't think so." Her decision made. She tries to slap him, but his large arm is up to quickly blocking her attack instinctively. Rising up in a blur too fast to see pulling her into his brawny hard arms. His handsome face hot with passion, excited and defiant. He's not going to let things end this way again sure that he can convince her. Bending his neck down to kiss her lips. Just one that is all he will need. Andor turns her face away from him furious and not ready to forgive. Her form dissolves leaving Enkil holding on to nothing but air. Wind gusts across the balcony carrying with it sand. Hitting him in the face. Everything wiped off the table sending it crashing to the floor. Royal Doulton china breaking along with Baccarat crystal glasses shattering as they hit the terrace floor.

Enkil bellows, "Why?" his frustration coming out. "Can't you just let it go! Five thousand years!" His bass voice more of a howl with anguish. Angrily stomping into the house slamming the French doors shut. Just as quickly they blow open from a blast of gale force wind. Whipping up the now torn white shears from debris with leaves. An unbroken saucer smacking into the back of Enkil's head breaking. Using his enormous powers he pushes the doors closed, but not before blasting them to pieces. Sending glass shards and wood outward. Andor already gone her storm dissipating rain falling softly. As always she has to have the last… Rubbing the back of his head where a lump was already rising up.

CHAPTER 80

MR. THORNBURG READING over Norma Campbell's last will and testament. Mary sits patiently across the mahogany desk from him. In one of two low backed leather chairs. Robert looks up from the last page. "It will take a couple of months to wrap up your aunt's estate. Once it has gone through probate you can dispose of the property as you see fit."

Mary, "Very good." Her accent proper English. "What about the furnishings and personal effects?"

Mr. Thornburg, "I don't usually involve myself with such inconsequentialities of a minor estate." Letting out a small breath. "You could donate clothing and personal effects to battered women's shelters. The furniture and bric-a-brac to local charities. I'm sure the nuns would be an excellent resource for who and where to donate those items. You are staying at the motherhouse are you not?"

Mary, "Yes. Until I leave for London. Where I will be staying with a close friend. Her family has graciously agreed to this until I start school at Eton in fall."

Mr. Thornburg, "Your aunt never mentioned you were going to college. Eton is a great university." Obviously impressed, "What is your major?"

Mary, "Political science with a minor in ancient languages."

Robert Thornburg taking a new view of her. "Good for you, a barrister. Criminal or civil?"

Mary, "I haven't decided yet." Robert evaluates her. *She seems a little naive for law, but nothing a few good professors won't dispense with. That should be a real eye-opener for her. Considering some of her associates.* Not a stretch to know whom he was thinking of, Marc and Camel.

Robert, "Criminal is where the money is at. Civil, most of them are guilty scum. It's a fast burnout." Having just decided to help her more. Opening his desk drawer to remove a business card. "This is a real estate agent I have used over the years." Handing her the card. "She is very good at staging homes to sell them. You don't want a home sitting on the market too long. You want every dollar you can get out of it."

Mary accepts the card. "Thank you. Is there anything I can do to expedite this process?" Preferring to get away from Marc and his twisted games.

Robert, "Start clearing the house out some. I'll send a contractor over this week to inspect it. If all it needs is some interior painting and a freshening up of exterior trim. It should sell fast being in a desirable neighborhood, East Irondequoit. It won't be on the market long."

Mary, "Good."

Robert, "Provided all goes well in probate with no unforeseen leans against the property. Which knowing your aunt as I do there will be no surprises."

Mary, "I'll make sure you have my address with additional contact numbers for outside London where I will be staying. If you need to contact me before I'm settled in at Eton this fall."

Robert stands up their meeting at an end. Offering his hand Mary accepts it shaking hands with him. "Make sure you get me that address before you leave town."

Mary, "I will." Pausing for a moment.

"Is there something else?" Robert says.

Mary takes the plunge. "What do you know about the Du Bois family?"

Robert, "Well, I can tell this much. They are an old respectable American family. We are talking prerevolutionary very wealthy. Enough money in trusts so that they need never work. Having business interests on five continents. Family all over North America. Of course that is all common knowledge. On a more personal note every family member that I have had the pleasure of working for is industrious. It is expected of their children to be studious with education and to be gainfully employed."

Mary, "Really?"

Robert, "Yes, there are no rich lay about playboys tolerated. They are a behind the scenes type of family. If you get my meaning." Suspecting where her thoughts were headed. "Except until now. I'm just not so sure about this next generation." Realizing another reason for her question. "Why?" Robert asks in his usual direct manner, concern veiled. *Has that damn boy gotten her in trouble?* His intelligent brown eyes watching her closely.

Mary, "Oh just curious is all. I spent the better part of the summer working for one. I couldn't figure him out." Mr. Thornburg looks at her intensely, sizing her up. Very pretty girl. Using his years of experience as a criminal attorney in dealing with clients. Rarely is what they say and what they are inquiring about the same. Mary picks up on this and feels prompted to elaborate. "Well, Marc just doesn't fit that conservative," hesitating, "proper mold."

Mr. Thornburg, not violating any attorney client privilege, "In my opinion no. He never has." Having been vocal about this very real fact with his family elders. Well, that of Theron and his parents. "I believe he is too wild. The blame resides squarely with his archeologist parents. Dragging him all over the planet.

Growing up with tribal peoples of the desert and natives in the rain forest." His disdain apparent. "He should have been raised more cultured, sophisticated."

Mary, encouraging him, "Boarding schools?"

Robert, "Yes. A good preparatory school in North America. It's a wonder he's not in prison somewhere."

Mary using gossip from Melinda, "Yes like his last brush with the International law, now that is fascinating."

Mr. Thornburg, raising his guard, "Very difficult. I would personally stay with one country."

Mary backs off. "Yes. Marc is rough around the edges. Yet he seems to fit in with the established families of this community." Her sarcasm missed.

Mr. Thornburg, "Well and good, but he still needs a strong moral direction in his life and home. That is why I enlisted my niece and your aunt. God rest her soul."

"All you can do is try," Mary says. Wanting some revenge against Marc. Looking an opportunity presenting itself.

Mr. Thornburg, "However he has been resistant to the potential employees I've been sending over. He keeps saying they are not what he is looking for."

Mary sees an opening to get a chance at revenge. "He really liked aunt Norma. She reminded him of one his mother's great-aunts or was it a grandmother."

"Really? I had no idea."

Mary, "He wouldn't admit that to you. Then he might have to admit you were right about something." Mr. Thornburg looks at her closely. "It's probably one of those young male things you know." Her green eyes round with innocence.

Mr. Thornburg, "That is not what he has been saying. Hm, his grandmother. What I know of her is only hearsay. From his father that she was strong willed. A force to be reckoned with. What else was it he said?" Trying to remember what Charles Du Bois had said. *She was a stitch? Or a witch?*

Mary, "That was aunt Norma a force to be dealt with. Why don't you speak with Melinda?"

Mr. Thornburg, "You mean that sweet girl he has been dating?"

Mary, "Yes. I have her cell number right here." Writing it down for him on a Post-it note.

Mr. Thornburg, "She's one of Angelique's friends. From the upper east side, Manhattan. Her father is an impeccable businessman and moral. He's a member of the Christian Coalition. Very outspoken on moral issues."

Mary, "Really, I'm not familiar with him. She doesn't speak much of him. Melinda is gorgeous isn't she?" More of a statement to redirect him.

Robert, "Yes she is and dresses like a model. Always wearing expensive designer clothes Dolce & Gabbana. That is a woman of breeding and culture. I can't imagine what she sees in him." Saying what he is thinking.

Mary, "He is handsome with those deep blue eyes." Remembering to back when they first met. How genuinely sweet and helpful he was. Her face softening.

Mr. Thornburg observes this. Reading into it so easy to spot after years of dealing with human behavior. "Young women are frequently attracted to if not seduced by the wrong man. For the wrong reasons. A simple act of kindness with a few well-chosen words." Mary blushes from his probative insight. "However misguided the sentiment. The idea is not sound. I'll give Angelique a call. She is the one that recommended your aunt Norma."

Mary now has her answer. *So Angelique was behind this*. Standing up to go. "Thank you for your time. I know it is valuable."

Mr. Thornburg, "It's always a pleasure to meet a young adult with strong direction and convictions. Stay the course, it will be difficult but the outcome will open your mind and so many doors." Shaking her hand.

CHAPTER 81

THE FOLLOWING DAY Robert Thornburg calls his favorite niece Angelique. Requesting her assistance with finding a suitable housekeeper for the Du Bois estate. After getting the usual cordialities out of the way. Robert couldn't be more pleased with his niece.

Angelique, "I'd be delighted to help. I'll go through my Rolodex. That is a large estate. Are you sure there isn't a need for more than one person?"

Robert, "Yes, I know it is large and could use a cleaning staff. But with only Marc living there for who knows how long. Before he is jetting off to Dubai. I just don't see the need for the added expenses."

Angelique, "Uncle Robert, if you weren't so frugal I would be concerned about you." Robert taking that as a compliment.

Robert, "Wealthy people keep their money by not squandering it. One man living alone in that large mansion doesn't need every room dusted. I would doubt if he notices more than the refrigerator is empty. So must his stomach be."

Angelique, "Harsh words but the truth I'm afraid. I have an idea that would save money for the estate."

"What is it, dear?"

"I believe my sorority has a couple of girls that could use the money for books and other expenses. My charity awards at least two scholarships each year. That way you would have a pair of eyes inside that house."

Robert, "That won't work this time. Apparently he's not the tool we thought him to be. He seems determined to hire a more docile housekeeper."

Angelique, "I see." Her tone disappointed.

Robert, "Your thought is a charitable one, but some of the rumors I've heard. I don't want to put fish in the barrel for him to shoot."

Angelique, "Well, I could warn them off." Trying again. "Maybe you could draw up a morals contract. Whereby inappropriate sexual relations would terminate their scholarship."

Robert, "That would need some work but it's not half bad. I'm afraid Marc and his friend Camel would just see them as a challenge. I don't want to put young women around there."

Angelique, "Why? You are holding something back, aren't you? What is it? I won't repeat it."

Robert takes pause. "This is in the strictest of confidences. I don't want anyone getting wind of this."

"Uncle Robert who would I tell. You know I would never betray a secret."

Robert, "Some rumors are circulating that Camel is a person of interest. In this string of young women's deaths. This is not something to trifle with. It's coming from the top level downtown."

Angelique smiles to herself. "I wasn't aware of that. Do you think it's possible?" Her voice almost a whisper.

Uncle Robert, "Are you still seeing him?"

Angelique, "Only socially, certainly not privately. He is like a bee. He wants to pollinate all the flowers in the garden. Something I will not tolerate." Uncle Robert is satisfied with her answer. A slight smile playing over his lips eyes twinkling with pride for his niece. Becoming stern again.

"What is this thing between Marc and his maid?"

"What do you mean?" Her best coy response.

Uncle Robert, "Don't be coy with me. There is something going on between those two. Mary speaks intelligently has a scholarship to an exceptional school. But she is a bit naive."

Angelique thinks to herself, *If I didn't know him I would believe him to be a witch. He has such good insights.* Finally giving him something. "You know how college men need to sow wild oats. Not any serious commitments. Take a young naive girl sheltered as she has been. Raised in parochial boarding schools by nuns. Marc would be naturally attractive to her. Presenting as a seasoned traveler, handsome. All too easy for her to become seduced. Then getting the wrong idea. Especially at such a vulnerable time in her life." Baiting her uncle to see what he knows.

Uncle Robert, "I certainly hope not. A child at this time would be disastrous for both of them."

Angelique, "Do you think it has gone that far? I would hope Marc would have enough sense to use protection. Certainly when cockling with a maid."

Uncle Robert, "Do you believe she would be on the pill? Being from a strict Catholic background, I doubt it."

Angelique, "She must have some family she could turn to." Her usual probative self. Finding it always good to double or even triple check what you know about someone you are corrupting. Especially when taking so much personal risk.

Uncle Robert, "I had this very discussion with her aunt Norma." Having missed part of what he said.

Angelique, "I feel so bad for her being all alone. Are you sure there isn't some distant relative?"

Robert, "I'm afraid not. That is why I have been helping her so closely with the estate. Well, not really an estate but certainly a small nest egg for her future if managed closely."

Angelique satisfied that her uncle is harmless. He hasn't exposed some detail that could be disastrous to her plans. Uncle Robert only knowing what is general knowledge to law enforcement authorities. "You will keep me apprised in regard to Mary, won't you? If there is anything I can do to assist just let me know."

Robert, "That is so kind of you. If I discover a need you will be the first person I go to. You always make me so proud of you, my dearest niece."

Angelique, "Thank you Uncle Rob."

Robert, "She seems to be holding it all together for one so young."

Angelique, "I'll talk to you soon." Taking a moment after she gets off the phone. *He is a strong litigator but as a relative easily glamoured*. As for as Mary she has presented with a few surprises, unexpected strengths. But then so has Marc. How difficult can it be to find some narrow minded Christian bitch. Another puppet from the family values group like Norma Campbell?

CHAPTER 82

DAYS HAVE PASSED without incident allowing Marc to fall back into his routine life for now. Melinda calls leaving messages to tempt him with her provocative suggestions to lure him back under her power. Their web of deception with its deadly spells of sexual corruption. Marc refuses to return her calls no matter how tempting she's managed to make them. Also enthralling him a time or two. His increased libido not withstanding her. Has not resolved leaving him horny. Wet dreams so vivid again waking him in climax some nights twice. His resolve still very strong to avoid their traps. Using his religion of Islam with prayer to stay the course.

Having been busy with the grounds and interviewing housekeepers to no avail. The ones Mr. Thornburg had sent over much too like their predecessor. Seeking one from the Islamic community as Camel had suggested in the first place. Nahadeina and her daughter for the time being were helping out at the manor. Marc finds them to be a fresh addition to his busy life. It was good to hear Arabic spoken at the manor. Making him less homesick for the Dubai. A sunny and hot tropical city bustling with activity. Its grand new palaces with the modern skyline rising up. Seeming to change every day as a new building would be completed. Rivaling if not surpassing European and American cities with new designs. Landmark buildings giving young new architects a chance. Marc anxious to be finished with a degree in hand to take his place at the Khalid Architectural Firm. He and Camel would soon be working together. In the process of drafts, designing his own signature high-rise with any luck. Not having to wait years for the chance. Marc having already begun one that would have numerous green features. Including xeriscape grounds and a forest park starting at the fifteenth floor. Giving Singapore a run for their money with those green design requirements.

The smell of lamb stew spiced with aromatic herbs gives him pause. Its aroma of home. Setting down his protractor looking over his multileveled drafts. Nahadeina herself being from the UAE has chosen this dish for him. The house beginning to sparkle with cleanliness that Ms. Campbell had never had time for. Even the library books were dusted. Plus they followed his directions with regard to the mirrors. Hearing the rustle of fabric Marc turns to see Aziza. "Lunch is ready."

Marc, "I'll be right there." His cell phone ringing taking the call. "Hello."

Camel, "Hi, I have a lead on their next intended male victims."

"That's great. How did you come across this information?"

"Enkil has someone on the inside of the coven."

Marc, "Do you know any of them?"

Camel, "One is a foreign exchange student here on an athletic scholarship Helmut Stein."

"Wow, you do have good intelligence."

"No. I've played soccer against him. He is a real tough son of a gun out there on the field. He's a very good player."

Marc, "I didn't know you still played football. When was this?"

Camel, "Before you arrived and all this trouble started. I was an alternate for a team that plays with an informal league."

"Hey, I didn't start the trouble." Marc's feeling a little sensitive. "Just what is that supposed to mean?"

Camel, "I'm sorry. I know you didn't bring this on us. I'm just becoming battle worn. You know? Wasn't intending to lash out at you."

Marc, "What's got you so edgy?" Knowing his brother too well.

Camel, "Apparently I'm the prime suspect for the homicides of several young women. That was the other information Enkil found out. While he was eavesdropping on Angelique."

"How would she know that?" Marc says.

"Her uncle Robert has connections downtown. Remember he is a criminal defense attorney?"

Marc, "Damn. Why you?"

Camel, "I'm the common thread between all of these women. I have a feeling that isn't just a coincidence. Besides the timing not long after that night. The night you met Melinda on your first date. Finding the old book that looked interesting. It wasn't just Angelique being jealous. She was setting me up to take a fall."

Marc, "You're sure about this?"

Camel, "Oh yeah. Angelique always has a contingency plan."

Marc, "Wow. This just keeps getting worse. It's never going to stop is it?"

Camel, "No. Not until she gets what she wants."

Marc, "What does she want? We're not their cockles anymore. We are onto them and cannot be used anymore."

Camel, "She won't rest until we're out of the way or dead. Both would make her the happiest, that I have no doubt of."

Marc, "We have to disrupt their plans. If we cannot stop them."

Camel, "I'm glad you said that because that is just what I plan for us do."

Marc, "Great, what is your plan?" Getting excited. "What can I do to help?"

Camel, "Helmut plays soccer at Saint John's on Sunday afternoon. He never misses, too much of a jock."

Marc, "Perfect I'll go over there this afternoon. Oh, do you want to come over for some lamb stew. It's Nahadeina's cooking."

Camel, "I can't." Knowing Marc's next question, he adds, "I have a lead on the other guy they are after. Maybe later, keep me posted."

Marc, "All right, I'll let you know how it goes. Good luck."

Camel, "You too."

CHAPTER 83

MARC IS SITTING up in the bleachers waiting for the soccer players to all arrive. Having taken Camel's place as an alternate waiting to see if he will get in the game. Himself a fair football player. Helmut already there warming up on the field. A husky build being one of those men you can't tell about until they lose their shirt. Wrapping on a blue bandana to hold back his blonde hair. Marc talking with the team he will be on, the opposing team. Hearing that Helmut is an aggressive player not above a sly foul to make a goal.

After the first round having seen a couple of serious fouls go unchallenged. Marc is convinced Helmut is only out to win at any cost. They collide with enough force, sending Marc bouncing on the damp ground. His hard buttocks the only cushion from the fall. The wind knocked out of him. His team mate Angus gives him a hand to pull him up to his feet. Marc's buttocks smarting along with his pride. Play resuming by now a small gathering of students are watching from the bleachers. Cheers coming up from a group made up of mostly females, encouraging Helmut on.

"Does he always have that when he plays?" Marc asks Angus.

"Yeah, he has a bleedin' fan club."

Ahmed, "It seems to be increasing over the past two weekends."

Angus, "I don't understand why? He is such a dirty player."

Marc intercepts the ball making a score to tie up the game. Helmut stares at him threateningly. Then flexes his chest pulling off his perspiration soaked tee shirt. Definitely all muscle with a dirty blonde hair matted down from sweat. Hard abdominal muscles like a washboard very visible. His strip of hair not as defined as Marc's but still full. All the way down to his waistband. Angelique's handiwork very apparent. Marc wonders, *Has he bothered to consider the physical changes that are happening to him?* He's an exceptional player without the excessive roughness. The ball in play lands close to the stands. Several of Helmut's female fans talking favorably about him. Yelling cheers of encouragement. Helmut quickly sets the ball up with his foot. Scoring again ending the Sunday afternoon game.

The small crowd in the stands coming down to greet the hero. Marc makes his way over to the edge of the field. Where a couple of Helmut's female fans are extolling his athletic abilities. Their faces familiar Marc not quite able to place where he has seen them before.

Marc deciding to make his more calling out to Helmut. "Hi, great move that last score. Do you have a minute to speak with me?" His hand outstretched Helmut takes it in a firm handshake.

"Do I know you?" Perspiration dripping off numerous peaks of hair from his chest and abdomen.

Marc, "Let's get out of the sun. I need to have a word with you." Indicating the shade trees, across the field heading over to them.

"I will be with you in a minute." Speaking to the three women giving them his best smile. Walking over to Marc with his masculine strut like a sprinter. The ladies watch him with his back turned. A great view as he walks away. Large gluteal muscles moving solidly with each step.

Helmut, "What is it you need to speak with me about?" Standing in the shade across from him. Marc trying to choose his words carefully then just takes the plunge. "We have some of the same acquaintances."

Helmut, "Ya. Go on."

Marc, "I saw you at the soiree Angelique was hosting."

Helmut uses his tee shirt to wipe the perspiration off of his thick stubble covered face. His beard blonde along with his eye lashes. Helmut snaps his fingers together his blue eyes having recognition. "Yes, you were the one the young ladies made the spectacle over." His English quite good now. Marc observes an accent from that of around Munich, making a mental note.

Marc, "Great," speaking under his breath. "Uh yeah, that was me."

Helmut, "They are wunderbar ladies making me feel so welcome. You should be more how you say, careful. You shouldn't get caught leading them on. That was so clumsy." Smiling his blue eyes twinkling. Giving Marc a knowing look. "You live and learn." Marc realizes this is going to be more difficult than he thought.

Marc, "Uh Yes, they are wonderful at first."

Helmut looks at Marc dubiously turning his head to the side questioningly. "What's not good? You went upstairs with that gorgeous redhead. She was just of age right? A virgin. How was she?" Not waiting for him to answer, "I personally would have taken both women. A blonde and a redhead."

Marc is becoming annoyed with the conversation getting off track. Trying another tactic. "Have you noticed any physical changes or lapses in memory?"

Helmut, "No." Searching Marc's face.

So Marc continues, "Has your hair always grown fast or your body been so hairy?"

Helmut, "Those are odd questions." His hand unconsciously rubbing his thick dirty blonde chest pelt. "I don't remember meeting you, but I have heard rumors about you and your close friend." Smirking for a second. His light blue eyes holding Marc's with a questioning yet serious expression.

"I am a man, we grow body hair. Since going to that party I have women calling me all the time. So many I have to turn some of them down." Feeling the need to explain himself. "I would be too tired for sports. If you know what I mean."

Marc, "Not really. I'm never too tired." Helmut's arrogance beginning to irritate him. Helmut picks up on this.

"Why are you so interested?"

Marc, "I'm not interested in that. I came to warn you. That you are in danger from those very women. I can help you."

Helmut, "Help me? What makes you think I want anything you have to offer." His eyes getting a little bigger. As a look of understanding crosses his face. Helmut reaches over tugging at the clump of dark hair curling over Marc's crew neck tee shirt. Marc's hand shoots up to push his hand away. Not before feeling the sting after Helmut releases it.

Helmut smiles at him. "I'm not how you say, down with that." Stepping back quickly ready to leave. Looking at a surprised Marc, stammering.

"You don't understand." Closing the distance between them.

Helmut, "I'm really not interested. The only cock I like is mine. If your Arab boyfriend isn't giving you what you need. I'm sure you will find some other man. Just not me." Helmut turns and walks away with a runner's strut. Confident Marc is watching his ass.

Marc follows him not ready to give up. "Wait! I'm not trying to pick you up." Helmut turns around to face him. In desperation Marc pulls his shirt off to expose his hirsute body muscular and hard. "I wasn't like this until I started having sex with those women. They are witches!"

Helmut gives him an incredulous look before speaking, "You have some crazy notions. Yes, you are as hairy as a bear. If it bothers you get laser therapy and some counseling. You Christian Americans worry too much about sex. It's natural, hormones and genetics make you hairy. Get over it and stop following me." His fists now clinched at his sides. Marc's also really wanting to punch this stupid idiot. His own stance centered ready for defense. Marc reads Helmut's body language and his own anger. Backing off it's not worth pursuing. They will just end up fist fighting and that was not why he came here. He won't listen; then he will get what is coming. Not that he wouldn't feel better getting some of his frustration out on Helmut's face. Stupid blonde watching Helmut strut away over to his three female fans waiting for him. Putting his arms around all three gathering them away.

Walking back to his blue Mustang. Wishing he had chosen another approach with Helmut. Give him some time after the spell has had a chance to work on him more. The physical changes will make him think differently. Perhaps Camel could reason with him. *If not him, then maybe I should try that running back with Camel's help. He might be easier to convince.* Climbing into the Mustang, turning its engine over a healthy rumble coming out. Pressing the accelerator a couple of times making it roar. Shifting into gear peeling away allowing his frustration that exit.

CHAPTER 84

MARC OPENS HIS cell phone memory thumbing down. Pressing Camel's name sending out the call. Camel's baritone, "Hello."

Before he can say more Marc goes off, "Dude, that lacrosse captain. What a cock!"

Camel, "I take it that it didn't go so well?"

Marc, "Yeah you could say that."

Camel, "What happened?" His voice a little too happy for Marc.

"He thought I was trying to pick him up." Camel bursts out laughing. "Keep laughing. He is under the impression we are together."

Camel still laughing drying his eyes becoming serious. "What do you mean?"

"It would seem your ex-girlfriend is doing some damage control. He thought we were lovers."

Camel is not laughing anymore. "Are you serious?" Marc recounts the story of his exchange with Helmut. Camel not angry. "They could be making up worse stories about us. Any woman that's been with us knows we are 100 percent heterosexual. I wouldn't take it too seriously." Knowing how his brother was.

Marc, "That's not what pissed me off. He had a logical explanation for everything I tried to warn him about."

Camel, "Let it go. You can only help those who want to be helped. It just may be kismet. You can't change that."

Calmer now, "It was just so frustrating," Marc says.

Camel, "I understand, but I didn't think you were going to have much luck with him. Consider his position. If some unknown guy came up to you. Giving you a strange story vague at best about a group of women. Gorgeous I have to say and you agree with that point. Being witches using him for his lusty sexual powers. Would you have stopped having hot mad sex with Melinda or Jadon for that matter." Marc thinks about it. "Come on! You know the answer," Camel says.

Marc, "I wouldn't have believed him."

Camel, "Right."

Marc, "I had to try."

Camel, "If Enkil hadn't been called upon, neither of us would have believed someone coming to us with such a story. Much less what to do to save ourselves."

Marc, "We should try the running back tonight. Maybe we could at least help him."

Camel, "We?"

"Yes you. Ask Enkil where we can find him. You know as soon as Angelique finds out about this she will be scorched with us. Meddling in her affairs, she will consider treachery. We both know how she deals with traitors. I have the scars to prove it." Marc thinking of Jadon certain the news story where two coeds were drown was her. Certain her death was his fault. Remembering details of the story death by drowning. Trapped inside the car what an awful way to die gasping for breath. Her choking and gagging with only water to fill her lungs. *How long was she conscious in the cold, dirty water?*

Camel, "Hey! Come back. You checked out there for a minute." Marc's face grief and guilt stricken.

"Yes I did." His voice sad.

"It wasn't your fault. There was nothing you could have done for her. She made the life choices that brought her down that path. Besides, if you hadn't done what you did would you still be alive? Or would you have changed into some animal good for a blood sacrifice?" Camel knowing his brother too well. "You are right. It's just... I really liked her. Jadon could have been the one." Enkil shimmers Camel over to Marc's side. Putting his hand on Marc's shoulder for comfort. Appreciating the comforting gesture from his brother. No longer startled by his sudden appearances.

Camel, "There will be other women. Hopefully not pursuing their hellish plans."

Marc stifling his melancholy changing the subject. "So where do we find him?"

Camel flashes his usual toothy grin. "Well, I hear he likes some of the strip clubs downtown."

"Now why does that not surprise me that you would know that."

Camel, "It seems he can't stay out of them for very long since his encounter with our special ladies. At least when he is not servicing them."

Marc, "Who gave you all the information?"

"A friend." Camel sounding coy.

Marc, "Now I know why you're so willing to help with this one."

Camel, "I'm crushed you would think of me as so shallow." Keeping a straight face.

Marc lifting an eyebrow, "Is that your story?"

Camel, "And I'm sticking to it. I knew you were going to involve me in this somehow. Robert our running back has developed a new interest in strip clubs. I have it on good advice that he will be out tonight. That is if our gals don't already have plans for him tonight."

Marc, "If your information is accurate this may be the only chance we have to get to him. Before they do, if they haven't already anticipated our next move."

Camel, "Helmut was unreachable it is already too late for him. Once they know and it will be soon enough they hear about your clumsy approach."

Marc, "What do think Angelique will do?"

Camel, "She will retaliate." Taking a moment to consider it. "It will be swift and something unexpected. She will do something to make us suffer." Marc feeling a tightness in his gut after that thought. "Have you heard from Mary?"

Marc, "No."

Camel, "It is a safe assumption she won't be returning your calls." Marc nodding his head. His long hair a mane now with it pulled back tied in two places. Before he can ask, Camel answers, "Yes, I called there also. Some nun answered the phone. She said my name wasn't on the list of people Mary wished to receive calls from.

"She said I was not to disturb the sanctity of the house by calling again."

Marc makes a punching sound popping his right fist out front. "Boom, TKO. I guess us heathens aren't on the list."

"I guess not." Camel sounding put off.

Marc, "Don't take it too personally. We already had the biggest strike against us, we're men. Never mind the religious aspect."

Camel, "They call us heathens?"

Marc, "We call them infidels. Besides, Muslim women at Hadassah wouldn't let us get through either." Camel accepts this with a nod of his head causing his thick wavy black hair to shimmer under the light of two chandeliers. "I'll call her cell again she just needs time to cool off. If she doesn't answer then maybe it's for the best."

Camel agreeing with Marc. "It would be safer for her to stay out of the mix. What are you doing for dinner Tuesday?"

Marc, "I don't have any plans."

Camel, "Good. Nahadeina is making our favorite. Moroccan chicken with lemon preserve."

Marc, "My mouth is almost watering. What time do you want me over?"

Camel, "How about six o'clock?"

"Great see you then." Camel shimmers and is gone. Leaving him sitting in the enormous dining room easily able to seat his immediate extended family. Longing for one of the other sibling the room so quiet.

CHAPTER 85

THAT TUESDAY EVENING at Camel's for dinner Nahadeina's niece Allia serves up the Moroccan chicken. Ladling the aromatic seasoned meat over couscous. Flavored with chives and dried apricots. Pilling on the portions steam rising up carrying its aroma. Being a young single woman her veil is in place with only her dark eyes visible. After their plates have been cleared with the second portions eaten. They retire to the private library.

Allia serves a strong sweetened hot tea good for after dinner. Drinking their tea in silence. Each man enjoys some time for personal thoughts. Marc finally notices Camel is too quiet. Reading his moods easily having been friends for the better part of two decades. Camel's handsome face serious even in this light his stubble covered jaw blue-black shadowed but it's his eyes they are troubled.

Marc, "All right what's really on your mind?" Camel shrugs his shoulders. A thinly veiled attempt at pushing off his concerns. "What is bothering you?"

Camel, "Enkil tells me they must be close to completion of their ritual."

Marc, "Go on."

"Whatever they are after it's big. To require so much power that they went after two more men. Each time they do this it increases their risk of being discovered." Marc's blue eyes serious dread increasing with each moment. He waits patiently for his lifelong friend to continue. "Enkil is sensing something very powerful is gathering. He has never been this close to exo-ecumenical forces.

Marc's tanned face turns ashen. "What are you saying?" Afraid to voice what he is thinking.

Enkil's deep bass voice takes over. "Forces of darkness are stirring. When that happens it will draw out other beings."

Marc, "You mean like angels or their counterparts?"

Enkil, "Yes, the fallen are gathering."

Marc, "Are you not one of them? The fallen." His voice unable to hide his fear. Never having dealt with any supernatural beings. That and having a healthy respect for Allah.

Enkil, "I am not!" His tone outraged. "I was once human as you are a man of flesh and blood." Not sure how to respond to this admission. Marc remains silent thus allowing Enkil to continue. "It is wise to be afraid." Picking up on Marc's waver in his baritone voice.

Marc, "I'm not afraid. I believe in Allah." Mounting his strength. Enkil gives him a hard look his yellow irises with their vertical pupils narrowed. Like a cat irritated with being disturbed.

Enkil, "Both sides have gone on alert. You have alerted the darker forces by that foolish attempt earlier today."

Marc defending himself, "I needed to try. If I could have just convinced him."

Enkil, "It is a dangerous time for the two of you. For that matter, all concerned."

Marc, "What does that mean?"

"Possibly you have endangered your families no...," correcting himself. Something he rarely ever did, "You are vulnerable through your families. Especially since you pursued that course of action."

Camel's voice mirrors Marc's. "How can we protect them?"

Enkil, "You can't. Use greater caution when you meet this Robert. Undoubtedly they will be watching for you." Looking into Marc's deep blue eyes. His own pupils slivers inside reptilian yellow eyes, cold and unfeeling.

Marc, "How are you so sure of this?"

Enkil's look is one of incredulity. "They conjured two creatures to aid them." Referring to himself and Andor without naming her. "Being human, power hungry and arrogant they have weaknesses. Added with believing themselves strong enough to control us. They have made some mistakes."

Marc, "We should be able to use that to our advantage."

Enkil, "There is a crack that can be put to use. Don't fool yourself into believing you launching a frontal assault against them would succeed. Their powers exceed anything in existence for centuries. If not at least fifteen hundred years." A cold chill spreads deep inside Marc. Hair rising up on his hackles and arms.

Camel speaks inside his mind to Enkil, *Why have you waited to apprise us of this?*

Enkil, "I wouldn't take that approach with me, son!"

Marc reading the silence. *He must be communicating with Camel.*

"I was not aware of this development until just recently myself." Enkil turns it back on both men. "You two have not been living righteously. Tell me you have been following the Five Pillars of Islam? Maybe it's the Christian doctrines, the Ten Commandments." Camel falls silent while Marc looks guilty his eyes downcast. Enkil satisfied with his effect on them continues, "You both unwittingly embraced the use of powers from an ancient religion. Allowing its darkest forms to come forth."

Marc, "We didn't know that was real. It was just some innocent fun."

His tone is too defensive for Enkil's liking. Yelling back at him, "Innocent! You were seeking to charm and seduce two daughters of dark magic. How innocent can you be?" Speaking to Camel so Marc hears him, "You destroyed innocence in your cavalier approach to self-gratification." Camel is quick to reject this reasoning. Enkil stops him. "Infidels? So it does not matter. Are you that self-centered as to believe that Allah would not care?"

Speaking to Marc again, "You taking innocence for granted. Destroying trust to satisfy your ever increasing lust." Marc swallowing his mouth very dry. Enkil continues his lecture not convinced Marc has been humbled enough. Anticipating Marc's next rationalization. "Not all of it was drug induced. You had a choice!" Raising his voice. "You were fully aware that she was enamored with you." Silencing his protest. "Will Allah or Jehovah look the other way when you are judged?" Both Marc and Camel give his words some thought. Enkil hears it in Camel's mind and partially his brother's. "Good! Now that I have both of you thinking. You need to stop using the primitive part of your brains and start using analytical parts. I understand as mortals you have weaknesses. They will use those weaknesses with cunning. Skillfully subverting your attempts to stop them. You will need to be three steps ahead of them. Since this plan has been in motion for decades. Do either of you really believe that you are going to prevent it from reaching its fruition without casualties?" Enkil leaves the two young men to consider his warning of their situation.

Camel speaks first, "What he is saying has a ring of truth. He has been alive for at least five millennia."

Marc acknowledges this in his own way. "We would be dead or worse by now."

Camel, "Yes, satyrs." His pupils round with thoughts of pleasing so many beautiful women. Marc reading his face briefly having the same thoughts. That and knowing his brother too well.

"That's what he means by weaknesses," Marc says. Then picking up his teacup sipping from it. "We don't know how long it takes to make the complete change."

Camel, "What happens to the men after their services are no longer needed?"

Enkil having returned as a shimmering form before them. Answers the question with a question. "What happens to any farm animal that is no longer of use? The coven is not going to keep them around."

Marc, "When we find Robert how do we convince him it is for his own safety?"

Enkil, "You will know rather quickly if he is changed mentally so much that he is unreachable."

Camel, "What then? Are we to wait and see their nefarious plans come to fruition?"

"We still don't know what they are after," Marc says.

Enkil gives his thoughts on it. "I have my suspicions, but to tell you would undoubtedly get you both killed quickly. If even a hint of it were accurate and it gets back to Angelique. She wouldn't hesitate to kill you both."

Camel, "So you are not going to tell me either?"

Enkil becomes irritated with him. "What did I just say!" His vertical pupils enlarging within the yellow irises frighteningly predatory. Staring back at him. "Consider yourself warned!" Abruptly leaving a gust of wind blowing open the French doors. Leading out onto the balcony overlooking the garden.

Camel makes an astute observation. "For something that is angry frequently. He seems to have taken a fondness for us. He seems genuinely concerned."

Marc annoyed with his brother changes the subject. "Have you noticed any changes back to normal?"

Camel, "How could I? Enkil is a womanizer. The men in my family are hairy, we're Middle Eastern." Marc nods his head. "What about you? Have you noticed any difference?" Camel asks.

Marc, "No."

Camel, "Enough of this tea. I want something stronger." Getting up moving over to a bookshelf. Pulling a wood panel forward causing a hidden compartment to pop open. Exposing a heavy crystal decanter. Pouring up two snifters of Hennessey brandy. Handing one to Marc. "Come on."

Marc gets up as Camel walks out though the open French doors onto the balcony. The night sky sparkling under a star covered clear night. Camel's well-tended gardens below. Marc takes in the peaceful sanctuary with the sound of water trickling. The garden illuminated by its own stars from the occasional low-voltage lights. Camel sits down at the table taking up his hookah puffing. While Marc sets his Baccarat snifter on the balustrade beside him. Admiring the subtlety of the lights playing over the mosaic-covered wall. As water weeps down it. Brought out of his silent wonder by the sweet smell of apples mixed with tobacco smoke. He turns around. "I didn't know you smoked," Marc says.

Camel takes another puff before responding. "Yes once in a while." Turning back to study the garden taking another sip of the brandy. Letting some air through his teeth to taste its fragrance. Both men reflecting on Enkil's warnings.

Those warnings having more of the tone from a concerned father rather than a king or a supernatural being.

Camel speaks after a couple of hearty puffs savoring the taste. "There is nothing better than Turkish tobacco and French brandy. It tastes good and helps me to relax." Marc agrees with him. Hiding his growing suspicions that Enkil's preferences were beginning to take root. Camel had never liked smokers. It was the one thing that would turn him off to woman. Smoking. He had always said their mouth tasted like an ashtray when he kissed them.

"Where do you want to start the search?" Marc asks.

Camel, "He is known to frequent a club downtown. You know a strip club with private viewing rooms."

Marc, "Yeah?"

Camel, "Yes, it's not that nice. The concrete floors are well, sticky."

Marc, "That private?"

Camel, "A good tip and you can arrange whatever you like."

Marc, "I had heard he was a polite Southern raised Evangelical. Not into decadent hedonism."

Camel, "Obviously that has been changed with good effect. At least from some people's way of thinking. Look at you."

Marc taking offence. "What's that supposed to mean?"

Camel, "Seriously? You have to ask? The poster child for European Islam."

Marc, "I was not that naive."

Camel, "Really? You had not been in a strip club before you were twenty."

Marc gives in unable to pretend to be worldly any longer. "Fine, we'll go to your choice."

Camel, "Isn't there a place near to you?" Checking to see what Marc would say. Knowing full well the answer to that one. The Barrel of Dolls, a topless dancers' club with lap dances. Tuesdays have drink specials are would be packed with local business men.

Marc, "Yes, the Barrel is conveniently located close to my home." Looking at him dryly. "But you already knew that. Why pretend ignorance?"

Camel, "I just wanted to see what you would say."

Marc, "Yes. I've been there a few times."

"I bet you have, big dog. Come on I want to see titties," Camel says smiling playfully.

"I can't argue with that," Marc agrees.

After searching several burlesque clubs without any luck except for a few phone numbers from female employees. Well, that and a couple of lap dances the two leave Henrietta to go back to the city. The Barrel of Dolls being their last stop for the night. Ordering a round of drinks. "Brittany was really aggressive. A free lap dance and her phone number," Marc says. Obviously still thinking of her. A Michelle Pfeiffer look-alike.

Camel rolls his eyes, "She is a hot blonde. All she kept telling me was how much she liked your tan skin and blue eyes. That we were both handsome."

Marc, "She wanted a ménage à trois?"

Camel, "I think so."

"We haven't had any luck finding Robert. He is probably doing what I want to be doing," Marc says while he watches Brittany dance provocatively onstage. Grasping the pole with her legs hanging outward. Looking past them confident she has his attention. Nursing his Glenlivet on the rocks. While fixing her baby blue eyes on Marc as she slides sensuously down her tool of trade. Her breasts pressed against the pole.

"Wasn't she at the other club?" Camel questions Marc. Not getting an answer he nudges him in the shoulder.

"Uh yes. This is her second job," Marc responds without taking his eyes off Brittany.

Camel, "Since you are so fascinated by her. Let her be your private dancer. I'm going to be busy soon." Getting his brother's attention with that comment. Sliding a fifty dollar bill in the muscular brunette's G-string, her name Nikki. "You would do well to entertain Brittany. I'm sure once you arrive at the cost of time and conversation, use a condom." Marc watches with masculine fascination. His thick lips almost a natural pout, five o'clock shadow dark. Giving him a rough yet handsome look added to his dark blue eyes. Almost black under the dim lighting of a burlesque club. His pupils so round. "I'll have to ask Enkil to help us with this but not tonight. I don't want him taking over. No sharing tonight." Marc does not hear Camel anymore. Both of their minds on other things after seeing all the scantily clad women tonight.

Brittany steps off the stage adjusting her G-string. Sitting on Marc's lap. "So what's up beside you?" she says. Wiggling her waist writhing her hips against him.

Marc feels her heat through his pants. Catching his breath. "I'll call you tomorrow. Let me know how your night turns out." Then turning his full attention to Brittany. "When are you off?"

Brittany, "In fifteen minutes." Camel slaps Marc on the back standing up to leave using his cell phone. Heading outside where it is quieter to make his call.

Brittany adds, "I should be able to get off a few minutes early. Give me a second and I'll see if it's all right to leave now. I was doing a friend a favor." Marc's expression inquisitive Brittany laughing. "For a girlfriend, she couldn't get a baby-sitter until now." Nodding her head toward an olive-complexioned dancer named Maria taking the stage now. Dropping her bikini top allowing generous breasts like ripe pomegranates to sway. Her male audience cheering loudly. Dividing Marc's attention causing Brittany to frown.

"Any more questions or do I need to wait to put my street clothes on?" Marc lifts a thick dark eyebrow. Picking up on her jealousy.

CHAPTER 86

THE FOLLOWING MORNING he wakes up to bright sunlight. Shining through the window of an unfamiliar bedroom, alone. On a pillow next to him with a note attached to it. After a quick assessment of the room, probably a Micro Motel. That and Brittany is gone. Picking up the note to read it.

"Thanx for last night. I really needed what you had to offer, repeatedly. Not many men can do that for me anymore. See you around. P.S. Last night wasn't for free lover boy. A girl has to make a living."

Marc having a moment of panic whipping off the sheet. Rolling out of bed his bare feet touching down on the carpeting. Snatching his pants up off the floor. Finding his wallet still in them. Pulling it out and checking it emptied of cash. Credit cards still present and accounted for. His heart still racing but the panic subsiding. Then noticing he's stepping on something cold and sticky. Lifting his foot off a used condom from last night. Wiping his foot on the carpet as he strolls into the bathroom to take a badly needed leak. Seeing another used condom half submerged floating in the toilet. One hand against the wall leaning, relief immediate.

Once on the road heading north on 590 Marc slides his cell phone out of his pocket. Thumbing over to preprogrammed numbers to call Camel. Expecting it to go into voice message being before noon. Speaking to the machine, "Hi it's me. You were right. She was almost as good as Melinda or Jadon. I guess I have become spoilt to women that are good in the boudoir. She could take a few lessons from a couple of witches. Talk to you later." *Click*, tapping the cell phone roughly to end the call. Not a moment too soon passing a state trooper. Cars pulled over to the side their drivers receiving tickets.

The blue 1968 Mustang rumbles into the driveway. Its windows down Marc's dark hair loose so incredibly thick and well past his shoulders close to mid-back. Another glorious summer day. Rochester having so many grey overcast days. You can't help but enjoy a sunny day rolling through the Porte cochere. By the time he sees Nahadeina she has already been at work for hours. Her sensible small car a Subaru parking next to it.

Marc sets about his own business. Passing the kitchen where the smell of Nahadeina's good cooking is wafting out into the hall. Making him feel at home back in the Emirates. Checking the answering machine first before going upstairs. The electronic device looking out of place on the Louis XVI desk with its delicate curves. Pressing the play button the female voice sounding more breathy than usual. "Three new messages."

Melinda's voice the first message: "Marc why haven't you called me? I've missed our times together." Turning his attention into fascination. Forcing himself to concentrate. *Yeah, you're not going to get your hooks into me again.* Ready to delete her message. "Have you heard from Mary?"

"No. Thanks to you," Marc speaking out loud to the machine.

"It's so sad about Jadon, isn't it?"

Marc, "Accident? What kind of accident could happen to your kind?"

Melinda, "A freak accident. *Moi petite se belle, so sad.* She was such a vibrant young woman, but no more." Realizing he was no longer listening to the machine but talking to Melinda.

"How did you do that?" Marc asks. A peal of laughter erupting from her.

"You still have to ask?" Not really a question. Anger burning inside him causing adrenaline to be released into his bloodstream. Melinda choosing to fill the silence. "Dumb as a box of blocks, but good for one thing. We both know what that is. Right Marc? Oh by the way Brittany says hi. She really enjoyed you last night."

Marc covering his surprise becoming more angry. "You only thought you played me."

Melinda, "All too easy, you and your brother. It's like putting food in front of starving Bedouins." Her insult getting to him.

"Really!" Marc's anger rises up making him speak through clinched teeth. Making his handsome face turned into a snarl. "You won't get away with this. I will see that you are stopped." Anger and frustration tongue tying him.

Melinda's eyes light up enjoying seeing him this way. Speaking. "Like you have so far?"

"If I have to kill you myself this will end." Marc's voice a low baritone rumble almost a growl.

Un-intimidated, even defiant, "Strong words for one who has been led around like a goat for stud," Melinda says. Beginning to laugh, delighting in his seeming helplessness from his loss of words. Marc gets that feeling when someone is staring at you from across a crowded room. Their eyes burning a hole in you. That's not possible, startled by movement at the periphery of his vision. Turning his head toward the mirror over the mantel. Melinda is staring back at him. Wearing her favorite designer Versace, the dress worth thousands. A small gold cross complementing the hypocrisy of her public persona. "I'll see you soon. Bye-bye, Marcus." Her image dissolving inside the mirror. His own reflection there staring back but almost as not his own. Seeing his face that of a

Cajun man. His olive skin darkened by the sun with those dark blue eyes. Long straight black hair well past his shoulders down his back. More than just hinting of his Native American heritage. Having not heard Nahadeina when she entered the room. He was still glaring at his own image.

Nahadeina, "Who are you talking to? I didn't know you had company." Glancing around the room to see whom he was talking to. An uneasy expression passing over her face.

Marc sees this. *Great collateral damage, not only will she be frightened of this place. She will be afraid of me.* Choosing not to answer her but going on the defensive. "I thought I left instructions that all of the mirrors in this estate were to be left untouched."

Nahadeina, "Everyone was given those instructions."

"That mirror was." Marc speaking Arabic, "Allia come here!" Switching back to English. "Have you been cleaning in here?"

Allia, "Yes." Seeing them both looking at the mirror. Adding in her defense, "It was uncovered and dirty so I cleaned it. Was that wrong?"

"Do not ever touch any of the mirrors in this house again. Do you understand me?" Marc's voice coming out loud and full of anger.

Allia obviously frightened by his outburst. Keeping her gaze low to avoid making eye contact. As you would a crazy man in the street. "Yes sir."

Nahadeina takes her away by the arm speaking softly, "Who was he speaking to?"

Allia whispering admits, "It was uncovered." Nahadeina acknowledges this with a nod of her head. "This place feels unholy," Allia says. Just to emphasize her comment a cold breeze rushes over them blowing their dresses. Allia shivers from the cold air seeing her own breath. Her silver-green eyes round with fear.

Nahadeina's eyes wide for a second. Searching for something not there. "We are being ridiculous. It's the central climate control." Not so sure whose benefit this was said for. "Get back to work and don't touch any of the mirrors as you have been instructed."

Marc approaching, Nahadeina speaks first, "This new young girl is not very conscientious for a daughter of Yemen."

Marc reads into what she is saying. "How well do you know her? Something is familiar about her." Smelling a fragrance too faint for a human to detect with his heightened olfactory senses. The sense of smell being a strong memory trigger in mammals. It tickles a memory just out of reach but having the desired effect on his endocrine system. Finding himself distracted by Allia. Not hearing Nahadeina.

"I will see to them more closely. Will there be anything else?" Covering the mirror.

Marc, "No that will be all thank you." Sitting down at the desk. Just then a thought occurs to him. Spiking a rush of panic coursing through him. Did Brittany do something to him? His thumb unconsciously rubs the protective ring. Inhaling and releasing his breath calming. Conscious of his heavy gold ring with its deep blue tanzanites glimmering under the light from the Tiffany desk lamp.

Looking closer at the ring bequeathed him by his late uncle Theron. It's almost as if they don't see it. His question forms. *Could it be a glamoured invisible to most witches?* Listening to the drumming of his pulse in his right ear. It's still up not sure whether from adrenaline or something else. Having been able to hear his heart rate pounding in the right ear since before preschool. Only then it kept him awake at night. Unaware of where that drumming sound was coming from then.

Deciding not to wait for his brother to call back he picks up his cell phone off the desk. Getting Camel's machine again. "It's Marc. Brittany the woman from last night she was a setup. Let me know if you are all right. I don't know but I think she was a warning that they can get to us anytime." Holding back from cussing. "They seem to have allies everywhere." Slamming the cell phone down. His suspicions growing of the new woman in the house, Allia. *I'll be watching you.*

Rustling sounds come from behind him. Up from his chair in a blur so fast. Marc turns into a fight stance with hands out and feet spread, adrenaline pumping. Ready for an assault against himself. Stopping immediately. Nahadeina drops a wet dust rag gasping. "I'm so sorry, I didn't mean to startle you."

Marc relaxing some, "It's okay. I didn't mean to scare you."

Her look of fright replaced by worry. *Something is going on in this house.* "I understand your request for the mirrors to be covered. A death in the family is always very difficult to get over, but when it is one so young...," pausing, "you think of all the accomplishments they will never achieve. I wanted to give my condolences."

"Thank you. The loss is really more for Mary. Ms. Campbell being her only known living relative. It is much harder on her being alone in the world now."

Nahadeina is silent for a moment swallowing. "If you wish I will come back to wash the mirror with mugwort."

"No it's all right go ahead. The sooner the better," Marc says.

"Your friend the blonde came by earlier," Nahadeina volunteers

"Who? Melinda? She's not a friend anymore."

Nahadeina, "No. That was not her name. It was French starting with an 'ang'?"

"Angelique? Was that her name?" Marc asks.

Nahadeina, "Yes that was it." Holding back reluctant to speak. Not wanting to be the bearer of bad news.

"Go on. What is it?" Marc encourages her. Starting to get a bad feeling about this.

Nahadeina, "She said… to tell you she was sorry for your loss. A young first cousin so much like a brother to you, he could never be replaced."

Marc becoming angry. "What cousin? No one else has died that I know of." Enkil's words of warning comes back to him. Bitter grief rising up inside his gut.

"Phillip would be like losing a younger brother to you." Nahadeina finishes Angelique's message It feeling like a knife twisting in his gut. The pain of sudden loss hurting him.

"It can't be Phillip. I just spoke to him the other day."

Nahadeina, "I am so sorry. I did not know you had not been told."

Marc, "There must be some kind of mistake. He can't be dead. How?"

Nahadeina, "That is all I was told. Again I am so sorry."

Marc is now speaking to her as much as himself. "No! She doesn't know my cousin. She has never met him." His eyes misting up visibly shaken. Nahadeina just stands there helpless bowing her head to leave. Marc rushes over to the answering machine. Pressing the play button.

"Hi Marc." Cousin Phillip's voice. "I have the final sections translated. It's incredible just in the detail historically. Let alone the machinations our ancestor was capable of. I'm talking about royal intrigue, treason…" Silence then static breaking up Phillip's call. "Wow that came up fast." Thunder booming in the background. "Did you hear that one? It was close." Static disrupting his call again. On Phillip's end rain is pouring off his roof in New Orleans. Having the second highest rainfall amount outside the American Northwest. Sometimes rainfall of up to nine inches in one hour causing flooding. Warm moisture laden air coming off the Gulf of Mexico carrying with it potential energy. Ripe for the taking. That is if you know how to tap into it.

Phillip's voice comes back in. "You won't believe what they are trying to do." Rain mixed with hail plinking off windows pounding against his roof. Drowning out his voice. Water inundating rain gutters coming so fast it washes over the outside of downspouts becoming waterfalls pouring three floors below. Marc anxiously turns the volume up on the answering machine to coax out a few more distinct words. Nervous energy pumping him up. Could they reach him that far away? No. They get monsoon rains there off the Gulf.

"Marc! You have to..." Phillip's voice fades in and out static howling. "It's dangerous." Lightning explodes its sound covering his voice followed by silence. A dial tone humming his call ended.

He frantically punches in Phillip's area code followed by the phone number. Waiting anxiously the seconds over long distance taking an eternity. A voice coming on an automated recording, "The number you are trying to reach is temporarily out of service. Please check the number you have entered and try again." Marc hangs the phone up pressing resend. Fear beginning to grip at his insides twisting them. Reality setting in where a numb cold feeling like that of death's hand passs over his skin. Hanging up again determined not to hear what is most likely the truth. Tears beginning to stream down his face. This was all his fault. He should have never involved Phillip in all of this. Grabbing for his cell phone unable to see the pad. Marc wipes his eyes to clear them enough to see. Waiting for a sound hearing the phone on the other end ringing. Letting his breath out not having noticed he was holding it. The phone still ringing on the other end.

"Pick up, pick up," Marc speaks into the phone.

"Bon jour come se vous."

"Phil! I'm here." Marc shouts at the recording of Phil's voice.

"That means you. Leave a message at the tone." Phillip's voice on the recording.

"Call me as soon as you get this message. It's Marc, okay? Call me." Marc finishes the phone call pressing end. Feeling some relief. *Maybe they are just torturing me*. Playing the next message.

"Marc it's your mother." Her voice calm. "What the hell have you and Camel gotten yourselves into this time?" Jumping right to the point angry, not good. "I had an unexpected visitor last night. She will rue the day they sent her to enchant me. That one is for another time when I'm actually able to reach you. And I do mean physically. Your father called. I had a message waiting at the embassy here in Lima for me. Someone has been threatening the Khalid family. I'll be here an extra day." Marc feels like he was eleven again. That was an order to call his mom.

Marc's cell phone chimes. Checking it for Phil's return call, the caller ID blocked. Who the heck could this be? Accepting the phone to accept the call. "Yes."

"Marc it's Camel, my brother Ibram called. Someone claiming to be jihadist for a pure Arabia. They are threatening my family because of its association with yours."

"I just received a message from Mom. Dad called her saying someone is threatening your family" Marc says

"This has gone on too long both of our families have be drawn into this. We should just tell them everything. To be forewarned is to be better prepared." Camel says.

Marc, "That is definitely a bad idea." His voice tightening up.

Camel, "Why do you sound as though you know it to be true."

"Because I—they killed Phil," Marc says.

Camel, "No? Are you sure?" After explaining what he had heard on the answering machine. Camel says, "Find out what your mother has to say. I will contact some Lebanese friends who have contacts in finance and construction in New Orleans. Someone there may be able to be our eyes and go to his home to check on him."

Marc, "If they have contacts all over the world. I've been thinking about this too small."

Camel, "Coven members," correcting him. "Find out what your mother knows but limit what you tell her for her own safety. Those women last night have strong connections with our coven."

"I know," Marc says.

Camel, "Why, what happened?" His deep voice concerned.

Marc, "You remember Brittany the dancer last night?"

Camel, "How could I forget?"

"She was a setup. To keep me busy so I wouldn't speak with Phil." Then adding, "Before they killed him." His voice having a hard edge to it. Which had never been there before.

"How, are you all right?" Camel says.

Marc understands his meaning. Answering him as truthfully as he could. "I think so. I have not changed any further." Looking at his ring. "I am pretty sure the tanzanite ring is protecting me."

Camel, "We have to put our heads together. This has gone far enough."

"I don't know what to do next." Marc says. "I'm just not one of those political manipulators."

Camel seeing red, "I'll be right over." Anger in his usually calm deep voice making it loud. Within the blink of an eye Camel's physical body shimmers into the manor in front of Marc standing there. Marc starts to speak but stops himself. For it is Enkil's yellow eyes with their vertical pupils and very angry.

Enkil, "You two have really mixed it up with some powerful, intelligent, and devious women. I warned you there could be repercussions."

Marc with his head down answers, "I know. I just thought—"

Enkil, "You just thought?" His bass voice booming inside Marc's chest and around the room. Out across the house rattling windowpanes even dishes in the kitchen. Causing both women in that room to take pause. "Do you understand now what you are up against?" Not a question more of an accusation.

Marc answers him as a stubborn son would his father. "I am beginning to." Snarling. "You have to keep your voice down." Enkil not used to taking orders from mortals. Certainly not one so weak in his eyes, but with strong potential. If he would ever be smart enough to harness them. Glaring at Marc ready to put him in check. Seeing Nahadeina and the other staff members rushing to the library. Believing an earthquake had just occurred not yet entering the room. "They know I was alone." Allowing his baritone voice to carry low so as only Enkil could hear him. Marc and Camel look at the women gathered in the doorway.

Marc speaks first to them, "It's all right a family discussion."

Allia, "What about the earthquake? Should we not prepare for aftershocks?" Looking around the room but not for damage.

Camel, "It was sound waves on a low frequency. They can jar small items like dishes and crystal." Surmising what had happened to bring them. That combined with loud male voices arguing. Glaring at Marc and him back at Camel. End of conversation the group disperses but not before Allia glances once more at the two men. Not believing their explanation.

Marc waits for them to get out of earshot before speaking. "We do not need the ecumenical community after us also." Going over pulling the library doors closed. Enkil's insulted expression lessening. "They will be calling for a trial of possession." Marc adds. Enkil shifts his weight on his feet. His face an unreadable mask with his anger under better control now.

Enkil speaks freely now that they are alone again. "It is that vengeance demon working with those witches. Have you not noticed that your every move is being anticipated. They are always two steps ahead. Trust no one."

Marc nods his head in agreement keeping his voice low speaking softly. "I, we determined that. It is why I called Camel." Feeling lame. Enkil becomes angry again causing Camel's face to become dusky. His yellow eyes like that of a snake fixed on its prey cold and ready to strike. The room temperature dropping some forty degrees. Too cold to be just air conditioning. Marc seeing his breath.

"I warned both of you about those sorceresses." Enkil saying it like it left a bad taste in his mouth. "The two of you act like some adolescent schoolboys. So easily manipulated by a couple of obvious whores, no less." Marc feeling worse if that was possible. Enkil continues not one to be interrupted with foolishness. Not that at that point Marc would have challenged him his right to speak. "They sent two witch whores to try and kill me last night. I gave them a send-off." Finality in his voice along with some satisfaction.

Marc afraid to ask but is itching to know. "What do you mean?"

Enkil, "I used the old Christian way of dealing with witches. I burned them." Shoving the newspaper across the desk at Marc. Its headline reading, "Tragic Motor Vehicle Accident?" Skimming down the story. Two students burnt to death in a tragic car accident on Highway 390. For just a moment he had begun to sound like his dad or an iman with that schoolboy stuff and the whores lecture. Just not quite so lethal. Marc takes back his comparison. "Need I say any more on that subject?"

Marc, "No, sir."

"I cannot protect you both all the time. This war has spread to many fronts." Enkil advises him.

Marc, "I know." Going on to explain about the threats made to both of their families.

All the while Enkil paces back and forth walking past Marc sitting at his Louis XVI desk. Concentrating on what is said. Having been a king during the Bronze Age. All too familiar with battle strategies but above including intimidation of one's enemies with smaller strikes. Fear is a good weapon of any age. Enkil stops his anger getting the better of him. Speaking in his bass voice a growl at first, "That damned Angelique with her consort Andor." His yellow irises with their vertical black pupils fixed on Marc's eyes. "She is a vengeance demon and the worst sort." As if Marc had a reference point for demons. Enkil being his first. "She is giving them reconnaissance mixed with her own brand of trouble. Jealous and unforgiving after millennia's." That last part almost under his breath. But with Marc's hearing having become more acute he hears it. One beneficial change wrought by the curse against him. Yes he can admit it now. It is a curse to be male and so easily subverted sexually by females. That and most women at least in this country do not like fur. Except on their clothes not their men.

"Are you listening to me?" Enkil searches his face.

"Uh yeah." His expression telling him otherwise. His hard reptilian eyes forcing Marc with just a look to sit up straight before continuing on.

"You need to be. The two of you have crossed paths with a very old and powerful coven. Some of its members are millennia's old back to the times of the magi. For those legends of old hold a grain of truth." This news causes the hair on Marc's arms to rise up a chill spreading over his body.

"You are telling me they can live forever?"

"A soul once turned to darkness can live off of others," Enkil says answering him.

"How are they able to do this?"

"By taking what is not theirs to take." Enkil's usually unreadable and stoic face solemn.

Marc pursues the answer. "How?"

Taking a deep breath before answering him, "By taking a man's soul." He says. His arrogant mask slipping for a moment. Marc able to read the sadness in Enkil's face. More questions coming to mind than he knows Enkil will answer. Suspecting he already knows the answer to this question but needing to hear it anyway.

"Are these ancient ones all over the world?"

Enkil takes a moment his angry arrogant expression returning before speaking. "They are not just in Rochester or North America."

Marc's panic rises. "How do we protect our families from them? Surely there must be something we can do to protect them."

Enkil, "Stay out of their way. Stop being duped into having sexual encounters with them. You are just pawns to be used and discarded once they are finished with you. You cannot save all the men they encounter." Marc feels extremely vulnerable twisting his tanzanite ring with its blue-purple stones sparkling. Catching Enkil's eyes giving him pause. A thought occuring to him. "I'm missing something here. Why would your family possess such a book of power?"

Marc, "I don't know."

"Even that ring pulses out a protective field around you. Subtle but effective. It is why you are not dead or perhaps an animal of the pastures for slaughter." Looking thoughtful before asking his new question to Marc. "Which relative was it passed down from to you?"

"My father's side so that would be his great-great-great-grandmother," Marc answers him questioningly.

Enkil, "That would be your paternal side. How long ago did she live?"

"She lived two centuries ago." Answering his question wondering where he was leading with all this. An unsettled feeling coming over him.

Enkil watches him closely as he asks the next question. "You know nothing from family lore about her?"

"That is what I went to cousin Phil about. He was calling me with the completed translations. A powerful electrical storm interrupted his message when he called."

"That was why you were concerned about him." Enkil becoming excited. "What did you learn from him?"

"Up until a few days ago not much." Marc feeling a little foolish.

"Come on out with it. So that was why you were concerned about him."

Marc, "You were reading my thoughts again?" Enkil looking very irritated but not seeing a discernible need to respond. Why should he? "Fine." Marc's own irritation coming out in his voice. "Phil said he spoke with our great-great-aunt just before she died. I didn't think much about it at the time. Her being one hundred and seven years old. Death was soon to come." His callousness not the Marc that was a few weeks ago. Enkil observes quietly. "She said her great-grandmother was an evil woman. Then the strangest thing happened. The clock on her mantel chimed thirteen times instead of one o'clock. She became very frightened and wouldn't say any more. Except that anything of her great-grandmother's should be destroyed. A good Christian would not keep such stuff of darkest evil. Then she became confused and then a nurse came in and stopped him from questioning her further. Saying it was upsetting her too much."

Enkil paces again spotting the fax light blinking. "Your machine needs paper. Maybe he sent you something."

"You are adjusting to the twenty-first century." Marc says while tearing open a ream of paper sliding out a stack to feed into the fax. Causing it to come on printing.

A knock at the door startles them both. Enkil pulls up his energy ready to kill. Before Marc can speak Nahadeina opens the door. "I heard voices. Hello Camel. I did not know you were still here. Can I get anything for the two of you?"

"Yes, strong hot tea." Enkil's deeper bass voice not Camel's. Having already turned back to the fax unconcerned with the servant.

Marc covers quickly. "That sounds like an excellent idea. Maybe it will help your throat Camel. Bring us a pot and thank you." Nahadeina backs out of the room having no expression on her face. Hiding any fear she might have.

Marc looks questioningly at him. "What? I don't care. He could be hoarse from hanging out in seedy places with smoky back rooms." Enkil disregarding his worry.

"Yeah and what about the accent?" says Marc.

Enkil ignores him. "Now we need a plan to keep Andor, *mon petite cheri,* busy."

Marc decides he has a past with Andor, *Mon petite cheri.* Not all bad venturing a guess.

"Andor from your past?" Enkil's yellow eyes seethe with anger staring at Marc. *Yes, there's hate in those eyes,* giving him a small thrill. Slowly this hard man to read has a layer peeled away. Not wanting to be on the receiving end of that hate. Enkil's silence is all the answer he needs.

Enkil finally answers him, "Yes. She was beautiful and we were in love. That was thousands of years ago." Changing the subject. "The first page is completed." The fax continuing to printing out more pages. Marc follows his lead and not wanting to push his luck further. At least not now; that subject could be explored more later. Accepting the change of subject.

"How does Mary fit into all this? I don't see why would they need her." Marc asks but the more important question for now. Why?

"Those are good questions. Tell me what you know about her leaving no detail out." Enkil says.

"She is hardworking, kind. Uh..."

"Not that. What is she to your family? Why bring her into the mix at all? Is she secretly in league with the coven?" Enkil digs deeper.

"No!" Marc practically shouts becoming defensive. "She is not working with them."

"How do you know this?" Enkil asks.

"Her aunt made her come here to work. Before that she lead a very sheltered life. At Saint Anne's Parochial School for Girls."

Enkil, "Where was this life before here?" Unimpressed or not understanding.

"She was on another continent at a religious boarding school." Marc says this slowly as it were another language.

Enkil gives him an insightful look. "A convent?"

"Yes, I guess so, managed by nuns." Marc agrees.

"Was she the innocent one?" Enkil asks. Watching Marc's face closely himself already knowing where this was heading.

"I did not know she was until—" Marc stops himself. Why revisit that old bit of news?

"Did she say she loved you?" Enkil asks. His pupils narrowing into slits with his jaw muscles tightening while the rest of his face remains unreadable as stone.

"Does everyone have to know that detail? Yes." Marc says. Enkil's reaction is immediate. Anger palpable spreading over the very air around Marc. His hair floating out on statically charged on the air with a hint of ozone smell to it. "What? Why are you becoming concerned now?" Marc asks.

Nahadeina knocks on one of the heavy pocket doors before entering with their hot tea. Served in a Georgian silver service with tray. Fine English bone china cups against saucers rattling. The sound almost tinkling like small bells. Feeling the tension between men. She sets the tray down at the nearby round table. Pouring up two cups of tea before taking her leave. Their silence not withstanding before she is out of the room.

"You fool! How has it that the world has forgotten something so important?" Enkil says.

"I don't know what you mean," Marc says.

"The gift of love and innocence are powerful magic alone." Enkil says. Marc is still holding the fax pages not looking at them. Passing them to Enkil but not before recognizing Phil's handwriting at the top.

"I need to check on Phil," Marc says, moving his apps across cell phone screen pressing the memory icon. Then getting the same recording: "Client out of service." Marc dials the land phone waiting impatiently. Phil had grown up around both Camel and himself. They were close being youngest of the three. He had been a tagalong at times in their desert adventures. That is until they almost lost him in the desert.

"I can't read these they are in some sort of gibberish," Enkil says. Ready to hand them back to Marc. Instead using his powers to gain the knowledge from his young associate's mind. The phone in Marc's hand with its message repeating out of service.

"It could be used in a resurrection or rebirth ritual. Both are similar, requiring a male descendant to defile innocence." Handing the pages back to Marc. Enkil's look of disgust causes him to cast his eyes down guiltily.

Marc rationalizes. "It was a party in June. I did not know she would be there."

"It was the summer solstice. A time of great fertility. This just gets worse as more comes out a piece at a time. Did you at least use protection?" Enkil asks, already suspecting the answer. Marc feeling like a trapped animal, his eyes round. "Did you both accept special drinks?" Enkil asks.

"I had begun to suspect we were drugged." Marc says.

"Do you need further convincing of that?" Enkil says.

Marc thinks back to that night. "Jadon and Melinda were bartending. Melinda was so jealous, downright cruel to Mary." Recounting that night along with a nagging realization beginning to set in. Of to just what level he had been manipulated. The older more experienced Enkil reads his face. That and picking up on his thoughts Marc's face so open. Shaking his head Camel's thick mane of dark curls so regal. His demeanor that of a leader.

"You two were easier to work than some foreign pilgrims on hajj, lost at Ramadan," Enkil says.

"We were all manipulated." Choosing now as good as any other time to tell Enkil about his presumption that Jadon had been murdered.

"If that is true, then Angelique is more desperate than I thought. She will stop at nothing to complete this ritual. Which makes them more dangerous for all of us."

"What is it they are after?" Marc asks.

"They use all the guile and finesse of true courtesans." Enkil having the beginnings of recognition. Their use of intrigue and power only too familiar.

Increasing his concerns for both Marc and Camel. "Did you at least use protection?"

Marc ducks his head. *He sounds more like a father all the time. Than some infinitely powerful, ageless being.* "Uh, I don't remember so much happened that night." Marc says.

Enkil scrutinizes Marc's face for the slightest tick of falsehood. Enkil's frustration rising. "You were too busy being the hero and then too horny to get inside to care, right?" Marc's silence all the answer he needs. "We have to keep that girl Mary away from those witches. Before they can complete their ritual." Enkil determines.

Marc volunteers. "She is leaving for London soon."

"I doubt even distance will be enough to protect her," Enkil says.

"Protect her from what? Melinda has already turned her against me." Marc says. Enkil's anger nears the boiling point. His energy becoming a solid force in the air around them shimmering as if it was heat across the desert sand. Marc uncomfortable from static charges stinging his skin as they crackle randomly over it.

"They intend to use her to bring back a more evil soul than Angelique's." Marc's face sobers, ignoring the stings from the static electricity. "That is a fertility spell with some sort of reincarnation ritual. It can pull a soul from the cull." Marc's blank expression pushes Enkil closer yet to rage. "That is a Christian term for where souls are kept in heaven. Until they are called upon to come back down to be reborn. As for whom, your great-great-great-grandmother. Who do you think brought down the House of Bourbon? All those salacious inflammatory rumors." Marc surprised first, then his guilt with fear for Mary not himself. Twisting up deep to his bones. Reaching all the way into his groin.

"That is not possible. She is barely mentioned in history books. Definitely not a cause of a revolution," Marc says with confidence.

Enkil regards Marc with his yellow irises, dilating the pupils to have that cold stare of a snake. "I was there, Marie and she never got along. Marie insulted her youth being her folly. Never considering an enemy once made is forever. Especially a courtesan of her father in law. Foolish indeed to think she was not of any significance. Marie was very wrong as history would prove."

"But how?" Marc asks.

Enkil looks at him incredulously. "Have you not learned?" His voice impatient. "She used a glamour. Then went on an expensive diamond jewelry buying spree. Enough to bankrupt the French treasury. A mere coincidence that a large blue diamond was sold from London. Days after no claim from the new French government could be made, after the revolution. The British hated the French before that. Making it all too easy to smuggle diamonds across the channel. Then starting a new life. By the way, where do you think some of that Du Bois fortune comes from?"

A knock on the library doors ends Enkil's story. Marc glad for the break having not liked where the direction of his history lesson was heading. Who wants to know old family money came from blood money? Even if it was two centuries ago.

Enkil drinks his tea, no longer hot, its cup made small by his large hands. Examining its pattern more closely something this time nudging his memory. Moving over to the table to see the saucer. Both have matching Celtic vines intertwined around them forming triangles of life. Noting the runes of the northern people. Enkil being from Sumerian people, not as familiar to them. But being educated as was a requirement of his father. Stretching his memory back almost having forgotten the language of the barbarians. He recognizes the protective runes forming the compass points of north, south, east, and west, reading them.

Marc advises Allia they were not ready for tea service to be removed. Herself taking an extra moment to look into the room at Camel. Her face not so blank, allowing him a glance at something well hidden on her, but the eyes tell the truth. Hate mixed with fear. Just as quickly her eyes look away before returning to his, blank again. "That will be all." Marc says, closing the door almost in her face.

Enkil speaks from across the room. "How well do you know your family history?"

Marc thinks to himself, *Here we go. This sounds all too familiar.* "Not well at all apparently. Why?" Hating to ask that question.

"No one ever discussed any of it with you?" Enkil asks.

"Until recently, I… was never very interested. My great-uncle Theron tried, Mom tried. She told me I needed to learn it." Enkil shakes his head with disappointment on his face. "I started. That is why I contacted my cousin Phil. He was always intrigued by it. If he didn't know, he knew whom to contact that did," Marc says.

Enkil speaks, "Basically this is your own negligence, all of this."

"Everyone loves a finger pointer." Marc's sarcasm not missed. Enkil just didn't get the analogy. Choosing instead to ignore his comment.

"Come here I want you to see these runes." Marc is hesitant at first but not really having any choice. "You would do well to watch your tone with me." Enkil growls in his deep bass voice, only loud enough for Marc to hear him. "These are runes used for calling the elements. To protect the witch from evildoers. Especially witches that use the darker powers. Not your Wiccan type with their 'harm none' philosophy," Enkil says. Then he adds, "Karma will exact a price for all of this." Marc's questioning expression concerns Enkil. How could he be this ignorant?

"Well, I don't really understand that expression." Marc says.

"Let me put it another way. When you use magic, whatever you send out there will come back to you times three." Marc's face still looks unsure so Enkil continues to explain. "Send bad things out against the innocent, as Angelique has. Her comeuppance will be a delight for me to watch happen." Enkil then adds, "It needs to be sooner than later."

Marc then asks, "But is not evil, evil's consort?"

Enkil, "The universe is neither good nor bad. She may be able to hide or even mask herself, but sooner or later karma will find a crack or I will."

"What would make them target us?" Marc says.

Enkil having his suspicions trying to decide how much to tell him. "The obvious choice being two young men of affluent families. That and their ignorance, shortsightedness, general inability to see what is in front of them." Marc's forehead furrowed changing from concentration to one with his Cupid's bow lips turned down. Enkil smirking at his reaction. "More importantly your family history, you have magic in your bloodline." Marc's dubious expression gives Enkil cause to be impatient.

"Magic is all around you. All you have to do is open your eyes. It's in the china pattern." Indicating the cup he was holding and drinking from. "It's in the ring you're wearing, it's in the garden's design. I can feel it in this house, echoes of your uncle's past enlightenment. Angelique is using it to tap into your genetic disposition." Having suspicions about more, but not ready to comment on that until he investigates further.

"I do not know anything about magic and I'm having trouble believing any of this." Marc says.

"Then you are either a fool or in denial. I doubt the latter," Enkil says. Not feeling the need to say more.

Marc tries hard to think back to what his great-uncle had said. "What is the point of knowing all this, if I can do nothing to stop them?" Marc says.

"Learn your family history, study these symbols. Combining the symbols with the rituals of protection will make it more difficult for Angelique and her coven to harm you," Enkil says.

"I am a Muslim. I do not use infidel rituals." Marc says.

"They will use whatever they have at their disposal against you. From some of the most ancient religions to your own system of beliefs. Make no mistake in that. I am not saying you should worship any other god than Allah." Marc takes in what he has said.

"You cannot prevent kismet, but you may be able to move it around, if you will." Enkil says.

"Move fate around if I choose?" Marc's question presented back to Enkil.

"Altering what will happen to you may change the outcome. You three, your lives are intertwined from now on. Thereby you have a past. Learn from your ancestor's past mistakes." Enkil says. Then moving to take his leave.

"Wait," Marc says. Enkil looks at him impatiently, as if to say, *What?* Clearly their conversation over. "How do we stop the vengeance demon from following us?" Marc says.

"I will create a few distractions for her but they will only be beneficial at key times." Looking at him squarely, ready to leave again.

"One other thing. What is a vengeance demon?" Marc asks.

Enkil sighs out loud before answering him. "In times past they—"

Marc interrupts him. "They?"

"There is only one here at work now. If you will let me finish. Yes, there are more. I do not know how many. Usually a woman scorned calls upon one of these to take revenge against her cheating lover." Enkil face sober, very matter of fact. "She kills the man horribly, disembowelment, burning body parts off. You get the general picture here of what I am saying."

Marc's tan face visibly paler shaken. "I have not been cheating on anyone." Marc says in his defense.

"That could be a matter of opinion. You are promiscuous." Raising his hand to stop Marc from denying it, choosing another tactic. "You sleep around a lot now. That combined with your ample size and your increased need to satisfy women. Slavishly, I might add in your bestial programming. It would not take much to get you into hot water. Ignoring the fact that you already are in over your head."

"I have not been cheating on anyone." Marc says again. This with less conviction. Thinking hard Melinda said she did not care. Jadon, not recalling her opinion on this subject and *Mary?*

"Originally Camel was the target because of Angelique. She found she could not control him bringing me into the mix. Believing herself strong enough to control yours truly." Indicating himself using Camel's large brown hands.

"Why change us into satyrs becoming angry when our behavior is what you wanted?" Marc says.

"Blind to the obvious. Having free will, you could do as you wanted. Also she did not count on both of you being so strong magically I would guess. However she is very resourceful. Having insights beyond an ordinary witch her age." Taking pause to reflect. Speaking more to himself than Marc. "It is almost as if she has someone else giving her directions, guidance." Enkil's expression slowly changes to one of guile. Foreign to Camel's openly honest face. Once again reminding Marc just how much trouble they were both in. Himself and Camel, that is. Enkil's yellow irises with their vertical pupils frighteningly mean especially once he was angry.

"Have you seen the face of this blonde you dream of?" Marc tries not to swallow, his mouth very dry. *What happened?*

"No. I have not yet. Almost." Not about to let Enkil see him sweat. The look Enkil gives him, no further verbal communication needed. He was expected to recount his dream.

"She has big hair, it must be a wig, white, coiffured high. Her face is powdered white, what I can see of it before she hides it behind the fan. The clothes she's wearing are expensive, from the eighteen hundreds." Unconsciously running his hand over the bicep that was scarred. "Her fingernails are long and sharp." Touching the horizontal scars on his arm. Her nails were more like talons at the ends of her fingers with bejeweled rings on each.

"She did that to you from a dream?" Enkil asks, watching Marc's hand rub the scars. For some reason they are now hurting.

"Yes."

"Why did you not say something about this? When did it happen?" Enkil asks.

"It was a couple of weeks ago and I thought I did tell Camel. A lot has been going on." Marc becoming defensive.

Enkil's bass voice soft as he asks his next question. Making him sound more like an attorney cross-examining his own witness. "What else? Has she spoken to you?"

"The last dream she was wearing a large blue diamond suspended on a heavy gold chain between her bosom." Marc taking his time to remember his dream's details. "She calls to me, 'Mon fils, don't be afraid.'" Enkil examines the scars made from the scratches. Where they had become infected. Treated for the infection now gone but for the pinkish keloid scars. Like a brand used to mark livestock showing ownership. Enkil remains silent through Marc's recount of his dreams, his expression unreadable.

"What did you think after you had this happen in a dream?" Enkil asks.

"Something about her has always been disturbing. Her presence felt," pausing, Marc stifling a shudder, "evil. She felt evil. Who is she?" Marc asks.

"Do you not already know her?" Marc pieces together his own suspicions. *No. It couldn't be.* Doubting himself. Enkil has had a good idea of who she was from their other conversations. "She is your progenitor." His bass voice soft with regret.

"What?" Marc says.

"Your distant ancestor, a great-great-great-grandmother if you will," Enkil snarls, baring Camel's white teeth at Marc. He hated her then and now. The memory still strong as it were yesterday. Marc pulls back from his anger, charging the room with tension.

"She intends to use me?" Marc asks.

"You are simply a means to an end. To get what she wants," Enkil says.

"How can she do that? She has been dead over two hundred years," Marc says.

"Death is not the end. Your spirit does not die," Enkil says.

"What could they want?" Marc asks.

"They are intending to bring about her reincarnation. Now it all makes sense." Enkil states out loud more for himself.

Marc thinks, *Not to me. What was she doing at the French court?*

"She was a courtesan." Enkil picking up on his open thoughts. Looking at Marc with disgust. *How could that witch have insinuated herself into so many bloodlines?*

"Are you saying she was a prostitute?" Marc asks.

"She was Louis XV's beloved mistress and identical twin sister to Madame du Barry. A bitter enemy of Marie Antoinette's. Make no mistake she was duplicitous, machinating, and cruel. Stopping at nothing to have what she sets her sights on. Court intrigue with rumors and lies of misdirection. All her tools of court. She used religious and political manipulation with an ease only matched in America and Iran. She destroyed a family with thousands of other lives to have her revenge. Changing a country forever. I cannot imagine what she would be capable of in this century."

Marc's insides twist up with cold dread rising up to fear. Will she stop at nothing? Destroying all of his family and Camel's to achieve her goals?

"Where will she turn up?" Marc asks, thinking ahead.

"She will seek a position of power. Perhaps posing as a family values advocate. The perfect Christian whore. Cutting the throats of anyone that opposes her. This country is ripe for the opportunity. A few well-chosen prostitutes mixed with greed and power. Free press will be to her advantage. Eagerly spreading salacious innuendoes and lies furthering her power mongering," Enkil says.

"There is no doubt sex and power cause a feeding frenzy where the press are concerned," Marc agrees.

"Since I have been in this new age. There is nothing more important and exciting to the biggest whores. The American press rumors and innuendoes mixed with a sexual scandal," Enkil says.

"A harsh description for something so important to fight against tyranny," Marc says.

"When people posing as ignorant claiming to be average going without being challenged for their actions are then allowed to promote dangerous self-serving deeds. Then your free press only serves those who are powerful enough to manipulate it. That my friend is not freedom but another form of repression," Enkil says.

"Freedom of speech and the press are civil liberties." Marc's temper rising. Thinking to himself, *All of that coming from a king or dictator, not much difference*. Enkil glares at him. Marc unsure as to whether his associate just read his thoughts or his face.

"Now I must leave. It will take some time to plan our next move. When our opponents are always two steps ahead of us. You would do well to keep that in mind, before you act unwisely. But then I would not want to be accused of making decisions for you. No matter how dangerous those choices could be to you. That could be construed as dictating." Looking Marc directly in the eyes. Forcing him to swallow self-consciously. Enkil turns to shimmer, irritated enough not to want to look at Marc's handsome but so very ignorant face.

"What about Andor?" Marc speaks quickly.

"I will distract her giving you chances. You should not keep saying her name. That will call her to you. She hears it each time it is used, especially at night," Enkil warns him.

"Would you leave Camel with me to help? Three heads are better to work together than two." Marc says.

"Only if the two minds are capable of intelligent thought. As you wish for now. Get prepared, things will start happening quickly. Wear your ring at all times be it on your hand or around your neck," Enkil says.

"I will."

"Good, you are going to need all the protection you can get." The air around him shimmers like summer heat waves. Enkil leaves, only Camel's physical form remaining.

Camel shudders slightly. "Wow, that feels so strange when he detaches from my mind."

Marc, "How so?"

"It's like a rush of wind blowing through the inside of my head. Along with a pulling sensation. Except I know that the sensation is not a physical one because I do not feel it on my skin," Camel says.

"Then it must be metaphysical. Your soul feels him when he leaves," Marc says.

"What is odder, I can hear some of his thoughts and even feel his emotions at the time." Feeling recovered from Enkil's ethereal pull. "I can smell him on my skin," Camel exclaims. Smelling his forearm.

"Now that is just weird."

"No worse than smelling like a goat herder and a men's locker room," Camel says, offended. His handsome square-jawed face with its rough stubble very serious.

"What?" Marc says, realizing he injured his brother. "I am sorry. I did not mean that to be insulting," Marc adds.

"It is forgotten." Camel says, easing up.

Marc, changing the subject, "You can tell Enkil and Andor have a past together."

"Yes that much is obvious. Do not use her name or you risk too much bringing her down on us." Camel says. Giving Marc a serious look.

"Right, right I will try not to let that happen again. So spill. What's the story there? She has a grudge against him. Why?" Marc says.

"There was a slave girl that wanted to bear a king's child. She enchanted and seduced him," Camel says very matter of factly.

"Come on! Seriously? I'm not falling for that story. That is totally lame." Marc says.

"No! It is true. She used magic to enchant him and then a glamour over herself. Then seducing him into bed as his wife. By the time anyone figured it out she was pregnant." Camel says. Marc's expression one of dubiousness. "This is his side of the story. It destroyed Enkil's relationship with Andor. There is more I can feel it, but it is too painful and personal for even him. Something happened that evokes some very strong guilt on his part. He keeps that truth locked up guarded if you will in a part of his mind walled off to me." Camel adds.

"So he has a complicated past." Marc says.

"It is what destroyed their relationship. From what I can gather she became a vengeance demon to get back at him for hurting her." Camel says.

"How did she get him back?" Marc asks.

"I am not sure but he is an immortal demon. That evil people call on for darker purposes. Would not that be revenge enough?" Camel says.

"Eternal damnation? Yes, I guess would even the score some." Marc says.

"Enkil blocks his thoughts and knowledge from me. It is only when he chooses or on a rare occasion that his guard is down. Then it is only bits and pieces of memories. Difficult to understand enough to put it all together," Camel says.

"I guess she didn't realize forever is a long time." Marc says.

"She did. They have been going up against each other for thousands of years." Camel says.

"Remind me to be less cavalier in my relationships with women." Camel adds. Marc nods his head in agreement. "Will you ever be free of him?"

"I don't know anymore. He is getting stronger and he likes being corporeal using my body to make love to women." Camel says.

"That can't be all bad," Marc says.

"It's not, I have learned a few things from him. But I still want him out. You cannot imagine what it's like to share everything inside my mind." Camel says.

"How difficult would it be to get him to leave?" Marc says.

"He is becoming a part of me." Camel says, putting his hand to his head. "He is always in there. The more carnal sensations he has the more he enjoys them."

"That is not good," Marc says.

"The upside it's like having an older brother with you to share unspoken thoughts. Plus he is a very smooth talker. When it comes to the ladies."

"For now why don't we focus on the immediate situation." Marc says, looking worried. Camel's expression grim. Both men silent with their thoughts to entertain or torture them. Depending on how you look at their positions.

Camel speaks what Marc is thinking. "I know. It is hard to believe even now all of this. That those...," at a loss for words. His throat tightening so much it is difficult to speak. His handsome face sad nearer to tears than Marc has seen ever. Reaching out to his brother he places a hand on Camel's large shoulder to comfort him.

"We will beat this big brother. I am not just going to watch you disappear. I won't let it happen." Marc's face serious, mature beyond his years.

Camel's expression softens. "What would I do without you?" Encouraged with renewed strength.

"We will keep searching for ways to keep ourselves safe and undo the work of darkness. These daughters of evil will not succeed." Marc says. Camel's resolve returning his poker face back in place.

"Let us pray to Allah, while we still may." Camel says. In their darkest hour both men face east kneeling to pray. Touching their foreheads to the centuries old Persian carpets. Woven with prayers in Arabic surrounding them. Not typical rugs sold to Westerners being Christians.

After finishing their prayers they resume their research. Reading through centuries old tomes to glean out the smallest bit of help.

CHAPTER 87

JUNE HAD TURNED to July. Life had settled back into its routine, not the one of normalcy as we had before. Even with the spell broken I could not see any changes within myself. I had accepted my new life of celibacy, grudgingly. Physically there was no change. My body was still retained the hair on my chest, thick and soft as mink narrowing down to a stripe like most men have down their abdomens. Only mine was silky soft and thick. The hair on my head I cut short. Donating it to a group that make wigs for children suffering with cancer. By the way, it still grows extremely fast. Apparently my physical response to self-gratification is no different than intimate relations with a female. Which I achingly miss. Being male and young, my endocrine hormones take over forcing my body to discharge what I will deny it. Waking me from erotic dreams of coitus at my climax. After a time it is just easier to handle matters myself. Plus it is a little embarrassing to have the maids changing my sheets every day.

Mary being strong willed and protected while living at the convent. Finally had left the sanctity of their stronghold and returned to London. Aunt Norma had provided for her with a death benefit small by some standards. Thus allowing for her to have a choice with regard to arrangements for a place to live. Once college started her life would settle back to studies. Not that college couldn't be routine. Leaving Rochester the sooner the better as far as she was concerned. After Melinda had outright lied, doing everything she could to destroy any friendship or trust Mary had in me. Mary still managed to be civil towards me. Which leads me to believe all is not ruined. She did allow me to see her one last time before her departure in July. Though I am not sure she would have appreciated some of my newest talents. Having learned a few tricks from our adversaries. Mirrors can be true windows into our lives.

After calling on the mirror (this exercise is for real), "Mirror, Mirror, in front of me. Bring forth the element of water. Allowing sight of what I so choose to see." Standing still to increase my mental concentration and focusing my mind on Mary. At first seeing only my own reflection. Then its image wavering as ripples on water spreading out with the reflection of the sky on its surface. Clouds moving rapidly toward my face as I pass through them. Like when one is on an airliner ascending into wisps of vaporous white heaven. "Voices bring my brush with grace back to earth." One voice British allowing a smile to soften my lips. Which I had not felt were drawn tight until now.

"It is all set. I'm leaving July 24. I can't wait to go home." Mary's accent British educated but softly feminine. Her expression happy. Not that she really had much to smile about of late. That with her aunt's tragic death and Marc's turning out to be a total scoundrel. Why she never listened to her aunt about that one, she would never get. Love being so damn blind wasting herself on him.

"I wish you wouldn't be so distant at times." Melinda's voice cold, educated American without an accent. Forcing her out of her deeply felt moment.

"I am not." Mary defending her privacy.

"Are you really sure about leaving?" Melinda asks.

"Yes," Mary answers.

"You don't have to be so quick to depart. You have the rest of summer. I could take you around to some of the colleges right here. Cornell is just an hour away. If you really are insistent on an Ivy League college."

"Come on. What is here for me?" Mary says. "A lot of painful memories. The only good to have come out of my stay here was you, and of course Angelique. If it were not for the two of you, I don't know how I would have gotten through this time and the sisters help." Mary says.

"You are too kind." Melinda says, trying her best to make it sound sincere. When all she can really feel is disdain mixed with jealousy for Mary.

Looking around her modest room with its pious effigy, Madonna with Child. On the opposite wall a crucifix. Her twin bed pushed against the other wall across from a small window. Too high to view the cloister garden without standing up. When you do look it is serene and almost forest like. Trees spread across its consecrated grounds towering. Having reached maturity at two hundred years old. Definitely rivaling the Du Bois or Khalid estates.

Melinda speaks, "There you go again. Where are you?"

"Besides, would you give up a full scholarship to Eton?" Mary being the voice of reason. This entire situation making her flushed, nausea pushing its way again to her attention. Not feeling that well hoping it isn't some stomach virus

"You don't have to decide today." Trying another tactic. "You are always welcome here if Eton is not to your taste. If it's not working out or you just need to get away to be with friends." Melinda on her game now. Her tone genuinely kind and nurturing. Smiling patiently to herself. All the while seething inside. How was it that this milky skinned bitch would be chosen and not me? Marc was perfect of breeding and privilege. Unlike this thing, the maid's bastard niece raised in poverty. Wrapping herself in chastity, nothing more than a ragamuffin. Mary's turn to notice Melinda is deep in her own thoughts. She looks very displeased. No angry. Jealous?

"A penny for your thoughts. Now who's being distant?" Mary says. Melinda glares back at her sharply. Causing Mary to cringe inside. So much anger behind that pretty face. Not the first young woman of privilege that she had seen so unhappy.

" It's nothing. I was thinking about fall classes and how glad I will be that this is my last year."

"I may be dense but that face was not for happy." Mary says. Melinda irritated with her insight and not keeping her own face masked. Allowing Mary the chance to see behind the expressions of sweetness with innocence. Revealing herself as she was the night of the party. Mary extremely skilled at not showing any reaction, her affect flat. Between the nuns and aunt Norma's cruel punishments. No one would ever be allowed to see the pain they had inflicted. Maybe Marc was right; Melinda isn't so nice. Still not having figured out why these privileged young women would befriend a maid.

Melinda recognizing her anger showing at the surface quickly covers it up. "Yes you are right. I was thinking about Marc. It's still very painful for me to think of him. Remembering how foolish I was to let him treat me the way he did."

"Maybe we should change the subject," Mary suggests.

"Right you are. How about we have a little going away party for you?" Melinda says.

"As nice as that would be I'm just not up to celebrating just yet," Mary says. "Besides yourself and Angelique with the exception of a few nuns. Who else would you invite?"

Melinda thinks about it. "Well, I don't think the nuns would be too interested in coming to a college type mixer. That would certainly put a damper on things. We could just think of them as chaperones, or as the guys would say, a cock block." Mary does not getting the colorful colloquial expression. Melinda rolls her eyes realizing Ms. Sheltered didn't get it.

"I don't know if I am up to drinking and being up late. I have been so easily tired lately," Mary says. Not wanting to sound like a child. "I have to think about it."

Melinda, "It's probably the stress you have been under. We could have a ladies' tea instead. That way it wouldn't be late." Melinda smiling now from her thoughts. *Wouldn't that be a laugh on Angelique? In front of the elders, an FAS baby. That would put a crimp in her plans.*

"I will have to get back to you on that one. But I'm glad to see you are in a better mood now," Mary says.

"Yes. Yes, I am," Melinda says, continuing to smile. "Let me know if you change your mind. I really do have to be going." Standing up to leave.

"I will," Mary says, walking her out.

CHAPTER 88

ENKIL CONJURING THE elements to contact Andor. Using the table outside on the balcony off Camel's master suite. Burning a mixture of herbs and powders. Stirring them together. Chanting softly at first, all the while infusing his energy into the task. Calling on the elementals to aid him in his need. To go forth and find her. Concentrating on Andor her olive complexion face of such beauty. Her almond shaped eyes their color silver-green with long dark hair naturally wavy as if it had been crimped, but not. That was just another gift from Mother Nature she was born with. Being a princess it was long almost to her hips when she did not braid it. A gentle summer breeze rises up blowing warm air over him. His loose white cotton shirt fluttering open bearing a dark haired muscular chest. Unbothered by such things as body hair being from a time when men were men. Not using steroid creams to block hair growth. *If I just close my eyes I can see home.*

Enkil is standing on their stone terrace back in time, the Sumerian city of Ur. The smell of fresh tilled earth in the air. Along with the scent of frankincense wafting from a censer across the terrace. Where the Altar of Enkar is set for the noon ritual of supplication. Andor comes up behind him stealthily. Jumping, Enkil turns quickly and with perfect timing catches her. Andor wraps her arms around his neck affectionately kissing his full lips deeply until they are juicy. Then she places her head against his chest in the crush of dark soft curly hair there, not like it is in the future a straight thick pelt. Enkil having smelt her being downwind. Jasmine oil its sweet scent on her body and hair. That being her favorite perfume. Having this particular fragrance imported from what would be known as India someday. Olive oil mixed with lanolin making her skin soft and supple. Basking in the heat of the noon sun with the feel of her perfumed brown skin against his. What more could a husband want from his new wife? So evocative, so real, this memory having pulled back time's veil.

Whispering in Enkil's ear, "Why have you called upon me?" Andor herself engulfed in his power, bending time to the past. Feeling herself a young woman again. Mortal, with all of her dreams before her with the man she would love forever.

Enkil no longer able to maintain its great amount of energy. The portal to their past closes blurring into the present surrounding them once again.

Hemlocks and cypresses swaying with the July breeze carrying subtle scents of the flowers four-o'clocks like perfume. Jasmine being a stronger fragrance of the two washing over them. Camel's serious expression alerting Andor to the importance of Enkil's request for her presence.

"I needed to speak with you on a matter of the gravest issue." His bass voice vibrating inside her chest.

"Yes? Enkil," Andor's breathy response. Her eyes so loving and passionate. His solid arms still embracing her. Pulling her tighter against his hard body. Brushing his thick lips over hers repeatedly before his tongue thrusts past her teeth meeting hers. Before she has time to remember to be angry with him. Andor uses her hands to push away from his muscular body. Not strongly enough to separate them. Her eyes asking the question.

"I need your help," Enkil says. His body responding to her closeness, hard, firmly pressing against her. Delighting in his maleness responding to her. Andor's eyes shade to a silvery green. Sparkling are the irises twinkling before Enkil's warm breath against her supple neck. Fearful of saying anything to ruin the moment with her. Her eyes taking in the set of his angular stubble-covered jaw. How strong he looks even in this physical form. Enkil's presence that of a king. Finally pushing him back away from her determined to keep the upper hand. Enkil unable for just a second to hide the hurt.

"With what?" Andor asks. Then continuing not letting him answer. "You have never asked a woman for anything. The great Enkil, except for physical pleasures. I doubt you ever had to ask for that either. You certainly didn't bring me here for pleasures, did you?" His silence her answer. "Not with all the women you have in and out of your bed." Enkil's brown eyes smoldering with passion. Searching her eyes deeply, cautious, not sure how to proceed. Andor senses this hesitancy. Not his normal take charge or the stone faced stare he often used. Blocking out any emotion or feelings making him unreadable. This usually incites her anger further.

"This really is important to you. What is it?" Andor asks. Loving concern spreading across her beautiful face at least for just a moment.

Enkil, *She is worried about me.* Saying, "I need you to stop interfering with these two mortals' lives." *Her almond-shaped eyes beautiful as the day I met her.* Andor looks up at him. Her eyes hardening turning to an olive green. Looking petulant with her lips becoming pouty. Enkil realizes he did not ask her as an equal but told her.

"And why should I do that? Because you demand it of me?"

"Because I am asking you," Enkil says beseechingly to her. Not a man who admits he was wrong, at least not easily. Giving her pause again, ready to rip into him. Instead keeping her voice calm for that she took a page out of his play book. Using less emotion and more control.

"I have not had to obey a man in thousands of years. You already know that. So tell me why?" Stepping back from Enkil. A gust of wind stronger than a breeze right on cue blowing his hair into his eyes.

"It would be best for both of us." Enkil deciding how much he could tell her. His suspicions gnawing at him. Wouldn't it be just like karma? The children suffer the sins of their parents.

"Are you threatening me?" Her once beautiful eyes flashing to their true state. Angry red irises with those vertical pupils, marquise shaped, with the same coldness of stone. Now more like that of a snake. Her body becoming ethereal, vaporous. Summer's warm breeze dead still leaving the air humid and charged. Just as before a severe electrical storm.

"No! I am not threatening you." Trying to sound reasonable. "Why go to all the trouble of having you come to my home?" Enkil says.

Andor's ethereal form solidifying again. "I'm listening," she says.

"Those witches are using us mostly you now." Andor listens, waiting to pass judgment on what he says. Enkil continues, "They can no longer control me directly." Andor decides to give him as little as possible, but to affirm what he already knows.

"Angelique conjured me to deal with Camel's betrayals."

"He was under influence of a spell causing him to behave promiscuously. She conjured yours truly first." Indicating himself. "Have you not recognized the hand of witchcraft at work here?" Andor is unmoved so he continues. "Both of these young men have had changes wrought to them to promote this kind of behavior. Yes, they have acted less than honorable, but not solely by choice," Enkil says.

"Camel is still alive." Andor tips her head toward Enkil. "That Marc is not any better if but by a hair. He is not dead. They both still live because of your protection. Angelique is working to change that as we speak. What I have said isn't new information is it now? As if you do not already know." Enkil nods, he is aware of this.

"Have you considered for whom you are doing their bidding for? I mean seriously? A coven of evil and malevolent practitioners. That are subverting innocent young people to dark purposes."

"I am a vengeance demon," she says. Forcing her to examine the true intentions behind their call for revenge. But also putting to the forefront another interesting question. *What is his real interest in those two?*

"When did you become concerned about the young and innocent?" Her question hanging on "innocent." Watching Enkil's face and body for any tick of emotion. To give her the answers he is not giving her willingly. Enkil maintains a passive face without moving a muscle. Not even allowing himself to take a deeper breath. Lest his nostrils flare and chest rises. Leaving her unable to read him. Beginning to annoy her as he always did. "I have not destroyed either of them yet," Andor says. Not that she hadn't tried.

Enkil takes a different tactic. "What about those causing harm to an innocent?"

"I have never… rarely." Correcting herself. "Once or twice in centuries taken vengeance against a female. Women get most of the blame for everything." Enkil waits quietly for Andor to have her say. "A woman gets raped. Her character, her virtue are always called into question. She must have been asking for it, right? Camel was quite the ladies' man before," pausing to let her point have weight, "you occupied his physical form. Has anything changed?"

"The two are not one and the same," Enkil says.

"Do not toy with me. You know exactly what I am not saying," Andor says. While keeping her emotions in check. Her face stern but not angry.

"I am not trying to right all the wrongs of the past. Just to protect and make a few right," Enkil says.

"Men are just easier targets in these matters. They are always into something or somewhere they shouldn't be. So weak of the flesh. Wouldn't you say?"

Enkil does not take Andor's bait. "These two men are innocent. Mere pawns of intrigue and subterfuge started long before they were born. Most definitely beyond their control or abilities to recognize such traps. Certainly they were used as surely as any woman could have been through a devious male." Enkil's defense of their behavior.

"There is nothing innocent about those two or they would not be in this situation given their religious edicts. Would they now?" His brown eyes implore her. The air sultry, no longer stirring out over the garden. More like the quiet before a destructive storm. In that instant the wind whips around the trees and shrubs rocking them. Andor's eyes glowing red embers. "And you would certainly know about that." Andor taking a swipe at him regarding their past.

Enkil again does not take the bait. Keeping his face neutral before speaking. "Only this time it is the men who were not given a choice." All sound of happy chirping from half a dozen or so bird species silenced. Not even a squawk from the noisy blue jay family. Watching from the safety of cover inside a cypress. The air becoming heavier yet with humidity and white noise humming so very still as if to exemplify the seriousness of the moment.

Andor speaks, "I will consider this. I'm just not sure what you get out of it." Looking at him inquisitively, knowing Enkil is holding something back. Tossing her hair back causing it to ripple like a waterfall, long well passed her mid-back. Her hair dark and thick with her head turned to the side casually. Sure that she has Enkil's attention. Her olive complexion exquisite with delicate features and high cheekbones. A true Sumerian princess. A slight catch in Enkil's breath the response she was looking for. His eyes wandering over her incredible beauty again in how many days had he seen her? When before that it had been centuries and now the veils of time momentarily parted. To reveal the young woman he so loved.

Enkil clears his throat to regain the present. "It is nice not to be at odds with you," Enkil says. Blinking slowly his naturally dark long lashes those that some men can have giving Andor pause. A ruggedly masculine man's man. Patiently waiting for her response. Getting lost in those silver-green eyes of hers, before she answers him.

"Yes it is." The leaves of the jasmine vines rustle from the exhaled breaths blowing over old adversaries.

Enkil stalling to make their moment in time together last longer says, "Once they are done with you surely they will try to send you back."

Andor looks him straight in the eyes with her silver-green ones. So vibrant the color green overtaking the silver. Her charm and beauty powerful enough for a weaker man to lose himself. Thus allowing her to enslave him to his death. In the manner and time she so chooses.

Andor speaks thus allowing her glamour over Enkil to fade. But not without using the last tendrils of her energy force to caress him in places sensitive enough to evoke a shiver of pleasure.

"We both know it doesn't work that way. I come and go as I please. There are still some women in this world that worship me. A few would still let lose my powers for vengeance against an unfaithful male. Besides, right now I'm enjoying helping these 'women' take control of this 'situation.' As you would put it. Plus I like seeing the three of you squirm." Smiling playfully at Enkil. He starts to speak in protest. Raising her hand to silence him Andor says, "I will think of what you are requesting of me." Moving gracefully away from him. Her form shimmers as heat energy with silver sparkles dancing as a cluster of lightning bugs.

Nahadeina pushes open the French doors to the balcony. Carrying on a silver tray a platter of sliced fruit and ripe figs. Along with a pitcher of ice-cold lemonade. Clearing her throat to get Camel's attention. Which is still focused where Andor had been. Speaking to fill the quiet, "I thought a storm was coming up the way the wind was gusting. Before that it was the kind of sultry heat right before a strong storm." Her dark eyes wary at finding him alone. Placing the tray on the table with its setting for two.

"No it has passed." Enkil answers in his deep bass voice definitely not Camel's. Nahadeina blinks up at him covering her reaction to his voice. Her expression neutral.

"That is a shame sometimes you need a storm to bring the calm. Will there be anything else?" Nahadeina asks. Enkil is still thinking of Andor with her scent of perfume lingering in the air. "No, that will be all." Speaking his native Sumerian with his deep bass voice. Nahadeina holding her rising fear and suspicion in check.

Iman Hussein steps out onto the balcony. "I have some information for you." Speaking Arabic. Enkil indicates for him to take a seat with his outstretched arm.

"Nahadeina set a place for the holy man." Andor's perfume still lingering on him. "Are you hungry? I was just sitting down to eat." Nahadeina anticipating what would be customary for an esteemed guest. Placing a dish in front of Iman Hussein. Pouring him a glass of lemonade with ice chunks clinking against the heavy crystal glass. The iman quietly watches listening.

Enkil dismisses Nahadeina with a wave of his hand. "That will be all. You may leave."

Her eyes downcast subserviently. "Yes sir." Backing away off the balcony.

"Why are you so harsh today? Is something wrong?" Iman Hussein says.

"What do you mean?" Enkil's voice less deep but not quite his normal baritone.

Iman Hussein chooses his words carefully. "You seem not quite yourself today. You dismissed her like an emir of old would a slave."

Enkil speaks, "Why is this mere servant so important to you?" Sounding defensive.

"She's not. It was not my intention to disturb you at home like this. It is your business how you treat your staff," Iman Hussein says. "You made this information sound of an urgent nature. That is why I came unannounced."

Camel takes over. "What is that you have for me?" Sounding more ingratiating with his voice back to his baritone. The iman glances around them nervously. Wanting their conversation to be private. Camel observes this. "You may speak freely we are alone."

Iman Hussein speaking softly, "What I have found is from ancient texts. So old they are not written on papyrus but on clay tablets in cuneiform." The holy man pauses.

Enkil listens closely his attention focused, "Go on."

Iman Hussein, "It is of old legends. So I do not know how much to believe. Added to this, I have not worked with translating these ancient scripts in years. If it were not for the increased security because of al-Qaeda. I would have more access to help for this work. With that said, this is the best that I can decipher from the cuneiform script."

"The best that you can do is certainly appreciated," Camel says.

"Now there are references to a demon of old. For even the time these tablets were written." Enkil, *Great*. Speaking to Camel silently in his mind. *You two keep endangering more people*. Iman Hussein infers Camel's silence to mean to go on. "It is a female vengeance demon. Jealous wives or spurned lovers would call upon this thing. To seek revenge against men. Do you follow me?" Iman Hussein says.

Camel already hearing the sermon in his mind, *About living right*. "Yes. I get it, promiscuous husbands and lovers are the targets of that creature. Is there anything else you have learned?" He asks.

"No. That is as far as we have gotten. I have enlisted Professor Du Bois to help in the translations. He has been invaluable in helping me with this undertaking. As I have said, I have not worked with this language in decades." Camels expression one of concern. "However some of it is coming back to me." Camel nods his head causing his thick mane of dark hair to move in waves. Though it is not long at all. Iman Hussein continues, "You do realize most of this script has never been translated. It is a dead language that has been lost to time. Until the last century and most recently the last few years."

"May I have a look at what you have?" Glancing over the pages of cuneiform script copied and on faxed sheets of paper.

"Are you able to read this?" Iman Hussein asks.

"Uh, no. Not really. I have seen it around being from the peninsula (almost using the Sumerian name). It is on ruins and broken pieces in the sand. Has not anyone that is Arabian seen it?"

His eyebrows raised, Iman Hussein gives Camel a look before speaking. "I would say not. I do not believe that many people have seen them. You make it sound as though everyone from Iraq to Yemen can read cuneiform because it is so commonly found."

"Well, I just meant it was not that rare," Camel says.

"It would be more unusual if regular people were familiar with this. Now." clearing his throat, "There are some references to pages in private collections held in Saudi Arabia and of course in Baghdad's National Museum of Antiquities. Well, that is before it was looted a few years ago. A Professor Du Bois has been instrumental in helping me locate some of these. He has extensive contacts throughout the archaeological and ancient antiquities literati." Camel is still reading over the pages. Recognizing Andor's name with mention of a counterforce to drive her back into her human form.

"Where is the other page?" Camel asks.

"What do you mean the other page? That is all I have so far. You make it appear that you are reading these," Iman Hussein says.

Camel speaks to Enkil, *You need to let me out. You are going to make him suspicious.* "No. It's all confusing. I just thought there would be more pages." Camel says, trying to cover for Enkil's comment.

Iman Hussein, "That is all I have." Finding Camel's statement disturbing but not quite sure why. Enkil reaches out with his power sending discreet amounts of energy. As in micron sized, just enough to tickle lost electrons in Iman Hussein's brain. Altering beta waves, thus making him forget minute amounts of short-term memory. "I...," pausing for just a second forgetting what had made him uneasy moments earlier. Then resuming his thoughts. "I have asked your father to help by working through diplomatic channels of the United Arab Emirates. He has considerable clout so he is trying to get photocopies from the Saudi Arabian portions in private collections."

"My father?" Camel asks.

Iman Hussein, "Yes, your father is a great resource. He has many contacts being a structural engineer and architect. Having built many buildings on the peninsula as you young people like to call it these days. They always need someone from National Antiquities. You cannot dig a hole without finding some history. I'm surprised you didn't think to call him, or one of your brothers for that matter."

"It did not occur to me," Camel says. While thinking, *Not that I would call Ibram, my oldest brother. He is too critical. Then he always asks more questions than answers,* having nine brothers including Marc.

"It is always important to stay in touch with your family, especially your father," Iman Hussein says, smiling broadly. Camel lifts an eyebrow getting the hint to call his father.

"I had no idea this would lead to home and my father. If there is anything I can do to expedite the acquisition of this information just let me know. And thank you, I will call Father." Iman Hussein nods. "I should have call Father. It's been months since we have spoken. I am sure that is what my father told you," Camel says.

"Yes it was. He wants to hear from you. Not just when his wayward son needs money." Camel's cheeks turn dusky being put on the spot. Then laughing with one of those deep, rich masculine sounds, both men laughing. Fathers no matter how old could manage to move their sons. Iman Hussein says, "Fathers have a way."

"Yes they do," Camel responds.

"He also said it would be good if you settled down and gave him a grandchild," Iman Hussein says.

"Now I know you have been talking to Dad. You sound just like him. I'm not ready to settle down yet. Does he want me happy or married?" Camel says.

"How about a wife and children would make you both happy," Iman Hussein says.

Enkil speaks to Camel out loud, "That is true."

Iman Hussein, "Oh? Your father will be so excited." Camel speaks to Enkil, *You are just ganging up on me. Now he will be ready to start setting us up with nice Islamic girls. He can be a real yenta* "Before I introduce you to the women. You will need to meet a couple of fathers. For a proper introduction and of course chaperoned. Whom I am sure will find you suitable for their daughters."

"Wait! You are going a little fast here. Give me some time to get used to the idea," Camel says.

"You are already backpedaling. There is nothing to be afraid of. Every man eventually has to come to this decision." Camel looks at the iman dubiously.

"You are not the one giving up your freedom," Camel says.

"You are gaining a wife and then hopefully with Allah's blessings you will have children," Iman Hussein says.

Enkil speaks up, "First there is more important business to attend to before we start choosing a suitable wife to start a family."

"Yes of course you are right," Iman Hussein says. Then he continues, "These women you have been having sexual relations with must stop. They are the absolute worst sort. True infidels. Hiding behind Christianity and from some of the most powerful families in this country. They are dangerous. If what the two of you are saying is true."

"I am afraid so." Camel says.

"Manipulating demons laid to rest thousands of years ago. You must cut all ties and stay away from them," Iman Hussein says. Camel nods his agreement with that fact. "It is of the utmost importance that you do this." His bearded face normally calm showing fear.

"I'm in the process of doing just that, but I also have to be able to defend myself against them," Camel says, his expression grim.

"It has gone that far has it?" Iman Hussein asks. Neither men having disclosed the full story to their iman. "This power of evil has roots that reach back to a time of the magi," Iman Hussein says.

Camel answers with Enkil's input, "Before the time of the magi."

"I fear this has gone too far. An ecumenical council of the elders in Tehran may be needed to sort this out. There are not many who read this language. Much less know how to counter such power and practices," Iman Hussein says.

"Is that really necessary? To involve Tehran in American Islamic issues? This could turn into a scandal of international proportions," taking over, Enkil says.

"Would not the American archdiocese contact the Vatican with such epic news?" Iman Hussein says.

Camel speaks to Enkil, *Do not touch him. I can hear the direction your mind is heading.*

Enkil, *Then you already know me too well. You would do better to stay out of my thoughts. Lest I lock you away or maybe you need a taste of what I can do to you.* Camel finds himself surrounded in the deepest of darks. Solitude without any light. Like that of only a sub-basement can produce. Musky earth its scent filling his nostrils. Without his first two senses to get his bearing he stands frozen. Then feeling a heavy breath against his shoulder. Unafraid waiting for his would be assailant. Skilled as a mixed martial arts combatant his reflexes are above average from years of training. Preparing his muscles tensing and then centering. Still nothing but the hot breath blowing down his back. A challenge of nerves to see who defensive and which will be offense. Camel beginning to surmise his opponent is a seasoned fighter. Making his decision to strike first. Crouching slightly as he pivots kicking out expecting to make contact, but connection with air. His anger rising nerves getting the better of him. "What is the matter you afraid I'll kick your ass?"

Dim light front torches ignite. A heavy oak paneled door appears in front of him. Swinging open, the only light in the cavernous room. Beyond the door dozens of foul yellow eyes those of night creatures boring back at him unblinking and angry. Camel feels a rush of air to late as he skewered from behind by razor-sharp talons. Stabbing into his broad back and shoulders. Frozen in place with shock from the pain going zero to ten. Ten being severe enough to take his breath away. Taking in small breaths with little gasps. Unable to yell out his pain strong. His opponent a red skinned demon lifting his two hundred and forty pounds of muscle off his feet. Camel's finally producing a scream of agony cut short. Being thrown against the threshold then slamming into the ground knocking the air out of his lungs. Seeing lights as his head repeatedly strikes the stone of the ground beneath him. This thing upon him with its crushing weight. Stopping allowing him lying there with lungs burning from trying to pull in enough air. Pain numbing his consciousness but a fighter. He forces himself up onto his feet slowly by pushing his wet back against the wall through which the doorway passes. This time talons lacerate the front of his muscular chest. Managing to punch this thing in its face. A solid contact. Unable to stop himself from falling forward, too weakened from blood loss. Falling on to the stone floor. Grasping his upper body the demon slowly pushes its thumb talons into his back. One piercing where the scar of his recent stab wound had been, complements of Angelique. Then digging its large claw deeper into the muscle intentionally pushing aside nerve cords. Camel's pain now like electricity coursing through his body making the muscles on that side of his body jump wildly and uncontrollably. Stopping for just a millisecond he grabs onto the wood doorjamb. Unable to hold on with one hand his evil opponent rips loss. He falls backward through the threshold tumbling across stone and hard-packed earth. Being allowed to see the door growing distant. As he is dragged away from it. Surrounded by angry yellow eyes all now appearing to be hungry for meat. Fighting amongst themselves The red demon drags him over to the edge of a wide fissure. Dropped over its edge falling darkness engulfing him as he falls. At least he will not be alive when they eat him. One more physical insult his body smashes onto the jagged rocks shattering bones. into total despair and suffering. But not losing consciousness before his pain so strong, unconsciousness taking him.

"Are you listening to me?" Iman Hussein says to Camel. "I find all this unseemly. It goes against the teachings of the Koran. I can no longer participate in this."

Enkil speaks, "Yes you will." Reaching out in a comforting gesture placing his large hand on the man's shoulder. Wind rising up scattering the pages off the table as if on cue. Iman Hussein unable to move looks up at the taller man in terror. His body frozen. Fear rising up in his umbilical area squeezing his stomach so hard he can taste bile at the back of his throat. His eyes watching the cypress trees in their magnificence whipping in the wind. Knowing certain death is coming. Enkil's voice in his mind whispering Hittite a language the iman can recognize. His heartbeat pounding in his ears. Enkil speaks in Arabic using a tone soothing and hypnotic. "You are no longer afraid. You will not remember anything sinister. There is no need to contact the Supreme Religious council for a fatwa" Electrical activity altered in his memory centers, Iman Hussein forgetting. "I am so glad to have you helping me with these translations," Camel says.

"Uh, yes," says Iman Hussein appearing confused.

"I will no longer need your help with translations of the cuneiform script. You may just fax over to me any new data that professor Du Bois sends to you. No, better yet give him my fax number," Enkil says through Camel, punished for defying him.

"As you wish," says Iman Hussein. Camel removes his hand from his shoulder. Iman Hussein looks oddly at him.

"You looked faint for a second there. Is everything all right with you?" Enkil says, thinking quickly.

"Yes, yes. I don't know what came over me," Iman Hussein says.

"Perhaps you should go home and lie down, rest for a while," Enkil says.

"I believe you are right. I will do that. Go with Allah my son," Iman Hussein says as Camel stands for him to leave.

CHAPTER 89

ANGELIQUE IS STANDING in her spell room. Conjuring Andor to aid her with a small task in mind. Andor shimmers into a dark form with only her red irises visible with their reptilian pupils. Glaring back hotly at the witch she had begun to despise. Silent to allow her presence time to become more threatening. Angelique is unwilling or too obsessed to recognize the danger before her.

"I summoned you for a small favor. Something that you could do easily. While I could not do it with the finesse you are able to."

"What would that be? You find so trifling that I may perform. Wasting my time," Andor responds.

"I need to keep Camel and Marc apart."

"Why don't you just use one of your whores for that purpose?" Andor says.

"If only it were that simple I would." Andor watches her unmoved. "Well, very good. I need you to cause a mechanical problem for a jet. Something that will detain it for a few hours," Angelique says.

"Why not have one of your minions do this. I'm a vengeance demon powerful beyond anything you will ever achieve. Why should I want to do this?"

"Because it will frustrate Enkil," Angelique says, becoming impatient. "It was I who conjured you. So you will do as you were told without question." Andor is not the least bit threatened by her. Angelique feeling the need to bully Andor as she does her underlings, says, "I brought you forth. So I'm telling you to do it!" Those unblinking red eyes only watch her. Their only tale Andor's pupils narrowing into slits as some large carnivorous cat close to pouncing. The rest of her body frozen. A pin could have dropped and been noisy. Andor savors the moment; she realizes that killing this insipid witch will bring her enormous satisfaction. Her lips curving just slightly giving the appearance of contentment. Only her red irises gleaming with their pupils narrowed into vertical slits. The only movement she gives to her opponent. Angelique foolishly believing this to mean acquiescence, continues speaking. "I don't want anything left to chance. By some balls-out demon interfering." Referring to Enkil. Andor is debating whether to kill this witch now or go along with her for a little longer.

"As long as it tortures Enkil I'll be more than happy to do this," Andor says, moving closer to Angelique her decision made. Their faces within inches of each other. Both females staring each other in the eyes. Andor's ethereal form having become solid outside the protective circle. Since she was not charged inside of it. A serious mistake on Angelique's part, combined with a break in both circles of protection that wasn't there before. Andor challenges her coolly. Watching her blue eyes become rounder, smelling her fear. "If you ever speak to me that way again as some common servant I will kill you right where you stand." Angelique swallows, regaining her composure. "Are you clear on that?" Andor's eyes unblinking her human form gone a vaporous clouds of blackness with greys surrounding Angelique blocking out all light.

"Yes," Angelique manages to say coolly. Stone-face only now her pupils are rounded wide. Clinching her teeth and hands to keep from shaking. Angelique channels her anger back up. Attempting to keep her opponent from knowing she is frightened. Andor not only able to smell fear but hear it. Listening to her heartbeats quickening. Such a feeble attempt from a feeble witch. Encouraged by her weakness to want to kill her more now. Allowing herself to be satisfied for now. Her effect on Angelique will have to do. Andor shimmers from the room but not before sensing another presence, decidedly human. Eavesdropping from behind the door.

Melinda pushes the door open slowly not too quietly. In time to see her teacher's mask down. Fear showing in her eyes.

"Can I help with any of the preparations?" Glancing around the room inquisitively. Melinda's facial expression one of satisfaction. Gone when she turns back to her taskmaster, or as Jadon liked to call her, "The Khan." Angelique's face already resuming its insanely angry expression with those round bulging eyes. Scorched by her crass invasion into what should have been a private work. Let alone appearing after a grave mistake combined with Andor's complete disrespect of her.

"Yes you can be of service." Melinda not liking her dig. "Come." Walking out of her darkened spell room. Moving on her five-inch stilettos as if she was born to them. Angelique whips back the black silk fabric covering her scrying mirror. The Louis XVI mirror with its bows carved from wood surrounding it. "Watch and learn young one." Angelique says, pushing her blonde hair back. Having recovered in all appearances. Visibly concentrating on her scrying mirror. Its surface rippling before she speaks. "Samir I need you, come forth."

At once a very handsome male's image comes into focus. His black mustache thick, dark brown eyes intelligent and piercing. Moving closer to his mirror.

His accent Lebanese, "*Moi bella,* bon jour. This could not have waited?" Melinda is enjoying the view from her angle. Samir's shirt open at the collar. A crush of black hair pushing out at the neck. Chest muscles bulging beneath the white cotton fabric. Much shorter than Marc or Camel. Every bit as masculine and handsome. If not more attractive than both younger men. Made more so by his man of thirty-something appearance, definitely not a boy.

"No," Angelique says.

"What is it you want?" Samir asks.

"I need a favor from you." Samir waits for her to continue. "I need a jet brought down. But it can't be obvious that magic was behind this. It must appear as mortal in design," Angelique says.

Samir smiles, his dimples making his face more handsome, if that was possible. Showing perfect white teeth beneath a large dark mustache neatly trimmed. Surmising what she was looking for.

"So you want by design what presents as an accident? Something from human actions causing the destruction of an airliner? Hum. Say, religious extremists? You know it's not that easy anymore. The Americans and Europeans are all over airport security these days," Samir says.

"Can't you just activate a sleeper cell or something? I don't care whether jihadist or right-wing Christian. Just as long it's taken care of." Angelique says.

"Any particular place you want this jet to go down." His question veiled, as if this was sending a message.

"No. I don't care." Then an idea forms. "Yes, on second thought why not." She smiles cruelly. Melinda knows that expression shuddering inside. How many need die to get her message across?

CHAPTER 90

LATER THAT EVENING Camel's older brother Ibram calls. He speaks his English with an Oxford accent. Being a successful cardiologist medically trained in Great Britain. Now has a large practice in Dubai. Having never been too impressed with his younger brother Camel's antics and brushes with the law.

"I'm calling to inform you that our father is in the hospital. Dubai General in guarded condition," Ibram says without waiting for the usual greetings.

"What happened to him? Is he all right?" Camel says in panic mixed with fear.

"I said he was in guarded condition." Taking a breath. "He is doing poorly. It was a myocardial infarction to the septal wall with atrial flutter as a result," Ibram says in his usual condescending tone.

"What did you just say? I'm not studying medicine." Camel says.

Ibram sighs bigger this time before answering. "He has had a heart attack and because of that is having dysrhythmia." Adjusting himself. "Rhythm problems that cause blood clots. Dr. Shah, his cardiologist has put him on a streptokinase drip. He is going to need a quadruple bypass."

"How could this happen? He has been healthy as a horse," Camel says.

"Yes, but his diet is high in fat. I reviewed his last echo-cardio. It did not demonstrate any blockages at the time. A blood clot can happen anytime. The other reason I called is because he is asking for you. Allah's name be praised if anything happened to him before you get here. You would feel so guilty. At least I would." Ibram says.

"I will be there as soon as I can, Allah willing." Camel says.

"I have already contacted the corporate jet. They are gassing up as we speak preparing for departure as soon as they get clearance. They will pick up the two of you." Meaning Marc also.

"It is good to hear from you. Even if it is a time of crisis for our family." Camel says.

"Yes it has been a while." his older brother says being more reserved. "Maybe now you will consider working for the family business. Assuming Father lives, he would be delighted to have his wayward son working for him. He has always wanted you there." Ibram says, not missing a chance to twist the knife of guilt in his brother's gut. Camel put off by Ibram's comment. The twinge of guilt right on target.

"Yes, well, I look forward to discussing that more when I'm there in person." Camel says. His eyes flashing to yellow and angry, his voice deepening. Ibram unfazed by his brother's threat or tone.

"I will see you soon." *Click*. Their call disconnecting before Camel can say more. Feeling his brother's disapproval of his choices. Not seeing behind it that Ibram was jealous. Camel was always their father Omar's favorite son.

Calling up Marc to apprise him of their father's condition. Marc answers on the first ring. "Hello." Concern in his voice.

"It's me. I have some grave news," Camel says.

"It can't be worse than mine," Marc says.

"Why? What has happened? Are you all right?" Camel asks. Too many bad things are going on.

"It's not me. It is cousin Phil. He is dead." Camel is quiet in stunned silence.

"How?" His only word. Now more bad news.

"It was a freak accident, lightning struck his home. While he was on the phone." Marc's anger simmering.

"Do you really believe that was just an accident?"

"No, but that is the official report. He was calling me to warn us. So what news do you have that is grave?" Marc asks.

Camel swallows. "Dad is in the hospital. He has had a heart attack. It's a bad one. Ibram called and is sending the jet for us." Marc feels the stab of grief for a second time. Ahmed is like a father to him also. Their silence allows each other time to take in the bad news. Ahmed had always treated him as one of his own sons. Encouraging religious and academic education.

"How soon are you leaving?" Marc says.

"Tomorrow sometime at least twelve hours from now give or take. How soon is the funeral?" Camel says.

"Tomorrow, I will know more later tonight or in the morning. I wish I could go with you." Marc says.

"I could send the jet for you," Camel offers.

"No that is okay. I will use a commercial airline. Is everyone else there already?" Meaning their other brothers and his sisters still living on the peninsula. All married to well off men, except Aziza, the youngest daughter of Ahmed. From his third wife in Sudan. Aziza still living in Dubai but in her own apartment very strong willed. A modern Muslim woman refusing to get married until after she finishes college. Secretly active for female rights. Defiant to the end sometimes refusing to cover her hair and face.

"Are you listening to me?" Camel says.

"I'm sorry the funeral services are tomorrow. I just received a text from Paul, cousin Phil's friend there in New Orleans." Camel not able to shake the feeling stunned by more bad news.

"I cannot believe he is gone. He was always the kid brother in a way."

"I know, a tagalong. We were always stuck with having to watch out for him." Marc says.

"He was a magnet to trouble. Keeping him out of harm's way was a full time job." Camel says. His jaw set teeth clinched for the wave of grief. Refusing to let it hurt more. "Please give his partner Paul my deepest sympathy. Let him know if I could be there to show my respect I would. You know that." Camel adds.

"I will. Paul will understand. After the funeral services I'll be on the next flight out that I can manage to get on." Marc's eyes misty with unshed tears. His throat tight and hurting from choking back grief.

Camel gives him a second before asking him, "Are you all right?"

"Do I have a choice?" Marc says.

"Don't you think the timing on all this is a little to extraordinary?" Camel says.

"Without a doubt. Our families were threatened and now this happens. We were warned. I'm just sorry it went this far so fast." Marc says.

"Could?" Camel not wanting to say it. "Could Dad be in the hospital because of me?" Managing to speak through his tightening throat grief its cause. Marc not answering him. That in itself his answer. Knowing his brother too well. That he would blame himself for what has happened to his dad. His own anger and frustration growing over their situation worsening by the day. "I spoke with Iman Hussein. He enlisted your father's help in finding the clay tablets we need." Camel says.

"My father?" Marc says with surprise. "I had not thought he would involve himself in our problems of poor judgment."

"He does not know that the translations along with the data is for us." Camel says. "Oh, and by the way, Iman Hussein was going to go to the ecumenical council in Tehran."

"What? This just keeps getting worse." Marc's alarmed voice loud. Camel pulling the phone away from his ear.

"Don't worry. Once he voiced his intentions Enkil erased part of his memory." Camel says.

"This keeps getting worse. Is there anything else?" Marc says.

"Nothing more than we already plan to do. Iman Hussein said we need to disengage ourselves from that coven. Otherwise these sort of tragedies would keep happening to us." Camel says.

"It's good he is able to see that." Marc says

"What he will remember of that is another story." Camel says.

"That probably is the best for us."

"Did you learn any more from Phillip?"

"He had completed the translations of Uncle Theron's grimoire and was in the process of faxing them to me. He called me to let me know what he was doing. I heard his last word.," Marc says. His throat tightening up so much it hurts. Holding back his grief unable to speak. Camel hears in the silence his brother's grief.

"We won't let his death be in vain. Enkil has read what was on the tablets. He knows who this demon is." Camel says.

"Are you sure?" Marc says.

"Oh yes. I am pretty sure they have a past together." Camel says.

"Really?" Marc's interest piqued "What sort of past as in relationship?"

"Not with such a good ending. She hates him." Camel says.

"She? Why does that not surprise me. How do you know this?" Marc says.

"He can't keep everything blocked from me. They were in love and when it was over the earth was scorched beneath their feet." Camel says.

"I have more news. Mom called me from Bolivia, South America." Marc says.

"Is she all right?" Camel asks.

"For now. She called to warn us after an apparition threatened her. Before you ask I don't know. The satellite connection was interrupted before she could finish. But knowing a lot more about the Du Bois family history. She said we have to protect ourselves." Marc says.

"More importantly our families, our loved ones." Camel says.

"They are using basic battle strategy to divide and conquer." Marc says while pushing his long hair out of his face. Grazing his hand against the thick stubble along his jaw.

"Will she be all right?" Camel asks.

"Mother is quite adept at taking care of herself. I have come to find out." Marc says.

"Yes?" Camel says, looking for more of an explanation.

"It is a story for Dubai. When we have more time. I will fill you in on some interesting facts about the Du Bois family history," Marc says.

"Sounds goo.," Camel says.

"In the meantime how do we stop them?" Rising frustration in his voice.

"We will." Camel says. His irises changing to yellow along with his voice deepening.

“Very soon I will have an ally to help me. This trip to Arabia could not come at a more opportune time.” Enkil says,

“What just happened?” Camel says.

“Enkil spoke he has an ally on the peninsula. You did not hear him?” Marc says.

“No. It is getting more difficult for me to come back into control. I fear I will loss myself.” His handsome face worried.

CHAPTER 91

AT THE SAME time, over at Angelique's home herself and Melinda are working another spell.

"Andor has been next to no help for reconnaissance with her vision being blocked by those two halfwits," Melinda says.

"Someone is teaching them white magic. She cannot see through all of the protective barriers." Angelique says frowning. Melinda follows her response appearing unhappy. "You on the other hand." Melinda feeling a sense of dread catching in her chest, "you are an absolute delight." Angelique says.

Melinda is smiling with relief. "Thank you."

"That was a touch of genius. To give Ahmed, Camel's father a little push. A blood clot. How unexpected yet subtle." Angelique says, giving Melinda a compliment.

"I'm yours to serve you." Melinda says.

"And well you do. Unlike that Turkish traitor." Angelique says.

"How appropriate, using an old way of dealing with a witch." Melinda says.

"Sometimes the old ways are still the best (meaning drowning).

"Once you are past your apprenticeship in a hundred years or so, you will start your own coven. Under my guidance of course." Angelique says.

"Absolutely." Melinda says.

"Do not overdo it there. A good leader doesn't want an ass-kissing sycophant. She wants a good soldier who can make good decisions without her. Am I clear on that?" Angelique's blue eyes icy and unblinking, looking into Melinda's.

"Yes." Melinda answers, not hiding her anger well. Finally making her face a neutral mask. While her thoughts are not so neutral. *Over a hundred years with this shrew of a witch. I think not. I will be away from her long before that happens.*

Angelique already speaking, "That is more like it. I want you to recruit that Evangelical from Montgomery. Such a beautiful young woman, blonde, with those deep blue eyes and an angel's face. She will be priceless, a natural villainess. Men will never see her coming until it is too late."

Melinda daring to ask, "Sara?"

"Yes of course. Were you not listening? Her family background alone would make her invaluable. So versed in scriptures, combined with an angelic face and rosy cheeks. Her skin so dewy. She has you beat for appearing innocent. Plus I bet she knows the Bible as well as any preacher." Angelique says.

"Her family does have strong roots in the church." Melinda says, ignoring the insult. Her jealousy aroused.

"Unimpeachable if you will," Angelique says. Smiling slyly, remembering her business deal in what was it, 1988? Dearest Monica Lewis. That was good for a hundred million dollars paid to the coven funds. A quite tidy sum for seemingly innocuous work behind the scenes. Poor girl, just not that bright, but when did a whore ever have to be intelligent? Just do what you are paid to do and not that well. Actually very cheaply. Only 2.3% of that amount. He was so easy, ripe for the scandal. It was like being paid twice. Once the conservatives got in office. Money well spent. *Right, boys?* "Yes, she will go far with an impeccable background and family. Who would ever think, let alone believe, with her hellfire and brimstone sermons. She could be playing for the other side, a dark witch. Only too good to be bad. Seeing why Camel and the other men were so easily seduced by her charms. Her comely face, beautiful and sensuous body." Angelique says, feeling content.

Melinda swallows her pride venturing cautiously. "This would be a good time to put the brimstone to the fire, don't you think?"

"Yes it's time to finish the summoning." Angelique says.

"Don't we need thirteen?" Melinda says, unable to keep an excited waver out of her voice. Knowing she would be asked to participate in this powerful summoning. Angelique irritated by her thinly veiled desire. Glaring at her as if she was some annoying and insipid child. Her lips stretched thin from her obvious displeasure.

"You will allure and seduce, use whatever wiles you have to bring Marc here. He will be the thirteenth." Her words sharp and insulting. Said as if she was some common Lyell Avenue whore. Melinda flushing with anger; never has anyone gotten away with treating her like that. Forcing herself to ignore the insult. Choosing instead to find a way to make it work for her. Just a glimmer of hope sparkling in her eyes. Hiding it quickly to prevent her face being read too easily. Allowing her hope to be followed by lust crossing her face. Masking her true feelings. Angelique reading her face oh so well, speaks. "You pathetic girl. Samir would not give you a second glance. You are not in his league. Certainly not enough power and what little you have is not focused. That will take a couple of centuries for you."

Melinda's cheeks flush with anger. "I am strong!" She says. Not loud but strong enough to be threatening. Angelique looks at Melinda in a new light. Glaring with eyes round with psychotic rage. Her blue eyes icy like the blue of glaciers, beautiful but deadly. Willing to kill at a moment's chance to have her way this time. No one would stop her. Calming herself for she still has need of Melinda's talents.

"I need the strongest witches for this to work. That is why the elders are coming. Only those few of us who can control their powers are needed for this to work. Marc with his familial blood ties' potency rivaling that of a djinn with powers unimagined. Then and only then will I ensure that the soul I'm intending to bring back will be amongst us again. That's right. The soul I am after has to be torn from the very cull, manifesting it here on earth again." Her words carrying so much power, shaking the house to its very foundations and into the earth. Triggering seismographs, making a pulse for a split second of ink jumping across their pages. Swaying wine in glasses at the lakefront estates. Melinda in quite awed from the amount of energy Angelique must have pulled off the earth to do that.

CHAPTER 92

"THANK YOU FOR being so understanding. Just meet me at Dad's. Ibram has already arranged for a driver to pick you up at Dubai International Airport. Besides, everyone is expecting you to be there. I know Aziza is looking forward to seeing you." Camel says.

"She is just a kid." Marc says.

"Actually she is not. She has grown into a beautiful dark-skinned woman just like her mother and as willful." Marc not surprised by this development.

"Aziza all grown up imagine that. She was always our second tagalong." Marc says.

"Dress accordingly." Meaning wearing robes, heads covered, use of tribal colors. As Marc is one of the family not needing to be told.

"Are the phone numbers the same?" Marc asks.

"Yes, well dads are. I'm not so sure about anyone else's," Camel says.

"You really have been out of touch for a while, haven't you?" Marc says.

"Like you stay in contact with everyone." Camel's tone defensive.

"That's not a criticism. Just an observation. We have both been busy with college and life." Massively understating their predicament.

"I'm sorry. Speaking with Ibram always puts me on the defensive. He already started that whole issue of me working for the family architectural firm, with the same old grind. Implying that I'm Dad's favorite and what a disappointment I have become. Unmarried and without grandchildren to show for." Marc lets him vent. He is a successful cardiologist, with clientele from Europe, India, even the royal family of Saudi Arabia. To name a few of his patients.

'"Yes, I've heard Prince Laden came to him a few years ago." Marc says.

"You would think he would not have gone into medicine if he so wanted dad's favor." Camel says, letting out a big sigh. Ibram always could make him feel guilty.

"Take a couple of deep breaths." Marc says to Camel. "This is not the time to let him get to you. We both have to put aside our family differences. Dad is too important to all of us."

"I know, he just knows which buttons to push. I try to be nice, ignoring his little comments but he just doesn't let up." Camel says.

"We are in a many sided war now. I have been getting dumped on from all sides. We have to be the stronger ones in this and take it, within reason. Do not let him get to you. You know he is jealous." Marc says.

"I know, I know. We have to put aside our differences for the sake of our families." Camel says.

"This is our last year of college. I would not be so quick to turn down an apprenticeship at Jalar. It is well known in Europe and Africa, not to mention across the peninsula. What would Dubai be without her modern landmark buildings? Jalar was there to set the trend for the new millennia by designing skylines, not just skyscrapers." Marc says.

"I have not ruled Jalar out. I am leaning toward accepting a position with them. What about you?" Camel says.

"I wouldn't mind going back. It's certainly more of a home than Rochester, with its grey overcast skies all the time. I might even see my dad once in a while." Marc acknowledges.

"The demand for architects who speak Hindi grows higher with each passing year. So much of the labor force is coming from there." Camel says.

"That is true. Namaste." Marc says.

"Hold on, what about Cantonese?" Camel says Marc agreeing with him. The need for speaking Chinese was rising faster. Then speaking to Nahadeina, "Put those in my carry-on bag." Camel says.

"I should let you go so you can get ready. That and I have not even started packing and my flight is in a couple of hours." Marc says.

"All right." Camel says.

"Keep me posted. If there are any changes, I want to know right away." Marc says.

"I will. Go with Allah my brother," Camel says.

"And you also." Marc says.

"Be careful, the sisterhood are very devious." Camel says. His own feelings of concern rising. Something is not right, but he just can't put his finger on it. Not wanting to concern Marc, so keeping it to himself.

"I will be, Brother."

After getting off the phone Marc cannot help but feel he should have said more to Camel. His own sense of warning tightening the muscles at the back of his neck. That with a feeling of loneliness. Already missing his brother. Sitting with the stillness of the house ringing in his ears. Pushing his full, dark hair, regrown to well down his muscular back. Knowing as long as he is cursed his haircuts won't last but for a short time. It will grow back only too quickly. Frightening his Arabian family or anyone else that knows him. Having always kept it cut short. What a difference they would find. Looking at him, the boyish innocence gone from his eyes. The face of a man now, with youthful curves changed to angular edges, handsome. Deciding he would need to tie his hair back to make it less obvious at a glance that it was so long. Ironic having something so basic and physically pleasing to females and all without an effort. Not that it would be a source of much attention with all of the restrictions and cautions he would be forced to bear. Almost like a female now, unable to live by the double standard that men are afforded. Unless he risked the curse, taking his life with every amorous encounter. What would others think of him? Zealot or believer?

Putting his earbuds, using music to relax to. Attached to his cell phone ringing almost immediately. Not bothering to check the incoming caller's identity. Assuming it had to be his brother calling back with some forgotten details. Marc pressing receive on his cell phone.

Speaking his tone playful. "What did you forget?" Assuming it was Camel.

"I didn't forget about you. Or how much I have missed our sessions." So very breathy, her voice. Catching Marc off guard. "Why haven't you called me back?" Melinda using her bedroom voice, so feminine, caressing his senses. Causing him to have trouble focusing.

"Besides destroying my life. What is it you want?" Marc says.

"I would never do anything to harm you. Why would you say such a thing?" Melinda's voice soft and breathy, her sensuality flowing over him. His better judgment yelling in his mind, *Hang up! Hang the phone up!* Too late, finding himself unable to do just that. Much less concentrate on keeping safe from her wiles.

"Oh, I don't know." Marc struggling to speak against her. "The spell you put on me has left changes. That will mark as deeply as any scars ever could." He finally gets out.

"Spell? I did nothing you did not allow me to do. You only allowed out the chord of your true self. Enabling us to make love with free ardor as it was intended. Did you not enjoy our hours of bliss? Each of us giving freely to another, ourselves." Melinda's voice melodious as a naiad, weaving her words skillfully, an adept enchantress her true gift. Tugging at Marc into enthrallment. Memories of their lovemaking to fill his mind. Her words as hands caressing, moving over his body physically. Pushing her natural energy field out, surrounding him as a gossamer blanket would. Intense, this energy flowing over his own aura into basal red chakra and next the orange one. Marc already having lost touch with common wisdom. His body heat radiating from the red chakra. Readily shedding his clothes, so heated with arousal, uncomfortably hard. Standing in all his male magnificence, muscle straining against the very air itself. His breaths shallow and fast with only one thing on his mind.

Struggling against Melinda's enthrallment over him, Marc finds his voice. "No! You would change me into some beast for slaughter." His words coming out in panting breaths. Having one last vestige of mental strength from the maternal line of the Du Bois side.

Melinda's voice soft and innocent as a child's. "I could never harm you. I might be a little jealous, but that is your fault."

"My fault?" Marc says. Regaining some ground.

"Yes. You tortured me, allowing me to see other women with you." Melinda says.

"Look, you said we should see other people and did." Marc says. Using his anger as a rock to hang on. Dangling out there from some high crag without a safety line. To lose his grip now would mean sure death. He would never recover this time. Knowing they would use him until a knife cut his throat, as any goat is drained during slaughter. Giving his mind a chance to focus. Her ethereal caressing diminishing, allowing his head to clear further.

Melinda sensing she is losing her control over him, grasps at her chance. "Can we at least meet, somewhere neutral? Perhaps near you. Then we could talk about this." Her voice feminine, so soft and hypnotic. Marc feeling himself being pulled back under her spell. Becoming light-headed and confused. Why was he angry with her? Finding himself wanting to see her. His pulse quickening with renewed heat flushing over his face. Making his cheeks dusky. Those dark blue eyes of his almost black the pupils so round. Running his hand down his chest pelt every bit of it as thick and fine as a black llama mink. All the way down to where it becomes course, as males are. The lone ring on its gold chain, his hand having just passed it. Protection so close but missed because it was buried deep in thick fur. Rubbing his hand back up his chest fur absently. This time his hand brushing against that very ring. Causing it to send out a burst of protection, radiating out around his aura. Affording him a chance to be reminded to put it on.

Melinda herself missing being stretched by him. Asks herself, was she really doing this as much for Angelique as she was for herself? One last time, a good-bye. Once again she was forced to think about why. Why was she the one always giving something up? Socially Marc was a good match, money connections, breeding, Islam aside. She could have lived with that flaw. After all, she was a Wasp. At least publicly. Every couple had a few secrets, right?

Marc's deep baritone voice soothing and very enticing. Using his curse-given abilities on her. To distract females into seduction as satyrs are known to do. Since sliding on his blue-purple tanzanite ring, sparkling, his eyes focusing with the mind clearing out. Concentration returning so strongly as it were with laser point precision, determined to crush her enchantment over him.

"I know what you and your group are. Infidels." Marc says. Sounding more like an old iman. Melinda snapped out of his ardor over her.

"And what is it you know?" Her voice acid.

"You are witches." His voice venomous with disgust. Melinda begins to laugh at him. Her tone becoming bitter and evil. Making the hair on his arms rise up. His anger for having been such a fool. To ever have believed she was anything more than vain, preoccupied with material possessions.

"We were just a means to an end. Man toys for you to use and then destroy." Melinda laughs heartily, taking great delight in Marc's misery.

"Right you are. All too easy. The Arabian boys of Islam, naive to the point of stupidity," Melinda says. Then she adds, "You had a chance, you should have used it. Now I know what strength you have in those satyr abilities." Speaking with her most educated accent-less American English.

Marc angry to the point of being incensed, says, "That would make me no better than you. I won't let you succeed!"

"We already have. You might as well roll over like some big dumb dog. So I can scratch your stomach. You should be careful or you just might get fleas. Then your master would have to keep you chained outside." Melinda saying just what she knows will insult and hurt Marc. Infuriating him into letting his guard down. Using renewed effort, she channels all the recently derived energy from other recent unwitting male victims she can muster into her renewed attack on him.

"Marc, I will give you my body with its warmth. You need release, I can feel you aching for my soft caresses against skin so taut, it weeps for my touch. Come to me anywhere of your choosing." Melinda's voice breathy, sensuous, and somehow melodic. Beginning to chant, no longer speaking English. Using a language long dead. Marc's eyes glazing over with deep lust the heady kind. His blood rush joining mind and groin; no amount of warning will separate the two. *She is doing it again.* Marc recognizing her attack. Fighting back mentally against her enthrallment, struggling to hold on. He unconsciously sets his angular dark-shadowed jaw in strengthening his resolve. Instinctually seeking the only things left to save him. Grabbing on to childhood memories of Camel with his other brothers. Their father and cousin Phil. This last two bring on a strong emotion, one of the strongest. Love being one of the most powerful of the emotions, releasing endorphins, spreading over his mind. Combined with happiness, his fond memories of those family members giving him the strength to overcome her bewitching. Marc's tanzanite ring sparkling with a fire from within it, gaining brightness as he gathers strength. His mother's words come to mind clearly as she was in the room.

"You have the power to fight them. It is all around you."

"I will come to you there. Where we have made some incredible passions beyond our dreams." Her words whispering across Marc's flushed cheeks, caressing him as though hands were rippling down his body. Sending rushes of delight down his spine into the primordial base chakra, tugging at him. Until his hard body is uncomfortably ready. His satyr within howling for release. In desperation, it shows him the runes of his more distant European past. Those before Christianity destroyed and demonized a decent practice. Intussusception spreading into his frontal lobes. Centers of written language, the runes for north, east, south, west. A circle of sea salt pouring out in a circle around them. Marc instinctively knowing this is a way for protection. Marc kneels facing east, beginning a prayer. Melinda realizing her endeavor is not working, uses a verbal trigger that was implanted during a highly suggestible state.

She whispers, "Listen to me. Veni, vidi, vici!" Using Caesar's famous words.

Marc yells in Arabic, "I will not listen to any more!"

Marc tearing out his earbuds. Melinda screaming at him. Using her rage to build energy before projecting it at him, to burn him. If he won't be under her control, then he will know pain. Releasing it at him. Marc remembers the ancient phrase, "As above, so below." Bowing his head to the floor in prayer, humbling himself before Allah. His eyes closed, not seeing energy skittering across the invisible protective sphere surrounding him. Its colors like that of the aurora borealis, greens and with electric blues streaking over just out of reach. Growing in intensity with Melinda's anger, mirrored by her attack on him. Sparks blue-white in color popping and crackling as her energy strikes against the once invisible sphere of protection. A static charge increasing with electrical potential to kill.

The hair on Marc's head floating up and out along with his chest pelt. Standing up straight out from his body. His hackles forced to rise, giving him that uncomfortable sensation. The cord to his earbuds stretching out taut before they are pulled free, shorting out. Picking up on a sensation, Marc feels a tremor begin to vibrate the hardwood floorboards. Its source not that of the hundred and fifty year old house. Solid with the earth having settled into the ground years ago as the original architect had intended. That of its source from the vicious inhuman attack against him. Soon to be more than a few but to become many over a lifetime. From a power so old written in cuneiform scripts on clay. Those lost to thousands of years of human wars. Leaders always so righteous in their conquests destroying older civilizations before them. Crushing their pasts before armies.

Marc's understanding and faith stronger than ever with Islam. His faith having protected him. Lying prone on the floor naked as the day he was born.

Slowly rising up to his knees. He would take his newfound insight, though at its infancy, with him into life.

Asking himself the question, *What were these pagan rites from old Europe, rooted long before Christianity?* Yet himself firmly entrenched with Islam now. Silence of his domicile ringing in his ears. Melinda's presence no longer there. She had failed yet again. Giving him a moment of satisfaction before caution, the better side of valor intercedes. He listens with an increased sense of hearing as any creature of the forest would. Another side effect of the curse, more acute hearing. Listening for any intruders, hearing only the sound of gear sprockets rhythmically coming together. Their source that of the stately grandfather clock from Vermont, built in 1730. Banging out the time of 10:00 p.m. Snapping Marc out of his silent reverie.

Jumping up from the floor, yelling, "No!" in grief. Phil's funeral is tomorrow. Anguish mixed with the pain of loss. This changing to a numbness dulling his feelings. Stepping out of the sea salt circle, his only light that of a solitary candle. Long having burned until its wax is pooled on the octagonal tabletop. Just enough light to cast long shadows across the library. Where the real nightmares began. Using his hand behind the flame to shield the table from more wax. Blowing out its lone candle in one quick breath. The splatter of hot wax not a bother to his calloused hand.

Marc chooses to use the main staircase, making a last minute check of the security alarm system. Yes, it needed to be activated. A wonder it didn't go off after everything that just happened. Moving methodically up the main staircase appreciating its beauty, a pied-à-terre. Every part as satisfying to view as a woman's legs in six-inch stilettos. Moving up the stairs with only exterior light from the large wrought iron chandelier of the porch. Shining through stained glass windows on each side of the heavy double doors. A craftsmanship achieving an elegance no longer found. Especially in the newer houses.

Marc unhurried moves up the stairs feeling as though a great weight had been lifted from his shoulders. Never mind he was still nude, clothes rolled into a bundle under one arm. Finding humor in the moment. If anyone looked in the windows, wouldn't they get a surprise. A muscular male with only a vest on and no other clothes. Nutty rich people. That is probably what it would look like at first glance, a fur vest; he is so very hirsute. Letting out a laugh. Oh well, after all, it was his home. He could do what he wanted in it now. It finally did feel like home.

After getting into the bathroom dumping his clothes on the floor. In need of a shower and a shave plus to save time for tomorrow morning.

Marc calls out, "Shower on, temperature ninety degrees, rainfall, light blue." Water comes on from the shower at ninety degrees. He steps under the rainfall setting. Blue lights glowing in the background. Standing under the water with both his hands pressed against the marble wall for support. Just letting it drench his hairy body, trying to relax. Finding it difficult to do. Though soothing, the water falls like a Southern summer shower. His thoughts keep returning to Melinda, and if not her, then other women. Flashing through his mind, causing him to respond as only a red blooded male could. Angered by his own physical weakness, arousal. Changing the shower jets. "Sharp spray." That with the increased PSI hitting him from multiple directions. "Maximum velocity!" Commanding. Water pounding against his thick hair first, then skin to get to the muscles beneath. Finishing with a water temperature of forty-five degrees. Completely ineffective in diminishing his heightened state of arousal.

After shaving, Marc's towel low slung, just hanging on his hips. It drops to the marble floor. Turning sideways to examine his back in the mirror. Unbelievable, looking like a thunderbird rock glyph except in black mink. How lasting are the side effects of this curse? Not seeing any changes since Jadon helped him end the spell. In doing so giving her life. What a tragic ending for a young woman. Not wanting to dwell on what could have been. If she hadn't been on the evil side.

Still the ever present Thunderbird tee of dark mink shoulder to shoulder, then running down his spine. His front the same as well. His broad chest covered, ending at the shoulders, then going all the way down in a wider band. Over rippling muscles of the abdomen still notable.

Shaking his head in disbelief. Will he be marked for life physically by this encounter with evil? His transgression into Western society. No. Not its society, but the inherent evil that can blossom into insatiable power of individuals left unchecked by God. Splashing on Tommy Hilfiger, burning, to take the sting out of shaving. Another archaic ritual still perpetuated—shaving, that is. He still takes two towels and a blow-dryer to get his body almost dry. Padding out of the bathroom over to the Chippendale highboy, circa 1730 New England, with broad curving feet on it. Pulling on a pair of boxer shorts. Dressing summer casual to go out for a bite to eat. Hunger forcing him out of the safety and comfort of home. Selecting a short-sleeved blue silk shirt and a pair of khaki Dockers with brown deck shoes. No socks. Marc unaware of how the blue in his shirt brings out the dark sapphire blue in his eyes. Nor that the ring of protection's tanzanites are glowing lightly again with red sparkles.

Debating whether to go to the valley by Panorama Trail, one of those restaurants there. Wanting a taste of some New Orleans food. Maybe it would be safer to eat near home. Staying farther away from Pittsford. Plus he was having craving for some home cooked food. Like Nahadeina would prepare. Since she hadn't been around for a few days. Deciding on Aladdin's Oasis restaurant. Mediterranean food would be good. Marc very sure Nahadeina is being kept busy with Camel's big appetite these days. So it would be a well-deserved rest for her while he is out of town. Choosing Aladdin's Oasis, which is closer to home, maybe not safer. Then he could have foods seasoned the way he was accustomed. Craving goat or lamb, his mouth almost watering. Setting the alarm system before exiting the side door. Noting that the protective charm was still in place around it. Preventing non- physical intruders from entering through the threshold.

Marc climbs into his '68 Mustang turning over the engine with a healthy rumble. Satisfied with the sound, turning around with his large arm draped down the side of the bucket seat, backing out one of five garage bays. Looking around for a sound made so softly he was not sure it was actually anything to be concerned over. Accelerating down the driveway turning east unconsciously. This time hearing the sound again, now with a sensation of mild euphoria. Melinda's soft voice whispering into his mind's ear.

"Make love to me. You are my chosen mate." Speaking French in her most seductive voice. Marc shakes his head, realizing he missed the turn for Aladdin's. Catching a red light because of her distraction.

"Get out of my head, witch!" Marc says. Glancing to see her watching him from his rearview mirror. Overheard by people on the sidewalk waiting for the crosswalk signal. All of them staring at the crazy man yelling alone in his car. Marc looks over feeling eyes on him. The group all look away, not wanting to make eye contact with the crazy man.

"What the—!" Marc says angrily. The light changes, giving him some relief from the embarrassing moment. Punching the gas pedal down with his foot making his tires spin from the sudden torque, squealing for a quick second. Arriving at Aladdin's Oasis right before they were to close. But since he and Camel being regulars there and friends with the owner's son Ali. He is graciously seated in a booth.

After a hot meal of heavily spiced lamb in a curried gravy. Served with couscous and dried apricots. Ali joins Marc for some hot milk tea. Ali talks with Marc about soccer and mosque politics. Helping to take his mind off Ahmed, his second father. Having been around more than his own dad. Who was frequently away at some remote location, often perilous. Within the Islamic community, news travels quickly, especially bad news of a member's poor health. Being a small community, Ali's family already knows of Camel's father's condition.

Marc goes home grateful for an uneventful evening. Settling into bed well after midnight, his reservations confirmed to New Orleans. A flight to Lebanon connecting to Dubai. The only flight of the week. How many people had made those flights daily in the seventies? When peoples from all over the Middle East traveled daily to the Crescent City. Long before Katrina, when oil was king.

Louisiana being one of two Southern states with a large petrochemical industry. Iranian students were by the thousands soaking up Western technologies and culture. Not that oil was not still king; just now it was no longer untarnished.

His flight scheduled and luggage packed, you think he would be able to sleep. Instead struggling to sleep, insomnia, fighting back with a mind that won't rest. All of his troubles seeking a voice. Turning over, frustrated punching his pillow. Marc finally slips into a fitful sleep. Hearing Melinda's voice whispering into his troubled mind, "If not tonight then another time, *moi amor.*"

Waking up with a start, knowing it's morning. The alarm clock annoying with that pulsing sound so loud. Ready to smash it. Only his sheets tangled around his waist and legs, unable to move. His own weight used against him. Preventing even his arms from being freed. Giving him the alarming sensation of being pinned down by others holding his legs and arms. Making him feel trapped. Struggling awake from a dream where he was tied down. So his heart could be cut out while he was alive. As punishment for his betrayal of the coven, death with severe pain. Female laughter echoing from voices he recognizes. Tumbling out of bed, hitting the floor hard. Tearing at the sheets, rolling across the floor, breaking free of them. Marc jumps up off the Persian rug beside the bed. Landing in a fighting stance, ready for an attack. Only no one is there, just the silent rush of air from the central climate control vent. Carrying on it the familiar scent of coitus and his own male musk in the air. Marc easing up but not relaxing, still guarded. Stopping the alarm clock from pulsing. How long had it been ringing?

Dressing hurriedly, his limousine already scheduled on its way, due to arrive soon. Marc rushes downstairs, taking two steps at a time. Wanting coffee at least before dealing with anyone. Pouring his strong brew, Columbian, black today. No milk in the refrigerator, closing the door. The doorbell ringing as he is putting the lid on his travel mug.

After an uneventful ride to the airport in blissful silence and posh comfort. At the airport, the exact opposite. Being singled out by security and practically strip-searched. Marc finally cleared security, almost missing his commercial flight. Settling into his first-class cabin seat, reasonably comfortable. Unavoidably checking out the tall blonde flight attendant. Herself accustomed to caring for front cabin guests, already noting him. Moving over, introducing herself as Ann. Giving the usual information about flight safety. "Air services will begin once we are safely airborne." If there was anything he needed prior to departure, of course as a first-class passenger, now would be good. Giving Marc a cool bottled water.

"You need to hydrate when you travel by air," Ann says. Marc thanks, her twisting open the water, taking a swig.

Marc still restless after the flight is under way. Ann being the consummate guest specialist notices this. Deciding to offer him some of her personal chai tea. Only after Marc had turned down all other beverages. Ann loosens her red scarf around her neck. Part of the uniform ensemble, never really caring for it. Leaning over, speaking to Marc.

"I keep an excellent mélange of chia tea. To help me relax when I'm laying over in some hotel. Sometimes it's difficult to settle in. I cannot help but notice that you are a little restless. Would you like some? Life can be hectic," Ann says. Ready to decline her offer. Ann, reading his body language, says, "Hot tea will help you relax. Sometimes I just sip it. That helps to ease my mind. If you know what I mean."

Marc did. "You know that does seem like a good idea."

"Very good, sir. I'll be right back," Ann says. Marc watches her glide as a model would into the kitchenette. Marc goes back to his Al Jazeera story on his laptop. Ann returns shortly with a steaming cup of chia tea. The aroma tinged with cardamom, with hints of cinnamon. Placing it next to Marc, using the empty seat's tray table. Then pulling out a pillow and blanket for him. Handing him the pillow.

"It helps to get comfortable," Ann says. Then she adds, "If you catch a nap, I will understand. These flights can be so boring."

"Thank you, but I doubt that will happen," Marc says.

Ann smiles. "You never know." Leaving him to sip his hot tea.

Ann, passing by later notes Marc's face. Handsome but masculine with that blue-black shadow, his muscles more relaxed. Those eyes dark blue with a aqua blue outer ring, not so intense as from earlier. Getting waft of his cologne. He smells so good. His body chemistry a good match for it, making him almost irresistible. Its scent very masculine, one that only a male could produce. Ann hands him another pillow, noting his ring as he accepts the pillow.

"That's really beautiful. A family heirloom?" Marc not really in the mood for conversation.

"Uh, yeah." No longer wound up. Thinking, *She has been nice to me.* "My uncle gave it to me." Stifling a yawn. Ann holds his hand admiring the ring. His blanket and pillows helping to make him warm and comfortable, relaxing further.

Another passenger approaches using his 4G thumbing the screen. Brushes by Ann a little too closely. His other hand reflexively slides over her bottom. Looking sharply up at him, her light blue eyes piercingly saying no. Moving herself over into the seat next to Marc. To avoid further unwanted attention. Speaking Arabic first, then switching to English. He apologizes offhandedly with a thick Lebanese accent. Shorter than Marc but every bit as handsome in his swarthy Mediterranean looks. To the point of being captivating. Straight black hair cut short but not clipped down, with a thick, full black mustache. Matching his dark eyes, intelligent, wise beyond the years of his face. Dressed in a grey Armani suit tailored to fit him. Broad shoulders and narrow wasted, completing his power executive look with a yellow silk tie knotted in a perfect Windsor. Looking every bit of Middle Eastern wealth down to his soft Italian leather shoes, Gucci.

Ann evaluating him before speaking. "No problem, sir." Her smile flashing, not matching her eyes. Turning her attention back to Marc. Her hand still on the ring, already sliding past his knuckle at the point of resistance. Letting his hand pull free, with the ring tumbling off. Lost in the folds of the blanket. As Marc shifts his body, moving in his sleep. Ann cusses under her breath, "Damn." Only a partial success. At least now without his ring to interfere, their schedule maintained. Closing the privacy curtains to his pod. Fortunately first-class only has two other passengers, keeping to themselves. Making it another uneventful flight. Ann smiles to herself while tying the red scarf back around her neck. Having used it to make a physical barrier between herself and his ring. Otherwise risking his supernatural ability to seduce women. His pheromones circulating in the air of the cockpit. Already making her heady and overtly attracted. That ring would protect him; at least with it off, he's fair game. She had done her part as agreed.

Light flickers in bands as though passing through venetian blinds behind Marc's closed eyelids. His sleep deepening into beta waves just before REM, leaving his body helpless. When the brain disengages from the somatic part, leaving you helpless, unable to move. He dreams of tumbling through clouds so thin and vaporous yet somehow damp. Unafraid, he falls with his arms outstretched. His shirt and pants rippling against the force of air rushing past. The feeling of exhilaration and freedom he has felt in the past when skydiving.

Marc opens his eyes. *How did I get here?* Standing in front of the oak double doors of Angelique's palatial colonial home with its columns behind him. Melinda opens both doors grandly.

"Come in. That blue shirt brings out the aqua color in your eyes." Unmoved by her cheerful approach. Melinda is wearing a black silk dress, shimmering as she moves. One that presents her decotage seductively. "You look so handsome. You've been getting a lot of sun." Wearing five-inch stiletto heels, still needing to lean up to kiss his rough cheek. Her expensive perfume intoxicating him more. "Come on. Let's go upstairs where it's more private." Marc's voice a breathy baritone rumble. Caution lost in a hot flush of a hard noun.

Her five-inch black Jimmy Choo's clicking across the marble foyer with its black-and-white alternating pattern. His eyes fixed on the hypnotic sway of fabric sliding over shapely hips. Familiar enough to more than just a promised paradise. Marc wondering how a dream can be so physically real. As he takes the stairs. Knowing the way to Angelique's private boudoir. Hearing the massive oak doors behind him close by themselves. Brass slide bolts snapping into place, locking them.

The door to Angelique's boudoir swings open. Melinda walks in ahead of Marc. Glancing over her shoulder to watch him saunter with his long legged strides, then pausing. Melinda going over to the bed, sitting up against the headboard. The duvet already turned down, allowing the red sheets to be visible. Which are embroidered with yellow gold silk threads, creating symbols inside two concentric circles. Melinda sits with her shapely legs crossed alluringly. Watching Marc from the doorway. Taking in his strong build. Even under a dress shirt his deltoids and pectorals visible. Rippling under it like some big cat. So very healthy. Smiling up at him appreciatively. Her calves pumped up exquisitely from wearing high heels. Sliding one shapely leg over the other, watching Marc. His eyes following their motion, licking his lips. Unaware of his less than subtle body language. Standing in the threshold several meters shy of the bed. Hesitant and untrusting of her motives, with good reason. Melinda arches one eyebrow in disapproval before speaking.

"Now don't be that way. If you don't choose of your own volition, I'll just force you to come to me anyway." Marc resolute in his refusal to move. His wide jaw tipping up ever so slightly in steadfast defiance to enter the room. This dream is so real. Almost believing she could do it.

"Very well, have it your way." Stretching her arm out in a reaching motion, curling her fingers like claws. Using her power hand, the left one. Marc's entire two hundred plus pound muscular frame lifted off the floor. Grabbing out frantically to hold on to the doorjamb a split second too late. Clutching at air, pitching forward off balance. Then tumbling as he is tossed across the room. Landing with a solid bounce against the mattress. Right at the center of the concentric circles of gold surrounded by red. On his back unable to move, held down by some invisible force. His look of surprise priceless. Brings a smile to Melinda's face but not a nice one. Looking absolutely evil before covering her power hungry expression with something more benign. Managing a more gracious expression, that of a good hostess. As though nothing had happened at all. Never mind the fact she had tossed a man across the room without touching him physically. Now held hostage in her bed. Lifting up her teacup, taking a sip out of fine bone china. Like nothing untoward had just happened. Setting it down with a clink. Turning to Marc.

"You're not in a dream now." His confident expression unchanged. Keeping his best poker face, the only tell a bead of perspiration forming at the side of his forehead. Willing himself to stay calm, forcing slow easy respirations. Finally one drop unavoidably slipping down the side of his face. Melinda's eyes following it.

"Would you like some? There is no alcohol in it." She offers innocuously, holding her cup out to him. Marc turns his head away, refusing. His angular jaw stubble covered blue-black set in defiance. Still not speaking to her because it is bad luck to speak to a witch in a dream. Melinda knows some of his beliefs.

"You can speak to me. Your luck cannot get any worse."

"Why are you doing this to me?" His sapphire blue eyes sparkling with anger.

"Take a little sip and maybe I will answer you," Melinda chides him.

"I don't think so. You haven't answered me. Why am I here?" Marc says.

"Those are very reasonable questions. Each leading to sound answers. I doubt either would encourage you to drink up. So let me put it to you another way. I'll give you a choice."

"What's that?" Marc asks. Glaring at her. Struggling furiously against his unseen restraints, perspiration beginning to bleed through his dress shirt. Melinda waits for him to settle down before continuing. Giving up for the moment, Marc looks at her, waiting for her to speak.

"Good, now I have your undivided attention. Someone close to you will die. Whom shall it be?" Marc panics, fighting with even more force against the power holding him to the bed. His shirt ripping at the seams. Where the sleeves come together at the shoulders. The shirt front splitting open, hair now exposed though the gaps. Smiling cruelly, Melinda rests a hand to her chin, thinking about it.

"I don't know how I ever could have thought you were the woman I could spend my life with. You are completely evil, to the core!" Melinda enjoying herself just a little too much. *Could he be right about me?*

"How about, hum, Mr. Khalid senior? Or one of your brothers, Camel perhaps." Melinda says.

"You need Camel so I know you won't harm him," Marc snarls.

"Oh? How right you are. And I thought you were just another handsome male for stud. How about your father? A tragic accident, collateral damage from an IED. Placed by one of your jihadist brethren." A tickle of fear making his heart race. Perspiration soaking though Marc's shirt, in several places joining.

"Mr. Khalid it is then." Her tone final. "He will have a setback. Being he is already on the coronary care unit. It wouldn't come as that big a surprise, now will it?" Not really speaking to Marc as much as to herself. Working out cause and effect in her mind. "Then I'll get the added bonus. Hurting and making you feel helpless. Don't you want to know what else, Marc? I'm used to getting what I want. You know that much about me now. Well, besides the obvious." Looking at him and knowing he is seething inside, internalizing all that anger. "What, from threats to reticence?"

"I'm just thinking how I would like to choke the life out of you." Marc snarls.

"Well, at least you're not being so boringly predictable." Smiling back at him before answering her own question. "That way Ibram will have the guilt of his father's death on his conscience. I'm sure we can come up with some sort of medical error. That will lead back to the cardiologist's poor judgment. Then I will get two Khalid's with one stroke. No, actually three, counting you, because you wouldn't cooperate."

Marc struggling with renewed ferocity against the unseen restraints. His wrists bruising already, beginning to bleed, with ankles excoriated, skin peeling up. But no closer to escape. Finally yelling in frustration. "Ahhhh! I will kill you!" Marc says.

"I love hate sex. It is some of the best, most passionate sex." Melinda says breathily, her eyes sparkling. "Are you willing now to acquiesce?" Her expression smug, one of having all the control. Marc held in bondage, trapped, and now backed into a corner with the lives of people he loves in danger. Their fates stretching out before him. The only clear choice left to him. Inhaling a deep breath of resolve, calming himself. Accepting blame for all of this. How could he ever have been so stupid? To have fallen for this infidel whore with her tricks. No matter how this turned out, he would always be scarred by them. It was a lose-lose situation for his side.

"Give me the drink." Speaking to her without making eye contact.

"Not so fast. I will hold on to the cup and you will drink first. I'm not going to let you up first." Melinda says.

"It was worth the try. Fine just get it over with." Marc says.

"Now that is more like it. Finally some cooperation." Melinda says gloatingly. She puts the cup to his Cupid's bow lips. Marc hesitating at the content's bitter scent.

"Drink it all down quickly. It makes it easier to tolerate the taste that way." Marc manages one last threatening glare. Melinda presses the cup against his thick bottom lip. As soon as he opens his mouth to drink, she grabs the back of his head by the hair. Pulling his hair hard, at the same time tipping the cup up. Surprising Marc and pouring the rest of the cup's contents into his mouth. Forcing him to gulp it down. The bitter concoction burning down his throat, hitting his stomach like a punch to the gut. Gagging on it.

Seconds later, a new sensation explodes through his body. Making him feel warm and euphoric. His head dropping to his chest, all of his resistance leaving him. Melinda releases her hold on his long hair. Letting his head drop back against the mattress. Having time to appreciate him, tractable now. So thick and long, Marc's hair more like that of a tousled mane on a rock star. Shaking his head from the bitter almond aftertaste. His dark hair no longer tied back but spread out loose around him, bunching up at his shoulders.

Looking to Melinda. "So what now, am I going to die a slow death? Tortured by you."

Melinda looks at him coldly. "I'm are not going to kill you. We have invested too much time and energy for that." Marc's body flows with the warmth of increasing euphoria. All too content to lie there. Tractable, it will be much easier to remove his clothing.

"So at least now you won't kill anyone close to me." Believing himself to have made the most beneficial move for his family.

Melinda smirks at him. "When did we reach that agreement?" Betrayal stabbing though his drug-confused mind. Already feeling the effects of poison, probably cyanide.

Marc whispers softly, "Come here." Melinda, unable to understand him, leans in closer to hear. Marc plants a wet kiss on her lips, forcing his tongue into her mouth. Giving her back some of her poison. *Let her die with me.* Melinda struggles back with her hands on his face. Her nails scraping his stubble-covered jaws, digging her thumbnails into the flesh under his chin. Instead of fighting him, she kisses him back forcefully. *Stupid witch. Now you can die with me,* Marc's last thought.

Instead of her shrinking away from him, she rips open what is left of the front of his dress shirt, sending buttons flying. Marc realizes somewhere in his hyperesthesia state (tactile senses heighten) that her reaction is wrong. Melinda nips his thick lower lip, drawing blood. Making him wince from pain but stirring something else in him more primal. His pants tight to the point of painful. An experience that only men frequently have.

Marc panting shallowly. "You daughter of a bitch!"

Melinda unfazed by his insult. "You better believe it."

Running her hand down his exposed abdomen while digging her nails through the hair. Sending rushes of pleasure though his desire crazed body. "Somehow I find those to be empty words. Let's look at the proof." Unbuckling his belt then tugging at his pants. Pulling them down by the bottoms of his pant legs, coming off not so easily. His shoes already having come off during his earlier struggles against his invisible restraints.

Exposure to open air allows heat to radiate out his body. Increasing his arousal. "You are one hot male. Even if you are planning on killing me." Melinda says. Marc experiences diplopia, his head dropping back against the mattress.

Where he is situated within the double concentric circles with their runes surrounding around his body.

"It is time to begin." Using her anthem to cut away and then tear off his boxer shorts. Allowing his hard body to be free from restraint, snapping up to his navel.

Marc hears voices coming from around the room. People shimmer into view out of thin air. The elders form a circle around the bed, chanting. Thus begun, the runes that are embroidered on the sheet rising up and out, off the sheet into the air. Becoming three-dimensional hovering there continuing to encircle his body. Voices carrying from all around the bed. Marc recognizes Angelique's and another one. Familiar, having heard that one recently. That of a Lebanese male. Marc attempts to focus his eyes on the source of that voice. Seeing at first a thick black mustache. Then those same intelligent dark eyes, the man from earlier. Looking back at him with compassion in those dark eyes of his for just a split second. Before his handsome face becomes a mask of indifference again. Marc remembering where he saw him from the jet they were on. That is impossible. Marc's mind rolling with his ethereal body so loosely attached now to his physical one. Making it difficult to concentrate.

Samir speaks to him in Arabic. A strong masculine baritone voice. "What does not kill us makes us stronger, my brother."

Marc calls out to him for help in Arabic. Samir disregarding Marc's plea. Being a natural leader and the eldest present. Who would dare to occasion one of the most dangerous and forbidden of rituals. One that could bring down the wrath of the archangels themselves to destroy them. Leaving only their ashes for the most ancient of their kind to bear witness knowing what truly had been brought against them. But himself not having any accountability for such an egregious work. His debt paid and his responsibility annulled on this day. How could he help Marc? Someone he did not know and at what personal cost? *So sorry, my young brother.* His decision made. Samir proceeds chanting.

Marc's mind begins to rove as in a dream state, moving into other centuries past. Peoples and places passing before his mind's eye, continuing further back in time. The ceiling to the room he is held in no longer there but the open sky in all its vastness. Stars scatter across a night sky in all of their glory, constellations moving through their seasons rapidly counterclockwise. Along with the moon cycles waxing and waning faster and faster until everything is a blur in the night sky. Then not so obvious at first, slowing down. Microseconds pass, the constellations have slowed, returning to an earlier sky at a different time on earth. When there was another, a thirteenth constellation, now unfamiliar to present day eyes. This constellation that of the serpent now back in its rightful apogee. Thus increasing the zodiac again to thirteen. Returning the serpent to the skies of thousands of years. Lost to the ever expanding universe present and future sky. Many constellation are destined to vanish from the skies of earth.

Only a few still able to remember the skies as they were millennia past. So many voices all at once calling out to Marc. Leading him back to his body. Able now to watch from above, seeing the gathered coven members. Their powers strong, keeping them suspended above the floor. All the while taking energy from the planet. Charging energy into the protective sphere around Marc's body on the bed. So surreal, watching this detached from his body, from above it. Seeing his body below on the bed with Melinda. Her astride his body, at that point seeing it all happen, aware of it but somehow detached. She is using him as the satyr.

Marc feels the silver cord tug him back, not truly sure of what was happening. Falling away from the ceiling through the scent of frankincense. A tenuous wisp of incense around him, past candles suspended in midair, blinking his eyes in the physical body again. Marc's sapphire blue eyes settling on a woman speaking Farsi. Her hair and face covered, with only her intense black eyes so beautiful visible. Then allowing her burka to slide down. Revealing her beautiful face, with long dark hair tossing it. Such a gorgeous face, a Persian woman maybe but definitely not Muslim. She couldn't be to behave so common. Others present but Marc can no longer be concerned with them. Her name is Allia. Melinda reaches out, grabbing a fistful of his chest pelt, tugging at it roughly. Forcefully pulling on it until she draws Marc's anger to her. While engulfing him in her satiny warmth. Making him groan with pure pleasure. Marc's eyes returning to Allia's direction. Melinda will not be second to any woman trailing her long nails around his hairy chest until she finds something tender. Closing her nails, clipper fashion, over his nipple, cutting in. Wincing, Marc's attention back to her face. As she leans over to whisper in his ear, hearing a voice not Melinda's.

What's she saying? Chanting voices growing louder, drowning out hers. Deep in his mind something dark reaches into it. Stroking the pleasure center of his brain. Sending endorphins rushing out on neurons affecting other parts of the brain. A guttural growl escapes his thick lips, coming from deep within his chest. Marc's muscular arms freed at that moment. He locks his hands around her small waist. Bucking with his hips, using all those muscles to increase thrusting force, pounding. Determined to find his release from the torture of the aphrodisiac. Having been left achingly aroused to the point of madness without achieving release. That being part of reason he was restrained to prevent release. Melinda screams with him, no longer caring what she was instructed to do. Himself no longer held back begins to growl, letting it out, howling into the night sky, spinning, with its stars blurring.

CHAPTER 93

FLIGHT 1821. THE jet touches down against the tarmac. A rough jarring motion and a loud screech of rubber hitting concrete. Marc becomes conscious, waking up to waves of warmth rushing over him. Sweet release pulsing. Shifting his legs uncomfortably. Having just had a wet dream one to never forget. Something that young men so frequently have, not really all that unusual. Passengers already disembarking. Hoping no one heard him when he was dreaming. Becoming aware that a wet area in his boxers has soaked through his pants. Creating a dark spot on his dress pants. Already turning cool and wet inside and down the leg of his boxers.

Marc stands up, stretching casually, looking down to check his pants. His ring rolling out of the crumpled blanket. Picking it up off the soft leather first-class seat. Jumping at a surprise hand patting him on the shoulder. Grabbing the hand defensively before realizing it's that of another passenger. Releasing it upon seeing a friendly face. The man looking amused, says, "That was some dream." Winking at him then moving on. Marc's cheeks becoming dusky. Sliding his ring back on. "Excuse me," A dark-haired man says. Being the other first class passenger.

"Oh, uh, sorry," Marc says, moving out of the way for the shorter man.

Glancing back at the first-class cabin, empty, with only a couple of stragglers remaining in coach. Marc pulls his carry on out of the overhead compartment. Swinging it over his shoulder. Walking down the gangway, all too conscious of needing to clean up. Seeking out the closest lavatory.

Stepping out of the cool air-conditioned terminal into the sunny New Orleans humidity. Perspiration already beading all over him. Wishing he had dressed for the tropics instead of covering his body in a Northeastern fashion. Noting the temperature in the upper nineties on the exterior temperature gauge. Sweat running down his back, dripping. The triple *H*'s—hot, humid, and hazy.

Using his hand to shield the sun from his eyes. Searching for his ride. Where is he?

Paul is waiting inside the baggage claim area. Believing he has missed Marc. Walking back outside to check with Marissa. Who is waiting in a late model compact with the motor running to keep the air conditioner on. Beads of perspiration running into his eyes, stinging them. Blinding him and frustrating at the same time. Pulling his shirt up to blot his eyes. At the same time exposing a well-developed set of abdominal muscles covered in a stripe. That is down the center dirty blonde colored. Letting go of his shirt dropping back in place. Nervously questioning, *Where is he?* Paul searches the immediate area quickly. Being able to do it fast even with it crowded. His six-foot-plus height giving him an advantage. That being not his only good fortune, being a dishwater blonde with silver-blue eyes. Giving him advantages in other ways not important right now.

Marissa opens her window partially, not wanting to let the cool air out and heat in.

Paul, "I can't find him." Marissa looks past Paul.

"Get a load of that one. GQ meets Cajun." Marissa comments

Paul turns as Marc puts his hand up to his forehead again. Shielding his eyes from the bright blazing afternoon sun. Perspiration already causing his shirt to stick to his body uncomfortably trapping heat. Paul waves at Marc, spotting him. As Marc approaches, Paul notices the difference from his photographs. Not boyish anymore, Paul decides.

Marc sees Paul's face drawn from grief, eyes bloodshot with dark circles around them.

Marissa chatters away. "That's him? What a babe." Pushing open the car door. Marc finds Paul looks just the way Phil described him. Ruggedly handsome in that outdoorsman kind of way. In that moment it hits him. They were more than just friends but lovers. 'Partners'

"Hi, I'm Phil's first cousin." Paul shakes Marc's hand with an iron crushing grip.

"Hi, I'm Phil's...," pausing, grief stopping him. Paul takes a second to recover his feelings.

"Phil has told me some about you. How long have you been partners?" Marc asks solidly.

"We have been living together for over a year. But dating two years before that," Paul says, with his face tightening up again with grief. His strong jaws covered in two days of blonde stubble, a very heavy growth. Looking more an outdoorsman than a former Jesuit priest. Having a natural build with low-twitch muscles. Which favor development when hard labor is applied. Paul having grown up on a ranch in Nebraska, digging postholes and baling hay. From a family of six siblings. All brothers and being a middle child, competition was tough. That and all of them were expected to work from early ages. As rural children often are. Added with a philosophy of "spare the rod, spoil the child." Paul definitely didn't look his educational stereotype.

Paul speaks up, "I have heard so much about you, and your escapades together." Looking Marc squarely in the eyes, sizing him as rough and tumble men do.

"I have to admit Phillip and I have been out of touch for a while. Not that we were not still close. You just get busy with life and colleg." Marc says. Feeling more than a little guilt for not having stayed in closer touch. Added to his involving Phil in what was becoming the epic mistake of his life. It got his younger cousin killed. Something that would define his character before it was over. Less the physical scars he would learn to deal with but the spiritual and psychological ones. Those were going to remain unclear until time presented them.

Paul recognizing survivor guilt, says, "Your picture doesn't do you justice. You have the same blue-colored eyes as Phil (dark blue)." Paul tearing up. Marc hugs him, needing to be strong for his cousin's partner. Holding his grief tinged guilt bitterly in check.

Marissa leans over, pushing the car door open again. "Are you two going to stand there and sweat? Get in the car before it overheats." A taxi driver leans on his horn, honking impatiently. Both men glare at him.

"We have to go," Paul says, climbing into the front seat. His knees against the dashboard.

"This is Marissa, one of Phil's undergraduate students."

Marissa, "Hi, gorgeous!" Paul closes the car door, Marc's knees jammed into the seat in front of him.

"Hi, nice to you, ma'am."

"It's not ma'am, darlin'." Just a hint of Ninth Ward accent coming out, making her sound like she's from Brooklyn.

"Don't scare him off." Paul cautions, cracking a smile. Marc smiles sheepishly back.

Marissa encouraged by having the attention of two handsome men. "Manners and a great smile." The taxi driver behind them is laying on his horn. Marissa revs the engine up, popping the clutch into first, peeling away from the curb. Cutting off another taxi blasting its horn. Forced to stop, tires squealing, with the front end dipping down. Marissa already gone before the sound of broken glass can reach them. The first cab rear-ended.

"I would like to get to the services in one piece." Paul says with both hands braced against the dash. His knees jammed into the hard plastic dash.

"Equally important to get there for the services, don't you think?" Marissa answers, already focused on traffic turning onto the highway heading east back toward New Orleans. The airport being squeezed into the suburb of Metairie.

Marc more concerned about the late model Toyota weaving in and out of traffic than what he is going to say.

"I can't believe Phil is gone."

"I know," Paul agrees, "He was working on a doctorate in Sanskrit linguistics."

"I didn't know that," Marc says.

"Yeah, we were planning on seeing Robert in Iraq next spring. Before heading to Mumbai. He had a visiting professor from Provence, France. Stepping in for the year while we were to be away." Paul's voice trailing off with the sight of the Saint Louis Cemetery on the left coming into view. Giving all of the occupants of the small compact a reminder of death. Spread out before them hundreds of marble mausoleums. Mute testament to life always coming to an end. Marissa usually bubbly and quick witted self, silenced. All three passengers given a time to internalize their thoughts on death. The hum of tires against pavement surrounding them, filling the void.

Marissa breaks the silence. "Okay, one of the two of you needs to talk. I can't take this silence." Turning on her signal to exit the highway before the Greater New Orleans Bridge takes them over the Mississippi River, away from the city proper.

The compact rolls to a stop for the red light at Saint Charles. Not a very pretty corner if you like the Garden District. Looking very industrial with the highway rising up to the bridge. Turning right onto Saint Charles, away from the Vieux Carré. Gradually the residential area becomes eloquent with its architecture from previous centuries. Stately oak trees once covered and shaded the street on both sides. Some well over a century old, if not older. All destroyed in the flooding aftermath of Hurricane Katrina. The worst tropical storm to hit North America. Of course not admitting to global warming combined with a lackadaisical federal government as responsible. Did what two wars between Spain and France could never do to the Crescent City.

"Where are the services being held?" The farther uptown Saint Charles they traveled, the more impressive the well-kept architecture.

"Loyola has a beautiful church. It's where he wanted his funeral. Phil always said it was from a time when the church showed its wealth. We both planned on this when we were old." Paul becoming quiet, his grief overcoming him. Marissa puts her hand on his shoulder for comfort. Their silence uncomfortable but understandable. Giving Paul some time to grieve quietly. He wipes at tears with the back of his hands. Getting his emotions under control.

Marissa glances in the rearview mirror, sneaking a look at Marc. Already attracted to him, unaware with the windows closed that her olfactory senses are surrounded by his heightened pheromones. Causing not so subtle responses in her brain chemistry. Thus her body responding to him.

"Your cologne. It smells so good. What is it?"

"Oh, uh, Tommy Hilfiger," Marc says, managing a weak smile. Returning to looking out the window. Passing through large open spaces. Where once magnificent oak trees shaded the grand boulevard that is Saint Charles. Preventing the hot subtropical sun from beating down making it hotter. Heat waves shimmering off the pavement under the unrelenting ninety-eight degree sun.

Sunlight passes through Marissa's dark auburn hair turning it a deep red. Marc admiring its beauty. "You don't look much like that picture Phil has of the three of you." Paul says.

"I'll say, downright swarthy." Marissa adds with a wicked smile. Paul ignores her just needing to talk. Turning his body around in the seat to face Marc.

"I thought I had a heavy beard. It's early afternoon and you already have a full five o'clock shadow."

Marc answers him. "I know, it's a curse. I have a shadow at nine in the morning."

"Your flight was an hour late. I was afraid we would have to leave and you would miss the services." Paul says.

"I was told about it by one of the pilots. Apparently I slept through all of it. They flew around the outer edges of a large storm. Even that was bumpy and rough. It must have affected my dreams."

Marissa, "Really? How so?"

"Well, what I can remember of any of it was the part where I was falling." Not about to go into details of how sexual that dream was. More embarrassing to discuss the outcome. An incredible way to wake up.

"I hate those kind of dreams," Marissa says.

"No. It wasn't like that. It was more like when I have gone skydiving. Actually it felt good having the wind rushing over my body, you know?"

"No. I have never jumped out of a plane. That is one thing I have no desire to. Joining the mile-high club, now that would be different." Marissa looks in the rearview mirror at Marc.

"What's the mile-high club?" Marc asks

"It's good you can sleep through anything. Phil was that way too." Paul says, only halfway listening to their conversation. Getting closer to Loyola, causing Paul to become more distracted.

"Some of my dreams were strangely erotic." Marc not having meant to say that out loud to a woman he just met.

"It is having hot sex on a jet. Usually in the lavatory." Marissa says.

Marc puzzled, "Why not just take a flight with a bedroom suite?"

"What are you two talking about?" Paul asks as Marissa pulls into the driveway at Loyola.

After parking the compact, they join the crowd of youth going up the steps into the church. Paul noting faculty members present to show their respect. The dean of students in attendance with his wife, nodding to Paul. Phillip had been young and well liked. So many in attendance, the church pews were full and the standing room at the back was packed. Unprepared for this many coming, the air-conditioning had not been adjusted. Marc's shirt was soaked through in places from perspiration. He was not the only one in this condition. Many of the women present had made the church fliers into fans. It looked like a movie scene out of *To Kill a Mockingbird*. A time before there was climate control. People in Southern states sweltering under summer's oppressive humidity. Two important things were different now. The student body was multiracial and not all Christians. Paul observes everything, his training so ingrained.

"I forgot how humid it can be here." His entire body damp. Running his hands back to lift up his thick mane. Trying to get some air to his hot neck. Not much help, his dark hair very thick and heavy. Now grown well past his shoulders. Its length increasing in the time of the flight.

"You will get used to it." Paul says.

"What he means is going from one air-conditioned place to the next." Marissa stops him to help out. Pulling some black ribbon out of her purse, offering to use that. Having him turn sideways in the pew to give her more access. After tying the first knot at the nape of his neck. Then stringing it down to a second area well below the shoulder blades. Admiring Marc's hair, so soft and straight like corn silk. Definitely Cajun with Native American heritage, giving him this gorgeous head of hair. Noting his solid back narrowing down to a much smaller waist. A natural wedge shape. Allowing her eyes to roam further to a nicely shaped bubble butt. Marissa captivated from prolonged exposure with close contact to Marc. She just doesn't have any defense against his satyr nature.

"That feels better. Does it look all right?" Marc asks. Not used to having long hair or tying it.

"Very good from here." Patting him lightly. Just as she expected, hard muscles. Men like him usually are. Nothing soft on him, except his hair. Not wanting to go any further with those thoughts. After all, they were in a church for a funeral of a dear friend. *When did I become so desperate?* Questioning herself and not with a little ting of guilt.

Marc having been fascinated with architecture since he can remember. Having grown up in places where buildings could have been constructed thousands of years ago to hundreds of years ago. Some of the world's most beautiful buildings, mosques. Hot climate designs allowing for high ceilings to draw heat up and away from the occupants. Entering the church through solid cypress doors. That being the wood of choice at one time. Its nave covered with mahogany paneling. The church afforded more lavish details by its wealthy uptown parishioners. Marble stairs rising up several steps to a podium exquisitely hand carved. Where its priest would be giving mass. Elevated, thus he could see down across the pews all the way to the back into the nave. Before the inner solid mahogany doors are closed. Marc admiring the craftsmanship of carpenters and stonemasons alike.

Being some of the last to arrive. A packed house, Phil being young and popular. The three of them walk up the center aisle to the front of the church. Where seats have been saved for family. Most of the faces unfamiliar except for a few older cousins he hasn't seen or spoken to since he was a child years ago. After they are seated with not a moment to spare. The priest comes in with his retinue. The lead altar boy carrying a large crucifix with the others carrying lighted candles. The priest himself carrying an arabesque brass censer smoldering with frankincense. Its strong fragrance easily recognized by most present, including Marc. Both iconic symbols of the religion's origins. The censer swings back and forth in his hand gently. Allowing smoke to waft across the air before the service begins. Pallbearers bring up the rear behind the priest, rolling the casket to center stage.

Phillip's last time to be so close to so many friends and loved ones. Marc's sad yet dark thoughts haunting him. His teeth set firmly together to stifle any grief threatening to rise up unexpectedly. So much grief right at the surface, the entire room is set to go up in tears. Most of those in attendance college age students. With of course faculty and a dean present to represent. Phillip was respected and well liked, even loved by his students. Being close in age, he was able to communicate and relate on their level.

After several well-chosen speakers give their eulogies. The choir follows with "Ave Maria," not a dry eye in the church. Paul weeping quietly, a teary eyed Marc puts his arm around his shoulder. When the pallbearers begin to remove the casket, it is all Marc can do to remain stoic. His strong jaw muscles tight, swallowing his grief. In an attempt to be strong for Paul. Emptiness threatening to engulf from his loss so deeply felt. Marissa's tears dripping off her face.

Marc becomes angry. Phil shouldn't be dead because of something he had involved him in. They were going to pay for this sometime. He would see to it. Having not noticed that everyone was filing out. Standing there still holding Paul crying into his chest with an almost iron gripped bear hug. Marissa gets his attention back to the present. The priest with his smoldering censer already to the nave.

CHAPTER 94

THE RIDE TO the cemetery in the limousine was silent except for occasional weeping. Now that the funeral procession was on track. After a glitch from so much traffic, backed up for over a mile. Which was unanticipated by New Orleans police escorting them.

Marc and Paul both long legged having room to stretch out. Marissa comforting Paul, sitting next to him. Marc sprawled out, letting the air-conditioning cool his overheated body. His tie loosened, shirt unbuttoned, allowing his thick haired chest to start drying out, finally getting comfortable.

Once in the cemetery, a second line band falls in behind the limousine. Playing jazz music soulfully at first. Paul having made sure Phil's request for a traditional New Orleans funeral was adhered to. Parking their cars, the funeral's entourage is followed by the second line band. Phillip's favorite song a the Mardi Gras second line song. The main one played for carnival time so cheerful. Trombones and trumpets playing loudly. Their musicians and some of the entourage breaking into second line steps. Their black umbrellas held up overhead taking lively steps. Making it difficult to feel sad. That in and of itself reason enough to feel sorrow. Marc reminded again that Phillip from now on would not be a part of his life. His children would never know how wonderful their cousin is. Was.

Their limousine ride back is silent, with only the sound of the road beneath them filling the void. Its passengers keeping their own solace. Paul being raised an outdoorsman. Hunting and running trout lines. Long before he was introduced to the softer part of life. He was used to solitude. Now having time finally to reflect inwardly. About all that had taken place. No longer having to consider the safety of a loved one. Reaching that point where some men feel they have nothing to lose. In a committed relationship that would have had years of happiness before it. Now only death as a companion. Paul's life empty and devoid of so many things they were going to do. Their trip to Mumbai for Phil to study Sanskrit, but first stopping off in Baghdad to see his uncle. Questioning himself, what does he need? What could give him a sense of justice? If to no longer have the joy of sharing and companionship.

Their driver takes a shorter route to up town Saint Charles. Its architecture Marc always loved studying even when just passing by. Now having time to do just that. What he and Phil had discussed he should do after graduation. A summer of New Orleans with Gulf Coast architecture. Appreciating some time to consider the city. Where older established homes were built on higher ground. Just as was the Vieux Carré (French Quarter). Being from another century, homes were built several feet above the ground. To avoid periodic flooding from the Mississippi River. Moving past exquisite nineteenth-century homes with stairs leading up to the first floor. Anywhere else, that would have been the second story. You always had to consider flooring. Let alone expect it. New Orleans was built by this mighty river. Surrounded on three sides by water. A river on the southern side, Lake Pontchartrain on the north side, and a swamp on the west side. The old levees weren't as effective as present day ones were supposed to be. But then it's not like everyone living in the twentieth century here hadn't heard speculation and rumors. That New Orleans would flood from a hurricane greater than a level three. The odds were moving in favor of it happening. How many times can a city dodge the proverbial bullet? Eventually water would breach the city's levees, flooding it. Another near miss. While everyone believed it happened again. Reports were coming in that Mississippi just a few miles away had taken the hit.

Marc puzzling this and the bigger question. Why is it that federal level people always wait and see? Why not spend a billion dollars preventing a disaster? As opposed to thirty or forty billion in cleaning it up. Now instead while being driven from Phillip's funeral left to consider why.

CHAPTER 95

THEIR LIMOUSINE EASES lightly to a cushioned stop. In front of Phil and Paul's Greek Revival home. Its white columns and grand porch set back deeply. To provide shade from the sun's intense heat. Before there was such a wonder as climate control. Built in 1872 by a well to do Cajun family. To be closer to the city. Marc admires the architecture. Noting a sapling live oak planted to replace its once grand predecessor. The only remaining marks left there are large cracks in the sidewalk. To bear witness where it once stood. Also bald cypresses strategically planted down the side yard to help block the morning sun. Those being a nod to the region's indigenous trees and common sense. Certainly another flood will come, and those trees won't be affected by a long stay underwater. That and the ferns that had already grown back. Hugging the shade of the porch's overhang.

After the last mourners had paid their respects and gone. Their home feels empty to Paul. By now they would have been uncorking a bottle of Bordeaux. Taken from the climate controlled wine room. The water table too close to the surface and the city slowly sinking below sea. A wine cellar not practical. Paul continues their practice out of routine. Like being on autopilot going through the motions. Pouring up glasses handing them to his companions Marissa and Marc. Twisting his own watching the wine's legs stream back down. His face intense focused on the wine. Needing a distraction from the home's solitude. Empty with only the tick of the clock from the mantel in the other room. Marissa uncomfortable with their somber mood makes conversation.

"A lot of people couldn't be employed anymore here. So they were forced to move away. It's also hotter without the canopy the native live oak trees created. Shading entire streets and homes."

Marc understanding her need, asks, "What happened to them?"

Paul injects, "They drown." Marissa lifts her eyebrows impatiently. Paul getting it. "It's all very sad, being some of the people that have remained. You see the devastation day in and day out. So many left, moved away, or just didn't bother to come back. For the past few years the cultural mix has been changing. So many immigrants moving in and replacing old families. Not that this is a bad thing. I mean it's good. Life is about change, right?"

Marc's luggage is piled in the living room. Able to see it from where he is sitting in the kitchen. Change being forced on him. "Uh, yeah." Not really feeling what Paul has said. Too much change already rocking his world. Forcing him to grow up faster.

"That picture of you Phil has in the study. It must be a few years old. You don't look like it that much," Marissa says. "You really don't come across as the same man as in that picture."

"How did you expect me to look?" Marc asks.

"Well, not so mysterious and swarthy. I like it," Marissa says.

Paul rolls his eyes at her before speaking. "I would say you were a handsome pretty boy. Now you are ruggedly handsome, mature."

"Yes, definitely manly. There's nothing boyish about you anymore." Marissa adds. Her green eyes twinkling invitingly. Marc finds himself easily drawn to her. His boxers tightening up uncomfortably. Clearing his throat, adjusting his package. Choosing to change the subject. "I believe I saw a hotel on Saint Charles. The Pontchartrain?"

"You are not staying at any hotel. There are five bedrooms in this house. I only need one." Paul objects vehemently.

Marissa excuses herself to go home. Giving Paul time to speak privately with Marc. He shows Marc to his room along with a tour of the house. "I wish there would have been more time for you to get settled after you arrived." Paul walks into a second floor guest bedroom with its own balcony. "You have your own private bathroom." Opening the bedroom's double French doors out onto one of the home's balconies. Facing its private garden.

Acknowledging Phil's creativity. "This was all Phil's imagination and design. We used telephone poles with cables left over from the wreckage. Debris pulled from piles to be wasted. To create a trellis system for wisteria and jasmine to climb. Screening the garden from the street and our neighbors three floors up."

Marc, "It's brilliant, getting a double use out of it." Paul and Phil had worked hard building the massive system. Down to every detail, considering how it would look in winter when the leaves were gone. Paul having grown up on a ranch, hard work and digging postholes was second nature. So what if they weighed hundreds of pounds. Requiring some heavy equipment. The results were impressive for two guys that didn't work construction. Marc places his hand on his cousin's partner's shoulder to comfort him. Able to read even the toughest poker face. Paul's square jawed face set tight beneath a blonde stubble of sandpaper growth.

"You must have set the posts and cables." Trying to distract Paul from the painful moment.

Paul looks at him, his blue eyes wet from unshed tears. "Yes, I have a knack for that kind thing. It's probably from having to string miles of barbwire."

New Orleans tropical temperatures combined with high rainfalls, a close second to the Northwest. Wisteria had grown into an effective screen. If not, almost jungle like in its strangler vine growth.

Paul notices Marc's shirt already wet in areas from perspiration. New Orleans in August is hot. September will be just another summer month here. Relief won't arrive until October. "I'll give you some time to relax and change into lighter clothes." Paul turns to go hearing the doorbell ring downstairs. "This bedroom has a private bath we had added during the renovation. From the looks of that shirt, you could at least use a change. I'll leave you to freshen up." Marc glances down his shirt. Dark areas increasing with heat rising. Lifting an eyebrow with a nod of his head in agreement.

"I forgot how oppressive the heat and humidity could be here this time of the year. I need more than a freshening up. A cleansing cold shower would be more like it."

"Make yourself at home. If you need anything just ask." The doorbell rings again.

"Go. I'll be fine." Marc says. Paul closes the French doors behind him. Leaving Marc to enjoy the view from his private balcony. Unbuttoning his shirt and pulling it out of his pants at the same time. After all, even warm, fresh air against your body feels better than clothing. Tossing his dress shirt to the side. Then stretching the solid muscles of his chest before interlacing his fingers. Reaching up and stretching his back and body languidly. Looking more like a big cat in the shadows with his dark pelt on his chest. Loosening up into wide bands of fur thus allowing airflow between them. Not consciously aware of what he had just done. Yet feeling some relief from the ninety-nine degree heat, with its 70 plus percent humidity.

Finally coming inside after completely undressing. His balcony totally private, enjoying the hot air nude as nature had intended it. The air almost cold after being outside. Remembering to hang his clothes out around the room on the furniture. Something you learn early on after being out in the Southern heat. To let the cool dehumidified air dry them out. Hanging his underwear on the bathroom doorknob. Feeling absolutely relaxed and energized at the same time. Making the time he stretches out on the bed nude. Letting the cool, dry air blow over him from the ceiling fan above like a propeller blade.

Able to gather his thoughts. Grateful for a chance to stop and not be on the go. Air flowing over him in ripples carried by the gentle breeze of the ceiling. Whirling above with a low swishing sound, drowning out any background noise. So very good this breeze and to be relaxing inside. Cool air caressing him. Thinking of Melinda speaking in her soft breathy voice. The last of the evening light dimming into pastels of pinks and lavender. Summer's sun passing low on the horizon. Marc begins to feel drowsy like he's slipping off to sleep and out of his body. Incredibly soothing her voice in his dream. Comforting and restful sleep overtaking him.

There she is with some of her consorts. Several young women are gathered around a hearth singing. No. Not a hearth but a smoldering pot. They are saying something but it is unclear. Marc tries to hear them more closely concentrating. Almost familiar the tone with its cadence even this place. Déjà vu echoing in his mind. How is that possible? After all, this is only a dream. A thought more like a string tugging at the back of his memory.

Their voices clear now. "Firelight burning in the dark." Fear reaching up inside him. They are chanting around a cauldron!

"Guide thee, oh powerful one. Bring forth one whose power we seek tonight. Bind him and obscure our purpose so he won't see. Until our deed is replete."

"Join hands and concentrate. On what your intentions are." Angelique's voice all too clear. Letting her hood fall back turning her head to the side searching the room. Her face exposed now with those blue eyes round and angry so full of suspicion.

"Who's there? Show yourself!" she says. Marc cringes inside. *They can't know I'm here. It's not possible.*

"We will not harm you. Come forth, we wish to see you." Melinda's voice sly with her obvious lie. Marc panics, *How do I get out of here?* Unable to move frozen no, trapped. Panic pumping up his adrenaline. Struggling in his mind to leave.

"Yes. He is a strong male. I can feel his strength." Her accent thick, Persian. It's Allia.

"He is familiar. Samir show yourself or there will be hell to pay!"

"For you that is." Melinda adds, snickering.

"Give me that censer." Angelique directs. "We will trap him in the circle." Its pungent scent carried on the smoke from it. Marc's adrenaline rushing, he panics inside his mind. Struggling to wake up. *I need to get out of here.* An odd sensation drawing at his umbilical area. Causing the center of his abdomen to tighten up. This sensation spreading over his entire body. Drawing him forward away from safety and observation. Right into the mists of them, dead center. Dragging the soles of his feet against the floor to slow his approach. Marc's arm flailing in the air with nothing to grab on to. Bare feet skidding against the smooth hardwood floors, not much resistance offered. His slide into the inside of their circle unavoidable. Adrenaline pumping, Marc crouches down like a skier, forcing more weight on his feet. It's not working unable to stop. His heart pounding in his ears. Marc yells, "Enkil! Yella!" Stumbling headfirst right between two of the young women into their surround.

"We got him now."

CHAPTER 96

PAUL COMES UPSTAIRS to offer Marc some dinner while it is hot. Marissa's mother having sent over hot food for Paul and Phil's cousin. Having liked both men after her daughter introduced them as a couple. Paul knocks on the bedroom door lightly at first. Ready to retreat without disturbing his guest. But hearing voices on the other side of the door. He knocks harder on the door. Then trying the cut glass knob turning it but the door is solidly unmoving. Hearing Marc's panicked voice speaking Arabic, "Yella! Yella! (Go! Go!)."

Paul lowers his shoulder hitting the door solidly with the weight of his body. Making it open only slowly causing its hinges to creek. The last glints of the westerly sun fading behind dark storm clouds. Paul's eyes adjust slowly to the increasing darkness.

Marc whispers, "No." Paul moves in the familiar darkness of his own home. Goes over to the nightstand switching on the lamp. Startled by what he sees but unable to look away for a few seconds staring. Surprise quickly spreading over his face. *What the heck?* No, saying it out loud. Marc's lying on his back, a sheet twisted in between his legs and around his waist. That's not the shocking part. Marc's chest covered in hair as dense as fur on a mink in winter. About four inches long narrowing down into a dark stripe all the way to the sheet disappearing below that.

Paul now understands why the urgency with the way Phil had worked at translating and seeking even his help for his close cousin. *Damn, he really was cursed.* Physically changed by this. The caregiver side of his mind takes over. Putting his hand on Marc's shoulder, gently shaking him to wake up. Not responding, Paul uses more force. "Wake up. Marc, it's all right, you are safe."

Paul hears women's voices. "Hold him there!"

Marc screaming, "No!" His body ripped, swinging his fists in a fight for his life. Thrashing under his grip back to consciousness here in the room in New Orleans. Throwing a punch with his right fist at his capturers. Paul just has time to block Marc's fist with his left forearm. Still taking a good hit. Paul rolls up and off the bedside.

"Come on!" Marc yells.

"Take it easy! You're safe now." Paul says. Marc's eyes open sitting up fast looking around the room for them. His fists clinched at the ready.

"It was just a nightmare. You're all right now." Paul says in a reassuring and calm tone. "Sorry, I didn't mean to scare you." Marc blinks back at him. Finally recognizing his surroundings.

Paul continues, "I came up to check on you. That must have been some kind of bad dream to have you this worked up. We have some hot food very good stuff it's homemade."

"Sorry I took a swing at you. I'm pretty sure that wasn't a bad dream. They had me trapped there."

Marc says. Pulling the sheet from between his legs which was also cutting into his waist. Needing to get more comfortable unself-conscious. You need to shower after a mixed martial arts fight. Paul having grown up with several brothers is equally unconcerned. Not the type to stare and most certainly coming off a man's man. Nothing obvious about his predisposition of being gay.

"What do you mean you were trapped? You were right here." Paul says.

"No. Part of me was there at Angelique's home, right there in Rochester, New York. If you hadn't woke me when you did. They were going to trap me in that circle of theirs." Marc explains.

"That would have been your astral body." Paul says, his blue eyes stern yet filled with concern. "They could have killed you by keeping your astral body trapped. Unable to return to your physical body. It would appear that you were in a comma while you were held there until your physical body died."

"You need protection when you sleep. We can discuss methods to keep you safe after supper. But first you need food to keep up your strength. Marissa brought over crawfish etouffee that her mother sent over for us. I'm sure you don't get much of that in Rochester." Paul says.

"That sounds great." Marc becomes a little self-conscious of his nudity. Having thrown his covers off moments earlier. When he was ready to fight.

Paul notices this now that Marc settled down. Averting his eyes. "I'll give you some time to dress."

"First I need a shower. Save me some of that etouffee." Marc says. Sliding over to the side of the bed.

"I will if you don't take too long in the shower. Otherwise I make no guarantees. Marissa's mother is one good cook." Paul says.

"In that case fast will be the shower." Marc says. His stomach growling and empty.

CHAPTER 97

AFTER HIS FAST shower hunger making it so Marc picks up his cell phone. Checking it for any missed messages. Having not had a chance to remember to do this since he arrived in New Orleans that early afternoon. Listening to Camel's message.

"The corporate jet was grounded in Madrid, Spain for mechanical repairs. So I switched to a commercial flight to Dubai that is nonstop. Naturally after the flight was airborne, I received the call that the repairs had been made. They were able to obtain new parts from Seville. So I directed the pilot to New Orleans to pick you up." Marc thinks, *Great,* because he hadn't confirmed with the local airline his seat. "Great isn't it?" Camel knowing his brother's mind so well.

"I'll see you soon little brother. Oh uh, I'm on flight 6312, in case someone needs to find me or you need to know for some reason. Uh, Ibram will have you picked up at the airport in Dudai. You know how in control he always has to be."

Marc nods. "Yes and you probably took commercial just to bedevil him." Marc says out loud.

Camel adds, "I did it just to mess with him. Bye, Allah protect you." Clicking off, the sound of emptiness gathering around him. A call ended too soon.

Marc pulls on a blue tee shirt XL and a pair of carpenter shorts. Choosing to go commando since he isn't going out of the house. Comfort the key to relaxation. Hurrying downstairs barefoot. His mouth already watering from the smell of crawfish etouffee carried in the air. Paul hearing him on the stairs calls out, "I'm in here." Marc follows the pop of an uncorked bottle of wine. Coming around the corner. Paul fills up two wine glasses with a Chenin Blanc. Nicely chilled, a gift one of the mourners had left earlier. Marc strolls into the kitchen barefooted. Marc's legs very hairy even his large feet have black hair on the toes, just like his knuckles.

"What time is it?" Marc asks.

"It's after eight o'clock." Paul says. Placing a dish heaped with white rice and topped with the creamy sauce of the etouffee full of crawfish. Marc inhales the light scent before shoveling in a forkful. So full of flavor and richness. No sound other than forks scrapping dishes. The best compliment a cook can get, silence. Both guys digging in only stopping long enough to tear off a hunk of French bread to dip in the sauce.

Marc having forgotten when he last ate, speaks first, "That is so good. You are right. I have never seen this in Rochester. I haven't had any in years."

"Good. Marissa's mom is a great cook. This wine should go well with it." Paul says, noticing Marc's sheepish look. "I'm sorry, you can't drink the wine because you're Muslim."

"No, it's all right now and then. It's just so much has been put into drinks that I wasn't aware of. I'll have some." Sipping the wine to get the bouquet. A light aftertaste of flower blossoms on his palate. "Where is Marissa?" Marc asks.

"She left." Paul answers, looking quizzically at Marc. Catching a scent he had smelled before. Able to recognize that it was Marc's heightened masculine scent. But not aware that it was full of pheromones. Making him attractive even to men on a subliminal level. Finding himself more than drawn to Marc. Paul's blue eyes sparkling with his pupils darkening them by enlarging. Enthrallment overtaking his mind replacing anguish from loss. Marc at first oblivious to Paul's unwavering eye contact. Then beginning to feel his attentions. That feeling you get when someone is undressing you with their eyes. Marc sets his fork down glancing up Paul looking away quickly. Convinced he wasn't just imagining this. The thought occurring to him. That his curse could have an effect on men, not just women.

"Look, I'm not exactly sure how to say this. So I'm just going to say it." Pausing. "You are being affected by this spell over me."

Paul does not say anything at first. Refusing to make eye contact, guilt raking his already hurt mental state. Unavoidably looking at Marc more like a hungry lion with his eyes fixed on its prey. His ruggedly handsome face going from sexy to realization. "I don't know what just happened." His breath catching in his throat. "I just buried my lover. How could I behave like this?"

Marc, "It's not you. It's how this spell works. I just didn't realize it could have an effect on masculine guys such as yourself." Paul shakes his head to clear it.

"It won't happen again. I'm sorry, I will be right back." Excusing himself to go upstairs. Retrieving his crucifix on its gold chain. Kissing it three times before putting it over his head around his neck. Confident that his faith combined by wearing this religious effigy will protect him. It was also blessed by a pious elderly priest. Making faith a strong force of protection. Coming back downstairs wearing it on the outside of his white tee shirt. Looking more like a longshoreman than an ex-priest. His chest and arms large and strong from years of hard work on a cattle ranch.

Marc nods his head in recognition of Paul's own protection. "Now where were we?" Paul says, sitting down at the black granite counter next to Marc. After heaping more food on both their plates. Marc waiting for Paul to start. "Dig in, you don't need to stand on ceremony." Paul says. Sliding a baguette of French bread between them. Tearing off a chunk dipping it in the etouffee sauce.

"I could just eat bread in sauce. You don't want to miss any of it." Marc follows suit, ripping off a hunk of bread. Eating with only the clinks of their forks against porcelain. Both men back to enjoying their meal in silence.

Paul remembering only two days ago sitting in this very spot. He and Phil were having a lively discussion about whether there really is power behind witchcraft. Over a meal of jambalaya. What Phil had always called "the death of a meal." Using up leftover meats like chicken, ham, or sausage to make it. Adding them to a red sauce served over white rice. Paul's throat tightens up until it hurts. Holding his pain in check on a strong but short chain. As his grief wells up threatening to choke him or overflow. Normally a very private man. Not prone to showing his emotions stoic to a fault. At least until Phil had broken through all those walls. Allowing him to begin expressing those feelings to him in the privacy of their home. Marc picks up on his unmoving host. Seeing in his eyes and face grief barely held in check. Setting his fork down leaning over, Marc bear hugs Paul. Pinning his arms to his sides Paul is stiff at first, then begins to shake. Until he trembles from holding in his pain. Sadness with overwhelming loss breaking through cracks in a dam pouring out of him. A deep seated pain twisting up in his insides. Barely a sound coming out of him. His father intolerant of showing any emotion of weakness. Tears quietly running down his cheeks covered in two days' growth of blonde stubble. Marc then releases him.

"I'm sorry. I didn't mean for that to happen." Paul apologizes. Having regained some of his composure back.

"You don't have to apologize for being normal. I certainly wouldn't." His own eyes misty from unshed tears. Keeping strong for Paul. After all, Phil was his closest relative outside Camel. He would want the same in return, not a spoken of favor but respect. Paul was family and you do that for family. Phil's death would leave a hole in all their lives for a long time.

Marc tries to make small talk to keep Paul distracted. Not very good at it, Paul finally tells him it's all right to stop talking. After finishing up their meal in silence. Paul suggests they sit outside in the courtyard. "I'll turn on the exterior ceiling fan. So it won't be so hot out there." Paul says.

"At least the air will be moving even if it is hot out." Marc agrees. Carrying their refreshed glasses of Chenin Blanc. Paul using a trick he picked up bartending in the Northwest. Keeping a couple of wineglasses in the freezer. That way if you're going to sit outside your wine will stay cooler longer. Especially in the Gulf Coast summer heat. Carrying their refreshed glasses of Chenin Blanc outside. Stepping through the French doors to their private courtyard. Taking their seat on the wrought iron furniture setting on a paved brick courtyard. Both Paul and Phil had taken bricks from demolished buildings from the turn of the last century. This color of brick pink and peach found only in and around the French Quarter. Marc studies the bricks, observing the spot on accuracy of the herringbone pattern the bricks are laid out in.

"It took us a couple of months to gather enough un-cracked bricks to do this. Not without a few arguments too." Paul admits. "You know, if you just relax and take it easy you won't get so hot." Looking at Marc. "Why am I telling you that? You should already know that coming from a hot weather climate. I've heard the United Arab Emirates gets pretty humid in the summer."

"Yes it does. I have learned that piece of truth, but sometimes you forget common sense." Paul waits for him to give his piece of wisdom. "Uh, you have to slow down and not stress over everything. Otherwise you only get hotter and more miserable." Marc acknowledges. Paul nods his head in agreement, then finishes up his wine.

"Do you smoke? I feel like having a cigar and some port wine." Marc declines. "Phil would never let me smoke one of my cigars in the house. He said they stunk it up too much. I'll be right back."

Paul returns with his cigar and two glasses of port. Puffing on out a cloud that the ceiling fan dissipates quickly. Their conversation moving easily to sports, soccer, with who will make into the World Cup finals. Between pauses in their rumbling male voiced conversation the cicadas fill in buzzing from the trees. Denoting the time of year as late summer. Marc becomes distracted and restless. Having a sensation of déjà vu becoming uneasy. That feeling of when something is wrong or bad is about to happen. He just couldn't quite recall, but a memory teasing at the edge of his mind. Trying harder still but eluding his conscious mind slipping further away. Dreams, that's it, almost having given up. How disturbing those dreams were.

"You look like you're getting bored. The news will be on in a few minutes. We can go in and watch it," Paul says.

"No. I'm not bored. I just had déjà vu that hit me in the gut like when you fall. You know how when you are free falling. Except this wasn't fun with me in control. There is something eluding me that I should be able to remember. It's just that I only get pieces of those dreams. Nothing clear coming back to me." Marc says.

"Everything that's been going on in your life. I really don't believe you were dreaming at all today." Paul's face showing his concern.

"How could it be anything else?" Marc asks.

"I'm not sure of the how, but they are able to pull your astral body out of your physical one."

"I don't see how that could be possible. What's coming back to me in part is vivid as regular memories. While other parts are like my dreams. Where normal physical laws of, say, gravity have no bearing." Marc concentrates on fragments that have surfaced. "If I am to understand you, it's like part of my soul was pulled out of my body?"

"Yes," Paul says "That's right." Marc tries to push his memory to retrieve a few more details. Attempting to glean even a little more information. Paul watches quietly to avoid interrupting him, causing the loss of memory fragments coming to the surface. Their recall quickening his pulse. Marc remembers parts that piece together fragments. Enough to know where he was. Angelique's home in Pittsford and that he was being held against his will. Along with his struggle to be freed. Ligature marks around his wrists and ankles. A deep seated fear of helplessness that every man feels squeezing his very intestines, a cold sensation. Caused when his family is threatened and he is unable to protect them. Then forced to partake in some infidel ritual at the most intimate level. Anger mixing with guilt at not having been able to stop them. Marc's face showing his rage only by his tight lips and his eyes. Their pupils narrowed to pinpoints. Paul reads his face. "You can't blame yourself."

"If all of what is coming back to me are true memories. Then everything that was done to me really happened?" His tan face turning dusky from embarrassment. Even under the dim outside lights it's obvious to Paul. What has happened to him sometime today. Marc swallows turning his head away from the other man.

"It's not your fault." Paul says.

"There has to be a way I could have prevented all of that from happening to me. I can't help myself. Plus, I'm the one that brought all of this down on us." Marc says.

"When I have counseled victims coming to me as a priest. They have always blamed themselves. You know what I would tell them?"

Marc, "It's not just that I was used for stud. They changed me physically. I need release from priapism so strong it makes me ache. No, hurt for release that only intercourse can bring. It's like going into a bazaar and smelling all the spices and foods. You get hungry for it but you are not allowed to have any." Paul listens patiently letting Marc vent his frustrations.

"I want intercourse so bad it's painful. Now throw on top of that once into their seduction, I become a rusk crazed animal. All I can do is seek to gratify a woman's needs. No matter how long it takes. Even though they have started threatening my family. Camel's father is in the hospital on a coronary care unit. Hell, they killed Phil." Paul reacts to his painful words.

"I'm sorry, I didn't mean to be so crass."

"It's the truth," Paul admits. His jaw so tightly tensed that muscles twitching in it. Automatically twisting his neck to the side making it crack. "I need to speak with an old professor of mine. He taught when I was in the seminary. The church was never too happy with his teachings of other religions. Especially the older religions of Europe. If anyone could help us in this fight it's him. Come on the news will be starting soon." Paul stands up. "Besides it's hot out here." Perspiration wicking over Paul's broad blonde stubble covered jaw. Marc stands up the back of his once dry tee-shirt with wet patches on it. No argument from him. As if on cue their neighbor's security lights come on. Knowing the time is 9:10 p.m. because the next door security lights are set on a timer. While they are on vacation. Shafts of light find a few openings through the wisteria's dense growth. Then his kitchen phone rings.

CHAPTER 98

WALKING INTO THE man cave that would have been a family room. Paul talking on the phone in the other room. Marc already impressed with the comfort of this room. Two large overstuffed recliners facing where a concealed television would be. The walls painted a medium shade of brown with dark chocolate blackout drapes covering the floor to ceiling windows, not pooled, just brushing the cypress hardwood floor. Old but restored nicely to a natural patina. The beautiful grains of the wood left uncovered by any rugs.

A Germantown Navaho blanket hung on one wall. On the opposite wall a large Picasso abstract with oranges and blacks of round flat circles. Definitely not from his cubist period. Marc stands in front of it appreciating it. Remembering his father telling him about this very painting. When Uncle Theron had bought it from an art dealer in the Vieux Carré in the eighties. A story told more than once by both men. How his uncle had found it buying at a steal for only ten thousand dollars. That and the fact that Uncle Theron gave it to Phil as one of his college graduation gifts.

Marc ready to sit down but before doing so he spots a baseball under the glass sitting on the mantel. Yep, World Series Yankees signed yellowed with age. Taking mental note of a black fabric–covered mirror above the fireplace. Coming into the room going right over to the dry bar. Pouring himself a rocks glass with three fingers of whiskey. Then dropping down into his recliner.

"Would you like something? I need a couple after I get off the phone. Talking with my dad." Paul says.

"Yeah sure. Do you have any scotch?" Marc says.

"You know it will Glenlivet do?" Paul asks.

"Absolutely." Marc says. "I got it." Getting up before Paul can. Pouring himself up three fingers straight. Taking the other recliner. Paul picks up the remote control. At the press of a button a large high-definition screen television is revealed from behind a panel that slides into the wall. Turning on the news Paul sets the remote on the table between the two recliners. Then pulls on his lever to raise his long legs and bare feet up to get more comfortable.

Local sports newscaster discusses the upcoming Saints lineup. Then moving on to college football talking about LSU's up and coming season. Paul already finished with his drink getting up to pour another one. Marc still on his first taking his time enjoying the scotch.

The news interrupted. "This just in, a commercial airliner has gone down."

"They need to get serious about safety. Start retiring some of those jets after so many miles." Paul says.

"Yes, it's official, a commercial airline has gone down in the United Arab Emirates. We're transferring over to one of our affiliates in Bahrain." The metal click of his recliner bangs. Marc sitting forward bare feet on the floor rising up from his chair with drink still in his hand. Reaching back to set his glass down. Missing the table completely his crystal rocks glass smashing against the hardwood floor. Sending chunks skidding over the floor.

"This is Omar Kaleef." His accent British. "It's official. A commercial jet airliner went down in United Arab Emirates. We are switching live to our news crew. In the city of Dubai."

"This is the BBC affiliate reporting from downtown Dubai. Where a column of black smoke is rising up from the gem of the Middle East. Reports are coming in from all over the city that multiple explosions have rocked the city. This footage just came in on You Tube. What appears to be an airliner. Descending at a steep decline clipping a high rise building with its left wing. Ripping out several floors of windows and shattering hundreds of others. Before listing sideways and then falling onto the streets below. Witnesses closer to the scene are describing it as fiery chunks. When pieces of the fuselage broke apart." The camera takes a close-up view. Showing hundreds of people streaming out of the building. Some running while others appear to be in shock. Moving slower covered in ashes and soot. The news crew pulls away in their helicopter to give a sweeping view of the downtown. Smoke and debris blowing across the city. Its background noise alarms ringing from fire trucks and air raid alarms. "Back to you, Omar."

"Are there any reported deaths from this tragic scene?"

"Not yet, but most certainly there will be. I have an update. It was flight 6312 that went down. Currently we do not have any reports as to why."

"So you have right here. This is Omar Kaleef, reporting from BBC affiliate in Bahrain."

Paul rushes back into the room. "What is it? Watching the replay of the You Tube recording in horror.

"This just in, all flights heading to the peninsula have been redirected. I can't believe what I have just seen. The United Arab Emirates has gone on high alert. Officials are requesting help from Saudi Arabia's military. Egypt is allowing military flights only. Jordan, Lebanon, and Israel have stopped all air traffic as well." Marc's cell phone rings. Jamming his hand into his pocket. Using his thumb to turn it on. His adrenaline pumping with his breath caught.

"Hello, Camel is that you?"

Edwards Brothers Malloy
Thorofare, NJ USA
June 18, 2012